THE COUNT
OF MONTE CRISTO

THE COUNT OF MONTE CRISTO

VOLUME I

Alexandre Dumas

Gateway Editions
REGNERY PUBLISHING, INC.
WASHINGTON, D.C.

Library of Congress Cataloging-in-Publication Data

Published in the United States by
Regnery Publishing, Inc.
An Eagle Publishing Company
One Massachusetts Avenue, NW
Washington, DC 20001

Distributed to the trade by
National Book Network
4720-A Boston Way
Lanham, MD 20706

Printed on acid-free paper.
Manufactured in the United States of America

10 9 8 7 6 5 4 3 2 1

Books are available in quantity for promotional or premium use. Write to Director of Special Sales, Regnery Publishing, Inc., One Massachusetts Avenue, NW, Washington, DC 20001, for information on discounts and terms or call (202) 216-0600.

CONTENTS

CONTENTS

A Note on the Films

The Count of Monte Cristo was filmed at least three times in the silent era. But the cinema classic is the 1934 version starring Robert Donat, which provided our cover art.

Two television series based on *The Count of Monte Cristo* were made, one in 1955, the next in 1973. A made-for-TV movie starring Richard Chamberlain, Trevor Howard, Kate Nelligan, and Tony Curtis was broadcast in 1975. And given the enduring popularity of Dumas's thrilling tale, there's no doubt his swashbucker will soon be filmed again.

Preface

BY UNIVERSAL CONSENT ALEXANDRE DUMAS is now acknowledged the most entertaining of the writers of romance. For variety of incidents, sprightliness of dialogue, and vividness of narrative no tales of adventure can compete with such works as the *The Three Musketeers*, or the *Count of Monte Cristo*. It is doubtful also, whether the life of any novelist comes as near as the life of Alexandre Dumas to what is expected of an entertaining work of fiction. Viewed as a hero of romance, the great novelist is almost as striking a figure as his picturesque and fascinating D'Artagnan, so that his *Memoirs* and the numerous volumes in which he relates the story of his travels seem to differ from his other narrative works only in the use, for the hero, of the first instead of the third person of the verb.

Romance, in fact, had begun in his family even before he was born. His father, a handsome mulatto, was the son of a French nobleman, Marquis Davy de la Paillettrie, and of a San Domingo slave woman. The circumstances of his birth did not deprive the young man of the advantages which in such an aristocratic society as France had, at the end of the eighteenth century, naturally belonged to a marquis' son. Although he could not be known by the family title, and called himself simply Alexandre Dumas, a name which was to be made illustrious by his son and grandson, he moved in the most brilliant circles, and in 1786 joined the select cavalry troop known as the Queen's Dragoons.

His opportunity, however, came with the French Revolution. His magnificent bravery rapidly raised him to the highest ranks in the armies of the Republic. In 1793, when only twenty-seven years of age, he was made a general, and he soon commanded in chief, first in the Pyrenees, then in the Alps. He afterwards served under General Bonaparte, with whom he formed a close friendship. He went with him to Egypt, distinguished himself again by conduct of extraordinary brilliancy, which gave him a great influence over the native population, but had to be sent back to Europe on account of the poor state of his health. On his way back he fell into the hands of the Neapolitan government, then bitterly hostile to France, was thrown into prison and treated with shameful inhumanity. It is even suspected that poison was mixed with his food, and that his death, which occurred in 1806, before he was forty-four years of age, was due to the attempt then made against his life. What is sure is that he left prison a wreck after the signing of the peace, and was never able to resume his military career.

He was living in retirement, in the small town of Villera-Cotterets, in the northeast of France, when on the 10th of Thermidor of the year X of the French Republic (July 24, 1802), he became the father of a boy destined to even greater fame and more striking adventures than his own.

With the education of that son he had nothing to do, as he died before the child was four years of age. The lad grew under the eyes of his mother, who never mustered courage enough to part with her son and send him to college. Thus what he learned during his childhood did not amount to much, at least so far as regards intellectual improvement. In everything connected with physical development, in every sort of country sport he soon excelled; he had inherited his father's herculean strength and delighted in nothing so much as in the display of physical power. He thus grew, almost ignorant of the manifold cares of life, until his twenty-first year, when he was suddenly informed by his mother that the family resources on which both had lived up to that time were completely exhausted and that upon him devolved henceforth the duty of providing for mother and son.

He was not unprepared for the announcement, and already had ambitions the fulfilment of which was rather helped than hindered by his new responsibilities. He determined at once to go to Paris and seek his fortune there, a step which his mother would never have assented to unless driven to it, as she then was, by the sternest of necessities. Although provided with a very scanty amount of book learning the young man knew the stirring events of his father's career. Like all his contemporaries, he had followed, on the bulletins of victories placarded against the walls of public buildings, the extraordinary career of Emperor Napoleon, and knew that between the great warrior and his father a tie of personal friendship had at one time existed. He dreamed of emulating the great men of the period which had just closed, and as the reëstablishment of European peace precluded any hope of obtaining glory at the head of victorious armies, literature, and especially poetry, which had just made famous the names of Alphonse de Lamartine and Victor Hugo, the latter a young man of almost exactly the same age as Alexandre Dumas, seemed the most natural field in which to seek distinction.

In Paris young Dumas sought his father's friends. Most of them were unwilling or unable to help him. Fortunately for him, the district from which he came was then represented in the Chamber of Deputies by a former general of the Napoleonic army, who was also a great orator and one of the most respected leaders of the Liberal Party, General Foy. Thanks to the friendly intercourse existing between the general and the Duc d'Orléans, a clerkship was obtained in the latter's employment for young Dumas, who happened to possess one of the most important requisites for the position, a beautiful handwriting. On being told of his appointment he said to his patron, "General, I am going to live by my handwriting, but I promise you that I shall some day live by my pen." The promise was redeemed.

It is, however, not as a novelist that Alexandre Dumas first became known to the world. He had been only a short time in the employ of the Duc d'Orléans when Paris was visited by a company of English players. Although then totally ignorant of English, he was so powerfully impressed by the grandeur and life-like movement of the Shakesperian dramas, that he at once resolved to enroll himself among those who were then trying to emancipate the French stage from servile submission to rules which had had their *raison d'être* in the seventeenth century, but which had then to a great extent outlived their usefulness. He was rewarded with success. The first performance of *Henri III. et sa Cour*, in February, 1829, is in the history of the French Romantic Drama an event second in importance only to the production of Victor Hugo's *Hernani* in February, 1830.

The revolution of 1830, which followed a few months later, somewhat interfered with Dumas' newly undertaken literary labors. His sympathies were naturally with the insurgents, and with their illustrions chief, Marquis de Lafayette. He fought for the reëstablishment in France of the tricolor flag, proscribed during the preceding period, and hailed with delight the accession to the throne, as Louis Philippe the First, King of the French, of his former patron, the Duc d'Orléans.

In spite of the time given to several political missions, and to his duties as a captain in the artillery of the National Guard, he managed to have no less than five dramas performed during the year 1831. One of these dramas, *Antony*, which is in many respects a chapter of an autobiography, was received with even greater applause than *Henri III. et sa Cour*.

This activity of the young dramatic writer in the year 1831 was the first sign given by him of the prodigious fertility of romantic invention by which he was soon to astonish the world, when to the labors of the dramatist he was to add those of the writer of romances.

His first works of a narrative character were books of travels and short stories. He did not undertake the composition of any extended work of imagination until 1840, the date of the publication of *Captain Paul*. The climax was soon reached. In 1844 and 1845 he published his two masterpieces, *The Three Musketeers* and *Monte Cristo*, soon followed by the two sequels of the former work, *Twenty Years After*, and *The Vicomte de Bragelonne*.

Nothing can give an idea of the feverish haste with which Dumas was then working. He was surrounded by a real army of secretaries and collaborators whom he filled with his own genius, his inventiveness, his method of conveying facts through crisp and bright dialogue. He revised what they wrote, and gave it a brilliancy that makes it indistinguishable from what he himself wrote. Some of his assistants were men of real parts, for instance, Auguste Maquet, who had no small part in the production of *The Three Musketeers*. Dumas was then attacked by a libellous writer, known by the nom de plume of Eugène de Mirecourt, who described what he called the firm of "Alexandre Dumas and Co., manufacturers of romances." In the trial that followed the publication of the libel it was demonstrated that Dumas' name during the year appeared on the title page of more novels than could be produced by one man unceasingly working at his desk day and night for the whole of the three hundred and sixty-five days! But what of it, if the whole of this production bore the indisputable stamp of the master who was subjecting others to the overlordship of his imperial mind? No small compliment was paid then to the great novelist and dramatist by the historian Michelet, who wrote to him: "Monsieur, I love you and admire you, for you are one of the forces of nature."

Lavish beyond conception of the productions of his brain, Dumas was unfortunately no less lavish of the princely income which these productions brought to him. His African blood undoubtedly manifested itself in his love of gorgeous display. His travels through Italy and Spain, related by him in some of his most entertaining volumes, were planned and carried out on a scale of expenditure such as almost appals the imagination, and the result of which was that he never could extricate himself completely from financial difficulties.

His activity on the field of the novel, where his rivals then were no smaller writers than Balzac and George Sand, did not cause him to desert the stage. One of his dramas, *The Tower of Nesle*, brought about a duel with one of the authors of the play, Fréderic Gaillardet, who was afterwards the editor of the French newspaper, *Le Courrier des États-Unis*, in New York. Another of his plays, *Le Chevalier de Maison Rouge*, the action of which takes place during the French Revolution; contained a song, *Mourir pour la patrie*, which became a sort of war cry during the months following the Revolution of 1848, and for a while almost rivalled the popularity of the "Marseillaise."

Dumas undoubtedly expected great results for himself to follow a political revolution which called to power a poet, Lamartine, and raised to the highest places men with whom he, on the whole, thoroughly sympathized. But he was hampered by the money obligations which resulted from his extravagant mode of living. When not Lamartine only, but Victor Hugo, Béranger, La Mennais, and a great many more of his literary friends triumphantly entered the National Assembly, he suffered a severe defeat and saw his political ambitions for the second time nipped in the bud. In fact, after a while he had to leave Paris, where he was harassed by his creditors, and to take refuge in Brussels, and there he resided for several years, until an old political friend, Noël Parfait, managed at last to straighten somewhat his business affairs.

But he was soon to leave Paris again under circumstances strangely appealing to his imagination.

In 1860 the Italian hero, Giuseppe Garibaldi, drove the Bourbon dynasty from the kingdom of Naples and sent word to the great French novelist to come and join him. Dumas answered the call and was soon in Naples. Just what he performed there is not exactly known. Officially he was simply the superintendent of the magnificent art museums of the city. But he seems to have had also a good deal to do with the political situation; perhaps a little less, however, than he would have had his countrymen believe. When speaking of himself he was always romancing. How could he help doing so? To invent the incidents of a narrative was the natural function of his brain. How could he be expected, simply because he was writing of himself, to confine himself to facts that had actually occurred? In fact, he hardly recognized any dividing line between the real and the imaginary and once boasted that he had "raised History to the dignity of the Novel."

He returned to Paris in 1864, and until the last months of his life maintained his literary activity, producing novels and plays as naturally and as regularly as a manufacturer his wares. But he had not acquired the financial wisdom of the business man. Fortunately for him, a watchful and loving eye was now looking after his comfort. His son, known as Alexandre Dumas fils, had acquired, through his success as a dramatist, both fortune and glory, and yielded to no one the privilege of attending to the needs of the father whom he loved and whose fame he considered his most priceless possession. His weaknesses he knew, but he could not find it in his heart to condemn the childlike great man who had never shown him anything but the most loving and indulgent smile. How he viewed these weaknesses is shown in his humorous play *The Prodigal Father*, an adaptation of which was shown on the English stage under the title of *My Awful Dad*.

When both body and mind began to weaken. Alexandre Dumas was carried to his son's country estate, at Puys near Dieppe, on the British channel. There, in total ignorance of what was happening in the outside world, he spent the terrible weeks of 1870 when France was suffering defeat after defeat, surrendering one army after another, and drinking to the dregs the cup of national disaster. The joyful chronicler of D'Artagnan knew nothing of the pitiful tale, though he did not breathe his last until the fifth of December, that is, two months after the surrender at Sedan.

His effigy is seen in France in many places. A superb bust shows his rugged features in the lower rotunda of the Théâtre Français. A statue tells the boys and girls of Villers-Cotterets of the most illustrious child of their native town. But what would most rejoice the heart of the indefatigable story-teller is a statue in Paris, facing a monument to his own son, in one of the most beautiful gardens of the beautiful city, which is soon to hold also the statue of the heroic general of the French Revolution and then to receive a new name,—the "Square of the Three Dumas."

II

WHAT SORT OF WORKS DID Dumas bring out during this eventful life, in which so much time was given to pleasure, to passion, to outside activity, that none seemed to be left for the intense labor of literary production? As has already been remarked, it is as a dramatist that Dumas first won distinction, and it is to be here noticed that he is one of the very few writers who attained a very high rank both as authors of novels and of dramatic works. In France itself, Balzac, George Sand, Daudet, Zola, the great rivals of Dumas on the field of romance, have done comparatively little for the stage, and that little is not of such high excellence as to add very much to the fame that they justly possess as novelists. Hugo alone towers above all, and his magnificent poetical gifts shine no less in *Les Misérables* and in *Ninety-Three* than in *Hernani* or *Ruy Blas*. Outside of France we know the novels of Thackeray, Dickens, George Eliot, Freytag, Sienkiewicz, Tolstoy, D'Annunzio; their names owe nothing, or next to nothing, to dramatic activity. Not so with Dumas. His dramas stand out by themselves, and his place in the literary history of

France would be a conspicuous one, even if not a single romance had ever come from his pen. The twenty volumes of his Theatre are filled with thrilling dramas, some of which, indeed, are simply dramatized romances, but the most striking of which were conceived by him originally as dramatic works, and have not been treated by him in the more extended form of the novel. In fact, Dumas conceived life as a drama: the conflict of human desires as expressed in human speech and revealed in human deeds; such is the all-absorbing theme of his thoughts, and in his hurried life he quite naturally chose for its manifestations, first the shorter, more condensed, and, let us add, more quickly remunerative form of the play. No wonder, therefore, that *action*, which is the chief element of the drama, should also be the main source of interest in his romances, and that his dialogue be the most telling and effective, perhaps, to be found in the works of any novelist.

It was fortunate for Dumas that he appeared at a moment when the time-honored formulas of French classical tragedy and comedy were about to undergo the furious onslaught of the Romanticists. His exuberant nature could not easily have been curbed and made to obey the rules laid down for the writers of a statelier age. There was a lawless element in him, which manifested itself in his life no less than in his books, and which, happily, was entirely free from any taint of malice, so that no one was ever harmed by it, except Dumas himself. His nature remained unsubdued to the last.

Thus it happened that *Henry III. and his Court* brought as much novelty on the French stage as Victor Hugo's *Hernani*, which it preceded by about a year, and that the dramatists of France are indebted for their emancipation to the author of *The Three Musketeers* hardly less than to the author of *Les Misérables*.

In the list of Dumas' plays we find, of course, a number of dramatized novels; and no wonder, for every scene of his novels has the stirring quality that is demanded of the drama, and it seems almost as if one might, by the simple omission of the narrative passages, at once make it ready for the stage. Indeed, Dumas' novels were, if we are not mistaken, the first novels that were bodily turned into plays; and to the success that greeted Dumas' characters, when actually walking in flesh and bone before a public which had already been delighted by the narrative of their deeds in the pages of the book, is due in no small measure the practice so prevalent today of turning into a play nearly every novel that has won the approval of the reading public.

But Dumas' best and greatest plays are those the subjects of which are not found in the long list of his romances. In writing them he was moved, not as in his novels, by the ambition of depicting a whole period of history, or reciting every incident of an eventful career, but by the desire of explaining a single act which might have been made known to him by a page of history, an incident of real life, or sometimes even as in his romantic drama of passion, *Antony*, by a supposition of his ever seething fancy.

Thus, for instance, he happened one day to read in the now discarded French History of Anquetil, that Duke Henry of Guise had murdered a nobleman by the name of Saint-Mégrin, a favorite of the King, after compelling his own wife, by a sheer display of physical force, to write a note inviting Saint-Mégrin to a love meeting; and thence the play of *Henry III. and his Court. Christian of Sweden* explains Monaldeschi's murder in the palace at Fontainebleau. *Mademoiselle de Belle-Isle*, Dumas' most successful comedy, owes more to fancy than to truth, but is also mainly the preparation and explanation of a single deed in the whole play.

One of the characteristics of Dumas' plays is the striking manner in which each act ends. Dumas possessed the faculty of compelling the spectator to ask himself: What will happen next? And it is perhaps the desire of causing this question to arise that kept Dumas for a while from producing works in which the answer might easily be found by simply turning over a few pages of a book. But he soon found a way of combining the exhilaration of keeping the public waiting for an answer to a riddle with the satisfaction of giving full play to one's own imagination, and leaving nothing unexplained which belongs to the writer of romance more than to the dramatist; and he became thus the creator of a kind of work of fiction in which he was to acquire his greatest glory, and to remain to this day unequalled, viz.: what the French call the Roman-Feuilleton.

III

WE HAVE CALLED ATTENTION already to the advantage for Dumas of having made his literary début at the same time as the great School of Romanticists. Another good fortune of this happy child of nature was to have lived at the time when the daily press was entering the period of extraordinary development which has made it one of the indispensable institutions of modern society. He conceived the idea of using the daily paper, not simply for the dissemination of the news of the day and of political speculations, but also for the satisfaction of the craving for the ideal, for the unreal and imaginary which exists in the human heart, and which has given us our great poets, our great dramatists, our great writers of romance; and he began to write and to dictate novels which were to appear before the public first not in the shape of volumes, but in daily instalments, of, say, from two to three thousand words, filling only the lower part of the first two pages of *La Presse* or *Le Journal des Débats*. Let it be well understood here that it never was Dumas' practice to hand to the newspaper editor a complete novel, allowing him to cut it in such a way as to fit the exigencies of the publishers, the character and quantity of news of the day, etc. Dumas composed his narrative day by day, his *copy* reached the printer's office usually just at the last moment, and he sent of it just as much as he wished to appear in the next issue. He had also a knack for placing the famous *to be continued* at such a place that the reader had to ask himself nearly every day the question which tickles the spectator of a stirring play at the end of every act: What will happen next?

And here we strike one of the causes of Dumas' extraordinary success. His works are not the result of cold calculation. They are instinct with life. Of all the faults which may exist in a literary work, the one which the reader is sure never to find in his romances is dulness. His heroes may be charged with a great many offences, but they are not lazy; they are always doing something, and always have to fight against something, against some danger by which they are threatened. We cannot help being interested in the never ending struggle which they have to carry against obstacles and odds which for any one except Dumas' heroes would be absolutely insuperable. They, however, triumph over everything. For them human strength and human endurance seem to have been stretched far beyond their usual limits without, however, giving the reader any impression of extravagance. We follow D'Artagnan or Monte Cristo through their extraordinary adventures with a feeling of exhilaration which makes us their companions and associates in the performance of their super-human feats and the enjoyment of their impossible success. Why?

Because they are filled with Dumas' own exuberant life. Strength was the most striking characteristic of the whole family. It had been noticeable in the father almost as much as it was in the heroes which came out of the son's inexhaustible imagination. During the wars of the Revolution at Brixen, in Tyrol, it was necessary for the French army to keep the Austrians from crossing a bridge. General Dumas managed to do it without any companions. His life seemed charmed. The enemies could not touch him. The deeds which, by their impossible character, gave the readers of Livy's first books their first doubts as to the historical accuracy of the narrative, were equalled by the Hercules-like mulatto chieftain, whom General Bonaparte saluted by the name of the Horatius Cocles of Tyrol. The impression that had been created by the warrior was repeated by the man of letters. The men by whom Alexandre Dumas was surrounded were struck by something like awe, at the sight of his display of vigor and indefatigableness either in work or pleasure. How could they have raised any doubt as to the possibility for his heroes of accomplishing the tasks he had set for them when he was constantly doing what, but for his doing it, they would have declared to be impossible? He is perhaps the only writer of extraordinary adventures whose tales are told with an accent of irresistible conviction. Even when indulging in the most extravagant flights of fancy his sincerity is undeniable. For a moment what he says seems possible not only to himself, but to every reader of his extraordinarily entertaining productions. His resourcefulness fills us with a feeling of security for those of his characters in whose favor the magician that he is has managed to enlist our sympathies. By whatever dangers they are encompassed we know that he will find a way out for them.

IV

TWO TYPES ARE TO BE found in Dumas' romances. On one side we find the works that have been put together under the collective titles of *The Valois romances* and the *D'Artagnan romances*, on the other those that belong to the same class as *Monte Cristo*. By what traits are these two types distinguished from each other?

The first class, the *Valois* and the *D'Artagnan* romances, are the outcome of a purpose early formed by Alexandre Dumas of narrating to the French, in an entertaining form, the whole of their national history. He had reached manhood with a very scanty stock of historical notions, and he experienced, in discovering how much romance there was in history, a feeling of delighted surprise and amazement which he determined to communicate to his contemporaries. He tells us himself in his memoirs of an incident which had a good deal to do in starting him on his career of reciter of historical tales.

While he was in the service of the Duc d'Orléans, the prince had once to set up a defence in a rather strange judicial contest. He was

charged by a kind of adventuress with not being at all a member of
the royal family, but with having been substituted for a girl baby
born to the Duchess at a time when it was necessary for the Orléans
branch of the Bourbon dynasty to possess a male heir. The Duke was
fond of composing himself the legal briefs to be used in his controversies, and to dictate them to his secretaries. On that occasion
young Dumas was selected by him on account of his beautiful handwriting as his amanuensis. Suddenly, while dictating, the Duke
noticed in the features of his secretary an expression of astonishment. He had just dictated the following sentence: "If, moreover, no
other proof existed, the striking likeness that is noticeable between
his Royal Highness the Duc d'Orléans and his illustrious ancestor,
Louis XIV., would be sufficient to establish his right to occupy his
place in the royal family of France." Dumas knew, of course, that the
Orléans branch was descended from Philippe d'Orléans, brother of
Louis XIV., while the older branch, then still on the throne, came
directly from the great King himself. What he did not know, and
what he would have known if better acquainted with history, was
that a marriage had taken place between members of the two
branches, that Louis XIV. had as much as compelled his nephew,
who became afterwards the Regent, during the minority of Louis
XV., to marry one of his numerous illegitimate daughters, Mademoiselle de Blois. The true condition of things dawned upon the
young man when he heard the Duke tell him in his deep basso
voice: "Learn, sir, that when a man is descended from Louis XIV.,
though it be through bastards, it is glorious enough for him to boast
of it." When back at his desk Dumas related the occurrence to his
colleagues, one of whom simply said to him: "You had better read
the memoirs of Saint-Simon." He followed the advice thus given,
and on reading the pages of the haughty nobleman was dum-
founded to discover that often history was very different in reality
from what it seemed to be in the official text-books written under
the eyes and published with the approval of the monarchical author-

ities. He at once decided to do for others what had been done for him through the occurrence just related, and the book *Gaul and France* was the first outcome of his ambition to make the French people acquainted with the true character of their annals. The cold reception of the book in no way disheartened him, and he went on, reading Memoirs, Souvenirs, Recollections, until one day, in the National Library, he stumbled upon a comparatively short work on the reigns of Louis XIII. and Louis XIV., *Memoirs of the Chevalier D'Artagnan.* There was enough of romance in the book to fire his imagination, and a new form of historical novel was created. Of this type of narrative the most celebrated are, following the sequence of historical events, *Queen Margot* (1845), *The Three Musketeers* (1844), with its two continuations, *Twenty Years After* (1845), and *The Vicomte de Bragelonne* (1848–50), and finally, *The Queen's Necklace* (1849–50). The common trait of all these works, and of the numerous other romances by which Dumas' novels are made to constitute, as it were, a continuous narrative, stretching from the time of the last Valois kings to the time of the Revolution, is the outward claim that the important thing in them consists in the narrative of the well-known facts of official history, such as the massacre of Saint Bartholomew's night, the murder of Buckingham, the disturbances of the Fronde, the trial of Cardinal de Rohan before the Parliament of Paris; while what will interest the reader is the imaginary explanation of how these things took place. In official history the important people seem to be Cardinal Richelieu, Cardinal Mazarin, General Monk, etc.; in Dumas' romances these great people seem to have been mere play-things, puppets in the hands of daring adventurers, known by, or rather hidden under, the names of Athos, Porthos, and Aramis; and the wonderful thing in them is the snug fit of truth with fiction which they present.

In the novels of the *Monte Cristo* type, the most remarkable of which, after the entrancing *Monte Cristo* itself, is *The Mohicans of Paris*, history provides only the background. They do not attempt to furnish explanations of historical events, and they place upon the stage no great historical characters. The Comte de Monte Cristo, or rather Edmond Dantès, M. de Villefort, The Comte de Morcerf are all offsprings of Dumas' inexhaustibly prolific brain, and their adventures are freed from the obligations of fitting in with facts already well known through the more dignified narratives due to the pen of historians; hence the more fantastic character of the occurrences with which they are filled.

But whether Dumas takes us through the halls and corridors of the Louvre, at the time of Catherine of Medici, Charles IX., or Henry III., to some treasure cave under the waters of the Mediterranean, to the Palais Royal, with Richelieu, or to the walls of Janina, with the terrible Ali-Pasha, he always holds us, wistfully listening to his wonderful story-telling, even with the look of the child carried away to fairy-land by the old tales of the nursery.

For the benefit of American readers let us add that Dumas' French style is almost the perfection of narrative style. It has no very striking personal traits; it tells its story swiftly, brightly, clearly, and therefore loses little, if anything, in passing through the hands of a clever and experienced translator.

ADOLPHE COHN.

Introduction

1815–1838

The Count of Monte Cristo is totally unlike any of Dumas'
other stories and in many respects is the strongest of all.
Even the D'Artagnan romances, though containing points
of superiority, must yield to this novel in interest and popularity.
Despite its obvious faults, which critics have analyzed repeatedly, it
has been placed by general consent in the list of the world's ten
greatest novels. This high position has been accorded it because it
has been found broad in sweep while narrow of theme, and con-
vincing in interest while melodramatic in its ideals.

The first departure from other Dumas stories made by *Monte
Cristo* lies in its freedom from historic relation. Dumas' lifelong purpose was to "elevate history to the rank of fiction," and his long list
of interest compelling novels and plays constructed closely upon
fact attests the realization of his purpose. But in *Monte Cristo* he
suddenly turns aside from established record to write a narrative of
unbridled fancy. Liberated from the trammels of history, he gives
free rein to his exuberant imagination, writing carelessly and
swiftly, but producing a story that will enthrall the attention as certainly as the reader has an answering imagination.

Nor is Dumas to be tempted into the field of history even
momentarily, notwithstanding the period is an alluring one to a man

of his temperament. The closing Hundred Days of the dynasty of Napoleon I., culminating with the Battle of Waterloo, is the first incident he passes over with a bare mention, whereas his contemporary Hugo turns aside in *Les Misérables* and devotes several chapters to Waterloo alone, although having to skip a period and break the thread of his story so to do. Other episodes about which the mysterious *Monte Cristo* or his enemies might have been personally interested are the reigns of Louis XVIII., Charles X., and Louis Philippe, and the Revolution of July. But none of these things are allowed to intrude upon the story proper, save in the most episodical way. The problem is now not the safety of thrones, but the oppression of a soul that lives to oppress other souls in its turn.

The motif indeed is not a lofty one. Revenge cannot be ennobled by the most elaborate system of counterweights. In the D'Artagnan romances it will be noticed that friendship is the compelling force—a friendship of man for man that dwarfs the love of sexes. In *Monte Cristo* it is not friendship but hatred of man for man—so strong that once again the love of man for woman becomes almost insignificant. Edmond Dantès, a simple sailor lad, frank, open-hearted, sunny, to whom the whole sky is blue, and the whole earth is glorified by his sweetheart's smile, falls the victim of cruel plots and devilish circumstances. Four men are instrumental in his complete undoing—Danglars being actuated by jealousy in rank; Mondego by rivalry in love; Caderousse by cowardly self-interest; and Villefort by political fear. On the eve of his wedding day Dantès is torn from his betrothed and sent to languish in a dungeon, while his four enemies are apparently triumphant. Years afterwards, when they have ceased to think of their victim, he escapes from prison armed with a store of worldly knowledge, possessed with the secret of an enormous wealth, and imbued with the spirit of an undying vengeance. Henceforth his life, his knowledge, his wealth, and every faculty of his nature are devoted to the culmination of his plans for revenge.

The plot takes on a fourfold aspect at this point, since the revenge contemplates four separate persons. Danglars has become a baron and a banker; he must be attacked through financial channels. The problem is one involving only time for a man of unlimited means. Mondego has become a count and has attained considerable wealth; but his war and private record conceals some doubtful actions of which his enemy has but to possess himself by patient investigation in order to work his ruin. Caderousse's cowardice and selfishness have brought their own reward—criminality—and his secret foe has little to do save abandon him to his evil nature, and wait patiently for the inevitable and terrible day when his name can be erased from the list. Villefort's case seems more perplexing at first. His official position as king's attorney does not readily present any culpable deeds that may be proven. A spot upon his private life is finally discovered and used with overwhelming effect against him.

But the four problems are by no means so simple as would appear from the above outline. They present subtleties and intricacies of wonderful scope. Villefort is not alone attacked officially. An insidious enemy to his domestic happiness is set at work within his home. The two catastrophes descend simultaneously, leaving the man crushed and demented. Danglars is attacked from two other sides beside the financial, so that his wife's social prestige and his daughter's happiness are overthrown at the same time with his flight. And in the same manner with the two others, every available influence is brought to bear upon them. The fourfold problem is accurately demonstrated and comprehensively outlined. It would also have been completely worked out but for the presence of an unexpected factor—the factor of a woman's recurring love. Dantès' sweetheart, Mercédès, has been won by Mondego after her lover's sudden and inexplicable disappearance. The subsequent revenge, therefore, against Mondego in order to be complete must include his wife and their son. The pitiless Dantès, or Count of Monte Cristo, as he is now called, is on the point of slaying the son after having practically accomplished the father's disgrace, when the wife, Mercédès, pierces the count's disguise, till then impenetrable, and implores him to pity in the name of their own former love. The man of bronze hesitates. The woman pleads and avows her love of the earlier days. The man and his beautifully wrought system of revenge is disturbed and thwarted because he has not succeeded in crushing out his heart. The incident comes as a blessed relief after many pages freighted with fatality. It relieves the figure of Monte Cristo which till then had seemed almost devoid of humanity and limued only by the darkness of an inflexible hatred.

Monte Cristo cannot appeal as an actual, living person. He is rather one of the forces of nature, hardly human in conception, and robed with an air of mystery that prevents a personal acquaintance. One cannot be attracted by his individuality, but is repelled instead by the qualities which he assiduously cultivates. He has transformed himself into an instrument of vengeance, and thus may neither expect nor desire sympathy. So insistently has this been brought out that, on the few rare occasions when his generosity or gratitude are revealed—as in the case of the Morrels, or in the interview with Mercédès—the reader feels almost as little personal sympathy for his actions as though they were of the opposite type. He is neither to be praised nor condemned for his treatment of his four enemies. In each case he merely directs their crimes against their own heads. He aids society by rooting out of its midst four evil weeds. But the conception of a man thus taking upon himself to save or punish is not consistent with our twentieth century ideals; and for this reason, if for no other, the figure of Monte Cristo will never seem real, but will keep company with such legendary characters as "Sinbad the Sailor." Viewed thus as a mythical hero imbued with supernatural qualities of foresight and omniscience and endowed with untold wealth, his figure is irresistibly attractive to younger minds. While with all, young or old, who have had vague longings for riches and power, and who have believed themselves capable of using wisely such fortune, Monte Cristo's actions will arouse the keenest interest.

The problem of the expenditure of resources is at all times alluring. Dumas himself became so attracted by the type he had created, that his own after life was influenced by Monte Cristo's career, living prodigally and spending lavishly.

Mercédès comes as a grateful change from the dark, conflicting passions of the book. She never loses her girlish charm. Her pathetic smile is a hint of a divine forgiveness, a promise of future benison. She is the real sufferer, but her suffering is not tinged by bitterness. Her devotion continues unchanged through all the varying fortunes of those it rests upon. Contrasted with the inflexible hatred of Dantès, her love becomes a symbol of the God-like attribute of mercy outweighing the demands of justice.

Another glint of sunshine is the courtship of Valentine and Maximilian. It stands out all the brighter from being outlined against a threatening sky. That Valentine the innocent was almost destroyed with her guilty parents simply shows the blindness of a humanly-instituted justice. The story of the two lovers, and the means by which they were united—through the agency of a sleeping potion—bears close resemblance to the tale of *Romeo and Juliet*.

The absence of humor will be noted. The plot is too sternly tragic to admit of it. The melodramatic dénouements are relieved by a naturalness of narration. The tremendous onward sweep of circumstance appeals principally to the intellect and to the logical sense. Dumas' spirit of generosity and chivalry, met with so abundantly elsewhere, is here replaced by a brutality, a harshness of tone, that hints of the barbaric blood still lingering in his veins. His magnificent Count of Monte Cristo may lay exulting claim to the world, but it is for him a world wherein he is to pursue his egoistic interests, and not an arena for the exploiting of a larger humanity.

J. WALKER McSPADDEN.

Cast of Characters

CAVALCANTI, MAJOR BARTOLOMEO, an Italian adventurer.

CHÂTEAU-RENAUD, COMTE DE, of Parisian society.

COCLÉS, cashier for Morrel & Sons.

CORNÉLIE, MLLE., maid to Mme. Danglars.

CUCUMETTO, chief of Italian brigands.

DANDRÉ, BARON, minister of police.

DANGLARS, supercargo of the "Pharaon;" afterwards Baron Danglars, a Paris banker.

DANGLARS, BARONNE HERMINE, wife of foregoing.

DANGLARS, MLLE. EUGÉNIE, daughter of foregoing.

DANTÈS, EDMOND, sailor of Marseilles, mate of the "Pharaon;" afterwards known as Comte de Monte Cristo; also assuming the names of Lord Wilmore, Abbé Busoni, and Sinbad the Sailor.

DANTÈS, LOUIS, a native of Marseilles.

D'ARMILLY, LOUISE, music-teacher, instructor of Mlle. Danglars.

D'AVRIGNY, DOCTOR, physician to Villefort.

DEBRAY, LUCIEN, private secretary to the Minister of the Interior.

D'ÉPIGNAY, FRANZ DE QUESNEL, BARON, of Parisian society.

DESCHAMPS, notary.

DIAVOLACCIO, of Cucumetto's hand of brigands.

ÉTIENNE, valet to Danglars.

FANNY, maid to Mlle. de Villefort.

FARIA, ABBÉ, prisoner in Château d'If.

FLORENTIN, valet to Albert de Morcerf.

GAETANO, Roman sailor.

GAUMARD, CAPTAIN, in service of Morrel & Sons.

GERMAIN, valet to Gérard de Villefort.

GERMAIN, valet to Albert de Morcerf.

GOVERNOR of the Château d'If.

GUICCIOLI, COMTESSE, an Italian.

HAIDEE, daughter of Ali Pasha; slave to Monte Cristo.

HERBAULT, EMMANUEL, clerk for Morrel & Sons.

HERBAULT, MME. JULIE (née Morrel), wife of foregoing

JACOPO, Genoese smuggler.

JAILOR of the Château d'If.

JOANNES, jeweller.

LOUIS XVIII., King of France.

MERCÉDÈS, a Catalan; afterwards Comtesse de Morcerf.

MONDEGO, FERNAND, a Catalan; afterwards Comte de Morcerf.

MONTE CRISTO, COMTE DE (see Edmond Dantès).

MORCERF, ALBERT, VICOMTE DE, of Parisian society.

MORREL, of Morrel & Sons, ship-owners of Marseilles.

MORREL, MME., wife of foregoing.

MORREL, MAXIMILIAN, son of foregoing.

NAPOLEON I., Emperor of France.

PAMPHILE, PÈRE, of La Réserve Inn.

PASTRINI, signor, of Hôtel de Londres, Rome.

PECAUD, hostler.

PENELON, sailor, in service of Morrel & Sons.

PEPPINO, Italian bandit.

RITA, Italian.

RONDOLA, ANDREA, Italian.

SAINT–MÉRAN, MARQUIS DE, Royalist.

SAINT–MÉRAN, MARQUISE DE, wife of foregoing.

SALVIEUX, COMTE DE, chamberlain to Comte d'Artois.

SALVIEUX, MLLE. DE, daughter of foregoing.

SAN–FELICE, COUNT OF, Roman nobleman.

TERESA, Italian.

TRINETTE, chambermaid.

VAMPA, LUIGI, chief of Italian banditti.

VILLEFORT, GÉRARD DE, procureur.

VILLEFORT, MME. RENÉE DE (née Saint-Méran), first wife of foregoing.

VILLEFORT, MLLE. VALENTINE DE, daughter of foregoing.

VILLEFORT, MME. HÉLOÏSE DE, second wife of Gérard de Villefort.

VILLEFORT, EDWARD DE, son of foregoing

VILLEFORT, EDWARD DE, son of foregoing.
VILLEFORT, NOIRTIER DE, Bonapartist.

THE COUNT
OF MONTE CRISTO

I

Marseilles—The Arrival

O N THE 24TH OF February, 1815, the look-out at Notre-Dame de la Garde signalled the three-master, the *Pharaon* from Smyrna, Trieste, and Naples.

As usual, a pilot put off immediately, and rounding the Château d'If, got on board the vessel between Cape Morgion and Rion island.

Immediately, and according to custom, the ramparts of Fort, Saint-Jean were covered with spectators; it is always an event at Marseilles for a ship to come into port, especially when this ship, like the *Pharaon*, has been built, rigged, and laden at the old Phocée docks, and belongs to an owner of the city.

The ship drew on and had safely passed the strait, which some volcanic shock has made between the Calasareigne and Jaros islands; had doubled Pomègue, and approached the harbor under topsails, jib, and spanker, but so slowly and sedately that the idlers, with that instinct which is the forerunner of evil, asked one another what misfortune could have happened on board. However, those experienced in navigation saw plainly that if any accident had occurred, it was not to the vessel herself, for she bore down with all the evidence of being skilfully handled, the anchor a-cockbill, the jib-boom guys already eased off, and standing by the side of the pilot, who was steering the *Pharaon* towards the narrow entrance of the inner port, was a young man, who, with activity and vigilant eye, watched every motion of the ship, and repeated each direction of the pilot.

The vague disquietude which prevailed among the spectators had so much affected one of the crowd that he did not await the arrival of the vessel in harbor, but jumping into a small skiff, desired to be pulled alongside the *Pharaon*, which he reached as she rounded into La Réserve basin.

When the young man on board saw this person approach, he left his station by the pilot, and, hat in hand, leaned over the ship's bulwarks.

He was a fine, tall, slim young fellow of eighteen or twenty, with black eyes, and hair as dark as a raven's wing; and his whole appearance bespoke that calmness and resolution peculiar to men accustomed from their cradle to contend with danger.

"Ah, is it you, Dantès?" cried the man in the skiff. "What's the matter? and why have you such an air of sadness aboard?"

"A great misfortune, M. Morrel," replied the young man,—"a great misfortune, for me especially! Off Civita Vecchia we lost our brave Captain Leclère."

"And the cargo?" inquired the owner, eagerly.

"Is all safe, M. Morrel; and I think you will be satisfied on that head. But poor Captain Leclère—"

"What happened to him?" asked the owner, with an air of considerable resignation. "What happened to the worthy captain?"—"He died."

"Fell into the sea?"

"No, sir, he died of brain-fever in dreadful agony." Then turning to the crew, he said, "Bear a hand there, to take in sail!"

All hands obeyed, and at once the eight or ten seamen who composed the crew, sprang to their respective stations at the spanker brails and outhaul, topsail sheets and halyards, the jib downhaul, and the topsail clewlines and buntlines. The young sailor gave a look to see that his orders were promptly and accurately obeyed, and then turned again to the owner.

"And how did this misfortune occur?" inquired the latter, resuming the interrupted conversation.

"Alas, sir, in the most unexpected manner. After a long talk with the harbor-master, Captain Leclère left Naples greatly disturbed in mind. In twenty-four hours he was attacked by a fever, and died three days afterwards. We performed the usual burial service, and he is at his rest, sewn up in his hammock with a thirty-six pound shot at his head and his heels, off El Giglio island. We bring to his widow his sword and cross of honor. It was worth while, truly," added the young man with a melancholy smile, "to make war against the English for ten years, and to die in his bed at last, like everybody else."

"Why, you see, Edmond," replied the owner, who appeared more comforted at every moment, "we are all mortal, and the old must make way for the young. If not, why, there would be no promotion; and since you assure me that the cargo—"

"Is all safe and sound, M. Morrel, take my word for it; and I advise you not to take 25,000 francs for the profits of the voyage."

Then, as they were just passing the Round Tower, the young man shouted: "Stand by there to lower the topsails and jib; brail up the spanker!"

The order was executed as promptly as it would have been on board a man-of-war.

"Let go—and clue up!" At this last command all the sails were lowered, and the vessel moved almost imperceptibly onwards.

"Now, if you will come on board, M. Morrel," said Dantès, observing the owner's impatience, "here is your supercargo, M. Danglars, coming out of his cabin, who will furnish you with every particular. As for me, I must look after the anchoring, and dress the ship in mourning."

The owner did not wait for a second invitation. He seized a rope which Dantès flung to him, and with an activity that would have done credit to a sailor, climbed up the side of the ship, while the young man, going to his task, left the conversation to Danglars, who now came towards the owner. He was a man of twenty-five or twenty-six years of age, of unprepossessing countenance, obsequious to his superiors, insolent to his subordinates; and this, in addition to his position as responsible agent on board, which is always obnoxious to the sailors, made him as much disliked by the crew as Edmond Dantès was beloved by them.

"Well, M. Morrel," said Danglars, "you have heard of the misfortune that has befallen us?"

"Yes—yes: poor Captain Leclère! He was a brave and an honest man."

"And a first-rate seaman, one who had seen long and honorable service, as became a man charged with the interests of a house so important as that of Morrel & Son," replied Danglars.

"But," replied the owner, glancing after Dantès, who was watching the anchoring of his vessel, "it seems to me that a sailor needs not be so old as you say, Danglars, to understand his business, for our friend Edmond seems to understand it thoroughly, and not to require instruction from any one."

"Yes," said Danglars, darting at Edmond a look gleaming with hate. "Yes, he is young, and youth is invariably self-confident. Scarcely was the captain's breath out of his body when he assumed the command without consulting any one, and he caused us to lose a day and a half at the Island of Elba, instead of making for Marseilles direct."

"As to taking command of the vessel," replied Morrel, "that was his duty as captain's mate; as to losing a day and a half off the Island of Elba, he was wrong, unless the vessel needed repairs."

"The vessel was in as good condition as I am, and as, I hope, you are, M. Morrel, and this day and a half was lost from pure whim, for the pleasure of going ashore, and nothing else."

"Dantès," said the shipowner, turning towards the young man, "come this way!"

"In a moment, sir," answered Dantès, "and I'm with you." Then calling to the crew, he said—"Let go!"

The anchor was instantly dropped, and the chain ran rattling through the port-hole. Dantès continued at his post in spite of the presence of the pilot, until this manœuvre was completed, and then he added, "Half-mast the colors, and square the yards!"

"You see," said Danglars, "he fancies himself captain already, upon my word."

"And so, in fact, he is," said the owner.

"Except your signature and your partner's, M. Morrel."

"And why should he not have this?" asked the owner; "he is young, it is true, but he seems to me a thorough seaman, and of full experience."

A cloud passed over Danglars' brow. "Your pardon, M. Morrel," said Dantès, approaching, "the vessel now rides at anchor, and I am at your service. You hailed me, I think?"

Danglars retreated a step or two. "I wished to inquire why you stopped at the Island of Elba?"

"I do not know, sir; it was to fulfil the last instructions of Captain Leclère, who, when dying, gave me a packet for Marshal Bertrand."

"Then did you see him, Edmond?"—"Who?"

"The marshal."—"Yes."

Morrel looked around him, and then, drawing Dantès on one side, he said suddenly—"And how is the emperor?"

"Very well, as far as I could judge from the sight of him."

"You saw the emperor, then?"

"He entered the marshal's apartment while I was there."

"And you spoke to him?"

"Why, it was he who spoke to me, sir," said Dantès, with a smile.

"And what did he say to you?"

"Asked me questions about the vessel, the time she left Marseilles, the course she had taken, and what was her cargo. I believe, if she had not been laden, and I had been her master, he would have bought her. But I told him I was only mate, and that she belonged to the firm of Morrel & Son. 'Ah, yes,' he said, 'I know them. The Morrels have been shipowners from father to son; and there was a Morrel who served in the same regiment with me when I was in garrison at Valence.'"

"*Pardieu*, and that is true!" cried the owner, greatly delighted. "And that was Policar Morrel, my uncle, who was afterwards a captain. Dantès, you must tell my uncle that the emperor remembered him, and you will see it will bring tears into the old soldier's eyes. Come, come," continued he, patting Edmond's shoulder kindly, "you did very right, Dantès, to follow Captain Leclère's instructions, and touch at Elba, although if it were known that you had conveyed a packet to the marshal, and had conversed with the emperor, it might bring you into trouble."

"How could that bring me into trouble, sir?" asked Dantès; "for I did not even know of what I was the bearer; and the emperor merely made such inquiries as he would of the first comer. But, pardon me, here are the health officers and the customs inspectors coming alongside." And the young man went to the gangway. As he departed, Danglars approached, and said,—

"Well, it appears that he has given you satisfactory reasons for his landing at Porto-Ferrajo?"

"Yes, most satisfactory, my dear Danglars."

"Well, so much the better," said the supercargo; "for it is not pleasant to think that a comrade has not done his duty."

"Dantès has done his," replied the owner, "and that is not saying much. It was Captain Leclère who gave orders for this delay."

"Talking of Captain Leclère, has not Dantès given you a letter from him?"

"To me?—no—was there one?"

"I believe that, besides the packet, Captain Leclère confided a letter to his care."

"Of what packet are you speaking, Danglars?"

"Why, that which Dantès left at Porto-Ferrajo."

"How do you know he had a packet to leave at Porto-Ferrajo?" Danglars turned very red.

"I was passing close to the door of the captain's cabin, which was half open, and I saw him give the packet and letter to Dantès."

"He did not speak to me of it," replied the shipowner; "but if there be any letter he will give it to me."

Danglars reflected for a moment. "Then, M. Morrel, I beg of you," said he, "not to say a word to Dantès on the subject. I may have been mistaken."

At this moment the young man returned; Danglars withdrew.

"Well, my dear Dantès, are you now free?" inquired the owner.—"Yes, sir."

"You have not been long detained."

"No. I gave the custom-house officers a copy of our bill of lading; and as to the other papers, they sent a man off with the pilot, to whom I gave them."

"Then you have nothing more to do here?"

"No—everything is all right now."

"Then you can come and dine with me?"

"I really must ask you to excuse me, M. Morrel. My first visit is due to my father, though I am not the less grateful for the honor you have done me."

"Right, Dantès, quite right. I always knew you were a good son."

"And," inquired Dantès, with some hesitation, "do you know how my father is?"

"Well, I believe, my dear Edmond, though I have not seen him lately."

"Yes, he likes to keep himself shut up in his little room."

"That proves, at least, that he has wanted for nothing during your absence."

Dantès smiled. "My father is proud, sir, and if he had not a meal left, I doubt if he would have asked anything from anyone, except from Heaven."

"Well, then, after this first visit has been made we shall count on you."

"I must again excuse myself, M. Morrel, for after this first visit has been paid I have another which I am most anxious to pay."

"True, Dantès, I forgot that there was at the Catalans some one who expects you no less impatiently than your father—the lovely Mercédès."

Dantès blushed.

"Ah, ha," said the shipowner, "I am not in the least surprised, for she has been to me three times, inquiring if there were any news of the *Pharaon*. *Peste*, Edmond, you have a very handsome mistress!"

"She is not my mistress," replied the young sailor, gravely; "she is my betrothed."

"Sometimes one and the same thing," said Morrel, with a smile.

"Not with us, sir," replied Dantès.

"Well, well, my dear Edmond," continued the owner, "don't let me detain you. You have managed my affairs so well that I ought to allow you all the time you require for your own. Do you want any money?"

"No, sir; I have all my pay to take—nearly three months' wages."

"You are a careful fellow, Edmond."

"Say I have a poor father, sir."

"Yes, yes, I know how good a son you are, so now hasten away to see your father. I have a son too, and I should be very wroth with those who detained him from me after a three months' voyage."

"Then I have your leave, sir?"

"Yes, if you have nothing more to say to me."—"Nothing."

"Captain Leclère did not, before he died, give you a letter for me?"

"He was unable to write, sir. But that reminds me that I must ask your leave of absence for some days."

"To get married?"—"Yes, first, and then to go to Paris."

"Very good; have what time you require, Dantès. It will take quite six weeks to unload the cargo, and we cannot get you ready for sea until three months after that; only be back again in three months, for the *Pharaon*," added the owner, patting the young sailor on the back, "cannot sail without her captain."

"Without her captain!" cried Dantès, his eyes sparkling with animation; "pray mind what you say, for you are touching on the most secret wishes of my heart. Is it really your intention to make me captain of the *Pharaon*?"

"If I were sole owner we'd shake hands on it now, my dear Dantès, and call it settled; but I have a partner, and you know the Italian proverb—*Chi ha compagno ha padrone*—'He who has a partner has a master.' But the thing is at least half done, as you have one out of two votes. Rely on me to procure you the other; I will do my best."

"Ah, M. Morrel," exclaimed the young seaman, with tears in his eyes, and grasping the owner's hand, "M. Morrel, I thank you in the name of my father and of Mercédès."

"That's all right, Edmond. There's a providence that watches over the deserving. Go to your father: go and see Mercédès, and afterwards come to me."

"Shall I row you ashore?"

"No, thank you; I shall remain and look over the accounts with Danglars. Have you been satisfied with him this voyage?"

"That is according to the sense you attach to the question, sir. Do you mean is he a good comrade? No, for I think he never liked me since the day when I was silly enough, after a little quarrel we had, to propose to him to stop for ten minutes at the island of Monte Cristo to settle the dispute—a proposition which I was wrong to suggest, and he quite right to refuse. If you mean as responsible agent when you ask me the question, I believe there is nothing to say against him, and that you will be content with the way in which he has performed his duty."

"But tell me, Dantès, if you had command of the *Pharaon* should you be glad to see Danglars remain?"

"Captain or mate, M. Morrel, I shall always have the greatest respect for those who possess the owners' confidence."

"That's right, that's right, Dantès! I see you are a thoroughly good fellow, and will detain you no longer. Go, for I see how impatient you are."

"Then I have leave?"—"Go, I tell you."

"May I have the use of your skiff?"—"Certainly."

"Then, for the present, M. Morrel, farewell, and a thousand thanks!"

"I hope soon to see you again, my dear Edmond. Good luck to you."

The young sailor jumped into the skiff, and sat down in the stern sheets, with the order that he be put ashore at La Canebière. The two oarsmen bent to their work, and the little boat glided away as rapidly as possible in the midst of the thousand vessels which choke up the narrow way which leads between the two rows of ships from the mouth of the harbor to the Quai d'Orléans.

The shipowner, smiling, followed him with his eyes until he saw him spring out on the quay and disappear in the midst of the throng, which from five o'clock in the morning until nine o'clock at night, swarms in the famous street of La Canebière,—a street of which the modern Phocæans are so proud that they say with all the gravity in the world, and with that accent which gives so much character to what is said, "If Paris had La Canebière, Paris would be a second Marseilles." On turning round the owner saw Danglars behind him, apparently awaiting orders, but in reality also watching the young sailor,—but there was a great difference in the expression of the two men who thus followed the movements of Edmond Dantès.

II

Father and Son

W E WILL LEAVE DANGLARS struggling with the demon of hatred, and endeavoring to insinuate in the ear of the ship owner some evil suspicions against his comrade, and follow Dantès, who, after having traversed La Canebière, took the Rue de Noailles, and entering a small house, on the left of the Allées de Meillan, rapidly ascended four flights of a dark staircase, holding the baluster with one hand, while with the other he repressed the beatings of his heart, and paused before a half-open door, from which he could see the whole of a small room.

This room was occupied by Dantès' father. The news of the arrival of the *Pharaon* had not yet reached the old man, who, mounted on a chair, was amusing himself by training with trembling hand the nasturtiums and sprays of clematis that clambered over the trellis at his window. Suddenly, he felt an arm thrown around his body, and a well-known voice behind him exclaimed, "Father—dear father!"

The old man uttered a cry, and turned round; then, seeing his son, he fell into his arms, pale and trembling.

"What ails you, my dearest father? Are you ill?" inquired the young man, much alarmed.

"No, no, my dear Edmond—my boy—my son!—no; but I did

not expect you; and joy, the surprise of seeing you so suddenly—Ah, I feel as if I were going to die."

"Come, come, cheer up, my dear father! 'Tis I—really I! They say joy never hurts, and so I came to you without any warning. Come now, do smile, instead of looking at me so solemnly. Here I am back again, and we are going to be happy."

"Yes, yes, my boy, so we will—so we will," replied the old man; "but how shall we be happy? Shall you never leave me again? Come, tell me all the good fortune that has befallen you."

"God forgive me," said the young man, "for rejoicing at happiness derived from the misery of others, but, Heaven knows, I did not seek this good fortune; it has happened, and I really cannot pretend to lament it. The good Captain Leclère is dead, father, and it is probable that, with the aid of M. Morrel, I shall have his place. Do you understand, father? Only imagine me a captain at twenty, with a hundred louis pay, and a share in the profits! Is this not more than a poor sailor like me could have hoped for?"

"Yes, my dear boy," replied the old man, "it is very fortunate."

"Well, then, with the first money I touch, I mean you to have a small house, with a garden in which to plant clematis, nasturtiums, and honeysuckle. But what ails you, father? Are you not well?"

"'Tis nothing, nothing; it will soon pass away"—and as he said so the old man's strength failed him, and he fell backwards.

"Come, come," said the young man, "a glass of wine, father, will revive you. Where do you keep your wine?"

"No, no; thanks. You need not look for it; I do not want it," said the old man.

"Yes, yes, father, tell me where it is," and he opened two or three cupboards.

"It is no use," said the old man, "there is no wine."

"What, no wine?" said Dantès, turning pale, and looking alternately at the hollow cheeks of the old man and the empty cupboards. "What, no wine? Have you wanted money, father?"

"I want nothing now that I have you," said the old man.

"Yet," stammered Dantès, wiping the perspiration from his brow,—"yet I gave you two hundred francs when I left, three months ago."

"Yes, yes, Edmond, that is true, but you forgot at that time a little debt to our neighbor, Caderousse. He reminded me of it, telling me if I did not pay for you, he would be paid by M. Morrel; and so, you see, lest he might do you an injury"—

"Well?"—"Why, I paid him."

"But," cried Dantès, "it was a hundred and forty francs I owed Caderousse."

"Yes," stammered the old man.

"And you paid him out of the two hundred francs I left you?" The old man nodded.

"So that you have lived for three months on sixty francs," muttered Edmond.

"You know how little I require," said the old man.

"Heaven pardon me," cried Edmond, falling on his knees before his father.

"What are you doing?"

"You have wounded me to the heart."

"Never mind it, for I see you once more," said the old man; "and now it's all over—everything is all right again."

"Yes, here I am," said the young man, "with a promising future and a little money. Here, father, here!" he said, "take this—take it, and send for something immediately." And he emptied his pockets on the table, the contents consisting of a dozen gold pieces, five or six five-franc pieces, and some smaller coin. The countenance of old Dantès brightened.

"Whom does this belong to?" he inquired.

"To me, to you, to us! Take it; buy some provisions; be happy, and to-morrow we shall have more."

"Gently, gently," said the old man, with a smile; "and by your leave I will use your purse moderately, for they would say, if they saw me buy too many things at a time, that I had been obliged to await your return, in order to be able to purchase them."

"Do as you please; but, first of all, pray have a servant, father. I will not have you left alone so long. I have some smuggled coffee and most capital tobacco, in a small chest in the hold, which you shall have to-morrow. But, hush, here comes somebody."

"'Tis Caderousse, who has heard of your arrival, and no doubt comes to congratulate you on your fortunate return."

"Ah, lips that say one thing, while the heart thinks another," murmured Edmond. "But, never mind, he is a neighbor who has done us a service on a time, so he's welcome."

As Edmond paused, the black and bearded head of Caderousse appeared at the door. He was a man of twenty-five or six, and held a piece of cloth, which, being a tailor, he was about to make into a coat-lining.

"What, is it you, Edmond, back again?" said he, with a broad Marseillaise accent, and a grin that displayed his ivory-white teeth.

"Yes, as you see, neighbor Caderousse; and ready to be agreeable to you in any and every way," replied Dantès, but ill-concealing his coldness under this cloak of civility.

"Thanks—thanks; but, fortunately, I do not want for anything; and it chances that at times there are others who have need of me." Dantès made a gesture. "I do not allude to you, my boy. No!—no! I lent you money, and you returned it; that's like good neighbors, and we are quits."

"We are never quits with those who oblige us," was Dantès' reply; "for when we do not owe them money, we owe them gratitude."

"What's the use of mentioning that? What is done is done. Let us talk of your happy return, my boy. I had gone on the quay to match a piece of mulberry cloth, when I met friend Danglars. 'You at Marseilles?'—'Yes,' says he.

"'I thought you were at Smyrna.'—'I was; but am now back again.'

"'And where is the dear boy, our little Edmond?'

"'Why, with his father, no doubt,' replied Danglars. And so I came," added Caderousse, "as fast as I could to have the pleasure of shaking hands with a friend."

"Worthy Caderousse!" said the old man, "he is so much attached to us."

"Yes, to be sure I am. I love and esteem you, because honest folks are so rare. But it seems you have come back rich, my boy," continued the tailor, looking askance at the handful of gold and silver which Dantès had thrown on the table.

The young man remarked the greedy glance which shone in the dark eyes of his neighbor. "Eh," he said, negligently, "this money is not mine. I was expressing to my father my fears that he had wanted many things in my absence, and to convince me he emptied his purse on the table. Come, father," added Dantès, "put this money back in your box—unless neighbor Caderousse wants anything, and in that case it is at his service."

"No, my boy, no," said Caderousse. "I am not in any want, thank God, my living is suited to my means. Keep your money—keep it, I say;—one never has too much;—but, at the same time, my boy, I am as much obliged by your offer as if I took advantage of it."

"It was offered with good will," said Dantès.

"No doubt, my boy; no doubt. Well, you stand well with M. Morrel I hear,—you insinuating dog, you!"

"M. Morrel has always been exceedingly kind to me," replied Dantès.

"Then you were wrong to refuse to dine with him."

"What, did you refuse to dine with him?" said old Dantès; "and did he invite you to dine?"

"Yes, my dear father," replied Edmond, smiling at his father's astonishment at the excessive honor paid to his son.

"And why did you refuse, my son?" inquired the old man.

"That I might the sooner see you again, my dear father," replied the young man. "I was most anxious to see you."

"But it must have vexed M. Morrel, good, worthy man," said Caderousse. "And when you are looking forward to be captain, it was wrong to annoy the owner."

"But I explained to him the cause of my refusal," replied Dantès, "and I hope he fully understood it."

"Yes, but to be captain one must do a little flattery to one's patrons."

"I hope to be captain without that," said Dantès.

"So much the better—so much the better! Nothing will give greater pleasure to all your old friends; and I know one down there behind the Saint Nicolas citadel who will not be sorry to hear it."

"Mercédès?" said the old man.

"Yes, my dear father, and with your permission, now I have seen you, and know you are well and have all you require, I will ask your consent to go and pay a visit to the Catalans."

"Go, my dear boy," said old Dantès: "and heaven bless you in your wife, as it has blessed me in my son!"

"His wife!" said Caderousse; "why, how fast you go on, father Dantès; she is not his wife yet, as it seems to me."

"No, but according to all probability she soon will be," replied Edmond.

"Yes—yes," said Caderousse; "but you were right to return as soon as possible, my boy."

"And why? "Because Mercédès is a very fine girl, and fine girls never lack followers; she particularly has them by dozens."

"Really?" answered Edmond, with a smile which had in it traces of slight uneasiness.

"Ah, yes," continued Caderousses, "and capital offers, too; but you know, you will be captain, and who could refuse you then?"

"Meaning to say," replied Dantès, with a smile which but ill-concealed his trouble, "that if I were not a captain"—

"Eh—eh!" said Caderousse, shaking his head.

"Come, come," said the sailor, "I have a better opinion than you of women in general, and of Mercédès in particular; and I am certain that, captain or not, she will remain ever faithful to me."

"So much the better—so much the better," said Caderousse. "When one is going to be married, there is nothing like implicit confidence; but never mind that, my boy,—go and announce your arrival, and let her know all your hopes and prospects."

"I will go directly," was Edmond's reply; and, embracing his father, and nodding to Caderousse, he left the apartment.

Caderousse lingered for a moment, then taking leave of old Dantès, he went downstairs to rejoin Danglars, who awaited him at the corner of the Rue Senac.

"Well," said Danglars, "did you see him?"

"I have just left him," answered Caderousse.

"Did he allude to his hope of being captain?"

"He spoke of it as a thing already decided."

"Indeed!" said Danglars, "he is in too much hurry, it appears to me."

"Why, it seems M. Morrel has promised him the thing."

"So that he is quite elated about it?"

"Why, yes, he is actually insolent over the matter—has already offered me his patronage, as if he were a grand personage, and proffered me a loan of money, as though he were a banker."

"Which you refused?"

"Most assuredly; although I might easily have accepted it, for it was I who put into his hands the first silver he ever earned; but now M. Dantès has no longer any occasion for assistance—he is about to become a captain."

"Pooh!" said Danglars, "he is not one yet."

"*Ma foi*, it will be as well if he is not," answered Caderousse; "for if he should be, there will be really no speaking to him."

"If we choose," replied Danglars, "he will remain what he is; and perhaps become even less than he is."

"What do you mean?"

"Nothing—I was speaking to myself. And is he still in love with the Catalane?"

"Over head and ears; but, unless I am much mistaken, there will be a storm in that quarter."—"Explain yourself."

"Why should I?"—"It is more important than you think, perhaps. You do not like Dantès?"

"I never like upstarts."—"Then tell me all you know about the Catalane."

"I know nothing for certain; only I have seen things which induce me to believe, as I told you, that the future captain will find some annoyance in the vicinity of the Vieilles Infirmeries."

"What have you seen?—come, tell me!"

"Well, every time I have seen Mercédès come into the city she has been accompanied by a tall, strapping, black-eyed Catalan, with a red complexion, brown skin, and fierce air, whom she calls cousin."

"Really; and you think this cousin pays her attentions?"

"I only suppose so. What else can a strapping chap of twenty-one mean with a fine wench of seventeen?"

"And you say that Dantès has gone to the Catalans?"

"He went before I came down."

"Let us go the same way; we will stop at La Réserve, and we can drink a glass of La Malgue, whilst we wait for news."

"Come along," said Caderousse; "but you pay the score."

"Of course," replied Danglars; and going quickly to the designated place, they called for a bottle of wine, and two glasses.

Père Pamphile had seen Dantès pass not ten minutes before; and assured that he was at the Catalans, they sat down under the budding foliage of the planes and sycamores, in the branches of which the birds were singing their welcome to one of the first days of spring.

III

The Catalans

BEYOND A BARE, WEATHER-WORN wall, about a hundred paces from the spot where the two friends sat looking and listening as they drank their wine, was the village of the Catalans. Long ago this mysterious colony quitted Spain, and settled on the tongue of land on which it is to this day. Whence it came no one knew, and it spoke an unknown tongue. One of its chiefs, who understood Provençal, begged the commune of Marseilles to give them this bare and barren promontory, where, like the sailors of old, they had run their boats ashore. The request was granted; and three months afterwards, around the twelve or fifteen small vessels which had brought these gypsies of the sea, a small village sprang up. This village, constructed in a singular and picturesque manner, half Moorish, half Spanish, still remains, and is inhabited by descendants of the first comers, who speak the language of their fathers. For three or four centuries they have remained upon this small promontory, on which they had settled like a flight of sea-birds, without mixing with the Marseillaise population, intermarrying, and preserving their original customs and the costume of their mother-country as they have preserved its language.

Our readers will follow us along the only street of this little village, and enter with us one of the houses, which is sun-burned to the beautiful dead-leaf color peculiar to the buildings of the country, and within coated with whitewash, like a Spanish posada. A young and beautiful girl, with hair as black as jet, her eyes as velvety as the gazelle's, was leaning with her back against the wainscot, rubbing in her slender delicately moulded fingers a bunch of heath blossoms, the flowers of which she was picking off and strewing on the floor; her arms, bare to the elbow, brown, and modelled after those of the Arlesian Venus, moved with a kind of restless impatience, and she tapped the earth with her arched and supple foot, so as to display the pure and full shape of her well-turned leg, in its red cotton, gray and blue clocked, stocking. At three paces from her, seated in a chair which he balanced on two legs, leaning his elbow on an old worm-eaten table, was a tall young man of twenty, or two-and-twenty, who was looking at her with an air in which vexation and uneasiness were mingled. He questioned her with his eyes, but the firm and steady gaze of the young girl controlled his look.

"You see, Mercédès," said the young man, "here is Easter come round again; tell me, is this the moment for a wedding?"

"I have answered you a hundred times, Fernand, and really you must be very stupid to ask me again."

"Well, repeat it,—repeat it, I beg of you, that I may at last believe it! Tell me for the hundredth time that you refuse my love, which had your mother's sanction. Make me understand once for all that you are trifling with my happiness, that my life or death are nothing to you. Ah, to have dreamed for ten years of being your husband, Mercédès, and to lose that hope, which was the only stay of my existence!"

"At least it was not I who ever encouraged you in that hope, Fernand," replied Mercédès; "you cannot reproach me with the slightest coquetry. I have always said to you, 'I love you as a brother; but do not ask from me more than sisterly affection, for my heart is another's.' Is not this true, Fernand?"

"Yes, that is very true, Mercédès," replied the young man. "Yes, you have been cruelly frank with me; but do you forget that it is among the Catalans a sacred law to intermarry?"

"You mistake, Fernand; it is not a law, but merely a custom, and, I pray of you, do not cite this custom in your favor. You are included in the conscription, Fernand, and are only at liberty on sufferance, liable at any moment to be called upon to take up arms. Once a soldier, what would you do with me, a poor orphan, forlorn, without fortune, with nothing but a half-ruined hut and a few ragged nets, the miserable inheritance left by my father to my mother, and by my mother to me? She has been dead a year, and you know, Fernand, I have subsisted almost entirely on public charity. Sometimes you pretend I am useful to you, and that is an excuse to share with me the produce of your fishing, and I accept it, Fernand, because you are the son of my father's brother, because we were brought up together, and still more because it would give you so much pain if I refuse. But I feel very deeply that this fish which I go and sell, and with the produce of which I buy the flax I spin,— I feel very keenly, Fernand, that this is charity."

"And if it were, Mercédès, poor and lone as you are, you suit me as well as the daughter of the first ship-owner or the richest banker of Marseilles! What do such as we desire but a good wife and careful housekeeper, and where can I look for these better than in you?"

"Fernand," answered Mercédès, shaking her head, "a woman becomes a bad manager, and who shall say she will remain an honest woman, when she loves another man better than her husband? Rest content with my friendship, for I say once more that is all I can promise, and I will promise no more than I can bestow."

"I understand," replied Fernand, "you can endure your own wretchedness patiently, but you are afraid to share mine. Well, Mercédès, beloved by you, I would tempt fortune; you would bring me good luck, and I should become rich. I could extend my occupation as a fisherman, might get a place as clerk in a warehouse, and become in time a dealer myself."

"You could do no such thing, Fernand; you are a soldier, and if you remain at the Catalans it is because there is no war; so remain a fisherman, and contented with my friendship, as I cannot give you more."

"Well, I will do better, Mercédès. I will be a sailor; instead of the costume of our fathers, which you despise, I will wear a varnished hat, a striped shirt, and a blue jacket, with an anchor on the buttons. Would not that dress please you?"

"What do you mean?" asked Mercédès, with an angry glance,—"what do you mean? I do not understand you?"

"I mean, Mercédès, that you are thus harsh and cruel with me, because you are expecting some one who is thus attired; but perhaps he whom you await is inconstant, or if he is not, the sea is so to him."

"Fernand," cried Mercédès, "I believed you were good-hearted, and I was mistaken! Fernand, you are wicked to call to your aid jealousy and the anger of God! Yes, I will not deny it, I do await, and I do love him of whom you speak; and, if he does not return, instead of accusing him of the inconstancy which you insinuate, I will tell you that he died loving me and me only." The young girl made a gesture of rage. "I understand you, Fernand; you would be revenged on him because I do not love you; you would cross your Catalan knife with his dirk. What end would that answer? To lose you my friendship if he were conquered, and see that friendship changed into hate if you were victor. Believe me, to seek a quarrel with a man is a bad method of pleasing the woman who loves that man. No, Fernand, you will not thus give way to evil thoughts. Unable to have me for your wife, you will content yourself with having me for your friend and sister; and besides," she added, her eyes troubled and moistened with tears, "wait, wait, Fernand; you said just now that the sea was treacherous, and he has been gone four months, and during these four months there have been some terrible storms."

Fernand made no reply, nor did he attempt to check the tears which flowed down the cheeks of Mereédès, although for each of these tears he would have shed his heart's blood; but these tears flowed for another. He arose, paced a while up and down the hut, and then, suddenly stopping before Mercédès, with his eyes glowing and his hands clinched,—"Say, Mercédès," he said, "once for all, is this your final determination?"

"I love Edmond Dantès," the young girl calmly replied, "and none but Edmond shall ever be my husband."

"And you will always love him?"—"As long as I live."

Fernand let fall his head like a defeated man, heaved a sigh that was like a groan, and then suddenly looking her full in the face, with clinched teeth and expanded nostrils, said,—"But if he is dead"—

"If he is dead, I shall die too."

"If he has forgotten you"—

"Mercédès!" called a joyous voice from without,—"Mercédès!"

"Ah," exclaimed the young girl, blushing with delight, and fairly leaping in excess of love, "you see he has not forgotten me, for here he is!" And rushing towards the door, she opened it, saying, "Here, Edmond, here I am!"

Fernand, pale and trembling, drew back, like a traveller at at the sight of a serpent, and fell into a chair beside him. Edmond and Mercédès were clasped in each other's arms. The burning Marseilles sun, which shot into the room through the open door, covered them with a flood of light. At first they saw nothing around them. Their intense happiness isolated them from all the rest of the world, and they only spoke in broken words, which are the tokens of a joy so extreme that they seem rather the expression of sorrow. Suddenly Edmond saw the gloomy, pale, and threatening countenance of Fernand, as it was defined in the shadow. By a movement for which he could scarcely account to himself, the young Catalan placed his hand on the knife at his belt.

"Ah, your pardon," said Dantès, frowning in his turn; "I did not perceive that there were three of us." Then, turning to Mercédès, he inquired, "Who is this gentleman?"

"One who will be your best friend, Dantès, for he is my friend, my cousin, my brother; it is Fernand—the man whom, after you, Edmond, I love the best in the world. Do you not remember him?"

"Yes!" said Dantès, and without relinquishing Mercédès' hand clasped in one of his own, he extended the other to the Catalan with a cordial air. But Fernand, instead of responding to this amiable gesture, remained mute and trembling. Edmond then cast his eyes scrutinizingly at the agitated and embarrassed Mercédès, and then again on the gloomy and menacing Fernand. This look told him all, and his anger waxed hot.

"I did not know, when I came with such haste to you, that I was to meet an enemy here."

"An enemy!" cried Mercédès, with an angry look at her cousin. "An enemy in my house, do you say, Edmond! If I believed that, I would place my arm under yours and go with you to Marseilles, leaving the house to return to it no more."

Fernand's eye darted lightning. "And should any misfortune occur to you, dear Edmond," she continued with the same calmness which proved to Fernand that the young girl had read the very innermost depths of his sinister thought, "if misfortune should occur to you, I would ascend the highest point of the Cape de Morgion and cast myself headlong from it."

Fernand became deadly pale. "But you are deceived, Edmond," she continued. "You have no enemy here—there is no one but Fernand, my brother, who will grasp your hand as a devoted friend."

And at these words the young girl fixed her imperious look on the Catalan, who, as if fascinated by it, came slowly towards Edmond, and offered him his hand. His hatred, like a powerless though furious wave, was broken against the strong ascendancy which Mercédès exercised over him. Scarcely, however, had he touched Edmond's hand than he felt he had done all he could do, and rushed hastily out of the house.

"Oh," he exclaimed, running furiously and tearing his hair—

"Oh, who will deliver me from this man? Wretched—wretched that I am!"

"Hallo, Catalan! Hallo, Fernand! where are you running to?" exclaimed a voice.

The young man stopped suddenly, looked around him, and perceived Caderousse sitting at table with Danglars, under an arbor.

"Well," said Caderousse, "why don't you come? Are you really in such a hurry that you have no time to pass the time of day with your friends?"

"Particularly when they have still a full bottle before them," added Danglars. Fernand looked at them both with a stupefied air, but did not say a word.

"He seems besotted," said Danglars, pushing Caderousse with his knee. "Are we mistaken, and is Dantès triumphant in spite of all we have believed?"

"Why, we must inquire into that," was Caderousse's reply; and turning towards the young man, said, "Well, Catalan, can't you make up your mind?"

Fernand wiped away the perspiration steaming from his brow, and slowly entered the arbor, whose shade seemed to restore somewhat of calmness to his senses, and whose coolness somewhat of refreshment to his exhausted body.

"Good-day," said he. "You called me, didn't you?" And he fell, rather than sat down, on one of the seats which surrounded the table.

"I called you because you were running like a madman, and I was afraid you would throw yourself into the sea," said Caderousse, laughing. "Why, when a man has friends, they are not only to offer him a glass of wine, but, moreover, to prevent his swallowing three or four pints of water unnecessarily!"

Fernand gave a groan, which resembled a sob, and dropped his head into his hands, his elbows leaning on the table.

"Well, Fernand, I must say," said Caderousse, beginning the conversation, with that brutality of the common people in which curiosity destroys all diplomacy, "you look uncommonly like a rejected lover;" and he burst into a hoarse laugh.

"Bah!" said Danglars, "a lad of his make was not born to be unhappy in love. You are laughing at him, Caderousse."

"No," he replied, "only hark how he sighs! Come, come, Fernand," said Caderousse, "hold up your head, and answer us. It's not polite not to reply to friends who ask news of your health."

"My health is well enough," said Fernand, clinching his hands without raising his head.

"Ah, you see, Danglars," said Caderousse, winking at his friend, "this is how it is; Fernand, whom you see here, is a good and brave Catalan, one of the best fishermen in Marseilles, and he is in love with a very fine girl, named Mercédès; but it appears, unfortunately, that the fine girl is in love with the mate of the *Pharaon*; and as the *Pharaon* arrived to-day—why, you understand!"

"No; I do not understand," said Danglars.

"Poor Fernand has been dismissed," continued Caderousse.

"Well, and what then?" said Fernand, lifting up his head, and looking at Caderousse like a man who looks for some one on whom to vent his anger; "Mercédès is not accountable to any person, is she? Is she not free to love whomsoever she will?"

"Oh, if you take it in that sense," said Caderousse, "it is another thing. But I thought you were a Catalan, and they told me the Catalans were not men to allow themselves to be supplanted by a rival. It was even told me that Fernand, especially, was terrible in his vengeance."

Fernand smiled piteously. "A lover is never terrible," he said.

"Poor fellow!" remarked Danglars, affecting to pity the young man from the bottom of his heart. "Why, you see, he did not expect to see Dantès return so suddenly—he thought he was dead, perhaps; or perchance faithless! These things always come on us more severely when they come suddenly."

"Ah, *ma foi*, under any circumstances," said Caderousse, who drank as he spoke, and on whom the fumes of the wine began to take effect,—"under any circumstances Fernand is not the only person put out by the fortunate arrival of Dantès; is he, Danglars?"

"No, you are right—and I should say that would bring him ill-luck."

"Well, never mind," answered Caderousse, pouring out a glass of wine for Fernand, and filling his own for the eighth or ninth time, while Danglars had merely sipped his. "Never mind—in the meantime he marries Mercédès—the lovely Mercédès—at least he returns to do that."

During this time Danglars fixed his piercing glance on the young man, on whose heart Caderousse's words fell like molten lead.

"And when is the wedding to be?" he asked.

"Oh, it is not yet fixed!" murmured Fernand.

"No, but it will be," said Caderousse, "as surely as Dantès will be captain of the *Pharaon*—eh, Danglars?"

Danglars shuddered at this unexpected attack, and turned to Caderousse, whose countenance he scrutinized, to try and detect whether the blow was premeditated; but he read nothing but envy in a countenance already rendered brutal and stupid by drunkenness.

"Well," said he, filling the glasses, "let us drink to Captain Edmond Dantès, husband of the beautiful Catalane!"

Caderousse raised his glass to his month with unsteady hand, and swallowed the contents at a gulp. Fernand dashed his on the ground.

"Eh, eh, eh!" stammered Caderousse. "What do I see down there by the wall, in the direction of the Catalans? Look, Fernand, your eyes are better than mine. I believe I see double. You know wine is a deceiver; but I should say it was two lovers walking side by side, and hand in hand. Heaven forgive me, they do not know that we can see them, and they are actually embracing!"

Danglars did not lose one pang that Fernand endured.

"Do you know them, Fernand?" he said.

"Yes," was the reply, in a low voice. "It is Edmond and Mercédès!"

"Ah, see there, now!" said Caderousse; "and I did not recognize them! Hallo, Dantès! hallo, lovely damsel! Come this way, and let us know when the wedding is to be, for Fernand here is so obstinate he will not tell us."

"Hold your tongue, will you?" said Danglars, pretending to restrain Caderousse, who, with the tenacity of drunkards, leaned out of the arbor. "Try to stand upright, and let the lovers make love without interruption. See, look at Fernand, and follow his example; he is well-behaved!"

Fernand, probably excited beyond bearing, pricked by Danglars, as the bull is by the bandilleros, was about to rush out; for he had risen from his seat, and seemed to be collecting himself to dash headlong upon his rival, when Mercédès, smiling and graceful, lifted up her lovely head, and looked at them with her clear and bright eyes. At this Fernand recollected her threat of dying if Edmond died, and dropped again heavily on his seat. Danglars looked at the two men, one after the other, the one brutalized by liquor, the other overwhelmed with love.

"I shall get nothing from these fools," he muttered; "and I am very much afraid of being here between a drunkard and a coward. Here's an envious fellow making himself boozy on wine when he ought to be nursing his wrath, and here is a fool who sees the woman he loves stolen from under his nose and takes on like a big baby. Yet this Catalan has eyes that glisten like those of the vengeful Spaniards, Sicilians, and Calabrians, and the other has fists big enough to crush an ox at one blow. Unquestionably, Edmond's star is in the ascendant, and he will marry the splendid girl—he will be captain, too, and laugh at us all, unless"—a sinister smile passed over Danglars' lips—"unless I take a hand in the affair," he added.

"Hallo!" continued Caderousse, half-rising, and with his fist on the table, "hallo, Edmond! do you not see your friends, or are you too proud to speak to them?"

"No, my dear fellow!" replied Dantès, "I am not proud, but I am happy, and happiness blinds, I think, more than pride."

"Ah, very well, that's an explanation!" said Caderousse. "How do you do, Madame Dantès?"

Mercédès courtesied gravely, and said—"That is not my name, and in my country it bodes ill fortune, they say, to call a young girl by the name of her betrothed before he becomes her husband. So call me Mercédès, if you please."

"We must excuse our worthy neighbor, Caderousse," said Dantès, "he is so easily mistaken."

"So, then, the wedding is to take place immediately, M. Dantès," said Danglars, bowing to the young couple.

"As soon as possible, M. Danglars; to-day all preliminaries will be arranged at my father's, and to-morrow, or next day at latest, the wedding festival here at La Réserve. My friends will be there. I hope; that is to say, you are invited, M. Danglars, and you, Caderousse."

"And Fernand," said Caderousse with a chuckle; "Fernand, too, is invited!"

"My wife's brother is my brother," said Edmond; "and we, Mercédès and I, should be very sorry if he were absent at such a time."

Fernand opened his mouth to reply, but his voice died on his lips, and he could not utter a word.

"To-day the preliminaries, to-morrow or next day the ceremony! You are in a hurry, captain!"

"Danglars," said Edmond, smiling, "I will say to you as Mercédès said just now to Caderousse, 'Do not give me a title which does not belong to me'; that may bring me bad luck."

"Your pardon," replied Danglars, "I merely said you seemed in a hurry, and we have lots of time; the *Pharaon* cannot be under weigh again in less than three months."

"We are always in a hurry to be happy, M. Danglars; for when we have suffered a long time, we have great difficulty in believing in good fortune. But it is not selfishness alone that makes me thus in haste; I must go to Paris."

"Ah, really?—to Paris! and will it be the first time you have ever been there, Dantès?"—"Yes"

"Have you business there?"—"Not of my own; the last commission of poor Captain Leclère; you know to what I allude, Danglars—it is sacred. Besides, I shall only take the time to go and return."

"Yes, yes, I understand," said Danglars, and then in a low tone, he added, "To Paris, no doubt to deliver the letter which the grand marshal gave him. Ah, this letter gives me an idea—a capital idea! Ah, Dantès, my friend, you are not yet registered number one on board the good ship *Pharaon*;" then turning towards Edmond, who was walking away, "A pleasant journey," he cried.

"Thank you," said Edmond with a friendly nod, and the two lovers continued on their way, as calm and joyous as if they were the very elect of heaven.

IV

Conspiracy

DANGLARS FOLLOWED EDMOND AND Mercédès with his eyes until the two lovers disappeared behind one of the angles of Fort Saint Nicolas, then turning round, he perceived Fernand, who had fallen, pale and trembling, into his chair, while Caderousse stammered out the words of a drinking-song.

"Well, my dear sir," said Danglars to Fernand, "here is a marriage which does not appear to make everybody happy."

"It drives me to despair," said Fernand.

"Do you, then, love Mercédès?"—"I adore her!"

"For long?"—"As long as I have known her—always."

"And you sit there, tearing your hair, instead of seeking to remedy your condition; I did not think that was the way of your people."

"What would you have me do?" said Fernand.

"How do I know? Is it my affair? I am not in love with Mademoiselle Mercédès; but for you—in the words of the gospel, seek, and you shall find."

"I have found already."—"What?"

"I would stab the man, but the woman told me that if any misfortune happened to her betrothed, she would kill herself."

"Pooh! Women say those things, but never do them."

"You do not know Mercédès; what she threatens she will do."

"Idiot!" muttered Danglars; "whether she kill herself or not, what matter, provided Dantès is not captain?"

"Before Mercédès should die," replied Fernand, with the accents of unshaken resolution, "I would die myself!"

"That's what I call love!" said Caderousse with a voice more tipsy than ever. "That's love, or I don't know what love is."

"Come," said Danglars, "you appear to me a good sort of fellow, and hang me, I should like to help you, but"—

"Yes," said Caderousse, "but how?"

"My dear fellow," replied Danglars, "you are three parts drunk; finish the bottle, and you will be completely so. Drink, then, and do not meddle with what we are discussing, for that requires all one's wit and cool judgment."

"I—drunk!" said Caderousse; "well that's a good one! I could drink four more such bottles; they are no bigger than cologne flasks. Père Pamphile, more wine!" and Caderousse rattled his glass upon the table.

"You were saying, sir"—said Fernand, awaiting with great anxiety the end of this interrupted remark.

"What was I saying? I forget. This drunken Caderousse has made me lose the thread of my sentence."

"Drunk, if you like; so much the worse for those who fear wine, for it is because they have bad thoughts which they are afraid the liquor will extract from their hearts;" and Caderousse began to sing the two last lines of a song very popular at the time,—

'Tous les méchants sont beuveurs d'eau;
C'est bien prouvé par le déluge.'[1]

"You said, sir, you would like to help me, but"—

"Yes; but I added, to help you it would be sufficient that Dantès did not marry her you love; and the marriage may easily be thwarted, methinks, and yet Dantès need not die."

[1]"The wicked are great drinkers of water, As the flood proved once for all."

"Death alone can separate them," remarked Fernand.

"You talk like a noodle, my friend," said Caderousse; "and here is Danglars, who is a wide-awake, clever, deep fellow, who will prove to you that you are wrong. Prove it, Danglars. I have answered for you. Say there is no need why Dantès should die; it would, indeed, be a pity he should. Dantès is a good fellow; I like Dantès. Dantès, your health."

Fernand rose impatiently. "Let him run on," said Danglars, restraining the young man; "drunk as he is, he is not much out in what he says. Absence severs as well as death, and if the walls of a prison were between Edmond and Mercédès they would be as effectually separated as if he lay under a tombstone."

"Yes; but one gets out of prison," said Caderousse, who, with what sense was left him, listened eagerly to the conversation, "and when one gets out and one's name is Edmond Dantès, one seeks revenge"—

"What matters that?" muttered Fernand.

"And why, I should like to know," persisted Caderousse, "should they put Dantès in prison? he had not robbed or killed or murdered."

"Hold your tongue!" said Danglars.

"I won't hold my tongue!" replied Caderousse; "I say I want to know why they should put Dantès in prison; I like Dantès; Dantès, your health!" and he swallowed another glass of wine.

Danglars saw in the muddled look of the tailor the progress of his intoxication, and turning towards Fernand, said, "Well, you understand there is no need to kill him."

"Certainly not, if, as you said just now, you have the means of having Dantès arrested. Have you that means?"

"It is to be found for the searching. But why should I meddle in the matter? it is no affair of mine."

"I know not why you meddle," said Fernand, seizing his arm; "but this I know, you have some motive of personal hatred against Dantès, for he who himself hates is never mistaken in the sentiments of others."

"I!—motives of hatred against Dantès? None, on my word! I saw you were unhappy, and your unhappiness interested me; that's all; but since you believe I act for my own account, adieu, my dear friend, get out of the affair as best you may;" and Danglars rose as if he meant to depart.

"No, no," said Fernand, restraining him, "stay! It is of very little consequence to me at the end of the matter whether you have any angry feeling or not against Dantès. I hate him! I confess it openly. Do you find the means, I will execute it, provided it is not to kill the man, for Mercédès has declared she will kill herself if Dantès is killed."

Caderousse, who had let his head drop on the table, now raised it, and looking at Fernand with his dull and fishy eyes, he said,—"Kill Dantès! who talks of killing Dantès? I won't have him killed—I won't! He's my friend, and this morning offered to share his money with me, as I shared mine with him. I won't have Dantès killed—I won't!"

"And who has said a word about killing him, muddlehead?" replied Danglars. "We were merely joking; drink to his health," he added, filling Caderousse's glass, "and do not interfere with us."

"Yes, yes, Dantès' good health!" said Caderousse, emptying his glass, "here's to his health! his health—hurrah!"

"But the means—the means?" said Fernand.—"Have you not hit upon any?" asked Danglars.

"No!—you undertook to do so."

"True," replied Danglars; "the French have the superiority over the Spaniards, that the Spaniards ruminate, while the French invent."

"Do you invent, then," said Fernand impatiently.

"Waiter," said Danglars, "pen, ink, and paper."—"Pen, ink, and paper," muttered Fernand.

"Yes; I am a supercargo; pen, ink, and paper are my tools, and without my tools I am fit for nothing."

"Pen, ink, and paper, then," called Fernand loudly.

"There's what you want on that table," said the waiter.

"Bring them here." The waiter did as he was desired.

"When one thinks," said Caderousse, letting his hand drop on the paper, "there is here wherewithal to kill a man more sure than if we waited at the corner of a wood to assasinate him! I have always had more dread of a pen, a bottle of ink, and a sheet of paper, than of a sword or pistol."

"The fellow is not so drunk as he appears to be," said Danglars. "Give him some more wine, Fernand." Fernand filled Caderousse's glass, who, like the confirmed toper he was, lifted his hand from the paper and seized the glass.

The Catalan watched him until Caderousse, almost overcome by this fresh assault on his senses, rested, or rather dropped, his glass upon the table.

"Well!" resumed the Catalan, as he saw the final glimmer of Caderousse's reason vanishing before the last glass of wine.

"Well, then, I should say, for instance," resumed Danglars, "that if after a voyage such as Dantès has just made, in which he touched at the Island of Elba, some one were to denounce him to the king's procureur as a Bonapartist agent"—

"I will denounce him!" exclaimed the young man hastily.

"Yes, but they will make you then sign your declaration, and confront you with him you have denounced; I will supply you with the means of supporting your accusation, for I know the fact well. But Dantès cannot remain forever in prison, and one day or other he will leave it, and the day when he comes out, woe betide him who was the cause of his incarceration!"

"Oh, I should wish nothing better than that he would come and seek a quarrel with me."

"Yes, and Mercédès! Mercédés, who will detest you if you have only the misfortune to scratch the skin of her dearly beloved Edmond!"

"True!" said Fernand.

"No, no," continued Danglars; "if we resolve on such a step, it would be much better to take, as I now do, this pen, dip it into this ink, and write with the left hand (that the writing may not be recognized) the denunciation we propose." And Danglars, uniting practice with theory, wrote with his left hand, and in a writing reversed from his usual style, and totally unlike it, the following lines, which he handed to Fernand, and which Fernand read in an undertone:—

"The honorable, the king's attorney, is informed by a friend of the throne and religion, that one Edmond Dantès, mate of the ship *Pharaon*, arrived this morning from Smyrna, after having touched at Naples and Porto-Ferrajo, has been intrusted by Murat with a letter for the usurper, and by the usurper with a letter for the Bonapartist committee in Paris. Proof of this crime will be found on arresting him, for the letter will be found upon him, or at his father's, or in his cabin on board the *Pharaon*."

"Very good," resumed Danglars; "now your revenge looks like common-sense, for in no way can it revert to yourself, and the matter will thus work its own way; there is nothing to do now but fold the letter as I am doing, and write upon it, 'To the king's attorney,' and that's all settled." And Danglars wrote the address as he spoke.

"Yes, and that's all settled!" exclaimed Caderousse, who, by a last effort of intellect, had followed the reading of the letter, and instinctively comprehended all the misery which such a denunciation must entail. "Yes, and that's all settled; only it will be an infamous shame;" and he stretched out his hand to reach the letter.

"Yes," said Danglars, taking it from beyond his reach; "and as what I say and do is merely in jest, and I, amongst the first and foremost, should be sorry if anything happened to Dantès—the worthy Dantès—look here!" And taking the letter, he squeezed it up in his hands and threw it into a corner of the arbor.

"All right!" said Caderousse. "Dantès is my friend, and I won't have him ill-used."

"And who thinks of using him ill? Certainly neither I nor Fernand," said Danglars, rising and looking at the young man, who still remained seated, but whose eye was fixed on the denunciatory sheet of paper flung into the corner.

"In this case," replied Caderousse, "let's have some more wine. I wish to drink to the health of Edmond and the lovely Mercédès."

"You have had too much already, drunkard," said Danglars; "and if you continue, you will be compelled to sleep here, because unable to stand on your legs."

"I?" said Caderousse, rising with all the offended dignity of a drunken man, "I can't keep on my legs? Why, I'll wager I can go up into the belfry of the Accoules, and without staggering, too!"

"Done!" said Danglars, "I'll take your bet; but to-morrow—to-day it is time to return. Give me your arm, and let us go."

"Very well, let us go," said Caderousse; "but I don't want your arm at all. Come, Fernand, won't you return to Marseilles with us?"

"No," said Fernand; "I shall return to the Catalans."

"You're wrong. Come with us to Marseilles—come along." — "I will not."

"What do you mean? you will not? Well, just as you like, my prince; there's liberty for all the world. Come along, Danglars, and let the young gentleman return to the Catalans if he chooses."

Danglars took advantage of Caderousse's temper at the moment, to take him off towards Marseilles by the Porte Saint-Victor, staggering as he went.

When they had advanced about twenty yards, Danglars looked back and saw Fernand stoop, pick up the crumpled paper, and putting it into his pocket then rush out of the arbor towards Pillon.

"Well," said Caderousse, "why, what a lie he told! He said he was going to the Catalans, and he is going to the city. Hallo, Fernand!"

"Oh, you don't see straight," said Danglars; "he's gone right enough."

"Well," said Caderousse, "I should have said not—how treacherous wine is!"

"Come, come," said Danglars to himself, "now the thing is at work and it will effect its purpose unassisted."

V

The Marriage-Feast

T HE MORNING'S SUN ROSE clear and resplendent, touching the foamy waves into a network of ruby-tinted light.

The feast had been made ready on the second floor at La Réserve, with whose arbor the reader is already familiar. The apartment destined for the purpose was spacious and lighted by a number of windows, over each of which was written in golden letters for some inexplicable reason the name of one of the principal cities of France; beneath these windows a wooden balcony extended the entire length of the house. And although the entertainment was fixed for twelve o'clock, an hour previous to that time the balcony was filled with impatient and expectant guests, consisting of the favored part of the crew of the *Pharaon*, and other personal friends of the bridegroom, the whole of whom had arrayed themselves in their choicest costumes, in order to do greater honor to the occasion.

Various rumors were afloat to the effect that the owners of the *Pharaon* had promised to attend the nuptial feast; but all seemed unanimous in doubting that an act of such rare and exceeding condescension could possibly be intended.

Danglars, however, who now made his appearance, accompanied by Caderousse, effectually confirmed the report, stating that he

had recently conversed with M. Morrel, who had himself assured
him of his intention to dine at La Réserve.

In fact, a moment later M. Morrel appeared and was saluted
with an enthusiastic burst of applause from the crew of the *Pharaon*,
who hailed the visit of the shipowner as a sure indication that the
man whose wedding feast he thus delighted to honor would ere
long be first in command of the ship; and as Dantès was universally
beloved on board his vessel, the sailors put no restraint on their
tumultuous joy at finding that the opinion and choice of their
superiors so exactly coincided with their own.

With the entrance of M. Morrel, Danglars and Caderousse were
despatched in search of the bridegroom to convey to him the intelligence of the arrival of the important personage whose coming had
created such a lively sensation, and to beseech him to make haste.

Danglars and Caderousse set off upon their errand at full speed;
but ere they had gone many steps they perceived a group advancing towards them, composed of the betrothed pair, a party of young
girls in attendance on the bride, by whose side walked Dantès'
father; the whole brought up by Fernand, whose lips wore their
usual sinister smile.

Neither Mercédès nor Edmond observed the strange expression
of his countenance; they were so happy that they were conscious
only of the sunshine and the presence of each other.

Having acquitted themselves of their errand, and exchanged a
hearty shake of the hand with Edmond, Danglars and Caderousse
took their places beside Fernand and old Dantès,—the latter of
whom attracted universal notice. The old man was attired in a suit of
glistening watered silk, trimmed with steel buttons, beautifully cut
and polished. His thin but wiry legs were arrayed in a pair of richly
embroidered clocked stockings, evidently of English manufacture,
while from his three-cornered hat depended a long streaming knot
of white and blue ribbons. Thus he came along, supporting himself
on a curiously carved stick, his aged countenance lit up with

happiness, looking for all the world like one of the aged dandies of 1796, parading the newly opened gardens of the Tuileries and Luxembourg. Beside him glided Caderousse, whose desire to partake of the good things provided for the wedding-party had induced him to become reconciled to the Dantès, father and son, although there still lingered in his mind a faint and imperfect recollection of the events of the preceding night; just as the brain retains on waking in the morning the dim and misty outline of a dream.

As Danglars approached the disappointed lover, he cast on him a look of deep meaning, while Fernand, as he slowly paced behind the happy pair, who seemed, in their own unmixed content, to have entirely forgotten that such a being as himself existed, was pale and abstracted; occasionally, however, a deep flush would overspread his countenance, and a nervous contraction distort his features, while, with an agitated and restless gaze, he would glance in the direction of Marseilles, like one who either anticipated or foresaw some great and important event.

Dantès himself was simply, but becomingly, clad in the dress peculiar to the merchant service—a costume somewhat between a military and a civil garb; and with his fine countenance, radiant with joy and happiness, a more perfect specimen of manly beauty could scarcely be imagined.

Lovely as the Greek girls of Cyprus or Chios, Mercédès boasted the same bright flashing eyes of jet, and ripe, round, coral lips. She moved with the light, free step of an Arlesienne or an Andalusian. One more practised in the arts of great cities would have hid her blushes beneath a veil, or, at least, have cast down her thickly fringed lashes, so as to have concealed the liquid lustre of her animated eyes; but, on the contrary, the delighted girl looked around her with a smile that seemed to say: "If you are my friends, rejoice with me, for I am very happy."

As soon as the bridal party came in sight of La Réserve, M. Morrel descended and came forth to meet it, followed by the soldiers and sailors there assembled, to whom he had repeated the promise already given, that Dantès should be the successor to the late Captain Leclère. Edmond, at the approach of his patron, respectfully placed the arm of his affianced bride within that of M. Morrel, who, forthwith conducting her up the flight of wooden steps leading to the chamber in which the feast was prepared, was gayly followed by the guests, beneath whose heavy tread the slight structure creaked and groaned for the space of several minutes.

"Father," said Mercédès, stopping when she had reached the centre of the table, "sit, I pray you, on my right hand; on my left I will place him who has ever been as a brother to me," pointing with a soft and gentle smile to Fernand; but her words and look seemed to inflict the direst torture on him, for his lips became ghastly pale, and even beneath the dark hue of his complexion the blood might be seen retreating as though some sudden pang drove it back to the heart.

During this time, Dantès, at the opposite side of the table, had been occupied in similarly placing his most honored guests. M. Morrel was seated at his right hand, Danglars at his left; while, at a sign from Edmond, the rest of the company ranged themselves as they found it most agreeable.

Then they began to pass around the dusky, piquant, Arlesian sausages, and lobsters in their dazzling red cuirasses, prawns of large size and brilliant color, the echinus with its prickly outside and dainty morsel within, the clovis, esteemed by the epicures of the South as more than rivalling the exquisite flavor of the oyster,—all the delicacies, in fact, that are cast up by the wash of waters on the sandy beach, and styled by the grateful fishermen "fruits of the sea."

"A pretty silence truly!" said the old father of the bridegroom, as he carried to his lips a glass of wine of the hue and brightness of the topaz, and which had just been placed before Mercédès herself. "Now, would anybody think that this room contained a happy, merry party, who desire nothing better than to laugh and dance the hours away?"

"Ah," sighed Caderousse, "a man cannot always feel happy because he is about to be married."

"The truth is," replied Dantès, "that I am too happy for noisy mirth; if that is what you meant by your observation, my worthy friend, you are right; joy takes a strange effect at times, it seems to oppress us almost the same as sorrow."

Danglars looked towards Fernand, whose excitable nature received and betrayed each fresh impression.

"Why, what ails you?" asked he of Edmond. "Do you fear any approaching evil? I should say that you were the happiest man alive at this instant."

"And that is the very thing that alarms me," returned Dantès. "Man does not appear to me to be intended to enjoy felicity so unmixed; happiness is like the enchanted palaces we read of in our childhood, where fierce, fiery dragons defend the entrance and approach; and monsters of all shapes and kinds, requiring to be overcome ere victory is ours. I own that I am lost in wonder to find myself promoted to an honor of which I feel myself unworthy—that of being the husband of Mercédès."

"Nay, nay!" cried Caderousse, smiling, "you have not attained that honor yet. Mercédès is not yet your wife. Just assume the tone and manner of a husband, and see how she will remand you that your hour is not yet come!"

The bride blushed, while Fernand, restless and uneasy, seemed to start at every fresh sound, and from time to time wiped away the large drops of perspiration that gathered on his brow.

"Well, never mind that, neighbor Caderousse; it is not worth while to contradict me for such a trifle as that. 'Tis true that Mercédès is not actually my wife; but," added he, drawing out his watch, "in an hour and a half she will be."

A general exclamation of surprise ran round the table, with the exception of the elder Dantès, whose laugh displayed the still perfect beauty of his large white teeth. Mercédès looked pleased and

gratified, while Fernand grasped the handle of his knife with a convulsive clutch.

"In an hour?" inquired Danglars, turning pale. "How is that, my
friend?"

"Why, thus it is," replied Dantès. "Thanks to the influence of
M. Morrel, to whom, next to my father, I owe every blessing I
enjoy, every difficulty has been removed. We have purchased permission to waive the usual delay; and at halfpast two o'clock the
mayor of Marseilles will be waiting for us at the city hall. Now, as
a quarter-past one has already struck, I do not consider I have
asserted too much in saying, that in another hour and thirty minutes Mercédès will have become Madame Dantès."

Fernand closed his eyes, a burning sensation passed across his
brow, and he was compelled to support himself by the table to prevent his falling from his chair; but in spite of all his efforts, he could
not refrain from uttering a deep groan, which, however, was lost
amid the noisy felicitations of the company.

"Upon my word," cried the old man, "you make short work of
this kind of affair. Arrived here only yesterday morning, and married to-day at three o'clock! Commend me to a sailor for going the
quick way to work!"

"But," asked Danglars, in a timid tone, "how did you manage
about the other formalities—the contract—the settlement?"

"The contract," answered Dantès, laughingly, "it didn't take long
to fix that. Mercédès has no fortune; I have none to settle on her. So,
you see, our papers were quickly written out, and certainly do not
come very expensive." This joke elicited a fresh burst of applause.

"So that what we presumed to be merely the betrothal feast
turns out to be the actual wedding dinner!" said Danglars.

"No, no," answered Dantès; "don't imagine I am going to put
you off in that shabby manner. To-morrow morning I start for
Paris; four days to go, and the same to return, with one day to
discharge the commission intrusted to me, is all the time I shall be

absent. I shall be back here by the first of March, and on the second I give my real marriage feast."

This prospect of fresh festivity redoubled the hilarity of the guests to such a degree, that the elder Dantès, who, at the commencement of the repast, had commented upon the silence that prevailed, now found it difficult, amid the general din of voices, to obtain a moment's tranquillity in which to drink to the health and prosperity of the bride and bridegroom.

Dantès, perceiving the affectionate eagerness of his father, responded by a look of grateful pleasure; while Mercédès glanced at the clock and made an expressive gesture to Edmond.

Around the table reigned that noisy hilarity which usually prevails at such a time among people sufficiently free from the demands of social position not to feel the trammels of etiquette. Such as at the commencement of the repast had not been able to seat themselves according to their inclination, rose unceremoniously, and sought out more agreeable companions. Everybody talked at once, without waiting for a reply and each one seemed to be contented with expressing his or her own thoughts.

Fernand's paleness appeared to have communicated itself to Danglars. As for Fernand himself, he seemed to be enduring the tortures of the damned; unable to rest, he was among the first to quit the table, and, as though seeking to avoid the hilarious mirth that rose in such deafening sounds, he continued, in utter silence, to pace the farther end of the salon.

Caderousse approached him just as Danglars, whom Fernand seemed most anxious to avoid, had joined him in a corner of the room.

"Upon my word," said Caderousse, from whose mind the friendly treatment of Dantès, united with the effect of the excellent wine he had partaken of, had effaced every feeling of envy or jealousy at Dantès' good fortune,—"upon my word, Dantès is a downright good fellow, and when I see him sitting there beside his pretty wife that is so soon to be, I cannot help thinking it would have been a great pity to have served him that trick you were planning yesterday."

"Oh, there was no harm meant," answered Danglars; "at first I certainly did feel somewhat uneasy as to what Fernand might be tempted to do; but when I saw how completely he had mastered his feelings, even so far as to become one of his rival's attendants, I knew there was no further cause for apprehension." Caderousse looked full at Fernand—he was ghastly pale.

"Certainly," continued Danglars, "the sacrifice was no trifling one, when the beauty of the bride is concerned. Upon my soul, that future captain of mine is a lucky dog! Gad, I only wish he would let me take his place."

"Shall we not set forth?" asked the sweet, silvery voice of Mercédès; "two o'clock has just struck, and you know we are expected in a quarter of an hour."

"To be sure!—to be sure!" cried Dantès, eagerly quitting the table; "let us go directly!"

His words were re-echoed by the whole party, with vociferous cheers.

At this moment Danglars, who had been incessantly observing every change in Fernand's look and manner, saw him stagger and fall back, with an almost convulsive spasm, against a seat placed near one of the open windows. At the same instant his ear caught a sort of indistinct sound on the stairs, followed by the measured tread of soldiery, with the clanking of swords and military accoutrements; then came a hum and buzz as of many voices, so as to deaden even the noisy mirth of the bridal party, among whom a vague feeling of curiosity and apprehension quelled every disposition to talk, and almost instantaneously the most deathlike stillness prevailed.

The sounds drew nearer. Three blows were struck upon the panel of the door. The company looked at each other in consternation.

"I demand admittance," said a loud voice outside the room, "in the name of the law!" As no attempt was made to prevent it, the door was opened, and a magistrate, wearing his official scarf, presented himself, followed by four soldiers and a corporal. Uneasiness now yielded to the most extreme dread on the part of those present.

"May I venture to inquire the reason of this unexpected visit?" said M. Morrel, addressing the magistrate, whom he evidently knew; "there is doubtless some mistake easily explained."

"If it be so," replied the magistrate, "rely upon every reparation being made; meanwhile, I am the bearer of an order of arrest, and although I most reluctantly perform the task assigned me, it must, nevertheless, be fulfilled. Who among the persons here assembled answers to the name of Edmond Dantès?" Every eye was turned towards the young man who, spite of the agitation he could not but feel, advanced with dignity, and said, in a firm voice, "I am he; what is your pleasure with me?"

"Edmond Dantès," replied the magistrate, "I arrest you in the name of the law!"—"Me!" repeated Edmond, slightly changing color, "and wherefore, I pray?"

"I cannot inform you, but you will be duly acquainted with the reasons that have rendered such a step necessary at the preliminary examination."

M. Morrel felt that further resistance or remonstrance was useless. He saw before him an officer delegated to enforce the law, and perfectly well knew that it would be as unavailing to seek pity from a magistrate decked with his official scarf, as to address a petition to some cold marble effigy. Old Dantès, however, sprang forward. There are situations which the heart of a father or a mother cannot be made to understand. He prayed and supplicated in terms so moving, that even the officer was touched; and, although firm in his duty, he kindly said, "My worthy friend, let me beg of you to calm your apprehensions. Your son has probably neglected some prescribed form or attention in registering his cargo, and it is more than probable he will be set at liberty directly he has given the information required, whether touching the health of his crew, or the value of his freight."

"What is the meaning of all this?" inquired Caderousse, frowningly, of Danglars, who had assumed an air of utter surprise.

"How can I tell you?" replied he; "I am, like yourself, utterly bewildered at all that is going on, and cannot in the least make out what it is about." Caderousse then looked around for Fernand, but he had disappeared.

The scene of the previous night now came back to his mind with startling clearness. The painful catastrophe he had just witnessed appeared effectually to have rent away the veil which the intoxication of the evening before had raised between himself and his memory.

"So, so," said he, in a hoarse and choking voice, to Danglars, "this, then, I suppose, is a part of the trick you were concerting yesterday? All I can say is, that if it be so, 'tis an ill turn, and well deserves to bring double evil on those who have projected it."

"Nonsense," returned Danglars, "I tell you again I have nothing whatever to do with it; besides, you know very well that I tore the paper to pieces."

"No, you did not!" answered Caderousse, "you merely threw it by—I saw it lying in a corner."—"Hold your tongue, you fool!— what should you know about it?—why, you were drunk!"

"Where is Fernand?" inquired Caderousse.—"How do I know?" replied Danglars; "gone, as every prudent man ought to be, to look after his own affairs, most likely. Never mind where he is, let you and I go and see what is to be done for our poor friends."

During this conversation, Dantès, after having exchanged a cheerful shake of the hand with all his sympathizing friends, had surrendered himself to the officer sent to arrest him, merely saying, "Make yourselves quite easy, my good fellows, there is some little mistake to clear up, that's all, depend upon it; and very likely I may not have to go so far as the prison to effect that."

"Oh, to be sure!" responded Danglars, who had now approached the group, "nothing more than a mistake, I feel quite certain."

Dantès descended the staircase, preceded by the magistrate, and followed by the soldiers. A carriage awaited him at the door; he got in, followed by two soldiers and the magistrate, and the vehicle drove off towards Marseilles.

"Adieu, adieu, dearest Edmond!" cried Mercédès, stretching out her arms to him from the balcony.

The prisoner heard the cry, which sounded like the sob of a broken heart, and leaning from the coach he called out, "Good-by, Mercédès—we shall soon meet again!" Then the vehicle disappeared round one of the turnings of Fort Saint-Nicolas.

"Wait for me here, all of you!" cried M. Morrel; "I will take the first conveyance I find, and hurry to Marseilles, whence I will bring you word how all is going on."

"That's right!" exclaimed a multitude of voices; "go, and return as quickly as you can!"

This second departure was followed by a long and fearful state of terrified silence on the part of those who were left behind. The old father and Mercédès remained for some time apart, each absorbed in grief; but at length the two poor victims of the same blow raised their eyes, and with a simultaneous burst of feeling rushed into each other's arms.

Meanwhile Fernand made his appearance, poured out for himself a glass of water with a trembling hand; then hastily swallowing it, went to sit down at the first vacant place, and this was, by mere chance, placed next to the seat on which poor Mercédès had fallen half fainting, when released from the warm and affectionate embrace of old Dantès. Instinctively Fernand drew back his chair.

"He is the cause of all this misery—I am quite sure of it," whispered Caderousse, who had never taken his eyes off Fernand, to Danglars.

"I don't think so," answered the other; he's too stupid to imagine such a scheme. I only hope the mischief will fall upon the head of whoever wrought it."

"You don't mention those who aided and abetted the deed," said Caderousse.

"Surely," answered Danglars, "one cannot be held responsible for every chance arrow shot into the air."

"You can, indeed, when the arrow lights point downward on somebody's head."

Meantime the subject of the arrest was being canvassed in every different form.

"What think you, Danglars," said one of the party, turning towards him, "of this event?"

"Why," replied he, "I think it just possible Dantès may have been detected with some trifling article on board ship considered here as contraband."

"But how could he have done so without your knowledge, Danglars, since you are the ship's supercargo?"

"Why, as for that, I could only know what I was told respecting the merchandise with which the vessel was laden. I know she was loaded with cotton, and that she took in her freight at Alexandria from Pastret's warehouse, and at Smyrna from Pascal's; that is all I was obliged to know, and I beg I may not be asked for any further particulars."

"Now I recollect," said the afflicted old father; "my poor boy told me yesterday he had got a small case of coffee, and another of tobacco for me!"

"There, you see," exclaimed Danglars. "Now the mischief is out; depend upon it the custom-house people went rummaging about the ship in our absence, and discovered poor Dantès' hidden treasures."

Mercédès, however, paid no heed to this explanation of her lover's arrest. Her grief, which she had hitherto tried to restrain, now burst out in a violent fit of hysterical sobbing.

"Come, come," said the old man, "be comforted, my poor child; there is still hope!"—"Hope!" repeated Danglars.

"Hope!" faintly murmured Fernand; but the word seemed to die away on his pale agitated lips, and a convulsive spasm passed over his countenance.

"Good news! good news!" shouted forth one of the party stationed in the balcony on the lookout. "Here comes M. Morrel back. No doubt, now, we shall hear that our friend is released!"

Mercédès and the old man rushed to meet the shipowner and greeted him at the door. He was very pale.

"What news?" exclaimed a general burst of voices.

"Alas, my friends," replied M. Morrel, with a mournful shake of his head, "the thing has assumed a more serious aspect than I expected."

"Oh, indeed—indeed, sir, he is innocent!" sobbed forth Mercédès.

"That I believe!" answered M. Morrel; "but still he is charged"—

"With what?" inquired the elder Dantès.

"With being an agent of the Bonapartist faction!" Many of my readers may be able to recollect how formidable such an accusation became in the period at which our story is dated.

A despairing cry escaped the pale lips of Mercédès; the old man sank into a chair.

"Ah, Danglars!" whispered Caderousse, "you have deceived me—the trick you spoke of last night has been played; but I cannot suffer a poor old man or an innocent girl to die of grief through your fault. I am determined to tell them all about it."

"Be silent, you simpleton!" cried Danglars, grasping him by the arm, "or I will not answer even for your own safety. Who can tell whether Dantès be innocent or guilty? The vessel did touch at Elba, where he quitted it, and passed a whole day in the island. Now, should any letters or other documents of a compromising character be found upon him, will it not be taken for granted that all who uphold him are his accomplices?"

With the rapid instinct of selfishness, Caderousse readily perceived the solidity of this mode of reasoning; he gazed, doubtfully, wistfully, on Danglars, and then caution supplanted generosity.

"Suppose we wait a while, and see what comes of it," said he, casting a bewildered look on his companion.

"To be sure!" answered Danglars. "Let us wait, by all means. If he be innocent, of course he will be set at liberty; if guilty, why, it is no use involving ourselves in a conspiracy."

"Let us go, then. I cannot stay here any longer."

"With all my heart!" replied Danglars, pleased to find the other so tractable. "Let us take ourselves out of the way, and leave things for the present to take their course."

After their departure, Fernand, who had now again become the friend and protector of Mercédès, led the girl to her home, while the friends of Dantès conducted the now half-fainting man back to his abode.

The rumor of Edmond's arrest as a Bonapartist agent was not slow in circulating throughout the city.

"Could you ever have credited such a thing, my dear Danglars?" asked M. Morrel, as, on his return to the port for the purpose of gleaning fresh tidings of Dantès, from M. de Villefort, the assistant procureur, he overtook his supercargo and Caderousse. "Could you have believed such a thing possible?"

"Why, you know I told you," replied Danglars, "that I considered the circumstance of his having anchored at the Island of Elba as a very suspicious circumstance."

"And did you mention these suspicions to any person beside myself?"

"Certainly not!" returned Danglars. Then added in a low whisper, "You understand that, on account of your uncle, M. Policar Morrel, who served under the other government, and who does not altogether conceal what he thinks on the subject, you are strongly suspected of regretting the abdication of Napoleon. I should have feared to injure both Edmond and yourself, had I divulged my own apprehensions to a soul. I am too well aware that though a subordinate, like myself, is bound to acquaint the shipowner with everything that occurs, there are many things he ought most carefully to conceal from all else."

"'Tis well, Danglars—'tis well!" replied M. Morrel. "You are a worthy fellow; and I had already thought of your interests in the event of poor Edmond having become captain of the *Pharaon*."— "Is it possible you were so kind?"

"Yes, indeed; I had previously inquired of Dantès what was his opinion of you, and if he should have any reluctance to continue you in your post, for somehow I have perceived a sort of coolness between you."—"And what was his reply?"

"That he certainly did think he had given you offence in an affair which he merely referred to without entering into particulars, but that whoever possessed the good opinion and confidence of the ship's owner would have his preference also."

"The hypocrite!" murmured Danglars.

"Poor Dantès!" said Caderousse. "No one can deny his being a noble-hearted young fellow."

"But meanwhile," continued M. Morrel, "here is the *Pharaon* without a captain."

"Oh," replied Danglars, "since we cannot leave this port for the next three months, let us hope that ere the expiration of that period Dantès will be set at liberty."—"No doubt; but in the meantime?"

"I am entirely at your service, M. Morrel," answered Danglars. "You know that I am as capable of managing a ship as the most experienced captain in the service; and it will be so far advantageous to you to accept my services, that upon Edmond's release from prison no further change will be requisite on board the *Pharaon* than for Dantès and myself each to resume our respective posts."

"Thanks, Danglars—that will smooth over all difficulties. I fully authorize you at once to assume the command of the *Pharaon*, and look carefully to the unloading of her freight. Private misfortunes must never be allowed to interfere with business."

"Be easy on that score, M. Morrel; but do you think we shall be permitted to see our poor Edmond?"

"I will let you know that directly I have seen M. de Villefort, whom I shall endeavor to interest in Edmond's favor. I am aware he is a furious royalist; but, in spite of that, and of his being king's attorney, he is a man like ourselves, and I fancy not a bad sort of one."

"Perhaps not," replied Danglars; "but I hear that he is ambitious, and that's rather against him."

"Well, well," returned M. Morrel, "we shall see. But now hasten on board, I will join you there ere long." So saying, the worthy shipowner quitted the two allies, and proceeded in the direction of the Palais de Justice.

"You see," said Danglars, addressing Caderousse, "the turn things have taken. Do you still feel any desire to stand up in his defence?"

"Not the slightest, but yet it seems to me a shocking thing that a mere joke should lead to such consequences."

"But who perpetrated that joke, let me ask? neither you nor myself, but Fernand; you knew very well that I threw the paper into a corner of the room—indeed, I fancied I had destroyed it."

"Oh, no," replied Caderousse, "that I can answer for, you did not. I only wish I could see it now as plainly as I saw it lying all crushed and crumpled in a corner of the arbor."

"Well, then, if you did, depend upon it, Fernand picked it up, and either copied it or caused it to be copied; perhaps, even, he did not take the trouble of recopying it. And now I think of it, by Heavens, he may have sent the letter itself! Fortunately, for me, the handwriting was disguised."

"Then you were aware of Dantès being engaged in a conspiracy?"

"Not I. As I before said, I thought the whole thing was a joke, nothing more. It seems, however, that I have unconsciously stumbled upon the truth."

"Still," argued Caderousse, "I would give a great deal if nothing of the kind had happened; or, at least, that I had had no hand in it. You will see, Danglars, that it will turn out an unlucky job for both of us."

"Nonsense! If any harm come of it, it should fall on the guilty person; and that, you know, is Fernand. How can we be implicated in any way? All we have got to do is, to keep our own counsel, and remain perfectly quiet, not breathing a word to any living soul; and you will see that the storm will pass away without in the least affecting us."

"Amen!" responded Caderousse, waving his hand in token of adieu to Danglars, and bending his steps towards the Allées de Meillan, moving his head to and fro, and muttering as he went, after the manner of one whose mind was overcharged with one absorbing idea.

"So far, then," said Danglars, mentally, "all has gone as I would have it. I am, temporarily, commander of the *Pharaon*, with the certainty of being permanently so, if that fool of a Caderousse can be persuaded to hold his tongue. My only fear is the chance of Dantès being released. But, there, he is in the hands of Justice; and," added he with a smile, "she will take her own." So saying, he leaped into a boat, desiring to be rowed on board the *Pharaon*, where M. Morrel had agreed to meet him.

VI

The Deputy Procureur du Roi

IN ONE OF THE aristocratic mansions built by Puget in the Rue du Grand Cours opposite the Medusa fountain, a second marriage feast was being celebrated, almost at the same hour with the nuptial repast given by Dantès. In this case, however, although the occasion of the entertainment was similar, the company was strikingly dissimilar. Instead of a rude mixture of sailors, soldiers, and those belonging to the humblest grade of life, the present assembly was composed of the very flower of Marseilles society,—magistrates who had resigned their office during the usurper's reign; officers who had deserted from the imperial army and joined forces with Condé; and younger members of families, brought up to hate and execrate the man whom five years of exile would convert into a martyr, and fifteen of restoration elevate to the rank of a god.

The guests were still at table, and the heated and energetic conversation that prevailed betrayed the violent and vindictive passions that then agitated each dweller of the South, where, unhappily, for five centuries religions strife had long given increased bitterness to the violence of party feeling.

The emperor, now king of the petty Island of Elba, after having held sovereign sway over one-half of the world, counting as his subjects a small population of five or six thousand souls,—after having been accustomed to hear the "*Vive Napoléons*" of a hundred and twenty millions of human beings, uttered in ten different languages,—was looked upon here as a ruined man, separated forever from any fresh connection with France or claim to her throne.

The magistrates freely discussed their political views; the military part of the company talked unreservedly of Moscow and Leipsic, while the women commented on the divorce of Josephine. It was not over the downfall of the man, but over the defeat of the Napoleonic idea, that they rejoiced, and in this they foresaw for themselves the bright and cheering prospect of a revivified political existence.

An old man, decorated with the cross of Saint Louis, now rose and proposed the health of King Louis XVIII. It was the Marquis de Saint-Méran. This toast, recalling at once the patient exile of Hartwell and the peace-loving King of France, excited universal enthusiasm; glasses were elevated in the air *à l'Anglais*, and the ladies, snatching their bouquets from their fair bosoms, strewed the table with their floral treasures. In a word, an almost poetical fervor prevailed.

"Ah," said the Marquise de Saint-Méran, a woman with a stern, forbidding eye, though still noble and distinguished in appearance, despite her fifty years—"ah, these revolutionists, who have driven us from those very possessions they afterwards purchased for a mere trifle during the Reign of Terror, would be compelled to own, were they here, that all true devotion was on our side, since we were content to follow the fortunes of a falling monarch, while they, on the contrary, made their fortune by worshipping the rising sun; yes, yes, they could not help admitting that the king, for whom we sacrificed rank, wealth, and station was truly our 'Louis the well-beloved,' while their wretched usurper has been, and ever will be, to them their evil genius, their 'Napoleon the accursed.' Am I not right, Villefort?"

"I beg your pardon, madame. I really must pray you to excuse me, but—in truth—I was not attending to the conversation."

"Marquise, marquise!" interposed the old nobleman who had proposed the toast, "let the young people alone; let me tell you, on one's wedding day there are more agreeable subjects of conversation than dry politics."

"Never mind, dearest mother," said a young and lovely girl, with a profusion of light brown hair, and eyes that seemed to float in liquid crystal, "'tis all my fault for seizing upon M. de Villefort, so as to prevent his listening to what you said. But there—now take him—he is your own for as long as you like. M. Villefort, I beg to remind you my mother speaks to you."

"If the marquise will deign to repeat the words I but imperfectly caught, I shall be delighted to answer," said M. de Villefort.

"Never mind, Renée," replied the marquise, with a look of tenderness that seemed out of keeping with her harsh dry features; but, however all other feelings may be withered in a woman's nature, there is always one bright smiling spot in the desert of her heart, and that is the shrine of maternal love. "I forgive you. What I was saying, Villefort, was, that the Bonapartists had not our sincerity, enthusiasm, or devotion."

"They had, however, what supplied the place of those fine qualities," replied the young man, "and that was fanaticism. Napoleon is the Mahomet of the West, and is worshipped by his commonplace but ambitious followers, not only as a leader and lawgiver, but also as the personification of equality."

"He!" cried the marquise; "Napoleon the type of equality! For mercy's sake, then, what would you call Robespierre? Come, come, do not strip the latter of his just rights to bestow them on the Corsican, who, to my mind, has usurped quite enough."

"Nay, madame; I would place each of these heroes on his right pedestal—that of Robespierre on his scaffold in the Place Louis Quinze; that of Napoleon on the column of the Place Vendôme. The only difference consists in the opposite character of the equality advocated by these two men; one is the equality that elevates, the other is the equality that degrades; one brings a king within reach of the guillotine, the other elevates the people to a level with the throne. Observe," said Villefort, smiling, "I do not mean to deny that both these men were revolutionary scoundrels, and that the 9th Thermidor and the 4th of April, in the year 1814, were lucky days for France, worthy of being gratefully remembered by every friend to monarchy and civil order; and that explains how it comes to pass that, fallen, as I trust he is forever, Napoleon has still retained a train of parasitical satellites. Still, marquise, it has been so with other usurpers—Cromwell, for instance, who was not half so bad as Napoleon, had his partisans and advocates."

"Do you know, Villefort, that you are talking in a most dreadfully revolutionary strain? But I excuse it; it is impossible to expect the son of a Girondin to be free from a small spice of the old leaven." A deep crimson suffused the countenance of Villefort.

"'Tis true, madame," answered he, "that my father was a Girondin, but he was not among the number of those who voted for the king's death; he was an equal sufferer with yourself during the Reign of Terror, and had well-nigh lost his head on the same scaffold on which your father perished."

"True," replied the marquise, without wincing in the slightest degree at the tragic remembrance thus called up; "but bear in mind, if you please, that our respective parents underwent persecution and proscription from diametrically opposite principles; in proof of which I may remark, that while my family remained among the stanchest adherents of the exiled princes, your father lost no time in joining the new government; and that while the Citizen Noirtier was a Girondin, the Count Noirtier became a senator."

"Dear mother," interposed Renée, "you know very well it was agreed that all these disagreeable reminiscences should forever be laid aside."

"Suffer me, also, madame," replied Villefort, "to add my earnest request to Mademoiselle de Saint-Méran's, that you will kindly allow the veil of oblivion to cover and conceal the past. What avails recrimination over matters wholly past recall? For my own part, I have laid aside even the name of my father, and altogether disown his political principles. He was—nay, probably may still be—a Bonapartist, and is called Noirtier; I, on the contrary, am a stanch royalist, and style myself de Villefort. Let what may remain of revolutionary sap exhaust itself and die away with the old trunk, and condescend only to regard the young shoot which has started up at a distance from the parent tree, without having the power, any more than the wish, to separate entirely from the stock from which it sprung."

"Bravo, Villefort!" cried the marquis; "excellently well said! Come, now, I have hopes of obtaining what I have been for years endeavoring to persuade the marquise to promise; namely, a perfect amnesty and forgetfulness of the past."

"With all my heart," replied the marquise; "let the past be forever forgotten. I promise you it affords *me* as little pleasure to revive it as it does you. All I ask is, that Villefort will be firm and inflexible for the future in his political principles. Remember, also, Villefort, that we have pledged ourselves to his majesty for your fealty and strict loyalty, and that at our recommendation the king consented to forget the past, as I do" (and here she extended to him her hand)—"as I now do at your entreaty. But bear in mind, that should there fall in your way any one guilty of conspiring against the government, you will be so much the more bound to visit the offence with rigorous punishment, as it is known you belong to a suspected family."

"Alas, madame," returned Villefort, "my profession, as well as the times in which we live, compels me to be severe. I have already successfully conducted several public prosecutions, and brought the offenders to merited punishment. But we have not done with the thing yet."

"Do you, indeed, think so?" inquired the marquise.

"I am, at least, fearful of it. Napoleon, in the Island of Elba, is too near France, and his proximity keeps up the hopes of his partisans. Marseilles is filled with half-pay officers, who are daily, under one frivolous pretext or other, getting up quarrels with the royalists; from hence arise continual and fatal duels among the higher classes of persons, and assassinations in the lower."

"You have heard, perhaps," said the Comte de Salvieux, one of M. de Saint-Méran's oldest friends, and chamberlain to the Comte d'Artois, "that the Holy Alliance purpose removing him from thence?"

"Yes; they were talking about it when we left Paris," said M. de Saint-Méran; "and where is it decided to transfer him?"—"To Saint Helena."

"For heaven's sake, where is that?" asked the marquise.

"An island situated on the other side of the equator, at least two thousand leagues from here," replied the count.

"So much the better. As Villefort observes, it is a great act of folly to have left such a man between Corsica, where he was born, and Naples, of which his brother-in-law is king, and face to face with Italy, the sovereignty of which he coveted for his son."

"Unfortunately," said Villefort, "there are the treaties of 1814, and we cannot molest Napoleon without breaking those compacts."

"Oh, well, we shall find some way out of it," responded M. de Salvieux. "There wasn't any trouble over treaties when it was a question of shooting the poor Duc d'Engbien."

"Well," said the marquise, "it seems probable that, by the aid of the Holy Alliance, we shall be rid of Napoleon; and we must trust to the vigilance of M. de Villefort to purify Marseilles of his partisans. The king is either a king or no king; if he be acknowledged as sovereign of France, he should be upheld in peace and tranquillity; and this can best be effected by employing the most inflexible agents to put down every attempt at conspiracy—'tis the best and surest means of preventing mischief."

"Unfortunately, madame," answered Villefort, "the strong arm of the law is not called upon to interfere until the evil has taken place."

"Then all he has got to do is to endeavor to repair it."

"Nay, madame, the law is frequently powerless to effect this; all it can do is to avenge the wrong done."

"Oh, M. de Villefort," cried a beautiful young creature, daughter to the Comte de Salvieux, and the cherished friend of Mademoiselle de Saint-Méran, "do try and get up some famous trial while we are at Marseilles. I never was in a law-court; I am told it is so very amusing!"

"Amusing, certainly," replied the young man, "inasmuch as, instead of shedding tears as at the fictitious tale of woe produced at a theatre, you behold in a law-court a case of real and genuine distress—a drama of life. The prisoner whom you there see pale, agitated, and alarmed, instead of—as is the case when a curtain falls on a tragedy—going home to sup peacefully with his family, and then retiring to rest, that he may recommence his mimic woes on the morrow,—is removed from your sight merely to be reconducted to his prison and delivered up to the executioner. I leave you to judge how far your nerves are calculated to bear you through such a scene. Of this, however, be assured, that should any favorable opportunity present itself, I will not fail to offer you the choice of being present."

"For shame, M. de Villefort!" said Renée, becoming quite pale; "don't you see how you are frightening us?—and yet you laugh."

"What would you have? 'Tis like a duel. I have already recorded sentence of death, five or six times, against the movers of political conspiracies, and who can say how many daggers may be ready sharpened, and only waiting a favorable opportunity to be buried in my heart?"

"Gracious heavens, M. de Villefort," said Renée, becoming more and more terrified; "you surely are not in earnest."

"Indeed I am," replied the young magistrate with a smile; "and in the interesting trial that young lady is anxious to witness, the case would only be still more aggravated. Suppose, for instance, the prisoner, as is more than probable, to have served under Napoleon—well, can you expect for an instant, that one accustomed, at the word of his commander, to rush fearlessly on the very bayonets of his foe, will scruple more to drive a stiletto into the heart of one he knows to be his personal enemy, than to slaughter his fellow-creatures, merely because bidden to do so by one he is bound to obey? Besides, one requires the excitement of being hateful in the eyes of the accused, in order to lash one's self into a state of sufficient vehemence and power. I would not choose to see the man against whom I pleaded smile, as though in mockery of my words. No; my pride is to see the accused pale, agitated, and as though beaten out of all composure by the fire of my eloquence." Renée uttered a smothered exclamation.

"Bravo!" cried one of the guests; "that is what I call talking to some purpose."

"Just the person we require at a time like the present," said a second.

"What a splendid business that last case of yours was, my dear Villefort!" remarked a third; "I mean the trial of the man for murdering his father. Upon my word, you killed him ere the executioner had laid his hand upon him."

"Oh, as for parricides, and such dreadful people as that," interposed Renée, "it matters very little what is done to them; but as regards poor unfortunate creatures whose only crime consists in having mixed themselves up in political intrigues"—

"Why, that is the very worst offence they could possibly commit; for, don't you see, Renée, the king is the father of his people, and he who shall plot or contrive aught against the life and safety of the parent of thirty-two millions of souls, is a parricide upon a fearfully great scale?"

"I don't know anything about that," replied Renée; "but, M. de Villefort, you have promised me—have you not?—always to show mercy to those I plead for."

"Make yourself quite easy on that point," answered Villefort, with one of his sweetest smiles; "you and I will always consult upon our verdicts."

"My love," said the marquise, "attend to your doves, your lap-dogs, and embroidery, but do not meddle with what you do not understand. Nowadays the military profession is in abeyance and the magisterial robe is the badge of honor. There is a wise Latin proverb that is very much in point."

"*Cedant arma togæ*," said Villefort with a bow.

"I cannot speak Latin," responded the marquise.

"Well," said Renée, "I cannot help regretting you had not chosen some other profession than your own—a physician, for instance. Do you know I always felt a shudder at the idea of even a *destroying* angel?"

"Dear, good Renée," whispered Villefort, as he gazed with unutterable tenderness on the lovely speaker.

"Let us hope, my child," cried the marquis, "that M. de Villefort may prove the moral and political physician of this province; if so, he will have achieved a noble work."

"And one which will go far to efface the recollection of his father's conduct," added the incorrigible marquise.

"Madame," replied Villefort, with a mournful smile, "I have already had the honor to observe that my father has—at least, I hope so—abjured his past errors, and that he is, at the present moment, a firm and zealous friend to religion and order—a better royalist, possibly, than his son; for he has to atone for past dereliction, while I have no other impulse than warm, decided preference and conviction." Having made this well-turned speech, Villefort looked carefully around to mark the effect of his oratory, much as he would have done had he been addressing the bench in open court.

"Do you know, my dear Villefort," cried the Comte de Salvieux, "that is exactly what I myself said the other day at the Tuileries, when questioned by his majesty's principal chamberlain touching the singularity of an alliance between the son of a Girondin and the daughter of an officer of the Duc de Condé; and I assure you he seemed fully to comprehend that this mode of reconciling political differences was based upon sound and excellent principles. Then the king, who, without our suspecting it, had overheard our conversation, interrupted us by saying, 'Villefort'—observe that the king did not pronounce the word Noirtier, but, on the contrary, placed considerable emphasis on that of Villefort—'Villefort,' said his majesty, 'is a young man of great judgment and discretion, who will be sure to make a figure in his profession; I like him much, and it gave me great pleasure to hear that he was about to become the son-in-law of the Marquis and Marquise de Saint-Méran. I should myself have recommended the match, had not the noble marquis anticipated my wishes by requesting my consent to it.'"

"Is it possible the king could have condescended so far as to express himself so favorably of me?" asked the enraptured Villefort.

"I give you his very words; and if the marquis chooses to be candid, he will confess that they perfectly agree with what his majesty said to him, when he went six months ago to consult him upon the subject of your espousing his daughter."

"That is true," answered the marquis.

"How much do I owe this gracious prince! What is there I would not do to evince my earnest gratitude!"

"That is right," cried the marquise. "I love to see you thus. Now, then, were a conspirator to fall into your hands, he would be most welcome."

"For my part, dear mother," interposed Renée, "I trust your wishes will not prosper, and that Providence will only permit petty offenders, poor debtors, and miserable cheats to fall into M. de Villefort's hands,—then I shall be contented."

"Just the same as though you prayed that a physician might only be called upon to prescribe for headaches, measles, and the stings of wasps, or any other slight affection of the epidermis. If you wish to see me the king's attorney, you must desire for me some of those violent and dangerous diseases from the cure of which so much honor redounds to the physician."

At this moment, and as though the utterance of Villefort's wish had sufficed to effect its accomplishment, a servant entered the room, and whispered a few words in his ear. Villefort immediately rose from table and quitted the room upon the plea of urgent business; he soon, however, returned, his whole face beaming with delight. Renée regarded him with fond affection; and certainly his handsome features, lit up as they then were with more than usual fire and animation, seemed formed to excite the innocent admiration with which she gazed on her graceful and intelligent lover.

"You were wishing just now." said Villefort, addressing her, "that I were a doctor instead of a lawyer. Well, I at least resemble the disciples of Esculapius in one thing—that of not being able to call a day my own, not even that of my betrothal."

"And wherefore were you called away just now?" asked Mademoiselle de Saint-Méran, with an air of deep interest

"For a very serious matter, which bids fair to make work for the executioner."

"How dreadful!" exclaimed Renée, turning pale.

"Is it possible?" burst simultaneously from all who were near enough to the magistrate to hear his words.

"Why, if my information prove correct, a sort of Bonaparte conspiracy has just been discovered.

"Can I believe my ears?" cried the marquise.

"I will read you the letter containing the accusation, at least," said Villefort:—

"'The king's attorney is informed by a friend to the throne and the religious institutions of his country, that one named Edmond Dantès, mate of the ship *Pharaon*, this day arrived from Smyrna, after having touched at Naples and Porto-Ferrajo, has been the bearer of a letter from Murat to the usurper, and again taken charge of another letter from the usurper to the Bonapartist club in Paris. Ample corroboration of this statement may be obtained by arresting the above-mentioned Edmond Dantès, who either carries the letter for Paris about with him, or has it at his father's abode. Should it not be found in the possession of father or son, then it will assuredly be discovered in the cabin belonging to the said Dantès on board the *Pharaon*.'"

"But," said Renée, "this letter, which, after all, is but an anonymous scrawl, is not even addressed to you, but to the king's attorney."

"True; but that gentleman being absent, his secretary, by his orders, opened his letters; thinking this one of importance, he sent for me, but not finding me, took upon himself to give the necessary orders for arresting the accused party."

"Then the guilty person is absolutely in custody?" said the marquise.

"Nay, dear mother, say the accused person. You know we cannot yet pronounce him guilty."

"He is in safe custody," answered Villefort; "and rely upon it, if the letter is found, he will not be likely to be trusted abroad again, unless he goes forth under the especial protection of the headsman."

"And where is the unfortunate being?" asked Renée.—"He is at my house."

"Come, come, my friend," interrupted the marquise, "do not neglect your duty to linger with us. You are the king's servant, and must go wherever that service calls you."

"O Villefort!" cried Renée, clasping her hands, and looking towards her lover with piteous earnestness, "be merciful on this the day of our betrothal."

The young man passed round to the side of the table where the fair pleader sat, and leaning over her chair said tenderly,—

"To give you pleasure, my sweet Renée, I promise to show all the lenity in my power; but if the charges brought against this

Bonapartist hero prove correct, why, then, you really must give me leave to order his head to be cut off." Renée shuddered.

"Never mind that foolish girl, Villefort," said the marquise. "She will soon get over these things." So saying, Madame de Saint-Méran extended her dry bony hand to Villefort, who, while imprinting a son-in-law's respectful salute on it, looked at Renée, as much as to say, "I must try and fancy 'tis your dear hand I kiss, as it should have been."

"These are mournful auspices to accompany a betrothal," sighed poor Renée.

"Upon my word, child!" exclaimed the angry marquise, "your folly exceeds all bounds. I should be glad to know what connection there can possibly be between your sickly sentimentality and the affairs of the state!"

"O mother!" murmured Renée.

"Nay, madame, I pray you pardon this little traitor. I promise you that to make up for her want of loyalty, I will be most inflexibly severe;" then casting an expressive glance at his betrothed, which seemed to say, "Fear not, for your dear sake my justice shall be tempered with mercy," and receiving a sweet and approving smile in return, Villefort quitted the room.

VII

The Examination

NO SOONER HAD VILLEFORT left the salon, than he assumed the grave air of a man who holds the balance of life and death in his hands. Now, in spite of the mobility of his countenance, the command of which, like a finished actor, he had carefully studied before the glass, it was by no means easy for him to assume an air of judicial severity. Except the recollection of the line of politics his father had adopted, and which might interfere, unless he acted with the greatest prudence, with his own career, Gerard de Villefort was as happy as a man could be. Already rich, he held a high official situation, though only twenty-seven. He was about to marry a young and charming woman, whom he loved, not passionately, but reasonably, as became a deputy attorney of the king; and besides her personal attractions, which were very great, Mademoiselle de Saint-Méran's family possessed considerable political influence, which they would, of course, exert in his favor. The dowry of his wife amounted to fifty thousand crowns, and he had, besides, the prospect of seeing her fortune increased to half a million at her father's death. These considerations naturally gave Villefort a feeling of such complete felicity that his mind was fairly dazzled in its contemplation.

At the door he met the commissary of police, who was waiting for him. The sight of this officer recalled Villefort from the third heaven to earth; he composed his face, as we have before described, and said, "I have read the letter, sir, and you have acted rightly in arresting this man; now inform me what you have discovered concerning him and the conspiracy."

"We know nothing as yet of the conspiracy, monsieur; all the papers found have been sealed up and placed on your desk. The prisoner himself is named Edmond Dantès, mate on board the three-master the *Pharaon*, trading in cotton with Alexandria and Smyrna, and belonging to Morrel & Son, of Marseilles."

"Before he entered the merchant service, had he ever served in the marines?"

"Oh, no, monsieur, he is very young."

"How old?"—"Nineteen or twenty at the most." At this moment, and as Villefort had arrived at the corner of the Rue des Conseils, a man, who seemed to have been waiting for him, approached; it was M. Morrel.

"Ah, M. de Villefort," cried he, "I am delighted to see you. Some of your people have committed the strangest mistake—they have just arrested Edmond Dantès, mate of my vessel."

"I know it, monsieur," replied Villefort, "and I am now going to examine him."

"Oh," said Morrel, carried away by his friendship, "you do not know him, and I do. He is the most estimable, the most trustworthy creature in the world, and I will venture to say, there is not a better seaman in all the merchant service. Oh, M. de Villefort, I beseech your indulgence for him."

Villefort, as we have seen, belonged to the aristocratic party at Marseilles, Morrel to the plebeian; the first was a royalist, the other suspected of Bonapartism. Villefort looked disdainfully at Morrel, and replied,—

"You are aware, monsieur, that a man may be estimable and trustworthy in private life, and the best seaman in the merchant service, and yet be, politically speaking, a great criminal. Is it not true?"

The magistrate laid emphasis on these words, as if he wished to apply them to the owner himself, while his eyes seemed to plunge into the heart of one who, interceding for another, had himself need of indulgence. Morrel reddened, for his own conscience was not quite clear on politics; besides, what Dantès had told him of his interview with the grand-marshal, and what the emperor had said to him, embarrassed him. He replied, however,—

"I entreat you, M. de Villefort, be, as you always are, kind and equitable, and give him back to us soon." This *give us* sounded revolutionary in the deputy's ears.

"Ah, ah," murmured he, "is Dantès then a member of some Carbonari society, that his protector thus employs the collective form? He was, if I recollect, arrested in a tavern, in company with a great many others." Then he added, "Monsieur, you may rest assured I shall perform my duty impartially, and that if he be innocent you shall not have appealed to me in vain; should he, however, be guilty, in this present epoch, impunity would furnish a dangerous example, and I must do my duty."

As he had now arrived at the door of his own house, which adjoined the Palais de Justice, he entered, after having coldly saluted the shipowner, who stood, as if petrified, on the spot where Villefort had left him. The antechamber was full of police agents and gendarmes, in the midst of whom, carefully watched, but calm and smiling, stood the prisoner. Villefort traversed the antechamber, cast a side glance at Dantès, and taking a packet which a gendarme offered him, disappeared, saying, "Bring in the prisoner."

Rapid as had been Villefort's glance, it had served to give him an idea of the man he was about to interrogate. He had recognized intelligence in the high forehead, courage in the dark eye and bent brow, and frankness in the thick lips that showed a set of pearly teeth. Villefort's first impression was favourable; but he had been so often warned to mistrust first impulses, that he applied the maxim to the impression, forgetting the difference between the two words.

He stifled, therefore, the feelings of compassion that were rising, composed his features, and sat down, grim and sombre, at his desk. An instant after Dantès entered. He was pale, but calm and collected, and saluting his judge with easy politeness, looked round for a seat, as if he had been in M. Morrel's salon. It was then that he encountered for the first time Villefort's look,—that look peculiar to the magistrate, who, while seeming to read the thoughts of others, betrays nothing of his own.

"Who and what are you?" demanded Villefort, turning over a pile of papers, containing information relative to the prisoner, that a police agent had given to him on his entry, and that, already, in an hour's time, had swelled to voluminous proportions, thanks to the corrupt espionage of which "the accused" is always made the victim.

"My name is Edmond Dantès," replied the young man calmly; "I am mate of the *Pharaon*, belonging to Messrs. Morrel & Son."

"Your age?" continued Villefort.—"Nineteen," returned Dantès.

"What were you doing at the moment you were arrested?"

"I was at the festival of my marriage, monsieur," said the young man, his voice slightly tremulous, so great was the contrast between that happy moment and the painful ceremony he was now undergoing; so great was the contrast between the sombre aspect of M. de Villefort and the radiant face of Mercédès.

"You were at the festival of your marriage?" said the deputy, shuddering in spite of himself.

"Yes, monsieur; I am on the point of marrying a young girl I have been attached to for three years." Villefort, impassive as he was, was struck with this coincidence; and the tremulous voice of Dantès, surprised in the midst of his happiness, struck a sympathetic chord in his own bosom—he also was on the point of being married, and he was summoned from his own happiness to destroy that of another. "This philosophie reflection," thought he, "will make a great sensation at M. de Saint Méran's;" and he arranged mentally, while Dantès awaited further questions, the antithesis by which orators often create a reputation for eloquence. When this speech was arranged, Villefort turned to Dantès.

"Go on, sir," said he.—"What would you have me say?"

"Give all the information in your power."

"Tell me on which point you desire information, and I will tell all I know; only," added he, with a smile, "I warn you I know very little."

"Have you served under the usurper?"—"I was about to be mustered into the Royal Marines when he fell."

"It is reported your political opinions are extreme," said Villefort, who had never heard anything of the kind, but was not sorry to make this inquiry, as if it were an accusation.

"My political opinions!" replied Dantès. "Alas, sir, I never had any opinions. I am hardly nineteen; I know nothing; I have no part to play. If I obtain the situation I desire, I shall owe it to M. Morrel. Thus all my opinions—I will not say public, but private—are confined to these three sentiment,—I love my father, I respect M. Morrel, and I adore Mercédès. This, sir, is all I can tell you, and you see how uninteresting it is." As Dantès spoke, Villefort gazed at his ingenuous and open countenance, and recollected the words of Renée, who, without knowing who the culprit was, had besought his indulgence for him. With the deputy's knowledge of crime and criminals, every word the young man uttered convinced him more and more of his innocence. This lad,—for he was scarcely a man,—simple, natural, eloquent with that eloquence of the heart never found when sought for; full of affection for everybody, because he was happy, and because happiness renders even the wicked good—extended his affection even to his judge, spite of Villefort's severe look and stern accent. Dantès seemed full of kindness.

"Pardieu," said Villefort, "he is a noble fellow. I hope I shall gain Renée's favor easily by obeying the first command she ever imposed on me. I shall have at least a pressure of the hand in public, and a sweet kiss in private." Full of this idea, Villefort's face became so joyous, that when he turned to Dantès, the latter, who had watched the change on his physiognomy, was smiling also.

"Sir," said Villefort, "have you any enemies, at least, that you know."

"I have enemies?" replied Dantès; "my position is not sufficiently elevated for that. As for my disposition, that is, perhaps, somewhat too hasty; but I have striven to repress it. I have had ten or twelve sailors under me, and if you question them, they will tell you that they love and respect me, not as a father, for I am too young, but as an elder brother."

"But you may have excited jealousy. You are about to become captain at nineteen—an elevated post; you are about to marry a pretty girl, who loves you; and these two pieces of good fortune may have excited the envy of some one."

"You are right; you know men better than I do, and what you say may possibly be the case, I confess; but if such persons are among my acquaintances I prefer not to know it, because then I should be forced to hate them."

"You are wrong; you should always strive to see clearly around you. You seem a worthy young man; I will depart from the strict line of my duty to aid you in discovering the author of this accusation. Here is the paper; do you know the writing?" As he spoke, Villefort drew the letter from his pocket, and presented it to Dantès. Dantès read it. A cloud passed over his brow as he said,—

"No, monsieur, I do not know the writing, and yet it is tolerably plain. Whoever did it writes well. I am very fortunate," added he, looking gratefully at Villefort, "to be examined by such a man as you; for this envious person is a real enemy." And by the rapid glance that the young man's eyes shot forth, Villefort saw how much energy lay hid beneath this mildness.

"Now," said the deputy, "answer me frankly, not as a prisoner to a judge, but as one man to another who takes an interest in him, what truth is there in the accusation contained in this anonymous letter?" And Villefort threw disdainfully on his desk the letter Dantès had just given back to him.

"None at all. I will tell you the real facts. I swear by my honor as a sailor, by my love for Mercédès, by the life of my father"—

"Speak, monsieur," said Villefort. Then, internally, "If Renée could see me, I hope she would be satisfied, and would no longer call me a decapitator."

"Well, when we quitted Naples, Captain Leclère was attacked with a brain fever. As we had no doctor on board, and he was so anxious to arrive at Elba, that he would not touch at any other port, his disorder rose to such a height, that at the end of the third day, feeling he was dying, he called me to him. 'My dear Dantès,' said he, 'swear to perform what I am going to tell you, for it is a matter of the deepest importance.'"

"'I swear, captain,' replied I.

"'Well, as after my death the command devolves on you as mate, assume the command, and bear up for the Island of Elba, disembark at Porto-Ferrajo, ask for the grand-marshal, give him this letter— perhaps they will give you another letter, and charge you with a commission. You will accomplish what I was to have done, and derive all the honor and profit from it.'

"'I will do it, captain; but perhaps I shall not be admitted to the grand marshal's presence as easily as you expect?'

"'Here is a ring that will obtain audience of him, and remove every difficulty,' said the captain. At these words he gave me a ring. It was time—two hours after he was delirious; the next day he died."

"And what did you do then?"

"What I ought to have done, and what every one would have done in my place. Everywhere the last requests of a dying man are sacred; but with a sailor the last requests of his superior are commands. I sailed for the Island of Elba, where I arrived the next day; I ordered everybody to remain on board, and went on shore alone. As I had expected, I found some difficulty in obtaining access to the grand-marshal; but I sent the ring I had received from the captain to him, and was instantly admitted. He questioned me concerning Captain Leclère's death; and, as the latter had told me, gave me a letter to carry on to a person in Paris. I undertook it because it was what my captain had bade me do. I landed here, regulated the affairs of the vessel, and hastened to visit my affianced bride, whom I found more lovely than ever. Thanks to M. Morrel, all the forms were got over; in a word, I was, as I told you, at my marriage-feast; and I should have been married in an hour, and to-morrow I intended to start for Paris, had I not been arrested on this charge which you as well as I now see to be unjust."

"Ah," said Villefort, "this seems to me the truth. If you have been culpable, it was imprudence, and this imprudence was in obedience to the orders of your captain. Give up this letter you have brought from Elba, and pass your word you will appear should you be required, and go and rejoin your friends."

"I am free, then, sir?" cried Dantès joyfully.—"Yes; but first give me this letter."

"You have it already, for it was taken from me with some others which I see in that packet."

"Stop a moment," said the deputy, as Dantès took his hat and gloves. "To whom is it addressed?"

"To Monsieur Noirtier, Rue Coq-Héron, Paris." Had a thunderbolt fallen into the room, Villefort could not have been more stupefied. He sank into his seat, and hastily turning over the packet, drew forth the fatal letter, at which he glanced with an expression of terror.

"M. Noirtier, Rue Coq-Héron, No. 13," murmured he, growing still paler.

"Yes," said Dantès; "do you know him?"

"No," replied Villefort; "a faithful servant of the king does not know conspirators."

"It is a conspiracy, then?" asked Dantès, who after believing himself free, now began to feel a tenfold alarm. "I have, however, already told you, sir, I was entirely ignorant of the contents of the letter."

"Yes; but you knew the name of the person to whom it was addressed," said Villefort.

"I was forced to read the address to know to whom to give it."

"Have you shown this letter to any one?" asked Villefort, becoming still more pale.—"To no one, on my honor."

"Everybody is ignorant that you are the bearer of a letter from the Island of Elba, and addressed to M. Noirtier?"—"Everybody, except the person who gave it to me."

"And that was too much, far too much," murmured Villefort. Villefort's brow darkened more and more, his white lips and clinched teeth filled Dantès with apprehension. After reading the letter, Villefort covered his face with his hands.

"Oh," said Dantès timidly, "what is the matter?" Villefort made no answer, but raised his head at the expiration of a few seconds, and again perused the letter.

"And you say that you are ignorant of the contents of this letter?"

"I give you my word of honor, sir," said Dantès; "but what is the matter? You are ill—shall I ring for assistance?—shall I call?"

"No," said Villefort, rising hastily; "stay where you are. It is for me to give orders here, and not you."

"Monsieur," replied Dantès proudly, "it was only to summon assistance for you."

"I want none; it was a temporary indisposition. Attend to yourself; answer me." Dantès waited, expecting a question, but in vain. Villefort fell back on his chair, passed his hand over his brow, moist with perspiration, and, for the third time, read the letter.

"Oh, if he knows the contents of this!" murmured he, "and that Noirtier is the father of Villefort, I am lost!" And he fixed his eyes upon Edmond as if he would have penetrated his thoughts.

"Oh, it is impossible to doubt it," cried he, suddenly.

"In heaven's name!" cried the unhappy young man, "if you doubt me, question me; I will answer you." Villefort made a violent effort, and in a tone he strove to render firm,—

"Sir," said he, "I am no longer able, as I had hoped, to restore you immediately to liberty; before doing so, I must consult the trial justice; what my own feeling is you already know."

"Oh, monsieur," cried Dantès, "you have been rather a friend than a judge."

"Well, I must detain you some time longer, but I will strive to make it as short as possible. The principal charge against you is this letter, and you see"—Villefort approached the fire, cast it in, and waited until it was entirely consumed.

"You see, I destroy it?"

"Oh," exclaimed Dantès, "you are goodness itself."

"Listen," continued Villefort; "you can now have confidence in me after what I have done."—"Oh, command, and I will obey."

"Listen; this is not a command, but advice I give you."

"Speak, and I will follow your advice."

"I shall detain you until this evening in the Palais de Justice. Should any one else interrogate you, say to him what you have said to me, but do not breathe a word of this letter."—"I promise." It was Villefort who seemed to entreat, and the prisoner who reassured him.

"You see," continued he, glancing toward the grate, where fragments of burnt paper fluttered in the flames, "the letter is destroyed; you and I alone know of its existence; should you, therefore, be questioned, deny all knowledge of it—deny it boldly, and you are saved."

"Be satisfied; I will deny it."

"It was the only letter you had?"—"It was."

"Swear it."—"I swear it." Villefort rang. A police agent entered. Villefort whispered some words in his ear, to which the officer replied by a motion of his head.

"Follow him," said Villefort to Dantès. Dantès saluted Villefort and retired. Hardly had the door closed when Villefort threw himself half-fainting into a chair.

"Alas, alas," murmured he, "if the procureur himself had been at Marseilles I should have been ruined. This accursed letter would have destroyed all my hopes. Oh, my father, must your past career always interfere with my successes?" Suddenly a light passed over his face, a smile played round his set mouth, and his haggard eyes were fixed in thought.

"This will do," said he, "and from this letter, which might have ruined me, I will make my fortune. Now to the work I have in hand." And after having assured himself that the prisoner was gone, the deputy procurcur hastened to the house of his betrothed.

VIII

The Château D'If

THE COMMISSARY OF POLICE, as he traversed the antechamber, made a sign to two gendarmes, who placed themselves one on Dantès' right and the other on his left. A door that communicated with the Palais de Justice was opened, and they went through a long range of gloomy corridors, whose appearance might have made even the boldest shudder. The Palais de Justice communicated with the prison,—a sombre edifice, that from its grated windows looks on the clock-tower of the Accoules. After numberless windings, Dantès saw a door with an iron wicket. The commissary took up an iron mallet and knocked thrice, every blow seeming to Dantès as if struck on his heart. The door opened, the two geudarmes gently pushed him forward, and the door closed with a loud sound behind him. The air he inhaled was no longer pure, but thick and mephitic,—he was in prison. He was conducted to a tolerably neat chamber, but grated and barred, and its appearance, therefore, did not greatly alarm him; besides, the words of Villefort, who seemed to interest himself so much, resounded still in his ears like a promise of freedom. It was four o'clock when Dantès was placed in this chamber. It was, as we have said, the 1st of March, and the prisoner was soon buried in darkness. The obscurity augmented the acuteness of his hearing; at the slightest sound

he rose and hastened to the door, convinced they were about to liberate him, but the sound died away, and Dantès sank again into his
seat. At last, about ten o'clock, and just as Dantès began to despair,
steps were heard in the corridor, a key turned in the lock, the bolts
creaked, the massy oaken door flew open, and a flood of light from
two torches pervaded the apartment. By the torchlight Dantès saw
the glittering sabres and carbines of four gendarmes. He had
advanced at first, but stopped at the sight of this display of force.

"Are you come to fetch me?" asked he.—"Yes," replied a
gendarme.

"By the orders of the deputy procureur?"—"I believe so." The
conviction that they came from M. de Villefort relieved all Dantès'
apprehensions; he advanced calmly, and placed himself in the centre of the escort. A carriage waited at the door, the coachman was
on the box, and a police officer sat beside him.

"Is this carriage for me?" said Dantès.—"It is for you," replied a
gendarme.

Dantès was about to speak; but feeling himself urged forward,
and having neither the power nor the intention to resist, he
mounted the steps, and was in an instant seated inside between two
gendarmes; the two others took their places opposite, and the carriage rolled heavily over the stones.

The prisoner glanced at the windows—they were grated; he
had changed his prison for another that was conveying him he
knew not whither. Through the grating, however, Dantès saw they
were passing through the Rue Caisserie, and by the Rue Saint-
Laurent and the Rue Taramis, to the port. Soon he saw the lights
of La Consigne.

The carriage stopped, the officer descended, approached the
guardhouse, a dozen soldiers came out and formed themselves in
order; Dantès saw the reflection of their muskets by the light of the
lamps on the quay.

"Can all this force be summoned on my account?" thought he.

The officer opened the door, which was locked, and, without speaking a word, answered Dantès' question; for he saw between the ranks of the soldiers a passage formed from the carriage to the port. The two gendarmes who were opposite to him descended first, then he was ordered to alight, and the gendarmes on each side of him followed his example. They advanced towards a boat, which a custom-house officer held by a chain, near the quay.

The soldiers looked at Dantès with an air of stupid curiosity. In an instant he was placed in the stern-sheets of the boat, between the gendarmes, while the officer stationed himself at the bow; a shove sent the boat adrift, and four sturdy oarsmen impelled it rapidly towards the Pilon. At a shout from the boat, the chain that closes the mouth of the port was lowered, and in a second they were, as Dantès knew, in the Frioul and outside the inner harbor.

The prisoner's first feeling was of joy at again breathing the pure air—for air is freedom; but he soon sighed, for he passed before La Réserve, where he had that morning been so happy, and now through the open windows came the laughter and revelry of a ball. Dantès folded his hands, raised his eyes to heaven, and prayed fervently.

The boat continued her voyage. They had passed the Tête de Morte, were now off the Anse du Pharo, and about to double the battery. This manœuvre was incomprehensible to Dantès.

"Whither are you taking me?" asked he.—"You will soon know."

"But still"——"We are forbidden to give you any explanation." Dantès, trained in discipline, knew that nothing would be more absurd than to question subordinates, who were forbidden to reply; and so he remained silent.

The most vague and wild thoughts passed through his mind. The boat they were in could not make a long voyage; there was no vessel at anchor outside the harbor; he thought, perhaps, they were going to leave him on some distant point. He was not bound, nor had they made any attempt to handcuff him; this seemed a good augury. Besides, had not the deputy, who had been so kind to him, told him that provided he did not pronounce the dreaded name of Noirtier, he had nothing to apprehend? Had not Villefort in his presence destroyed the fatal letter, the only proof against him? He waited silently, striving to pierce through the darkness.

They had left the Ile Ratonneau, where the lighthouse stood, on the right, and were now opposite the Point des Catalans. It seemed to the prisoner that he could distinguish a feminine form on the beach, for it was there Mercédès dwelt. How was it that a presentiment did not warn Mercédès that her lover was within three hundred yards of her?

One light alone was visible; and Dantès saw that it came from Mercédès' chamber. Mercédès was the only one awake in the whole settlement. A loud cry could be heard by her. But pride restrained him and he did not utter it. What would his guards think if they heard him shout like a madman?

He remained silent, his eyes fixed upon the light; the boat went on, but the prisoner thought only of Mercédès. An intervening elevation of land hid the light. Dantès turned and perceived that they had got out to sea. While he had been absorbed in thought, they had shipped their oars and hoisted sail; the boat was now moving with the wind.

In spite of his repugnance to address the guards, Dantès turned to the nearest gendarme, and taking his hand,—

"Comrade," said he, "I adjure you, as a Christian and a soldier, to tell me where we are going. I am Captain Dantès, a loyal Frenchman, though accused of treason; tell me where you are conducting me, and I promise you on my honor I will submit to my fate."

The gendarme looked irresolutely at his companion, who returned for answer a sign that said, "I see no great harm in telling him now," and the gendarme replied,—

"You are a native of Marseilles, and a sailor, and yet you do not know where you are going?"—"On my honor, I have no idea."

"Have you no idea whatever?"

"None at all."

"That is impossible."—"I swear to you it is true. Tell me, I entreat."

"But my orders."—"Your orders do not forbid your telling me what I must know in ten minutes, in half an hour, or an hour. You see I cannot escape, even if I intended."

"Unless you are blind, or have never been outside the harbor, you must know."—"I do not."

"Look round you then." Dantès rose and looked forward, when he saw rise within a hundred yards of him the black and frowning rock on which stands the Château d'If. This gloomy fortress, which has for more than three hundred years furnished food for so many wild legends, seemed to Dantès like a scaffold to a malefactor.

"The Château d'If?" cried he, "what are we going there for?" The gendarme smiled.

"I am not going there to be imprisoned," said Dantès; "it is only used for political prisoners. I have committed no crime. Are there any magistrates or judges at the Château d'If?"

"There are only," said the gendarme, "a governor, a garrison, turnkeys, and good thick walls. Come, come, do not look so astonished, or you will make me think you are laughing at me in return for my good nature." Dantès pressed the gendarme's hand as though he would crush it.

"You think, then," said he, "that I am taken to the Château d'If to be imprisoned there?"

"It is probable; but there is no occasion to squeeze so hard."

"Without any inquiry, without any formality?"—"All the formalities have been gone through; the inquiry is already made."

"And so, in spite of M. de Villefort's promises?"—"I do not know what M. de Villefort promised you," said the gendarme, "but I know we are taking you to the Château d'If. But what are you doing? Help, comrades, help!"

By a rapid movement, which the gendarme's practised eye had

perceived, Dantès sprang forward to precipitate himself into the sea; but four vigorous arms seized him as his feet quitted the bottom of the boat. He fell back cursing with rage.

"Good!" said the gendarme, placing his knee on his chest; "believe soft-spoken gentlemen again! Harkye, my friend, I have disobeyed my first order, but I will not disobey the second; and if you move, I will blow your brains out." And he levelled his carbine at Dantès, who felt the muzzle against his temple.

For a moment the idea of struggling crossed his mind, and of so ending the unexpected evil that had overtaken him. But he bethought him of M. de Villefort's promise; and, besides, death in a boat from the hand of a gendarme seemed too terrible. He remained motionless, but gnashing his teeth and wringing his hands with fury.

At this moment the boat came to a landing with a violent shock. One of the sailors leaped on shore, a cord creaked as it ran through a pulley, and Dantès guessed they were at the end of the voyage, and that they were mooring the boat.

His guards, taking him by the arms and coat-collar, forced him to rise, and dragged him towards the steps that lead to the gate of the fortress, while the police officer carrying a musket with fixed bayonet followed behind.

Dantès made no resistance; he was like a man in a dream: he saw soldiers drawn up on the embankment; he knew vaguely that he was ascending a flight of steps; he was conscious that he passed through a door, and that the door closed behind him; but all this indistinctly as through a mist. He did not even see the ocean, that terrible barrier against freedom, which the prisoners look upon with utter despair.

They halted for a minute, during which he strove to collect his thoughts. He looked around; he was in a court surrounded by high walls; he heard the measured tread of sentinels, and as they passed before the light he saw the barrels of their muskets shine.

They waited upwards of ten minutes. Certain Dantès could not escape, the gendarmes released him. They seemed awaiting orders. The orders came.

"Where is the prisoner?" said a voice.—"Here," replied the gendarmes.

"Let him follow me; I will take him to his cell."

"Go!" said the gendarmes, thrusting Dantès forward.

The prisoner followed his guide, who led him into a room almost under ground, whose bare and reeking walls seemed as though impregnated with tears; a lamp placed on a stool illumined the apartment faintly, and showed Dantès the features of his conductor, an under-jailer, ill-clothed, and of sullen appearance.

"Here is your chamber for to-night," said he. "It is late, and the governor is asleep. To-morrow, perhaps, he may change you. In the meantime there is bread, water, and fresh straw; and that is all a prisoner can wish for. Goodnight." And before Dantès could open his mouth—before he had noticed where the jailer placed his bread or the water—before he had glanced towards the corner where the straw was, the jailer disappeared, taking with him the lamp and closing the door, leaving stamped upon the prisoner's mind the dim reflection of the dripping walls of his dungeon.

Dantès was alone in darkness and in silence—cold as the shadows that he felt breathe on his burning forehead. With the first dawn of day the jailer returned, with orders to leave Dantès where he was. He found the prisoner in the same position, as if fixed there, his eyes swollen with weeping. He had passed the night standing, and without sleep. The jailer advanced; Dantès appeared not to perceive him. He touched him on the shoulder. Edmond started.

"Have you not slept?" said the jailer.—"I do not know," replied Dantès. The jailer stared.

"Are you hungry?" continued he.—"I do not know."

"Do you wish for anything?"—"I wish to see the governor." The jailer shrugged his shoulders and left the chamber.

Dantès followed him with his eyes, and stretched forth his hands towards the open door; but the door closed. All his emotion then burst forth; he cast himself on the ground, weeping bitterly, and asking himself what crime he had committed that he was thus punished.

The day passed thus; he scarcely tasted food, but walked round and round the cell like a wild beast in its cage. One thought in particular tormented him; namely, that during his journey hither he had sat so still, whereas he might, a dozen times, have plunged into the sea, and, thanks to his powers of swimming, for which he was famous, have gained the shore, concealed himself until the arrival of a Genoese or Spanish vessel, escaped to Spain or Italy, where Mercédès and his father could have joined him. He had no fears as to how he should live—good seamen are welcome everywhere. He spoke Italian like a Tuscan, and Spanish like a Castilian; he would have been free, and happy with Mercédès and his father, whereas he was now confined in the Château d'If, that impregnable fortress, ignorant of the future destiny of his father and Mercédès; and all this because he had trusted to Villefort's promise. The thought was maddening, and Dantès threw himself furiously down on his straw. The next morning at the same hour, the jailer came again.

"Well," said the jailer, "are you more reasonable to-day?" Dantès made no reply.

"Come, cheer up; is there anything that I can do for you?"

"I wish to see the governor."

"I have already told you it was impossible."

"Why so?"—"Because it is against prison rules, and prisoners must not even ask for it."

"What is allowed, then?"—"Better fare, if you pay for it, books, and leave to walk about."

"I do not want books, I am satisfied with my food, and I do not care to walk about; but I wish to see the governor."

"If you worry me by repeating the same thing, I will not bring you any more to eat."

"Well, then," said Edmond, "if you do not, I shall die of

hunger—that is all."

The jailer saw by his tone he would be happy to die; and as every prisoner is worth ten sous a day to his jailer, he replied in a more subdued tone,

"What you ask is impossible; but if you are very well behaved you will be allowed to walk about, and some day you will meet the governor; and if he chooses to reply, that is his affair."

"But," asked Dantès, "how long shall I have to wait?"

"Ah, a month—six months—a year."

"It is too long a time. I wish to see him at once."

"Ah," said the jailer, "do not always brood over what is impossible, or you will be mad in a fortnight."

"You think so?"—"Yes; we have an instance here; it was by always offering a million of francs to the governor for his liberty that an abbé became mad, who was in this chamber before you."

"How long has he left it?"—"Two years."

"Was he liberated, then?"—"No; he was put in a dungeon."

"Listen!" said Dantès. "I am not an abbé, I am not mad; perhaps I shall be, but at present, unfortunately, I am not. I will make you another offer."

"What is that?"

"I do not offer you a million, because I have it not; but I will give you a hundred crowns if, the first time you go to Marseilles, you will seek out a young girl named Mercédès, at the Catalans, and give her two lines from me."

"If I took them, and were detected, I should lose my place, which is worth two thousand francs a year; so that I should be a great fool to run such a risk for three hundred."

"Well," said Dantès, "mark this; if you refuse at least to tell Mercédès I am here, I will some day hide myself behind the door, and when you enter I will dash out your brains with this stool."

"Threats!" cried the jailer, retreating and putting himself on the defensive; "you are certainly going mad. The abbé began like you, and in three days you will be like him, mad enough to tie up; but, fortunately, there are dungeons here." Dantès whirled the stool round his head.

"All right, all right," said the jailer; "all right, since you will have it so. I will send word to the governor."

"Very well," returned Dantès, dropping the stool and sitting on it as if he were in reality mad. The jailer went out, and returned in an instant with a corporal and four soldiers.

"By the governor's orders," said he, "conduct the prisoner to the tier beneath."

"To the dungeon, then," said the corporal.

"Yes; we must put the madman with the madmen." The soldiers seized Dantès, who followed passively.

He descended fifteen steps, and the door of a dungeon was opened, and he was thrust in. The door closed, and Dantès advanced with outstretched hands until he touched the wall; he then sat down in the corner until his eyes became accustomed to the darkness. The jailer was right; Dantès wanted but little of being utterly mad.

IX

The Evening of the Betrothal

VILLEFORT HAD, AS WE have said, hastened back to Madame de Saint-Méran's in the Place du Grand Cours, and on entering the house found that the guests whom he had left at table were taking coffee in the salon. Renée was, with all the rest of the company, anxiously awaiting him, and his entrance was followed by a general exclamation.

"Well, Decapitator, Guardian of the State, Royalist, Brutus, what is the matter?" said one. "Speak out."

"Are we threatened with a fresh Reign of Terror?" asked another.

"Has the Corsican ogre broken loose?" cried a third.

"Marquise," said Villefort, approaching his future mother-in-law, "I request your pardon for thus leaving you. Will the marquis honor me by a few moments' private conversation?"

"Ah, it is really a serious matter, then?" asked the marquis, remarking the cloud on Villefort's brow.

"So serious that I must take leave of you for a few days; so," added he, turning to Renée, "judge for yourself if it be not important."

"You are going to leave us?" cried Renée, unable to hide her emotion at this unexpected announcement.

"Alas," returned Villefort, "I must!"

"Where, then, are you going?" asked the marquise.

"That, madame, is an official secret; but if you have any commissions for Paris, a friend of mine is going there to-night, and will with pleasure undertake them." The guests looked at each other.

"You wish to speak to me alone?" said the marquis.

"Yes, let us go to the library, please." The marquis took his arm, and they left the salon.

"Well," asked he, as soon as they were by themselves, "tell me what it is?"

"An affair of the greatest importance, that demands my immediate presence in Paris. Now, excuse the indiscretion, marquis, but have you any funded property?"

"All my fortune is in the funds; seven or eight hundred thousand francs."

"Then sell out—sell out, marquis, or you will lose it all."

"But how can I sell out here?"

"You have a broker, have you not?"—"Yes."

"Then give me a letter to him, and tell him to sell out without an instant's delay, perhaps even now I shall arrive too late."

"The deuce you say!" replied the marquis, "let us lose no time, then!"

And, sitting down, he wrote a letter to his broker, ordering him to sell out at the market price.

"Now, then," said Villefort, placing the letter in his pocketbook, "I must have another!"

"To whom?"—"To the king."

"To the king?"

"Yes."

"I dare not write to his majesty."

"I do not ask you to write to his majesty, but ask M. de Salvieux to do so. I want a letter that will enable me to reach the king's presence without all the formalities of demanding an audience; that would occasion a loss of precious time."

"But address yourself to the keeper of the seals; he has the right of entry at the Tuileries, and can procure you audience at any hour of the day or night."

"Doubtless; but there is no occasion to divide the honors of my discovery with him. The keeper would leave me in the background, and take all the glory to himself. I tell you, marquis, my fortune is made if I only reach the Tuileries the first, for the king will not forget the service I do him."

"In that case go and get ready. I will call Salvieux and make him write the letter."

"Be as quick as possible, I must be on the road in a quarter of an hour."

"Tell your coachman to stop at the door."

"You will present my excuses to the marquise and Mademoiselle Renée, whom I leave on such a day with great regret."

"You will find them both here, and can make your farewells in person."

"A thousand thanks—and now for the letter."

The marquis rang, a servant entered.

"Say to the Comte de Salvieux that I would like to see him."

"Now, then, go," said the marquis.—"I shall be gone only a few moments."

Villefort hastily quitted the apartment, but reflecting that the sight of the deputy procureur running through the streets would be enough to throw the whole city into confusion, he resumed his ordinary pace. At his door he perceived a figure in the shadow that seemed to wait for him. It was Mercédès, who, hearing no news of her lover, had come unobserved to inquire after him.

As Villefort drew near, she advanced and stood before him. Dantès had spoken of Mercédès, and Villefort instantly recognized her. Her beauty and high bearing surprised him, and when she inquired what had become of her lover, it seemed to him that she was the judge, and he the accused.

"The young man you speak of," said Villefort abruptly, "is a great criminal, and I can do nothing for him, mademoiselle." Mercédès burst into tears, and, as Villefort strove to pass her, again addressed him.

"But, at least, tell me where he is, that I may know whether he is alive or dead," said she.

"I do not know; he is no longer in my hands," replied Villefort.

And desirous of putting an end to the interview, he pushed by her, and closed the door, as if to exclude the pain he felt. But remorse is not thus banished; like Virgil's wounded hero, he carried the arrow in his wound, and, arrived at the salon, Villefort uttered a sigh that was almost a sob, and sank into a chair.

Then the first pangs of an unending torture seized upon his heart. The man he sacrificed to his ambition, that innocent victim immolated on the altar of his father's faults, appeared to him pale and threatening, leading his affianced bride by the hand, and bringing with him remorse, not such as the ancients figured, furious and terrible, but that slow and consuming agony whose pangs are intensified from hour to hour up to the very moment of death. Then he had a moment's hesitation. He had frequently called for capital punishment on criminals, and owing to his irresistible eloquence they had been condemned, and yet the slightest shadow of remorse had never clouded Villefort's brow, because they were guilty; at least, he believed so; but here was an innocent man whose happiness he had destroyed: in this case he was not the judge, but the executioner.

As he thus reflected, he felt the sensation we have described, and which had hitherto been unknown to him, arise in his bosom, and fill him with vague apprehensions. It is thus that a wounded man trembles instinctively at the approach of the finger to his wound until it be healed, but Villefort's was one of those that never close, or if they do, only close to reopen more agonizing than ever. If at this moment the sweet voice of Renée had sounded in his ears pleading for mercy, or the fair Mercédès had entered and said, "In the name of God, I conjure you to restore me my affianced husband," his cold and trembling hands would have signed his release; but no voice broke the stillness of the chamber, and the door was opened only by Villefort's valet, who came to tell him that the travelling carriage was in readiness.

Villefort rose, or rather sprang, from his chair, hastily opened one of the drawers of his desk, emptied all the gold it contained into his pocket, stood motionless an instant, his hand pressed to his head, muttered a few inarticulate sounds, and then, perceiving that his servant had placed his cloak on his shoulders, he sprang into the carriage, ordering the postilions to drive to M. de Saint-Méran's. The hapless Dantès was doomed.

As the marquis had promised, Villefort found the marquise and Renée in waiting. He started when he saw Renée, for he fancied she was again about to plead for Dantès. Alas, her emotions were wholly personal: she was thinking only of Villefort's departure.

She loved Villefort, and he left her at the moment he was about to become her husband. Villefort knew not when he should return, and Renée, far from pleading for Dantès, hated the man whose crime separated her from her lover.

Meanwhile what of Mercédès? She had met Fernand at the corner of the Rue de la Loge; she had returned to the Catalaus, and had despairingly cast herself on her couch. Fernand, kneeling by her side, took her hand, and covered it with kisses that Mercédès did not even feel. She passed the night thus. The lamp went out for want of oil, but she paid no heed to the darkness, and dawn came, but she knew not that it was day. Grief had made her blind to all but one object—that was Edmond.

"Ah, you are there," said she, at length, turning towards Fernand.

"I have not quitted you since yesterday," returned Fernand sorrowfully.

M. Morrel had not readily given up the fight. He had learned that Dantès had been taken to prison, and he had gone to all his friends, and the influential persons of the city; but the report was already in circulation that Dantès was arrested as a Bonapartist agent; and as the most sanguine looked upon any attempt of Napoleon to remount the throne as impossible, he met with nothing but refusal, and had returned home in despair, declaring that the matter was serious and that nothing more could be done.

Caderousse was equally restless and uneasy, but instead of seeking, like M. Morrel, to aid Dantès, he had shut himself up with two bottles of black currant brandy, in the hope of drowning reflection. But he did not succeed, and became too intoxicated to fetch any more drink, and yet not so intoxicated as to forget what had happened. With his elbows on the table he sat between the two empty bottles, while spectres danced in the light of the unsnuffed candle—spectres such as Hoffmann strews over his punch-drenched pages, like black, fantastic dust.

Danglars alone was content and joyous—he had got rid of an enemy and made his own situation on the *Pharaon* secure. Danglars was one of those men born with a pen behind the ear, and an inkstand in place of a heart. Everything with him was multiplication or subtraction. The life of a man was to him of far less value than a numeral, especially when, by taking it away, he could increase the sum total of his own desires. He went to bed at his usual hour, and slept in peace.

Villefort, after having received M. de Salvieux' letter, embraced Renée, kissed the marquise's hand, and shaken that of the marquis, started for Paris along the Aix road.

Old Dantès was dying with anxiety to know what had become of Edmond. But we know very well what had become of Edmond.

X

The King's Closet at the Tuileries

W E WILL LEAVE VILLEFORT on the road to Paris, travelling—thanks to trebled fees—with all speed, and passing through two or three apartments, enter at the Tuileries the little room with the arched window, so well known as having been the favorite closet of Napoleon and Louis XVIII., and now of Louis Philippe.

There, seated before a walnut table he had brought with him from Hartwell, and to which, from one of those fancies not uncommon to great people, he was particularly attached, the king, Louis XVIII., was carelessly listening to a man of fifty or fifty-two years of age, with gray hair, aristocratic bearing, and exceedingly gentlemanly attire, and meanwhile making a marginal note in a volume of Gryphius's rather inaccurate, but much sought-after, edition of Horace—a work which was much indebted to the sagacious observations of the philosophical monarch.

"You say, sir"—said the king.

"That I am exceedingly disquieted, sire."

"Really, have you had a vision of the seven fat kine and the seven lean kine?"

"No, sire, for that would only betoken for us seven years of plenty and seven years of scarcity; and with a king as full of foresight as your majesty, scarcity is not a thing to be feared."

"Then of what other scourge are you afraid, my dear Blacas?"

"Sire, I have every reason to believe that a storm is brewing in the south."

"Well, my dear duke," replied Louis XVIII., "I think you are wrongly informed, and know positively that, on the contrary, it is very fine weather in that direction." Man of ability as he was, Louis XVIII. liked a pleasant jest.

"Sire," continued M. de Blacas, "if it only be to reassure a faithful servant, will your majesty send into Languedoc, Provence, and Dauphiné, trusty men, who will bring you back a faithful report as to the feeling in these three provinces?"

"*Caninus surdis*," replied the king, continuing the annotations in his Horace.

"Sire," replied the courtier, laughing, in order that he might seem to comprehend the quotation, "your majesty may be perfectly right in relying on the good feeling of France, but I fear I am not altogether wrong in dreading some desperate attempt."

"By whom?"—"By Bonaparte, or, at least, by his adherents."

"My dear Blacas," said the king, "you with your alarms prevent me from working."

"And you, sire, prevent me from sleeping with your security."

"Wait, my dear sir, wait a moment; for I have such a delightful note on the *Pastor quum traheret*—wait, and I will listen to you afterwards."

There was a brief pause, during which Louis XVIII. wrote, in a hand as small as possible, another note on the margin of his Horace, and then looking at the duke with the air of a man who thinks he has an idea of his own, while he is only commenting upon the idea of another, said,—

"Go on, my dear duke, go on—I listen."

"Sire," said Blacas, who had for a moment the hope of sacrificing Villefort to his own profit, "I am compelled to tell you that these are not mere rumors destitute of foundation which thus disquiet me; but a serious-minded man, deserving all my confidence, and charged by me to watch over the south" (the duke hesitated as he pronounced these words), "has arrived by post to tell me that a great peril threatens the king, and so I hastened to you, sire."

"*Mala ducis avi domum*," continued Louis XVIII., still annotating.

"Does your majesty wish me to drop the subject?"

"By no means, my dear duke; but just stretch out your hand."

"Which?"—"Whichever you please—there to the left."

"Here, sire?"

"I tell you to the left, and you are looking to the right; I mean on my left—yes, there. You will find yesterday's report of the minister of police. But here is M. Dandré himself;" and M. Dandré, announced by the chamberlain-in-waiting, entered.

"Come in," said Louis XVIII., with repressed smile, "come in, baron, and tell the duke all you know—the latest news of M. de Bonaparte; do not conceal anything, however serious,—let us see, the Island of Elba is a volcano, and we may expect to have issuing thence flaming and bristling war—*bella, horrida bella*." M. Dandré leaned very respectfully on the back of a chair with his two hands, and said,—

"Has your majesty perused yesterday's report?"

"Yes, yes; but tell the duke himself, who cannot find anything, what the report contains—give him the particulars of what the usurper is doing in his islet."

"Monsieur," said the baron to the duke, "all the servants of his majesty must approve of the latest intelligence which we have from the Island of Elba. Bonaparte"—M. Dandré looked at Louis XVIII., who, employed in writing a note, did not even raise his head. "Bonaparte," continued the baron, "is mortally wearied, and passes whole days in watching his miners at work at Porto-Longone."

"And scratches himself for amusement," added the king.

"Scratches himself?" inquired the duke, "what does your majesty mean?"

"Yes, indeed, my dear duke. Did you forget that this great man, this hero, this demigod, is attacked with a malady of the skin which worries him to death, *prurigo?*"

"And, moreover, my dear duke," continued the minister of police, "we are almost assured that, in a very short time, the usurper will be insane."

"Insane?"

"Raving mad; his head becomes weaker. Sometimes he weeps bitterly, sometimes laughs boisterously; at other times he passes hours on the seashore, flinging stones in the water, and when the flint makes 'duck-and-drake' five or six times, he appears as delighted as if he had gained another Marengo or Austerlitz. Now, you must agree that these are indubitable symptoms of insanity."

"Or of wisdom, my dear baron—or of wisdom," said Louis XVIII., laughing; "the greatest captains of antiquity amused themselves by casting pebbles into the ocean—see Plutarch's life of Scipio Africanus."

M. de Blacas pondered deeply between the confident monarch and the truthful minister. Villefort, who did not choose to reveal the whole secret, lest another should reap all the benefit of the disclosure, had yet communicated enough to cause him the greatest uneasiness.

"Well, well, Dandré," said Louis XVIII., "Blacas is not yet convinced; let us proceed, therefore, to the usurper's conversion." The minister of police bowed.

"The usurper's conversion!" murmured the duke, looking at the king and Dandré, who spoke alternately, like Virgil's shepherds. "The usurper converted!"

"Decidedly, my dear duke."

"In what way converted?"—"To good principles. Tell him all about it, baron."

"Why, this is the way of it," said the minister, with the gravest air in the world: "Napoleon lately had a review, and as two or three of his old veterans expressed a desire to return to France, he gave them their dismissal, and exhorted them to 'serve the good king'. These were his own words, of that I am certain."

"Well, Blacas, what think you of this?" inquired the king triumphantly, and pausing for a moment from the voluminous scholiast before him.

"I say, sire, that the minister of police is greatly deceived or I am; and as it is impossible it can be the minister of police, as he has the guardianship of the safety and honor of your majesty, it is probable that I am in error. However, sire, if I might advise, your majesty will interrogate the person of whom I spoke to you, and I will urge your majesty to do him this honor."

"Most willingly, duke; under your auspices I will receive any person you please, but you must not expect me to be too confiding. Baron, have you any report more recent than this, dated the 20th February.—this is the 4th of March?"

"No, sire, but I am hourly expecting one; it may have arrived since I left my office."

"Go thither, and if there be none—well, well," continued Louis XVIII., "make one; that is the usual way, is it not?" and the king laughed facetiously.

"Oh, sire," replied the minister, "we have no occasion to invent any; every day our desks are loaded with most circumstantial denunciations, coming from hosts of people who hope for some return for services which they seek to render, but cannot; they trust to fortune, and rely upon some unexpected event in some way to justify their predictions."

"Well, sir, go," said Louis XVIII., "and remember that I am waiting for you."

"I will but go and return, sire; I shall be back in ten minutes."

"And I, sire," said M. de Blacas, "will go and find my messenger."

"Wait, sir, wait," said Louis XVIII. "Really, M. de Blacas, I must change your armorial bearings; I will give you an eagle with outstretched wings, holding in its claws a prey which tries in vain to escape, and bearing this device—*Tenax*."

"Sire, I listen," said De Blacas, biting his nails with impatience.

"I wish to consult you on this passage, '*Molli fugiens anhelitu*,' you know it refers to a stag flying from a wolf. Are you not a sportsman and a great wolf-hunter? Well, then, what do you think of the *molli anhelitu*?"

"Admirable, sire; but my messenger is like the stag you refer to, for he has posted two hundred and twenty leagues in scarcely three days."

"Which is undergoing great fatigue and anxiety, my dear duke, when we have a telegraph which transmits messages in three or four hours, and that without getting in the least out of breath."

"Ah, sire, you recompense but badly this poor young man, who has come so far, and with so much ardor, to give your majesty useful information. If only for the sake of M. de Salvieux, who recommends him to me, I entreat your majesty to receive him graciously."

"M. de Salvieux, my brother's chamberlain?"—"Yes, sire."

"He is at Marseilles."—"And writes me thence."

"Does he speak to you of this conspiracy?"—"No; but strongly recommends M. de Villefort, and begs me to present him to your majesty."

"M. de Villefort!" cried the king, "is the messenger's name M. de Villefort?"—"Yes, sire."

"And he comes from Marseilles?"—"In person."

"Why did you not mention his name at once?" replied the king, betraying some uneasiness.

"Sire, I thought his name was unknown to your majesty."

"No, no, Blacas; he is a man of strong and elevated understanding, ambitious, too, and, pardieu, you know his father's name!"

"His father?"—"Yes, Noirtier."

"Noirtier the Girondin?—Noirtier the senator?"—"He himself."

"And your majesty has employed the son of such a man?"

"Blacas, my friend, you have but limited comprehension. I told you Villefort was ambitious, and to attain this ambition Villefort would sacrifice everything, even his father."

"Then, sire, may I present him?"—"This instant, duke! Where is he?"

"Waiting below, in my carriage."—"Seek him at once."

"I hasten to do so." The duke left the royal presence with the speed of a young man; his really sincere royalism made him youthful again. Louis XVIII. remained alone, and turning his eyes on his half-opened Horace, muttered,—

"Justum et tenacem propositi virum."

M. de Blacas returned as speedily as he had departed, but in the antechamber he was forced to appeal to the king's authority. Villefort's dusty garb, his costume, which was not of courtly cut, excited the susceptibility of M. de Brézé, who was all astonishment at finding that this young man had the audacity to enter before the king in such attire. The duke, however, overcame all difficulties with a word—his majesty's order; and, in spite of the protestations which the master of ceremonies made for the honor of his office and principles, Villefort was introduced.

The king was seated in the same place where the duke had left him. On opening the door, Villefort found himself facing him, and the young magistrate's first impulse was to panse.

"Come in, M. de Villefort," said the king, "come in." Villefort bowed, and advancing a few steps, waited until the king should interrogate him.

"M. de Villefort," said Louis XVIII., "the Due de Blacas assures me you have some interesting information to communicate."

"Sire, the duke is right, and I believe your majesty will think it equally important."

"In the first place, and before everthing else, sir, is the news as bad in your opinion as I am asked to believe?"

"Sire, I believe it to be most urgent, but I hope, by the speed I have used, that it is not irreparable."

"Speak as fully as you please, sir," said the king, who began to give way to the emotion which had showed itself in Blacas's face and affected Villefort's voice. "Speak, sir, and pray begin at the beginning; I like order in everything."

"Sire," said Villefort, "I will render a faithful report to your majesty, but I must entreat your forgiveness if my anxiety leads to some obscurity in my language." A glance at the king after this discreet and subtle exordium, assured Villefort of the benignity of his august auditor, and he went on:—

"Sire, I have come as rapidly to Paris as possible, to inform your majesty that I have discovered, in the exercise of my duties, not a commonplace and insignificant plot, such as is every day got up in the lower ranks of the people and in the army, but an actual conspiracy— a storm which menaces no less than your majesty's throne. Sire, the usurper is arming three ships, he meditates some project, which, however mad, is yet, perhaps, terrible. At this moment he will have left Elba, to go whither I know not, but assuredly to attempt a landing either at Naples, or on the coast of Tuscany, or perhaps on the shores of France. Your majesty is well aware that the sovereign of the Island of Elba has maintained his relations with Italy and France?"

"I am, sir," said the king, much agitated; "and recently we have had information that the Bonapartist clubs have had meetings in the Rue Saint-Jacques. But proceed, I beg of you. How did you obtain these details?"

"Sire, they are the results of an examination which I have made of a man of Marseilles, whom I have watched for some time, and arrested on the day of my departure. This person, a sailor, of turbulent character, and whom I suspected of Bonapartism, has been secretly to the Island of Elba. There he saw the grand-marshal, who charged him with an oral message to a Bonapartist in Paris, whose name I could not extract from him; but this mission was to prepare men's minds for a return (it is the man who says this, sire)—a return which will soon occur."

"And where is this man?"—"In prison, sire."

"And the matter seems serious to you?"

"So serious, sire, that when the circumstance surprised me in the midst of a family festival, on the very day of my betrothal, I left my bride and friends, postponing everything, that I might hasten to lay at your majesty's feet the fears which impressed me, and the assurance of my devotion."

"True," said Louis XVIII., "was there not a marriage engagement between you and Mademoiselle de Saint-Méran?"

"Daughter of one of your majesty's most faithful servants."

"Yes, yes; but let us talk of this plot, M. de Villefort."

"Sire, I fear it is more than a plot; I fear it is a conspiracy."

"A conspiracy in these times," said Louis XVIII., smiling, "is a thing very easy to meditate, but more difficult to conduct to an end, inasmuch as, re-established so recently on the throne of our ancestors, we have our eyes open at once upon the past, the present, and the future. For the last ten months my ministers have redoubled their vigilance, in order to watch the shore of the Mediterranean. If Bonaparte landed at Naples, the whole coalition would be on foot before he could even reach Piomoino; if he land in Tuscany, he will be in an unfriendly territory; if he land in France, it must be with a handful of men, and the result of that is easily foretold, execrated as he is by the population. Take courage, sir; but at the same time rely on our royal gratitude."

"Ah, here is M. Dandré!" cried de Blacas. At this instant the minister of police appeared at the door, pale, trembling, and as if ready to faint. Villefort was about to retire, but M. de Blacas, taking his hand, restrained him.

XI

The Corsican Ogre

A T THE SIGHT OF THIS AGITATION Louis XVIII. pushed from him violently the table at which he was sitting.

"What ails you, baron?" he exclaimed. "You appear quite aghast. Has your uneasiness anything to do with what M. de Blacas has told me, and M. de Villefort has just confirmed?" M. de Blacas moved suddenly towards the baron, but the fright of the courtier pleaded for the forbearance of the statesman; and besides, as matters were, it was much more to his advantage that the prefect of police should triumph over him than that he should humiliate the prefect.

"Sire"—stammered the baron.

"Well, what is it?" asked Louis XVIII. The minister of police, giving way to an impulse of despair, was about to throw himself at the feet of Louis XVIII., who retreated a step and frowned.

"Will you speak?" he said.

"Oh, sire, what a dreadful misfortune! I am, indeed, to be pitied. I can never forgive myself!"

"Monsieur," said Louis XVIII., "I command you to speak."

"Well, sire, the usurper left Elba on the 26th February, and landed on the 1st of March."

"And where? In Italy?" asked the king eagerly.

"In France, sire,—at a small port, near Antibes, in the Gulf of Juan."

"The usurper landed in France, near Antibes, in the Gulf of Juan, two hundred and fifty leagues from Paris, on the 1st of March, and you only acquired this information to-day, the 4th of March! Well, sir, what you tell me is impossible. You must have received a false report, or you have gone mad."

"Alas, sire, it is but too true!" Louis made a gesture of indescribable anger and alarm, and then drew himself up as if this sudden blow had struck him at the same moment in heart and countenance.

"In France!" he cried, "the usurper in France! Then they did not watch over this man. Who knows? they were, perhaps, in league with him."

"Oh, sire," exclaimed the Duc de Blacas, "M. Dandré is not a man to be accused of treason! Sire, we have all been blind, and the minister of police has shared the general blindness, that is all."

"But"—said Villefort, and then suddenly checking himself, he was silent; then he continued, "Your pardon, sire," he said, bowing, "my zeal carried me away. Will your majesty deign to excuse me?"

"Speak, sir, speak boldly," replied Louis. "You alone forewarned us of the evil; now try and aid us with the remedy."

"Sire," said Villefort, "the usurper is detested in the south; and it seems to me that if he ventured into the south, it would be easy to raise Languedoe and Provence against him."

"Yes, assuredly," replied the minister; "but he is advancing by Gap and Sisteron."

"Advancing—he is advancing!" said Louis XVIII. "Is he then advancing on Paris?" The minister of police maintained a silence which was equivalent to a complete avowal.

"And Dauphiné, sir?" inquired the king, of Villefort. "Do you think it possible to rouse that as well as Provence?"

"Sire, I am sorry to tell your majesty a cruel fact; but the feeling in Dauphiné is quite the reverse of that in Provence or Languedoc. The mountaineers are Bonapartists, sire."

"Then," murmured Louis, "he was well informed. And how many men had he with him?"

"I do not know, sire," answered the minister of police.

"What, you do not know! Have you neglected to obtain information on that point? Of course it is of no consequence," he added, with a withering smile.

"Sire, it was impossible to learn; the despatch simply stated the fact of the landing and the route taken by the usurper."

"And how did this despatch reach you?" inquired the king. The minister bowed his head, and while a deep color overspread his cheeks, he stammered out,—

"By the telegraph, sire."—Louis XVIII. advanced a step, and folded his arms over his chest as Napoleon would have done.

"So then," he exclaimed, turning pale with anger, "seven conjoined and allied armies overthrew that man. A miracle of heaven replaced me on the throne of my fathers after five-and-twenty years of exile. I have, during those five-and-twenty years, spared no pains to understand the people of France and the interests which were confided to me; and now, when I see the fruition of my wishes almost within reach, the power I hold in my hands bursts, and shatters me to atoms!"

"Sire, it is fatality!" murmured the minister, feeling that the pressure of circumstances, however light a thing to destiny, was too much for any human strength to endure.

"What our enemies say of us is then true. We have learnt nothing, forgotten nothing! If I were betrayed as he was, I would console myself; but to be in the midst of persons elevated by myself to places of honor, who ought to watch over me more carefully than over themselves,—for my fortune is theirs—before me they were nothing—after me they will be nothing, and perish miserably from ineapaeity—ineptitude! Oh, yes, sir, you are right—it is fatality!"

The minister quailed before this outburst of sareasm. M. de Blacas wiped the moisture from his brow. Villefort smiled within himself, for he felt his increased importance.

"To fall," continued King Louis, who at the first glance had sounded the abyss on which the monarchy hung suspended,—"to fall, and learn of that fall by telegraph! Oh, I would rather mount the scaffold of my brother, Louis XVI., than thus descend the staircase at the Tuileries driven away by ridicule. Ridicule, sir—why, you know not its power in France, and yet you ought to know it!"

"Sire, sire," murmured the minister, "for pity's"—

"Approach, M. de Villefort," resumed the king, addressing the young man, who, motionless and breathless, was listening to a conversation on which depended the destiny of a kingdom. "Approach, and tell monsieur that it is possible to know beforehand all that he has not known."

"Sire, it was really impossible to learn secrets which that man concealed from all the world."

"Really impossible! Yes—that is a great word, sir. Unfortunately, there are great words, as there are great men; I have measured them. Really impossible for a minister who has an office, agents, spies, and fifteen hundred thousand francs for secret service money, to know what is going on at sixty leagues from the coast of France! Well, then, see, here is a gentleman who had none of these resources at his disposal—a gentleman, only a simple magistrate, who learned more than you with all your police, and who would have saved my crown, if, like you, he had the power of directing a telegraph." The look of the minister of police was turned with concentrated spite on Villefort, who bent his head in modest triumph.

"I do not mean that for you, Blacas," continued Louis XVIII.; "for if you have discovered nothing, at least you have had the good sense to persevere in your suspicions. Any other than yourself would have considered the disclosure of M. de Villefort insignificant, or else dictated by venal ambition." These words were an allusion to the sentiments which the minister of police had uttered with so much confidence an hour before.

Villefort understood the king's intent. Any other person would, perhaps, have been overcome by such an intoxicating draught of praise; but he feared to make for himself a mortal enemy of the police minister, although he saw that Dandrè was irrevocably lost. In fact, the minister, who, in the plenitude of his power, had been unable to unearth Napoleon's secret, might in despair at his own downfall interrogate Dantès and so lay bare the motives of Villefort's plot. Realizing this, Villefort came to the rescue of the crestfallen minister, instead of aiding to crush him.

"Sire," said Villefort, "the suddenness of this event must prove to your majesty that the issue is in the hands of Providence; what your majesty is pleased to attribute to me as profound perspicacity is simply owing to chance, and I have profited by that chance, like a good and devoted servant—that's all. Do not attribute to me more than I deserve, sire, that your majesty may never have occasion to recall the first opinion you have been pleased to form of me." The minister of police thanked the young man by an eloquent look, and Villefort understood that he had succeeded in his design; that is to say, that without forfeiting the gratitude of the king, he had made a friend of one on whom, in case of necessity, he might rely.

"'Tis well," resumed the king. "And now, gentlemen," he continued, turning towards M. de Blacas and the minister of police, "I have no further occasion for you, and you may retire; what now remains to do is in the department of the minister of war."

"Fortunately, sire," said M. de Blacas, "we can rely on the army; your majesty knows how every report confirms their loyalty and attachment."

"Do not mention reports, duke, to me, for I know now what confidence to place in them. Yet, speaking of reports, baron, what have you learned with regard to the affair in the Rue Saint-Jacques?"

"The affair in the Rue Saint-Jacques!" exclaimed Villefort, unable to repress an exclamation. Then, suddenly pausing, he added, "Your pardon, sire; but my devotion to your majesty has made me forget, not the respect I have, for that is too deeply engraven in my heart, but the rules of etiquette."

"Go on, go on, sir," replied the king; "you have to-day earned the right to make inquiries here."

"Sire," interposed the minister of police, "I came a moment ago to give your majesty fresh information which I had obtained on this head, when your majesty's attention was attracted by the terrible event that has occurred in the gulf, and now these facts will cease to interest your majesty."

"On the contrary, sir,—on the contrary," said Louis XVIII., "this affair seems to me to have a decided connection with that which occupies our attention, and the death of General Quesnel will, perhaps, put us on the direct track of a great internal conspiracy." At the name of General Quesnel, Villefort trembled.

"Everything points to the conclusion, sire," said the minister of police, "that death was not the result of suicide, as we first believed, but of assassination. General Quesnel, it appears, had just left a Bonapartist club when he disappeared. An unknown person had been with him that morning, and made an appointment with him in the Rue Saint-Jacques; unfortunately, the general's valet, who was dressing his hair at the moment when the stranger entered, heard the street mentioned, but did not catch the number." As the police minister related this to the king, Villefort, who looked as if his very life hung on the speaker's lips, turned alternately red and pale. The king looked towards him.

"Do you not think with me, M. de Villefort, that General Quesnel, whom they believed attached to the usurper, but who was really entirely devoted to me, has perished the victim of a Bonapartist ambush?"

"It is probable, sire," replied Villefort. "But is this all that is known?"

"They are on the track of the man who appointed the meeting with him."

"On his track?" said Villefort.

"Yes, the servant has given his description. He is a man of from fifty to fifty-two years of age, dark, with black eyes covered with shaggy eyebrows, and a thick mustache. He was dressed in a blue frock-coat, buttoned up to the chin, and wore at his button-hole the rosette of an officer of the Legion of Honor. Yesterday a person exactly corresponding with this description was followed, but he was lost sight of at the corner of the Rue de la Jussienne and the Rue Coq-Héron." Villefort leaned on the back of an arm-chair, for as the minister of police went on speaking he felt his legs bend under him; but when he learned that the unknown had escaped the vigilance of the agent who followed him, he breathed again.

"Continue to seek for this man, sir," said the king to the minister of police; "for if, as I am all but convinced, General Quesnel, who would have been so useful to us at this moment, has been murdered, his assassins, Bonapartists or not, shall be cruelly punished." It required all Villefort's coolness not to betray the terror with which this declaration of the king inspired him.

"How strange," continued the king, with some asperity; "the police think that they have disposed of the whole matter when they say, "A murder has been committed,' and especially so when they can add, "And we are on the track of the guilty persons."'

"Sire, your majesty will, I trust, be amply satisfied on this point at least."

"We shall see. I will no longer detain you, M. de Villefort, for you must be fatigued after so long a journey; go and rest. Of course you stopped at your father's?" A feeling of faintness came over Villefort.

"No, sire," he replied, "I alighted at the Hôtel de Madrid, in the Rue de Tournon."

"But you have seen him?"—"Sire, I went straight to the Duc de Blacas."

"But you will see him, then?"—"I think not, sire."

"Ah, I forgot," said Louis, smiling in a manner which proved that all these questions were not made without a motive; "I forgot you and M. Noirtier are not on the best terms possible, and that is another sacrifice made to the royal cause, and for which you should be recompensed."

"Sire, the kindness your majesty deigns to evince towards me is a recompense which so far surpasses my utmost ambition that I have nothing more to ask for."

"Never mind, sir, we will not forget you; make your mind easy. In the meanwhile" (the king here detached the cross of the Legion of Honor which he usually wore over his blue coat, near the cross of St. Louis, above the order of Notre-Dame-du-Mont-Carmel and St. Lazare, and gave it to Villefort)—"in the meanwhile take this cross."

"Sire," said Villefort, "your majesty mistakes; this is an officer's cross."

"Ma foi," said Louis XVIII., "take it, such as it is, for I have not the time to procure you another. Blacas, let it be your care to see that the brevet is made out and sent to M. de Villefort." Villefort's eyes were filled with tears of joy and pride; he took the cross and kissed it.

"And now," he said, "may I inquire what are the orders with which your majesty deigns to honor me?"

"Take what rest you require, and remember that if you are not able to serve me here in Paris, you may be of the greatest service to me at Marseilles."

"Sire," replied Villefort, bowing, "in an hour I shall have quitted Paris."

"Go, sir," said the king; "and should I forget you (kings' memories are short), do not be afraid to bring yourself to my recollection. Baron, send for the minister of war. Blacas, remain."

"Ah, sir," said the minister of police to Villefort, as they left the Tuileries, "you entered by luck's door—your fortune is made."

"Will it be long first?" muttered Villefort, saluting the minister, whose career was ended, and looking about him for a hackney-coach. One passed at the moment, which he hailed; he gave his address to the driver, and springing in, threw himself on the seat, and gave loose to dreams of ambition.

Ten minutes afterwards Villefort reached his hotel, ordered horses to be ready in two hours, and asked to have his breakfast brought to him. He was about to begin his repast when the sound of the bell rang sharp and loud. The valet opened the door, and Villefort heard some one speak his name.

"Who could know that I was here already?" said the young man. The valet entered.

"Well," said Villefort, "what is it?—Who rang?—Who asked for me?"

"A stranger who will not send in his name."

"A stranger who will not send in his name! What can he want with me?"

"He wishes to speak to you."

"To me?"—"Yes."

"Did he mention my name?"—"Yes."

"What sort of person is he?"—"Why, sir, a man of about fifty."

"Short or tall?"—"About your own height, sir."

"Dark or fair?"—"Dark,—very dark; with black eyes, black hair, black eyebrows."

"And how dressed?" asked Villefort quickly.—"In a blue frock-coat, buttoned up close, decorated with the Legion of Honor."

"It is he!" said Villefort, turning pale.

"Eh, pardieu," said the individual whose description we have twice given, entering the door, "what a great deal of ceremony! Is it the custom in Marseilles for sons to keep their fathers waiting in their anterooms?"

"Father!" cried Villefort, "then I was not deceived; I felt sure it must be you."

"Well, then, if you felt so sure," replied the new-comer, putting his cane in a corner and his hat on a chair, "allow me to say, my dear

Gérard, that it was not very filial of you to keep me waiting at the door."

"Leave us, Germain," said Villefort. The servant quitted the apartment with evident signs of astonishment.

XII

Father and Son

M. NOIRTIER—FOR IT WAS, indeed, he who entered—looked after the servant until the door was closed, and then, fearing, no doubt, that he might be overheard in the antechamber, he opened the door again, nor was the precaution useless, as appeared from the rapid retreat of Germain, who proved that he was not exempt from the sin which ruined our first parents. M. Noirtier then took the trouble to close and bolt the antechamber door, then that of the bed-chamber, and then extended his hand to Villefort, who had followed all his motions with surprise which he could not conceal.

"Well, now, my dear Gérard," said he to the young man, with a very significant look, "do you know, you seem as if you were not very glad to see me?"

"My dear father," said Villefort, "I am, on the contrary, delighted; but I so little expected your visit, that it has somewhat overcome me."

"But, my dear fellow," replied M. Noirtier, seating himself, "I might say the same thing to you, when you announce to me your wedding for the 28th of February, and on the 3rd of March you turn up here in Paris."

"And if I have come, my dear father," said Gérard, drawing

closer to M. Noirtier, "do not complain, for it is for you that I came, and my journey will be your salvation."

"Ah, indeed!" said M. Noirtier, stretching himself out at his ease in the chair. "Really, pray tell me all about it, for it must be interesting."

"Father, you have heard speak of a certain Bonapartist club in the Rue Saint-Jacques?"

"No. 53; yes, I am vice-president."

"Father, your coolness makes me shudder."

"Why, my dear boy, when a man has been proscribed by the mountaineers, has escaped from Paris in a hay-cart, been hunted over the plains of Bordeaux by Robespierre's blood-hounds, he becomes accustomed to most things. But go on, what about the club in the Rue Saint-Jacques?"

"Why, they induced General Quesnel to go there, and General Quesnel, who quitted his own house at nine o'clock in the evening, was found the next day in the Seine."

"And who told you this fine story?"—"The king himself."

"Well, then, in return for your story," continued Noirtier, "I will tell you another."

"My dear father, I think I already know what you are about to tell me."

"Ah, you have heard of the landing of the emperor?"

"Not so loud, father, I entreat of you—for your own sake as well as mine. Yes, I heard this news, and knew it even before you could; for three days ago I posted from Marseilles to Paris with all possible speed, half-desperate at the enforced delay."

"Three days ago? You are crazy. Why, three days ago the emperor had not landed."—"No matter; I was aware of his intention."

"How did you know about it?"—"By a letter addressed to you from the Island of Elba."

"To me?"—"To you; and which I discovered in the pocket-book of the messenger. Had that letter fallen into the hands of another, you, my dear father, would probably ere this have been shot." Villefort's father laughed.

"Come, come," said he, "will the Restoration adopt imperial methods so promptly? Shot, my dear boy? What an idea! Where is the letter you speak of? I know you too well to suppose you would allow such a thing to pass you."

"I burnt it, for fear that even a fragment should remain; for that letter must have led to your condemnation."

"And the destruction of your future prospects," replied Noirtier; "yes, I can easily comprehend that. But I have nothing to fear while I have you to protect me."

"I do better than that, sir—I save you."

"You do? why, really, the thing becomes more and more dramatic—explain yourself."

"I must refer again to the club in the Rue Saint-Jacques."

"It appears that this club is rather a bore to the police. Why didn't they search more vigilantly? they would have found"—

"They have not found; but they are on the track."

"Yes, that's the usual phrase; I am quite familiar with it. When the police is at fault, it declares that it is on the track; and the government patiently awaits the day when it comes to say, with a sneaking air, that the track is lost."

"Yes, but they have found a corpse; the general has been killed, and in all countries they call that a murder."

"A murder do you call it? why, there is nothing to prove that the general was murdered. People are found every day in the Seine, having thrown themselves in, or having been drowned from not knowing how to swim."

"Father, you know very well that the general was not a man to drown himself in despair, and people do not bathe in the Seine in the month of January. No, no, do not be deceived; this was murder in every sense of the word."

"And who thus designated it?"—"The king himself."

"The king! I thought he was philosopher enough to allow that there was no murder in politics. In politics, my dear fellow, you know, as well as I do, there are no men, but ideas—no feelings, but interests; in politics we do not kill a man, we only remove an obstacle, that is all. Would you like to know how matters have progressed? Well, I will tell you. It was thought reliance might be placed in General Quesnel; he was recommended to us from the Island of Elba; one of us went to him, and invited him to the Rue Saint-Jacques, where he would find some friends. He came there, and the plan was unfolded to him for leaving Elba, the projected landing, etc. When he had heard and comprehended all to the fullest extent, he replied that he was a royalist. Then all looked at each other,—he was made to take an oath, and did so, but with such an ill grace that it was really tempting Providence to swear him, and yet, in spite of that, the general was allowed to depart free—perfectly free. Yet he did not return home. What could that mean? why, my dear fellow, that on leaving us he lost his way, that's all. A murder? really, Villefort, you surprise me. You, a deputy procureur, to found an acussation on such bad premises! Did I ever say to you, when you were fulfilling your character as a royalist, and cut off the head of one of my party, 'My son, you have committed a murder?' No, I said, 'Very well, sir, you have gained the victory; to-morrow, perchance, it will be our turn.'"

"But, father, take care; when our turn comes, our revenge will be sweeping."

"I do not understand you."

"You rely on the usurper's return?"—"We do."

"You are mistaken; he will not advance two leagues into the interior of France without being followed, tracked, and caught like a wild beast."

"My dear fellow, the emperor is at this moment on the way to Grenoble; on the 10th or 12th he will be at Lyons, and on the 20th or 25th at Paris."

"The people will rise."—"Yes, to go and meet him."

"He has but a handful of men with him, and armies will be despatched against him."

"Yes, to escort him into the capital. Really, my dear Gérard, you are but a child; you think yourself well informed because the telegraph has told you, three days after the landing, 'The usurper has landed at Cannes with several men. He is pursued.' But where is he? what is he doing? You do not know at all; and in this way they will chase him to Paris, without drawing a trigger."

"Grenoble and Lyons are faithful cities, and will oppose to him an impassable barrier."

"Grenoble will open her gates to him with enthusiasm—all Lyons will hasten to welcome him. Believe me, we are as well informed as you, and our police are as good as your own. Would you like a proof of it? well, you wished to conceal your journey from me, and yet I knew of your arrival half an hour after you had passed the barrier. You gave your direction to no one but your position, yet I have your address, and in proof I am here the very instant you are going to sit at table. Ring, then, if you please, for a second knife, fork, and plate, and we will dine together."

"Indeed!" replied Villefort, looking at his father with astonishment, "you really do seem very well informed."

"Eh? the thing is simple enough. You who are in power have only the means that money produces—we who are in expectation, have those which devotion prompts."

"Devotion!" said Villefort, with a sneer.

"Yes, devotion; for that is, I believe, the phrase for hopeful ambition."

And Villefort's father extended his hand to the bell-rope, to summon the servant whom his son had not called. Villefort caught his arm.

"Wait, my dear father," said the young man; "one word more."

"Say on."

"However stupid the royalist police may be, they do know one terrible thing."

"What is that?"

"The description of the man who, on the morning of the day when General Quesnel disappeared, presented himself at his house."

"Oh, the admirable police have found that out, have they? And what may be that description?"

"Dark complexion; hair, eyebrows, and whiskers, black; blue frock-coat, buttoned up to the chin; rosette of an officer of the Legion of Honor in his button-hole; a hat with wide brim, and a cane."

"Ah, ha, that's it, is it?" said Noirtier; "and why, then, have they not laid hands on him?"

"Because yesterday, or the day before, they lost sight of him at the corner of the Rue Coq-Héron."

"Didn't I say that your police were good for nothing?"

"Yes; but they may catch him yet."

"True," said Noirtier, looking carelessly around him, "true, if this person were not on his guard, as he is;" and he added with a smile, "he will consequently make a few changes in his personal appearance." At these words he rose, and put off his frock-coat and cravat, went towards a table on which lay his son's toilet articles, lathered his face, took a razor, and, with a firm hand, cut off the compromising whiskers. Villefort watched him with alarm not devoid of admiration.

His whiskers cut off, Noirtier gave another turn to his hair; took, instead of his black cravat, a colored neckerchief which lay at the top of an open portmanteau; put on, in lieu of his blue and high-buttoned frock-coat, a coat of Villefort's of dark brown, and cut away in front; tried on before the glass a narrow-brimmed hat of his son's, which appeared to fit him perfectly, and, leaving his cane in the corner where he had deposited it, he took up a small bamboo switch, cut the air with it once or twice, and walked about with that easy swagger which was one of his principal characteristics.

"Well," he said, turning towards his wondering son, when this disguise was completed, "well, do you think your police will recognize me now."

"No, father," stammered Villefort; "at least, I hope not."

"And now, my dear boy," continued Noirtier, "I rely on your prudence to remove all the things which I leave in your care."

"Oh, rely on me," said Villefort.

"Yes, yes; and now I believe you are right, and that you have really saved my life; be assured I will return the favor hereafter." Villefort shook his head.

"You are not convinced yet?"—"I hope, at least, that you may be mistaken."

"Shall you see the king again?"—"Perhaps."

"Would you pass in his eyes for a prophet?"—"Prophets of evil are not in favor at the court, father."

"True, but some day they do them justice; and supposing a second restoration, you would then pass for a great man."

"Well, what should I say to the king?"

"Say this to him: 'Sire, you are deceived as to the feeling in France, as to the opinions of the towns, and the prejudices of the army; he whom in Paris you call the Corsican ogre, who at Nevers is styled the usurper, is already saluted as Bonaparte at Lyons, and emperor at Grenoble. You think he is tracked, pursued, captured; he is advancing as rapidly as his own eagles. The soldiers you believe to be dying with hunger, worn out with fatigue, ready to desert, gather like atoms of snow about the rolling ball as it hastens onward. Sire, go, leave France to its real master, to him who acquired it, not by purchase, but by right of conquest; go, sire, not that you incur any risk, for your adversary is powerful enough to show you mercy, but because it would be humiliating for a grandson of Saint Louis to owe his life to the man of Arcola, Marengo, Austerlitz.' Tell him this, Gérard; or, rather, tell him nothing. Keep your journey a secret; do not boast of what you have come to Paris to do, or have done; return with all speed; enter Marseilles at night, and your house by the back-door, and there remain, quiet, submissive, secret, and, above all, inoffensive; for this time, I swear to you, we shall act like powerful men who know their enemies. Go, my son—go, my dear Gérard, and by your obedience to my paternal orders, or, if you prefer it, friendly counsels, we will keep you in your place. This will be," added Noirtier, with a smile, "one means by which you may a second time save me, if the political balance should some day take another turn, and cast you aloft while hurling me down. Adieu, my dear Gérard, and at your next journey alight at my door." Noirtier left the room when he had finished, with the same calmness that had characterized him during the whole of this remarkable and trying conversation. Villefort, pale and agitated, ran to the window, put aside the curtain, and saw him pass, cool and collected, by two or three ill-looking men at the corner of the street, who were there, perhaps, to arrest a man with black whiskers, and a blue frock-coat, and hat with broad brim.

Villefort stood watching, breathless, until his father had disappeared at the Rue Bussy. Then he turned to the various articles he had left behind him, put the black cravat and blue frock-coat at the bottom of the portmanteau, threw the hat into a dark closet, broke the cane into small bits and flung it in the fire, put on his travelling-cap, and calling his valet, checked with a look the thousand questions he was ready to ask, paid his bill, sprang into his carriage, which was ready, learned at Lyons that Bonaparte had entered Greuoble, and in the midst of the tumult which prevailed along the road, at length reached Marseilles, a prey to all the hopes and fears which enter into the heart of man with ambition and its first successes.

XIII

The Hundred Days

M. NOIRTIER WAS A TRUE prophet, and things progressed rapidly, as he had predicted. Every one knows the history of the famous return from Elba, a return which was unprecedented in the past, and will probably remain without a counterpart in the future.

Louis XVIII. made but a faint attempt to parry this unexpected blow; the monarchy he had scarcely reconstructed tottered on its precarious foundation, and at a sign from the emperor the incongruous structure of ancient prejudices and new ideas fell to the ground. Villefort, therefore, gained nothing save the king's gratitude (which was rather likely to injure him at the present time) and the cross of the Legion of Honor, which he had the prudence not to wear, although M. de Blacas had duly forwarded the brevet.

Napoleon would, doubtless, have deprived Villefort of his office had it not been for Noirtier, who was all powerful at court, and thus the Girondin of '93 and the Senator of 1806 protected him who so lately had been his protector. All Villefort's influence barely enabled him to stifle the secret Dantès had so nearly divulged. The king's procureur alone was deprived of his office, being suspected of royalism.

However, scarcely was the imperial power established—that is, scarcely had the emperor re-entered the Tuileries and begun to issue

orders from the closet into which we have introduced our readers,—
he found on the table there Louis XVIII.'s half-filled snuff-box,—
scarcely had this occurred when Marseilles began, in spite of the
authorities, to rekindle the flames of civil war, always smouldering in
the south, and it required but little to excite the populace to acts of
far greater violence than the shouts and insults with which they
assailed the royalists whenever they ventured abroad.

Owing to this change, the worthy shipowner became at that
moment—we will not say all powerful, because Morrel was a prudent and rather a timid man, so much so, that many of the most
zealous partisans of Bonaparte accused him of "moderation"—but
sufficiently influential to make a demand in favor of Dantès.

Villefort retained his place, but his marriage was put off until a
more favorable opportunity. If the emperor remained on the throne,
Gérard required a different alliance to aid his career; if Louis XVIII.
returned, the influence of M. de Saint-Méran, like his own, could be
vastly increased, and the marriage be still more suitable. The deputy-
procureur was, therefore, the first magistrate of Marseilles, when one
morning his door opened, and M. Morrel was announced.

Any one else would have hastened to receive him; but Villefort
was a man of ability, and he knew this would be a sign of weakness.
He made Morrel wait in the antechamber, although he had no one
with him, for the simple reason that the king's procureur always
makes every one wait, and after passing a quarter of an hour in
reading the papers, he ordered M. Morrel to be admitted.

Morrel expected Villefort would be dejected; he found him as
he had found him six weeks before, calm, firm, and full of that
glacial politeness, that most insurmountable barrier which separates
the well-bred from the vulgar man.

He had entered Villefort's office expecting that the magistrate
would tremble at the sight of him; on the contrary, he felt a cold
shudder all over him when he saw Villefort sitting there with his
elbow on his desk, and his head leaning on his hand. He stopped at

the door; Villefort gazed at him as if he had some difficulty in recognizing him; then, after a brief interval, during which the honest shipowner turned his hat in his hands,—

"M. Morrel, I believe?" said Villefort.—"Yes, sir."

"Come nearer," said the magistrate, with a patronizing wave of the hand, "and tell me to what circumstance I owe the honor of this visit."

"Do you not guess, monsieur?" asked Morrel.

"Not in the least; but if I can serve you in any way I shall be delighted."

"Everything depends on you."—"Explain yourself, pray."

"Monsieur," said Morrel, recovering his assurance as he proceeded, "do you recollect that a few days before the landing of his majesty the emperor, I came to intercede for a young man, the mate of my ship, who was accused of being concerned in correspondence with the Island of Elba? What was the other day a crime is to-day a title to favor. You then served Louis XVIII., and you did not show any favor—it was your duty; to-day you serve Napoleon, and you ought to protect him—it is equally your duty; I come, therefore, to ask what has become of him?"

Villefort by a strong effort sought to control himself. "What is his name?" said he. "Tell me his name."

"Edmond Dantès."

Villefort would probably have rather stood opposite the muzzle of a pistol at five-and-twenty paces than have heard this name spoken; but he did not blanch.

"Dantès," repeated he, "Edmond Dantès."—"Yes, monsieur." Villefort opened a large register, then went to a table, from the table turned to his registers, and then, turning to Morrel,—

"Are you quite sure you are not mistaken, monsieur?" said he, in the most natural tone in the world.

Had Morrel been a more quick-sighted man, or better versed in these matters, he would have been surprised at the king's procureur answering him on such a subject, instead of referring him to the governors of the prison or the prefect of the department. But Morrel, disappointed in his expectations of exciting fear, was conscious only of the other's condescension. Villefort had calculated rightly.

"No," said Morrel; "I am not mistaken. I have known him for ten years, the last four of which he was in my service. Do not you recollect, I came about six weeks ago to plead for clemency, as I come to-day to plead for justice. You received me very coldly. Oh, the royalists were very severe with the Bonapartists in those days."

"Monsieur," returned Villefort, "I was then a royalist, because I believed the Bourbons not only the heirs to the throne, but the chosen of the nation. The miraculous return of Napoleon has conquered me; the legitimate monarch is he who is loved by his people."

"That's right!" cried Morrel. "I like to hear you speak thus, and I augur well for Edmond from it."

"Wait a moment," said Villefort, turning over the leaves of a register; "I have it—a sailor, who was about to marry a young Catalan girl. I recollect now; it was a very serious charge."—"How so?"

"You know that when he left here he was taken to the Palais de Justice."—"Well?"

"I made my report to the authorities at Paris, and a week after he was carried off."

"Carried off!" said Morrel. "What can they have done with him?"

"Oh, he has been taken to Fenestrelles, to Pignerol, or to the Sainte-Marguérite islands. Some fine morning he will return to take command of your vessel."

"Come when he will, it shall be kept for him. But how is it he is not already returned? It seems to me the first care of government should be to set at liberty those who have suffered for their adherence to it."

"Do not be too hasty, M. Morrel," replied Villefort. "The order of imprisonment came from high authority, and the order for his liberation must proceed from the same source; and, as Napoleon has scarcely been reinstated a fortnight, the letters have not yet been forwarded."

"But," said Morrel, "is there no way of expediting all these formalities—of releasing him from arrest?"

"There has been no arrest."—"How?"

"It is sometimes essential to government to cause a man's disappearance without leaving any traces, so that no written forms or documents may defeat their wishes."

"It might be so under the Bourbons, but at present"—

"It has always been so, my dear Morrel, since the reign of Louis XIV. The emperor is more strict in prison discipline than even Louis himself, and the number of prisoners whose names are not on the register is incalculable." Had Morrel even any suspicions, so much kindness would have dispelled them.

"Well, M. de Villefort, how would you advise me to act?" asked he.

"Petition the minister."

"Oh, I know what that is; the minister receives two hundred petitions every day, and does not read three."

"That is true; but he will read a petition countersigned and presented by me."

"And will you undertake to deliver it?"

"With the greatest pleasure. Dantès was then guilty, and now he is innocent, and it is as much my duty to free him as it was to condemn him." Villefort thus forestalled any danger of an inquiry, which, however improbable it might be, if it did take place would leave him defenceless.

"But how shall I address the minister?"

"Sit down there," said Villefort, giving up his place to Morrel, "and write what I dictate."—"Will you be so good?"

"Certainly. But lose no time; we have lost too much already."

"That is true. Only think what the poor fellow may even now be suffering." Villefort shuddered at the suggestion; but he had gone too far to draw back. Dantès must be crushed to gratify Villefort's ambition.

Villefort dictated a petition, in which, from an excellent intention, no doubt, Dantès patriotic services were exaggerated, and he was made out one of the most active agents of Napoleon's return. It was evident that at the sight of this document the minister would instantly release him. The petition finished, Villefort read it aloud.

"That will do," said he; "leave the rest to me."

"Will the petition go soon?"—"To-day."

"Countersigned by you?"—"The best thing I can do will be to certify the truth of the contents of your petition." And, sitting down, Villefort wrote the certificate at the bottom.

"What more is to be done?"—"I will do whatever is necessary." This assurance delighted Morrel, who took leave of Villefort, and hastened to announce to old Dantès that he would soon see his son.

As for Villefort, instead of sending to Paris, he carefully preserved the petition that so fearfully compromised Dantès, in the hopes of an event that seemed not unlikely,—that is, a second restoration. Dantès remained a prisoner, and heard not the noise of the fall of Louis XVIII.'s throne, or the still more tragic destruction of the empire.

Twice during the Hundred Days had Morrel renewed his demand, and twice had Villefort soothed him with promises. At last there was Waterloo, and Morrel came no more; he had done all that was in his power, and any fresh attempt would only compromise himself uselessly.

Louis XVIII. remounted the throne; Villefort, to whom Marseilles had become filled with remorseful memories, sought and obtained the situation of king's procureur at Toulouse, and a fortnight afterwards he married Mademoiselle de Saint-Méran, whose father now stood higher at court than ever.

And so Dantès, after the Hundred Days and after Waterloo, remained in his dungeon, forgotten of earth and heaven. Danglars comprehended the full extent of the wretched fate that overwhelmed Dantès; and, when Napoleon returned to France, he, after the manner of mediocre minds, termed the coincidence, "a decree of Providence." But when Napoleon returned to Paris, Danglars' heart failed him, and he lived in constant fear of Dantès' return on a mission of vengeance. He therefore informed M. Morrel of his wish to quit the sea, and obtained a recommendation from him to a Spanish merchant, into whose service he entered at the end of March, that is, ten or twelve days after Napoleon's return. He then left for Madrid, and was no more heard of.

Fernand understood nothing except that Dantès was absent. What had become of him he cared not to inquire. Only, during the respite the absence of his rival afforded him, he reflected, partly on the means of deceiving Mercédès as to the cause of his absence, partly on plans of emigration and abduction, as from time to time he sat sad and motionless on the summit of Cape Pharo, at the spot from whence Marseilles and the Catalans are visible, watching for the apparition of a young and handsome man, who was for him also the messenger of vengeance. Fernand's mind was made up; he would shoot Dantès, and then kill himself. But Fernand was mistaken; a man of his disposition never kills himself, for he constantly hopes.

During this time the empire made its last conscription, and every man in France capable of bearing arms rushed to obey the summons of the emperor. Fernand departed with the rest, bearing with him the terrible thought that while he was away his rival would perhaps return and marry Mercédès. Had Fernand really meant to kill himself, he would have done so when he parted from Mercédès. His devotion, and the compassion he showed for her misfortunes, produced the effect they always produce on noble minds—Mercédès had always had a sincere regard for Fernand, and this was now strengthened by gratitude.

"My brother," said she as she placed his knapsack on his shoulders, "be careful of yourself, for if you are killed, I shall be alone in the world." These words carried a ray of hope into Fernand's heart. Should Dantès not return, Mercédès might one day be his.

Mercédès was left alone face to face with the vast plain that had never seemed so barren, and the sea that had never seemed so vast. Bathed in tears she wandered about the Catalan village. Sometimes she stood mute and motionless as a statue, looking towards Marseilles, at other times gazing on the sea, and debating as to whether it were not better to cast herself into the abyss of the ocean, and thus end her woes. It was not want of courage that prevented her putting this resolution into execution; but her religious feelings came to her aid and saved her. Caderousse was, like Fernand, enrolled in the army, but, being married and eight years older, he was merely sent to the frontier. Old Dantès, who was only sustained by hope, lost all hope at Napoleon's downfall. Five months after he had been separated from his son, and almost at the hour of his arrest, he breathed his last in Mercédès' arms. M. Morrel paid the expenses of his funeral, and a few small debts the poor old man had contracted.

There was more than benevolence in this action; there was courage; the south was aflame, and to assist, even on his death-bed, the father of so dangerous a Bonapartist as Dantès, was stigmatized as a crime.

XIV

The Two Prisoners

A YEAR AFTER LOUIS XVIII.'s restoration, a visit was made by the inspector-general of prisons. Dantès in his cell heard the noise of preparation,—sounds that at the depth where he lay would have been inaudible to any but the ear of a prisoner, who could hear the plash of the drop of water that every hour fell from the roof of his dungeon. He guessed something uncommon was passing among the living; but he had so long ceased to have any intercourse with the world, that he looked upon himself as dead.

The inspector visited, one after another, the cells and dungeons of several of the prisoners, whose good behavior or stupidity recommended them to the clemency of the government. He inquired how they were fed, and if they had any request to make. The universal response was, that the fare was detestable, and that they wanted to be set free.

The inspector asked if they had anything else to ask for. They shook their heads. What could they desire beyond their liberty? The inspector turned smilingly to the governor.

"I do not know what reason government can assign for these useless visits; when you see one prisoner, you see all,—always the same thing,—ill fed and innocent. Are there any others?"

"Yes; the dangerous and mad prisoners are in the dungeons."

"Let us visit them," said the inspector with an air of fatigue. "We must play the farce to the end. Let us see the dungeons."

"Let us first send for two soldiers," said the governor. "The prisoners sometimes, through mere uneasiness of life, and in order to be sentenced to death, commit acts of useless violence, and you might fall a victim."

"Take all needful precautions," replied the inspector.

Two soldiers were accordingly sent for, and the inspector descended a stairway, so foul, so humid, so dark, as to be loathsome to sight, smell, and respiration.

"Oh," cried the inspector, "who can live here?"

"A most dangerous conspirator, a man we are ordered to keep the most strict watch over, as he is daring and resolute."

"He is alone?"—"Certainly."

"How long has he been there?"—"Nearly a year."

"Was he placed here when he first arrived?"—"No; not until he attempted to kill the turnkey, who took his food to him."

"To kill the turnkey?"—"Yes, the very one who is lighting us. Is it not true, Autoine?" asked the governor.

"True enough; he wanted to kill me!" returned the turnkey.

"He must be mad," said the inspector.

"He is worse than that,—he is a devil!" returned the turnkey.

"Shall I complain of him?" demanded the inspector.

"Oh, no; it is useless. Besides, he is almost mad now, and in another year he will be quite so."

"So much the better for him,—he will suffer less," said the inspector. He was, as this remark shows, a man full of philanthropy, and in every way fit for his office.

"You are right, sir," replied the governor; "and this remark proves that you have deeply considered the subject. Now we have in a dungeon about twenty feet distant, and to which you descend by another stair, an abbé, formerly leader of a party in Italy, who has been here since 1811, and in 1813 he went mad, and the change is astonishing. He used to weep, he now laughs; he grew thin, he now grows fat. You had better see him, for his madness is amusing."

"I will see them both," returned the inspector; "I must conscientiously perform my duty." This was the inspector's first visit; he wished to display his authority.

"Let us visit this one first," added he.

"By all means," replied the governor; and he signed to the turnkey to open the door. At the sound of the key turning in the lock, and the creaking of the hinges, Dantès, who was crouched in a corner of the dungeon, whence he could see the ray of light that came through a narrow iron grating above, raised his head. Seeing a stranger, escorted by two turnkeys holding torches and accompanied by two soldiers, and to whom the governor spoke bareheaded, Dantès, who guessed the truth, and that the moment to address himself to the superior authorities was come, sprang forward with clasped hands.

The soldiers interposed their bayonets, for they thought that he was about to attack the inspector, and the latter recoiled two or three steps. Dantès saw that he was looked upon as dangerous. Then, infusing all the humility he possessed into his eyes and voice, he addressed the inspector, and sought to inspire him with pity.

The inspector listened attentively; then, turning to the governor, observed, "He will become religious—he is already more gentle; he is afraid, and retreated before the bayonets—madmen are not afraid of anything; I made some curious observations on this at Charenton." Then, turning to the prisoner, "What is it you want?" said he.

"I want to know what crime I have committed—to be tried; and if I am guilty, to be shot; if innocent, to be set at liberty."

"Are you well fed?" said the inspector.

"I believe so; I don't know; it's of no consequence. What matters really, not only to me, but to officers of justice and the king, is that an innocent man should languish in prison, the victim of an infamous denunciation, to die here cursing his executioners."

"You are very humble to-day," remarked the governor; "you are not so always; the other day, for instance, when you tried to kill the turnkey."

"It is true, sir, and I beg his pardon, for he has always been very good to me; but I was mad."

"And you are not so any longer?"

"No; captivity has subdued me—I have been here so long."

"So long?—when were you arrested, then?" asked the inspector.

"The 28th of February, 1815, at half-past two in the afternoon."

"To-day is the 30th of July, 1816,—why it is but seventeen months."

"Only seventeen months," replied Dantès. "Oh, you do not know what is seventeen months in prison!—seventeen ages rather, especially to a man who, like me, had arrived at the summit of his ambition—to a man, who, like me, was on the point of marrying a woman he adored, who saw an honorable career opened before him, and who loses all in an instant—who sees his prospects destroyed, and is ignorant of the fate of his affianced wife, and whether his aged father be still living! Seventeen months captivity to a sailor accustomed to the boundless ocean, is a worse punishment than human crime ever merited. Have pity on me, then, and ask for me, not indulgence, but a trial; not pardon, but a verdict—a trial, sir, I ask only for a trial; that, surely, cannot be denied to one who is accused."

"We shall see," said the inspector; then, turning to the governor, "On my word, the poor devil touches me. You must show me the proofs against him."

"Certainly; but you will find terrible charges."

"Monsieur," continued Dantès, "I know it is not in your power to release me; but you can plead for me—you can have me tried—and that is all I ask. Let me know my crime, and the reason why I was condemned. Uncertainty is worse than all."

"Go on with the lights," said the inspector.

"Monsieur," cried Dantès, "I can tell by your voice you are touched with pity; tell me at least to hope."

"I cannot tell you that," replied the inspector; "I can only promise to examine into your case."—"Oh, I am free—then I am saved!"

"Who arrested you?"—"M. Villefort. See him, and hear what he says."

"M. Villefort is no longer at Marseilles; he is now at Toulouse."

"I am no longer surprised at my detention," murmured Dantès, "since my only protector is removed."

"Had M. de Villefort any cause of personal dislike to you?"

"None; on the contrary, he was very kind to me."

"I can, then, rely on the notes he has left concerning you?"— "Entirely."

"That is well; wait patiently, then." Dantès fell on his knees, and prayed earnestly. The door closed; but this time a fresh inmate was left with Dantès—hope.

"Will you see the register at once," asked the governor, "or proceed to the other cell?"

"Let us visit them all," said the inspector. "If I once went up those stairs, I should never have the courage to come down again."

"Ah, this one is not like the other, and his madness is less affecting than this one's display of reason."

"What is his folly?"

"He fancies he possesses an immense treasure. The first year he offered government a million of Francs for his release; the second, two; the third, three; and so on progressively. He is now in his fifth year of captivity; he will ask to speak to you in private, and offer you five millions."

"How curious!—what is his name?"—"The Abbé Faria."

"No. 27," said the inspector.

"It is here; unlock the door, Antoine." The turnkey obeyed, and the inspector gazed curiously into the chamber of the "mad abbé."

In the centre of the cell, in a circle traced with a fragment of plaster detached from the wall, sat a man whose tattered garments scarcely covered him. He was drawing in this circle geometrical lines, and seemed as much absorbed in his problem as Archimedes was when the soldier of Marcellus slew him.

He did not move at the sound of the door, and continued his calculations until the flash of the torches lighted up with an unwonted glare the sombre walls of his cell; then, raising his head, he perceived with astonishment the number of persons present. He hastily seized the coverlet of his bed, and wrapped it round him.

"What is it you want?" said the inspector.

"I, monsieur," replied the abbé with an air of surprise—"I want nothing."

"You do not understand," continued the inspector; "I am sent here by government to visit the prison, and hear the requests of the prisoners."

"Oh, that is different," cried the abbé; "and we shall understand each other, I hope."

"There, now," whispered the governor, "it is just as I told you."

"Monsieur," continued the prisoner, "I am the Abbé Faria, born at Rome. I was for twenty years Cardinal Spada's secretary; I was arrested, why, I know not, toward the beginning of the year 1811; since then I have demanded my liberty from the Italian and French government."

"Why from the French government?"

"Because I was arrested at Piombino, and I presume that, like Milan and Florence, Piombino has become the capital of some French department."

"Ah," said the inspector, "you have not the latest news from Italy?"

"My information dates from the day on which I was arrested," returned the Abbé Faria; "and as the emperor had created the kingdom of Rome for his infant son, I presume that he has realized the dream of Machiavelli and Cæsar Borgia, which was to make Italy a united kingdom."

"Monsieur," returned the inspector, "providence has changed this gigantic plan you advocate so warmly."

"It is the only means of rendering Italy strong, happy, and independent."

"Very possibly; only I am not come to discuss politics, but to inquire if you have anything to ask or to complain of."

"The food is the same as in other prisons,—that is, very bad; the lodging is very unhealthful, but, on the whole, passable for a dungeon; but it is not that which I wish to speak of, but a secret I have to reveal of the greatest importance."

"We are coming to the point," whispered the governor.

"It is for that reason I am delighted to see you," continued the abbé, "although you have disturbed me in a most important calculation, which, if it succeeded, would possibly change Newton's system. Could you allow me a few words in private."

"What did I tell you?" said the governor.

"You knew him," returned the inspector with a smile.

"What you ask is impossible, monsieur," continued he, addressing Faria.

"But," said the abbé, "I would speak to you of a large sum, amounting to five millions."

"The very sum you named," whispered the inspector in his turn.

"However," continued Faria, seeing that the inspector was about to depart, "it is not absolutely necessary for us to be alone; the governor can be present."

"Unfortunately," said the governor, "I know beforehand what you are about to say; it concerns your treasures, does it not?" Faria fixed his eyes on him with an expression that would have convinced any one else of his sanity.

"Of course," said he; "of what else should I speak?"

"Mr. Inspector," continued the governor, "I can tell you the story as well as he, for it has been dinned in my ears for the last four or five years."

"That proves," returned the abbé, "that you are like those of Holy Writ, who having ears hear not, and having eyes see not."

"My dear sir, the government is rich and does not want your treasures," replied the inspector; "keep them until you are liberated." The abbé's eyes glistened; he seized the inspector's hand.

"But what if I am not liberated," cried he, "and am detained here until my death? this treasure will be lost. Had not government better profit by it? I will offer six millions, and I will content myself with the rest, if they will only give me my liberty."

"On my word," said the inspector in a low tone, "had I not been told beforehand that this man was mad, I should believe what he says."

"I am not mad," replied Faria, with that acuteness of hearing peculiar to prisoners. "The treasure I speak of really exists, and I offer to sign an agreement with you, in which I promise to lead you to the spot where you shall dig; and if I deceive you, bring me here again,—I ask no more."

The governor laughed. "Is the spot far from here?"—"A hundred leagues."

"It is not ill-planned," said the governor. "If all the prisoners took it into their heads to travel a hundred leagues, and their guardians consented to accompany them, they would have a capital chance of escaping."

"The scheme is well known," said the inspector; "and the abbé's plan has not even the merit of originality."

Then turning to Faria—"I inquired if you are well fed?" said he.

"Swear to me," replied Faria, "to free me if what I tell you prove true, and I will stay here while you go to the spot."

"Are you well fed?" repeated the inspector.

"Monsieur, you run no risk, for, as I told you, I will stay here; so there is no chance of my escaping."

"You do not reply to my question," replied the inspector impatiently.

"Nor you to mine," cried the abbé. "You will not accept my gold; I will keep it for myself. You refuse me my liberty; God will give it me." And the abbé, casting away his coverlet, resumed his place, and continued his calculations.

"What is he doing there?" said the inspector.

"Counting his treasures," replied the governor.

Faria replied to this sarcasm with a glance of profound comtempt. They went out. The turnkey closed the door behind them.

"He was wealthy once, perhaps?" said the inspector.

"Or dreamed he was, and awoke mad."

"After all," said the inspector, "if he had been rich, he would not have been here." So the matter ended for the Abbé Faria. He remained in his cell, and this visit only increased the belief in his insanity.

Caligula or Nero, those treasure-seekers, those desirers of the impossible, would have accorded to the poor wretch, in exchange for his wealth, the liberty he so earnestly prayed for. But the kings of modern times, restrained by the limits of mere probability, have neither courage nor desire. They fear the ear that hears their orders, and the eye that scrutinizes their actions. Formerly they believed themselves sprung from Jupiter, and shielded by their birth; but nowadays they are not inviolable.

It has always been against the policy of despotic governments to suffer the victims of their persecutions to reappear. As the Inquisition rarely allowed its victims to be seen with their limbs distorted and their flesh lacerated by torture, so madness is always concealed in its cell, from whence, should it depart, it is conveyed to some gloomy hospital, where the doctor has no thought for man or mind in the mutilated being the jailer delivers to him. The very madness of the Abbé Faria, gone mad in prison, condemned him to perpetual captivity.

The inspector kept his word with Dantès; he examined the register, and found the following note concerning him:—

EDMOND DANTÈS }Violent Bonapartist; took an active part in the return from Elba.

The greatest watchfulness and care to be exercised.

This note was in a different hand from the rest, which showed that it had been added since his confinement. The inspector could not contend against this accusation; he simply wrote,—"Nothing to be done."

This visit had infused new vigor into Dantès; he had, till then, forgotten the date; but now, with a fragment of plaster, he wrote the date, 30th July, 1816, and made a mark every day, in order not to lose his reckoning again. Days and weeks passed away, then months—Dantès still waited; he at first expected to be freed in a fortnight. This fortnight expired, he decided that the inspector would do nothing until his return to Paris, and that he would not reach there until his circuit was finished, he therefore fixed three months; three months passed away, then six more. Finally ten months and a half had gone by and no favorable change had taken place, and Dantès began to fancy the inspector's visit but a dream, an illusion of the brain.

At the expiration of a year the governor was transferred; he had obtained charge of the fortress at Ham. He took with him several of his subordinates, and amongst them Dantès' jailer. A new governor arrived; it would have been too tedious to acquire the names of the prisoners; he learned their numbers instead. This horrible place contained fifty cells; their inhabitants were designated by the numbers of their cell, and the unhappy young man was no longer called Edmond Dantès—he was now number 34.

XV

Number 34 and Number 27

D ANTÈS PASSED THROUGH ALL the stages of torture natural to prisoners in suspense. He was sustained at first by that pride of conscious innocence which is the sequence to hope; then he began to doubt his own innocence, which justified in some measure the governor's belief in his mental alienation; and then, relaxing his sentiment of pride, he addressed his supplications, not to God, but to man. God is always the last resource. Unfortunates, who ought to begin with God, do not have any hope in him till they have exhausted all other means of deliverance.

Dantès asked to be removed from his present dungeon into another; for a change, however disadvantageous, was still a change, and would afford him some amusement. He entreated to be allowed to walk about, to have fresh air, books, and writing materials. His requests were not granted, but he went on asking all the same. He accustomed himself to speaking to the new jailer, although the latter was, if possible, more taciturn than the old one; but still, to speak to a man, even though mute, was something. Dantès spoke for the sake of hearing his own voice; he had tried to speak when alone, but the sound of his voice terrified him. Often, before his captivity, Dantès' mind had revolted at the idea of assemblages of prisoners, made up of thieves, vagabonds, and murderers.

He now wished to be amongst them, in order to see some other face besides that of his jailer; he sighed for the galleys, with the infamous costume, the chain, and the brand on the shoulder. The galley-slaves breathed the fresh air of heaven, and saw each other. They were very happy. He besought the jailer one day to let him have a companion, were it even the mad abbé.

The jailer, though rough and hardened by the contrast sight of so much suffering, was yet a man. At the bottom of his heart he had often had a feeling of pity for this unhappy young man who suffered so; and he laid the request of number 34 before the governor; but the latter sapiently imagined that Dantès wished to conspire or attempt an escape, and refused his request. Dantès had exhausted all human resources, and he then turned to God.

All the pious ideas that had been so long forgotten, returned; he recollected the prayers his mother had taught him, and discovered a new meaning in every word; for in prosperity prayers seem but a mere medley of words, until misfortune comes and the unhappy sufferer first understands the meaning of the sublime language in which he invokes the pity of heaven! He prayed, and prayed aloud, no longer terrified at the sound of his own voice, for he fell into a sort of ecstasy. He laid every action of his life before the Almighty, proposed tasks to accomplish, and at the end of every prayer introduced the entreaty oftener addressed to man than to God: "Forgive us our trespasses as we forgive them that trespass against us." Yet in spite of his earnest prayers, Dantès remained a prisoner.

Then gloom settled heavily upon him. Dantès was a man of great simplicity of thought, and without education; he could not, therefore, in the solitude of his dungeon, traverse in mental vision the history of the ages, bring to life the nations that had perished, and rebuild the ancient cities so vast and stupendous in the light of the imagination, and that pass before the eye glowing with celestial colors in Martin's Babylonian pictures. He could not do this, he whose past life was so short, whose present so melancholy, and his future so doubtful.

Nineteen years of light to reflect upon in eternal darkness! No distraction could come to his aid; his energetic spirit, that would have exulted in thus revisiting the past, was imprisoned like an eagle in a cage. He clung to one idea—that of his happiness, destroyed, without apparent cause, by an unheard-of fatality; he considered and reconsidered this idea, devoured it (so to speak), as the implacable Ugolino devours the skull of Archbishop Roger in the Inferno of Dante.

Rage supplanted religious fervor. Dantès uttered blasphemies that made his jailer recoil with horror, dashed himself furiously against the walls of his prison, wreaked his anger upon everything, and chiefly upon himself, so that the least thing,—a grain of sand, a straw, or a breath of air that annoyed him, led to paroxysms of fury. Then the letter that Villefort had showed to him recurred to his mind, and every line gleamed forth in fiery letters on the wall like the *mene tekel upharsin* of Belshazzar. He told himself that it was the enmity of man, and not the vengeance of heaven, that had thus plunged him into the deepest misery. He consigned his unknown persecutors to the most horrible tortures he could imagine, and found them all insufficient, because after torture came death, and after death, if not repose, at least the boon of unconsciousness.

By dint of constantly dwelling on the idea that tranquillity was death, and if punishment were the end in view other tortures than death must be invented, he began to reflect on suicide. Unhappy he, who, on the brink of misfortune, broods over ideas like these!

Before him is a dead sea that stretches in azure calm before the eye; but he who unwarily ventures within its embrace finds himself struggling with a monster that would drag him down to perdition. Once thus ensnared, unless the protecting hand of God snatch him thence, all is over, and his struggles but tend to hasten his destruction. This state of mental anguish is, however, less terrible than the sufferings that precede or the punishment that possibly will follow. There is a sort of consolation at the contemplation of the yawning abyss, at the bottom of which lie darkness and obscurity.

Edmond found some solace in these ideas. All his sorrows, all his sufferings, with their train of gloomy spectres, fled from his cell when the angel of death seemed about to enter. Dantès reviewed his past life with composure, and, looking forward with terror to his future existence, chose that middle line that seemed to afford him a refuge.

"Sometimes," said he, "in my voyages, when I was a man and commanded other men, I have seen the heavens overcast, the sea rage and foam, the storm arise, and, like a monstrous bird, beating the two horizons with its wings. Then I felt that my vessel was a vain refuge that trembled and shook before the tempest. Soon the fury of the waves and the sight of the sharp rocks announced the approach of death, and death then terrified me, and I used all my skill and intelligence as a man and a sailor to struggle against the wrath of God. But I did so because I was happy, because I had not courted death, because to be cast upon a bed of rocks and seaweed seemed terrible, because I was unwilling that I, a creature made for the service of God, should serve for food to the gulls and ravens. But now it is different; I have lost all that bound me to life; death smiles and invites me to repose; I die after my own manner, I die exhausted and broken-spirited, as I fall asleep when I have paced three thousand times round my cell."

No sooner had this idea taken possession of him than he became more composed, arranged his couch to the best of his power, ate little and slept less, and found existence almost supportable, because he felt that he could throw it off at pleasure, like a worn-out garment. Two methods of self-destruction were at his disposal. He could hang himself with his handkerchief to the window bars, or refuse food and die of starvation. But the first was repugnant to him. Dantès had always entertained the greatest horror of pirates, who are hung up to the yard-arm; he would not die by what seemed an infamous death. He resolved to adopt the second, and began that day to carry out his resolve. Nearly four years had passed away; at the end of the second he had ceased to mark the lapse of time.

Dantès said, "I wish to die," and had chosen the manner of his death, and fearful of changing his mind, he had taken an oath to die. "When my morning and evening meals are brought," thought he, "I will cast them out of the window, and they will think that I have eaten them."

He kept his word; twice a day he cast out, through the barred aperture, the provisions his jailer brought him—at first gayly, then with deliberation, and at last with regret. Nothing but the recollection of his oath gave him strength to proceed. Hunger made viands once repugnant, now acceptable; he held the plate in his hand for an hour at a time, and gazed thoughtfully at the morsel of bad meat, of tainted fish, of black and mouldy bread. It was the last yearning for life contending with the resolution of despair; then his dungeon seemed less sombre, his prospects less desperate. He was still young—he was only four or five and twenty—he had nearly fifty years to live. What unforseen events might not open his prison door, and restore him to liberty? Then he raised to his lips the repast that, like a voluntary Tantalus, he refused himself; but he thought of his oath, and he would not break it. He persisted until, at last, he had not sufficient strength to rise and cast his supper out of the loophole. The next morning he could not see or hear; the jailer feared he was dangerously ill. Edmond hoped he was dying.

Thus the day passed away. Edmond felt a sort of stupor creeping over him which brought with it a feeling almost of content; the gnawing pain at his stomach had ceased; his thirst had abated; when he closed his eyes he saw myriads of lights dancing before them like the will-o'-the-wisps that play about the marshes. It was the twilight of that mysterious country called Death!

Suddenly, about nine o'clock in the evening, Edmond heard a hollow sound in the wall against which he was lying.

So many loathsome animals inhabited the prison, that their noise did not, in general, awake him; but whether abstinence had quickened his faculties, or whether the noise was really louder than usual, Edmond raised his head and listened. It was a continual scratching, as if made by a huge claw, a powerful tooth, or some iron instrument attacking the stones.

Although weakened, the young man's brain instantly responded to the idea that haunts all prisoners—liberty! It seemed to him that heaven had at length taken pity on him, and had sent this noise to warn him on the very brink of the abyss. Perhaps one of those beloved ones he had so often thought of was thinking of him, and striving to diminish the distance that separated them.

No, no, doubtless he was deceived, and it was but one of those dreams that forerun death!

Edmond still heard the sound. It lasted nearly three hours; he then heard a noise of something falling, and all was silent.

Some hours afterwards it began again, nearer and more distinct. Edmond was intensely interested. Suddenly the jailer entered.

For a week since he had resolved to die, and during the four days that he had been carrying out his purpose, Edmond had not spoken to the attendant, had not answered him when he inquired what was the matter with him, and turned his face to the wall when he looked too curiously at him; but now the jailer might hear the noise and put an end to it, and so destroy a ray of something like hope that soothed his last moments.

The jailer brought him his breakfast. Dantès raised himself up and began to talk about everything; about the bad quality of the food, about the coldness of his dungeon, grumbling and complaining, in order to have an excuse for speaking louder, and wearying the patience of his jailer, who out of kindness of heart had brought broth and white bread for his prisoner.

Fortunately, he fancied that Dantès was delirious; and placing the food on the rickety table, he withdrew. Edmond listened, and the sound became more and more distinct.

"There can be no doubt about it," thought he; "it is some prisoner who is striving to obtain his freedom. Oh, if I were only there to help him!" Suddenly another idea took possession of his mind, so used to misfortune, that it was scarcely capable of hope—the idea that the noise was made by workmen the governor had ordered to repair the neighboring dungeon.

It was easy to ascertain this; but how could he risk the question? It was easy to call his jailer's attention to the noise, and watch his countenance as he listened; but might he not by this means destroy hopes far more important than the short-lived satisfaction of his own curiosity? Unfortunately, Edmond's brain was still so feeble that he could not bend his thoughts to anything in particular.

He saw but one means of restoring lucidity and clearness to his judgment. He turned his eyes towards the soup which the jailer had brought, rose, staggered towards it, raised the vessel to his lips, and drank off the contents with a feeling of indescribable pleasure. He had often heard that shipwrecked persons had died through having eagerly devoured too much food. Edmond replaced on the table the bread he was about to devour, and returned to his couch—he did not wish to die. He soon felt that his ideas became again collected—he could think, and strengthen his thoughts by reasoning. Then he said to himself, "I must put this to the test, but without compromising anybody. If it is a workman, I need but knock against the wall, and he will cease to work, in order to find out who is knocking, and why he does so; but as his occupation is sanctioned by the governor, he will soon resume it. If, on the contrary, it is a prisoner, the noise I make will alarm him, he will cease, and not begin again until he thinks every one is asleep."

Edmond rose again, but this time his legs did not tremble, and his sight was clear; he went to a corner of his dungeon, detached a stone, and with it knocked against the wall where the sound came. He struck thrice. At the first blow the sound ceased, as if by magic.

Edmond listened intently; an hour passed, two hours passed, and no sound was heard from the wall—all was silent there.

Full of hope, Edmond swallowed a few mouthfuls of bread and

water, and, thanks to the vigor of his constitution, found himself well-nigh recovered.

The day passed away in utter silence—night came without recurrence of the noise.

"It is a prisoner," said Edmond joyfully. The night passed in perfect silence. Edmond did not close his eyes.

In the morning the jailer brought him fresh provisions—he had already devoured those of the previous day; he ate these, listening anxiously for the sound, walking round and round his cell, shaking the iron bars of the loophole, restoring vigor and agility to his limbs by exercise, and so preparing himself for his future destiny. At intervals he listened to learn if the noise had not begun again, and grew impatient at the prudence of the prisoner, who did not guess he had been disturbed by a captive as anxious for liberty as himself.

Three days passed—seventy-two long tedious hours which he counted off by minutes!

At length one evening, as the jailer was visiting him for the last time that night, Dantès, with his ear for the hundredth time at the wall, fancied he heard an almost imperceptible movement among the stones. He moved away, walked up and down his cell to collect his thoughts, and then went back and listened.

The matter was no longer doubtful. Something was at work on the other side of the wall; the prisoner had discovered the danger, and had substituted a lever for a chisel.

Encouraged by this discovery, Edmond determined to assist the indefatigable laborer. He began by moving his bed, and looked around for anything with which he could pierce the wall, penetrate the moist cement, and displace a stone.

He saw nothing, he had no knife or sharp instrument, the window grating was of iron, but he had too often assured himself of its solidity. All his furniture consisted of a bed, a chair, a table, a pail, and a jug. The bed had iron clamps, but they were screwed to the wood, and it would have required a screw-driver to take them off.

The table and chair had nothing, the pail had once possessed a handle, but that had been removed.

Dantès had but one resource, which was to break the jug, and with one of the sharp fragments attack the wall. He let the jug fall on the floor, and it broke in pieces.

Dantès concealed two or three of the sharpest fragments in his bed, leaving the rest on the floor. The breaking of his jug was too natural an accident to excite suspicion. Edmond had all the night to work in, but in the darkness he could not do much, and he soon felt that he was working against something very hard; he pushed back his bed, and waited for day.

All night he heard the subterranean workman, who continued to mine his way. Day came, the jailer entered. Dantès told him that the jug had fallen from his hands while he was drinking, and the jailer went grumblingly to fetch another, without giving himself the trouble to remove the fragments of the broken one. He returned speedily, advised the prisoner to be more careful, and departed.

Dantès heard joyfully the key grate in the lock; he listened until the sound of steps died away, and then, hastily displacing his bed, saw by the faint light that penetrated into his cell, that he had labored uselessly the previous evening in attacking the stone instead of removing the plaster that surrounded it.

The damp had rendered it friable, and Dantès was able to break it off—in small morsels, it is true, but at the end of half an hour he had scraped off a handful; a mathematician might have calculated that in two years, supposing that the rock was not encountered, a passage twenty feet long and two feet broad, might be formed.

The prisoner reproached himself with not having thus employed the hours he had passed in vain hopes, prayer, and despondency. During the six years that he had been imprisoned, what might he not have accomplished?

In three days he had succeeded, with the utmost precaution, in removing the cement, and exposing the stone-work. The wall was built of rough stones, among which, to give strength to the structure, blocks of hewn stone were at intervals imbedded. It was one of these he had uncovered, and which he must remove from its socket.

Dantès strove to do this with his nails, but they were too weak. The fragments of the jug broke, and after an hour of useless toil, he paused.

Was he to be thus stopped at the beginning, and was he to wait inactive until his fellow-workman had completed his task? Suddenly an idea occurred to him—he smiled, and the perspiration dried on his forehead.

The jailer always brought Dantès' soup in an iron saucepan; this saucepan contained soup for both prisoners, for Dantès had noticed that it was either quite full, or half empty, according as the turnkey gave it to him or to his companion first.

The handle of this saucepan was of iron; Dantès would have give ten years of his life in exchange for it.

The jailer was accustomed to pour the contents of the saucepan into Dantès' plate, and Dantès, after eating his soup with a wooden spoon, washed the plate, which thus served for every day. Now when evening came Dantès put his plate on the ground near the door; the jailer, as he entered, stepped on it and broke it.

This time he could not blame Dantès. He was wrong to leave it there, but the jailer was wrong not to have looked before him.

The jailer, therefore, only grumbled. Then he looked about for something to pour the soup into; Dantès' entire dinner service consisted of one plate—there was no alternative.

"Leave the saucepan," said Dantès; "you can take it away when you bring me my breakfast." This advice was to the jailer's taste, as it spared him the necessity of making another trip. He left the saucepan.

Dantès was beside himself with joy. He rapidly devoured his food, and after waiting an hour, lest the jailer should change his mind and return, he removed his bed, took the handle of the saucepan, inserted the point between the hewn stone and rough stones of the wall, and employed it as a lever. A slight oscillation showed Dantès that all went well. At the end of an hour the stone was extricated from the wall, leaving a cavity a foot and a half in diameter.

Dantès carefully collected the plaster, carried it into the corner of his cell, and covered it with earth. Then, wishing to make the best use of his time while he had the means of labor, he continued to work without ceasing. At the dawn of day he replaced the stone, pushed his bed against the wall, and lay down. The breakfast consisted of a piece of bread; the jailer entered and placed the bread on the table.

"Well, don't you intend to bring me another plate?" said Dantès.

"No," replied the turnkey; "you destroy everything. First you break your jug, then you make me break your plate; if all the prisoners followed your example, the government would be ruined. I shall leave you the saucepan, and pour your soup into that. So for the future I hope you will not be so destructive."

Dantès raised his eyes to heaven and clasped his hands beneath the coverlet. He felt more gratitude for the possession of this piece of iron than he had ever felt for anything. He had noticed, however, that the prisoner on the other side had ceased to labor; no matter, this was a greater reason for proceeding—if his neighbor would not come to him, he would go to his neighbor. All day he toiled on untiringly, and by the evening he had succeeded in extracting ten handfuls of plaster and fragments of stone. When the hour for his jailer's visit arrived, Dantès straightened the handle of the saucepan as well as he could, and placed it in its accustomed place. The turnkey poured his ration of soup into it, together with the fish— for thrice a week the prisoners were deprived of meat. This would have been a method of reckoning time, had not Dantès long ceased to do so. Having poured out the soup, the turnkey retired. Dantès wished to ascertain whether his neighbor had really ceased to work. He listened—all was silent, as it had been for the last three days. Dantès sighed; it was evident that his neighbor distrusted him. However, he toiled on all the night without being discouraged; but after two or three hours he encountered an obstacle. The iron made no impression, but met with a smooth surface; Dantès touched it, and found that it was a beam. This beam crossed, or rather blocked up, the hole Dantès had made; it was necessary, therefore, to dig above or under it. The unhappy young man had not thought of this. "O my God, my God!" murmured he, "I have so earnestly prayed to you, that I hoped my prayers had been heard. After having deprived me of my liberty, after having deprived me of death, after having recalled me to existence, my God, have pity on me, and do not let me die in despair!"

"Who talks of God and despair at the same time?" said a voice that seemed to come from beneath the earth, and, deadened by the distance, sounded hollow and sepulchral in the young man's ears. Edmond's hair stood on end, and he rose to his knees.

"Ah," said he, "I hear a human voice." Edmond had not heard any one speak save his jailer for four or five years; and a jailer is no man to a prisoner—he is a living door, a barrier of flesh and blood adding strength to restraints of oak and iron.

"In the name of heaven," cried Dantès, "speak again, though the sound of your voice terrifies me. Who are you?"

"Who are you?" said the voice.

"An unhappy prisoner," replied Dantès, who made no hesitation in answering.

"Of what country?"—"A Frenchman."

"Your name?"—"Edmond Dantès."

"Your profession?"—"A sailor."

"How long have you been here?"—"Since the 28th of February, 1815."

"Your crime?"—"I am innocent."

"But of what are you accused?"—"Of having conspired to aid the emperor's return."

"What! For the emperor's return?—the emperor is no longer on the throne, then?"

"He abdicated at Fontainebleau in 1814, and was sent to the Island of Elba. But how long have you been here that you are ignorant of all this?"—"Since 1811."

Dantès shuddered; this man had been four years longer than himself in prison.

"Do not dig any more," said the voice; "only tell me how high up is your excavation?"—"On a level with the floor."

"How is it concealed?"—"Behind my bed."

"Has your bed been moved since you have been a prisoner?"—"No."

"What does your chamber open on?"—"A corridor."

"And the corridor?"—"On a court."

"Alas!" murmured the voice.

"Oh, what is the matter?" cried Dantès.—"I have made a mistake owing to an error in my plans. I took the wrong angle, and have come out fifteen feet from where I intended. I took the wall you are mining for the outer wall of the fortress."

"But then you would be close to the sea?"—"That is what I hoped."

"And supposing you had succeeded?"—"I should have thrown myself into the sea, gained one of the islands near here—the Isle de Daume or the Isle de Tibonlen—and then I should have been safe."

"Could you have swum so far?"—"Heaven would have given me strength; but now all is lost."

"All?"—"Yes; stop up your excavation carefully, do not work any more, and wait until you hear from me."

"Tell me, at least, who you are?"—"I am—I am No. 27."

"You mistrust me, then," said Dantès. Edmond fancied he heard a bitter laugh resounding from the depths.

"Oh, I am a Christian," cried Dantès, guessing instinctively that this man meant to abandon him. "I swear to you by him who died for us that naught shall induce me to breathe one syllable to my jailers; but I conjure you do not abandon me. If you do, I swear to you, for I have got to the end of my strength, that I will dash my brains out against the wall, and you will have my death to reproach yourself with."

"How old are you? Your voice is that of a young man."

"I do not know my age, for I have not counted the years I have been here. All I do know is, that I was just nineteen when I was arrested, the 28th of February, 1815."

"Not quite twenty-six!" murmured the voice; "at that age he cannot be a traitor."

"Oh, no, no," cried Dantès. "I swear to you again, rather than betray you, I would allow myself to be hacked in pieces!"

"You have done well to speak to me, and ask for my assistance, for I was about to form another plan, and leave you; but your age reassures me. I will not forget you. Wait."

"How long?"

"I must calculate our chances; I will give you the signal."

"But you will not leave me; you will come to me, or you will let me come to you. We will escape, and if we cannot escape we will talk; you of those whom you love, and I of those whom I love. You must love somebody?"

"No, I am alone in the world."

"Then you will love me. If you are young, I will be your comrade; if you are old, I will be your son. I have a father who is seventy if he yet lives; I only love him and a young girl called Mercédès. My father has not yet forgotten me, I am sure, but God alone knows if she loves me still; I shall love you as I loved my father."

"It is well," returned the voice; "to-morrow."

These few words were uttered with an accent that left no doubt of his sincerity; Dantès rose, dispersed the fragments with the same precaution as before, and pushed his bed back against the wall. He then gave himself up to his happiness. He would no longer be alone.

He was, perhaps, about to regain his liberty; at the worst, he would have a companion, and captivity that is shared is but half captivity. Plaints made in common are almost prayers, and prayers where two or three are gathered together invoke the mercy of heaven.

All day Dantès walked up and down his cell. He sat down occasionally on his bed, pressing his hand on his heart. At the slightest noise he bounded towards the door. Once or twice the thought crossed his mind that he might be separated from this unknown, whom he loved already; and then his mind was made up—when the jailer moved his bed and stooped to examine the opening, he would kill him with his water jug. He would be condemned to die, but he was about to die of grief and despair when this miraculous noise recalled him to life.

The jailer came in the evening. Dantès was on his bed. It seemed to him that thus he better guarded the unfinished opening. Doubtless there was a strange expression in his eyes, for the jailer said, "Come, are you going mad again?"

Dantès did not answer; he feared that the emotion of his voice would betray him. The jailer went away shaking his head. Night came; Dantès hoped that his neighbor would profit by the silence to address him, but he was mistaken. The next morning, however, just as he removed his bed from the wall, he heard three knocks; he threw himself on his knees.

"Is it you?" said he; "I am here."—"Is your jailer gone?"

"Yes," said Dantès; "he will not return until the evening; so that we have twelve hours before us."

"I can work, then?" said the voice.—"Oh, yes, yes; this instant, I entreat you."

In a moment that part of the floor on which Dantès was resting his two hands, as he knelt with his head in the opening, suddenly gave way; he drew back smartly, while a mass of stones and earth disappeared in a hole that opened beneath the aperture he himself had formed. Then from the bottom of this passage, the depth of which it was impossible to measure, he saw appear, first the head, then the shoulders, and lastly the body of a man, who sprang lightly into his cell.

XVI

A Learned Italian

SEIZING IN HIS ARMS the friend so long and ardently desired, Dantès almost carried him towards the window, in order to obtain a better view of his features by the aid of the imperfect light that struggled through the grating.

He was a man of small stature, with hair blanched rather by suffering and sorrow than by age. He had a deep-set, penetrating eye, almost buried beneath the thick gray eyebrow, and a long (and still black) beard reaching down to his breast. His thin face, deeply furrowed by care, and the bold outline of his strongly marked features, betokened a man more accustomed to exercise his mental faculties than his physical strength. Large drops of perspiration were now standing on his brow, while the garments that hung about him were so ragged that one could only guess at the pattern upon which they had originally been fashioned.

The stranger might have numbered sixty or sixty-five years; but a certain briskness and appearance of vigor in his movements made it probable that he was aged more from captivity than the course of time. He received the enthusiastic greeting of his young acquaintance with evident pleasure, as though his chilled affections were rekindled and invigorated by his contact with one so warm and ardent. He thanked him with grateful cordiality for his kindly welcome, although he must at that moment have been suffering bitterly to find another dungeon where he had fondly reckoned on discovering a means of regaining his liberty.

"Let us first see," said he, "whether it is possible to remove the traces of my entrance here—our future tranquillity depends upon our jailers being entirely ignorant of it." Advancing to the opening, he stooped and raised the stone easily in spite of its weight; then, fitting it into its place, he said,—

"You removed this stone very carelessly; but I suppose you had no tools to aid you."

"Why," exclaimed Dantès, with astonishment, "do you possess any?"

"I made myself some; and with the exception of a file, I have all that are necessary,—a chisel, pineers, and lever."

"Oh, how I should like to see these products of your industry and patience."

"Well, in the first place, here is my chisel." So saying, he displayed a sharp strong blade, with a handle made of beechwood.

"And with what did you contrive to make that?" inquired Dantès.

"With one of the clamps of my bedstead; and this very tool has sufficed me to hollow out the road by which I came hither, a distance of about fifty feet."

"Fifty feet!" responded Dantès, almost terrified.

"Do not speak so loud, young man—don't speak so loud. It frequently occurs in a state prison like this, that persons are stationed outside the doors of the cells purposely to overhear the conversation of the prisoners."

"But they believe I am shut up alone here."

"That makes no difference."

"And you say that you dug your way a distance of fifty feet to get here?"

"I do; that is about the distance that separates your chamber from mine; only, unfortunately, I did not curve aright; for want of the necessary geometrical instruments to calculate my scale of proportion, instead of taking an ellipsis of forty feet, I made it fifty. I expected, as I told you, to reach the outer wall, pierce through it, and throw myself into the sea; I have, however, kept along the corridor on which your chamber opens, instead of going beneath it. My labor is all in vain, for I find that the corridor looks into a courtyard filled with soldiers."

"That's true," said Dantès; "but the corridor you speak of only bounds *one* side of my cell; there are three others—do you know anything of their situation?"

"This one is built against the solid rock, and it would take ten experienced miners, duly furnished with the requisite tools, as many years to perforate it. This adjoins the lower part of the governor's apartments, and were we to work our way through, we should only get into some lock-up cellars, where we must necessarily be recaptured. The fourth and last side of your cell faces on—faces on—stop a minute, now where does it face?"

The wall of which he spoke was the one in which was fixed the loophole by which light was admitted to the chamber. This loophole, which gradually diminished in size as it approached the outside, to an opening through which a child could not have passed, was, for better security, furnished with three iron bars, so as to quiet all apprehensions even in the mind of the most suspicious jailer as to the possibility of a prisoner's escape. As the stranger asked the question, he dragged the table beneath the window.

"Climb up," said he to Dantès. The young man obeyed, mounted on the table, and, divining the wishes of his companion, placed his back securely against the wall and held out both hands. The stranger, whom as yet Dantès knew only by the number of his cell, sprang up with an agility by no means to be expected in a person of his years, and, light and steady on his feet as a cat or a lizard, climbed from the table to the outstretched hands of Dantès, and from them to his shoulders; then, bending double, for the ceiling of the dungeon prevented him from holding himself erect, he managed to slip his head between the upper bars of the window, so as to be able to command a perfect view from top to bottom.

An instant afterwards he hastily drew back his head, saying, "I thought so!" and sliding from the shoulders of Dantès as dexterously as he had ascended, he nimbly leaped from the table to the ground.

"What was it that you thought?" asked the young man anxiously, in his turn descending from the table.

The elder prisoner pondered the matter. "Yes," said he at length, "it is so. This side of your chamber looks out upon a kind of open gallery, where patrols are continually passing, and sentries keep watch day and night."

"Are you quite sure of that?"

"Certain. I saw the soldier's shako and the top of his musket; that made me draw in my head so quickly, for I was fearful he might also see me."

"Well?" inquired Dantès.

"You perceive then the utter impossibility of escaping through your dungeon?"

"Then," pursued the young man eagerly—

"Then," answered the elder prisoner, "the will of God be done!" and as the old man slowly pronounced those words, an air of profound resignation spread itself over his careworn countenance. Dantès gazed on the man who could thus philosophically resign hopes so long and ardently nourished with an astonishment mingled with admiration.

"Tell me, I entreat of you, who and what you are?" said he at length; "never have I met with so remarkable a person as yourself."

"Willingly," answered the stranger; "if, indeed, you feel any curiosity respecting one, now, alas, powerless to aid you in any way."

"Say not so; you can console and support me by the strength of your own powerful mind. Pray let me know who you really are?"

The stranger smiled a melancholy smile. "Then listen," said he. "I am the Abbé Faria, and have been imprisoned as you know in this Château d'If since the year 1811; previously to which I had been confined for three years in the fortress of Fenestrelle. In the year 1811 I was transferred to Piedmont in France. It was at this period I learned that the destiny which seemed subservient to every wish formed by Napoleon, had bestowed on him a son, named king of Rome even in his cradle. I was very far then from expecting the change you have just informed me of; namely, that four years afterwards, this colossus of power would be overthrown. Then who reigns in France at this moment—Napoleon II.?"

"No, Louis XVIII."

"The brother of Louis XVII.! How inscrutable are the ways of providence—for what great and mysterious purpose has it pleased heaven to abase the man once so elevated, and raise up him who was so abased?"

Dantès' whole attention was riveted on a man who could thus forget his own misfortunes while occupying himself with the destinies of others.

"Yes, yes," continued he, "'Twill be the same as it was in England. After Charles I., Cromwell; after Cromwell, Charles II., and then James II., and then some son-in-law or relation, some Prince of Orange, a stadtholder who becomes a king. Then new concessions to the people, then a constitution, then liberty. Ah, my friend!" said the abbé, turning towards Dantès, and surveying him with the kindling gaze of a prophet, "you are young, you will see all this come to pass."

"Probably, if ever I get out of prison!"

"True," replied Faria, "we are prisoners; but I forget this sometimes, and there are even moments when my mental vision transports me beyond these walls, and I fancy myself at liberty."

"But wherefore are you here?"

"Because in 1807 I dreamed of the very plan Napoleon tried to

realize in 1811; because, like Machiavelli, I desired to alter the political face of Italy, and instead of allowing it to be split up into a
quantity of pretty principalities, each held by some weak or tyran-
nical ruler, I sought to form one large, compact, and powerful
empire; and, lastly, because I fancied I had found my Cæsar Borgia
in a crowned simpleton, who feigned to enter into my views only
to betray me. It was the plan of Alexander VI. and Clement VII., but
it will never succeed now, for they attempted it fruitlessly, and
Napoleon was unable to complete his work. Italy seems fated to
misfortune." And the old man bowed his head.

Dantès could not understand a man risking his life for such
matters. Napoleon certainly he knew something of, inasmuch as he
had seen and spoken with him; but of Clement VII, and Alexander
VI, he knew nothing.

"Are you not," he asked, "the priest who here in the Château
d'If is generally thought to be—ill?"

"Mad, you mean, don't you?"

"I did not like to say so," answered Dantès, smiling.

"Well, then," resumed Faria with a bitter smile, "let me answer
your question in full, by acknowledging that I am the poor mad
prisoner of the Château d'If, for many years permitted to amuse the
different visitors with what is said to be my insanity; and, in all
probability, I should be promoted to the honor of making sport for
the children, if such innocent beings could be found in an abode
devoted like this to suffering and despair."

Dantès remained for a short time mute and motionless; at length
he said,—"Then you abandon all hope of escape?"

"I perceive its utter impossibility; and I consider it impious to
attempt that which the Almighty evidently does not approve."

"Nay, be not discouraged. Would it not be expecting too much
to hope to succeed at your first attempt? Why not try to find an
opening in another direction from that which has so unfortunately
failed?"

"Alas, it shows how little notion you can have of all it has cost me to effect a purpose so unexpectedly frustrated, that you talk of beginning over again. In the first place, I was four years making the tools I possess, and have been two years scraping and digging out earth, hard as granite itself; then what toil and fatigue has it not been to remove huge stones I should once have deemed impossible to loosen. Whole days have I passed in these Titanic efforts, considering my labor well repaid if, by night-time I had contrived to carry away a square inch of this hard-bound cement, changed by ages into a substance unyielding as the stones themselves; then to conceal the mass of earth and rubbish I dug up, I was compelled to break through a staircase, and throw the fruits of my labor into the hollow part of it; but the well is now so completely choked up, that I scarcely think it would be possible to add another handful of dust without leading to discovery. Consider also that I fully believed I had accomplished the end and aim of my undertaking, for which I had so exactly husbanded my strength as to make it just hold out to the termination of my enterprise; and now, at the moment when I reckoned upon success, my hopes are forever dashed from me. No, I repeat again, that nothing shall induce me to renew attempts evidently at variance with the Almighty's pleasure."

Dantès held down his head, that the other might not see how joy at the thought of having a companion outweighed the sympathy he felt for the failure of the abbé's plans.

The abbé sank upon Edmond's bed, while Edmond himself remained standing. Escape had never once occurred to him. There are, indeed, some things which appear so impossible that the mind does not dwell on them for an instant. To undermine the ground for fifty feet—to devote three years to a labor which, if successful, would conduct you to a precipice overhanging the sea—to plunge into the waves from the height of fifty, sixty, perhaps a hundred feet, at the risk of being dashed to pieces against the rocks, should you have been fortunate enough to have escaped the fire of the sentinels; and even, supposing all these perils past, then to have to swim for your life a distance of at least three miles ere you could reach the shore—were difficulties so startling and formidable that Dantès had never even dreamed of such a scheme, resigning himself rather to death. But the sight of an old man clinging to life with so desperate a courage, gave a fresh turn to his ideas, and inspired him with new courage. Another, older and less strong than he, had attempted what he had not had sufficient resolution to undertake, and had failed only because of an error in calculation. This same person, with almost incredible patience and perseverance, had contrived to provide himself with tools requisite for so unparalleled an attempt. Another had done all this; why, then, was it impossible to Dantès? Faria had dug his way through fifty feet, Dantès would dig a hundred; Faria, at the age of fifty, had devoted three years to the task; he, who was but half as old, would sacrifice six; Faria, a priest and savant, had not shrunk from the idea of risking his life by trying to swim a distance of three miles to one of the islands—Daume, Rattonneau, or Lemaire; should a hardy sailor, an experienced diver, like himself, shrink from a similar task; should he, who had so often for mere amusement's sake plunged to the bottom of the sea to fetch up the bright coral branch, hesitate to entertain the same project? He could do it in an hour, and how many times had he, for pure pastime, continued in the water for more than twice as long! At once Dantès resolved to follow the brave example of his energetic companion, and to remember that what has once been done may be done again.

After continuing some time in profound meditation, the young man suddenly exclaimed, "I have found what you were in search of!"

Faria started: "Have you, indeed?" cried he, raising his head with quick anxiety; "pray, let me know what it is you have discovered?"

"The corridor through which you have bored your way from the cell you occupy here, extends in the same direction as the outer gallery, does it not?"—"It does."

"And is not above fifteen feet from it?"—"About that."

"Well, then, I will tell you what we must do. We must pierce through the corridor by forming a side opening about the middle, as it were the top part of a cross. This time you will lay your plans more accurately; we shall get out into the gallery you have described; kill the sentinel who guards it, and make our escape. All we require to insure success is courage, and that you possess, and strength, which I am not deficient in; as for patience, you have abundantly proved yours—you shall now see me prove mine."

"One instant, my dear friend," replied the abbé; "it is clear you do not understand the nature of the courage with which I am endowed, and what use I intend making of my strength. As for patience, I consider that I have abundantly exercised that in beginning every morning the task of the night before, and every night renewing the task of the day. But then, young man (and I pray of you to give me your full attention), then I thought I could not be doing anything displeasing to the Almighty in trying to set an innocent being at liberty—one who had committed no offence, and merited not condemnation."

"And have your notions changed?" asked Dantès with much surprise; "do you think yourself more guilty in making the attempt since you have encountered me?"

"No; neither do I wish to incur guilt. Hitherto I have fancied myself merely waging war against circumstances, not men. I have thought it no sin to bore through a wall, or destroy a staircase; but I cannot so easily persuade myself to pierce a heart or take away a life." A slight movement of surprise escaped Dantès.

"Is it possible," said he, "that where your liberty is at stake you can allow any such scruple to deter you from obtaining it?"

"Tell me," replied Faria, "what has hindered you from knocking down your jailer with a piece of wood torn from your bedstead, dressing yourself in his clothes, and endeavoring to escape?"

"Simply the fact that the idea never occurred to me," answered Dantès.

"Because," said the old man, "the natural repugnance to the commission of such a crime prevented you from thinking of it; and so it ever is because in simple and allowable things our natural instincts keep us from deviating from the strict line of duty. The tiger, whose nature teaches him to delight in shedding blood, needs but the sense of smell to show him when his prey is within his reach, and by following this instinct he is enabled to measure the leap necessary to permit him to spring on his victim; but man, on the contrary, loathes the idea of blood—it is not alone that the laws of social life inspire him with a shrinking dread of taking life; his natural construction and physiological formation"—

Dantès was confused and silent at this explanation of the thoughts which had unconsciously been working in his mind, or rather soul; for there are two distinct sorts of ideas, those that proceed from the head and those that emanate from the heart.

"Since my imprisonment," said Faria, "I have thought over all the most celebrated cases of escape on record. They have rarely been successful. Those that have been crowned with full success have been long meditated upon, and carefully arranged; such, for instance, as the escape of the Duc de Beaufort from the Château de Vincennes, that of the Abbé Dubuquoi from For l'Evêque; of Latude from the Bastille. Then there are those for which chance sometimes affords opportunity, and those are the best of all. Let us, therefore, wait patiently for some favorable moment, and when it presents itself, profit by it."

"Ah," said Dantès, "you might well endure the tedious delay; you were constantly employed in the task you set yourself, and when weary with toil, you had your hopes to refresh and encourage you."

"I assure you," replied the old man, "I did not turn to that source for recreation or support."

"What did you do then?"—"I wrote or studied."

"Were you then permitted the use of pens, ink, and paper?"

"Oh, no," answered the abbé; "I had none but what I made for myself."

"You made paper, pens and ink?"

"Yes."

Dantès gazed with admiration, but he had some difficulty in believing. Faria saw this.

"When you pay me a visit in my cell, my young friend," said he, "I will show you an entire work, the fruits of the thoughts and reflections of my whole life; many of them meditated over in the shades of the Coliseum at Rome, at the foot of St. Mark's column at Venice, and on the borders of the Arno at Florence, little imagining at the time that they would be arranged in order within the walls of the Château d'If. The work I speak of is called 'A Treatise on the Possibility of a General Monarchy in Italy,' and will make one large quarto volume."

"And on what have you written all this?"

"On two of my shirts. I invented a preparation that makes linen as smooth and as easy to write on as parchment."

"You are, then, a chemist?"—"Somewhat; I know Lavoisier, and was the intimate friend of Cabanis."

"But for such a work you must have needed books—had you any?"

"I had nearly five thousand volumes in my library at Rome; but after reading them over many times, I found out that with one hundred and fifty well-chosen books a man possesses, if not a complete summary of all human knowledge, at least all that a man need really know. I devoted three years of my life to reading and studying these one hundred and fifty volumes, till I knew them nearly by heart; so that since I have been in prison, a very slight effort of memory has enabled me to recall their contents as readily as though the pages were open before me. I could recite you the whole of Thucydides, Xenophon, Plutarch, Titus Livius, Tacitus, Strada, Jornandes, Dante, Montaigne, Shakespeare, Spinoza, Machiavelli, and Bossuet. I name only the most important."

"You are, doubtless, acquainted with a variety of languages, so as to have been able to read all these?"

"Yes, I speak five of the modern tongues—that is to say, German, French, Italian, English, and Spanish; by the aid of ancient Greek I learned modern Greek—I don't speak it so well as I could wish, but I am still trying to improve myself."

"Improve yourself!" repeated Dantès; "why, how can you manage to do so?"

"Why, I made a vocabulary of the words I knew; turned, returned, and arranged them, so as to enable me to express my thoughts through their medium. I know nearly one thousand words, which is all that is absolutely necessary, although I believe there are nearly one hundred thousand in the dictionaries. I cannot hope to be very fluent, but I certainly should have no difficulty in explaining my wants and wishes; and that would be quite as much as I should ever require."

Stronger grew the wonder of Dantès, who almost fancied he had to do with one gifted with supernatural powers; still hoping to find some imperfection which might bring him down to a level with human beings, he added, "Then if you were not furnished with pens, how did you manage to write the work you speak of?"

"I made myself some excellent ones, which would be universally preferred to all others if once known. You are aware what huge whitings are served to us on maigre days. Well, I selected the cartilages of the heads of these fishes, and you can scarcely imagine the delight with which I welcomed the arrival of each Wednesday, Friday, and Saturday, as affording me the means of increasing my stock of pens; for I will freely confess that my historical labors have been my greatest solace and relief. While retracing the past, I forget the present; and traversing at will the path of history I cease to remember that I am myself a prisoner."

"But the ink," said Dantès; "of what did you make your ink?"

"There was formerly a fireplace in my dungeon," replied Faria, "but it was closed up long ere I became an occupant of this prison. Still, it must have been many years in use, for it was thickly covered with a coating of soot; this soot I dissolved in a portion of the wine brought to me every Sunday, and I assure you a better ink cannot be desired. For very important notes, for which closer attention is required, I pricked one of my fingers, and wrote with my own blood."

"And when," asked Dantès, "may I see all this?"

"Whenever you please," replied the abbé.

"Oh, then let it be directly!" exclaimed the young man.

"Follow me, then," said the abbé, as he re-entered the subterranean passage, in which he soon disappeared, followed by Dantès.

XVII

The Abbé's Chamber

AFTER HAVING PASSED WITH tolerable ease through the subterranean passage, which, however, did not admit of their holding themselves erect, the two friends reached the further end of the corridor, into which the abbés cell opened; from that point the passage became much narrower, and barely permitted one to creep through on hands and knees. The floor of the abbé's cell was paved, and it had been by raising one of the stones in the most obscure corner that Faria had been able to commence the laborious task of which Dantès had witnessed the completion.

As he entered the chamber of his friend, Dantès cast around one eager and searching glance in quest of the expected marvels, but nothing more than common met his view.

"It is well," said the abbé; "we have some hours before us—it is now just a quarter past twelve o'clock." Instinctively Dantès turned round to observe by what watch or clock the abbé had been able so accurately to specify the hour.

"Look at this ray of light which enters by my window," said the abbé, "and then observe the lines traced on the wall. Well, by means of these lines, which are in accordance with the double motion of the earth, and the ellipse it describes round the sun, I am enabled to ascertain the precise hour with more minuteness than if I possessed a watch; for that might be broken or deranged in its movements, while the sun and earth never vary in their appointed paths."

This last explanation was wholly lost upon Dantès, who had always imagined, from seeing the sun rise from behind the mountains and set in the Mediterranean, that it moved, and not the earth. A double movement of the globe he inhabited, and of which he could feel nothing, appeared to him perfectly impossible. Each word that fell from his companion's lips seemed fraught with the mysteries of science, as worthy of digging out as the gold and diamonds in the mines of Guzerat and Golconda, which he could just recollect having visited during a voyage made in his earliest youth.

"Come," said he to the abbé, "I am anxious to see your treasures."

The abbé smiled, and, proceeding to the disused fireplace, raised, by the help of his chisel, a long stone, which had doubtless been the hearth, beneath which was a cavity of considerable depth, serving as a safe depository of the articles mentioned to Dantès.

"What do you wish to see first?" asked the abbé.

"Oh, your great work on the monarchy of Italy!"

Faria then drew forth from his hiding-place three or four rolls of linen, laid one over the other, like folds of papyrus. These rolls consisted of slips of cloth about four inches wide and eighteen long; they were all carefully numbered and closely covered with writing, so legible that Dantès could easily read it, as well as make out the sense—it being in Italian, a language he, as a Provençal, perfectly understood.

"There," said he, "there is the work complete. I wrote the word *finis* at the end of the sixty-eighth strip about a week ago. I have torn up two of my shirts, and as many handkerchiefs as I was master of, to complete the precious pages. Should I ever get out of prison and find in all Italy a printer courageous enough to publish what I have composed, my literary reputation is forever secured."

"I see," answered Dantès. "Now let me behold the curious pens with which you have written your work."

"Look!" said Faria, showing to the young man a slender stick about six inches long, and much resembling the size of the handle of a fine painting-brush, to the end of which was tied, by a piece of thread, one of those cartilages of which the abbé had before spoken to Dantès; it was pointed, and divided at the nib like an ordinary pen. Dantès examined it with intense admiration, then looked around to see the instrument with which it had been shaped so correctly into form.

"Ah, yes," said Faria; "the penknife. That's my masterpiece. I made it, as well as this larger knife, out of an old iron candlestick." The penknife was sharp and keen as a razor; as for the other knife, it would serve a double purpose, and with it one could cut and thrust.

Dantès examined the various articles shown to him with the same attention that he had bestowed on the curiosities and strange tools exhibited in the shops at Marseilles as the works of the savages in the South Seas from whence they had been brought by the different trading vessels.

"As for the ink," said Faria, "I told you how I managed to obtain that—and I only just make it from time to time, as I require it."

"One thing still puzzles me," observed Dantès, "and that is how you managed to do all this by daylight?"

"I worked at night also," replied Faria.

"Night!—why, for heaven's sake, are your eyes like cats', that you can see to work in the dark?"

"Indeed they are not; but God has supplied man with the intelligence that enables him to overcome the limitations of natural conditions. I furnished myself with a light."

"You did? Pray tell me how."

"I separated the fat from the meat served to me, melted it, and so made oil—here is my lamp." So saying, the abbé exhibited a sort of torch very similar to those used in public illuminations.

"But light?"

"Here are two flints and a piece of burnt linen."

"And matches?"

"I pretended that I had a disorder of the skin, and asked for a little sulphur, which was readily supplied." Dantès laid the different things he had been looking at on the table, and stood with his head drooping on his breast, as though overwhelmed by the perseverance and strength of Faria's mind.

"You have not seen all yet," continued Faria, "for I did not think it wise to trust all my treasures in the same hiding-place. Let us shut this one up." They put the stone back in its place; the abbé sprinkled a little dust over it to conceal the traces of its having been removed, rubbed his foot well on it to make it assume the same appearance as the other, and then, going towards his bed, he removed it from the spot it stood in. Behind the head of the bed, and concealed by a stone fitting in so closely as to defy all suspicion, was a hollow space, and in this space a ladder of cords between twenty-five and thirty feet in length. Dantès closely and eagerly examined it; he found it firm, solid, and compact enough to bear any weight.

"Who supplied you with the materials for making this wonderful work?"

"I tore up several of my shirts, and ripped out the seams in the sheets of my bed, during my three years' imprisonment at Fenestrelle; and when I was removed to the Château d'If, I managed to bring the ravellings with me, so that I have been able to finish my work here."

"And was it not discovered that your sheets were unhemmed?"

"Oh, no, for when I had taken out the thread I required, I hemmed the edges over again."—"With what?"

"With this needle," said the abbé, as, opening his ragged vestments, he showed Dantès a long, sharp fish-bone, with a small perforated eye for the thread, a small portion of which still remained in it. "I once thought," continued Faria, "of removing these iron bars, and letting myself down from the window, which, as you see, is somewhat wider than yours, although I should have enlarged it still more preparatory to my flight; however, I discovered that I should merely have dropped into a sort of inner court, and I therefore renounced the project altogether as too full of risk and danger. Nevertheless, I carefully preserved my ladder against one of those unforeseen opportunities of which I spoke just now, and which sudden chance frequently brings about." While affecting to be deeply engaged in examining the ladder, the mind of Dantès was, in fact, busily occupied by the idea that a person so intelligent, ingenious, and clearsighted as the abbé, might probably be able to solve the dark mystery of his own misfortunes, where he himself could see nothing.

"What are you thinking of?" asked the abbé smilingly, imputing the deep abstraction in which his visitor was plunged to the excess of his awe and wonder.

"I was reflecting, in the first place," replied Dantès, "upon the enormous degree of intelligence and ability you must have employed to reach the high perfection to which you have attained. What would you not have accomplished if you had been free?"

"Possibly nothing at all; the overflow of my brain would probably, in a state of freedom, have evaporated in a thousand follies; misfortune is needed to bring to light the treasures of the human intellect. Compression is needed to explode gunpowder. Captivity has brought my mental faculties to a focus; and you are well aware that from the collision of clouds electricity is produced—from electricity, lightning, from lightning, illumination."

"No," replied Dantès. "I know nothing. Some of your words are to me quite empty of meaning. You must be blessed indeed to possess the knowledge you have."

The abbé smiled. "Well," said he, "but you had another subject for your thoughts; did you not say so just now?"—"I did!"

"You have told me as yet but one of them—let me hear the other."

"It was this,—that while you had related to me all the particulars of your past life, you were perfectly unacquainted with mine."

"Your life, my young friend, has not been of sufficient length to admit of your having passed through any very important events."

"It has been long enough to inflict on me a great and undeserved misfortune. I would fain fix the source of it on man that I may no longer vent reproaches upon heaven."

"Then you profess ignorance of the crime with which you are charged?"

"I do, indeed; and this I swear by the two beings most dear to me upon earth,—my father and Mercédès."

"Come," said the abbé, closing his hiding-place, and pushing the bed back to its original situation, "let me hear your story."

Dantès obeyed, and commenced what he called his history, but which consisted only of the account of a voyage to India, and two or three voyages to the Levant, until he arrived at the recital of his last cruise, with the death of Captain Leclère, and the receipt of a packet to be delivered by himself to the grand marshal; his interview with that personage, and his receiving, in place of the packet brought, a letter addressed to a Monsieur Noirtier—his arrival at Marseilles, and interview with his father—his affection for Mercédès, and their nuptial feast—his arrest and subsequent examination, his temporary detention at the Palais de Justice, and his final imprisonment in the Château d'If. From this point everything was a blank to Dantès—he knew nothing more, not even the length of time he had been imprisoned. His recital finished, the abbé reflected long and earnestly.

"There is," said he, at the end of his meditations, "a clever maxim, which bears upon what I was saying to you some little while ago, and that is, that unless wicked ideas take root in a naturally depraved mind, human nature, in a right and wholesome state, revolts at crime. Still, from an artificial civilization have originated wants, vices, and false tastes, which occasionally become so powerful as to stifle within us all good feelings, and ultimately to lead us into guilt and wickedness. From this view of things, then, comes the axiom that if you wish to discover the author of any bad action, seek first to discover the person to whom the perpetration of that bad action could be in any way advantageous. Now, to apply it in your case,—to whom could your disappearance have been serviceable?"

"To no one, by heaven! I was a very insignificant person."

"Do not speak thus, for your reply evinces neither logic nor philosophy; everything is relative, my dear young friend, from the king who stands in the way of his successor, to the employee who keeps his rival out of a place. Now, in the event of the king's death, his successor inherits a crown,—when the employee dies, the supernumerary steps into his shoes, and receives his salary of twelve thousand livres. Well, these twelve thousand livres are his civil list, and are as essential to him as the twelve millions of a king. Every one, from the highest to the lowest degree, has his place on the social ladder, and is beset by stormy passions and conflicting interests, as in Descartes' theory of pressure and impulsion. But these forces increase as we go higher, so that we have a spiral which in defiance of reason rests upon the apex and not on the base. Now let us return to your particular world. You say you were on the point of being made captain of the *Pharaon?*"—"Yes."

"And about to become the husband of a young and lovely girl?"—"Yes."

"Now, could any one have had any interest in preventing the accomplishment of these two things? But let us first settle the question as to its being the interest of any one to hinder you from being captain of the *Pharaon*. What say you?"

"I cannot believe such was the case. I was generally liked on board, and had the sailors possessed the right of selecting a captain themselves, I feel convinced their choice would have fallen on me. There was only one person among the crew who had any feeling of ill-will towards me. I had quarrelled with him some time previously, and had even challenged him to fight me; but he refused."

"Now we are getting on. And what was this man's name?"—"Danglars."

"What rank did he hold on board?"—"He was super-cargo."

"And had you been captain, should you have retained him in his employment?"

"Not if the choice had remained with me, for I had frequently observed inaccuracies in his accounts."

"Good again! Now then, tell me, was any person present during your last conversation with Captain Leclère?"—"No; we were quite alone."

"Could your conversation have been overheard by any one?"

"It might, for the cabin door was open—and—stay; now I recollect,—Danglars himself passed by just as Captain Leclère was giving me the packet for the grand marshal."

"That's better," cried the abbé; "now we are on the right scent. Did you take anybody with you when you put into the port of Elba?"—"Nobody."

"Somebody there received your packet, and gave you a letter in place of it, I think?"—"Yes; the grand marshal did."

"And what did you do with that letter?"—"Put it into my portfolio."

"You had your portfolio with you, then? Now, how could a sailor find room in his pocket for a portfolio large enough to contain an official letter?"

"You are right; it was left on board."

"Then it was not till your return to the ship that you put the letter in the portfolio?"—"No."

"And what did you do with this same letter while returning from Porto-Ferrajo to the vessel?"—"I carried it in my hand."

"So that when you went on board the *Pharaon*, everybody could see that you held a letter in your hand?"—"Yes."

"Danglars, as well as the rest?"—"Danglars, as well as others."

"Now, listen to me, and try to recall every circumstance attending your arrest. Do you recollect the words in which the information against you was formulated?"

"Oh, yes, I read it over three times, and the words sank deeply into my memory."—"Repeat it to me."

Dantès paused a moment, then said, "This is it, word for word: 'The king's attorney is informed by a friend to the throne and religion, that one Edmond Dantès, mate on board the *Pharaon*, this day arrived from Smyrna, after having touched at Naples and Porto-Ferrajo, has been intrusted by Murat with a packet for the usurper; again, by the usurper, with a letter for the Bonapartist Club in Paris. This proof of his guilt may be procured by his immediate arrest, as the letter will be found either about his person, at his father's residence, or in his cabin on board the *Pharaon*.'" The abbé shrugged his shoulders. "The thing is clear as day," said he; "and you must have had a very confiding nature, as well as a good heart, not to have suspected the origin of the whole affair."

"Do you really think so? Ah, that would indeed be infamous."

"How did Danglars usually write?"—"In a handsome, running hand."

"And how was the anonymous letter written?"

"Backhanded." Again the abbé smiled. "Disguised."—"It was very boldly written, if disguised."

"Stop a bit," said the abbé, taking up what he called his pen, and, after dipping it into the ink, he wrote on a piece of prepared linen, with his left hand, the first two or three words of the accusation. Dantès drew back, and gazed on the abbé with a sensation almost amounting to terror.

"How very astonishing!" cried he at length. "Why your writing exactly resembles that of the accusation."

"Simply because that accusation had been written with the left hand; and I have noticed that"—

"What?"—"That while the writing of different persons done with the right hand varies, that performed with the left hand is invariably uniform."

"You have evidently seen and observed everything."

"Let us proceed."—"Oh, yes, yes!"

"Now as regards the second question."

"I am listening."

"Was there any person whose interest it was to prevent your marriage with Mercédès?"

"Yes; a young man who loved her."—"And his name was"—

"Fernand."

"That is a Spanish name, I think?"—"He was a Catalan."

"You imagine him capable of writing the letter?"

"Oh, no; he would more likely have got rid of me by sticking a knife into me."

"That is in strict accordance with the Spanish character; an assassination they will unhesitatingly commit, but an act of cowardice, never."

"Besides," said Dantès, "the various circumstances mentioned in the letter were wholly unknown to him."

"You had never spoken of them yourself to any one?"

"To no one."

"Not even to your mistress?"—"No, not even to my betrothed."

"Then it is Danglars."—"I feel quite sure of it now."

"Wait a little. Pray, was Danglars acquainted with Fernand?"

"No—yes, he was. Now I recollect"—

"What?"—"To have seen them both sitting at table together under an arbor at Père Pamphile's the evening before the day fixed for my wedding. They were in earnest conversation. Danglars was joking in a friendly way, but Fernand looked pale and agitated."

"Were they alone?"—"There was a third person with them whom I knew perfectly well, and who had, in all probability made their acquaintance; he was a tailor named Caderousse, but he was very drunk. Stay!—stay!—How strange that it should not have occurred to me before! Now I remember quite well, that on the table round which they were sitting were pens, ink, and paper. Oh, the heartless, treacherous scoundrels!" exclaimed Dantès, pressing his hand to his throbbing brows.

"Is there anything else I can assist you in discovering, besides the villany of your friends?" inquired the abbé with a laugh.

"Yes, yes," replied Dantès eagerly; "I would beg of you, who see so completely to the depths of things, and to whom the greatest mystery seems but an easy riddle, to explain to me how it was that I underwent no second examination, was never brought to trial, and, above all, was condemned without every having had sentence passed on me?"

"That is altogether a different and more serious matter," responded the abbé. "The ways of justice are frequently too dark and mysterious to be easily penetrated. All we have hitherto done in the matter has been child's play. If you wish me to enter upon the more difficult part of the business, you must assist me by the most minute information on every point."

"Pray ask me whatever questions you please; for, in good truth, you see more clearly into my life than I do myself."

"In the first place, then, who examined you,—the king's attorney, his deputy, or a magistrate?"—"The deputy."

"Was he young or old?"—"About six or seven and twenty years of age, I should say."

"So!" answered the abbé. "Old enough to be ambitious, but too young to be corrupt. And how did he treat you?"

"With more of mildness than severity."

"Did you tell him your whole story?"—"I did."

"And did his conduct change at all in the course of your examination?"

"He did appear much disturbed when he read the letter that had brought me into this scrape. He seemed quite overcome by my misfortune."

"By your misfortune?"—"Yes."

"Then you feel quite sure that it was your misfortune he deplored?"

"He gave me one great proof of his sympathy, at any rate."

"And that?"

"He burnt the sole evidence that could at all have criminated me."

"What? the accusation?"

"No; the letter."

"Are you sure?"—"I saw it done."

"That alters the case. This man might, after all, be a greater scoundrel than you have thought possible."

"Upon my word," said Dantès, "you make me shudder. Is the world filled with tigers and crocodiles?"

"Yes; and remember that two-legged tigers and crocodiles are more dangerous than the others."

"Never mind; let us go on."

"With all my heart! You tell me he burned the letter?"

"He did; saying at the same time, 'You see I thus destroy the only proof existing against you.'"

"This action is somewhat too sublime to be natural."

"You think so?"

"I am sure of it. To whom was this letter addressed?"

"To M. Noirtier, No. 13 Coq-Héron, Paris."

"Now can you conceive of any interest that your heroic deputy could possibly have had in the destruction of that letter?"

"Why, it is not altogether impossible he might have had, for he made me promise several times never to speak of that letter to any one, assuring me he so advised me for my own interest; and, more than this, he insisted on my taking a solemn oath never to utter the name mentioned in the address."

"Noirtier!" repeated the abbé; "Noirtier!—I knew a person of that name at the court of the Queen of Etruria,—a Noirtier, who had been a Girondin during the Revolution! What was your deputy called?"

"De Villefort!" The abbé burst into a fit of laughter, while Dantès gazed on him in utter astonishment.

"What ails you?" said he at length.

"Do you see that ray of sunlight?"—"I do."

"Well, the whole thing is more clear to me than that sunbeam is to you. Poor fellow! poor young man! And you tell me this magistrate expressed great sympathy and commiseration for you?"— "He did."

"And the worthy man destroyed your compromising letter?"

"Yes."

"And then made you swear never to utter the name of Noirtier?"

"Yes."

"Why, you poor short-sighted simpleton, can you not guess who this Noirtier was, whose very name he was so careful to keep concealed? Noirtier was his father."

Had a thunderbolt fallen at the feet of Dantès, or hell opened its yawning gulf before him, he could not have been more completely transfixed with horror than he was at the sound of these unexpected words. Starting up, he clasped his hands around his head as though to prevent his very brain from bursting, and exclaimed, "His father! his father!"

"Yes, his father," replied the abbé; "his right name was Noirtier de Villefort." At this instant a bright light shot through the mind of Dantès, and cleared up all that had been dark and obscure before. The change that had come over Villefort during the examination, the destruction of the letter, the exacted promise, the almost supplicating tones of the magistrate, who seemed rather to implore mercy than to pronounce punishment,—all returned with a stunning force to his memory. He cried out, and staggered against the wall like a drunken man; then he hurried to the opening that led from the abbé's cell to his own, and said, "I must be alone, to think over all this."

When he regained his dungeon, he threw himself on his bed, where the turnkey found him in the evening visit, sitting with fixed gaze and contracted features, dumb and motionless as a statue. During these hours of profound meditation, which to him had seemed only minutes, he had formed a fearful resolution, and bound himself to its fulfilment by a solemn oath.

Dantès was at length roused from his revery by the voice of Faria, who, having also been visited by his jailer, had come to invite his fellow-sufferer to share his supper. The reputation of being out of his mind, though harmlessly and even amusingly so, had procured for the abbé unusual privileges. He was supplied with bread of a finer, whiter quality than the usual prison fare, and even regaled each Sunday with a small quantity of wine. Now this was a Sunday, and the abbé had come to ask his young companion to share the luxuries with him. Dantès followed; his features were no longer contracted, and now wore their usual expression, but there was that in his whole appearance that bespoke one who had come to a fixed and desperate resolve. Faria bent on him his penetrating eye: "I regret now," said he, "having helped you in your late inquiries, or having given you the information I did."

"Why so?" inquired Dantès.—"Because it has instilled a new passion in your heart—that of vengeance."

Dantès smiled. "Let us talk of something else," said he.

Again the abbé looked at him, then mournfully shook his head; but in accordance with Dantès' request, he began to speak of other matters. The elder prisoner was one of those persons whose conversation, like that of all who have experienced many trials, contained many useful and important hints as well as sound information; but it was never egotistical, for the unfortunate man never alluded to his own sorrows. Dantès listened with admiring attention to all he said; some of his remarks corresponded with what he already knew, or applied to the sort of knowledge his nautical life had enabled him to acquire. A part of the good abbé's words, however, were wholly incomprehensible to him; but, like the aurora which guides the navigator in northern latitudes, opened new vistas to the inquiring mind of the listener, and gave fantastic glimpses of new horizons, enabling him justly to estimate the delight an intellectual mind would have in following one so richly gifted as Faria along the heights of truth, where he was so much at home.

"You must teach me a small part of what you know," said Dantès, "if only to prevent your growing weary of me. I can well believe that so learned a person as yourself would prefer absolute solitude to being tormented with the company of one as ignorant and uninformed as myself. If you will only agree to my request, I promise you never to mention another word about escaping." The abbé smiled. "Alas, my boy," said he, "human knowledge is confined within very narrow limits; and when I have taught you mathematics, physics, history, and the three or four modern languages with which I am acquainted, you will know as much as I do myself. Now, it will scarcely require two years for me to communicate to you the stock of learning I possess."

"Two years!" exclaimed Dantès; "do you really believe I can acquire all these things in so short a time?"—"Not their application, certainly, but their principles you may; to learn is not to know; there are the learners and the learned. Memory makes the one, philosophy the other."

"But cannot one learn philosophy?"

"Philosophy cannot be taught; it is the application of the sciences to truth; it is like the golden cloud in which the Messiah went up into heaven."

"Well, then," said Dantès, "what shall you teach me first? I am in a hurry to begin. I want to learn."

"Everything," said the abbé. And that very evening the prisoners sketched a plan of education, to be entered upon the following day. Dantès possessed a prodigious memory, combined with an astonishing quickness and readiness of conception; the mathematical turn of his mind rendered him apt at all kinds of calculation, while his naturally poetical feelings threw a light and pleasing veil over the dry reality of arithmetical computation, or the rigid severity of geometry. He already knew Italian, and had also picked up a little of the Romaic dialect during voyages to the East; and by the aid of these two languages he easily comprehended the construction of all the others, so that at the end of six months he began to speak Spanish, English, and German. In strict accordance with the promise made to the abbé, Dantès spoke no more of escape. Perhaps the delight his studies afforded him left no room for such thoughts; perhaps the recollection that he had pledged his word (on which his sense of honor was keen) kept him from referring in any way to the possibilities of flight. Days, even months, passed by unheeded in one rapid and instructive course. At the end of a year Dantès was a new man. Dantès observed, however, that Faria, in spite of the relief his society afforded, daily grew sadder; one thought seemed incessantly to harass and distract his mind. Sometimes he would fall into long reveries, sigh heavily and involuntarily, then suddenly rise, and, with folded arms, begin pacing the confined space of his dungeon. One day he stopped all at once, and exclaimed, "Ah, if there were no sentinel!"

"There shall not be one a minute longer than you please," said Dantès, who had followed the working of his thoughts as accurately as though his brain were enclosed in crystal so clear as to display its minutest operations.

"I have already told you," answered the abbé, "that I loathe the idea of shedding blood."

"And yet the murder, if you choose to call it so, would be simply a measure of self-preservation."

"No matter! I could never agree to it."

"Still, you have thought of it?"—"Incessantly, alas!" cried the abbé.

"And you have discovered a means of regaining our freedom, have you not?" asked Dantès eagerly.—"I have; if it were only possible to place a deaf and blind sentinel in the gallery beyond us."

"He shall be both blind and deaf," replied the young man, with an air of determination that made his companion shudder.

"No, no," cried the abbé; "impossible!" Dantès endeavored to renew the subject; the abbé shook his head in token of disapproval, and refused to make any further response. Three months passed away.

"Are you strong?" the abbé asked one day of Dantès. The young man, in reply, took up the chisel, bent it into the form of a horse-shoe, and then as readily straightened it.

"And will you engage not to do any harm to the sentry, except as a last resort?"

"I promise on my honor."

"Then," said the abbé, "we may hope to put our design into execution."—"And how long shall we be in accomplishing the necessary work?"—"At least a year."

"And shall we begin at once?"—"At once."

"We have lost a year to no purpose!" cried Dantès.

"Do you consider the last twelve months to have been wasted?" asked the abbé.—"Forgive me!" cried Edmond, blushing deeply.

"Tut, tut!" answered the abbé, "man is but man after all, and you are about the best specimen of the genus I have ever known. Come, let me show you my plan." The abbé then showed Dantès the sketch he had made for their escape. It consisted of a plan of his own cell and that of Dantès, with the passage which united them. In this passage he proposed to drive a level as they do in mines; this level would bring the two prisoners immediately beneath the gallery where the sentry kept watch; once there, a large excavation would be made, and one of the flag-stones with which the gallery was paved be so completely loosened that at the desired moment it would give way beneath the feet of the soldier, who, stunned by his fall, would be immediately bound and gagged by Dantès before he had power to offer any resistance. The prisoners were then to make their way through one of the gallery windows, and to let themselves down from the outer walls by means of the abbé's ladder of cords. Dantès' eyes sparkled with joy, and he rubbed his hands with delight at the idea of a plan so simple, yet apparently so certain to succeed.

That very day the miners began their labors, with a vigor and alacrity proportionate to their long rest from fatigue and their hopes of ultimate success. Nothing interrupted the progress of the work except the necessity that each was under of returning to his cell in anticipation of the turnkey's visits. They had learned to distinguish the almost imperceptible sound of his footsteps as he descended towards their dungeons, and happily, never failed of being prepared for his coming. The fresh earth excavated during their present work, and which would have entirely blocked up the old passage, was thrown, by degrees and with the utmost precaution, out of the window in either Faria's or Dantès' cell, the rubbish being first pulverized so finely that the night wind carried it far away without permitting the smallest trace to remain. More than a year had been consumed in this undertaking, the only tools for which had been a chisel, a knife, and a wooden lever; Faria still continuing to instruct Dantès by conversing with him, sometimes in one language, sometimes in another; at others, relating to him the history of nations and great men who from time to time have risen to fame and trodden the path of glory.

The abbé was a man of the world, and had, moreover, mixed in the first society of the day; he wore an air of melancholy dignity which Dantès, thanks to the imitative powers bestowed on him by nature, easily acquired, as well as that outward polish and politeness he had before been wanting in, and which is seldom possessed except by those who have been placed in constant intercourse with persons of high birth and breeding. At the end of fifteen months the level was finished, and the excavation completed beneath the gallery, and the two workmen could distinctly hear the measured tread of the sentinel as he paced to and fro over their heads.

Compelled, as they were, to await a night sufficiently dark to favor their flight, they were obliged to defer their final attempt till that auspicious moment should arrive; their greatest dread now was lest the stone through which the sentry was doomed to fall should give way before its right time, and this they had in some measure provided against by propping it up with a small beam which they had discovered in the walls through which they had worked their way. Dantès was occupied in arranging this piece of wood when he heard Faria, who had remained in Edmond's cell for the purpose of cutting a peg to secure their rope-ladder, call to him in a tone indicative of great suffering. Dantès hastened to his dungeon, where he found him standing in the middle of the room, pale as death, his forehead streaming with perspiration, and his hands clinched tightly together.

"Gracious heavens!" exclaimed Dantès, "what is the matter? what has happened?"

"Quick! quick!" returned the abbé, "listen to what I have to say." Dantès looked in fear and wonder at the livid countenance of Faria, whose eyes, already dull and sunken, were surrounded by purple circles, while his lips were white as those of a corpse, and his very hair seemed to stand on end.

"Tell me, I beseech you, what ails you?" cried Dantès, letting his chisel fall to the floor.

"Alas," faltered out the abbé, "all is over with me. I am seized with a terrible, perhaps mortal illness; I can feel that the paroxysm is fast approaching. I had a similar attack the year previous to my imprisonment. This malady admits but of one remedy; I will tell you what that is. Go into my cell as quickly as you can; draw out one of the feet that support the bed; you will find it has been hollowed out for the purpose of containing a small phial you will see there half-filled with a red-looking fluid. Bring it to me—or rather—no, no!—I may be found here, therefore help me back to my room while I have the strength to drag myself along. Who knows what may happen, or how long the attack may last?"

In spite of the magnitude of the misfortune which thus suddenly frustrated his hopes, Dantès did not lose his presence of mind, but descended into the passage, dragging his unfortunate companion with him; then, half-carrying, half-supporting him, he managed to reach the abbé's chamber, when he immediately laid the sufferer on his bed.

"Thanks," said the poor abbé, shivering as though his veins were filled with ice. "I am about to be seized with a fit of catalepsy; when it comes to its height I shall probably lie still and motionless as though dead, uttering neither sigh nor groan. On the other hand, the symptoms may be much more violent, and cause me to fall into fearful convulsions, foam at the mouth, and cry out loudly. Take care my cries are not heard, for if they are it is more than probable I should be removed to another part of the prison, and we be separated forever. When I become quite motionless, cold, and rigid as a corpse, then, and not before,—be careful about this,—force open my teeth with the knife, pour from eight to ten drops of the liquor contained in the phial down my throat, and I may perhaps revive."

"Perhaps!" exclaimed Dantès in grief-stricken tones.

"Help! help!" cried the abbé, "I—I—die—I"—

So sudden and violent was the fit that the unfortunate prisoner was unable to complete the sentence; a violent convulsion shook his whole frame, his eyes started from their sockets, his mouth was drawn on one side, his cheeks became purple, he struggled, foamed, dashed himself about, and uttered the most dreadful cries, which, however, Dantès prevented from being heard by covering his head with the blanket. The fit lasted two hours; then, more helpless than an infant, and colder and paler than marble, more crushed and broken than a reed trampled under foot, he fell back, doubled up in one last convulsion, and became as rigid as a corpse.

Edmond waited till life seemed extinct in the body of his friend, then, taking up the knife, he with difficulty forced open the closely fixed jaws, carefully administered the appointed number of drops, and anxiously awaited the result. An hour passed away and the old man gave no sign of returning animation. Dantès began to fear he had delayed too long ere he administered the remedy, and, thrusting his hands into his hair, continued gazing on the lifeless features of his friend. At length a slight color tinged the livid cheeks, consciousness returned to the dull, open eyeballs, a faint sigh issued from the lips, and the sufferer made a feeble effort to move.

"He is saved! he is saved!" cried Dantès in a paroxysm of delight.

The sick man was not yet able to speak, but he pointed with evident anxiety towards the door. Dantès listened, and plainly distinguished the approaching steps of the jailer. It was therefore near seven o'clock; but Edmond's anxiety had put all thoughts of time out of his head. The young man sprang to the entrance, darted through it, carefully drawing the stone over the opening, and hurried to his cell. He had scarcely done so before the door opened, and the jailer saw the prisoner seated as usual on the side of his bed. Almost before the key had turned in the lock, and before the departing steps of the jailer had died away in the long corridor he had to traverse, Dantès, whose restless anxiety concerning his friend left him no desire to touch the food brought him, hurried back to the abbé's chamber, and raising the stone by pressing his head against it, was soon beside the sick man's couch. Faria had now fully regained his consciousness, but he still lay helpless and exhausted.

"I did not expect to see you again," said he feebly, to Dantès.

"And why not?" asked the young man. "Did you fancy yourself dying?"

"No, I had no such idea; but, knowing that all was ready for flight, I thought you might have made your escape." The deep glow of indignation suffused the cheeks of Dantès.

"Without you? Did you really think me capable of that?"

"At least," said the abbé, "I now see how wrong such an opinion would have been. Alas, alas! I am fearfully exhausted and debilitated by this attack."

"Be of good cheer," replied Dantès; "your strength will return." And as he spoke he seated himself near the bed beside Faria, and took his hands. The abbé shook his head.

"The last attack I had," said he, "lasted but half an hour, and after it I was hungry, and got up without help; now I can move neither my right arm nor leg, and my head seems uncomfortable, which shows that there has been a suffusion of blood on the brain. The third attack will either carry me off, or leave me paralyzed for life."

"No, no," cried Dantès; "you are mistaken—you will not die! And your third attack (if, indeed, you should have another) will find you at liberty. We shall save you another time, as we have done this, only with a better chance of success, because we shall be able to command every requisite assistance."

"My good Edmond," answered the abbé, "be not deceived. The attack which has just passed away, condemns me forever to the walls of a prison. None can fly from a dungeon who cannot walk."

"Well, we will wait,—a week, a month, two months, if need be,—and meanwhile your strength will return. Everything is in readiness for our flight, and we can select any time we choose. As soon as you feel able to swim we will go."

"I shall never swim again," replied Faria. "This arm is paralyzed; not for a time, but forever. Lift it, and judge if I am mistaken." The young man raised the arm, which fell back by its own weight, perfectly inanimate and helpless. A sigh escaped him.

"You are convinced now, Edmond, are you not?" asked the abbé. "Depend upon it, I know what I say. Since the first attack I experienced of this malady, I have continually reflected on it. Indeed, I expected it, for it is a family inheritance; both my father and grandfather died of it in a third attack. The physician who prepared for me the remedy I have twice successfully taken, was no other than the celebrated Cabanis, and he predicted a similar end for me."

"The physician may be mistaken!" exclaimed Dantès. "And as for your poor arm, what difference will that make? I can take you on my shoulders, and swim for both of us."

"My son," said the abbé, "you, who are a sailor and a swimmer, must know as well as I do that a man so loaded would sink before he had done fifty strokes. Cease, then, to allow yourself to be duped by vain hopes, that even your own excellent heart refuses to believe in. Here I shall remain till the hour of my deliverance arrives, and that, in all human probability, will be the hour of my death. As for you, who are young and active, delay not on my account, but fly—go—I give you back your promise."

"It is well," said Dantès. "Then I shall also remain." Then, rising and extending his hand with an air of solemnity over the old man's head, he slowly added, "By the blood of Christ I swear never to leave you while you live."

Faria gazed fondly on his noble-minded, single-hearted, high-principled young friend, and read in his countenance ample confirmation of the sincerity of his devotion and the loyalty of his purpose.

"Thanks," murmured the invalid, extending one hand. "I accept. You may one of these days reap the reward of your disinterested devotion. But as I cannot, and you will not, quit this place, it becomes necessary to fill up the excavation beneath the soldier's gallery; he might, by chance, hear the hollow sound of his footsteps, and call the attention of his officer to the circumstance. That would bring about a discovery which would inevitably lead to our being separated. Go, then, and set about this work, in which, unhappily, I can offer you no assistance; keep at it all night, if necessary, and do not return here to-morrow till after the jailer has visited me. I shall have something of the greatest importance to communicate to you."

Dantès took the hand of the abbè in his, and affectionately pressed it. Faria smiled encouragingly on him, and the young man retired to his task, in the spirit of obedience and respect which he had sworn to show towards his aged friend.

XVIII

The Treasure

WHEN DANTÈS RETURNED NEXT morning to the chamber of his companion in captivity, he found Faria seated and looking composed. In the ray of light which entered by the narrow window of his cell, he held open in his left hand, of which alone, it will be recollected, he retained the use, a sheet of paper, which, from being constantly rolled into a small compass, had the form of a cylinder, and was not easily kept open. He did not speak, but showed the paper to Dantès.

"What is that?" he inquired.—"Look at it," said the abbè with a smile.

"I have looked at it with all possible attention," said Dantès, "and I only see a half-burnt paper, on which are traces of Gothic characters inscribed with a peculiar kind of ink."

"This paper, my friend," said Faria, "I may now avow to you, since I have the proof of your fidelity—this paper is my treasure, of which, from this day forth, one-half belongs to you."

The sweat started forth on Dantès brow. Until this day—and for how long a time!—he had refrained from talking of the treasure, which had brought upon the abbè the accusation of madness. With his instinctive delicacy Edmond had preferred avoiding any touch on this painful chord, and Faria had been equally silent. He had taken the silence of the old man for a return to reason; and now these few words uttered by Faria, after so painful a crisis, seemed to indicate a serious relapse into mental alienation.

"Your treasure?" stammered Dantès. Faria smiled.

"Yes," said he. "You have, indeed, a noble nature, Edmond, and I see by your paleness and agitation what is passing in your heart at this moment. No, be assured, I am not mad. This treasure exists, Dantès, and if I have not been allowed to possess it, you will. Yes— you. No one would listen or believe me, because everyone thought me mad; but you, who must know that I am not, listen to me, and believe me so afterwards if you will."

"Alas," murmured Edmond to himself, "this is a terrible relapse! There was only this blow wanting." Then he said aloud, "My dear friend, your attack has, perhaps, fatigued you; had you not better repose awhile? To-morrow, if you will, I will hear your narrative; but to-day I wish to nurse you carefully. Besides," he said, "a treasure is not a thing we need hurry about."

"On the contrary, it is a matter of the utmost importance, Edmond!" replied the old man. "Who knows if to-morrow, or the next day after, the third attack may not come on? and then must not all be over? Yes, indeed, I have often thought with a bitter joy that these riches, which would make the wealth of a dozen families, will be for-ever lost to those men who persecute me. This idea was one of vengeance to me, and I tasted it slowly in the night of my dungeon and the despair of my captivity. But now I have forgiven the world for the love of you; now that I see you, young and with a promising future,— now that I think of all that may result to you in the good fortune of such a disclosure, I shudder at any delay, and tremble lest I should not assure to one as worthy as yourself the possession of so vast an amount of hidden wealth." Edmond turned away his head with a sigh.

"You persist in your incredulity, Edmond," continued Faria. "My words have not convinced you. I see you require proofs. Well, then, read this paper, which I have never shown to any one."

"To-morrow, my dear friend," said Edmond, desirous of not yielding to the old man's madness. "I thought it was understood that we should not talk of that until to-morrow."—"Then we will not talk of it until to-morrow; but read this paper to-day."

"I will not irritate him," thought Edmond, and taking the paper, of which half was wanting,—having been burnt, no doubt, by some accident,—he read:—

"This treasure, which may amount to two...

of Roman crowns in the most distant a...

of the second opening wh...

declare to belong to him alo...

heir.

"25th April, 149"

"Well!" said Faria, when the young man had finished reading it.

"Why," replied Dantès, "I see nothing but broken lines and unconnected words, which are rendered illegible by fire."

"Yes, to you, my friend, who read them for the first time; but not for me, who have grown pale over them by many nights' study, and have reconstructed every phrase, completed every thought."

"And do you believe you have discovered the hidden meaning?"

"I am sure I have, and you shall judge for yourself; but first listen to the history of this paper."

"Silence!" exclaimed Dantès. "Steps approach—I go—adieu."

And Dantès, happy to escape the history and explanation which would be sure to confirm his belief in his friend's mental instability, glided like a snake along the narrow passage; while Faria, restored by his alarm to a certain amount of activity, pushed the stone into place with his foot, and covered it with a mat in order the more effectually to avoid discovery.

It was the governor, who, hearing of Faria's illness from the jailer, had come in person to see him.

Faria sat up to receive him, avoiding all gestures in order that he might conceal from the governor the paralysis that had already half stricken him with death. His fear was lest the governor, touched with pity, might order him to be removed to better quarters, and thus separate him from his young companion. But fortunately this was not the case, and the governor left him, convinced that the poor madman, for whom in his heart he felt a kind of affection, was only troubled with a slight indisposition.

During this time, Edmond, seated on his bed with his head in his hands, tried to collect his scattered thoughts. Faria, since their first acquaintance, had been on all points so rational and logical, so wonderfully sagacious, in fact, that he could not understand how so much wisdom on all points could be allied with madness. Was Faria deceived as to his treasure, or was all the world deceived as to Faria?

Dantès remained in his cell all day, not daring to return to his friend, thinking thus to defer the moment when he should be convinced, once for all, that the abbé was mad—such a conviction would be so terrible!

But, towards the evening after the hour for the customary visit had gone by, Faria, not seeing the young man appear, tried to move and get over the distance which separated them. Edmond shuddered when he heard the painful efforts which the old man made to drag himself along; his leg was inert, and he could no longer make use of one arm. Edmond was obliged to assist him, for otherwise he would not have been able to enter by the small aperture which led to Dantès' chamber.

"Here I am, pursuing you remorselessly," he said with a benignant smile. "You thought to escape my munificence, but it is in vain. Listen to me."

Edmond saw there was no escape, and placing the old man on his bed, he seated himself on the stool beside him.

"You know," said the abbé, "that I was the secretary and intimate friend of Cardinal Spada, the last of the princes of that name. I owe to this worthy lord all the happiness I ever knew. He was not rich, although the wealth of his family had passed into a proverb, and I heard the phrase very often, 'As rich as a Spada.' But he, like public rumor, lived on this reputation for wealth; his palace was my paradise. I was tutor to his nephews, who are dead; and when he was alone in the world, I tried by absolute devotion to his will, to make up to him all he had done for me during ten years of unremitting kindness. The cardinal's house had no secrets for me. I had often seen my noble patron annotating ancient volumes, and eagerly searching amongst dusty family manuscripts. One day when I was reproaching him for his unavailing searches, and deploring the prostration of mind that followed them, he looked at me, and, smiling bitterly, opened a volume relating to the History of the City of Rome. There, in the twentieth chapter of the Life of Pope Alexander VI., were the following lines, which I can never forget:—

"'The great wars of Romagna had ended; Cæsar Borgia, who had completed his conquest, had need of money to purchase all Italy. The pope had also need of money to bring matters to an end with Louis XII. King of France, who was formidable still in spite of his recent reverses; and it was necessary, therefore, to have recourse to some profitable scheme, which was a matter of great difficulty in the impoverished condition of exhausted Italy. His holiness had an idea. He determined to make two cardinals.'

"By choosing two of the greatest personages of Rome, especially rich men—*this* was the return the holy father looked for. In the first place, he could sell the great appointments and splendid offices which the cardinals already held; and then he had the two hats to sell besides. There was a third point in view, which will appear hereafter. The pope and Cæsar Borgia first found the two future cardinals; they were Giovanni Rospigliosi, who held four of the highest dignities of the Holy See, and Cæsar Spada, one of the noblest and richest of the Roman nobility; both felt the high honor of such a favor from the pope. They were ambitious, and Cæsar Borgia soon found purchasers for their appointments. The result was, that Rospigliosi and Spada paid for being cardinals, and eight other persons paid for the offices the cardinals held before their elevation, and thus eight hundred thousand crowns entered into the coffers of the speculators.

"It is time now to proceed to the last part of the speculation. The pope heaped attentions upon Rospigliosi and Spada, conferred upon them the insignia of the cardinalate, and induced them to arrange their affairs and take up their residence at Rome. Then the pope and Cæsar Borgia invited the two cardinals to dinner. This was a matter of dispute between the holy father and his son. Cæsar thought they could make use of one of the means which he always had ready for his friends, that is to say, in the first place, the famous key which was given to certain persons with the request that they go and open a designated cupboard. This key was furnished with a small iron point,—a negligence on the part of the locksmith. When this was pressed to effect the opening of the cupboard, of which the lock was difficult, the person was pricked by this small point, and died next day. Then there was the ring with the lion's head, which Cæsar wore when he wanted to greet his friends with a clasp of the hand. The lion bit the hand thus favored, and at the end of twenty-four hours, the bite was mortal. Cæsar proposed to his father, that they should either ask the cardinals to open the cupboard, or shake hands with them; but Alexander VI., replied: 'Now as to the worthy cardinals, Spada and Rospigliosi, let us ask both of them to dinner. Something tells me that we shall get that money back. Besides, you forget, Cæsar, an indigestion declares itself immediately, while a prick or a bite occasions a delay of a day or two.' Cæsar gave way before such cogent reasoning, and the cardinals were consequently invited to dinner.

"The table was laid in a vineyard belonging to the pope, near San Pierdarena, a charming retreat which the cardinals knew very well by report. Rospigliosi, quite set up with his new dignities, went with a good appetite and his most ingratiating manner. Spada, a prudent man, and greatly attached to his only nephew, a young captain of the highest promise, took paper and pen, and made his will. He then sent word to his nephew to wait for him near the vineyard; but it appeared the servant did not find him.

"Spada knew what these invitations meant; since Christianity, so eminently civilizing, had made progress in Rome, it was no longer a centurion who came from the tyrant with a message, 'Caesar wills that you die,' but it was a legate *à latere*, who came with a smile on his lips to say from the pope, 'His holiness requests you to dine with him.'

"Spada set out about two o'clock to San Pierdarena. The pope awaited him. The first sight that attracted the eyes of Spada was that of his nephew, in full costume, and Cæsar Borgia paying him most marked attentions. Spada turned pale, as Cæsar looked at him with an ironical air, which proved that he had anticipated all, and that the snare was well spread. They began dinner, and Spada was only able to inquire of his nephew if he had received his message. The nephew replied no; perfectly comprehending the meaning of the question. It was too late, for he had already drunk a glass of excellent wine, placed for him expressly by the pope's butler. Spada at the same moment saw another bottle approach him, which he was pressed to taste. An hour afterwards a physician declared they were both poisoned through eating mushrooms. Spada died on the threshold of the vineyard; the nephew expired at his own door, making signs which his wife could not comprehend.

"Then Cæsar and the pope hastened to lay hands on the heritage, under pretence of seeking for the papers of the dead man. But the inheritance consisted in this only, a scrap of paper on which Spada had written:—'I bequeath to my beloved nephew my coffers, my books, and, amongst others, my breviary with the gold corners, which I beg he will preserve in remembrance of his affectionate uncle.'

"The heirs sought everywhere, admired the breviary, laid hands on the furniture, and were greatly astonished that Spada, the rich man, was really the most miserable of uncles—no treasures—unless they were those of science, contained in the library and laboratories. That was all. Cæsar and his father searched, examined, scrutinized, but found nothing, or at least very little; not exceeding a few thousand crowns in plate, and about the same in ready money; but the nephew had time to say to his wife before he expired: 'Look well among my uncle's papers; there is a will.'

"They sought even more thoroughly than the august heirs had done, but it was fruitless. There were two palaces and a vineyard behind the Palatine Hill; but in these days landed property had not much value, and the two palaces and the vineyard remained to the family since they were beneath the rapacity of the pope and his son. Months and years rolled on. Alexander VI. died, poisoned,—you know by what mistake. Cæsar, poisoned at the same time, escaped by shedding his skin like a shake; but the new skin was spotted by the poison till it looked like a tiger's. Then, compelled to quit Rome, he went and got himself obscurely killed in a night skirmish, scarcely noticed in history. After the pope's death and his son's exile, it was supposed that the Spada family would resume the splendid position they had held before the cardinal's time; but this was not the case. The Spadas remained in doubtful ease, a mystery hung over this dark affair, and the public rumor was, that Cæsar, a better politician than his father, had carried off from the pope the fortune of the two cardinals. I say the two, because Cardinal Rospigliosi, who had not taken any precaution, was completely despoiled.

"Up to this point," said Faria, interrupting the thread of his narrative, "this seems to you very meaningless, no doubt, eh?"

"Oh, my friend," cried Dantès, "on the contrary, it seems as if I were reading a most interesting narrative; go on, I beg of you."— "I will."

"The family began to get accustomed to their obscurity. Years rolled on, and amongst the descendants some were soldiers, others diplomatists; some churchmen, some bankers; some grew rich, and

some were ruined. I come now to the last of the family, whose secretary I was—the Count of Spada. I had often heard him complain
of the disproportion of his rank with his fortune; and I advised him
to invest all he had in an annuity. He did so, and thus doubled his
income. The celebrated breviary remained in the family, and was in
the count's possession. It had been handed down from father to son;
for the singular clause of the only will that had been found, had
caused it to be regarded as a genuine relic, preserved in the family
with superstitious veneration. It was an illuminated book, with
beautiful Gothic characters, and so weighty with gold, that a servant always carried it before the cardinal on days of great solemnity.

"At the sight of papers of all sorts,—titles, contracts, parchments,
which were kept in the archives of the family, all descending from the
poisoned cardinal, I in my turn examined the immense bundles of
documents, like twenty servitors, stewards, secretaries before me; but
in spite of the most exhaustive researches, I found—nothing. Yet I
had read, I had even written a precise history of the Borgia family,
for the sole purpose of assuring myself whether any increase of fortune had occurred to them on the death of the Cardinal Cæsar
Spada; but could only trace the acquisition of the property of the
Cardinal Rospigliosi, his companion in misfortune.

"I was then almost assured that the inheritance had neither
profited the Borgias nor the family, but had remained unpossessed
like the treasures of the Arabian Nights, which slept in the bosom
of the earth under the eyes of the genie. I searched, ransacked,
counted, calculated a thousand and a thousand times the income
and expenditure of the family for three hundred years. It was useless. I remained in my ignorance, and the Count of Spada in his
poverty. My patron died. He had reserved from his annuity his family papers, his library, composed of five thousand volumes, and his
famous breviary. All these he bequeathed to me, with a thousand
Roman crowns, which he had in ready money, on condition that I
would have anniversary masses said for the repose of his soul, and

that I would draw up a genealogical tree and history of his house. All this I did scrupulously. Be easy, my dear Edmond, we are near the conclusion.

"In 1807, a month before I was arrested, and a fortnight after the death of the Count of Spada, on the 25th of December (you will see presently how the date became fixed in my memory), I was reading, for the thousandth time, the papers I was arranging, for the palace was sold to a stranger, and I was going to leave Rome and settle at Florence, intending to take with me twelve thousand francs I possessed, my library, and the famous breviary, when, tired with my constant labor at the same thing, and overcome by a heavy dinner I had eaten, my head dropped on my hands, and I fell asleep about three o'clock in the afternoon. I awoke as the clock was striking six. I raised my head; I was in utter darkness. I rang for a light, but as no one came, I determined to find one for myself. It was indeed but anticipating the simple manners which I should soon be under the necessity of adopting. I took a waxcandle in one hand, and with the other groped about for a piece of paper (my match-box being empty), with which I proposed to get a light from the small flame still playing on the embers. Fearing, however, to make use of any valuable piece of paper, I hesitated for a moment, then recollected that I had seen in the famous breviary, which was on the table beside me, an old paper quite yellow with age, and which had served as a marker for centuries, kept there by the request of the heirs. I felt for it, found it, twisted it up together, and putting it into the expiring flame, set light to it.

"But beneath my fingers, as if by magic, in proportion as the fire ascended, I saw yellowish characters appear on the paper. I grasped it in my hand, put out the flame as quickly as I could, lighted my taper in the fire itself, and opened the crumpled paper with inexpressible emotion, recognizing, when I had done so, that these characters had been traced in mysterious and sympathetic ink, only appearing when exposed to the fire; nearly one-third of the paper had been consumed by the flame. It was that paper you read this morning; read it again, Dantès, and then I will complete for you the incomplete words and unconnected sense."

Faria, with an air of triumph, offered the paper to Dantès, who this time read the following words, traced with an ink of a reddish color resembling rust:—

> *"This 25th day of April, 1498, be...*
> *Alexander VI., and fearing that not...*
> *he may desire to become my heir, and re...*
> *and Bentivoglio, who were poisoned,...*
> *my sole heir, that I have bu...*
> *and has visited with me, that is, in...*
> *Island of Monte Cristo, all I poss...*
> *jewels, diamonds, gems; that I alone...*
> *may amount to nearly two mil...*
> *will find on raising the twentieth ro...*
> *creek to the east in a right line. Two open...*
> *in these caves; the treasure is in the furthest a...*
> *which treasre I bequeath and leave en...*
> *as my sole heir.*
> *"25th April, 1498. "CÆS...*

"And Now," said the abbé, "read this other paper;" and he presented to Dantès a second leaf with fragments of lines written on it, which Edmond read as follows:—

> *"...ing invited to dine by his Holiness*
> *...content with making me pay for my hat,*
> *...serves for me the fate of Cardinals Caprara*
> *...I declare to my nephew, Guido Spada*
> *...ried in a place he knows*
> *...the caves of the small*

> *...essed of ingots, gold, money,*
> *...know of the existence of this treasure, which*
> *...lions of Roman crowns, and which he*
> *...ck from the small*
> *...ings have been made*
> *...ngle in the second;*
> *...tire to him*
> *...*AR † SPADA."

Faria followed him with an excited look. "And now," he said, when he saw that Dantès had read the last line, "put the two fragments together, and judge for yourself." Dantès obeyed, and the conjoined pieces gave the following:—

"This 25th day of April, 1498, be ... ing invited to dine by his Holiness Alexander IV., and fearing that not ... content with making me pay for my hat, he may desire to become my heir, and re ... serves for me the fate of Cardinals Caprara and Bentivoglio, who were poisoned ... I declare to my nephew, Guido Spada, my sole heir, that I have bu ... ried in a place he knows and has visited with me, that is, in ... the caves of the small Island of Monto Cristo, all I poss ... essed of ingots, gold, money, jewels, diamonds, gems; that I alone ... know of the existence of this treasure, which may amount to nearly two mil ... lions of Roman crowns, and which he will find on raising the twentieth ro ... ck from the small creek to the east in a right line. Two open ... ings have been made in these caves; the treasure is in the furthest a ... ngle in the second; which treasure I bequeath and leave en ... tire to him as my sole heir.

"25th April, 1498.

"CÆS ... AR † SPADA."

"Well, do you comprehend now?" inquired Faria.

"It is the declaration of Cardinal Spada, and the will so long sought for," replied Edmond, still incredulous.

"Yes; a thousand times, yes!"—"And who completed it as it now is?"

"I did. Aided by the remaining fragment, I guessed the rest; measuring the length of the lines by those of the paper, and divining the hidden meaning by means of what was in part revealed, as we are guided in a cavern by the small ray of light above us."

"And what did you do when you arrived at this conclusion?"

"I resolved to set out, and did set out at that very instant, carrying with me the beginning of my great work, the unity of the Italian kingdom; but for some time the imperial police (who at this period, quite contrary to what Napoleon desired so soon as he had a son born to him, wished for a partition of provinces) had their eyes on me; and my hasty departure, the cause of which they were unable to guess, having aroused their suspicions, I was arrested at the very moment I was leaving Piombino.

"Now," continued Faria, addressing Dantès with an almost paternal expression, "now, my dear fellow, you know as much as I do myself. If we ever escape together, half this treasure is yours; if I die here, and you escape alone, the whole belongs to you."

"But," inquired Dantès hesitating, "has this treasure no more legitimate possessor in the world than ourselves?"

"No, no, be easy on that score; the family is extinct. The last Count of Spada, moreover, made me his heir; bequeathing to me this symbolic breviary, he bequeathed to me all it contained; no, no, make your mind satisfied on that point. If we lay hands on this fortune, we may enjoy it without remorse."

"And you say this treasure amounts to"—

"Two millions of Roman crowns; nearly thirteen millions of our money."[1]

"Impossible!" said Dantès, staggered at the enormous amount.

"Impossible? and why?" asked the old man. "The Spada family

[1] 2,600,000

was one of the oldest and most powerful families of the fifteenth century; and in those times, when other opportunities for investment were wanting, such accumulations of gold and jewels were by no means rare; there are at this day Roman families perishing of hunger, though possessed of nearly a million in diamonds and jewels, handed down by entail, and which they cannot touch." Edmond thought he was in a dream—he wavered between incredulity and joy.

"I have only kept this secret so long from you," continued Faria, "that I might test your character, and then surprise you. Had we escaped before my attack of catalepsy, I should have conducted you to Monte Cristo; now," he added, with a sigh, "it is you who will conduct me thither. Well, Dantès, you do not thank me?"

"This treasure belongs to you, my dear friend," replied Dantès, "and to you only. I have no right to it. I am no relation of yours."

"You are my son, Dantès," exclaimed the old man. "You are the child of my captivity. My profession condemns me to celibacy. God has sent you to me to console, at one and the same time, the man who could not be a father, and the prisoner who could not get free." And Faria extended the arm of which alone the use remained to him to the young man who threw himself upon his neck and wept.

XIX

The Third Attack

NOW THAT THIS TREASURE, which had so long been the object of the abbé's meditations, could insure the future happiness of him whom Faria really loved as a son, it had doubled its value in his eyes, and every day he expatiated on the amount, explaining to Dantès all the good which, with thirteen or fourteen millions of francs, a man could do in these days to his friends; and then Dantès' countenance became gloomy, for the oath of vengeance he had taken recurred to his memory, and he reflected how much ill, in these times, a man with thirteen or fourteen millions could do to his enemies.

The abbé did not know the Island of Monte Cristo; but Dantès knew it, and had often passed it, situated twenty-five miles from Pianosa, between Corsica and the Island of Elba, and had once touched there. This island was, always had been, and still is, completely deserted. It is a rock of almost conical form, which looks as though it had been thrust up by volcanic force from the depth to the surface of the ocean. Dantès drew a plan of the island for Faria, and Faria gave Dantès advice as to the means he should employ to recover the treasure. But Dantès was far from being as enthusiastic and confident as the old man. It was past a question now that Faria was not a lunatic, and the way in which he had achieved the discovery, which had given rise to the suspicion of his madness, increased Edmond's admiration of him; but at the same time Dantès could not believe that the deposit, supposing it had ever existed, still existed; and though he considered the treasure as by no means chimerical, he yet believed it was no longer there.

However, as if fate resolved on depriving the prisoners of their last chance, and making them understand that they were condemned to perpetual imprisonment, a new misfortune befell them; the gallery on the sea side, which had long been in ruins, was rebuilt. They had repaired it completely, and stopped up with vast masses of stone the hole Dantès had partly filled in. But for this precaution, which, it will be remembered, the abbé had made to Edmond, the misfortune would have been still greater, for their attempt to escape would have been detected, and they would undoubtedly have been separated. Thus a new, a stronger, and more inexorable barrier was interposed to cut off the realization of their hopes.

"You see," said the young man, with an air of sorrowful resignation, to Faria, "that God deems it right to take from me any claim to merit for what you call my devotion to you. I have promised to remain forever with you, and now I could not break my promise if I would. The treasure will be no more mine than yours, and neither of us will quit this prison. But my real treasure is not that, my dear friend, which awaits me beneath the sombre rocks of Monte Cristo, it is your presence, our living together five or six hours a day, in spite of our jailers; it is the rays of intelligence you have elicited from my brain, the languages you have implanted in my memory, and which have taken root there with all their philological ramifications. These different sciences that you have made so easy to me by the depth of the knowledge you possess of them, and the clearness of the principles to which you have reduced them—this is my treasure, my beloved friend, and with this you have made me rich and happy. Believe me, and take comfort, this is better for me than tons of gold and cases of diamonds, even were they not as problematical as the clouds we see in the morning floating over the sea, which we take for *terra firma*, and which evaporate and vanish as we draw near to them. To have you as long as possible near me, to hear your eloquent speech,—which embellishes my mind, strengthens my soul, and makes my whole frame capable of great and terrible things, if I should ever be free,—so fills my whole existence, that the despair to which I was just on the point of yielding when I knew you, has no longer any hold over me; and this—this is my fortune—not chimerical, but actual. I owe you my real good, my present happiness; and all the sovereigns of the earth, even Cæsar Borgia himself, could not deprive me of this."

Thus, if not actually happy, yet the days these two unfortunates passed together went quickly. Faria, who for so long a time had kept silence as to the treasure, now perpetually talked of it. As he had prophesied would be the case, he remained paralyzed in the right arm and the left leg, and had given up all hope of ever enjoying it himself. But he was continually thinking over some means of escape for his young companion, and anticipating the pleasure he would enjoy. For fear the letter might be some day lost or stolen, he compelled Dantès to learn it by heart; and Dantès knew it from the first to the last word. Then he destroyed the second portion, assured that if the first were seized, no one would be able to discover its real meaning. Whole hours sometimes passed while Faria was giving instructions to Dantès,—instructions which were to serve him when he was at liberty. Then, once free, from the day and hour and moment when he was so, he could have but one only thought, which was, to gain Monte Cristo by some means, and remain there alone under some pretext which would arouse no suspicions; and once there, to endeavor to find the wonderful caverns, and search in the appointed spot,—the appointed spot, be it remembered, being the farthest angle in the second opening.

In the meanwhile the hours passed, if not rapidly, at least tolerably. Faria, as we have said, without having recovered the use of his hand and foot, had regained all the clearness of his understanding, and had gradually, besides the moral instructions we have detailed, taught his youthful companion the patient and sublime duty of a prisoner, who learns to make something from nothing. They were thus perpetually employed,—Faria, that he might not see himself grow old; Dantès, for fear of recalling the almost extinct past which now only floated in his memory like a distant light wandering in the night. So life went on for them as it does for those who are not victims of misfortune and whose activities glide along mechanically and tranquilly beneath the eye of providence.

But beneath this superficial calm there were in the heart of the young man, and perhaps in that of the old man, many repressed desires, many stifled sighs, which found vent when Faria was left alone, and when Edmond returned to his cell. One night Edmond awoke suddenly, believing that he heard some one calling him. He opened his eyes upon utter darkness. His name, or rather a plaintive voice which essayed to pronounce his name, reached him. He sat up in bed and a cold sweat broke out upon his brow. Undoubtedly the call came from Faria's dungeon. "Alas," murmured Edmond; "can it be?"

He moved his bed, drew up the stone, rushed into the passage, and reached the opposite extremity; the secret entrance was open. By the light of the wretched and wavering lamp, of which we have spoken, Dantès saw the old man, pale, but yet erect, clinging to the bedstead. His features were writhing with those horrible symptoms which he already knew, and which had so seriously alarmed him when he saw them for the first time.

"Alas, my dear friend," said Faria in a resigned tone, "you understand, do you not, and I need not attempt to explain to you?"

Edmond uttered a cry of agony, and, quite out of his senses, rushed towards the door, exclaiming, "Help, help!" Faria had just sufficient strength to restrain him.

"Silence," he said, "or you are lost. We must now only think of you, my dear friend, and so act as to render your captivity supportable or your flight possible. It would require years to do again what I have done here, and the results would be instantly destroyed if our jailers knew we had communicated with each other. Besides, be assured, my dear Edmond, the dungeon I am about to leave will not long remain empty; some other unfortunate being will soon take my place, and to him you will appear like an angel of salvation. Perhaps he will be young, strong, and enduring, like yourself, and will aid you in your escape, while I have been but a hindrance. You will no longer have half a dead body tied to you as a drag to all your movements. At length providence has done something for you; he restores to you more than he takes away, and it was time I should die."

Edmond could only clasp his hands and exclaim, "Oh, my friend, my friend, speak not thus!" and then resuming all his presence of mind, which had for a moment staggered under this blow, and his strength, which had failed at the words of the old man, he said, "Oh, I have saved you once, and I will save you a second time!" And raising the foot of the bed, he drew out the phial, still a third filled with the red liquor.

"See," he exclaimed, "there remains still some of the magic draught. Quick, quick! tell me what I must do this time; are there any fresh instructions? Speak, my friend; I listen."

"There is not a hope," replied Faria, shaking his head; "but no matter; God wills it that man whom he has created, and in whose heart he has so profoundly rooted the love of life, should do all in his power to preserve that existence, which, however painful it may be, is yet always so dear."

"Oh, yes, yes!" exclaimed Dantès; "and I tell you that I will save you yet."

"Well, then, try. The cold gains upon me. I feel the blood flowing towards my brain. These horrible chills, which make my teeth chatter and seem to dislocate my bones, begin to pervade my whole frame; in five minutes the malady will reach its height, and in a quarter of an hour there will be nothing left of me but a corpse."

"Oh!" exclaimed Dantès, his heart wrung with anguish.

"Do as you did before, only do not wait so long. All the springs of life are now exhausted in me, and death," he continued, looking at his paralyzed arm and leg, "has but half its work to do. If, after having made me swallow twelve drops instead of ten, you see that I do not recover, then pour the rest down my throat. Now lift me on my bed, for I can no longer support myself."

Edmond took the old man in his arms, and laid him on the bed.

"And now, my dear friend," said Faria, "sole consolation of my wretched existence,—you whom heaven gave me somewhat late, but still gave me, a priceless gift, and for which I am most grateful,—at the moment of separating from you forever, I wish you all the happiness and all the prosperity you so well deserve. My son, I bless thee!" The young man cast himself on his knees, leaning his head against the old man's bed.

"Listen, now, to what I say in this my dying moment. The treasure of the Spadas exists. God grants me the boon of vision unrestricted by time or space. I see it in the depths of the inner cavern. My eyes pierce the inmost recesses of the earth, and are dazzled at the sight of so much riches. If you do escape, remember that the poor abbé, whom all the world called mad, was not so. Hasten to Monte Cristo—avail yourself of the fortune—for you have indeed suffered long enough." A violent convulsion attacked the old man. Dantès raised his head and saw Faria's eyes injected with blood. It seemed as if a flow of blood had ascended from the chest to the head.

"Adieu, adieu!" murmured the old man, clasping Edmond's hand convulsively—"adieu!"

"Oh, no,—no, not yet," he cried; "do not forsake me! Oh, succor him! Help—help—help!"

"Hush—hush!" murmured the dying man, "that they may not separate us if you save me!"

"You are right. Oh, yes, yes; be assured I shall save you! Besides, although you suffer much, you do not seem to be in such agony as you were before."

"Do not mistake. I suffer less because there is in me less strength to endure. At your age we have faith in life; it is the privilege of youth to believe and hope, but old men see death more clearly. Oh, 'tis here—'tis here—'tis over—my sight is gone—my senses fail! Your hand, Dantès! Adieu—adieu!" And raising himself by a final effort, in which he summoned all his faculties, he said,—"Monte Cristo, forget not Monte Cristo!" And he fell back on the bed. The crisis was terrible, and a rigid form with twisted limbs, swollen eyelids, and lips flecked with bloody foam, lay on the bed of torture, in place of the intellectual being who so lately rested there.

Dantès took the lamp, placed it on a projecting stone above the bed, whence its tremulous light fell with strange and fantastic ray on the distorted countenance and motionless, stiffened body. With steady gaze he awaited confidently the moment for administering the restorative.

When he believed that the right moment had arrived, he took the knife, pried open the teeth, which offered less resistance than before, counted one after the other twelve drops, and watched; the phial contained, perhaps, twice as much more. He waited ten minutes, a quarter of an hour, half an hour,—no change took place. Trembling, his hair erect, his brow bathed with perspiration, he counted the seconds by the beating of his heart. Then he thought it was time to make the last trial, and he put the phial to the purple lips of Faria, and without having occasion to force open his jaws, which had remained extended, he poured the whole of the liquid down his throat.

The draught produced a galvanic effect, a violent trembling pervaded the old man's limbs, his eyes opened until it was fearful to gaze upon them, he heaved a sigh which resembled a shriek, and then his convulsed body returned gradually to its former immobility, the eyes remaining open.

Half an hour, an hour, an hour and a half elapsed, and during this period of anguish, Edmond leaned over his friend, his hand applied to his heart, and felt the body gradually grow cold, and the heart's pulsation become more and more deep and dull, until at length it stopped; the last movement of the heart ceased, the face became livid, the eyes remained open, but the eyeballs were glazed. It was six o'clock in the morning, the dawn was just breaking, and its feeble ray came into the dungeon, and paled the ineffectual light of the lamp. Strange shadows passed over the countenance of the dead man, and at times gave it the appearance of life. While the struggle between day and night lasted, Dantès still doubted; but as soon as the daylight gained the pre-eminence, he saw that he was alone with a corpse. Then an invincible and extreme terror seized upon him, and he dared not again press the hand that hung out of bed, he dared no longer to gaze on those fixed and vacant eyes, which he tried many times to close, but in vain—they opened again as soon as shut. He extinguished the lamp, carefully concealed it, and then went away, closing as well as he could the entrance to the secret passage by the large stone as he descended.

It was time, for the jailer was coming. On this occasion he began his rounds at Dantès' cell, and on leaving him he went on to Faria's dungeon, taking thither breakfast and some linen. Nothing betokened that the man knew anything of what had occurred. He went on his way.

Dantès was then seized with an indescribable desire to know what was going on in the dungeon of his unfortunate friend. He therefore returned by the subterraneous gallery, and arrived in time to hear the exclamations of the turnkey, who called out for help. Other turnkeys came, and then was heard the regular tramp of soldiers. Last of all came the governor.

Edmond heard the creaking of the bed as they moved the corpse, heard the voice of the governor, who asked them to throw water on the dead man's face; and seeing that, in spite of this application, the prisoner did not recover, they sent for the doctor. The governor then went out, and words of pity fell on Dantès' listening ears, mingled with brutal laughter.

"Well, well," said one, "the madman has gone to look after his treasure. Good journey to him!"

"With all his millions, he will not have enough to pay for his shroud!" said another.—"Oh," added a third voice, "the shrouds of the Château d'If are not dear!"

"Perhaps," said one of the previous speakers, "as he was a churchman, they may go to some expense in his behalf."

"They may give him the honors of the sack."

Edmond did not lose a word, but comprehended very little of what was said. The voices soon ceased, and it seemed to him as if every one had left the cell. Still he dared not to enter, as they might have left some turnkey to watch the dead. He remained, therefore, mute and motionless, hardly venturing to breathe. At the end of an hour, he heard a faint noise, which increased. It was the governor who returned, followed by the doctor and other attendants. There was a moment's silence,—it was evident that the doctor was examining the dead body. The inquiries soon commenced.

The doctor analyzed the symptoms of the malady to which the prisoner had succumbed, and declared that he was dead. Questions and answers followed in a nonchalant manner that made Dantès indignant, for he felt that all the world should have for the poor abbé a love and respect equal to his own.

"I am very sorry for what you tell me," said the governor, replying to the assurance of the doctor, "that the old man is really dead; for he was a quiet, inoffensive prisoner, happy in his folly, and required no watching."

"Ah," added the turnkey, "there was no occasion for watching him; he would have stayed here fifty years, I'll answer for it, without any attempt to escape."

"Still," said the governor, "I believe it will be requisite, notwithstanding your certainty, and not that I doubt your science, but in discharge of my official duty, that we should be perfectly assured that the prisoner is dead." There was a moment of complete silence, during which Dantès, still listening, knew that the doctor was examining the corpse a second time.

"You may make your mind easy," said the doctor; "he is dead. I will answer for that."

"You know, sir," said the governor, persisting, "that we are not content in such cases as this with such a simple examination. In spite of all appearances, be so kind, therefore, as to finish your duty by fulfilling the formalities prescribed by law."

"Let the irons be heated," said the doctor; "but really it is a useless precaution." This order to heat the irons made Dantès shudder. He heard hasty steps, the creaking of a door, people going and coming, and some minutes afterwards a turnkey entered, saying,—

"Here is the brazier, lighted." There was a moment's silence, and then was heard the crackling of burning flesh, of which the peculiar and nauseous smell penetrated even behind the wall where Dantès was listening in horror. The perspiration poured forth upon the young man's brow, and he felt as if he should faint.

"You see, sir, he is really dead," said the doctor; "this burn in the heel is decisive. The poor fool is cured of his folly, and delivered from his captivity."

"Wasn't his name Faria?" inquired one of the officers who accompanied the governor.—"Yes, sir; and, as he said, it was an ancient name. He was, too, very learned, and rational enough on all points which did not relate to his treasure; but on that, indeed, he was intractable."

"It is the sort of malady which we call monomania," said the doctor.

"You had never anything to complain of?" said the governor to the jailer who had charge of the abbé.

"Never, sir," replied the jailer, "never; on the contrary, he sometimes amused me very much by telling me stories. One day, too, when my wife was ill, he gave me a prescription which cured her."

"Ah, ah!" said the doctor, "I did not know that I had a rival; but I hope, governor, that you will show him all proper respect."

"Yes, yes, make your mind easy; he shall be decently interred in the newest sack we can find. Will that satisfy you?"

"Must this last formality take place in your presence, sir?" inquired a turnkey.

"Certainly. But make haste—I cannot stay here all day." Other footsteps, going and coming, were now heard, and a moment afterwards the noise of rustling canvas reached Dantès' ears, the bed creaked, and the heavy footfall of a man who lifts a weight sounded on the floor; then the bed again creaked under the weight deposited upon it.

"This evening," said the governor.

"Will there be any mass?" asked one of the attendants.

"That is impossible," replied the governor. "The chaplain of the château came to me yesterday to beg for leave of absence, in order to take a trip to Hyères for a week. I told him I would attend to the prisoners in his absence. If the poor abbé had not been in such a hurry, he might have had his requiem."

"Pooh, pooh;" said the doctor, with the impiety usual in persons of his profession; "he is a churchman. God will respect his profession, and not give the devil the wicked delight of sending him a priest." A shout of laughter followed this brutal jest. Meanwhile the operation of putting the body in the sack was going on.

"This evening," said the governor, when the task was ended.

"At what hour?" inquired a turnkey.—"Why, about ten or eleven o'clock."

"Shall we watch by the corpse?"—"Of what use would it be? Shut the dungeon as if he were alive—that is all." Then the steps retreated, and the voices died away in the distance; the noise of the door, with its creaking hinges and bolts ceased, and a silence more sombre than that of solitude ensued,—the silence of death, which was all-pervasive, and struck its icy chill to the very soul of Dantès.

Then he raised the flagstone cautiously with his head, and looked carefully around the chamber. It was empty, and Dantès emerged from the tunnel.

XX

The Cemetery of
the Château D'If

O N THE BED, AT full length, and faintly illuminated by the pale light that came from the window, lay a sack of canvas, and under its rude folds was stretched a long and stiffened form; it was Faria's last winding-sheet,—a winding-sheet which, as the turnkey said, cost so little. Everything was in readiness. A barrier had been placed between Dantès and his old friend. No longer could Edmond look into those wide-open eyes which had seemed to be penetrating the mysteries of death; no longer could he clasp the hand which had done so much to make his existence blessed. Faria, the beneficent and cheerful companion, with whom he was accustomed to live so intimately, no longer breathed. He seated himself on the edge of that terrible bed, and fell into melancholy and gloomy revery.

Alone—he was alone again—again condemned to silence—again face to face with nothingness! Alone!—never again to see the face, never again to hear the voice of the only human being who united him to earth! Was not Faria's fate the better, after all—to solve the problem of life at its source, even at the risk of horrible suffering? The idea of suicide, which his friend had driven away and kept away by his cheerful presence, now hovered like a phantom over the abbé's dead body.

"If I could die," he said, "I should go where he goes, and should assuredly find him again. But how to die? It is very easy," he went on with a smile; "I will remain here, rush on the first person that opens the door, strangle him, and then they will guillotine me." But excessive grief is like a storm at sea, where the frail bark is tossed from the depths to the top of the wave. Dantès recoiled from the idea of so infamous a death, and passed suddenly from despair to an ardent desire for life and liberty.

"Die? oh, no," he exclaimed—"not die now, after having lived and suffered so long and so much! Die? yes, had I died years ago; but now to die would be, indeed, to give way to the sarcasm of destiny. No, I want to live; I shall struggle to the very last; I will yet win back the happiness of which I have been deprived. Before I die I must not forget that I have my executioners to punish, and perhaps, too, who knows, some friends to reward. Yet they will forget me here, and I shall die in my dungeon like Faria." As he said this, he became silent and gazed straight before him like one overwhelmed with a strange and amazing thought. Suddenly he arose, lifted his hand to his brow as if his brain were giddy, paced twice or thrice round the dungeon, and then paused abruptly by the bed.

"Just God!" he muttered, "whence comes this thought? Is it from thee? Since none but the dead pass freely from this dungeon, let me take the place of the dead!" Without giving himself time to reconsider his decision, and, indeed, that he might not allow his thoughts to be distracted from his desperate resolution, he bent over the appalling shroud, opened it with the knife which Faria had made, drew the corpse from the sack, and bore it along the tunnel to his own chamber, laid it on his couch, tied around its head the rag he wore at night around his own, covered it with his counterpane, once again kissed the ice-cold brow, and tried vainly to close the resisting eyes, which glared horribly, turned the head towards the wall, so that the jailer might, when he brought the evening meal, believe that he was asleep, as was his frequent custom; entered the tunnel again, drew the bed against the wall, returned to the other cell, took from the hiding-place the needle and thread, flung off his rags, that they might feel only naked flesh beneath the coarse canvas, and getting inside the sack, placed himself in the posture in which the dead body had been laid, and sewed up the mouth of the sack from the inside.

He would have been discovered by the beating of his heart, if by any mischance the jailers had entered at that moment. Dantès might have waited until the evening visit was over, but he was afraid that the governor would change his mind, and order the dead body to be removed earlier. In that case his last hope would have been destroyed. Now his plans were fully made, and this is what he intended to do. If while he was being carried out the grave-diggers should discover that they were bearing a live instead of a dead body, Dantès did not intend to give them time to recognize him, but with a sudden cut of the knife, he meant to open the sack from top to bottom, and, profiting by their alarm, escape; if they tried to catch him, he would use his knife to better purpose.

If they took him to the cemetery and laid him in a grave, he would allow himself to be covered with earth, and then, as it was night, the grave-diggers could scarcely have turned their backs before he would have worked his way through the yielding soil and escaped. He hoped that the weight of earth would not be so great that he could not overcome it. If he was detected in this, and the earth proved too heavy, he would be stifled, and then,—so much the better, all would be over. Dantès had not eaten since the preceding evening, but he had not thought of hunger, nor did he think of it now. His situation was too precarious to allow him even time to reflect on any thought but one.

The first risk that Dantès ran was, that the jailer, when he brought him his supper at seven o'clock, might perceive the change that had been made; fortunately, twenty times at least, from misanthropy or fatigue, Dantès had received his jailer in bed, and then the man placed his bread and soup on the table, and went away without saying a word. This time the jailer might not be as silent as usual, but speak to Dantès, and seeing that he received no reply, go to the bed, and thus discover all.

When seven o'clock came, Dantès' agony really began. His hand placed upon his heart was unable to repress its throbbings, while, with the other he wiped the perspiration from his temples. From time to time chills ran through his whole body, and clutched his heart in a grasp of ice. Then he thought he was going to die. Yet the hours passed on without any unusual disturbance, and Dantès knew that he had escaped the first peril. It was a good augury. At length, about the hour the governor had appointed, footsteps were heard on the stairs. Edmond felt that the moment had arrived, summoned up all his courage, held his breath, and would have been happy if at the same time he could have repressed the throbbing of his veins. The footsteps—they were double—paused at the door—and Dantès guessed that the two grave-diggers had come to seek him—this idea was soon converted into certainty, when he heard the noise they made in putting down the hand-bier. The door opened, and a dim light reached Dantès' eyes through the coarse sack that covered him; he saw two shadows approach his bed, a third remaining at the door with a torch in its hand. The two men, approaching the ends of the bed, took the sack by its extremities.

"He's heavy though for an old and thin man," said one, as he raised the head.

"They say every year adds half a pound to the weight of the bones," said another, lifting the feet.

"Have you tied the knot?" inquired the first speaker.

"What would be the use of carrying so much more weight?" was the reply; "I can do that when we get there."

"Yes, you're right," replied the companion.

"What's the knot for?" thought Dantès.

They deposited the supposed corpse on the bier. Edmond

stiffened himself in order to play the part of a dead man, and then the party, lighted by the man with the torch, who went first, ascended the stairs. Suddenly he felt the fresh and sharp night air, and Dantès knew that the mistral was blowing. It was a sensation in which pleasure and pain were strangely mingled. The bearers went on for twenty paces, then stopped, putting the bier down on the ground. One of them went away, and Dantès heard his shoes striking on the pavement.

"Where am I?" he asked himself.

"Really, he is by no means a light load!" said the other bearer, sitting on the edge of the hand-barrow. Dantès' first impulse was to escape, but fortunately he did not attempt it.

"Give us a light," said the other bearer, "or I shall never find what I am looking for." The man with the torch complied, although not asked in the most polite terms.

"What can he be looking for?" thought Edmond. "The spade, perhaps." An exclamation of satisfaction indicated that the grave-digger had found the object of his search. "Here it is at last," he said, "not without some trouble though."

"Yes," was the answer, "but it has lost nothing by waiting."

As he said this, the man came towards Edmond, who heard a heavy metallic substance laid down beside him, and at the same moment a cord was fastened round his feet with sudden and painful violence.

"Well, have you tied the knot?" inquired the grave-digger, who was looking on.

"Yes, and pretty tight too, I can tell you," was the answer.

"Move on, then." And the bier was lifted once more, and they proceeded.

They advanced fifty paces farther, and then stopped to open a door, then went forward again. The noise of the waves dashing against the rocks on which the château is built, reached Dantès' ear distinctly as they went forward.

"Bad weather!" observed one of the bearers; "not a pleasant night for a dip in the sea."

"Why, yes, the abbé runs a chance of being wet," said the other; and then there was a burst of brutal laughter. Dantès did not comprehend the jest, but his hair stood erect on his head.

"Well, here we are at last," said one of them. "A little farther— a little farther," said the other. "You know very well that the last was stopped on his way, dashed on the rocks, and the governor told us next day that we were careless fellows."

They ascended five or six more steps, and then Dantès felt that they took him, one by the head and the other by the heels, and swung him to and fro. "One!" said the gravediggers, "two! three!" And at the same instant Dantès felt himself flung into the air like a wounded bird, falling, falling with a rapidity that made his blood curdle. Although drawn downwards by the heavy weight which hastened his rapid descent, it seemed to him as if the fall lasted for a century. At last, with a horrible splash, he darted like an arrow into the ice-cold water, and as he did so he uttered a shrill cry, stifled in a moment by his immersion beneath the waves.

Dantès had been flung into the sea, and was dragged into its depths by a thirty-six pound shot tied to his feet. The sea is the cemetery of the Château d'If.

XXI

The Island of Tiboulen

D ANTÈS, ALTHOUGH STUNNED AND almost suffocated, had sufficient presence of mind to hold his breath, and as his right
hand (prepared as he was for every chance) held his knife
open, he rapidly ripped up the sack, extricated his arm, and then his
body; but in spite of all his efforts to free himself from the shot, he
felt it dragging him down still lower. He then bent his body, and by
a desperate effort severed the cord that bound his legs, at the
moment when it seemed as if he were actually strangled. With a
mighty leap he rose to the surface of the sea, while the shot dragged
down to the depths the sack that had so nearly become his shroud.

Dantès waited only to get breath, and then dived, in order to
avoid being seen. When he arose a second time, he was fifty paces
from where he had first sunk. He saw overhead a black and tem-
pestuous sky, across which the wind was driving clouds that occasionally suffered a twinkling star to appear; before him was the vast
expanse of waters, sombre and terrible, whose waves foamed and
roared as if before the approach of a storm. Behind him, blacker
than the sea, blacker than the sky, rose phantom-like the vast stone
structure, whose projecting crags seemed like arms extended to
seize their prey, and on the highest rock was a torch lighting two
figures. He fancied that these two forms were looking at the sea;

doubtless these strange grave-diggers had heard his cry. Dantès dived again, and remained a long time beneath the water. This was an easy feat to him, for he usually attracted a crowd of spectators in the bay before the light house at Marseilles when he swam there, and was unanimously declared to be the best swimmer in the port. When he came up again the light had disappeared.

He must now get his bearings. Ratonneau and Pomègue are the nearest islands of all those that surround the Château d'If; but Ratonneau and Pomègue are inhabited, as is also the islet of Daume; Tiboulen and Lemaire were therefore the safest for Dantès' venture. The islands of Tiboulen and Lemaire are a league from the Château d'If; Dantès, nevertheless, determined to make for them. But how could he find his way in the darkness of the night? At this moment he saw the light of Planier, gleaming in front of him like a star. By leaving this light on the right, he kept the Island of Tiboulen a little on the left; by turning to the left, therefore, he would find it. But, as we have said, it was at least a league from the Château d'If to this island. Often in prison Faria had said to him, when he saw him idle and inactive, "Dantès, you must not give way to this listlessness; you will be drowned if you seek to escape, and your strength has not been properly exercised and prepared for exertion." These words rang in Dantès' ears, even beneath the waves; he hastened to cleave his way through them to see if he had not lost his strength. He found with pleasure that his captivity had taken away nothing of his power, and that he was still master of that element on whose bosom he had so often sported as a boy.

Fear, that relentless pursuer, clogged Dantès' efforts. He listened for any sound that might be audible, and every time that he rose to the top of a wave he scanned the horizon, and strove to penetrate the darkness. He fancied that every wave behind him was a pursuing boat, and he redoubled his exertions, increasing rapidly his distance from the château, but exhausting his strength. He swam on still, and already the terrible château had disappeared in the darkness. He could not see it, but he *felt* its presence. An hour passed, during which Dantès, excited by the feeling of freedom, continued to cleave the waves. "Let us see," said he, "I have swum above an hour, but as the wind is against me, that has retarded my speed; however, if I am not mistaken, I must be close to Tiboulen. But what if I were mistaken?" A shudder passed over him. He sought to tread water, in order to rest himself; but the sea was too violent, and he felt that he could not make use of this means of recuperation.

"Well," said he, "I will swim on until I am worn out, or the cramp seizes me, and then I shall sink;" and he struck out with the energy of despair.

Suddenly the sky seemed to him to become still darker and more dense, and heavy clouds seemed to sweep down towards him; at the same time he felt a sharp pain in his knee. He fancied for a moment that he had been shot, and listened for the report; but he heard nothing. Then he put out his hand, and encountered an obstacle and with another stroke knew that he had gained the shore.

Before him rose a grotesque mass of rocks, that resembled nothing so much as a vast fire petrified at the moment of its most fervent combustion. It was the Island of Tiboulen. Dantès rose, advanced a few steps, and, with a fervent prayer of gratitude, stretched himself on the granite, which seemed to him softer than down. Then in spite of the wind and rain he fell into the deep, sweet sleep of utter exhaustion. At the expiration of an hour Edmond was awakened by the roar of thunder. The tempest was let loose and beating the atmosphere with its mighty wings; from time to time a flash of lightning stretched across the heavens like a fiery serpent, lighting up the clouds that rolled on in vast chaotic waves.

Dantès had not been deceived—he had reached the first of the two islands, which was, in fact, Tiboulen. He knew that it was barren and without shelter; but when the sea became more calm, he resolved to plunge into its waves again, and swim to Lemaire, equally arid, but larger, and consequently better adapted for concealment.

An overhanging rock offered him a temporary shelter, and scarcely had he availed himself of it when the tempest burst forth in all its fury. Edmond felt the trembling of the rock beneath which he lay; the waves, dashing themselves against it, wetted him with their spray. He was safely sheltered, and yet he felt dizzy in the midst of the warring of the elements and the dazzling brightness of the lightning. It seemed to him that the island trembled to its base, and that it would, like a vessel at anchor, break moorings, and bear him off into the centre of the storm. He then recollected that he had not eaten or drunk for four-and-twenty hours. He extended his hands, and drank greedily of the rainwater that had lodged in a hollow of the rock.

As he rose, a flash of lightning, that seemed to rive the remotest heights of heaven, illumined the darkness. By its light, between the Island of Lemaire and Cape Croiselle, a quarter of a league distant, Dantès saw a fishing-boat driven rapidly like a spectre before the power of winds and waves. A second after, he saw it again, approaching with frightful rapidly. Dantès cried at the top of his voice to warn them of their danger, but they saw it themselves. Another flash showed him four men clinging to the shattered mast and the rigging, while a fifth clung to the broken rudder.

The men he beheld saw him undoubtedly, for their cries were carried to his ears by the wind. Above the splintered mast a sail rent to tatters was waving; suddenly the ropes that still held it gave way, and it disappeared in the darkness of the night like a vast sea-bird. At the same moment a violent crash was heard, and cries of distress. Dantès from his rocky perch saw the shattered vessel, and among the fragments the floating forms of the hapless sailors. Then all was dark again.

Dantès ran down the rocks at the risk of being himself dashed to pieces; he listened, he groped about, but he heard and saw nothing—the cries had ceased, and the tempest continued to rage. By degrees the wind abated, vast gray clouds rolled towards the west, and the blue firmament appeared studded with bright stars. Soon a red streak became visible in the horizon, the waves whitened, a light played over them, and gilded their foaming crests with gold. It was day.

Dantès stood mute and motionless before this majestic spectacle, as if he now beheld it for the first time; and indeed since his captivity in the Château d'If he had forgotten that such scenes were ever to be witnessed. He turned towards the fortress, and looked at both sea and laud. The gloomy building rose from the bosom of the ocean with imposing majesty and seemed to dominate the scene. It was about five o'clock. The sea continued to get calmer.

"In two or three hours," thought Dantès, "the turnkey will enter my chamber, find the body of my poor friend, recognize it, seek for me in vain, and give the alarm. Then the tunnel will be discovered; the men who cast me into the sea, and who must have heard the cry I uttered, will be questioned. Then boats filled with armed soldiers will pursue the wretched fugitive. The cannon will warn every one to refuse shelter to a man wandering about naked and famished. The police of Marseilles will be on the alert by land, whilst the governor pursues me by sea. I am cold, I am hungry. I have lost even the knife that saved me. O my God, I have suffered enough surely! Have pity on me, and do for me what I am unable to do for myself."

"As Dantès (his eyes turned in the direction of the Château d'If) uttered this prayer, he saw off the farther point of the Island of Pomègue a small vessel with lateen sail skimming the sea like a gull in search of prey; and with his sailor's eye he knew it to be a Genoese tartan. She was coming out of Marseilles harbor, and was standing out to sea rapidly, her sharp prow cleaving through the waves. "Oh," cried Edmond, "to think that in half an hour I could join her, did I not fear being questioned, detected, and conveyed back to Marseilles! What can I do? What story can I invent? Under pretext of trading along the coast, these men, who are in reality smugglers, will prefer selling me to doing a good action. I must wait. But I cannot—I am starving. In a few hours my strength will be utterly exhausted; besides, perhaps I have not been missed at the fortress. I can pass as one of the sailors wrecked last night. My story will be accepted, for there is no one left to contradict me."

As he spoke, Dantès looked toward the spot where the fishing-vessel had been wrecked, and started. The red cap of one of the sailors hung to a point of the rock, and some timbers that had formed part of the vessel's keel, floated at the foot of the crag. It an instant Dantès plan was formed. He swam to the cap, placed it on his head, seized one of the timbers, and struck out so as to cut across the course the vessel was taking.

"I am saved!" murmured he. And this conviction restored his strength.

He soon saw that the vessel, with the wind dead ahead, was tacking between the Château d'If and the tower of Planier. For an instant he feared lest, instead of keeping in shore, she should stand out to sea; but he soon saw that she would pass, like most vessels bound for Italy, between the islands of Jaros and Calaseraigne. However, the vessel and the swimmer insensibly neared one another, and in one of its tacks the tartan bore down within a quarter of a mile of him. He rose on the waves, making signs of distress; but no one on board saw him, and the vessel stood on another tack. Dantès would have shouted, but he knew that the wind would drown his voice.

It was then he rejoiced at his precaution in taking the timber, for without it he would have been unable, perhaps, to reach the vessel—certainly to return to shore, should he be unsuccessful in attracting attention.

Dantès, though almost sure as to what course the vessel would take, had yet watched it anxiously until it tacked and stood towards him. Then he advanced; but before they could meet, the vessel again changed her course. By a violent effort he rose half out of the water, waving his cap, and uttering a loud shout peculiar to sailors. This time he was both seen and heard, and the tartan instantly steered towards him. At the same time, he saw they were about to lower the boat.

An instant after, the boat, rowed by two men, advanced rapidly towards him. Dantès let go of the timber, which he now thought to be useless, and swam vigorously to meet them. But he had reckoned too much upon his strength, and then he realized how serviceable the timber had been to him. His arms became stiff, his legs lost their flexibility, and he was almost breathless.

He shouted again. The two sailors redoubled their efforts, and one of them cried in Italian, "Courage!"

The word reached his ear as a wave which he no longer had the strength to surmount passed over his head. He rose again to the surface, struggled with the last desperate effort of a drowning man, uttered a third cry, and felt himself sinking, as if the fatal cannon shot were again tied to his feet. The water passed over his head, and the sky turned gray. A convulsive movement again brought him to the surface. He felt himself seized by the hair, then he saw and heard nothing. He had fainted.

When he opened his eyes Dantès found himself on the deck of the tartan. His first care was to see what course they were taking. They were rapidly leaving the Château d'If behind. Dantès was so exhausted that the exclamation of joy he uttered was mistaken for a sigh.

As we have said, he was lying on the deck. A sailor was rubbing his limbs with a woollen cloth; another, whom he recognized as the one who had cried out "Courage!" held a gourd full of rum to his mouth; while the third, an old sailor, at once the pilot and captain, looked on with that egotistical pity men feel for a misfortune that they have escaped yesterday, and which may overtake them tomorrow.

A few drops of the rum restored suspended animation, while the friction of his limbs restored their elasticity.

"Who are you?" said the pilot in bad French.—"I am," replied Dantès, in bad Italian, "a Maltese sailor. We were coming from

Syracuse laden with grain. The storm of last night overtook us at Cape Morgion, and we were wrecked on these rocks."

"Where do you come from?"—"From these rocks that I had the good luck to cling to while our captain and the rest of the crew were all lost. I saw your vessel, and fearful of being left to perish on the desolate island, I swam off on a piece of wreckage to try and intercept your course. You have saved my life, and I thank you," continued Dantès. "I was lost when one of your sailors caught hold of my hair."

"It was I," said a sailor of a frank and manly appearance; "and it was time, for you were sinking."

"Yes," returned Dantès, holding out his hand, "I thank you again."

"I almost hesitated, though," replied the sailor; "you looked more like a brigand than an honest man, with your beard six inches, and your hair a foot long." Dantès recollected that his hair and beard had not been cut all the time he was at the Château d'If.

"Yes," said he, "I made a vow to our Lady of the Grotto not to cut my hair or beard for ten years if I were saved in a moment of danger; but to-day the vow expires."—"Now what are we to do with you?" said the captain.

"Alas, anything you please. My captain is dead; I have barely escaped; but I am a good sailor. Leave me at the first port you make; I shall be sure to find employment."

"Do you know the Mediterranean?"—"I have sailed over it since my childhood."

"You know the best harbors?"—"There are few ports that I could not enter or leave with a bandage over my eyes."

"I say, captain," said the sailor who had cried "Courage!" to Dantès, "if what he says is true, what hinders his staying with us?"

"If he says true," said the captain doubtingly. "But in his present condition he will promise anything, and take his chance of keeping it afterwards."

"I will do more than I promise," said Dantès.

"We shall see," returned the other, smiling.

"Where are you going?" asked Dantès.—"To Leghorn."

"Then why, instead of tacking so frequently, do you not sail nearer the wind?"—"Because we should run straight on to the Island of Rion."

"You shall pass it by twenty fathoms."—"Take the helm, and let us see what you know." The young man took the helm, felt to see if the vessel answered the rudder promptly, and seeing that, without being a first-rate sailer, she yet was tolerably obedient,—

"To the sheets," said he. The four seamen, who composed the crew, obeyed, while the pilot looked on. "Haul taut."—They obeyed.

"Belay." This order was also executed; and the vessel passed, as Dantès had predicted, twenty fathoms to windward.

"Bravo!" said the captain.—"Bravo!" repeated the sailors. And they all looked with astonishment at this man, whose eye now disclosed an intelligence and his body a vigor they had not thought him capable of showing.

"You see," said Dantès, quitting the helm, "I shall be of some use to you, at least during the voyage. If you do not want me at Leghorn, you can leave me there, and I will pay you out of the first wages I get, for my food and the clothes you lend me."

"Ah," said the captain, "we can agree very well, if you are reasonable."—"Give me what you give the others, and it will be all right," returned Dantès.

"That's not fair," said the seaman who had saved Dantès; "for you know more than we do."

"What is that to you, Jacopo?" returned the captain. "Every one is free to ask what he pleases."—"That's true," replied Jacopo; "I only make a remark."

"Well, you would do much better to lend him a jacket and a pair of trousers, if you have them."

"No," said Jacopo; "but I have a shirt and a pair of trousers."

"That is all I want," interrupted Dantès. Jacopo dived into the hold and soon returned with what Edmond wanted.

"Now, then, do you wish for anything else?" said the patron.

"A piece of bread and another glass of the capital rum I tasted, for I have not eaten or drunk for a long time." He had not tasted food for forty hours. A piece of bread was brought, and Jacopo offered him the gourd.

"Larboard your helm," cried the captain to the steersman. Dantès glanced that way as he lifted the gourd to his mouth; then paused with hand in mid-air.

"Hollo! what's the matter at the Château d'If?" said the captain.

A small white cloud, which had attracted Dantès' attention, crowned the summit of the bastion of the Château d'If. At the same moment the faint report of a gun was heard. The sailors looked at one another.

"What is this?" asked the captain.

"A prisoner has escaped from the Château d'If, and they are firing the alarm gun," replied Dantès. The captain glanced at him, but he had lifted the run to his lips, and was drinking it with so much composure, that suspicions, if the captain had any, died away.

"At any rate," murmured he, "if it be, so much the better, for I have made a rare acquisition." Under pretence of being fatigued, Dantès asked to take the helm; the steersman, glad to be relieved, looked at the captain, and the latter by a sign indicated that he might abandon it to his new comrade. Dantès could thus keep his eyes on Marseilles.

"What is the day of the month?" asked he of Jacopo, who sat down beside him.—"The 28th of February."

"In what year?"—"In what year—you ask me in what year?"

"Yes," replied the young man, "I ask you in what year!"—"You have forgotten then?"

"I got such a fright last night," replied Dantès, smiling, "that I have almost lost my memory. I ask you what year is it?"

"The year 1829," returned Jacopo. It was fourteen years day for day since Dantès' arrest. He was nineteen when he entered the Château d'If; he was thirty-three when he escaped. A sorrowful smile passed over his face; he asked himself what had become of Mercédès, who must believe him dead. Then his eyes lighted up with hatred as he thought of the three men who had caused him so long and wretched a captivity. He renewed against Danglers, Fernand, and Villefort the oath of implacable vengeance he had made in his dungeon. This oath was no longer a vain menace; for the fastest sailer in the Mediterranean would have been unable to overtake the little tartan, that with every stitch of canvas set was flying before the wind to Leghorn.

XXII

The Smugglers

D ANTÈS HAD NOT BEEN a day on board before he had a very clear idea of the men with whom his lot had been cast. Without having been in the school of the Abbé Faria, the worthy master of *The Young Amelia* (the name of the Genoese tartan) knew a smattering of all the tongues spoken on the shores of that large lake called the Mediterranean, from the Arabic to the Provençal; and this, while it spared him interpreters, persons always troublesome and frequently indiscreet, gave him great facilities of communication, either with the vessels he met at sea, with the small boats sailing along the coast, or with the people without name, country, or occupation, who are always seen on the quays of seaports, and who live by hidden and mysterious means which we must suppose to be a direct gift of providence, as they have no visible means of support. It is fair to assume that Dantès was on board a smuggler.

At first the captain had received Dantès on board with a certain degree of distrust. He was very well known to the customs officers of the coast; and as there was between these worthies and himself a perpetual battle of wits, he had at first thought that Dantès might be an emissary of these illustrious guardians of rights and duties, who perhaps employed this ingenious means of learning some of the secrets of his trade. But the skillful manner in which Dantès had handled the lugger had entirely reassured him; and then, when he saw the light plume of smoke floating above the bastion of the Château d'If, and heard the distant report, he was instantly struck with the idea that he had on board his vessel one whose coming and going, like that of kings, was accompanied with salutes of artillery. This made him less uneasy, it must be owned, than if the new-comer had proved to be a customs officer; but this supposition also disappeared like the first, when he beheld the perfect tranquillity of his recruit.

Edmond thus had the advantage of knowing what the owner was, without the owner knowing who he was; and however the old sailor and his crew tried to "pump" him, they extracted nothing more from him; he gave accurate descriptions of Naples and Malta, which he knew as well as Marseilles, and held stoutly to his first story. Thus the Genoese, subtle as he was, was duped by Edmond, in whose favor his mild demeanor, his nautical skill, and his admirable dissimulation, pleaded. Moreover, it is possible that the Genoese was one of those shrewd persons who know nothing but what they should know, and believe nothing but what they should believe.

In this state of mutual understanding, they reached Leghorn. Here Edmond was to undergo another trial; he was to find out whether he could recognize himself, as he had not seen his own face for fourteen years. He had preserved a tolerably good remembrance of what the youth had been, and was now to find out what the man had become. His comrades believed that his vow was fulfilled. As he had twenty times touched at Leghorn, he remembered a barber in St. Ferdinand Street; he went there to have his beard and hair cut. The barber gazed in amazement at this man with the long, thick and black hair and beard, which gave his head the appearance of one of Titian's portraits. At this period it was not the fashion to wear so large a beard and hair so long; now a barber would only be surprised if a man gifted with such advantages should consent voluntarily to deprive himself of them. The Leghorn barber said nothing and went to work.

When the operation was concluded, and Edmond felt that his chin was completely smooth, and his hair reduced to its usual length, he asked for a hand-glass. He was now, as we have said, three-and-thirty years of age, and his fourteen years' imprisonment had produced a great transformation in his appearance. Dantès had entered the Château d'If with the round, open, smiling face of a young and happy man, with whom the early paths of life have been smooth, and who anticipates a future corresponding with his past. This was now all changed. The oval face was lengthened, his smiling mouth had assumed the firm and marked lines which betoken resolution; his eyebrows were arched beneath a brow furrowed with thought; his eyes were full of melancholy, and from their depths occasionally sparkled gloomy fires of misanthropy and hatred; his complexion, so long kept from the sun, had now that pale color which produces, when the features are encircled with black hair, the aristocratic beauty of the man of the north; the profound learning he had acquired had besides diffused over his features a refined intellectual expression; and he had also acquired, being naturally of a goodly stature, that vigor which a frame possesses which has so long concentrated all its force within itself.

To the elegance of a nervous and slight form had succeeded the solidity of a rounded and muscular figure. As to his voice, prayers, sobs, and imprecations had changed it so that at times it was of a singularly penetrating sweetness, and at others rough and almost hoarse. Moreover, from being so long in twilight or darkness, his eyes had acquired the faculty of distinguishing objects in the night, common to the hyena and the wolf. Edmond smiled when he beheld himself: it was impossible that his best friend—if, indeed, he had any friend left—could recognize him; he could not recognize himself.

The master of *The Young Amelia*, who was very desirous of retaining amongst his crew a man of Edmond's value, had offered to advance him funds out of his future profits, which Edmond had accepted. His next care on leaving the barber's who had achieved his first metamorphosis was to enter a shop and buy a complete sailor's suit—a garb, as we all know, very simple, and consisting of white trousers, a striped shirt, and a cap. It was in this costume, and bringing back to Jacopo the shirt and trousers he had lent him, that Edmond reappeared before the captain of the lugger, who had made him tell his story over and over again before he could believe him, or recognize in the neat and trim sailor the man with thick and matted beard, hair tangled with seaweed, and body soaking in seabrine, whom he had picked up naked and nearly drowned. Attracted by his prepossessing appearance, he renewed his offers of an engagement to Dantès; but Dantès, who had his own projects, would not agree for a longer time than three months.

The Young Amelia had a very active crew, very obedient to their captain, who lost as little time as possible. He had scarcely been a week at Leghorn before the hold of his vessel was filled with printed muslins, contraband cottons, English powder, and tobacco on which the excise had forgotten to put its mark. The master was to get all this out of Leghorn free of duties, and land it on the shores of Corsica, where certain speculators undertook to forward the cargo to France. They sailed; Edmond was again cleaving the azure sea which had been the first horizon of his youth, and which he had so often dreamed of in prison. He left Gorgone on his right and La Pianosa on his left, and went towards the country of Paoli and Napoleon. The next morning going on deck, as he always did at an early hour, the patron found Dantès leaning against the bulwarks gazing with intense earnestness at a pile of granite rocks, which the rising sun tinged with rosy light. It was the Island of Monte Cristo. *The Young Amelia* left it three-quarters of a league to the larboard, and kept on for Corsica.

Dantès thought, as they passed so closely to the island whose name was so interesting to him, that he had only to leap into the sea and in half an hour be at the promised land. But then what could he do without instruments to discover his treasure, without arms to defend himself? Besides, what would the sailors say? What would the patron think? He must wait.

Fortunately, Dantès had learned how to wait; he had waited fourteen years for his liberty, and now he was free he could wait at least six months or a year for wealth. Would he not have accepted liberty without riches if it had been offered to him? Besides, were not those riches chimerical?—offspring of the brain of the poor Abbé Faria, had they not died with him? It is true, the letter of the Cardinal Spada was singularly circumstantial, and Dantès repeated it to himself, from one end to the other, for he had not forgotten a word.

Evening came, and Edmond saw the island tinged with the shades of twilight, and then disappear in the darkness from all eyes but his own; for he, with vision accustomed to the gloom of a prison, continued to behold it last of all, for he remained alone upon deck. The next morn broke off the coast of Aleria; all day they coasted, and in the evening saw fires lighted on land; the position of these was no doubt a signal for landing, for a ship's lantern was hung up at the mast-head instead of the steamer, and they came to within a gunshot of the shore. Dantès noticed that the captain of *The Young Amelia* had, as he neared the land, mounted two small culverins, which, without making much noise, can throw a four ounce ball a thousand paces or so.

But on this occasion the precaution was superfluous, and everything proceeded with the utmost smoothness and politeness. Four shallops came off with very little noise alongside the lugger, which, no doubt, in acknowledgment of the compliment, lowered her own shallop into the sea, and the five boats worked so well that by two o'clock in the morning all the cargo was out of *The Young Amelia* and on *terra firma*. The same night, such a man of regularity was the patron of *The Young Amelia*, the profits were divided, and each man had a hundred Tuscan livres, or about eighty frances. But the voyage was not ended. They turned the bowsprit towards Sardinia, where they intended to take in a cargo, which was to replace what had been discharged. The second operation was as successful as the first, *The Young Amelia* was in luck. This new cargo was destined for the coast of the Duchy of Lucca, and consisted almost entirely of Havana cigars, sherry, and Malaga wines.

There they had a bit of a skirmish in getting rid of the duties; the excise was, in truth, the everlasting enemy of the patron of *The Young Amelia*. A customs officer was laid low, and two sailors wounded; Dantès was one of the latter, a ball having touched him in the left shoulder. Dantès was almost glad of this affray, and almost pleased at being wounded, for they were rude lessons which taught him with what eye he could view danger, and with what endurance he could bear suffering. He had contemplated danger with a smile, and when wounded had exclaimed with the great philosopher, "Pain, thou art not an evil." He had, moreover, looked upon the customs officer wounded to death, and, whether from heat of blood produced by the encounter, or the chill of human sentiment, this sight had made but slight impression upon him. Dantès was on the way he desired to follow, and was moving towards the end he wished to achieve; his heart was in a fair way of petrifying in his bosom. Jacopo, seeing him fall, had believed him killed, and rushing towards him raised him up, and then attended to him with all the kindness of a devoted comrade.

This world was not then so good as Doctor Pangloss believed it, neither was it so wicked as Dantès thought it, since this man, who had nothing to expect from his comrade but the inheritance of his share of the prize-money, manifested so much sorrow when he saw him fall. Fortunately, as we have said, Edmond was only wounded, and with certain herbs gathered at certain seasons, and sold to the smugglers by the old Sardinian women, the wound soon closed. Edmond then resolved to try Jacopo, and offered him in return for his attention a share of his prize-money, but Jacopo refused it indignantly.

As a result of the sympathetic devotion which Jacopo had from the first bestowed on Edmond, the latter was moved to a certain degree of affection. But this sufficed for Jacopo, who instinctively felt that Edmond had a right to superiority of position—a superiority which Edmond had concealed from all others. And from this time the kindness which Edmond showed him was enough for the brave seaman.

Then in the long days on board ship, when the vessel, gliding on with security over the azure sea, required no care but the hand of the helmsman, thanks to the favorable winds that swelled her sails, Edmond, with a chart in his hand, became the instructor of Jacopo, as the poor Abbé Faria had been his tutor. He pointed out to him the bearings of the coast, explained to him the variations of the compass, and taught him to read in that vast book opened over our heads which they call heaven, and where God writes in azure with letters of diamonds. And when Jacopo inquired of him, "What is the use of teaching all these things to a poor sailor like me?" Edmond replied, "Who knows? You may one day be the captain of a vessel. Your fellow-countryman, Bonaparte, became emperor." We had forgotten to say that Jacopo was a Corsican.

Two months and a half elapsed in these trips, and Edmond had become as skilful a coaster as he had been a hardy seaman; he had formed an acquaintance with all the smugglers on the coast, and learned all the Masonic signs by which these half pirates recognize each other. He had passed and re-passed his Island of Monte Cristo twenty times, but not once had he found an opportunity of landing there. He then formed a resolution. As soon as his engagement with the patron of *The Young Amelia* ended, he would hire a small vessel on his own account—for in his several voyages he had amassed a hundred piastres—and under some pretext land at the Island of Monte Cristo. Then he would be free to make his researches, not perhaps entirely at liberty, for he would be doubtless watched by those who accompanied him. But in this world we must risk something. Prison had made Edmond prudent, and he was desirous of running no risk whatever. But in vain did he rack his imagination; fertile as it was, he could not devise any plan for reaching the island without companionship.

Dantès was tossed about on these doubts and wishes, when the patron, who had great confidence in him, and was very desirous of retaining him in his service, took him by the arm one evening and led him to a tavern on the Via del' Oglio, where the leading smugglers of Leghorn used to congregate and discuss affairs connected with their trade. Already Dantès had visited this maritime Bourse two or three times, and seeing all these hardy free-traders, who supplied the whole coast for nearly two hundred leagues in extent, he had asked himself what power might not that man attain who should give the impulse of his will to all these contrary and diverging minds. This time it was a great matter that was under discussion, connected with a vessel laden with Turkey carpets, stuffs of the Levant, and cashmeres. It was necessary to find some neutral ground on which an exchange could be made, and then to try and land these goods on the coast of France. If the venture was successful the profit would be enormous, there would be a gain of fifty or sixty piastres each for the crew.

The patron of *The Young Amelia* proposed as a place of landing the Island of Monte Cristo, which being completely deserted, and having neither soldiers nor revenue officers, seemed to have been placed in the midst of the ocean since the time of the heathen Olympus by Mercury, the god of merchants and robbers, classes of mankind which we in modern times have separated if not made distinct, but which antiquity appears to have included in the same category. At the mention of Monte Cristo Dantès started with joy; he rose to conceal his emotion, and took a turn around the smoky tavern, where all the languages of the known world were jumbled in a *lingua franca*. When he again joined the two persons who had been discussing the matter, it had been decided that they should touch at Monte Cristo, and set out on the following night. Edmond, being consulted, was of opinion that the island afforded every possible security, and that great enterprises to be well done should be done quickly. Nothing then was altered in the plan, and orders were given to get under weigh next night, and, wind and weather permitting, to make the neutral island by the following day.

XXIII

The Island of Monte Cristo

THUS, AT LENGTH, BY one of the unexpected strokes of fortune which sometimes befall those who have for a long time been the victims of an evil destiny, Dantès was about to secure the opportunity he wished for, by simple and natural means, and land on the island without incurring any suspicion. One night more and he would be on his way.

The night was one of feverish distraction, and in its progress visions good and evil passed through Dantès' mind. If he closed his eyes, he saw Cardinal Spada's letter written on the wall in characters of flame—if he slept for a moment the wildest dreams haunted his brain. He ascended into grottos paved with emeralds, with panels of rubies, and the roof glowing with diamond stalactites. Pearls fell drop by drop, as subterranean waters filter in their caves. Edmond, amazed, wonderstruck, filled his pockets with the radiant gems and then returned to daylight, when he discovered that his prizes had all changed into common pebbles. He then endeavored to re-enter the marvellous grottos, but they had suddenly receded, and now the path became a labyrinth, and then the entrance vanished, and in vain did he tax his memory for the magic and mysterious word which opened the splendid caverns of Ali Baba to the Arabian fisherman. All was useless, the treasure disappeared, and had again reverted to the genii from whom for a moment he had hoped to carry it off. The day came at length, and was almost as feverish as the night had been, but it brought reason to the aid of imagination, and Dantès was then enabled to arrange a plan which had hitherto been vague and unsettled in his brain. Night came, and with it the preparation for departure, and these preparations served to conceal Dantès' agitation. He had by degrees assumed such authority over his companions that he was almost like a commander on board; and as his orders were always clear, distinct, and easy of execution, his comrades obeyed him with celerity and pleasure.

The old patron did not interfere, for he too had recognized the superiority of Dantès over the crew and himself. He saw in the young man his natural successor, and regretted that he had not a daughter, that he might have bound Edmond to him by a more secure alliance. At seven o'clock in the evening all was ready, and at ten minutes past seven they doubled the lighthouse just as the beacon was kindled. The sea was calm, and, with a fresh breeze from the south-east, they sailed beneath a bright blue sky, in which God also lighted up in turn his beacon lights, each of which is a world. Dantès told them that all hands might turn in, and he would take the helm. When the Maltese (for so they called Dantès) had said this, it was sufficient, and all went to their bunks contentedly. This frequently happened. Dantès, cast from solitude into the world, frequently experienced an imperious desire for solitude; and what solitude is more complete, or more poetical, than that of a ship floating in isolation on the sea during the obscurity of the night, in the silence of immensity, and under the eye of heaven?

Now this solitude was peopled with his thoughts, the night lighted up by his illusions, and the silence animated by his anticipations. When the patron awoke, the vessel was hurrying on with every sail set, and every sail full with the breeze. They were making nearly ten knots an hour. The Island of Monte Cristo loomed large in the horizon. Edmond resigned the lugger to the master's care, and went and lay down in his hammock; but, in spite of a sleepless night, he could not close his eyes for a moment. Two hours afterwards he came on deck, as the boat was about to double the Island of Elba. They were just abreast of Mareciana, and beyond the flat but verdant Island of La Pianosa. The peak of Monte Cristo, reddened by the burning sun, was seen against the azure sky. Dantès ordered the helmsman to put down his helm, in order to leave La Pianosa to starboard, as he knew that he should shorten his course by two or three knots. About five o'clock in the evening the island was distinct, and everything on it was plainly perceptible, owing to that clearness of the atmosphere peculiar to the light which the rays of the sun cast at its setting.

Edmond gazed very earnestly at the mass of rocks which gave out all the variety of twilight colors, from the brightest pink to the deepest blue; and from time to time his cheeks flushed, his brow darkened, and a mist passed over his eyes. Never did gamester, whose whole fortune is staked on one cast of the die, experience the anguish which Edmond felt in his paroxysms of hope. Night came, and at ten o'clock they anchored. *The Young Amelia* was first at the rendezvous. In spite of his usual command over himself, Dantès could not restrain his impetuosity. He was the first to jump on shore; and had he dared, he would, like Lucius Brutus, have "kissed his mother earth." It was dark, but at eleven o'clock the moon rose in the midst of the ocean, whose every wave she silvered, and then, "ascending high," played in floods of pale light on the rocky hills of this second Pelion.

The island was familiar to the crew of *The Young Amelia*,—it was one of her regular haunts. As to Dantès, he had passed it on his voyage too and from the Levant, but never touched at it. He questioned Jacopo. "Where shall we pass the night?" he inquired.

"Why, on board the tartan," replied the sailor.

"Should we not do better in the grottos?"—"What grottos?"

"Why, the grottos—caves of the island."

"I do not know of any grottos," replied Jacopo. The cold sweat sprang forth on Dantès' brow.—"What, are there no grottos at Monte Cristo?" he asked.—"None."

For a moment Dantès was speechless; then he remembered that these caves might have been filled up by some accident, or even stopped up, for the sake of greater security, by Cardinal Spada. The point was, then, to discover the hidden entrance. It was useless to search at night, and Dantès therefore delayed all investigation until the morning. Besides, a signal made half a league out at sea, and to which *The Young Amelia* replied by a similar signal, indicated that the moment for business had come. The boat that now arrived, assured by the answering signal that all was well, soon came in sight, white and silent as a phantom, and cast anchor within a cable's length of shore.

Then the landing began. Dantès reflected, as he worked, on the shout of joy which, with a single word, he could evoke from all these men, if he gave utterance to the one unchanging thought that pervaded his heart; but, far from disclosing this precious secret, he almost feared that he had already said too much, and by his restlessness and continual questions, his minute observations and evident pre-occupation, aroused suspicions. Fortunately, as regarded this circumstance at least, his painful past gave to his countenance an indelible sadness, and the glimmerings of gayety seen beneath this cloud were indeed but transitory.

No one had the slightest suspicion; and when next day, taking a fowling-piece, powder, and shot, Dantès declared his intention to go and kill some of the wild goats that were seen springing from rock to rock, his wish was construed into a love of sport, or a desire for solitude. However, Jacopo insisted on following him, and Dantès did not oppose this, fearing if he did so that he might incur distrust. Scarcely, however, had they gone a quarter of a league when, having killed a kid, he begged Jacopo to take it to his comrades, and request them to cook it, and when ready to let him know by firing a gun. This and some dried fruits and a flask of Monte Pulciano, was the bill of fare. Dantès went on, looking from time to time behind and around about him. Having reached the summit of a rock, he saw, a thousand feet beneath him, his companions, whom Jacopo had rejoined, and who were all busy preparing the repast which Edmond's skill as a marksman had augmented with a capital dish.

Edmond looked at them for a moment with the sad and gentle smile of a man superior to his fellows. "In two hours' time," said he, "these persons will depart richer by fifty piastres each, to go and risk their lives again by endeavoring to gain fifty more; then they will return with a fortune of six hundred francs, and waste this treasure in some city with the pride of sultans and the insolence of nabobs. At this moment hope makes me despise their riches, which seem to me contemptible. Yet perchance to-morrow deception will so act on me, that I shall, on compulsion, consider such a contemptible possession as the utmost happiness. Oh, no!" exclaimed Edmond, "that will not be. The wise, unerring Faria could not be mistaken in this one thing. Besides, it were better to die than to continue to lead this low and wretched life." Thus Dantès, who but three months before had no desire but liberty, had now not liberty enough, and panted for wealth. The cause was not in Dantès, but in providence, who, while limiting the power of man, has filled him with boundless desires.

Meanwhile, by a cleft between two walls of rock, following a path worn by a torrent, and which, in all human probability, human foot had never before trod, Dantès approached the spot where he supposed the grottos must have existed. Keeping along the shore, and examining the smallest object with serious attention, he thought he could trace, on certain rocks, marks made by the hand of man.

Time, which encrusts all physical substances with its mossy mantle, as it invests all things of the mind with forgetfulness, seemed to have respected these signs, which apparently had been made with some degree of regularity, and probably with a definite purpose.

Occasionally the marks were hidden under tufts of myrtle, which spread into large bushes laden with blossoms, or beneath parasitical lichen. So Edmond had to separate the branches or brush away the moss to know where the guide-marks were. The sight of marks renewed Edmond's fondest hopes. Might it not have been the cardinal himself who had first traced them, in order that they might serve as a guide for his nephew in the event of a catastrophe, which he could not foresee would have been so complete. This solitary place was precisely suited to the requirements of a man desirous of burying treasure. Only, might not these betraying marks have attracted other eyes than those for whom they were made? and had the dark and wondrous island indeed faithfully guarded its precious secret?

It seemed, however, to Edmond, who was hidden from his comrades by the inequalities of the ground, that at sixty paces from the harbor the marks ceased; nor did they terminate at any grotto. A large round rock, placed solidly on its base, was the only spot to which they seemed to lead. Edmond concluded that perhaps instead of having reached the end of the route he had only explored its beginning, and he therefore turned round and retraced his steps.

Meanwhile his comrades had prepared the repast, had got some water from a spring, spread out the fruit and bread, and cooked the kid. Just at the moment when they were taking the dainty animal from the spit, they saw Edmond springing with the boldness of a chamois from rock to rock, and they fired the signal agreed upon. The sportsman instantly changed his direction, and ran quickly towards them. But even while they watched his daring progress, Edmond's foot slipped, and they saw him stagger on the edge of a rock and disappear. They all rushed towards him, for all loved Edmond in spite of his superiority; yet Jacopo reached him first.

He found Edmond lying prone, bleeding, and almost senseless. He had rolled down a declivity of twelve or fifteen feet. They poured a little rum down his throat, and this remedy, which had before been so beneficial to him, produced the same effect as formerly. Edmond opened his eyes, complained of great pain in his knee, a feeling of heaviness in his head, and severe pains in his loins. They wished to carry him to the shore; but when they touched him, although under Jacopo's directions, he declared, with heavy groans, that he could not bear to be moved.

It may be supposed that Dantès did not now think of his dinner, but he insisted that his comrades, who had not his reasons for fasting, should have their meal. As for himself, he declared that he had only need of a little rest, and that when they returned he should be easier. The sailors did not require much urging. They were hungry, and the smell of the roasted kid was very savory, and your tars are not very ceremonious. An hour afterwards they returned. All that Edmond had been able to do was to drag himself about a dozen paces forward to lean against a moss-grown rock.

But, instead of growing easier, Dantès' pains appeared to increase in violence. The old patron, who was obliged to sail in the morning in order to land his cargo on the frontiers of Piedmont and France, between Nice and Fréjus, urged Dantès to try and rise. Edmond made great exertions in order to comply; but at each effort he fell back, moaning and turning pale.

"He has broken his ribs," said the commander, in a low voice. "No matter; he is an excellent fellow, and we must not leave him. We will try and carry him on board the tartan." Dantès declared, however, that he would rather die where he was than undergo the agony which the slightest movement cost him. "Well," said the patron, "let what may happen, it shall never be said that we deserted a good comrade like you. We will not go till evening." This very much astonished the sailors, although not one opposed it. The patron was so strict that this was the first time they had ever seen him give up an enterprise, or even delay in its execution. Dantès would not allow that any such infraction of regular and proper rules should be made in his favor. "No, no," he said to the patron, "I was awkward, and it is just that I pay the penalty of my clumsiness.

Leave me a small supply of biscuit, a gun, powder, and balls, to kill the kids or defend myself at need, and a pickaxe, that I may build a shelter if you delay in coming back for me."

"But you'll die of hunger," said the patron.—"I would rather do so," was Edmond's reply, "than suffer the inexpressible agonies which the slightest movement causes me." The patron turned towards his vessel, which was rolling on the swell in the little harbor, and, with sails partly set, would be ready for sea when her toilet should be completed.

"What are we to do, Maltese?" asked the captain. "We cannot leave you here so, and yet we cannot stay."—"Go, go!" exclaimed Dantès.

"We shall be absent at least a week," said the patron, "and then we must run out of our course to come here and take you up again."

"Why," said Dantès, "if in two or three days you hail any fishing-boat, desire them to come here to me. I will pay twenty-five piastres for my passage back to Leghorn. If you do not come across one, return for me." The patron shook his head.

"Listen, Captain Baldi; there's one way of settling this," said Jacopo. "Do you go, and I will stay and take care of the wounded man."

"And give up your share of the venture," said Edmond, "to remain with me?"—"Yes," said Jacopo, "and without any hesitation."

"You are a good fellow and a kind-hearted messmate," replied Edmond, "and heaven will recompense you for your generous intentions; but I do not wish any one to stay with me. A day or two of rest will set me up, and I hope I shall find among the rocks certain herbs most excellent for bruises."

A peculiar smile passed over Dantès' lips; he squeezed Jacopo's hand warmly, but nothing could shake his determination to remain—and remain alone. The smugglers left with Edmond what he had requested and set sail, but not without turning about several times, and each time making signs of a cordial farewell, to which Edmond replied with his hand only, as if he could not move the rest of his body. Then, when they had disappeared, he said with a smile,—"'Tis strange that it should be among such men that we find proofs of friendship and devotion." Then he dragged himself cautiously to the top of a rock, from which he had a full view of the sea, and thence he saw the tartan complete her preparations for sailing, weigh anchor, and, balancing herself as gracefully as a water-fowl ere it takes to the wing, set sail. At the end of an hour she was completely out of sight; at least, it was impossible for the wounded man to see her any longer from the spot where he was. Then Dantès rose more agile and light than the kid among the myrtles and shrubs of these wild rocks, took his gun in one hand, his pickaxe in the other, and hastened towards the rock on which the marks he had noted terminated. "And now," he exclaimed, remembering the tale of the Arabian fisherman, which Faria had related to him, "now, open sesame!"

XXIV

The Secret Cave

THE SUN HAD NEARLY reached the meridian, and his scorching rays fell full on the rocks, which seemed themselves sensible of the heat. Thousands of grasshoppers, hidden in the bushes, chirped with a monotonous and dull note; the leaves of the myrtle and olive trees waved and rustled in the wind. At every step that Edmond took he disturbed the lizards glittering with the hues of the emerald; afar off he saw the wild goats bounding from crag to crag. In a word, the island was inhabited, yet Edmond felt himself alone, guided by the hand of God. He felt an indescribable sensation somewhat akin to dread—that dread of the daylight which even in the desert makes us fear we are watched and observed. This feeling was so strong, that at the moment when Edmond was about to begin his labor, he stopped, laid down his pickaxe, seized his gun, mounted to the summit of the highest rock, and from thence gazed round in every direction.

But it was not upon Corsica, the very houses of which he could distinguish; or on Sardinia; or on the Island of Elba, with its historical associations; or upon the almost imperceptible line that to the experienced eye of a sailor alone revealed the coast of Genoa the proud, and Leghorn the commercial, that he gazed. It was at the brigantine that had left in the morning, and the tartan that had just set sail, that Edmond fixed his eyes. The first was just disappearing in the straits of Bonifacio; the other, following an opposite direction, was about to round the Island of Corsica. This sight reassured him. He then looked at the objects near him. He saw that he was on the highest point of the island,—a statue on this vast pedestal of granite, nothing human appearing in sight, while the blue ocean beat against the base of the island, and covered it with a fringe of foam. Then he descended with cautious and slow step, for he dreaded lest an accident similar to that he had so adroitly feigned should happen in reality.

Dantès, as we have said, had traced the marks along the rocks, and he had noticed that they led to a small creek, which was hidden like the bath of some ancient nymph. This creek was sufficiently wide at its mouth, and deep in the centre, to admit of the entrance of a small vessel of the lugger class, which would be perfectly concealed from observation.

Then following the clew that, in the hands of the Abbé Faria, had been so skilfully used to guide him through the Dædalian labyrinth of probabilities, he thought that the Cardinal Spada, anxious not to be watched, had entered the creek, concealed his little barque, followed the line marked by the notches in the rock, and at the end of it had buried his treasure. It was this idea that had brought Dantès back to the circular rock. One thing only perplexed Edmond, and destroyed his theory. How could this rock, which weighed several tons, have been lifted to this spot, without the aid of many men? Suddenly an idea flashed across his mind. Instead of raising it, thought he, they have lowered it. And he sprang from the rock in order to inspect the base on which it had formerly stood. He soon perceived that a slope had been formed, and the rock had slid along this until it stopped at the spot it now occupied. A large stone had served as a wedge; flints and pebbles had been inserted around it, so as to conceal the orifice; this species of masonry had been covered with earth, and grass and weeds had grown there, moss had clung to the stones, myrtle-bushes had taken root, and the old rock seemed fixed to the earth.

Dantès dug away the earth carefully, and detected, or fancied he detected, the ingenious artifice. He attacked this wall, cemented by the hand of time, with his pickaxe. After ten minutes' labor the wall gave way, and a hole large enough to insert the arm was opened. Dantès went and cut the strongest olive-tree he could find, stripped off its branches, inserted it in the hole, and used it as a lever. But the rock was too heavy, and too firmly wedged, to be moved by any one man, were he Hercules himself. Dantès saw that he must attack the wedge. But how? He cast his eyes around, and saw the horn full of powder which his friend Jacopo had left him. He smiled; the infernal invention would serve him for this purpose. With the aid of his pickaxe, Dantès after the manner of a labor-saving pioneer, dug a mine between the upper rock and the one that supported it, filled it with powder, then made a match by rolling his handkerchief in saltpetre. He lighted it and retired. The explosion soon followed; the upper rock was lifted from its base by the terrific force of the powder; the lower one flew into pieces; thousands of insects escaped from the aperture Dantès had previously formed, and a huge snake, like the guardian demon of the treasure, rolled himself along in darkening coils, and disappeared.

Dantès approached the upper rock, which now, without any support, leaned towards the sea. The intrepid treasure-seeker walked round it, and, selecting the spot from whence it appeared most susceptible to attack, placed his lever in one of the crevices, and strained every nerve to move the mass. The rock, already shaken by the explosion, tottered on its base. Dantès redoubled his efforts; he seemed like one of the ancient Titans, who uprooted the mountains to hurl against the father of the gods. The rock yielded, rolled over, bounded from point to point, and finally disappeared in the ocean.

On the spot it had occupied was a circular space, exposing an iron ring let into a square flag-stone. Dantès uttered a cry of joy and surprise; never had a first attempt been crowned with more perfect success. He would fain have continued, but his knees trembled, and his heart beat so violently, and his sight became so dim, that he was forced to pause. This feeling lasted but for a moment. Edmond inserted his lever in the ring and exerted all his strength; the flagstone yielded, and disclosed steps that descended until they were lost in the obscurity of a subterraneous grotto. Any one else would have rushed on with a cry of joy. Dantès turned pale, hesitated, and reflected. "Come," said he to himself, "be a man. I am accustomed to adversity. I must not be cast down by the discovery that I have been deceived. What, then, would be the use of all I have suffered? The heart breaks when, after having been elated by flattering hopes, it sees all its illusions destroyed. Faria has dreamed this; the Cardinal Spada buried no treasure here; perhaps he never came here, or if he did, Cæsar Borgia, the intrepid adventurer, the stealthy and indefatigable plunderer, has followed him, discovered his traces, pursued them as I have done, raised the stone, and descending before me, has left me nothing." He remained motionless and pensive, his eyes fixed on the gloomy aperture that was open at his feet.

"Now that I expect nothing, now that I no longer entertain the slightest hopes, the end of this adventure becomes simply a matter of curiosity." And he remained again motionless and thoughtful.

"Yes, yes; this is an adventure worthy a place in the varied career of that royal bandit. This fabulous event formed but a link in a long chain of marvels. Yes, Borgia has been here, a torch in one hand, a sword in the other, and within twenty paces, at the foot of this rock, perhaps two guards kept watch on land and sea, while their master descended, as I am about to descend, dispelling the darkness before his awe-inspiring progress."

"But what was the fate of the guards who thus possessed his secret?" asked Dantès of himself.

"The fate," replied he, smiling, "of those who buried Alaric."

"Yet, had he come," thought Dantès, "he would have found the treasure, and Borgia, he who compared Italy to an artichoke, which he could devour leaf by leaf, knew too well the value of time to waste it in replacing this rock. I will go down."

Then he descended, a smile on his lips, and murmuring that last word of human philosophy, "Perhaps!" But instead of the darkness, and the thick and mephitic atmosphere he had expected to find, Dantès saw a dim and bluish light, which, as well as the air, entered, not merely by the aperture he had just formed, but by the interstices and crevices of the rock which were visible from without, and through which he could distinguish the blue sky and the waving branches of the evergreen oaks, and the tendrils of the creepers that grew from the rocks. After having stood a few minutes in the cavern, the atmosphere of which was rather warm than damp, Dantès' eye, habituated as it was to darkness, could pierce even to the remotest angles of the cavern, which was of granite that sparkled like diamonds. "Alas," said Edmond, smiling, "these are the treasures the cardinal has left; and the good abbé, seeing in a dream these glittering walls, has indulged in fallacious hopes."

But he called to mind the words of the will, which he knew by heart. "In the farthest angle of the second opening," said the cardinal's will. He had only found the first grotto; he had now to seek the second. Dantès continued his search. He reflected that this second grotto must penetrate deeper into the island; he examined the stones, and sounded one part of the wall where he fancied the opening existed, masked for precaution's sake. The pickaxe struck for a moment with a dull sound that drew out on Dantès' forehead large drops of perspiration. At last it seemed to him that one part of the wall gave forth a more hollow and deeper echo; he eagerly advanced, and with the quickness of perception that no one but a prisoner possesses, saw that there, in all probability, the opening must be.

However, he, like Cæsar Borgia, knew the value of time; and, in order to avoid fruitless toil, he sounded all the other walls with his pickaxe, struck the earth with the butt of his gun, and finding nothing that appeared suspicious, returned to that part of the wall whence issued the consoling sound he had before heard. He again struck it, and with greater force. Then a singular thing occurred. As he struck the wall, pieces of stucco similar to that used in the ground work of arabesques broke off, and fell to the ground in flakes, exposing a large white stone. The aperture of the rock had been closed with stones, then this stucco had been applied, and painted to imitate granite. Dantès struck with the sharp end of his pickaxe, which entered some way between the interstices. It was there he must dig. But by some strange play of emotion, in proportion as the proofs that Faria had not been deceived became stronger, so did his heart give way, and a feeling of discouragement stole over him. This last proof, instead of giving him fresh strength, deprived him of it; the pickaxe descended, or rather fell; he placed it on the ground, passed his hand over his brow, and remounted the stairs, alleging to himself, as an excuse, a desire to be assured that no one was watching him, but in reality because he felt that he was about to faint. The island was deserted, and the sun seemed to cover it with its fiery glance; afar off a few small fishing-boats studded the bosom of the blue ocean.

Dantès had tasted nothing, but he thought not of hunger at such a moment; he hastily swallowed a few drops of rum, and again entered the cavern. The pickaxe that had seemed so heavy, was now like a feather in his grasp; he seized it, and attacked the wall. After several blows he perceived that the stones were not cemented, but had been merely placed one upon the other, and covered with stucco; he inserted the point of his pickaxe, and using the handle as a lever, with joy soon saw the stone turn as if on hinges, and fall at his feet. He had nothing more to do now, but with the iron tooth of the pickaxe to draw the stones towards him one by one. The aperture was already sufficiently large for him to enter, but by waiting, he could still cling to hope, and retard the certainty of deception. At last, after renewed hesitation, Dantès entered the second grotto. The second grotto was lower and more gloomy than the first; the air that could only enter by the newly formed opening had the mephitic smell Dantès was surprised not to find in the outer cavern. He waited in order to allow pure air to displace the foul atmosphere, and then went on. At the left of the opening was a dark and deep angle. But to Dantès' eye there was no darkness. He glanced around this second grotto; it was, like the first, empty.

The treasure, if it existed, was buried in this corner. The time had at length arrived; two feet of earth removed, and Dantès' fate would be decided. He advanced towards the angle, and summoning all his resolution, attacked the ground with the pickaxe. At the fifth or sixth blow the pickaxe struck against an iron substance. Never did funeral knell, never did alarm-bell, produce a greater effect on the hearer. Had Dantès found nothing he could not have become more ghastly pale. He again struck his pickaxe into the earth, and encountered the same resistance, but not the same sound. "It is a casket of wood bound with iron," thought he. At this moment a shadow passed rapidly before the opening; Dantès seized his gun, sprang through the opening, and mounted the stair. A wild goat had passed before the mouth of the cave, and was feeding at a little distance. This would have been a favorable occasion to secure his dinner; but Dantès feared lest the report of his gun should attract attention.

He thought a moment, cut a branch of a resinous tree, lighted it at the fire at which the smugglers had prepared their breakfast, and descended with this torch. He wished to see everything. He approached the hole he had dug, and now, with the aid of the torch, saw that his pickaxe had in reality struck against iron and wood. He planted his torch in the ground and resumed his labor. In an instant a space three feet long by two feet broad was cleared, and Dantès could see an oaken coffer, bound with cut steel; in the middle of the lid he saw engraved on a silver plate, which was still untarnished, the arms of the Spada family—viz., a sword, *pale*, on an oval shield, like all the Italian armorial bearings, and surmounted by a cardinal's hat; Dantès easily recognized them, Faria had so often drawn them for him. There was no longer any doubt: the treasure was there—no one would have been at such pains to conceal an empty casket. In an instant he had cleared every obstacle away, and he saw successively the lock, placed between two padlocks, and the two handles at each end, all carved as things were carved at that epoch, when art rendered the commonest metals precious. Dantès seized the handles, and strove to lift the coffer; it was impossible. He sought to open it; lock and padlock were fastened; these faithful guardians seemed unwilling to surrender their trust. Dantès inserted the sharp end of the pickaxe between the coffer and the lid, and pressing with all his force on the handle, burst open the fastenings. The hinges yielded in their turn and fell, still holding in their grasp fragments of the wood, and the chest was open.

Edmond was seized with vertigo; he cocked his gun and laid it beside him. He then closed his eyes as children do in order that they may see in the resplendent night of their own imagination more stars than are visible in the firmament; then he re-opened them, and stood motionless with amazement. Three compartments divided the coffer. In the first, blazed piles of golden coin; in the second, were ranged bars of unpolished gold, which possessed nothing attractive save their value; in the third, Edmond grasped handfuls of diamonds, pearls, and rubies, which, as they fell on one another, sounded like hail against glass. After having touched, felt, examined these treasures, Edmond rushed through the caverns like a man seized with frenzy; he leaped on a rock, from whence he could behold the sea. He was alone—alone with these countless, these unheard-of treasures! Was he awake, or was it but a dream?

He would fain have gazed upon his gold, and yet he had not strength enough; for an instant he leaned his head in his hands as if to prevent his senses from leaving him, and then rushed madly about the rocks of Monte Cristo, terrifying the wild goats and scaring the sea-fowls with his wild cries and gestures; then he returned, and, still unable to believe the evidence of his senses, rushed into the grotto, and found himself before this mine of gold and jewels. This time he fell on his knees, and, clasping his hands convulsively, uttered a prayer intelligible to God alone. He soon became calmer and more happy, for only now did he begin to realize his felicity. He then set himself to work to count his fortune. There were a thousand ingots of gold, each weighing from two to three pounds; then he piled up twenty-five thousand crowns, each worth about eighty francs of our money, and bearing the effigies of Alexander VI. and his predecessors; and he saw that the compartment was not half empty. And he measured ten double handfuls of pearls, diamonds, and other gems, many of which, mounted by the most famous workmen, were valuable beyond their intrinsic worth. Dantès saw the light gradually disappear, and fearing to be surprised in the cavern, left it, his gun in his hand. A piece of biscuit and a small quantity of rum formed his supper, and he snatched a few hours' sleep, lying over the mouth of the cave.

It was a night of joy and terror, such as this man of stupendous emotions had already experienced twice or thrice in his lifetime.

XXV

The Unknown

DAY, FOR WHICH DANTÈS had so eagerly and impatiently
waited with open eyes, again dawned. With the first light
Dantès resumed his search. Again he climbed the rocky
height he had ascended the previous evening, and strained his view
to catch every peculiarity of the landscape; but it wore the same
wild, barren aspect when seen by the rays of the morning sun
which it had done when surveyed by the fading glimmer of eve.
Descending into the grotto, he lifted the stone, filled his pockets
with gems, put the box together as well and securely as he could,
sprinkled fresh sand over the spot from which it had been taken,
and then carefully trod down the earth to give it everywhere a uniform appearance; then, quitting the grotto, he replaced the stone,
heaping on it broken masses of rocks and rough fragments of crum-
bling granite, filling the interstices with earth, into which he deftly
inserted rapidly growing plants, such as the wild myrtle and flow-
ering thorn; then carefully watering these new plantations, he
scrupulously effaced every trace of footsteps, leaving the approach
to the cavern as savage-looking and untrodden as he had found it.
This done, he impatiently awaited the return of his companions. To
wait at Monte Cristo for the purpose of watching like a dragon
over the almost incalculable riches that had thus fallen into his

possession satisfied not the cravings of his heart, which yearned to
return to dwell among mankind, and to assume the rank, power,
and influence which are always accorded to wealth—that first and
greatest of all the forces within the grasp of man.

On the sixth day the smugglers returned. From a distance Dantès recognized the rig and handling of *The Young Amelia*, and dragging himself with affected difficulty towards the landing-place, he
met his companions with an assurance that, although considerably
better than when they quitted him, he still suffered acutely from his
late accident. He then inquired how they had fared in their trip. To
this question the smugglers replied that, although successful in
landing their cargo in safety, they had searcely done so when they
received intelligence that a guard-ship had just quitted the port of
Toulon, and was crowding all sail towards them; this obliged them
to make all the speed they could to evade the enemy, when they
could but lament the absence of Dantès, whose superior skill in the
management of a vessel would have availed them so materially. In
fact, the pursuing vessel had almost overtaken them when, fortunately, night came on, and enabled them to double the Cape of
Corsica, and so elude all further pursuit. Upon the whole, however,
the trip had been sufficiently successful to satisfy all concerned;
while the crew, and particularly Jacopo, expressed great regrets that
Dantès had not been an equal sharer with themselves in the profits, which amounted to no less a sum than fifty piastres each.

Edmond preserved the most admirable self-command, not suffering the faintest indication of a smile to escape him at the enumeration of all the benefits he would have reaped had he been able to quit
the island; but as *The Young Amelia* had merely come to Monte Cristo
to fetch him away, he embarked that same evening, and proceeded
with the captain to Leghorn. Arrived at Leghorn, he repaired to the
house of a Jew, a dealer in precious stones, to whom he disposed of
four of his smallest diamonds for five thousand frances each. Dantès
half feared that such valuable jewels in the hands of a poor sailor like

himself might excite suspicion; but the cunning purchaser asked no troublesome questions concerning a bargain by which he gained a round profit of at least eighty per cent.

The following day Dantès presented Jacopo with an entirely new vessel, accompanying the gift by a donation of one hundred piastres, that he might provide himself with a suitable crew and other requisites for his outfit, upon condition that he would go at once to Marseilles for the purpose of inquiring after an old man named Louis Dantès, residing in the Allées de Meillan, and also a young woman called Mercédès, an inhabitant of the Catalan village. Jacopo could scarcely believe his senses at receiving this munificent present, which Dantès hastened to account for by saying that he had merely been a sailor from whim and a desire to spite his family, who did not allow him as much money as he liked to spend; but that on his arrival at Leghorn he had come into possession of a large fortune, left him by an uncle, whose sole heir he was. The superior education of Dantès gave an air of such extreme probability to this statement that it never once occurred to Jacopo to doubt its accuracy. The term for which Edmond had engaged to serve on board *The Young Amelia* having expired, Dantès took leave of the captain, who at first tried all his powers of persuasion to induce him to remain as one of the crew, but having been told the history of the legacy, he ceased to importune him further. The following morning Jacopo set sail for Marseilles, with directions from Dantès to join him at the Island of Monte Cristo.

Having seen Jacopo fairly out of the harbor, Dantès proceeded to make his final adieus on board *The Young Amelia*, distributing so liberal a gratuity among her crew as to secure for him the good wishes of all, and expressions of cordial interest in all that concerned him. To the captain he promised to write when he had made up his mind as to his future plans. Then Dantès departed for Genoa. At the moment of his arrival a small yacht was under trial in the bay; this yacht had been built by order of an Englishman, who, having heard that the Genoese excelled all other builders along the shores of the Mediterranean in the construction of fast-sailing vessels, was desirous of possessing a specimen of their skill; the price agreed upon between the Englishman and the Genoese builder was forty thousand francs. Dantès, struck with the beauty and capability of the little vessel, applied to its owner to transfer it to him, offering sixty thousand francs, upon condition that he should be allowed to take immediate possession. The proposal was too advantageous to be refused, the more so as the person for whom the yacht was intended had gone upon a tour through Switzerland, and was not expected back in less than three weeks or a month, by which time the builder reckoned upon being able to complete another. A bargain was therefore struck. Dantès led the owner of the yacht to the dwelling of a Jew; retired with the latter for a few minutes to a small back parlor, and upon their return the Jew counted out to the shipbuilder the sum of sixty thousand frances in bright gold pieces.

The delighted builder then offered his services in providing a suitable crew for the little vessel, but this Dantès declined with many thanks, saying he was accustomed to cruise about quite alone, and his principal pleasure consisted in managing his yacht himself; the only thing the builder could oblige him in would be to con-trive a sort of secret closet in the cabin at his bed's head, the closet to contain three divisions, so constructed as to be concealed from all but himself. The builder cheerfully undertook the commission, and promised to have these secret places completed by the next day, Dantès furnishing the dimensions and plan in accordance with which they were to be constructed.

The following day Dantès sailed with his yacht from Genoa, under the inspection of an immense crowd, drawn together by curiosity to see the rich Spanish nobleman who preferred manag-ing his own yacht. But their wonder was soon changed to admira-tion at seeing the perfect skill with which Dantès handled the helm. The boat, indeed, seemed to be animated with almost human intelligence, so promptly did it obey the slightest touch; and Dantès required but a short trial of his beautiful craft to acknowledge that the Genoese had not without reason attained their high reputation in the art of shipbuilding. The spectators followed the little vessel with their eyes as long as it remained visible; they then turned their conjectures upon her probable destination. Some insisted she was making for Corsica, others the Island of Elba; bets were offered to any amount that she was bound for Spain; while Africa was positively reported by many persons as her intended course; but no one thought of Monte Cristo. Yet thither it was that Dantès guided his vessel, and at Monte Cristo he arrived at the close of the second day; his boat had proved herself a first-class sailer, and had come the distance from Genoa in thirty-five hours. Dantès had carefully noted the general appearance of the shore, and, instead of landing at the usual place, he dropped anchor in the little creek. The island was utterly deserted, and bore no evidence of having been visited since he went away; his treasure was just as he had left it. Early on the following morning he commenced the removal of his riches, and ere nightfall the whole of his immense wealth was safely deposited in the compartments of the secret locker.

A week passed by. Dantès employed it in manœuvring his yacht round the island, studying it as a skilful horseman would the animal he destined for some important service, till at the end of that time he was perfectly conversant with its good and bad qualities. The former Dantès proposed to augment, the latter to remedy.

Upon the eighth day he discerned a small vessel under full sail approaching Monte Cristo. As it drew near, he recognized it as the boat he had given to Jacopo. He immediately signalled it. His signal was returned, and in two hours afterwards the newcomer lay at anchor beside the yacht. A mournful answer awaited each of Edmond's eager inquiries as to the information Jacopo had obtained. Old Dantès was dead, and Mercédès had disappeared.

Dantès listened to these melancholy tidings with outward calmness; but, leaping lightly ashore, he signified his desire to be quite alone. In a couple of hours he returned. Two of the men from Jacopo's boat came on board the yacht to assist in navigating it, and he gave orders that she should be steered direct to Marseilles. For his father's death he was in some manner prepared; but he knew not how to account for the mysterious disappearance of Mercédès.

Without divulging his secret, Dantès could not give sufficiently clear instructions to an agent. There were, besides, other particulars he was desirous of ascertaining, and those were of a nature he alone could investigate in a manner satisfactory to himself. His looking-glass had assured him, during his stay at Leghorn, that he ran no risk of recognition; moreover, he had now the means of adopting any disguise he thought proper. One fine morning, then, his yacht, followed by the little fishing-boat, boldly entered the port of Marseilles, and anchored exactly opposite the spot from whence, on the never-to-be-forgotten night of his departure for the Château d'If, he had been put on board the boat destined to convey him thither. Still Dantès could not view without a shudder the approach of a gendarme who accompanied the officers deputed to demand his bill of health ere the yacht was permitted to hold communication with the shore; but with that perfect self-possession he had acquired during his acquaintance with Faria, Dantès coolly presented an English passport he had obtained from Leghorn, and as this gave him a standing which a French passport would not have afforded, he was informed that there existed no obstacle to his immediate debarkation.

The first person to attract the attention of Dantès, as he landed on the Canebière, was one of the crew belonging to the *Pharaon*. Edmond welcomed the meeting with this fellow—who had been one of his own sailors—as a sure means of testing the extent of the change which time had worked in his own appearance. Going straight towards him, he propounded a variety of questions on different subjects, carefully watching the man's countenance as he did so; but not a word or look implied that he had the slightest idea of ever having seen before the person with whom he was then conversing. Giving the sailor a piece of money in return for his civility, Dantès proceeded onwards; but ere he had gone many steps he heard the man loudly calling him to stop. Dantès instantly turned to meet him. "I beg your pardon, sir," said the honest fellow, in almost breathless haste, "but I believe you made a mistake; you intended to give me a two-franc piece, and see, you gave me a double Napoleon."—"Thank you, my good friend. I see that I have made a trifling mistake, as you say; but by way of rewarding your honesty I give you another double Napoleon, that you may drink to my health, and be able to ask your messmates to join you."

So extreme was the surprise of the sailor, that he was unable even to thank Edmond, whose receding figure he continued to gaze after in speechless astonishment. "Some nabob from India," was his comment.

Dantès, meanwhile, went on his way. Each step he trod oppressed his heart with fresh emotion; his first and most indelible recollections were there; not a tree, not a street, that he passed but seemed filled with dear and cherished memories. And thus he proceeded onwards till he arrived at the end of the Rue de Noailles, from whence a full view of the Allées de Meillan was obtained. At this spot, so pregnant with fond and filial remembrances, his heart beat almost to bursting, his knees tottered under him, a mist floated over his sight, and had he not clung for support to one of the trees, he would inevitably have fallen to the ground and been crushed beneath the many vehicles continually passing there. Recovering himself, however, he wiped the perspiration from his brows, and stopped not again till he found himself at the door of the house in which his father had lived.

The nasturtiums and other plants, which his father had delighted to train before his window, had all disappeared from the upper part of the house. Leaning against the tree, he gazed thoughtfully for a time

at the upper stories of the shabby little house. Then he advanced to
the door, and asked whether there were any rooms to be let. Though
answered in the negative, he begged so earnestly to be permitted to
visit those on the fifth floor, that, in despite of the oft-repeated assurance of the *concièrge* that they were occupied, Dantès succeeded in
inducing the man to go up to the tenants, and ask permission for a
gentleman to be allowed to look at them. The tenants of the humble
lodging were a young couple who had been scarcely married a week;
and seeing them, Dantès sighed heavily. Nothing in the two small
chambers forming the apartments remained as it had been in the time
of the elder Dantès; the very paper was different, while the articles of
antiquated furniture with which the rooms had been filled in
Edmond's time had all disappeared; the four walls alone remained as
he had left them. The bed belonging to the present occupants was
placed as the former owner of the chamber had been accustomed to
have his; and, in spite of his efforts to prevent it, the eyes of Edmond
were suffused in tears as he reflected that on that spot the old man had
breathed his last, vainly calling for his son. The young couple gazed
with astonishment at the sight of their visitor's emotion, and won-
dered to see the large tears silently chasing each other down his otherwise stern and immovable features; but they felt the sacredness of his
grief, and kindly refrained from questioning him as to its cause, while,
with instinctive delicacy, they left him to indulge his sorrow alone.
When he withdrew from the scene of his painful recollections, they
both accompanied him downstairs, reiterating their hope that he
would come again whenever he pleased, and assuring him that their
poor dwelling would ever be open to him. As Edmond passed the
door on the fourth floor, he paused to inquire whether Caderousse
the tailor still dwelt there; but he received for reply, that the person in
question had got into difficulties, and at the present time kept a small
inn on the route from Bellegarde to Beaucaire.

Having obtained the address of the person to whom the house in
the Allèes de Meillan belonged, Dantès next proceeded thither, and,

under the name of Lord Wilmore (the name and title inscribed on his passport), purchased the small dwelling for the sum of twenty-five thousand francs, at least ten thousand more than it was worth; but had its owner asked half a million, it would unhesitatingly have been given. The very same day the occupants of the apartments on the fifth floor of the house, now become the property of Dantès, were duly informed by the notary who had arranged the necessary transfer of deeds, etc., that the new landlord gave them their choice of any of the rooms in the house, without the least augmentation of rent, upon condition of their giving instant possession of the two small chambers they at present inhabited.

This strange event aroused great wonder and curiosity in the neighborhood of the Allées de Meillan, and a multitude of theories were afloat, none of which was anywhere near the truth. But what raised public astonishment to a climax, and set all conjecture at defiance, was the knowledge that the same stranger who had in the morning visited the Allèes de Meillan had been seen in the evening walking in the little village of the Catalans, and afterwards observed to enter a poor fisherman's hut, and to pass more than an hour in inquiring after persons who had either been dead or gone away for more than fifteen or sixteen years. But on the following day the family from whom all these particulars had been asked received a handsome present, consisting of an entirely new fishing-boat, with two seines and a tender. The delighted recipients of these munificent gifts would gladly have poured out their thanks to their generous benefactor; but they had seen him, upon quitting the hut, merely give some orders to a sailor, and then, springing lightly on horseback, leave Marseilles by the Porte d'Aix.

XXVI

The Pont du Gard Inn

S UCH OF MY READERS as have made a pedestrian excursion to the south of France may perchance have noticed, about midway between the town of Beaucaire and the village of Bellegarde,—a little nearer to the former than to the latter,—a small roadside inn, from the front of which hung, creaking and flapping in the wind, a sheet of tin covered with a grotesque representation of the Pont du Gard. This modern place of entertainment stood on the left-hand side of the post road, and backed upon the Rhone. It also boasted of what in Languedoc is styled a garden, consisting of a small plot of ground, on the side opposite to the main entrance reserved for the reception of guests. A few dingy olives and stunted fig-trees struggled hard for existence, but their withered dusty foliage abundantly proved how unequal was the conflict. Between these sickly shrubs grew a scanty supply of garlic, tomatoes, and eschalots; while, lone and solitary, like a forgotten sentinel, a tall pine raised its melancholy head in one of the corners of this unattractive spot, and displayed its flexible stem and fanshaped summit dried and cracked by the fierce heat of the subtropical sun.

In the surrounding plain, which more resembled a dusty lake than solid ground, were scattered a few miserable stalks of wheat,

the effect, no doubt, of a curious desire on the part of the agricul-
turists of the country to see whether such a thing as the raising of
grain in those parched regions was practicable. Each stalk served as
a perch for a grasshopper, which regaled the passers by through this
Egyptian scene with its strident, monotonous note.

For about seven or eight years the little tavern had been kept by
a man and his wife, with two servants,—a chambermaid named
Trinette, and a hostler called Pecaud. This small staff was quite equal
to all the requirements, for a canal between Beaucaire and Aiguemortes had revolutionized transportation by substituting boats for
the cart and the stagecoach. And, as though to add to the daily
misery which this prosperous canal inflicted on the unfortunate
innkeeper, whose utter ruin it was fast accomplishing, it was situated between the Rhone from which it had its source and the post-
road it had depleted, not a hundred steps from the inn, of which we
have given a brief but faithful description.

The innkeeper himself was a man of from forty to fifty-five years
of age, tall, strong, and bony, a perfect specimen of the natives of those
southern latitudes; he had dark, sparkling, and deep-set eyes, hooked
nose, and teeth white as those of a carnivorous animal; his hair, like his
beard, which he wore under his chin, was thick and curly, and in spite
of his age but slightly interspersed with a few silvery threads. His naturally dark complexion had assumed a still further shade of brown
from the habit the unfortunate man had acquired of stationing himself from morning till eve at the threshold of his door, on the lookout
for guests who seldom came, yet there he stood, day after day, exposed
to the meridional rays of a burning sun, with no other protection for
his head than a red handkerchief twisted around it, after the manner
of the Spanish muleteers. This man was our old acquaintance, Gaspard
Caderousse. His wife, on the contrary, whose maiden name had been
Madeleine Radelle, was pale, meagre, and sickly-looking. Born in the
neighborhood of Arles, she had shared in the beauty for which its
women are proverbial; but that beauty had gradually withered beneath

the devastating influence of the slow fever so prevalent among dwellers by the ponds of Aiguemortes and the marshes of Camargue. She remained nearly always in her second-floor chamber, shivering in her chair, or stretched languid and feeble on her bed, while her husband kept his daily watch at the door—a duty he performed with so much the greater willingness, as it saved him the necessity of listening to the endless plaints and murmurs of his helpmate, who never saw him without breaking out into bitter invectives against fate; to all of which her husband would calmly return an unvarying reply, in these philosophic words:—

"Hush, La Carconte. It is God's pleasure that things should be so."

The sobriquet of La Carconte had been bestowed on Madeleine Radelle from the fact that she had been born in a village so called, situated between Salon and Lambèse; and as a custom existed among the inhabitants of that part of France where Caderousse lived of styling every person by some particular and distinctive appellation, her husband had bestowed on her the name of La Carconte in place of her sweet and euphonious name of Madeleine, which, in all probability, his rude guttural language would not have enabled him to pronounce. Still, let it not be supposed that amid this affected resignation to the will of Providence, the unfortunate innkeeper did not writhe under the double misery of seeing the hateful canal carry off his customers and his profits, and the daily infliction of his peevish partner's murmurs and lamentations.

Like other dwellers in the south, he was a man of sober habits and moderate desires, but fond of external show, vain, and addicted to display. During the days of his prosperity, not a festivity took place without himself and wife being among the spectators. He dressed in the picturesque costume worn upon grand occasions by the inhabitants of the south of France, bearing equal resemblance to the style adopted both by the Catalans and Andalusians; while La Carconte displayed the charming fashion prevalent among the women of Arles, a mode of attire borrowed equally from Greece and Arabia. But, by degrees, watch-chains, necklaces, parti-colored scarfs, embroidered bodies, velvet vests, elegantly worked stockings, striped gaiters, and silver buckles for the shoes, all disappeared; and Gaspard Caderousse, unable to appear abroad in his pristine splendor, had given up any further participation in these pomps and vanities, both for himself and wife, although a bitter feeling of envious discontent filled his mind as the sound of mirth and merry music from the joyous revellers reached even the miserable hostelry to which he still clung, more for the shelter than the profit it afforded.

Caderousse, then, was, as usual, at his place of observation before the door, his eyes glancing listlessly from a piece of closely shaven grass—on which some fowls were industriously, though fruitlessly, endeavoring to turn up some grain or insect suited to their palate—to the deserted road, which led away to the north and south, when he was aroused by the shrill voice of his wife, and grumbling to himself as he went, he mounted to her chamber, first taking care, however, to set the entrance door wide open, as an invitation to any chance traveller who might be passing.

At the moment Caderousse quitted his sentry-like watch before the door, the road on which he so eagerly strained his sight was void and lonely as a desert at mid-day. There it lay stretching out into one interminable line of dust and sand, with its sides bordered by tall, meagre trees, altogether presenting so uninviting an appearance, that no one in his senses could have imagined that any traveller, at liberty to regulate his hours for journeying, would choose to expose himself in such a formidable Sahara. Nevertheless, had Caderousse but retained his post a few minutes longer, he might have caught a dim outline of something approaching from the direction of Bellegarde; as the moving object drew nearer, he would easily have perceived that it consisted of a man and horse, between whom the kindest and most amiable understanding appeared to exist. The horse was of Hungarian breed, and ambled along at an easy pace. His rider was a priest, dressed in black, and wearing a three-cornered hat; and, spite of the ardent rays of a noonday sun, the pair came on with a fair degree of rapidity.

Having arrived before the Pont du Gard, the horse stopped, but whether for his own pleasure or that of his rider would have been difficult to say. However that might have been, the priest, dismounting, led his steed by the bridle in search of some place to which he could secure him. Availing himself of a handle that projected from a half-fallen door, he tied the animal safely, and having drawn a red cotton handkerchief from his pocket, wiped away the perspiration that streamed from his brow, then, advancing to the door, struck thrice with the end of his iron-shod stick. At this unusual sound, a huge black dog came rushing to meet the daring assailant of his ordinarily tranquil abode, snarling and displaying his sharp white teeth with a determined hostility that abundantly proved how little he was accustomed to society. At that moment a heavy footstep was heard descending the wooden staircase that led from the upper floor, and, with many bows and courteous smiles, mine host of the Pont du Gard besought his guest to enter.

"You are welcome, sir, most welcome!" repeated the astonished Caderousse. "Now, then, Margotin," cried he, speaking to the dog, "will you be quiet? Pray don't heed him, sir!—he only barks, he never bites. I make no doubt a glass of good wine would be acceptable this dreadfully hot day." Then perceiving for the first time the garb of the traveller he had to entertain, Caderousse hastily exclaimed: "A thousand pardons! I really did not observe whom I had the honor to receive under my poor roof. What would the abbé please to have? What refreshment can I offer? All I have is at his service."

The priest gazed on the person addressing him with a long and searching gaze—there even seemed a disposition on his part to court a similar scrutiny on the part of the innkeeper; then, observing in the countenance of the latter no other expression than extreme surprise at his own want of attention to an inquiry so courteously worded, he deemed it as well to terminate this dumb show, and therefore said, speaking with a strong Italian accent, "You are, I presume, M. Caderousse?"—"Yes, sir," answered the host, even more surprised at the question than he had been by the silence which had preceded it; "I am Gaspard Caderousse, at your service."

"Gaspard Caderousse," rejoined the priest. "Yes,—Christian and surname are the same. You formerly lived, I believe, in the Allées de Meillan, on the fourth floor?"—"I did."

"And you followed the business of a tailor?"—"True, I was a tailor, till the trade fell off. It is so hot at Marseilles, that really I believe that the respectable inhabitants will in time go without any clothing whatever. But talking of heat, is there nothing I can offer you by way of refreshment?"

"Yes; let me have a bottle of your best wine, and then, with your permission, we will resume our conversation from where we left off."

"As you please, sir," said Caderousse, who, anxious not to lose the present opportunity of finding a customer for one of the few bottles of Cahors still remaining in his possession, hastily raised a trap-door in the floor of the apartment they were in, which served both as parlor and kitchen. Upon issuing forth from his subterranean retreat at the expiration of five minutes, he found the abbé seated upon a wooden stool, leaning his elbow on a table, while Margotin, whose animosity seemed appeased by the unusual command of the traveller for refreshments, had crept up to him, and had established himself very comfortably between his knees, his long, skinny neck resting on his lap, while his dim eye was fixed earnestly on the traveller's face.

"Are you quite alone?" inquired the guest, as Caderousse placed before him the bottle of wine and a glass.—"Quite, quite alone," replied the man—"or, at least, practically so; for my poor wife, who is the only person in the house besides myself, is laid up with illness, and unable to render me the least assistance, poor thing!"

"You are married, then?" said the priest, with a show of interest, glancing round as he spoke at the scanty furnishings of the apartment.

"Ah, sir," said Caderousse with a sigh, "it is easy to perceive I am not a rich man; but in this world a man does not thrive the better for being honest." The abbé fixed on him a searching, penetrating glance.

"Yes, honest—I can certainly say that much for myself," continued the innkeeper, fairly sustaining the scrutiny of the abbé gaze; "I can boast with truth of being an honest man; and," continued he significantly, with a hand on his breast and shaking his head, "that is more than every one can say nowadays."—"So much the better for you, if what you assert be true," said the abbé; "for I am firmly persuaded that, sooner or later, the good will be rewarded, and the wicked punished."

"Such words as those belong to your profession," answered Caderousse, "and you do well to repeat them; but," added he, with a bitter expression of countenance, "one is free to believe them or not, as one pleases."

"You are wrong to speak thus," said the abbé; "and perhaps I may, in my own person, be able to prove to you how completely you are in error."

"What mean you?" inquired Caderousse with a look of surprise.

"In the first place, I must be satisfied that you are the person I am in search of."

"What proofs do you require?"—"Did you, in the year 1814 or 1815, know anything of a young sailor named Dantès?"

"Dantès? Did I know poor dear Edmond? Why, Edmond Dantès and myself were intimate friends!" exclaimed Caderousse, whose countenance flushed darkly as he caught the penetrating gaze of the abbé fixed on him, while the clear, calm eye of the questioner seemed to dilate with feverish scrutiny.

"You remind me," said the priest, "that the young man concerning whom I asked you was said to bear the name of Edmond."

"Said to bear the name!" repeated Caderousse, becoming excited and eager. "Why, he was so called as truly as I myself bore the appellation of Gaspard Caderousse; but tell me, I pray, what has become of poor Edmond? Did you know him? Is he alive and at liberty? Is he prosperous and happy?"

"He died a more wretched, hopeless, heart-broken prisoner than the felons who pay the penalty of their crimes at the galleys of Toulon."

A deadly pallor followed the flush on the countenance of Caderousse, who turned away, and the priest saw him wiping the tears from his eyes with the corner of the red handkerchief twisted round his head.

"Poor fellow, poor fellow!" murmured Caderousse. "Well, there, sir, is another proof that good people are never rewarded on this earth, and that none but the wicked prosper. Ah," continued Caderousse, speaking in the highly colored language of the south, "the world grows worse and worse. Why does not God, if he really hates the wicked, as he is said to do, send down brimstone and fire, and consume them altogether?"

"You speak as though you had loved this young Dantès," observed the abbé, without taking any notice of his companion's vehemence.—"And so I did," replied Caderousse; "though once, I confess, I envied him his good fortune. But I swear to you, sir, I swear to you, by everything a man holds dear, I have, since then, deeply and sincerely lamented his unhappy fate." There was a brief silence, during which the fixed, searching eye of the abbé was employed in scrutinizing the agitated features of the innkeeper.

"You knew the poor lad, then?" continued Caderousse.

"I was called to see him on his dying bed, that I might administer to him the consolations of religion."

"And of what did he die?" asked Caderousse in a choking voice.

"Of what, think you, do young and strong men die in prison, when they have scarcely numbered their thirtieth year, unless it be of imprisonment?" Caderousse wiped away the large beads of perspiration that gathered on his brow.

"But the strangest part of the story is," resumed the abbé, "that

Dantès, even in his dying moments, swore by his crucified Redeemer, that he was utterly ignorant of the cause of his detention."

"And so he was," murmured Caderousse. "How should he have been otherwise? Ah, sir, the poor fellow told you the truth."

"And for that reason, he besought me to try and clear up a mystery he had never been able to penetrate, and to clear his memory should any foul spot or stain have fallen on it."

And here the look of the abbé, becoming more and more fixed, seemed to rest with ill-concealed satisfaction on the gloomy depression which was rapidly spreading over the countenance of Caderousse.

"A rich Englishman," continued the abbé, "who had been his companion in misfortune, but had been released from prison during the second restoration, was possessed of a diamond of immense value; this jewel he bestowed on Dantès upon himself quitting the prison, as a mark of his gratitude for the kindness and brotherly care with which Dantès had nursed him in a severe illness he underwent during his confinement. Instead of employing this diamond in attempting to bribe his jailers, who might only have taken it and then betrayed him to the governor, Dantès carefully preserved it, that in the event of his getting out of prison he might have wherewithal to live, for the sale of such a diamond would have quite sufficed to make his fortune."

"Then, I suppose," asked Caderousse, with eager, glowing looks, "that it was a stone of immense value?"—"Why, everything is relative," answered the abbé. "To one in Edmond's position the diamond certainly was of great value. It was estimated at fifty thousand francs."

"Bless me!" exclaimed Caderousse, "fifty thousand francs! Surely the diamond was as large as a nut to be worth all that."—"No," replied the abbé, "it was not of such a size as that; but you shall judge for yourself. I have it with me."

The sharp gaze of Caderousse was instantly directed towards the priest's garments, as though hoping to discover the location of the treasure. Calmly drawing forth from his pocket a small box covered with black shargreen, the abbé opened it, and displayed to the dazzled eyes of Caderousse the sparkling jewel it contained, set in a ring of admirable workmanship. "And that diamond," cried Caderousse, almost breathless with eager admiration, "you say, is worth fifty thousand francs?"

"It is, without the setting, which is also valuable," replied the abbé, as he closed the box, and returned it to his pocket, while its brilliant hues seemed still to dance before the eyes of the fascinated innkeeper.

"But how comes the diamond in your possession, sir? Did Edmond make you his heir?"—"No, merely his testamentary executor. 'I once possessed four dear and faithful friends, besides the maiden to whom I was betrothed' he said; 'and I feel convinced they have all unfeignedly grieved over my loss. The name of one of the four friends is Caderousse.'" The innkeeper shivered.

"'Another of the number,'" continued the abbé, without seeming to notice the emotion of Caderousse, "'is called Danglars; and the third, in spite of being my rival, entertained a very sincere affection for me.'" A fiendish smile played over the features of Caderousse, who was about to break in upon the abbé's speech, when the latter, waving his hand, said, "Allow me to finish first, and then if you have any observations to make, you can do so afterwards. 'The third of my friends, although my rival, was much attached to me,—his name was Fernand; that of my betrothed was'—Stay, stay," continued the abbé, "I have forgotten what he called her."—"Mercédès," said Caderousse eagerly.

"True," said the abbé, with a stifled sigh, "Mercédès it was."

"Go on," urged Caderousse.

"Bring me a carafe of water," said the abbé.

Caderousse quickly performed the stranger's bidding; and after pouring some into a glass, and slowly swallowing its contents, the abbé, resuming his usual placidity of manner, said, as he placed his empty glass on the table,—"Where did we leave off?"

"The name of Edmond's betrothed was Mercédès."

"To be sure. 'You will go to Marseilles,' said Dantès,—for you understand, I repeat his words just as he uttered them. Do you understand?"—"Perfectly."

"'You will sell this diamond; you will divide the money into five equal parts, and give an equal portion to these good friends, the only persons who have loved me upon earth.'"—"But why into five parts?" asked Caderousse; "you only mentioned four persons."

"Because the fifth is dead, as I hear. The fifth sharer in Edmond's bequest was his own father."—"Too true, too true!" ejaculated Caderousse, almost suffocated by the contending passions which assailed him, "the poor old man did die."

"I learned so much at Marseilles," replied the abbé, making a strong effort to appear indifferent; "but from the length of time that has elapsed since the death of the elder Dantès, I was unable to obtain any particulars of his end. Can you enlighten me on that point?"

"I do not know who could if I could not," said Caderousse. "Why, I lived almost on the same floor with the poor old man. Ah, yes, about a year after the disappearance of his son the poor old man died."

"Of what did he die?"

"Why, the doctors called his complaint gastro-enteritis, I believe; his acquaintances say he died of grief; but I, who saw him in his dying moments, I say he died of"—Caderousse paused.

"Of what?" asked the priest, anxiously and eagerly.

"Why, of downright starvation."—"Starvation!" exclaimed the abbé, springing from his seat. "Why, the vilest animals are not suffered to die by such a death as that. The very dogs that wander houseless and homeless in the streets find some pitying hand to cast them a mouthful of bread; and that a man, a Christian, should be allowed to perish of hunger in the midst of other men who call themselves Christians, is too horrible for belief. Oh, it is impossible—utterly impossible!"

"What I have said, I have said," answered Caderousse.

"And you are a fool for having said anything about it," said a voice from the top of the stairs. "Why should you meddle with what does not concern you?"

The two men turned quickly, and saw the sickly countenance of La Carconte peering between the baluster rails; attracted by the sound of voices, she had feebly dragged herself down the stairs, and, seated on the lower step, head on knees, she had listened to the foregoing conversation. "Mind your own business, wife," replied Caderousse sharply. "This gentleman asks me for information, which common politeness will not permit me to refuse."— "Politeness, you simpleton!" retorted La Carconte. "What have you to do with politeness, I should like to know? Better study a little common prudence. How do you know the motives that person may have for trying to extract all he can from you?"

"I pledge you my word, madam," said the abbé, "that my intentions are good; and that your husband can incur no risk, provided he answers me candidly."

"Ah, that's all very fine," retorted the woman. "Nothing is easier than to begin with fair promises and assurances of nothing to fear; but when poor, silly folks, like my husband there, have been persuaded to tell all they know, the promises and assurances of safety are quickly forgotten; and at some moment when nobody is expecting it, behold trouble and misery, and all sorts of persecutions, are heaped on the unfortunate wretches, who cannot even see whence all their afflictions come."

"Nay, nay, my good woman, make yourself perfectly easy, I beg of you. Whatever evils may befall you, they will not be occasioned by my instrumentality, that I solemnly promise you."

La Carconte muttered a few inarticulate words, then let her head again drop upon her knees, and went into a fit of ague, leaving the two speakers to resume the conversation, but remaining so as to be able to hear every word they uttered. Again the abbé had been obliged to swallow a draught of water to calm the emotions that threatened to overpower him. When he had sufficiently recovered himself, he said, "It appears, then, that the miserable old man you were telling me of was forsaken by every one. Surely, had not such been the case, he would not have perished by so dreadful a death."

"Why, he was not altogether forsaken," continued Caderousse, "for Mercédès the Catalan and Monsieur Morrel were very kind to him; but somehow the poor old man had contracted a profound hatred for Fernand—the very person," added Caderousse with a bitter smile, "that you named just now as being one of Dantès' faithful and attached friends."

"And was he not so?" asked the abbé.

"Gaspard, Gaspard!" murmured the woman, from her seat on the stairs, "mind what you are saying!" Caderousse made no reply to these words, though evidently irritated and annoyed by the interruption, but, addressing the abbé, said, "Can a man be faithful to another whose wife he covets and desires for himself? But Dantès was so honorable and true in his own nature, that he believed everybody's professions of friendship. Poor Edmond, he was cruelly deceived; but it was fortunate that he never knew, or he might have found it more difficult, when on his deathbed, to pardon his enemies. And, whatever people may say," continued Caderousse, in his native language, which was not altogether devoid of rude poetry, "I cannot help being more frightened at the idea of the malediction of the dead than the hatred of the living."—"Imbecile!" exclaimed La Carconte.

"Do you, then, know in what manner Fernand injured Dantès?" inquired the abbé of Caderousse.

"Do I? No one better."—"Speak out then, say what it was!"

"Gaspard!" cried La Carconte, "do as you will; you are master—but if you take my advice you'll hold your tongue."—"Well, wife," replied Caderoussse, "I don't know but what you're right!"

"So you will say nothing?" asked the abbé.—"Why, what good

would it do?" asked Caderousse. "If the poor lad were living, and came to me and begged that I would candidly tell which were his true and which his false friends, why, perhaps, I should not hesitate. But you tell me he is no more, and therefore can have nothing to do with hatred or revenge; so let all such feeling be buried with him."

"You prefer, then," said the abbé, "that I should bestow on men you say are false and treacherous, the reward intended for faithful friendship?"

"That is true enough," returned Caderousse. "You say truly, the gift of poor Edmond was not meant for such traitors as Fernand and Danglars; besides, what would it be to them? no more than a drop of water in the ocean."—"Remember," chimed in La Carconte, "those two could crush you at a single blow!"

"How so?" inquired the abbé. "Are these persons, then, so rich and powerful?"—"Do you not know their history?"

"I do not. Pray relate it to me!" Caderousse seemed to reflect for a few moments, then said, "No, truly, it would take up too much time."

"Well, my good friend," returned the abbé, in a tone that indicated utter indifference on his part, "you are at liberty either to speak or be silent, just as you please; for my own part, I respect your scruples and admire your sentiments; so let the matter end. I shall do my duty as conscientiously as I can, and fulfil my promise to the dying man. My first business will be to dispose of this diamond." So saying, the abbé again drew the small box from his pocket, opened it, and contrived to hold it in such a light, that a bright flash of brilliant hues passed before the dazzled gaze of Caderousse.

"Wife, wife!" cried he in a hoarse voice, "come here!"—"Diamond!" exclaimed La Carconte, rising and descending to the chamber with a tolerably firm step; "what diamond are you talking about?"

"Why, did you not hear all we said?" inquired Caderousse. "It is a beautiful diamond left by poor Edmond Dantès, to be sold, and the money divided between his father, Mercédès, his betrothed bride, Fernand, Danglars, and myself. The jewel is worth at least fifty thousand francs."

"Oh, what a magnificent jewel!" cried the astonished woman.

"The fifth part of the profits from this stone belongs to us, then, does it not?" asked Caderousse.

"It does," replied the abbé; "with the addition of an equal division of that part intended for the elder Dantès, which I believe myself at liberty to divide equally with the four survivors."

"And why among us four?" inquired Caderousse.

"As being the friends Edmond esteemed most faithful and devoted to him."—"I don't call those friends who betray and ruin you," murmured the wife in her turn, in a low, muttering voice.

"Of course not!" rejoined Caderousse quickly; "no more do I, and that was what I was observing to this gentleman just now. I said I looked upon it as a sacrilegious profanation to reward treachery, perhaps crime."

"Remember," answered the abbé calmly, as he replaced the jewel and its case in the pocket of his cassock, "it is your fault, not mine, that I do so. You will have the goodness to furnish me with the address of both Fernand and Danglars, in order that I may execute Edmond's last wishes." The agitation of Caderousse became extreme, and large drops of perspiration rolled from his heated brow. As he saw the abbé rise from his seat and go towards the door, as though to ascertain if his horse were sufficiently refreshed to continue his journey, Caderousse and his wife exchanged looks of deep meaning.

"There, you see, wife," said the former, "this splendid diamond might all be ours, if we chose!"—"Do you believe it?"

"Why, surely a man of his holy profession would not deceive us!"

"Well," replied La Carconte, "do as you like. For my part, I wash my hands of the affair." So saying, she once more climbed the staircase leading to her chamber, her body convulsed with chills, and her teeth rattling in her head, in spite of the intense heat of the weather. Arrived at the top stair, she turned round, and called out, in a warning tone, to her husband, "Gaspard, consider well what you are about to do!"—"I have both reflected and decided," answered he. La Carconte then entered her chamber, the flooring of which creaked beneath her heavy, uncertain tread, as she proceeded towards her arm-chair, into which she fell as though exhausted.

"Well," asked the abbé, as he returned to the apartment below, "what have you made up your mind to do?"

"To tell you all I know," was the reply.

"I certainly think you act wisely in so doing," said the priest. "Not because I have the least desire to learn anything you may please to conceal from me, but simply that if, through your assistance, I could distribute the legacy according to the wishes of the testator, why, so much the better, that is all."—"I hope it may be so," replied Caderousse, his face flushed with cupidity.

"I am all attention," said the abbé.—"Stop a minute," answered Caderousse; "we might be interrupted in the most interesting part of my story, which would be a pity; and it is as well that your visit hither should be made known only to ourselves." With these words he went stealthily to the door, which he closed, and, by way of still greater precaution, bolted and barred it, as he was accustomed to do at night. During this time the abbé had chosen his place for listening at his ease. He removed his seat into a corner of the room, where he himself would be in deep shadow, while the light would be fully thrown on the narrator; then, with head bent down and hands clasped, or rather clinched together, he prepared to give his whole attention to Caderousse, who seated himself on the little stool, exactly opposite to him.

"Remember, this is no affair of mine," said the trembling voice of La Carconte, as though through the flooring of her chamber she viewed the scene that was enacting below.

"Enough, enough!" replied Caderousse; "say no more about it; I will take all the consequences upon myself." And he began his story.

XXVII

The Story

"FIRST, SIR," SAID CADEROUSSE, "you must make me a promise."

"What is that?" inquired the abbé.

"Why, if you ever make use of the details I am about to give you, that you will never let any one know that it was I who supplied them; for the persons of whom I am about to talk are rich and powerful, and if they only laid the tips of their fingers on me, I should break to pieces like glass."

"Make yourself easy, my friend," replied the abbé. "I am a priest, and confessions die in my breast. Recollect, our only desire is to carry out, in a fitting manner, the last wishes of our friend. Speak, then, without reserve, as without hatred; tell the truth, the whole truth; I do not know, never may know, the persons of whom you are about to speak; besides, I am an Italian, and not a Frenchman, and belong to God, and not to man, and I shall shortly retire to my convent, which I have only quitted to fulfil the last wishes of a dying man." This positive assurance seemed to give Caderousse a little courage.

"Well, then, under these circumstances," said Caderousse, "I will, I even believe I ought to undeceive you as to the friendship which poor Edmond thought so sincere and unquestionable."—"Begin with his father, if you please," said the abbé; "Edmond talked to me a great deal about the old man, for whom he had the deepest love."

"The history is a sad one, sir," said Caderousse, shaking his head; "perhaps you know all the earlier part of it?"—"Yes," answered the abbé; "Edmond related to me everything until the moment when he was arrested in a small cabaret close to Marseilles."

"At La Réserve! Oh, yes; I can see it all before me this moment."

"Was it not his betrothal feast?"—"It was; and the feast that began so gayly had a very sorrowful ending; a police commissary, followed by four soldiers, entered, and Dantès was arrested."

"Yes, and up to this point I know all," said the priest. "Dantès himself only knew that which personally concerned him, for he never beheld again the five persons I have named to you, or heard mention of any one of them."

"Well, when Dantès was arrested, Monsieur Morrel hastened to obtain the particulars, and they were very sad. The old man returned alone to his home, folded up his wedding suit with tears in his eyes, and paced up and down his chamber the whole day, and would not go to bed at all, for I was underneath him and heard him walking the whole night; and for myself, I assure you I could not sleep either, for the grief of the poor father gave me great uneasiness, and every step he took went to my heart as really as if his foot had pressed against my breast. The next day Mercédès came to implore the protection of M. de Villefort; she did not obtain it, however, and went to visit the old man; when she saw him so miserable and heart-broken, having passed a sleepless night, and not touched food since the previous day, she wished him to go with her that she might take care of him; but the old man would not consent. 'No,' was the old man's reply, 'I will not leave this house, for my poor dear boy loves me better than anything in the world; and if he gets out of prison he will come and see me the first thing, and what would he think if I did not wait here for him?' I heard all this from the window, for I was anxious that Mercédès should persuade the old man to accompany her, for his footsteps over my head night and day did not leave me a moment's repose."

"But did you not go up-stairs and try to console the poor old man?" asked the abbé.—"Ah, sir," replied Caderousse, "we cannot console those who will not be consoled, and he was one of these; besides, I know not why, but he seemed to dislike seeing me. One night, however, I heard his sobs, and I could not resist my desire to go up to him, but when I reached his door he was no longer weeping but praying. I cannot now repeat to you, sir, all the eloquent words and imploring language he made use of; it was more than piety, it was more than grief, and I, who am no canter, and hate the Jesuits, said then to myself, 'It is really well, and I am very glad that I have not any children; for if I were a father and felt such excessive grief as the old man does, and did not find in my memory or heart all he is now saying, I should throw myself into the sea at once, for I could not bear it.'"

"Poor father!" murmured the priest.

"From day to day he lived on alone, and more and more solitary. M. Morrel and Mercédès came to see him, but his door was closed; and, although I was certain he was at home, he would not make any answer. One day, when, contrary to his custom, he had admitted Mercédès, and the poor girl, in spite of her own grief and despair, endeavored to console him, he said to her,—'Be assured, my dear daughter, he is dead; and instead of expecting him, it is he who is awaiting us; I am quite happy, for I am the oldest, and of course shall see him first.' However well disposed a person may be, why you see we leave off after a time seeing persons who are in sorrow, they make one melancholy; and so at last old Dantès was left all to himself, and I only saw from time to time strangers go up to him and come down again with some bundle they tried to hide; but I guessed what these bundles were, and that he sold by degrees what he had to pay for his subsistence. At length the poor old fellow reached the end of all he had; he owed three quarters' rent, and they threatened to turn him out; he begged for another week, which was granted to him. I know this, because the landlord came into my apartment when he left his. For the first three days I heard him walking about as usual, but on the fourth I heard nothing. I then resolved to go up to him at all risks. The door was closed, but I looked through the keyhole, and saw him so pale and haggard, that believing him very ill, I went and told M. Morrel and then ran on to Mercédès. They both came immediately, M. Morrel bringing a doctor, and the doctor said it was inflammation of the bowels, and ordered him a limited diet. I was there, too, and I never shall forget the old man's smile at this prescription. From that time he received all who came; he had an excuse for not eating any more; the doctor had put him on a diet." The abbé uttered a kind of groan. "The story interests you, does it not, sir?" inquired Caderousse.—"Yes," replied the abbé, "it is very affecting."

"Mercédès came again, and she found him so altered that she was even more anxious than before to have him taken to her own home. This was M. Morrel's wish also, who would fain have conveyed the old man against his consent; but the old man resisted, and cried so that they were actually frightened. Mercédès remained, therefore, by his bedside, and M. Morrel went away, making a sign to the Catalane that he had left his purse on the chimney-piece. But availing himself of the doctor's order, the old man would not take any sustenance; at length (after nine days of despair and fasting), the old man died, cursing those who had caused his misery, and saying to Mercédès, 'If you ever see my Edmond again, tell him I die blessing him.'" The abbé rose from his chair, made two turns round the chamber, and pressed his trembling hand against his parched throat. "And you believe he died"—

"Of hunger, sir, of hunger," said Caderousse. "I am as certain of it as that we two are Christians."

The abbé, with a shaking hand, seized a glass of water that was standing by him half-full, swallowed it at one gulp, and then resumed his seat, with red eyes and pale cheeks. "This was, indeed, a horrid event," said he in a hoarse voice.

"The more so, sir, as it was men's and not God's doing."—"Tell me of those men," said the abbé, "and remember too," he added in an almost menacing tone, "you have promised to tell me everything. Tell me, therefore, who are these men who killed the son with despair, and the father with famine?"—"Two men jealous of him, sir; one from love, and the other from ambition,—Fernand and Danglars."

"How was this jealousy manifested? Speak on."

"They denounced Edmond as a Bonapartist agent."

"Which of the two denounced him? Which was the real delinquent?"

"Both, sir; one with a letter, and the other put it in the post."

"And where was this letter written?"

"At La Réserve, the day before the betrothal feast."

"'Twas so, then—'twas so, then," murmured the abbé. "Oh, Faria, Faria, how well did you judge men and things!"

"What did you please to say, sir?" asked Caderousse.

"Nothing, nothing," replied the priest; "go on."

"It was Danglars who wrote the denunciation with his left hand, that his writing might not be recognized, and Fernand who put it in the post."

"But," exclaimed the abbé suddenly, "you were there yourself."

"I!" said Caderousse, astonished; "who told you I was there?"

The abbé saw he had overshot the mark, and he added quickly,—"No one; but in order to have known everything so well, you must have been an eye-witness."—"True, true!" said Caderousse in a choking voice, "I was there."

"And did you not remonstrate against such infamy?" asked the abbé; "if not, you were an accomplice."—"Sir," replied Caderousse, "they had made me drink to such an excess that I nearly lost all perception. I had only an indistinct understanding of what was passing around me. I said all that a man in such a state could say; but they both assured me that it was a jest they were carrying on, and perfectly harmless."

"Next day—next day, sir, you must have seen plain enough what they had been doing, yet you said nothing, though you were present when Dantès was arrested."—"Yes, sir, I was there, and very anxious to speak; but Danglars restrained me. 'If he should really be guilty,' said he, 'and did really put in to the Island of Elba; if he is really charged with a letter for the Bonapartist committee at Paris, and if they find this letter upon him, those who have supported him will pass for his accomplices.' I confess I had my fears, in the state in which politics then were, and I held my tongue. It was cowardly, I confess, but it was not criminal."

"I understand—you allowed matters to take their course, that was all."—"Yes, sir," answered Caderousse; "and remorse preys on me night and day. I often ask pardon of God, I swear to you, because this action, the only one with which I have seriously to reproach myself in all my life, is no doubt the cause of my abject condition. I am expiating a moment of selfishness, and so I always say to La Carconte, when she complains, 'Hold your tongue, woman; it is the will of God.'" And Caderousse bowed his head with every sign of real repentance.

"Well, sir," said the abbé, "you have spoken unreservedly; and thus to accuse yourself is to deserve pardon."—"Unfortunately, Edmond is dead, and has not pardoned me."—"He did not know," said the abbé.

"But he knows it all now," interrupted Caderousse; "they say the dead know everything." There was a brief silence; the abbé rose and paced up and down pensively, and then resumed his seat. "You have two or three times mentioned a M. Morrel," he said; "who was he?"—"The owner of the *Pharaon* and patron of Dantès."

"And what part did he play in this sad drama?" inquired the abbé.

"The part of an honest man, full of courage and real regard. Twenty times he interceded for Edmond. When the emperor returned, he wrote, implored, threatened, and so energetically, that on the second restoration he was persecuted as a Bonapartist. Ten times, as I told you, he came to see Dantès' father, and offered to receive him in his own house; and the night or two before his death, as I have already said, he left his purse on the mantelpiece, with which they paid the old man's debts, and buried him decently; and so Edmond's father died, as he had lived, without doing harm to any one. I have the purse still by me—a large one, made of red silk."

"And," asked the abbé, "is M. Morrel still alive?"—"Yes," replied Caderousse.

"In that case," replied the abbé, "he should be rich, happy." Caderousse smiled bitterly. "Yes, happy as myself," said he.

"What! M. Morrel unhappy?" exclaimed the abbé.

"He is reduced almost to the last extremity—nay, he is almost at the point of dishonor."—"How?"

"Yes," continued Caderousse, "so it is; after five and twenty years of labor, after having acquired a most honorable name in the trade of Marseilles, M. Morrel is utterly ruined; he has lost five ships in two years, has suffered by the bankruptcy of three large houses, and his only hope now is in that very *Pharaon* which poor Dantès commanded, and which is expected from the Indies with a cargo of cochineal and indigo. If this ship founders, like the others, he is a ruined man."—"And has the unfortunate man wife or children?" inquired the abbé.

"Yes, he has a wife, who through everything has behaved like an angel; he has a daughter, who was about to marry the man she loved, but whose family now will not allow him to wed the daughter of a ruined man; he has, besides, a son, a lieutenant in the army; and, as you may suppose, all this, instead of lessening, only augments his sorrows. If he were alone in the world he would blow out his brains, and there would be an end."

"Horrible!" ejaculated the priest.

"And it is thus heaven recompenses virtue, sir," added Caderousse. "You see, I, who never did a bad action but that I have told
you of—am in destitution, with my poor wife dying of fever before
my very eyes, and I unable to do anything in the world for her; I
shall die of hunger, as old Dantès did, while Fernand and Danglars
are rolling in wealth."

"How is that?"—"Because their deeds have brought them good
fortune, while honest men have been reduced to misery."

"What has become of Danglars, the instigator, and therefore the
most guilty?"—"What has become of him? Why, he left Marseilles,
and was taken, on the recommendation of M. Morrel, who did not
know his crime, as cashier into a Spanish bank. During the war
with Spain he was employed in the commissariat of the French
army, and made a fortune; then with that money he speculated in
the funds, and trebled or quadrupled his capital; and, having first
married his banker's daughter, who left him a widower, he has married a second time, a widow, a Madame de Nargonne, daughter of
M. de Servieux, the king's chamberlain, who is in high favor at
court. He is a millionaire, and they have made him a baron, and
now he is the Baron Danglars, with a fine residence in the Rue de
Mont-Blanc, with ten horses in his stables, six footmen in his
antechamber, and I know not how many millions in his strongbox."

"Ah!" said the abbé, in a peculiar tone, "he is happy."

"Happy? Who can answer for that? Happiness or unhappiness is
the secret known but to one's self and the walls—walls have ears but
no tongue; but if a large fortune produces happiness, Danglars is
happy."

"And Fernand?"—"Fernand? Why, much the same story."

"But how could a poor Catalan fisher-boy, without education
or resources, make a fortune? I confess this staggers me."—"And it
has staggered everybody. There must have been in his life some
strange secret that no one knows."

"But, then, by what visible steps has he attained this high fortune or high position?"

"Both, sir—he has both fortune and position—both."

"This must be impossible!"

"It would seem so; but listen, and you will understand. Some days before the return of the emperor, Fernand was drafted. The Bourbons left him quietly enough at the Catalans, but Napoleon returned, a special levy was made, and Fernand was compelled to join. I went too; but as I was older than Fernand, and had just married my poor wife, I was only sent to the coast. Fernand was enrolled in the active troop, went to the frontier with his regiment, and was at the battle of Ligny. The night after that battle he was sentry at the door of a general who carried on a secret correspondence with the enemy. That same night the general was to go over to the English. He proposed to Fernand to accompany him; Fernand agreed to do so, deserted his post, and followed the general. Fernand would have been court-martialed if Napoleon had remained on the throne, but his action was rewarded by the Bourbons. He returned to France with the epaulet of sub-lieutenant, and as the protection of the general, who is in the highest favor, was accorded to him, he was a captain in 1823, during the Spanish war—that is to say, at the time when Danglars made his early speculations. Fernand was a Spaniard, and being sent to Spain to ascertain the feeling of his fellow-countrymen, found Danglars there, got on very intimate terms with him, won over the support of the royalists at the capital and in the provinces, received promises and made pledges on his own part, guided his regiment by paths known to himself alone through the mountain gorges which were held by the royalists, and, in fact, rendered such services in this brief campaign that, after the taking of Trocadero, he was made colonel, and received the title of count and the cross of an officer of the Legion of Honor."

"Destiny! destiny!" murmured the abbé.

"Yes, but listen; this was not all. The war with Spain being ended, Fernand's career was checked by the long peace which seemed likely to endure throughout Europe. Greece only had risen against Turkey, and had begun her war of independence; all eyes were turned towards Athens—it was the fashion to pity and support the Greeks. The French government, without protecting them openly, as you know, gave countenance to volunteer assistance. Fernand sought and obtained leave to go and serve in Greece, still having his name kept on the army roll. Some time after, it was stated that the Comte de Morcerf (this was the name he bore) had entered the service of Ali Pasha with the rank of instructor-general. Ali Pasha was killed, as you know; but before he died he recompensed the services of Fernand by leaving him a considerable sum, with which he returned to France, when he was gazetted lieutenant-general."—"So that now?"—inquired the abbé.

"So that now," continued Caderousse, "he owns a magnificent house—No. 27, Rue du Helder, Paris." The abbé opened his mouth, hesitated for a moment, then, making an effort at self-control, he said, "And Mercédès—they tell me that she has disappeared?"

"Disappeared," said Caderousse, "yes, as the sun disappears, to rise the next day with still more splendor."—"Has she made a fortune also?" inquired the abbé, with an ironical smile.

"Mercédès is at this moment one of the greatest ladies in Paris," replied Caderousse.

"Go on," said the abbé; "it seems as if I were listening to the story of a dream. But I have seen things so extraordinary, that what you tell me seems less astonishing than it otherwise might."

"Mercédès was at first in the deepest despair at the blow which deprived her of Edmond. I have told you of her attempts to propitiate M. de Villefort, her devotion to the elder Dantès. In the midst of her despair, a new affliction overtook her. This was the departure of Fernand—of Fernand, whose crime she did not know, and whom she regarded as her brother. Fernand went, and Mercédès remained alone. Three months passed and still she wept—no news of Edmond, no news of Fernand, no companionship save that of an old man who was dying with despair. One evening, after a day of accustomed vigil at the angle of two roads leading to Marseilles from the Catalans, she returned to her home more depressed than ever. Suddenly she heard a step she knew, turned anxiously around, the door opened, and Fernand, dressed in the uniform of a sub-lieutenant, stood before her. It was not the one she wished for most, but it seemed as if a part of her past life had returned to her. Mercédès seized Fernand's hands with a transport which he took for love, but which was only joy at being no longer alone in the world, and seeing at last a friend, after long hours of solitary sorrow. And then, it must be confessed, Fernand had never been hated—he was only not precisely loved. Another possessed all Mercédès' heart; that other was absent, had disappeared, perhaps was dead. At this last thought Mercédès burst into a flood of tears, and wrung her hands in agony; but the thought, which she had always repelled before when it was suggested to her by another, came now in full force upon her mind; and then, too, old Dantès incessantly said to her, 'Our Edmond is dead; if he were not, he would return to us.' The old man died, as I have told you; had he lived, Mercédès, perchance, had not become the wife of another, for he would have been there to reproach her infidelity. Fernand saw this, and when he learned of the old man's death he returned. He was now a lieutenant. At his first coming he had not said a word of love to Mercédès; at the second he reminded her that he loved her. Mercédès begged for six months more in which to await and mourn for Edmond."

"So that," said the abbé, with a bitter smile, "that makes eighteen months in all. What more could the most devoted lover desire?" Then he murmured the words of the English poet, "'Frailty, thy name is woman.'"

"Six months afterwards," continued Caderousse, "the marriage took place in the church of Accoules."—"The very church in which she was to have married Edmond," murmured the priest; "there was only a change of bridegrooms."

"Well, Mercédès was married," proceeded Caderousse; "but although in the eyes of the world she appeared calm, she nearly fainted as she passed La Réserve, where, eighteen months before, the betrothal had been celebrated with him whom she might have known she still loved had she looked to the bottom of her heart. Fernand, more happy, but not more at his ease—for I saw at this time he was in constant dread of Edmond's return—Fernand was very anxious to get his wife away, and to depart himself. There were too many unpleasant possibilities associated with the Catalans, and eight days after the wedding they left Marseilles."—"Did you ever see Mercédès again?" inquired the priest.

"Yes, during the Spanish war, at Perpignan, where Fernand had left her; she was attending to the education of her son." The abbé started. "Her son?" said he.—"Yes," replied Caderousse, "little Albert."—"But, then, to be able to instruct her child," continued the abbé, "she must have received an education herself. I understood from Edmond that she was the daughter of a simple fisherman, beautiful but uneducated."

"Oh," replied Caderousse, "did he know so little of his lovely betrothed? Mercédès might have been a queen, sir, if the crown were to be placed on the heads of the loveliest and most intelligent. Fernand's fortune was already waxing great, and she developed with his growing fortune. She learned drawing, music—everything. Besides, I believe, between ourselves, she did this in order to distract her mind, that she might forget; and she only filled her head in order to alleviate the weight on her heart. But now her position in life is assured," continued Caderousse; "no doubt fortune and honors have comforted her; she is rich, a countess, and yet"—Caderousse paused.

"And yet what?" asked the abbé.

"Yet, I am sure, she is not happy," said Caderousse.

"What makes you believe this?"—"Why, when I found myself utterly destitute, I thought my old friends would, perhaps, assist me. So I went to Dauglars, who would not even receive me. I called on Fernand, who sent me a hundred francs by his valet-de-chambre."

"Then you did not see either of them?"

"No; but Madame de Morcerf saw me."

"How was that?"—"As I went away a purse fell at my feet—it contained five and twenty louis; I raised my head quickly, and saw Mercédès, who at once shut the blind."

"And M. de Villefort?" asked the abbé.—"Oh, he never was a friend of mine, I did not know him, and I had nothing to ask of him."

"Do you not know what became of him, and the share he had in Edmond's misfortunes?"—"No; I only know that some time after Edmond's arrest, he married Mademoiselle de Saint-Méran, and soon after left Marseilles; no doubt he has been as lucky as the rest; no doubt he is as rich as Danglars, as high in station as Fernand. I only, as you see, have remained poor, wretched, and forgotten."

"You are mistaken, my friend," replied the abbé; "God may seem sometimes to forget for a time, while his justice reposes, but there always comes a moment when he remembers—and behold—a proof!" As he spoke, the abbé took the diamond from his pocket, and giving it to Caderousse, said,—"Here, my friend, take this diamond, it is yours."

"What, for me only?" cried Caderousse; "ah, sir, do not jest with me!"

"This diamond was to have been shared among his friends. Edmond had one friend only, and thus it cannot be divided. Take the diamond, then, and sell it; it is worth fifty thousand francs, and I repeat my wish that this sum may suffice to release you from your wretchedness."

"Oh, sir," said Caderousse, putting out one hand timidly, and with the other wiping away the perspiration which bedewed his brow,—"Oh, sir, do not make a jest of the happiness or despair of a man."

"I know what happiness and what despair are, and I never make a jest of such feelings. Take it, then, but in exchange—"

Caderousse, who touched the diamond, withdrew his hand. The abbé smiled. "In exchange," he continued, "give me the red silk purse that M. Morrel left on old Dantès' chimney-piece, and which you tell me is still in your hands." Caderousse, more and more astonished, went toward a large oaken cupboard, opened it, and gave the abbé a long purse of faded red silk, round which were two copper runners that had once been gilt. The abbé took it, and in return gave Caderousse the diamond.

"Oh, you are a man of God, sir," cried Caderousse; "for no one knew that Edmond had given you this diamond, and you might have kept it."—"Which," said the abbé to himself, "you would have done." The abbé rose, took his hat and gloves. "Well," he said, "all you have told me is perfectly true, then, and I may believe it in every particular."—"See, sir," replied Caderousse, "in this corner is a crucifix in holy wood—here on this shelf is my wife's testament; open this book, and I will swear upon it with my hand on the crucifix. I will swear to you by my soul's salvation, my faith as a Christian, I have told everything to you as it occurred, and as the recording angel will tell it to the ear of God at the day of the last judgment!"

"'Tis well," said the abbé, convinced by his manner and tone that Caderousse spoke the truth. "'Tis well, and may this money profit you! Adieu; I go far from men who thus so bitterly injure each other." The abbé with difficulty got away from the enthusiastic thanks of Caderousse, opened the door himself, got out and mounted his horse, once more saluted the innkeeper, who kept uttering his loud farewells, and then returned by the road he had travelled in coming. When Caderousse turned around, he saw behind him La Carconte, paler and trembling more than ever. "Is, then, all that I have heard really true?" she inquired.—"What? That he has given the diamond to us only?" she inquired Caderousse, half bewildered with joy; "yes, nothing more true! See, here it is." The woman gazed at it a moment, and then said, in a gloomy voice, "Suppose it's false?" Caderousse started and turned pale. "False!" he muttered. "False! Why should that man give me a false diamond?"—"To get your secret without paying for it, you blockhead!"

Caderousse remained for a moment aghast under the weight of such an idea. "Oh!" he said, taking up his hat, which he placed on the red handkerchief tied round his head, "we will soon find out."—"In what way?"—"Why, the fair is on at Beaucaire, there are always jewellers from Paris there, and I will show it to them. Look after the house, wife, and I shall be back in two hours," and Caderousse left the house in haste, and ran rapidly in the direction opposite to that which the priest had taken. "Fifty thousand francs!" muttered La Carconte when left alone; "it is a large sum of money, but it is not a fortune."

XXVIII

The Prison Register

THE DAY AFTER THAT in which the scene we have just described had taken place on the road between Bellegarde and Beaucaire, a man of about thirty or two and thirty, dressed in a bright blue frock coat, nankeen trousers, and a white waistcoat, having the appearance and accent of an Englishman, presented himself before the mayor of Marseilles. "Sir," said he, "I am chief clerk of the house of Thomson & French, of Rome. We are, and have been these ten years, connected with the house of Morrel & Son, of Marseilles. We have a hundred thousand francs or thereabouts loaned on their securities, and we are a little uneasy at reports that have reached us that the firm is on the brink of ruin. I have come, therefore, express from Rome, to ask you for information."

"Sir," replied the mayor, "I know very well that during the last four or five years misfortune has seemed to pursue M. Morrel. He has lost four or five vessels, and suffered by three or four bankruptcies; but it is not for me, although I am a creditor myself to the amount of ten thousand francs, to give any information as to the state of his finances. Ask of me, as mayor, what is my opinion of M. Morrel, and I shall say that he is a man honorable to the last degree, and who has up to this time fulfilled every engagement with scrupulous punctuality. This is all I can say, sir; if you wish to learn more, address yourself to M. de Boville, the inspector of prisons, No. 15, Rue de Nouailles; he has, I believe, two hundred thousand francs in Morrel's hands, and if there be any grounds for apprehension, as this is a greater amount than mine, you will most probably find him better informed than myself."

The Englishman seemed to appreciate this extreme delicacy, made his bow and went away, proceeding with a characteristic British stride towards the street mentioned. M. de Boville was in his private room, and the Englishman, on perceiving him, made a gesture of surprise, which seemed to indicate that it was not the first time he had been in his presence. As to M. de Boville, he was in such a state of despair, that it was evident all the faculties of his mind, absorbed in the thought which occupied him at the moment, did not allow either his memory or his imagination to stray to the past. The Englishman, with the coolness of his nation, addressed him in terms nearly similar to those with which he had accosted the mayor of Marseilles. "Oh, sir," exclaimed M. de Boville, "your fears are unfortunately but too well founded, and you see before you a man in despair. I had two hundred thousand francs placed in the hands of Morrel & Son; these two hundred thousand francs were the dowry of my daughter, who was to be married in a fortnight, and these two hundred thousand francs were payable, half on the 15th of this month, and the other half on the 15th of next month. I had informed M. Morrel of my desire to have these payments punctually, and he has been here within the last half-hour to tell me that if his ship, the *Pharaon*, did not come into port on the 15th, he would be wholly unable to make this payment."

"But," said the Englishman, "this looks very much like a suspension of payment."—"It looks more like bankruptcy!" exclaimed M. de Boville despairingly.

The Englishman appeared to reflect a moment, and then said,—"From which it would appear, sir, that this credit inspires you with considerable apprehension?"—"To tell you the truth, I consider it lost."

"Well, then, I will buy it of you!"—"You?"

"Yes, I!"—"But at a tremendous discount, of course?"

"No, for two hundred thousand francs. Our house," added the Englishman with a laugh, "does not do things in that way."

"And you will pay"—

"Ready money." And the Englishman drew from his pocket a bundle of bank-notes, which might have been twice the sum M. de Boville feared to lose. A ray of joy passed across M. de Boville's countenance, yet he made an effort at self-control, and said,—"Sir, I ought to tell you that, in all probability, you will not realize six per cent of this sum."—"That's no affair of mine," replied the Englishman, "that is the affair of the house of Thomson & French, in whose name I act. They have, perhaps, some motive to serve in hastening the ruin of a rival firm. But all I know, sir, is, that I am ready to hand you over this sum in exchange for your assignment of the debt. I only ask a brokerage."

"Of course, that is perfectly just," cried M. de Boville. "The commission is usually one and a half; will you have two—three—five per cent, or even more? Whatever you say."—"Sir," replied the Englishman, laughing, "I am like my house, and do not do such things—no, the commission I ask is quite different."

"Name it, sir, I beg."—"You are the inspector of prisons?"

"I have been so these fourteen years."

"You keep the registers of entries and departures?"—"I do."

"To these registers there are added notes relative to the prisoners?"

"There are special reports on every prisoner."—"Well, sir, I was educated at Rome by a poor devil of an abbé, who disappeared suddenly. I have since learned that he was confined in the Château d'If, and I should like to learn some particulars of his death."

"What was his name?"—"The Abbé Faria."

"Oh, I recollect him perfectly," cried M. de Boville; "he was crazy."

"So they said."—"Oh, he was, decidedly."

"Very possibly; but what sort of madness was it?"

"He pretended to know of an immense treasure, and offered vast sums to the government if they would liberate him."

"Poor devil!—and he is dead?"

"Yes, sir; five or six months ago—last February."

"You have a good memory, sir, to recollect dates so well."

"I recollect this, because the poor devil's death was accompanied by a singular incident."

"May I ask what that was?" said the Englishman with an expression of curiosity, which a close observer would have been astonished at discovering in his phlegmatic countenance.—"Oh dear, yes, sir; the abbé's dungeon was forty or fifty feet distant from that of one of Bonaparte's emissaries,—one of those who had contributed the most to the return of the usurper in 1815,—a very resolute and very dangerous man."

"Indeed!" said the Englishman.

"Yes," replied M. de Boville; "I myself had occasion to see this man in 1816 or 1817, and we could only go into his dungeon with a file of soldiers. That man made a deep impression on me; I shall never forget his countenance!" The Englishman smiled imperceptibly.—"And you say, sir," he interposed, "that the two dungeons"—

"Were separated by a distance of fifty feet; but it appears that this Edmond Dantès"—

"This dangerous man's name was"—

"Edmond Dantès. It appears, sir, that this Edmond Dantès had procured tools, or made them, for they found a tunnel through which the prisoners held communication with one another."

"This tunnel was dug, no doubt, with an intention of escape?"

"No doubt; but unfortunately for the prisoners, the Abbé Faria had an attack of catalepsy, and died."

"That must have cut short the projects of escape."

"For the dead man, yes," replied M. de Boville, "but not for the survivor; on the contrary, this Dantès saw a means of accelerating his escape. He, no doubt, thought that prisoners who died in the Château d'If were interred in an ordinary burial-ground, and he conveyed the dead man into his own cell, took his place in the sack in which they had sewed up the corpse, and awaited the moment of interment."—"It was a bold step, and one that showed some courage," remarked the Englishman.

"As I have already told you, sir, he was a very dangerous man; and, fortunately, by his own act disembarrassed the government of the fears it had on his account."—"How was that?"

"How? Do you not comprehend?"—"No."

"The Château d'If has no cemetery, and they simply throw the dead into the sea, after fastening a thirty-six pound cannon-ball to their feet."—"Well," observed the Englishman as if he were slow of comprehension.

"Well, they fastened a thirty-six pound ball to his feet, and threw him into the sea."—"Really!" exclaimed the Englishman.

"Yes, sir," continued the inspector of prisons. "You may imagine the amazement of the fugitive when he found himself flung head-long over the rocks! I should like to have seen his face at that moment."

"That would have been difficult."—"No matter," replied De Boville, in supreme good-humor at the certainty of recovering his two hundred thousand francs,—"no matter, I can fancy it." And he shouted with laughter.

"So can I," said the Englishman, and he laughed too; but he laughed as the English do, "at the end of his teeth." "And so," continued the Englishman who first gained his composure, "he was drowned?"

"Unquestionably."

"So that the governor got rid of the dangerous and the crazy prisoner at the same time?"—"Precisely."

"But some official document was drawn up as to this affair, I suppose?" inquired the Englishman.

"Yes, yes, the mortuary deposition. You understand, Dantès' relations, if he had any, might have some interest in knowing if he were dead or alive."—"So that now, if there were anything to inherit from him, they may do so with easy conscience. He is dead, and no mistake about it."

"Oh, yes; and they may have the fact attested whenever they please."

"So be it," said the Englishman. "But to return to these registers."

"True, this story has diverted our attention from them. Excuse me."

"Excuse you for what? For the story? By no means; it really seems to me very curious."—"Yes, indeed. So, sir, you wish to see all relating to the poor abbé, who really was gentleness itself."

"Yes, you will much oblige me."—"Go into my study here, and I will show it to you." And they both entered M. de Boville's study. Everything was here arranged in perfect order; each register had its number, each file of papers its place. The inspector begged the Englishman to seat himself in an arm-chair, and placed before him the register and documents relative to the Château d'If, giving him all the time he desired for the examination, while De Boville seated himself in a corner, and began to read his newspaper. The Englishman easily found the entries relative to the Abbé Faria; but it seemed that the history which the inspector had related interested him greatly, for after having perused the first documents he turned over the leaves until he reached the deposition respecting Edmond Dantès. There he found everything arranged in due order,—the accusation, examination, Morrel's petition, M. de Villefort's marginal notes. He folded up the accusation quietly, and put it as quietly in his pocket; read the examination, and saw that the name of Noirtier was not mentioned in it; perused, too, the application dated 10th April, 1815, in which Morrel, by the deputy procureur's advice, exaggerated with the best intentions (for Napoleon was then on the throne) the services Dantès had rendered to the imperial cause—services which Villefort's certificates rendered indispensable. Then he saw through the whole thing. This petition to Napoleon, kept back by Villefort, had become, under the second restoration, a terrible weapon against him in the hands of the king's attorney. He was no longer astonished when he searched on to find in the register this note, placed in a bracket against his name:—

Edmond Dantès.

An inveterate Bonapartist; took an active part in
    the return from the Island of Elba.

To be kept in strict solitary confinement, and to
    to be closely watched and guarded.

Beneath these lines was written in another hand: "See note above—nothing can be done." He compared the writing in the bracket with the writing of the certificate placed beneath Morrel's petition, and discovered that the note in the bracket was the same writing as the certificate—that is to say, was in Villefort's handwriting. As to the note which accompanied this, the Englishman understood that it might have been added by some inspector who had taken a momentary interest in Dantès' situation, but who had, from the remarks we have quoted, found it impossible to give any effect to the interest he had felt.

As we have said, the inspector, from discretion, and that he might not disturb the Abbé Faria's pupil in his researches, had seated himself in a corner, and was reading *Le Drapeau Blanc*. He did not see the Englishman fold up and place in in his pocket the accusation written by Danglars under the arbor of La Réserve, and which had the postmark, "Marseilles, 27th Feb., delivery 6 o'clock, P.M.". But it must be said that if he had seen it, he attached so little importance to this scrap of paper, and so much importance to his two hundred thousand francs, that he would not have opposed whatever the Englishman might do, however irregular it might be.

"Thanks," said the latter, closing the register with a slam, "I have all I want; now it is for me to perform my promise. Give me a simple assignment of your debt; acknowledge therein the receipt of the cash, and I will hand you over the money." He rose, gave his seat to M. de Boville, who took it without ceremony, and quickly drew up the required assignment, while the Englishman counted out the bank-notes on the other side of the desk.

XXIX

The House of Morrel & Son

ANY ONE WHO HAD quitted Marseilles a few years previously, well acquainted with the interior of Morrel's warehouse, and had returned at this date, would have found a great change. Instead of that air of life, of comfort, and of happiness that permeates a flourishing and prosperous business establishment—instead of merry faces at the windows, busy clerks hurrying to and fro in the long corridors—instead of the court filled with bales of goods, re-echoing with the cries and the jokes of porters, one would have immediately perceived an aspect of sadness and gloom. Out of all the numerous clerks that used to fill the deserted corridor and the empty office, but two remained. One was a young man of three or four and twenty, who was in love with M. Morrel's daughter, and had remained with him in spite of the efforts of his friends to induce him to withdraw; the other was an old one-eyed cashier, called "Coclès," or "Cock-eye," a nickname given him by the young men who used to throng this vast now almost deserted bee-hive, and which had so completely replaced his real name that he would not, in all probability, have replied to any one who addressed him by it.

Coclès remained in M. Morrel's service, and a most singular change had taken place in his position; he had at the same time risen to the rank of cashier, and sunk to the rank of a servant. He was, however, the same Coclès, good, patient, devoted, but inflexible on the subject of arithmetic, the only point on which he would have stood firm against the world, even against M. Morrel; and strong in the multiplication-table, which he had at his fingers' ends, no matter what scheme or what trap was laid to catch him. In the midst of the disasters that befell the house, Coelès was the only one unmoved. But this did not arise from a want of affection; on the contrary, from a firm conviction. Like the rats that one by one forsake the doomed ship even before the vessel weighs anchor, so all the numerous clerks had by degrees deserted the office and the warehouse. Coclès had seen them go without thinking of inquiring the cause of their departure. Everything was, as we have said, a question of arithmetic to Coclès, and during twenty years he had always seen all payments made with such exactitude, that it seemed as impossible to him that the house should stop payment, as it would to a miller that the river that had so long turned his mill should cease to flow.

Nothing had as yet occurred to shake Coclès' belief; the last month's payment had been made with the most scrupulous exactitude; Coclès had detected an overbalance of fourteen sous in his cash, and the same evening he had brought them to M. Morrel, who, with a melancholy smile, threw them into an almost empty drawer, saying:—

"Thanks, Coclès; you are the pearl of cashiers."

Coclès went away perfectly happy, for this eulogium of M. Morrel, himself the pearl of the honest men of Marseilles, flattered him more than a present of fifty crowns. But since the end of the month M. Morrel had passed many an anxious hour. In order to meet the payments then due, he had collected all his resources, and, fearing lest the report of his distress should get bruited abroad at Marseilles when he was known to be reduced to such an extremity, he went to the Beaucaire fair to sell his wife's and daughter's jewels and a portion of his plate. By this means the end of the month was passed, but his resources were now exhausted. Credit, owing to the reports afloat, was no longer to be had; and to meet the one hundred thousand francs due on the 15th of the present month, and the one hundred thousand francs due on the 15th of the next month to M. de Boville, M. Morrel had, in reality, no hope but the return of the *Pharaon*, of whose departure he had learnt from a vessel which had weighed anchor at the same time, and which had already arrived in harbor. But this vessel which, like the *Pharaon*, came from Calcutta, had been in for a fortnight, while no intelligence had been received of the *Pharaon*.

Such was the state of affairs when, the day after his interview with M. de Boville, the confidential clerk of the house of Thomson & French of Rome, presented himself at M. Morrel's. Emmanuel received him; this young man was alarmed by the appearance of every new face, for every new face might be that of a new creditor, come in anxiety to question the head of the house. The young man, wishing to spare his employer the pain of this interview, questioned the new-comer; but the stranger declared that he had nothing to say to M. Emmanuel, and that his business was with M. Morrel in person. Emmanuel sighed, and summoned Coclès. Coclès appeared, and the young man bade him conduct the stranger to M. Morrel's apartment. Coclès went first, and the stranger followed him. On the staircase they met a beautiful girl of sixteen or seventeen, who looked with anxiety at the stranger.

"M. Morrel is in his room, is he not, Mademoiselle Julie?" said the cashier.

"Yes; I think so, at least," said the young girl hesitatingly. "Go and see, Coclès, and if my father is there, announce this gentleman."

"It will be useless to announce me, mademoiselle," returned the Englishman. "M. Morrel does not know my name; this worthy gentleman has only to announce the confidential clerk of the house of Thomson & French of Rome, with whom your father does business."

The young girl turned pale and continued to descend, while the stranger and Coclès continued to mount the staircase. She entered the office where Emmanuel was, while Coclès, by the aid of a key he possessed, opened a door in the corner of a landing-place on the second staircase, conducted the stranger into an antechamber, opened a second door, which he closed behind him, and after having left the clerk of the house of Thomson & French alone, returned and signed to him that he could enter. The Englishman entered, and found Morrel seated at a table, turning over the formidable columns of his ledger, which contained the list of his liabilities. At the sight of the stranger, M. Morrel closed the ledger, arose, and offered a seat to the stranger; and when he had seen him seated, resumed his own chair. Fourteen years had changed the worthy merchant, who, in his thirty-sixth year at the opening of this history, was now in his fiftieth; his hair had turned white, time and sorrow had ploughed deep furrows on his brow, and his look, once so firm and penetrating, was now irresolute and wandering, as if he feared being forced to fix his attention on some particular thought or person. The Englishman looked at him with an air of curiosity, evidently mingled with interest. "Monsieur," said Morrel, whose uneasiness was increased by this examination, "you wish to speak to me?"

"Yes, monsieur; you are aware from whom I come?"

"The house of Thomson & French; at least, so my cashier tells me."

"He has told you rightly. The house of Thomson & French had 300,000 or 400,000 francs to pay this month in France; and, knowing your strict punctuality, have collected all the bills bearing your signature, and charged me as they became due to present them, and to employ the money otherwise." Morrel sighed deeply, and passed his hand over his forehead, which was covered with perspiration.

"So then, sir," said Morrel, "you hold bills of mine?"

"Yes, and for a considerable sum."—"What is the amount?" asked Morrel with a voice he strove to render firm.

"Here is," said the Englishman, taking a quantity of papers from his pocket, "an assignment of 200,000 francs to our house by M. de Boville, the inspector of prisons, to whom they are due. You acknowledge, of course, that you owe this sum to him?"

"Yes; he placed the money in my hands at four and a half per cent nearly five years ago."—"When are you to pay?"

"Half the 15th of this month, half the 15th of next."

"Just so; and now here are 32,500 francs payable shortly; they are all signed by you, and assigned to our house by the holders."

"I recognize them," said Morrel, whose face was suffused, as he thought that, for the first time in his life, he would be unable to honor his own signature. "Is this all?"—"No, I have for the end of the month these bills which have been assigned to us by the house of Pascal, and the house of Wild & Turner of Marseilles, amounting to nearly 55,000 francs; in all, 287,500 francs." It is impossible to describe what Morrel suffered during this enumeration. "Two hundred and eighty-seven thousand five hundred francs," repeated he.—"Yes, sir," replied the Englishman. "I will not," continued he, after a moment's silence, "conceal from you, that while your probity and exactitude up to this moment are universally acknowledged, yet the report is current in Marseilles that you are not able to meet your liabilities." At this almost brutal speech Morrel turned deathly pale. "Sir," said he, "up to this time—and it is now more than four and twenty years since I received the direction of this house from my father, who had himself conducted it for five and thirty years—never has anything bearing the signature of Morrel & Son been dishonored."

"I know that," replied the Englishman. "But as a man of honor should answer another, tell me fairly, shall you pay these with the same punctuality?" Morrel shuddered, and looked at the man, who spoke with more assurance than he had hitherto shown. "To questions frankly put," said he, "a straightforward answer should be given. Yes, I shall pay, if, as I hope, my vessel arrives safely; for its arrival will again procure me the credit which the numerous accidents, of which I have been the victim, have deprived me; but if the *Pharaon* should be lost, and this last resource be gone"—the poor man's eyes filled with tears.—"Well," said the other "if this last resource fail you?"—"Well," returned Morrel, "it is a cruel thing to be forced to say, but, already used to misfortune, I must habituate myself to shame. I fear I shall be forced to suspend payment."

"Have you no friends who could assist you?" Morrel smiled mournfully. "In business, sir," said he, "one has no friends, only correspondents."—"It is true," murmured the Englishman; "then you have but one hope."

"But one."—"The last?"

"The last."—"So that if this fail"—

"I am ruined,—completely ruined!"

"As I was on my way here, a vessel was coming into port."—"I know it, sir; a young man, who still adheres to my fallen fortunes, passes a part of his time in a belvidere at the top of the house, in hopes of being the first to announce good news to me; he has informed me of the arrival of this ship."

"And it is not yours?"—"No, she is a Bordeaux vessel, *La Gironde*; she comes from India also; but she is not mine."

"Perhaps she has spoken the *Pharaon*, and brings you some tidings of her?"

"Shall I tell you plainly one thing, sir? I dread almost as much to receive any tidings of my vessel as to remain in doubt. Uncertainty is still hope." Then in a low voice Morrel added,—"This delay is not natural. The *Pharaon* left Calcutta the 5th February; she ought to have been here a month ago."—"What is that?" said the Englishman. "What is the meaning of that noise?"

"Oh, oh!" cried Morrel, turning pale, "what is it?" A loud noise was heard on the stairs of people moving hastily, and half-stifled sobs. Morrel rose and advanced to the door; but his strength failed him and he sank into a chair. The two men remained opposite one another, Morrel trembling in every limb, the stranger gazing at him with an air of profound pity. The noise had ceased; but it seemed that Morrel expected something—something had occasioned the noise, and something must follow. The stranger fancied he heard footsteps on the stairs; and that the footsteps, which were those of several persons, stopped at the door. A key was inserted in the lock of the first door, and the creaking of hinges was audible.

"There are only two persons who have the key to that door," murmured Morrel, "Coclès and Julie." At this instant the second door opened, and the young girl, her eyes bathed with tears, appeared. Morrel rose tremblingly, supporting himself by the arm of the chair. He would have spoken, but his voice failed him. "Oh, father!" said she, clasping her hands, "forgive your child for being the bearer of evil tidings."

Morrel again changed color. Julie threw herself into his arms.

"Oh, father, father!" murmured she, "courage!"—"The *Pharaon* has gone down, then?" said Morrel in a hoarse voice. The young girl did not speak; but she made an affirmative sign with her head as she lay on her father's breast.

"And the crew?" asked Morrel.—"Saved," said the girl; "saved by the crew of the vessel that has just entered the harbor." Morrel raised his two hands to heaven with an expression of resignation and sublime gratitude. "Thanks, my God," said he, "at least thou strikest but me alone." A tear moistened the eye of the phlegmatic Englishman.

"Come in, come in," said Morrel, "for I presume you are all at the door."

Scarcely had he uttered those words than Madame Morrel entered weeping bitterly, Emmanuel followed her, and in the antechamber were visible the rough faces of seven or eight half-naked sailors. At the sight of these men the Englishman started and advanced a step; then restrained himself, and retired into the farthest and most obscure corner of the apartment. Madame Morrel sat down by her husband and took one of his hands in hers, Julie still lay with her head on his shoulder, Emmanuel stood in the centre of the chamber and seemed to form the link between Morrel's family and the sailors at the door.

"How did this happen?" said Morrel.

"Draw nearer, Penelon," said the young man, "and tell us all about it."

An old seaman, bronzed by the tropical sun, advanced, twirling the remains of a tarpaulin between his hands. "Goodday, M. Morrel," said he, as if he had just quitted Marseilles the previous evening, and had just returned from Aix or Toulon.

"Good-day, Penelon," returned Morrel, who could not refrain from smiling through his tears, "where is the captain?"—"The captain, M. Morrel,—he has stayed behind sick at Palma; but please God, it won't be much, and you will see him in a few days all alive and hearty."

"Well, now tell your story, Penelon."

Penelon rolled his quid in his cheek, placed his hand before his mouth, turned his head, and sent a long jet of tobacco-juice into the antechamber, advanced his foot, balanced himself, and began,— "You see, M. Morrel," said he, "we were somewhere between Cape Blanc and Cape Boyador, sailing with a fair breeze, south-south-west after a week's calm, when Captain Gaumard comes up to me—I was at the helm I should tell you—and says, 'Penelon, what do you think of those clouds coming up over there?' I was just then looking at them myself. 'What do I think, captain? Why I think that they are rising faster than they have any business to do, and that they would not be so black if they didn't mean mischief.'—'That's my opinion too,' said the captain, 'and I'll take precautions accordingly. We are carrying too much canvas. Avast, there, all hands! Take in the studding-sl's and stow the flying jib.' It was time; the squall was on us, and the vessel began to heel. 'Ah,' said the captain, 'we have still too much canvas set; all hands lower the mains'll!' Five minutes after, it was down; and we sailed under mizzen-tops'ls and to'gall'nt sails. 'Well, Penelon,' said the captain, 'what makes you shake your head?''Why,' I says,'I still think you've got too much on.' 'I think you're right,' answered he, 'we shall have a gale.' 'A gale? More than that, we shall have a tempest, or I don't know what's what.'You could see the wind coming like the dust at Montredon; luckily the captain understood his business. 'Take in two reefs in the tops'ls,' cried the captain; 'let go the bowlin's, haul the brace, lower the to'gall'nt sails, haul out the reef-tackles on the yards.'"

"That was not enough for those latitudes," said the Englishman; "I should have taken four reefs in the topsails and furled the spanker."

His firm, sonorous, and unexpected voice made every one start. Penelon put his hand over his eyes, and then stared at the man who thus criticized the manœuvres of his captain. "We did better than that, sir," said the old sailor respectfully; "we put the helm up to run before the tempest; ten minutes after we struck our tops'ls and scudded under bare poles."

"The vessel was very old to risk that," said the Englishman.

"Eh, it was that that did the business; after pitching heavily for twelve hours we sprung a leak. 'Penelon,' said the captain, 'I think we are sinking, give me the helm, and go down into the hold.' I gave him the helm, and descended; there was already three feet of water. 'All hands to the pumps!' I shouted; but it was too late, and it seemed the more we pumped the more came in. 'Ah,' said I, after four hours' work, 'since we are sinking, let us sink; we can die but once.' 'That's the example you set, Penclon,' cries the captain; 'very well, wait a minute.' He went into his cabin and came back with a brace of pistols. 'I will blow the brains out of the first man who leaves the pump,' said he."—"Well done!" said the Englishman.

"There's nothing gives you so much courage as good reasons," continued the sailor; "and during that time the wind had abated, and the sea gone down, but the water kept rising; not much, only two inches an hour, but still it rose. Two inches an hour does not seem much, but in twelve hours that makes two feet, and three we had before, that makes five. 'Come,' said the captain, 'we have done all in our power, and M. Morrel will have nothing to reproach us with; we have tried to save the ship, let us now save ourselves. To the boats, my lads, as quick as you can.' Now," continued Penclon, "you see, M. Morrel, a sailor is attached to his ship, but still more to his life, so we did not wait to be told twice; the more so, that the ship was sinking under us, and seemed to say, 'Get along—save yourselves.' We soon launched the boat, and all eight of us got into it. The captain descended last, or rather, he did not descend, he would not quit the vessel; so I took him round the waist, and threw him into the boat, and then I jumped after him. It was time, for just as I jumped the deck burst with a noise like the broadside of a man-of-war. Ten minutes after she pitched for'ard, then the other way, spun round and round, and then good-by to the *Pharaon*. As for us, we were three days without anything to eat or drink, so that we began to think of drawing lots who should feed the rest, when we saw *La Gironde*; we made signals of distress, she perceived us, made for us, and took us all on board. There now, M. Morrel, that's the whole truth, on the honor of a sailor; is not it true, you fellows there?" A general murmur of approbation showed that the narrator had faithfully detailed their misfortunes and sufferings.

"Well, well," said M. Morrel, "I know there was no one in fault but destiny. It was the will of God that this should happen, blessed be his name. What wages are due to you?"

"Oh, don't let us talk of that, M. Morrel."

"Yes, but we will talk of it."

"Well, then, three months," said Penelon.

"Coelès, pay two hundred francs to each of these good fellows." said Morrel. "At another time," added he, "I should have said, Give them, besides, two hundred francs over as a present; but times are changed, and the little money that remains to me is not my own."

Penelon turned to his companions, and exchanged a few words with them.

"As for that, M. Morrel," said he, again turning his quid, "as for that"—

"As for what?"—"The money."—"Well"—

"Well, we all say that fifty francs will be enough for us at present, and that we will wait for the rest."—"Thanks, my friends, thanks!" cried Morrel gratefully; "take it—take it; and if you can find another employer, enter his service; you are free to do so." These last words produced a prodigious effect on the seaman. Penelon nearly swallowed his quid; fortunately he recovered. "What, M. Morrel!" said he in a low voice, "you send us away; you are then angry with us!"

"No, no," said M. Morrel, "I am not angry, quite the contrary, and I do not send you away; but I have no more ships, and therefore I do not want any sailors."—"No more ships!" returned Penelon; "well, then, you'll build some; we'll wait for you."

"I have no money to build ships with, Penelon," said the poor owner mournfully, "so I cannot accept your kind offer."—"No more money? Then you must not pay us; we can send, like the *Pharaon*, under bare poles."

"Enough, enough!" cried Morrel, almost overpowered; "leave me, I pray you; we shall meet again in a happier time. Emmanuel, go with them, and see that my orders are executed."—"At least, we shall see each other again, M. Morrel?" asked Penelon.

"Yes; I hope so, at least. Now go." He made a sign to Coclès, who went first; the seamen followed him, and Emmanuel brought up the rear. "Now," said the owner to his wife and daughter, "leave me; I wish to speak with this gentleman." And he glanced towards the clerk of Thomson & French, who had remained motionless in the corner during this scene, in which he had taken no part, except the few words we have mentioned. The two women looked at this person whose presence they had entirely forgotten, and retired; but, as she left the apartment, Julie gave the stranger a supplicating glance, to which he replied by a smile that an indifferent spectator would have been surprised to see on his stern features. The two men were left alone. "Well, sir," said Morrel, sinking into a chair, "you have heard all, and I have nothing further to tell you."

"I see," returned the Englishman, "that a fresh and unmerited misfortune has overwhelmed you, and this only increases my desire to serve you."—"Oh, sir!" cried Morrel.

"Let me see," continued the stranger, "I am one of your largest creditors."—"Your bills, at least, are the first that will fall due."

"Do you wish for time to pay?"

"A delay would save my honor, and consequently my life."

"How long a delay do you wish for?"—Morrel reflected. "Two months," said he.

"I will give you three," replied the stranger.

"But," asked Morrel, "will the house of Thomson & French consent?"

"Oh, I take everything on myself. To-day is the 5th of June."—"Yes."

"Well, renew these bills up to the 5th of September; and on the 5th of September at eleven o'clock (the hand of the clock pointed to eleven), I shall come to receive the money."—"I shall expect you," returned Morrel; "and I will pay you—or I shall be dead." These last words were uttered in so low a tone that the stranger could not hear them. The bills were renewed, the old ones destroyed, and the poor shipowner found himself with three months before him to collect his resources. The Englishman received his thanks with the phlegm peculiar to his nation; and Morrel, overwhelming him with grateful blessings, conducted him to the staircase. The stranger met Julie on the stairs; she pretended to be descending, but in reality she was waiting for him. "Oh, sir"—said she, clasping her hands.

"Mademoiselle," said the stranger, "one day you will receive a letter signed 'Sinbad the Sailor.' Do exactly what the letter bids you, however strange it may appear,"—"Yes, sir," returned Julie.

"Do you promise?"—"I swear to you I will."

"It is well. Adieu, mademoiselle. Continue to be the good, sweet girl you are at present, and I have great hopes that heaven will reward you by giving you Emmanuel for a husband."

Julie uttered a faint cry, blushed like a rose, and leaned against the baluster. The stranger waved his hand, and continued to descend. In the court he found Penelon, who, with a rouleau of a hundred francs in either hand, seemed unable to make up his mind to retain them. "Come with me, my friend," said the Englishman; "I wish to speak to you."

XXX

The Fifth of September

THE EXTENSION PROVIDED FOR by the agent of Thomson & French, at the moment when Morrel expected it least, was to the poor shipowner so decided a stroke of good fortune that he almost dared to believe that fate was at length grown weary of wasting her spite upon him. The same day he told his wife, Emmanuel, and his daughter all that had occurred; and a ray of hope, if not of tranquillity, returned to the family. Unfortunately, however, Morrel had not only engagements with the house of Thomson & French, who had shown themselves so considerate towards him; and, as he had said, in business he had correspondents, and not friends. When he thought the matter over, he could by no means account for this generous conduct on the part of Thomson & French towards him; and could only attribute it to some such selfish argument as this:—'We had better help a man who owes us nearly 300,000 francs, and have those 300,000 francs at the end of three months than hasten his ruin, and get only six or eight per cent of our money back again." Unfortunately, whether through envy or stupidity, all Morrel's correspondents did not take this view; and some even came to a contrary decision. The bills signed by Morrel were presented at his office with scrupulous exactitude, and, thanks to the delay granted by the Englishman, were paid by Coclès with equal punctuality. Coclès thus remained in his accustomed tranquility. It was Morrel alone who remembered with alarm, that if he had to repay on the 15th the 50,000 francs of M. de Boville, and on the 30th the 32,500 francs of bills, for which, as well as the debt due to the inspector of prisons, he had time granted, he must be a ruined man.

The opinion of all the commercial men was that, under the reverses which had successively weighed down Morrel, it was impossible for him to remain solvent. Great therefore, was the astonishment when at the end of the month, he cancelled all his obligations with his usual punctuality. Still confidence was not restored to all minds, and the general opinion was that the complete ruin of the unfortunate shipowner had been postponed only until the end of the month. The month passed, and Morrel made extraordinary efforts to get in all his resources. Formerly his paper, at any date, was taken with confidence, and was even in request. Morrel now tried to negotiate bills at ninety days only, and none of the banks would give him credit. Fortunately, Morrel had some funds coming in on which he could rely; and, as they reached him, he found himself in a condition to meet his engagements when the end of July came. The agent of Thomson & French had not been again seen at Marseilles; the day after, or two days after his visit to Morrel, he had disappeared; and as in that city he had had no intercourse but with the mayor, the inspector of prisons, and M. Morrel, his departure left no trace except in the memories of these three persons. As to the sailors of the *Pharaon*, they must have found snug berths elsewhere, for they also had disappeared.

Captain Ganmard, recovered from his illness, had returned from Palma. He delayed presenting himself at Morrel's, but the owner, hearing of his arrival, went to see him. The worthy shipowner knew, from Penelon's recital, of the captain's brave conduct during the storm, and tried to console him. He brought him also the amount of his wages, which Captain Gaumard had not dared to apply for. As he descended the staircase, Morrel met Penelon, who was going up. Penelon had, it would seem, made good use of his money, for he was newly clad. When he saw his employer, the worthy tar seemed much embarrassed, drew on one side into the corner of the landing-place, passed his quid from one cheek to the other, stared stupidly with his great eyes, and only acknowledged the squeeze of the hand which Morrel as usual gave him by a slight pressure in return. Morrel attributed Penelon's embarrassment to the elegance of his attire; it was evident the good fellow had not gone to such an expense on his own account; he was, no doubt, engaged on board some other vessel, and thus his bashfulness arose from the fact of his not having, if we may so express ourselves, worn mourning for the *Pharaon* longer. Perhaps he had come to tell Captain Gaumard of his good luck, and to offer him employment from his new master. "Worthy fellows!" said Morrel, as he went away, "may your new master love you as I loved you, and be more fortunate than I have been!"

August rolled by in unceasing efforts on the part of Morrel to renew his credit or revive the old. On the 20th of August it was known at Marseilles that he had left town in the mailcoach, and then it was said that the bills would go to protest at the end of the month, and that Morrel had gone away and left his chief clerk Emmanuel, and his cashier Coclès, to meet the creditors. But, contrary to all expectation, when the 31st of August came, the house opened as usual, and Coclès appeared behind the grating of the counter, examined all bills presented with the usual scrutiny, and, from first to last, paid all with the usual precision. There came in, moreover, two drafts which M. Morrel had fully anticipated, and which Coclès paid as punctually as the bills which the shipowner had accepted. All this was incomprehensible, and then, with the tenacity peculiar to prophets of bad news, the failure was put off until the end of September. On the 1st, Morrel returned; he was awaited by his family with extreme anxiety, for from this journey to Paris they hoped great things. Morrel had thought of Danglars, who was now immensely rich, and had lain under great obligations to Morrel in former days, since to him it was owing that Danglars entered the service of the Spanish banker, with whom he had laid the foundations of his vast wealth. It was said at this moment that Danglars was worth from six to eight millions of francs, and had unlimited credit. Danglars, then, without taking a crown from his pocket, could save Morrel; he had but to pass his word for a loan, and Morrel was saved. Morrel had long thought of Danglars, but had kept away from some instinctive motive, and had delayed as long as possible availing himself of this last resource. And Morrel was right, for he returned home crushed by the humiliation of a refusal. Yet, on his arrival, Morrel did not utter a complaint, or say one harsh word. He embraced his weeping wife and daughter, pressed Emmanuel's hand with friendly warmth, and then going to his private room on the second floor had sent for Coclès. "Then," said the two women to Emmanuel, "we are indeed ruined."

It was agreed in a brief council held among them, that Julie should write to her brother, who was in garrison at Nimes, to come to them as speedily as possible. The poor women felt instinctively that they required all their strength to support the blow that impended. Besides, Maximilian Morrel, though hardly two and twenty, had great influence over his father. He was a strong-minded, upright young man. At the time when he decided on his profession his father had no desire to choose for him, but had consulted young Maximilian's taste. He had at once declared for a military life, and had in consequence studied hard, passed brilliantly through the Polytechnic School, and left it as sub-lieutenant of the 53d of the line. For a year he had held this rank, and expected promotion on the first vacancy. In his regiment Maximilian Morrel was noted for his rigid observance, not only of the obligations imposed on a soldier, but also of the duties of a man; and he thus gained the name of "the stoic." We need hardly say that many of those who gave him this epithet repeated it because they had heard it, and did not even know what it meant. This was the young man whom his mother and sister called to their aid to sustain them under the serious trial which they felt they would soon have to endure. They had not mistaken the gravity of this event, for the moment after Morrel had entered his private office with Coclès, Julie saw the latter leave it pale, trembling, and his features betraying the utmost consternation. She would have questioned him as he passed by her, but the worthy creature hastened down the staircase with unusual precipitation, and only raised his hands to heaven and exclaimed, "Oh, mademoiselle, mademoiselle, what a dreadful misfortune! Who could ever have believed it!" A moment afterwards Julie saw him go up-stairs carrying two or three heavy ledgers, a portfolio, and a bag of money.

Morrel examined the ledgers, opened the portfolio, and counted the money. All his funds amounted to 6,000, or 8,000 francs, his bills receivable up to the 5th to 4,000 or 5,000, which, making the best of everything gave him 14,000 francs to meet debts amounting to 287,500 francs. He had not even the means for making a possible settlement on account. However, when Morrel went down to his dinner, he appeared very calm. This calmness was more alarming to the two women than the deepest dejection would have been. After dinner Morrel usually went out, and used to take his coffee at the Phocæan club, and read the *Semaphore*; this day he did not leave the house, but returned to his office.

As to Coclès, he seemed completely bewildered. For part of the day he went into the court-yard, seated himself on a stone with his head bare and exposed to the blazing sun. Emmanuel tried to comfort the women, but his eloquence faltered. The young man was too well acquainted with the business of the house, not to feel that a great catastrophe hung over the Morrel family. Night came, the two women had watched, hoping that when he left his room Morrel would come to them, but they heard him pass before their door, and trying to conceal the noise of his footsteps. They listened; he went into his sleeping-room, and fastened the door inside. Madame Morrel sent her daughter to bed, and half an hour after Julie had retired, she rose, took off her shoes, and went stealthily along the passage, to see through the keyhole what her husband was doing. In the passage she saw a retreating shadow; it was Julie, who, uneasy herself, had anticipated her mother. The young lady went towards Madame Morrel—"He is writing," she said. They had understood each other without speaking. Madame Morrel looked again through the keyhole, Morrel was writing; but Madame Morrel remarked, what her daughter had not observed, that her husband was writing on stamped paper. The terrible idea that he was writing his will flashed across her; she shuddered, and yet had not strength to utter a word. Next day M. Morrel seemed as calm as ever, went into his office as usual, came to his breakfast punctually, and then, after dinner, he placed his daughter beside him, took her head in his arms, and held her for a long time against his bosom. In the evening, Julie told her mother, that although he was apparently so calm, she had noticed that her father's heart beat violently. The next two days passed in much the same way. On the evening of the 4th of September, M. Morrel asked his daughter for the key of his study. Julie trembled at this request, which seemed to her of bad omen. Why did her father ask for this key which she always kept, and which was only taken from her in childhood as a punishment? The young girl looked at Morrel.

"What have I done wrong, father," she said, "that you should take this key from me?"—"Nothing, my dear," replied the unhappy man, the tears starting to his eyes at this simple question,—"nothing, only I want it." Julie made a pretence to feel for the key. "I must have left it in my room," she said. And she went out, but instead of going to her apartment she hastened to consult Emmanuel. "Do not give this key to your father," said he, "and to-morrow morning, if possible, do not quit him for a moment." She questioned Emmanuel, but he knew nothing, or would not say what he knew. During the night,

between the 4th and 5th of September, Madame Morrel remained
listening for every sound, and, until three o'clock in the morning, she
heard her husband pacing the room in great agitation. It was three
o'clock when he threw himself on the bed. The mother and daughter passed the night together. They had expected Maximilian since
the previous evening. At eight o'clock in the morning Morrel
entered their chamber. He was calm; but the agitation of the night
was legible in his pale and careworn visage. They did not dare to ask
him how he had slept. Morrel was kinder to his wife, more affectionate to his daughter, than he had ever been. He could not cease
gazing at and kissing the sweet girl. Julie, mindful of Emmanuel's
request, was following her father when he quitted the room, but he
said to her quickly,—"Remain with your mother, dearest." Julie
wished to accompany him. "I wish you to do so," said he.

This was the first time Morrel had ever so spoken, but he said
it in a tone of paternal kindness, and Julie did not dare to disobey.
She remained at the same spot standing mute and motionless. An
instant afterwards the door opened, she felt two arms encircle her,
and a mouth pressed her forehead. She looked up and uttered an
exclamation of joy.

"Maximilian, my dearest brother!" she cried. At these words
Madame Morrel rose, and threw herself into her son's arms.
"Mother," said the young man, looking alternately at Madame
Morrel and her daughter, "what has occurred—what has hap-
pened? Your letter has frightened me, and I have come hither with
all speed."

"Julie," said Madame Morrel, making a sign to the young man,
"go and tell your father that Maximilian has just arrived." The
young lady rushed out of the apartment, but on the first step of the
staircase she found a man holding a letter in his hand.

"Are you not Mademoiselle Julie Morrel?" inquired the man,
with a strong Italian accent.

"Yes, sir," replied Julie with hesitation; "what is your pleasure? I do not know you."—"Read this letter," he said, handing it to her. Julie hesitated. "It concerns the best interests of your father," said the messenger.

The young girl hastily took the letter from him. She opened it quickly and read:—

"Go this moment to the Allécs de Mcillan, enter the house No. 15, ask the porter for the key of the room on the fifth floor, enter the apartment, take from the corner of the mantelpiece a purse netted in red silk, and give it to your father. It is important that he should receive it before eleven o'clock. You promised to obey me implicitly. Remember your oath.

"SINBAD THE SAILOR."

The young girl uttered a joyful cry, raised her eyes, looked round to question the messenger, but he had disappeared. She cast her eyes again over the note to peruse it a second time, and saw there was a postscript. She read:—

"It is important that you should fulfil this mission in person and alone. If you go accompanied by any other person, or should any one else go in your place, the porter will reply that he does not know anything about it."

This postscript decreased greatly the young girl's happiness. Was there nothing to fear? was there not some snare laid for her? Her innocence had kept her in ignorance of the dangers that might assail a young girl of her age. But there is no need to know danger in order to fear it; indeed, it may be observed, that it is usually unknown perils that inspire the greatest terror.

Julie hesitated, and resolved to take counsel. Yet, through a singular impulse, it was neither to her mother nor her brother that she applied, but to Emmanuel. She hastened down and told him what had occurred on the day when the agent of Thomson & French had come to her father's, related the scene on the staircase, repeated the promise she had made, and showed him the letter. "You must go, then, mademoiselle," said Emmanuel.

"Go there?" murmured Julie.

"Yes; I will accompany you."

"But did you not read that I must be alone?" said Julie.

"And you shall be alone," replied the young man. "I will await you at the corner of the Rue de Musée, and if you are so long absent as to make me uneasy, I will hasten to rejoin you, and woe to him of whom you shall have cause to complain to me!"

"Then, Emmanuel," said the young girl with hesitation. "it is your opinion that I should obey this invitation?"—"Yes. Did not the messenger say your father's safety depended upon it?"

"But what danger threatens him, then, Emmanuel?" she asked.

Emmanuel hesitated a moment, but his desire to make Julie decide immediately made him reply.

"Listen," he said; "to-day is the 5th of September, is it not?"

"Yes."—"To-day, then, at eleven o'clock, your father has nearly three hundred thousand francs to pay?"

"Yes, we know that."—"Well, then," continued Emmanuel, "we have not fifteen thousand francs in the house."

"What will happen then?"—"Why, if to-day before eleven o'clock your father has not found some one who will come to his aid, he will be compelled at twelve o'clock to declare himself a bankrupt."

"Oh, come, then, come!" cried she, hastening away with the young man. During this time, Madame Morrel had told her son everything. The young man knew quite well that, after the succession of misfortunes which had befallen his father, great changes had taken place in the style of living and housekeeping; but he did not know that matters had reached such a point. He was thunderstruck. Then, rushing hastily out of the apartment, he ran up-stairs, expecting to find his father in his study, but he rapped there in vain. While he was yet at the door of the study he heard the bedroom door open, turned, and saw his father. Instead of going direct to his study, M. Morrel had returned to his bedchamber, which he was only this moment quitting. Morrel uttered a cry of surprise at the sight of his son, of whose arrival he was ignorant. He remained motionless on the spot, pressing with his left hand something he had concealed under his coat. Maximilian sprang down the staircase, and threw his arms round his father's neck; but suddenly he recoiled, and placed his right hand on Morrel's breast. "Father." he exclaimed, turning pale as death, "what are you going to do with that brace of pistols under your coat?"

"Oh, this is what I feared!" said Morrel.

"Father, father, in heaven's name," exclaimed the young man, "what are these weapons for?"—"Maximilian," replied Morrel, looking fixedly at his son, "you are a man, and a man of honor. Come, and I will explain to you."

And with a firm step Morrel went up to his study, while Maximilian followed him, trembling as he went. Morrel opened the door, and closed it behind his son; then, crossing the anteroom, went to his desk on which he placed the pistols, and pointed with his finger to an open ledger. In this ledger was made out an exact balance-sheet of his affairs. Morrel had to pay, within half an hour, 287,500 francs. All he possessed was 15,257 francs. "Read!" said Morrel.

The young man was overwhelmed as he read. Morrel said not a word. What could he say? What need he add to such a desperate proof in figures? "And have you done all that is possible, father, to meet this disastrous result?" asked the young man, after a moment's panse. "I have," replied Morrel.

"You have no money coming in on which you can rely?"—"None."

"You have exhausted every resource?"—"All."

"And in half an hour," said Maximilian in a gloomy voice, "our name is dishonored!"—"Blood washes out dishonor," said Morrel.

"You are right, father; I understand you." Then extending his hand towards one of the pistols, he said, "There is one for you and

one for me—thanks!" Morrel caught his hand. "Your mother—
your sister! Who will support them?" A shudder ran through the
young man's frame. "Father," he said, "do you reflect that you are
bidding me to live?"—"Yes, I do so bid you," answered Morrel; "it
is your duty. You have a calm, strong mind, Maximilian. Maximilian, you are no ordinary man. I make no requests or commands; I
only ask you to examine my position as if it were your own, and
then judge for yourself."

The young man reflected for a moment, then an expression of
sublime resignation appeared in his eyes, and with a slow and sad
gesture he took off his two epaulets, the insignia of his rank. "Be it
so, then, my father," he said, extending his hand to Morrel, "die in
peace, my father; I will live." Morrel was about to cast himself on
his knees before his son, but Maximilian caught him in his arms,
and those two noble hearts were pressed against each other for a
moment. "You know it is not my fault," said Morrel. Maximilian
smiled. "I know, father, you are the most honorable man I have ever
known."—"Good, my son. And now there is no more to be said;
go and rejoin your mother and sister."

"My father," said the young man, bending his knee, "bless me!"
Morrel took the head of his son between his two hands, drew him
forward, and kissing his forehead several times, said, "Oh, yes, yes, I
bless you in my own name, and in the name of three generations of
irreproachable men, who say through me, 'The edifice which misfortune has destroyed, providence may build up again.' On seeing
me die such a death, the most inexorable will have pity on you. To
you, perhaps, they will accord the time they have refused to me.
Then do your best to keep our name free from dishonor. Go to
work, labor, young man, struggle ardently and courageously; live,
yourself, your mother and sister, with the most rigid economy, so
that from day to day the property of those whom I leave in your
hands may augment and fructify. Reflect how glorious a day it will
be, how grand, how solemn, that day of complete restoration, on

which you will say in this very office, 'My father died because he could not do what I have this day done; but he died calmly and peaceably, because in dying he knew what I should do.'"

"My father, my father!" cried the young man, "why should you not live?"—"If I live, all would be changed; if I live, interest would be converted into doubt, pity into hostility; if I live. I am only a man who has broken his word, failed in his engagements—in fact, only a bankrupt. If, on the contrary, I die, remember, Maximilian, my corpse is that of an honest but unfortunate man. Living, my best friends would avoid my house; dead, all Marseilles will follow me in tears to my last home. Living, you would feel shame at my name; dead, you may raise your head and say, 'I am the son of him you killed, because, for the first time, he has been compelled to break his word.'"

The young man uttered a groan, but appeared resigned.

"And now," said Morrel, "leave me alone, and endeavor to keep your mother and sister away."—"Will you not see my sister once more?" asked Maximilian. A last but final hope was concealed by the young man in the effect of this interview, and therefore he had suggested it. Morrel shook his head. "I saw her this morning, and bade her adieu."

"Have you no particular commands to leave with me, my father?" inquired Maximilian in a faltering voice.

"Yes, my son, and a sacred command."—"Say it, my father."

"The house of Thomson & French is the only one who, from humanity, or, it may be, selfishness—it is not for me to read men's hearts—has had any pity for me. Its agent, who will in ten minutes present himself to receive the amount of a bill of 287,500 francs, I will not say granted, but offered me three months. Let this house be the first repaid, my son, and respect this man."—"Father, I will," said Maximilian.

"And now, once more, adieu," said Morrel. "Go, leave me; I would be alone. You will find my will in the secretary in my bedroom."

The young man remained standing and motionless, having but the force of will and not the power of execution.

"Hear me, Maximilian," said his father. "Suppose I was a soldier like you, and ordered to carry a certain redoubt, and you knew I must be killed in the assault, would you not say to me, as you said just now, 'Go, father; for you are dishonored by delay, and death is preferable to shame!'"

"Yes, yes!" said the young man, "yes;" and once again embracing his father with convulsive pressure, he said, "Be it so, my father."

And he rushed out of the study. When his son had left him, Morrel remained an instant standing with his eyes fixed on the door; then putting forth his arm, he pulled the bell. After a moment's interval, Coclès appeared.

It was no longer the same man—the fearful revelations of the three last days had crushed him. This thought—the house of Morrel is about to stop payment—bent him to the earth more than twenty years would otherwise have done.

"My worthy Coclès," said Morrel in a tone impossible to describe, "do you remain in the antechamber. When the gentleman who came three months ago—the agent of Thomson & French—arrives, announce his arrival to me." Coclès made no reply; he made a sign with his head, went into the anteroom, and seated himself. Morrel fell back in his chair, his eyes fixed on the clock; there were seven minutes left, that was all. The hand moved on with incredible rapidity; he seemed to see its motion.

What passed in the mind of this man at the supreme moment of his agony cannot be told in words. He was still comparatively young, he was surrounded by the loving care of a devoted family, but he had convinced himself by a course of reasoning, illogical perhaps, yet certainly plausible, that he must separate himself from all he held dear in the world, even life itself. To form the slightest idea of his feelings, one must have seen his face with its expression of enforced resignation, and its tear-moistened eyes raised to heaven. The minute hand moved on. The pistols were loaded; he stretched forth his hand, took one up, and murmured his daughter's name. Then he laid it down, seized his pen, and wrote a few words. It seemed to him as if he had not taken a sufficient farewell of his beloved daughter. Then he turned again to the clock, counting time now not by minutes, but by seconds. He took up the deadly weapon again, his lips parted and his eyes fixed on the clock, and then shuddered at the click of the trigger as he cocked the pistol. At this moment of mortal anguish the cold sweat came forth upon his brow, a pang stronger than death clutched at his heart strings. He heard the door of the staircase creak on its hinges—the clock gave its warning to strike eleven—the door of his study opened; Morrel did not turn round—he expected these words of Coclès, "The agent of Thomson & French."

He placed the muzzle of the pistol between his teeth. Suddenly he heard a cry—it was his daughter's voice. He turned and saw Julie. The pistol fell from his hands. "My father!" cried the young girl, out of breath, and half dead with joy—"saved, you are saved!" And she threw herself into his arms, holding in her extended hand a red, netted silk purse.

"Saved, my child!" said Morrel; "what do you mean?"

"Yes, saved—saved! See, see!" said the young girl.

Morrel took the purse, and started as he did so, for a vague remembrance reminded him that it once belonged to himself. At one end was the receipted bill for the 287,500 francs, and at the other was a diamond as large as a hazel-nut, with these words on a small slip of parchment:—*Julie's Dowry.*

Morrel passed his hand over his brows; it seemed to him a dream. At this moment the clock struck eleven. He felt as if each stroke of the hammer fell upon his heart. "Explain, my child," he said, "explain—where did you find this purse?"

"In a house in the Allées de Meillan, No. 15, on the corner of a mantelpiece in a small room on the fifth floor."

"But," cried Morrel, "this purse is not yours!" Julie handed to her father the letter she had received in the morning.

"And did you go alone?" asked Morrel, after he had read it.

"Emmanuel accompanied me, father. He was to have waited for me at the corner of the Rue de Musée, but, strange to say, he was not there when I returned."—"Monsieur Morrel!" exclaimed a voice on the stairs.—"Monsieur Morrel!"

"It is his voice!" said Julie. At this moment Emmanuel entered, his countenance full of animation and joy. "The *Pharaon!*" he cried; "the *Pharaon!*"

"What—what—the *Pharaon!* Are you mad, Emmanuel? You know the vessel is lost."—"The *Pharaon*, sir—they signal the *Pharaon!* The *Pharaon* is entering the harbor!" Morrel fell back in his chair, his strength was failing him; his understanding, weakened by such events, refused to comprehend such incredible, unheard of, fabulous facts. But his son came in. "Father," cried Maximilian, "how could you say the *Pharaon* was lost? The lookout has signalled her, and they say she is now coming into port."

"My dear friends," said Morrel, "if this be so, it must be a miracle of heaven! Impossible, impossible!"

But what was real and not less incredible was the purse he held in his hand, the acceptance receipted—the splendid diamond.

"Ah, sir," exclaimed Coclès, "what can it mean?—the *Pharaon?*"

"Come, dear ones," said Morrel, rising from his seat, "let us go and see, and heaven have pity upon us if it be false intelligence!" They all went out, and on the stairs met Madame Morrel, who had been afraid to go up into the study. In a moment they were at the Cannebière. There was a crowd on the pier. All the crowd gave way before Morrel. "The *Pharaon*, the *Pharaon!*" said every voice.

And, wonderful to see, in front of the tower of Saint-Jean, was a ship bearing on her stern these words, printed in white letters, "The *Pharaon*, Morrel & Son, of Marseilles." She was the exact duplicate of the other *Pharaon*, and loaded, as that had been, with cochineal and indigo. She cast anchor, clued up sails, and on the deck was Captain Gaumard giving orders, and good old Penelon making signals to M. Morrel. To doubt any longer was impossible; there was the evidence of the senses, and ten thousand persons who came to corroborate the testimony. As Morrel and his son embraced on the pier-head, in the presence and amid the applause of the whole city witnessing this event, a man, with his face half-covered by a black beard, and who, concealed behind the sentry-box, watched the scene with delight, uttered these words in a low tone: "Be happy, noble heart, be blessed for all the good thon hast done and wilt do hereafter, and let my gratitude remain in obscurity like your good deeds."

And with a smile expressive of supreme content, he left his hiding-place, and without being observed, descended one of the flights of steps provided for debarkation, and hailing three times, shouted "Jacopo, Jacopo, Jacopo!" Then a launch came to shore, took him on board, and conveyed him to a yacht splendidly fitted up, on whose deck he sprung with the activity of a sailor; thence he once again looked towards Morrel, who, weeping with joy, was shaking hands most cordially with all the crowd around him, and thanking with a look the unknown benefactor whom he seemed to be seeking in the skies. "And now," said the unknown, "farewell kindness, humanity, and gratitude! Farewell to all the feelings that expand the heart! I have been heaven's substitute to recompense the good—now the god of vengeance yields to me his power to punish the wicked!" At these words he gave a signal, and, as if only awaiting this signal, the yacht instantly put out to sea.

XXXI

Italy: Sinbad the Sailor

TOWARDS THE BEGINNING OF the year 1838, two young men belonging to the first society of Paris, the Vicomte Albert de Morcerf and the Baron Franz d'Epinay, were at Florence. They had agreed to see the Carnival at Rome that year, and that Franz, who for the last three or four years had inhabited Italy, should act as *cicerone* to Albert. As it is no inconsiderable affair to spend the Carnival at Rome, especially when you have no great desire to sleep on the Piazza del Popolo, or the Campo Vaccino, they wrote to Signor Pastrini, the proprietor of the Hotel de Londres, Piazza di Spagna, to reserve comfortable apartments for them. Signor Pastrini replied that he had only two rooms and a parlor on the third floor, which he offered at the low charge of a louis per diem. They accepted his offer; but wishing to make the best use of the time that was left, Albert started for Naples. As for Franz, he remained at Florence, and after having passed a few days in exploring the paradise of the Caseine, and spending two or three evenings at the houses of the Florentine nobility, he took a fancy into his head (having already visited Corsica, the cradle of Bonaparte) to visit Elba, the halting-place of Napoleon.

One evening he cast off the painter of a sailboat from the iron ring that secured it to the dock at Leghorn, wrapped himself in his

coat and lay down, and said to the crew,—"To the Island of Elba!"
The boat shot out of the harbor like a bird, and the next morning
Franz disembarked at Porto-Ferrajo. He traversed the island, after
having followed the traces which the footsteps of the giant have
left, and re-embarked for Marciana. Two hours after he again landed
at Pianosa, where he was assured that red partridges abounded. The
sport was had; Franz only succeeded in killing a few partridges, and,
like every unsuccessful sportsman, he returned to the boat very
much out of temper. "Ah, if your excellency chose," said the
captain, "you might have capital sport."

"Where?"

"Do you see that island?" continued the captain, pointing to a
conical pile rising from the indigo sea.

"Well, what is this island?"—"The Island of Monto Cristo."

"But I have no permission to shoot over this island."

"Your excellency does not require a permit, for the island is
uninhabited."—"Ah, indeed!" said the young man. "A desert island
in the midst of the Mediterranean must be a curiosity."

"It is very natural; this island is a mass of rocks, and does not
contain an acre of land capable of cultivation."

"To whom does this island belong?"—"To Tuscany."

"What game shall I find there?"—"Thousands of wild goats."

"Who live upon the stones, I suppose," said Franz with an
incredulous smile.

"No, but by browsing the shrubs and trees that grow out of the
crevices of the rocks."—"Where can I sleep?"

"On shore in the grottos, or on board in your cloak; besides, if
your excellency pleases, we can leave as soon as you like—we can sail
as well by night as by day, and if the wind drops we can use our oars."

As Franz had sufficient time, and his apartments at Rome were
not yet available, he accepted the proposition. Upon his answer in
the affirmative, the sailors exchanged a few words together in a low
tone. "Well," asked he, "what now? Is there any difficulty in the

way?"—"No," replied the captain, "but we must warn your excellency that the island is an infected port."

"What do you mean?"—"Monte Cristo, although uninhabited, yet serves occasionally as a refuge for the smugglers and pirates who come from Corsica, Sardinia, and Africa, and if it becomes known that we have been there, we shall have to perform quarantine for six days on our return to Leghorn."

"The deuce! That puts a different face on the matter. Six days! Why, that's as long as the Almighty took to make the world! Too long a wait—too long."

"But who will say your excellency has been to Monte Cristo?"

"Oh, I shall not," cried Franz.

"Nor I, nor I," chorused the sailors.

"Then steer for Monte Cristo."

The captain gave his orders, the helm was put up, and the boat was soon sailing in the direction of the island. Franz waited until all was in order, and when the sail was filled, and the four sailors had taken their places—three forward, and one at the helm—he resumed the conversation. "Gaetano," said he to the captain, "you tell me Monte Cristo serves as a refuge for pirates, who are, it seems to me, a very different kind of game from the goats."—"Yes, your excellency, and it is true."

"I knew there were smugglers, but I thought that since the capture of Algiers, and the destruction of the regency, pirates existed only in the romances of Cooper and Captain Marryat."

"Your excellency is mistaken; there are pirates, like the bandits who were believed to have been exterminated by Pope Leo XII., and who yet, every day, rob travellers at the gates of Rome. Has not your excellency heard that the French *chargé d'affaires* was robbed six months ago within five hundred paces of Velletri?"

"Oh, yes, I heard that."—"Well, then, if, like us, your excellency lived at Leghorn, you would hear, from time to time, that a little merchant vessel, or an English yacht that was expected at Bustia, at

Porto-Ferrajo, or at Civita Vecchia, has not arrived; no one knows what has become of it, but, doubtless, it has struck on a rock and foundered. Now this rock it has met has been a long and narrow boat, manned by six or eight men, who have surprised and plundered it, some dark and stormy night, near some desert and gloomy island, as bandits plunder a carriage in the recesses of a forest."

"But," asked Franz, who lay wrapped in his cloak at the bottom of the boat, "why do not those who have been plundered complain to the French, Sardinian, or Tuscan governments?"

"Why?" said Gaetano with a smile.

"Yes, why?"—"Because, in the first place, they transfer from the vessel to their own boat whatever they think worth taking, then they bind the crew hand and foot, they attach to every one's neck a four and twenty pound ball, a large hole is chopped in the vessel's bottom, and then they leave her. At the end of ten minutes the vessel begins to roll heavily and settle down. First one gun'l goes under, then the other. Then they lift and sink again, and both go under at once. All at once there's a noise like a cannon—that's the air blowing up the deck. Soon the water rushes out of the scupper-holes like a whale spouting, the vessel gives a last groan, spins round and round, and disappears, forming a vast whirlpool in the ocean, and then all is over, so that in five minutes nothing but the eye of God can see the vessel where she lies at the bottom of the sea. Do you understand now," said the captain, "why no complaints are made to the government, and why the vessel never reaches port?"

It is probable that if Gaetano had related this previous to proposing the expedition. Franz would have hesitated, but now that they had started, he thought it would be cowardly to draw back. He was one of those men who do not rashly court danger, but if danger presents itself, combat it with the most unalterable coolness. Calm and resolute, he treated any peril as he would an adversary in a duel,—calculated its probable method of approach; retreated, if at all, as a point of strategy and not from cowardice; was quick to see an opening for attack, and won victory at a single thrust. "Bah!" said he, "I have travelled through Sicily and Calabria—I have sailed two months in the Archipelago, and yet I never saw even the shadow of a bandit or a pirate."

"I did not tell your excellency this to deter you from your project," replied Gaetano, "but you questioned me, and I have answered; that's all."

"Yes, and your conversation is most interesting; and as I wish to enjoy it as long as possible, steer for Monte Cristo."

The wind blew strongly, the boat made six or seven knots an hour, and they were rapidly reaching the end of their voyage. As they drew near the island seemed to lift from the sea, and the air was so clear that they could already distinguish the rocks heaped on one another, like cannon balls in an arsenal, with green bushes and trees growing in the crevices. As for the sailors, although they appeared perfectly tranquil yet it was evident that they were on the alert, and that they carefully watched the glassy surface over which they were sailing, and on which a few fishing-boats, with their white sails, were alone visible. They were within fifteen miles of Monte Cristo when the sun began to set behind Corsica, whose mountains appeared against the sky, showing their rugged peaks in bold relief; this mass of rock, like the giant Adamastor, rose dead ahead, a formidable barrier, and intercepting the light that gilded its massive peaks so that the voyagers were in shadow. Little by little the shadow rose higher and seemed to drive before it the last rays of the expiring day; at last the reflection rested on the summit of the mountain, where it paused an instant, like the fiery crest of a volcano, then gloom gradually covered the summit as it had covered the base, and the island now only appeared to be a gray mountain that grew continually darker; half an hour after, the night was quite dark.

Fortunately, the mariners were used to these latitudes, and knew every rock in the Tuscan Archipelago; for in the midst of this obscurity Franz was not without uneasiness—Corsica had long since disappeared, and Monte Cristo itself was invisible; but the sailors seemed, like the lynx, to see in the dark, and the pilot who steered did not evince the slightest hesitation. An hour had passed since the sun had set, when Franz fancied he saw, at a quarter of a mile to the left, a dark mass, but he could not precisely make out what it was, and fearing to excite the mirth of the sailors by mistaking a floating cloud for land, he remained silent; suddenly a great light appeared on the strand; land might resemble a cloud, but the fire was not a meteor. "What is this light?" asked he.

"Hush!" said the captain; "it is a fire."

"But you told me the island was uninhabited?"

"I said there were no fixed habitations on it, but I said also that it served sometimes as a harbor for smugglers."

"And for pirates?"—"And for pirates," returned Gaetano, repeating Franz's words. "It is for that reason I have given orders to pass the island, for, as you see, the fire is behind us."

"But this fire?" continued Franz. "It seems to me rather reassuring than otherwise; men who did not wish to be seen would not light a fire."—"Oh, that goes for nothing," said Gaetano. "If you can guess the position of the island in the darkness, you will see that the fire cannot be seen from the side or from Pianosa, but only from the sea."

"You think, then, this fire indicates the presence of unpleasant neighbors?"

"That is what we must find out," returned Gaetano, fixing his eyes on this terrestrial star.

"How can you find out?"—"You shall see." Gaetano consulted with his companions, and after five minutes' discussion a manœuvre was executed which caused the vessel to lack about, they returned the way they had come, and in a few minutes the fire disappeared, hidden by an elevation of the land. The pilot again changed the course of the boat, which rapidly approached the island, and was soon within fifty paces of it. Gaetano lowered the sail, and the boat came to rest. All this was done in silence, and from the moment that their course was changed not a word was spoken.

Gaetano, who had proposed the expedition, had taken all the responsibility on himself; the four sailors fixed their eyes on him, while they got out their oars and held themselves in readiness to row away, which, thanks to the darkness, would not be difficult. As for Franz, he examined his arms with the utmost coolness; he had two double-barrelled guns and a rifle; he loaded them, looked at the priming, and waited quietly. During this time the captain had thrown off his vest and shirt, and secured his trousers round his waist; his feet were naked, so he had no shoes and stockings to take off; after these preparations he placed his finger on his lips, and lowering himself noiselessly into the sea, swam towards the shore with such precaution that it was impossible to hear the slightest sound; he could only be traced by the phosphorescent line in his wake. This track soon disappeared; it was evident that he had touched the shore. Every one on board remained motionless for half an hour, when the same luminous track was again observed, and the swimmer was soon on board. "Well?" exclaimed Franz and the sailors in unison.

"They are Spanish smugglers," said he; "they have with them two Corsican bandits."—"And what are these Corsican bandits doing here with Spanish smugglers?"

"Alas," returned the captain with an accent of the most profound pity, "we ought always to help one another. Very often the bandits are hard pressed by gendarmes or carbineers; well, they see a vessel, and good fellows like us on board, they come and demand hospitality of us; you can't refuse help to a poor hunted devil; we receive them, and for greater security we stand out to sea. This costs us nothing, and saves the life, or at least the liberty, of a fellow-creature, who on the first occasion returns the service by pointing out some safe spot where we can land our goods without interruption."

"Ah!" said Franz, "then you are a smuggler occasionally,

Gaetano?"—"Your excellency, we must live somehow," returned the other, smiling impenetrably.

"Then you know the men who are now on Monte Cristo?"—"Oh, yes, we sailors are like freemasons, and recognize each other by signs."

"And do you think we have nothing to fear if we land?"

"Nothing at all; smugglers are not thieves."

"But these two Corsican bandits?" said Franz, calculating the chances of peril.

"It is not their fault that they are bandits, but that of the authorities."

"How so?"—"Because they are pursued for having made a stiff, as if it was not in a Corsican's nature to revenge himself."

"What do you mean by having made a stiff?—having assassinated a man?" said Franz, continuing his investigation.—"I mean that they have killed an enemy, which is a very different thing," returned the captain.

"Well," said the young man, "let us demand hospitality of these smugglers and bandits. Do you think they will grant it?"

"Without doubt."—"How many are they?"

"Four, and the two bandits make six."

"Just our number, so that if they prove troublesome, we shall be able to hold them in check; so, for the last time, steer to Monte Cristo."

"Yes, but your excellency will permit us to take all due precautions."

"By all means, be as wise as Nestor and as prudent as Ulysses; I do more than permit, I exhort you."—"Silence, then!" said Gaetano.

Every one obeyed. For a man who, like Franz, viewed his position in its true light, it was a grave one. He was alone in the darkness with sailors whom he did not know, and who had no reason to be devoted to him; who knew that he had several thousand francs in his belt, and who had often examined his weapons,—which were very beautiful,—if not with envy, at least with curiosity. On the other hand, he was about to land, without any other escort than these men, on an island which had, indeed, a very religious name, but which did not seem to Franz likely to afford him much hospitality, thanks to the smugglers and bandits. The history of the scuttled vessels, which had appeared improbable during the day, seemed very probable at night; placed as he was between two possible sources of danger, he kept his eye on the crew, and his gun in his hand. The sailors had again hoisted sail, and the vessel was once more cleaving the waves. Through the darkness Franz, whose eyes were now more accustomed to it, could see the looming shore along which the boat was sailing, and then, as they rounded a rocky point, he saw the fire more brilliant than ever, and about it five or six persons seated. The blaze illumined the sea for a hundred paces around. Gaetano skirted the light, carefully keeping the boat in the shadow; then, when they were opposite the fire, he steered to the centre of the circle, singing a fishing song, of which his companions sung the chorus. At the first words of the song the men seated round the fire arose and approached the landing-place, their eyes fixed on the boat, evidently seeking to know who the new comers were and what were their intentions. They soon appeared satisfied and returned (with the exception of one, who remained at the shore) to their fire, at which the carcass of a goat was roasting. When the boat was within twenty paces of the shore, the man on the beach, who carried a carbine, presented arms after the manner of a sentinel, and cried, "Who comes there?" in Sardinian. Franz coolly cocked both barrels. Gaetano then exchanged a few words with this man, which the traveller did not understand, but which evidently concerned him. "Will your excellency give your name, or remain *incognito*?" asked the captain.

"My name must rest unknown,—merely say I am a Frenchman travelling for pleasure." As soon as Gaetano had transmitted this answer, the sentinel gave an order to one of the men seated round the fire, who rose and disappeared among the rocks. Not a word was spoken, every one seemed occupied, Franz with his disembarkment, the sailors with their sails, the smugglers with their goat; but in the midst of all this carelessness it was evident that they mutually observed each other. The man who had disappeared returned suddenly on the opposite side to that by which he had left; he made a sign with his head to the sentinel, who, turning to the boat, said, *S'accommodi.*"[1] The Italian *s'accommodi* is untranslatable; it means at once, "Come, enter, you are welcome; make yourself at home; you are the master." It is like that Turkish phrase of Mohère's that so astonished the bourgeois gentleman by the number of things implied in its utterance. The sailors did not wait for a second invitation; four strokes of the oar brought them to land; Gaetano sprang to shore, exchanged a few words with the sentinel, then his comrades disembarked, and lastly came Franz. One of his guns was swung over his shoulder, Gaetano had the other, and a sailor held his rifle; his dress, half artist, half dandy, did not excite any suspicion, and, consequently, no disquietude. The boat was moored to the shore, and they advanced a few paces to find a comfortable bivouac; but, doubtless, the spot they chose did not suit the smuggler who filled the post of sentinel, for he cried out, "Not that way, if you please."

Gaetano faltered an excuse, and advanced to the opposite side, while two sailors kindled torches at the fire to light them on their way. They advanced about thirty paces, and then stopped at a small esplanade surrounded with rocks, in which seats had been cut, not unlike sentry-boxes. Around in the crevices of the rocks grew a few dwarf oaks and thick bushes of myrtles. Franz lowered a torch, and saw by the mass of cinders that had accumulated that he was not the first to discover this retreat, which was, doubtless, one of the halting places of the wandering visitors of Monte Cristo. As for his suspicions, once on *terra firma*, once that he had seen the indifferent, if not friendly, appearance of his hosts, his anxiety had quite

[1] So spelled in the original.—*Ed.*

disappeared, or rather, at sight of the goat, had turned to appetite. He mentioned this to Gaetano, who replied that nothing could be more easy than to prepare a supper when they had in their boat, bread, wine, half a dozen partridges, and a good fire to roast them by. "Besides," added he, "if the smell of their roast meat tempts you, I will go and offer them two of our birds for a slice."

"You are a born diplomat," returned Franz; "go and try."

Meanwhile the sailors had collected dried sticks and branches with which they made a fire. Franz waited impatiently, inhaling the aroma of the roasted meat, when the captain returned with a mysterious air.—"Well," said Franz, "anything new? —do they refuse?"—"On the contrary," returned Gaetano, "the chief, who was told you were a young Frenchman, invites you to sup with him."

"Well," observed Franz, "this chief is very polite, and I see no objection—the more so as I bring my share of the supper." —"Oh, it is not that; he has plenty, and to spare, for supper; but he makes one condition, and rather a peculiar one, before he will receive you at his house."

"His house? Has he built one here, then?"

"No; but he has a very comfortable one all the same, so they say."

"You know this chief, then?"—"I have heard talk of him."

"Favorably or otherwise?"—"Both."

"The deuce!—and what is this condition?"

"That you are blindfolded, and do not take off the bandage until he himself bids you." Franz looked at Gaetano, to see, if possible, what he thought of this proposal. "Ah," replied he, guessing Franz's thought, "I know this is a serious matter."

"What should you do in my place?"

"I, who have nothing to lose,—I should go."

"You would accept?"—"Yes, were it only out of curiosity."

"There is something very peculiar about this chief, then?"

"Listen," said Gaetano, lowering his voice, "I do not know if what they say is true"—He stopped to see if any one was near.

"What do they say?"

"That this chief inhabits a cavern to which the Pitti Palace is nothing."

"What nonsense!" said Franz, reseating himself.

"It is no nonsense; it is quite true. Cama, the pilot of the *Saint Ferdinand*, went in once, and he came back amazed, vowing that such treasures were only to be heard of in fairy tales."—"Do you know," observed Franz, "that with such stories you make me think of Ali Baba's enchanted cavern?"

"I tell you what I have been told."—"Then you advise me to accept?"

"Oh, I don't say that; your excellency will do as you please; I should be sorry to advise you in the matter." Franz pondered the matter for a few moments, concluded that a man so rich could not have any intention of plundering him of what little he had, and seeing only the prospect of a good supper, accepted. Gaetano departed with the reply. Franz was prudent, and wished to learn all he possibly could concerning his host. He turned towards the sailor, who, during this dialogue, had sat gravely plucking the partridges with the air of a man proud of his office, and asked him how these men had landed, as no vessel of any kind was visible.

"Never mind that," returned the sailor, "I know their vessel."

"Is it a very beautiful vessel?"

"I would not wish for a better to sail round the world."

"Of what burden is she?"—"About a hundred tons; but she is built to stand any weather. She is what the English call a yacht."

"Where was she built?"

"I know not; but my own opinion is she is a Genoese."

"And how did a leader of smugglers," continued Franz, "venture to build a vessel designed for such a purpose at Genoa?"

"I did not say that the owner was a smuggler," replied the sailor.

"No; but Gaetano did, I thought."—"Gaetano had only seen the vessel from a distance, he had not then spoken to any one."

"And if this person be not a smuggler, who is he?"

"A wealthy signor, who travels for his pleasure."

"Come," thought Franz, "he is still more mysterious, since the two accounts do not agree."—"What is his name?"— "If you ask him he says Sinbad the Sailor; but I doubt if it be his real name."

"Sinbad the Sailor?"—"Yes."

"And where does he reside?"—"On the sea."

"What country does he come from?"—"I do not know."

"Have you ever seen him?"—"Sometimes."

"What sort of a man is he?"—"Your excellency will judge for yourself."

"Where will he receive me?"

"No doubt in the subterranean palace Gaetano told you of."

"Have you never had the curiosity, when you have landed and found this island deserted, to seek for this enchanted palace?"

"Oh, yes, more than once, but always in vain; we examined the grotto all over, but we never could find the slightest trace of any opening; they say that the door is not opened by a key, but a magic word."

"Decidedly," muttered Franz, "this is an Arabian Nights' adventure."—"His excellency waits for you," said a voice, which he recognized as that of the sentinel. He was accompanied by two of the yacht's crew. Franz drew his handkerchief from his pocket, and presented it to the man who had spoken to him. Without uttering a word, they bandaged his eyes with a care that showed their apprehensions of his committing some indiscretion. Afterwards he was made to promise that he would not make the least attempt to raise the bandage. He promised. Then his two guides took his arms, and he went on, guided by them, and preceded by the sentinel. After going about thirty paces, he smelt the appetizing odor of the kid that was roasting, and knew thus that he was passing the bivouac; they then led him on about fifty paces farther, evidently advancing towards that part of the shore where they would not allow Gaetano to go—a refusal he could now comprehend. Presently, by a change in the atmosphere, he knew that they were entering a cave; after going on for a few seconds more he heard a crackling, and it seemed to him as though the atmosphere again changed, and became balmy and perfumed. At length his feet touched on a thick and soft carpet, and his guides let go their hold of him. There was a moment's silence, and then a voice, in excellent French, although with a foreign accent, said, "Welcome, sir. I beg you will remove your bandage." It may be supposed, then, Franz did not wait for a repetition of this permission, but took off the handkerchief, and found himself in the presence of a man from thirty-eight to forty years of age, dressed in a Tunisian costume—that is to say, a red cap with a long blue silk tassel, a vest of black cloth embroidered with gold, pantaloons of deep red, large and full gaiters of the same color, embroidered with gold like the vest, and yellow slippers; he had a splendid cashmere round his waist, and a small sharp and crooked cangiar was passed through his girdle. Although of a paleness that was almost livid, this man had a remarkably handsome face; his eyes were penetrating and sparkling, his nose, quite straight, and projecting direct from the brow, was of the pure Greek type, while his teeth, as white as pearls, were set off to admiration by the black mustache that encircled them.

His pallor was so peculiar, that it seemed to pertain to one who had been long entombed, and who was incapable of resuming the healthy glow and hue of life. He was not particularly tall, but extremely well made, and, like the men of the south, had small hands and feet. But what astonished Franz, who had treated Gaetano's description as a fable, was the splendor of the apartment in which he found himself. The entire chamber was lined with crimson brocade, worked with flowers of gold. In a recess was a kind of divan, surmounted with a stand of Arabian swords in silver scabbards, and the handles resplendent with gems; from the ceiling hung a lamp of Venetian glass, of beautiful shape and color, while the feet rested on a Turkey carpet, in which they sunk to the instep; tapestry hung before the door by which Franz had entered, and also in front of another door, leading into a second apartment which seemed to be brilliantly illuminated. The host gave Franz time to recover from his surprise, and, moreover, returned look for look, not even taking his eyes off him. "Sir," he said, after a pause, "a thousand excuses for the precaution taken in your introduction hither; but as, during the greater portion of the year, this island is deserted, if the secret of this abode were discovered. I should, doubtless, find on my return my temporary retirement in a state of great disorder, which would be exceedingly annoying, not for the loss it occasioned me, but because I should not have the certainty I now possess of separating myself from all the rest of mankind at pleasure. Let me now endeavor to make you forget this temporary unpleasantness, and offer you what no doubt you did not expect to find here—that is to say, a tolerable supper and pretty comfortable beds."—"*Ma fui*, my dear sir," replied Franz, "make no apologies. I have always observed that they bandage people's eyes who penetrate enchanted palaces, for instance, those of Raoul in the 'Huguenots,' and really I have nothing to complain of, for what I see makes me think of the wonders of the 'Arabian Nights.'"

"Alas, I may say with Lucullus, if I could have anticipated the honor of your visit, I would have prepared for it. But such as is my hermitage, it is at your disposal; such as is my supper, it is yours to share, if you will. Ali, is the supper ready?" At this moment the tapestry moved aside, and a Nubian, black as ebony, and dressed in a plain white tunic, made a sign to his master that all was prepared in the dining-room. "Now," said the unknown to Franz, "I do not know if you are of my opinion, but I think nothing is more annoying than to remain two or three hours together without knowing by name or appellation how to address one another. Pray observe, that I too much respect the laws of hospitality to ask your name or title. I only request you to give me one by which I may have the pleasure of addressing you. As for myself, that I may put you at your ease, I tell you that I am generally called 'Sinbad the Sailor.'"

"And I," replied Franz, "will tell you, as I only require his wonderful lamp to make me precisely like Aladdin, that I see no reason why at this moment, I should not be called Aladdin. That will keep us from going away from the East, whither I am tempted to think I have been conveyed by some good genius."—"Well, then, Signor Aladdin," replied the singular amphitryon, "you heard our repast announced; will you now take the trouble to enter the dining-room, your humble servant going first to show the way?" At these words, moving aside the tapestry, Sinbad preceded his guest. Franz now looked upon another scene of enchantment; the table was splendidly covered, and once convinced of this important point, he cast his eyes around him. The dining-room was scarcely less striking than the room he had just left; it was entirely of marble, with antique bas-reliefs of priceless value; and at the four corners of this apartment, which was oblong, were four magnificent statues, having baskets in their hands. These baskets contained four pyramids of most splendid fruit; there were Sicily pine-apples, pomegranates from Malaga, oranges from the Balearic Isles, peaches from France, and dates from Tunis. The supper consisted of a roast pheasant garnished with Corsican black-birds; a boar's ham with jelly, a quarter of a kid with tartar sauce, a glorious turbot, and a gigantic lobster. Between these large dishes were smaller ones containing various dainties. The dishes were of silver, and the plates of Japanese china.

Franz rubbed his eyes in order to assure himself that this was not a dream. Ali alone was present to wait at table, and acquitted himself so admirably, that the guest complimented his host thereupon. "Yes," replied he, while he did the honors of the supper with much ease and grace—"yes, he is a poor devil who is much devoted to me, and does all he can to prove it. He remembers that I saved his life, and as he has a regard for his head, he feels some gratitude towards me for having kept it on his shoulders." Ali approached his master, took his hand, and kissed it.

"Would it be impertinent, Signor Sinbad," said Franz, "to ask you the particulars of this kindness?"

"Oh, they are simple enough," replied the host. "It seems the fellow had been caught wandering nearer to the harem of the Bey of Tunis than etiquette permits to one of his color, and he was condemned by the bey to have his tongue cut out, and his hand and head cut off; the tongue the first day, the hand the second, and the head the third. I always had a desire to have a mute in my service, so learning the day his tongue was cut out, I went to the bey, and proposed to give him for Ali a splendid double-barrelled gun which I knew he was very desirous of having. He hesitated a moment, he was so very desirous to complete the poor devil's punishment. But when I added to the gun an English cutlass with which I had shivered his highness's yataghan to pieces, the bey yielded, and agreed to forgive the hand and head, but on condition that the poor fellow never again set foot in Tunis. This was a useless clause in the bargain, for whenever the coward sees the first glimpse of the shores of Africa, he runs down below, and can only be induced to appear again when we are out of sight of that quarter of the globe."

Franz remained a moment silent and pensive, hardly knowing what to think of the half-kindness, half-cruelty, with which his host related the brief narrative. "And like the celebrated sailor whose name you have assumed," he said, by way of changing the conversation, "you pass your life in travelling?"

"Yes. I made a vow at a time when I little thought. I should ever be able to accomplish it," said the unknown with a singular smile; "and I made some others also, which I hope I may fulfil in due season." Although Sinbad pronounced these words with much calmness, his eyes gave forth gleams of extraordinary ferocity.

"You have suffered a great deal, sir?" said Franz inquiringly.

Sinbad started and looked fixedly at him, as he replied. "What makes you suppose so?"—"Everything," answered Franz,—"your voice, your look, your pallid complexion, and even the life you lead."

"I?—I live the happiest life possible, the real life of a pasha. I am king of all creation. I am pleased with one place, and stay there; I get tired of it, and leave it; I am free as a bird, and have wings like one; my attendants obey my slightest wish. Sometimes I amuse myself by delivering some bandit or criminal from the bonds of the law. Then I have my mode of dispensing justice, silent and sure, without respite or appeal, which condemns or pardons, and which no one sees. Ah, if you had tasted my life, you would not desire any other, and would never return to the world unless you had some great project to accomplish there."—"Revenge, for instance!" observed Franz.

The unknown fixed on the young man one of those looks which penetrate into the depth of the heart and thoughts. "And why revenge?" he asked.

"Because," replied Franz, "you seem to me like a man who, persecuted by society, has a fearful account to settle with it."

"Ah," responded Sinbad, laughing with his singular laugh which displayed his white and sharp teeth. "You have not guessed rightly. Such as you see me I am, a sort of philosopher, and one day perhaps I shall go to Paris to rival Monsieur Appert, and the little man in the blue cloak."

"And will that be the first time you ever took that journey?"

"Yes; it will. I must seem to you by no means curious, but I assure you that it is not my fault I have delayed it so long—it will happen one day or the other."

"And do you propose to make this journey very shortly?"

"I do not know; it depends on circumstances which depend on certain arrangements."

"I should like to be there at the time you come, and I will endeavor to repay you, as far as lies in my power, for your liberal hospitality displayed to me at Monte Cristo."—"I should avail myself of your offer with pleasure," replied the host, "but, unfortunately, if I go there, it will be, in all probability, *incognito*."

The supper appeared to have been supplied solely for Franz, for the unknown scarcely touched one or two dishes of the splendid banquet to which his guest did ample justice. Then Ali brought on the dessert, or rather took the baskets from the hands of the statues and placed them on the table. Between the two baskets he placed a small silver cup with a silver cover. The care with which Ali placed this cup on the table roused Franz's curiosity. He raised the cover and saw a kind of greenish paste, something like preserved angelica, but which was perfectly unknown to him. He replaced the lid, as ignorant of what the cup contained as he was before he had looked at it, and then casting his eyes towards his host he saw him smile at his disappointment. "You cannot guess," said he, "what there is in that small vase, can you?"

"No, I really cannot."

"Well, then, that green preserve is nothing less than the ambrosia which Hebe served at the table of Jupiter."—"But," replied Franz, "this ambrosia, no doubt, in passing through mortal hands has lost its heavenly appellation and assumed a human name; in vulgar phrase, what may you term this composition, for which, to tell the truth, I do not feel any particular desire?"

"Ah, thus it is that our material origin is revealed," cried Sinbad; "we frequently pass so near to happiness without seeing, without regarding it, or if we do see and regard it, yet without recognizing it. Are you a man for the substantials, and is gold your god? taste this, and the mines of Pern, Guzerat, and Golcomla are opened to you. Are you a man of imagination—a poet? taste this, and the boundaries of possibility disappear; the fields of infinite space open to you, you advance free in heart, free in mind, into the boundless realms of unfettered revery. Are you ambitious, and do you seek after the greatnesses of the earth? taste this, and in an hour you will be a king, not a king of a petty kingdom hidden in some corner of Europe like France, Spain, or England, but king of the world, king of the universe, king of creation; without bowing at the feet of

Satan, you will be king and master of all the kingdoms of the earth. Is it not tempting what I offer you, and is it not an easy thing, since it is only to do thus? look!" At these words he uncovered the small cup which contained the substance so lauded, took a teaspoonful of the magic sweetmeat, raised it to his lips, and swallowed it slowly, with his eyes half shut and his head bent backwards. Franz did not disturb him whilst he absorbed his favorite sweetmeat, but when he had finished, he inquired,—"What, then, is this precious stuff?"

"Did you ever hear," he replied, "of the Old Man of the Mountain, who attempted to assassinate Philip Augustus?"—"Of course I have."—"Well, you know he reigned over a rich valley which was overhung by the mountain whence he derived his picturesque name. In this valley were magnificent gardens planted by Hassen-ben-Sabah, and in these gardens isolated pavilions. Into these pavilions he admitted the elect; and there, says Marco Polo, gave them to eat a certain herb, which transported them to Paradise, in the midst of ever-blooming shrubs, ever-ripe fruit, and ever-lovely virgins. What these happy persons took for reality was but a dream; but it was a dream so soft, so voluptuous, so enthralling, that they sold themselves body and soul to him who gave it to them, and obedient to his orders as to those of a deity, struck down the designated victim, died in torture without a murmur, believing that the death they underwent was but a quick transition to that life of delights of which the holy herb, now before you, had given them a slight foretaste."

"Then," cried Franz, "it is hashish! I know that—by name at least."

"That is it precisely, Signor Aladdin; it is hashish—the purest and most unadulterated hashish of Alexandria,—the hashish of Abou-Gor, the celebrated maker, the only man, the man to whom there should be built a palace, inscribed with these words, 'A grateful world to the dealer in happiness.'"

"Do you know," said Franz, "I have a very great inclination to judge for myself of the truth or exaggeration of your eulogies."

"Judge for yourself, Signor Aladdin—judge, but do not confine yourself to one trial. Like everything else, we must habituate the senses to a fresh impression, gentle or violent, sad or joyous. There is a struggle in nature against this divine substance,—in nature which is not made for joy and clings to pain. Nature subdued must yield in the combat, the dream must succeed to reality, and then the dream reigns supreme, then the dream becomes life, and life becomes the dream. But what changes occur! It is only by comparing the pains of actual being with the joys of the assumed existence, that you would desire to live no longer, but to dream thus forever. When you return to this mundane sphere from your visionary world, you would seem to leave a Neapolitan spring for a Lapland winter—to quit paradise for earth—heaven for hell! Taste the hashish, guest of mine—taste the hashish."

Franz's only reply was to take a teaspoonful of the marvellous preparation, about as much in quantity as his host had eaten, and lift it to his mouth. "*Diable!*" he said, after having swallowed the divine preserve. "I do not know if the result will be as agreeable as you describe, but the thing does not appear to me as palatable as you say."

"Because your palate has not yet been attuned to the sublimity of the substances it flavors. Tell me, the first time you tasted oysters, tea, porter, truffles, and sundry other dainties which you now adore, did you like them? Could you comprehend how the Romans stuffed their pheasants with assafœtida, and the Chinese eat swallows' nests? Eh? no! Well, it is the same with hashish; only eat for a week, and nothing in the world will seem to you to equal the delicacy of its flavor, which now appears to you flat and distasteful. Let us now go into the adjoining chamber, which is your apartment, and Ali will bring us coffee and pipes." They both arose, and while he who called himself Sinbad—and whom we have occasionally named so, that we might, like his guest, have some title by which to distinguish him—gave some orders to the servant, Franz entered still another apartment. It was simply yet richly furnished. It was round, and a large divan completely encircled it. Divan, walls, ceiling, floor, were all covered with magnificent skins as soft and downy as the richest carpets; there were heavy maned lion-skins from Atlas, striped tiger-skins from Bengal; panther-skins from the Cape, spotted beautifully, like those that appeared to Dante; bear-skins from Siberia, fox-skins from Norway, and so on; and all these skins were strewn in profusion one on the other, so that it seemed like walking over the most mossy turf, or reclining on the most lux-urious bed. Both laid themselves down on the divan; chibouques with jasmine tubes and amber mouthpieces were within reach, and all prepared so that there was no need to smoke the same pipe twice. Each of them took one, which Ali lighted and then retired to prepare the coffee. There was a moment's silence, during which Sinbad gave himself up to thoughts that seemed to occupy him incessantly, even in the midst of his conversation; and Franz aban-doned himself to that mute revery, into which we always sink when smoking excellent tobacco, which seems to remove with its fume all the troubles of the mind, and to give the smoker in exchange all the visions of the soul. Ali brought in the coffee. "How do you take it?" inquired the unknown; "in the French or Turkish style, strong or weak, sugar or none, cool or boiling? As you please; it is ready in all ways."—"I will take it in the Turkish style," replied Franz.

"And you are right," said his host; "it shows you have a tendency for an Oriental life. Ah, those Orientals; they are the only men who know how to live. As for me," he added, with one of those singular smiles which did not escape the young man, "when I have completed my affairs in Paris, I shall go and die in the East; and should you wish to see me again, you must seek me at Cairo, Bagdad, or Ispahan."

"*Ma foi*," said Franz, "it would be the easiest thing in the world; for I feel eagle's wings springing out at my shoulders, and with these wings I could make a tour of the world in four and twenty hours."

"Ah, yes, the hashish is beginning its work. Well, unfurl your wings, and fly into superhuman regions; fear nothing, there is a watch over you; and if your wings, like those of Icarus, melt before the sun, we are here to case your fall." He then said something in Arabic to Ali, who made a sign of obedience and withdrew, but not to any distance. As to Franz, a strange transformation had taken place in him. All the bodily fatigue of the day, all the preoccupation of mind which the events of the evening had brought on, disappeared as they do at the first approach of sleep, when we are still sufficiently conscious to be aware of the coming of slumber. His body seemed to acquire an airy lightness, his perception brightened in a remarkable manner, his senses seemed to redouble their power, the horizon continued to expand; but it was not the gloomy horizon of vague alarms, and which he had seen before he slept, but a blue, transparent, unbounded horizon, with all the blue of the ocean, all the spangles of the sun, all the perfumes of the summer breeze; then, in the midst of the songs of his sailors,—songs so clear and sonorous, that they would have made a divine harmony had their notes been taken down,—he saw the Island of Monte Cristo, no longer as a threatening rock in the midst of the waves, but as an oasis in the desert; then, as his boat drew nearer, the songs became louder, for an enchanting and mysterious harmony rose to heaven, as if some Loreley had decreed to attract a soul thither, or Amphion, the enchanter, intended there to build a city.

At length the boat touched the shore, but without effort, without shock, as lips touch lips; and he entered the grotto amidst continued strains of most delicious melody. He descended, or rather seemed to descend, several steps, inhaling the fresh and balmy air, like that which may be supposed to reign around the grotto of Circe, formed from such perfumes as set the mind a dreaming, and such fires as burn the very senses; and he saw again all he had seen before his sleep, from Sinbad, his singular host, to Ali, the mute attendant; then all seemed to fade away and become confused before his eyes, like the last shadows of the magic lantern before it is extinguished, and he was again in the chamber of statues, lighted only by one of those pale and antique lamps which watch in the dead of the night over the sleep of pleasure. They were the same statues, rich in form, in attraction, and poesy, with eyes of fascination, smiles of love, and bright and flowing hair. They were Phryne, Cleopatra, Messalina, those three celebrated courtesans. Then among them glided like a pure ray, like a Christian angel in the midst of Olympus, one of those chaste figures, those calm shadows, those soft visions, which seemed to veil its virgin brow before these marble wantons. Then the three statues advanced towards him with looks of love, and approached the conch on which he was reposing, their feet hidden in their long white tunics, their throats bare, hair flowing like waves, and assuming attitudes which the gods could not resist, but which saints withstood, and looks inflexible and ardent like those with which the serpent charms the bird; and then he gave way before looks that held him in a torturing grasp and delighted his senses as with a voluptuous kiss. It seemed to Franz that he closed his eyes, and in a last look about him saw the vision of modesty completely veiled; and then followed a dream of passion like that promised by the Prophet to the elect. Lips of stone turned to flame, breasts of ice became like heated lava, so that to Franz, yielding for the first time to the sway of the drug, love was a sorrow and voluptuousness a torture, as burning mouths were pressed to his thirsty lips, and he was held in cool serpent-like embraces. The more he strove against this unhallowed passion the more his senses yielded to its thrall, and at length, weary of a struggle that taxed his very soul, he gave way and sank back breathless and exhausted beneath the kisses of these marble goddesses, and the enchantment of his marvellous dream.

XXXII

The Waking

WHEN FRANZ RETURNED TO himself, he seemed still to be in a dream. He thought himself in a sepulchre, into which a ray of sunlight in pity scarcely penetrated. He stretched forth his hand, and touched stone; he rose to his seat, and found himself lying on his bournous in a bed of dry heather, very soft and odoriferous. The vision had fled; and as if the statues had been but shadows from the tomb, they had vanished at his waking. He advanced several paces towards the point whence the light came, and to all the excitement of his dream succeeded the calmness of reality. He found that he was in a grotto, went towards the opening, and through a kind of fanlight saw a blue sea and an azure sky. The air and water were shining in the beams of the morning sun; on the shore the sailors were sitting, chatting and laughing; and at ten yards from them the boat was at anchor, undulating gracefully on the water. There for some time he enjoyed the fresh breeze which played on his brow, and listened to the dash of the waves on the beach, that left against the rocks a lace of foam as white as silver. He was for some time without reflection or thought for the divine charm which is in the things of nature, specially after a fantastic dream; then gradually this view of the outer world, so calm, so pure, so grand, reminded him of the illusiveness of his vision, and once more awakened memory. He recalled his arrival on the island, his presentation to a smuggler chief, a subterranean palace full of splendor, an excellent supper, and a spoonful of hashish. It seemed, however, even in the very face of open day, that at least a year had elapsed since all these things had passed, so deep was the impression made in his mind by the dream, and so strong a hold had it taken of his imagination. Thus every now and then he saw in fancy amid the sailors, seated on a rock, or undulating in the vessel, one of the shadows which had shared his dream with looks and kisses. Otherwise, his head was perfectly clear, and his body refreshed; he was free from the slightest headache; on the contrary, he felt a certain degree of lightness, a faculty for absorbing the pure air, and enjoying the bright sunshine more vividly than ever.

He went gayly up to the sailors, who rose as soon as they perceived him; and the patron, accosting him, said, "The Signor Sinbad has left his compliments for your excellency, and desires us to express the regret he feels at not being able to take his leave in person; but he trusts you will excuse him, as very important business calls him to Malaga."

"So, then, Gaetano," said Franz, "this is, then, all reality; there exists a man who has received me in this island, entertained me right royally, and has departed while I was asleep?"

"He exists as certainly as that you may see his small yacht with all her sails spread; and if you will use your glass, you will, in all probability, recognize your host in the midst of his crew." So saying, Gaetano pointed in a direction in which a small vessel was making sail towards the southern point of Corsica. Franz adjusted his telescope, and directed it towards the yacht. Gaetano was not mistaken. At the stern the mysterious stranger was standing up looking towards the shore, and holding a spy-glass in his hand. He was attired as he had been on the previous evening, and waved his pocket-handkerchief to his guest in token of adieu. Franz returned the salute by shaking his handkerchief as an exchange of signals.

After a second, a slight cloud of smoke was seen at the stern of the vessel, which rose gracefully as it expanded in the air, and then Franz heard a slight report. "There, do you hear?" observed Gaetano; "he is bidding you adieu." The young man took his carbine and fired it in the air, but without any idea that the noise could be heard at the distance which separated the yacht from the shore.

"What are your excellency's orders?" inquired Gaetano.

"In the first place, light me a torch."—"Ah, yes, I understand," replied the patron, "to find the entrance to the enchanted apartment. With much pleasure, your excellency, if it would amuse you; and I will get you the torch you ask for. But I too have had the idea you have, and two or three times the same fancy has come over me; but I have always given it up. Giovanni, light a torch," he added, "and give it to his excellency."

Giovanni obeyed. Franz took the lamp, and entered the subterranean grotto, followed by Gaetano. He recognized the place where he had awaked by the bed of heather that was there; but it was in vain that he carried his torch all round the exterior surface of the grotto. He saw nothing, unless that, by traces of smoke, others had before him attempted the same thing, and, like him, in vain. Yet he did not leave a foot of this granite wall, as impenetrable as futurity, without strict scrutiny; he did not see a fissure without introducing the blade of his hunting sword into it, or a projecting point on which he did not lean and press in the hopes it would give way. All was vain; and he lost two hours in his attempts, which were at last utterly useless. At the end of this time he gave up his search, and Gaetano smiled.

When Franz appeared again on the shore, the yacht only seemed like a small white speck on the horizon. He looked again through his glass, but even then he could not distinguish anything. Gaetano reminded him that he had come for the purpose of shooting goats, which he had utterly forgotten. He took his fowling-piece, and began to hunt over the island with the air of a man who is fulfilling a duty, rather than enjoying a pleasure; and at the end of a quarter of an hour he had killed a goat and two kids. These animals, though wild and agile as chamois, were too much like domestic goats, and Franz could not consider them as game. Moreover, other ideas, much more enthralling, occupied his mind. Since the evening before, he had really been the hero of one of the tales of the "Thousand and One Nights," and he was irresistibly attracted towards the grotto. Then, in spite of the failure of his first search, he began a second, after having told Gaetano to roast one of the two kids. The second visit was a long one, and when he returned the kid was roasted and the repast ready. Franz was sitting on the spot where he was on the previous evening when his mysterious host had invited him to supper; and he saw the little yacht, now like a sea-gull on the wave, continuing her flight towards Corsiea. "Why," he remarked to Gaetano, "you told me that Signor Sinbad was going to Malaga, while it seems he is in the direction of Porto-Veechio."

"Don't you remember," said the patron, "I told you that among the crew there were two Corsican brigands?"

"True; and he is going to land them," added Franz.

"Precisely so," replied Gaetano. "Ah, he is one who fears neither God nor Satan, they say, and would at any time run fifty leagues out of his course to do a poor devil a service."

"But such services as these might involve him with the authorities of the country in which he practises this kind of philanthropy," said Franz.

"And what cares he for that," replied Gaetano with a laugh, "or any authorities? He smiles at them. Let them try to pursue him! Why, in the first place, his yacht is not a ship, but a bird, and he would beat any frigate three knots in every nine; and if he were to throw himself on the coast, why, is he not certain of finding friends everywhere?"

It was perfectly clear that the Signor Sinbad, Franz's host, had the honor of being on excellent terms with the smugglers and bandits along the whole coast of the Mediterranean, and so enjoyed

exceptional privileges. As to Franz, he had no longer any induce-
ment to remain at Monte Cristo. He had lost all hope of detecting
the secret of the grotto; he consequently dispatched his breakfast,
and, his boat being ready, he hastened on board, and they were soon
under way. At the moment the boat began her course they lost sight
of the yacht, as it disappeared in the gulf of Porto-Vecchio. With it
was effaced the last trace of the preceding night; and then supper,
Sinbad, hashish, statues,—all became a dream for Franz. The boat
sailed on all day and all night, and next morning, when the sun rose,
they had lost sight of Monte Cristo. When Franz had once again set
foot on shore, he forgot, for the moment at least, the events which
had just passed, while he finished his affairs of pleasure at Florence,
and then thought of nothing but how he should rejoin his companion, who was awaiting him at Rome.

He set out, and on the Saturday evening reached the Eternal City
by the mail-coach. An apartment, as we have said, had been retained
beforehand, and thus he had but to go to Signor Pastrini's hotel. But
this was not so easy a matter, for the streets were thronged with people, and Rome was already a prey to that low and feverish murmur
which precedes all great events; and at Rome there are four great
events in every year,—the Carnival, Holy Week, Corpus Christi, and
the Feast of St. Peter. All the rest of the year the city is in that state of
dull apathy, between life and death, which renders it similar to a kind
of station between this world and the next—a sublime spot, a resting-
place full of poetry and character, and at which Franz had already
halted five or six times, and at each time found it more marvellous and
striking. At last he made his way through the mob, which was continually increasing and getting more and more turbulent, and reached
the hotel. On his first inquiry he was told, with the impertinence
peculiar to hired hackney-coachmen and innkeepers with their
houses full, that there was no room for him at the Hôtel de Londres.
Then he sent his card to Signor Pastrini, and asked for Albert de
Morcerf. This plan succeeded; and Signor Pastrini himself ran to him,

excusing himself for having made his excellency wait, scolding the waiters, taking the candlestick from the porter, who was ready to pounce on the traveller, and was about to lead him to Albert, when Morcerf himself appeared. The apartment consisted of two small rooms and a parlor. The two rooms looked onto the street—a fact which Signor Pastrini commented upon as an inappreciable advantage. The rest of the floor was hired by a very rich gentleman, who was supposed to be a Sicilian or Maltese; but the host was unable to decide to which of the two nations the traveller belonged. "Very good, Signor Pastrini," said Franz; "but we must have some supper instantly, and a carriage for tomorrow and the following days."—"As to supper," replied the landlord, "you shall be served immediately; but as for the carriage"—

"What as to the carriage?" exclaimed Albert. "Come, come, Signor Pastrini, no joking; we must have a carriage."

"Sir," replied the host, "we will do all in our power to procure you one—this is all I can say."

"And when shall we know?" inquired Franz.

"To-morrow morning," answered the innkeeper.

"Oh, the deuce! then we shall pay the more, that's all, I see plainly enough. At Drake's or Aaron's one pays twenty-five lire for common days, and thirty or thirty-five lire a day more for Sundays and feast days; add five lire a day more for extras, that will make forty, and there's an end of it."

"I am afraid if we offer them double that we shall not procure a carriage."

"Then they must put horses to mine. It is a little worse for the journey, but that's no matter."—"There are no horses." Albert looked at Franz like a man who hears a reply he does not understand.

"Do you understand that, my dear Franz—no horses?" he said; "but can't we have post-horses?"

"They have been all hired this fortnight, and there are none left but those absolutely requisite for posting."

"What are we to say to this?" asked Franz.

"I say, that when a thing completely surpasses my comprehension, I am accustomed not to dwell on that thing, but to pass to another. Is supper ready, Signor Pastrini?"—"Yes, your excellency."—"Well, then, let us sup."

"But the carriage and horses?" said Franz.

"Be easy, my dear boy; they will come in due season; it is only a question of how much shall be charged for them." Morcerf then, with that delighted philosophy which believes that nothing is impossible to a full purse or well-lined pocketbook, supped, went to bed, slept soundly, and dreamed he was racing all over Rome at Carnival time in a coach with six horses.

XXXIII

Roman Bandits

T HE NEXT MORNING FRANZ woke first, and instantly rang the bell. The sound had not yet died away when Signor Pastrini himself entered.

"Well, excellency," said the landlord triumphantly, and without waiting for Franz to question him, "I feared yesterday, when I would not promise you anything, that you were too late—there is not a single carriage to be had—that is, for the last three days of the carnival."

"Yes," returned Franz, "for the very three days it is most needed."

"What is the matter?" said Albert, entering; "no carriage to be had?"

"Just so," returned Franz, "you have guessed it."

"Well, your Eternal City is a nice sort of place."

"That is to say, excellency," replied Pastrini, who was desirous of keeping up the dignity of the capital of the Christian world in the eyes of his guest, "that there are no carriages to be had from Sunday to Tuesday evening, but from now till Sunday you can have fifty if you please."

"Ah, that is something," said Albert; "to-day is Thursday, and who knows what may arrive between this and Sunday?"

"Ten or twelve thousand travellers will arrive," replied Franz, "which will make it still more difficult."

"My friend," said Morcerf, "let us enjoy the present without gloomy forebodings for the future."——"At least we can have a window?"

"Where?"——"In the Corso."

"Ah, a window!" exclaimed Signor Pastrini,——"utterly impossible; there was only one left on the fifth floor of the Doria Palace, and that has been let to a Russian prince for twenty sequins a day."

The two young men looked at each other with an air of stupefaction.

"Well," said Franz to Albert, "do you know what is the best thing we can do? It is to pass the Carnival at Venice; there we are sure of obtaining gondolas if we cannot have carriages."

"Ah, the devil, no," cried Albert; "I came to Rome to see the Carnival, and I will, though I see it on stilts."

"Bravo! an excellent idea. We will disguise ourselves as monster pulchinellos or shepherds of the Landes, and we shall have complete success."

"Do your excellencies still wish for a carriage from now to Sunday morning?"——"*Parbleu!*" said Albert, "do you think we are going to run about on foot in the streets of Rome, like lawyer's clerks?"

"I hasten to comply with your excellencies' wishes; only, I tell you beforehand, the carriage will cost you six piastres a day."

"And, as I am not a millionaire, like the gentleman in the next apartments," said Franz, "I warn you, that as I have been four times before at Rome, I know the prices of all the carriages; we will give you twelve piastres for to-day, tomorrow, and the day after, and then you will make a good profit."

"But, excellency"—said Pastrini, still striving to gain his point.

"Now go," returned Franz, "or I shall go myself and bargain with your *affettatore*,[1] who is mine also; he is an old friend of mine, who has plundered me pretty well already, and, in the hope of

---

[1] So in original. *Affittatore*, one who lets for hire, is meant.—*Ed*.

making more out of me, he will take a less price than the one I offer you; you will lose the preference, and that will be your fault."

"Do not give yourselves the trouble, excellency," returned Signor Pastrini, with the smile peculiar to the Italian speculator when he confesses defeat; "I will do all I can, and I hope you will be satisfied."

"And now we understand each other."

"When do you wish the carriage to be here?"—"In an hour."

"In an hour it will be at the door."

An hour after the vehicle was at the door; it was a hack conveyance which was elevated to the rank of a private carriage in honor of the occasion, but, in spite of its humble exterior, the young men would have thought themselves happy to have secured it for the last three days of the Carnival. "Excellency," cried the *cicerone*, seeing Franz approach the window, "shall I bring the carriage nearer to the palace?"

Accustomed as Franz was to the Italian phraseology, his first impulse was to look round him, but these words were addressed to him. Franz was the "excellency," the vehicle was the "carriage," and the Hôtel de Londres was the "palace." The genius for landation characteristic of the race was in that phrase.

Franz and Albert descended; the carriage approached the palace; their excellencies stretched their legs along the seats; the *cicerone* sprang into the seat behind. "Where do your excellencies wish to go?" asked he.—"To Saint Peter's first, and then to the Colosseum," returned Albert. But Albert did not know that it takes a day to see Saint Peter's, and a month to study it. The day was passed at Saint Peter's alone. Suddenly the daylight began to fade away; Franz took out his watch—it was half-past four. They returned to the hotel; at the door Franz ordered the coachman to be ready at eight. He wished to show Albert the Colosseum by moonlight, as he had shown him Saint Peter's by daylight. When we show a friend a city one has already visited, we feel the same pride as when we poin out a woman whose lover we have been. He was to leave the city by the Porta del Popolo, skirt the outer wall, and re-enter by the Porta San Giovanni; thus they would behold the Colosseum without finding their impressions dulled by first looking on the Capitol, the Forum, the Arch of Septimus Severus, the Temple of Antoninus and Faustina, and the Via Saera. They sat down to dinner. Signor Pastrini had promised them a banquet; he gave them a tolerable repast. At the end of the dinner he entered in person. Franz thought that he came to hear his dinner praised, and began accordingly, but at the first words he was interrupted. "Excellency," said Pastrini, "I am delighted to have your approbation, but it was not for that I came."—"Did you come to tell us you have procured a carriage?" asked Albert, lighting his cigar.

"No; and your excellencies will do well not to think of that any longer; at Rome things can or cannot be done; when you are told anything cannot be done, there is an end of it."—"It is much more convenient at Paris,—when anything cannot be done, you pay double, and it is done directly."

"That is what all the French say," returned Signor Pastrini, somewhat piqued; "for that reason, I do not understand why they travel."

"But," said Albert, emitting a volume of smoke and balancing his chair on its hind legs, "only madmen, or blockheads like us, ever do travel. Men in their senses do not quit their hotel in the Rue du Helder, their walk on the Boulevard de Gand, and the Café de Paris." It is of course understood that Albert resided in the aforesaid street, appeared every day on the fashionable walk, and dined frequently at the only restaurant where you can really dine, that is, if you are on good terms with its frequenters. Signor Pastrini remained silent a short time; it was evident that he was musing over this answer, which did not seem very clear. "But," said Franz in his turn interrupting his host's meditations, "you had some motive for coming here, may I beg to know what it was?"

"Ah, yes; you have ordered your carriage at eight o'clock precisely?"

"I have."—"You intend visiting *Il Colosseo.*"—"You mean the Colosseum?"—"It is the same thing. You have told your coachman to leave the city by the Porta del Popolo, to drive round the walls, and re-enter by the Porta San Giovanni?"—"These are my words exactly."

"Well, this route is impossible."—"Impossible!"

"Very dangerous, to say the least."—"Dangerous!—and why?"

"On account of the famous Luigi Vampa."

"Pray, who may this famous Luigi Vampa be?" inquired Albert; "he may be very famous at Rome, but I can assure you he is quite unknown at Paris."—"What! do you not know him?"

"I have not that honor."

"You have never heard his name?"—"Never."

"Well, then, he is a bandit, compared to whom the Decesaris and the Gasparones were mere children."

"Now then, Albert," cried Franz, "here is a bandit for you at last."

"I forewarn you, Signor Pastrini, that I shall not believe one word of what you are going to tell us; having told you this, begin."

"Once upon a time"—

"Well, go on." Signor Pastrini turned toward Franz, who seemed to him the more reasonable of the two; we must do him justice,—he had had a great many Frenchmen in his house, but had never been able to comprehend them. "Excellency," said he gravely, addressing Franz, "if you look upon me as a liar, it is useless for me to say anything; it was for your interest I"—

"Albert does not say you are a liar, Signor Pastrini," said Franz, "but that he will not believe what you are going to tell us,—but I will believe all you say; so proceed."

"But if your excellency doubt my veracity"—

"Signor Pastrini," returned Franz, "you are more susceptible than Cassandra, who was a prophetess, and yet no one believed her; while you, at least, are sure of the credence of half your audience.

Come, sit down, and tell us all about this Signor Vampa."—"I had told your excellency he is the most famous bandit we have had since the days of Mastrilla."

"Well, what has this bandit to do with the order I have given the coachman to leave the city by the Porta del Popolo, and to re-enter by the Porta San Giovanni?"—"This," replied Signor Pastrini, "that you will go out by one, but I very much doubt your returning by the other."

"Why?" asked Franz.

"Because, after nightfall, you are not safe fifty yards from the gates."

"On your honor is that true?" cried Albert.

"Count," returned Signor Pastrini, hurt at Albert's repeated doubts of the truth of his assertions, "I do not say this to you, but to your companion, who knows Rome, and knows, too, that these things are not to be laughed at."—"My dear fellow," said Albert, turning to Franz, "here is an admirable adventure; we will fill our carriage with pistols, blunderbusses, and double-barrelled guns. Luigi Vampa comes to take us, and we take him—we bring him back to Rome, and present him to his holiness the Pope, who asks how he can repay so great a service; then we merely ask for a carriage and a pair of horses, and we see the Carnival in the carriage, and doubtless the Roman people will crown us at the Capitol, and proclaim us, like Curtius and the veiled Horatius, the preservers of their country." Whilst Albert proposed this scheme, Signor Pastrini's face assumed an expression impossible to describe.

"And pray," asked Franz, "where are these pistols, blunderbusses, and other deadly weapons with which you intend filling the carriage?"

"Not out of my armory, for at Terracina I was plundered even of my hunting-knife."

"I shared the same fate at Aquapendente."

"Do you know, Signor Pastrini," said Albert, lighting a second cigar at the first, "that this practice is very convenient for bandits, and that it seems to be due to an arrangement of their own." Doubtless Signor Pastrini found this pleasantry compromising, for he only answered half the question, and then he spoke to Franz, as the only one likely to listen with attention. "Your excellency knows that it is not customary to defend yourself when attacked by bandits."

"What!" cried Albert, whose courage revolted at the idea of being plundered tamely, "not make any resistance!"—"No, for it would be useless. What could you do against a dozen bandits who spring out of some pit, ruin, or aqueduct, and level their pieces at you?"

"Eh, *parbleu!*—they should kill me."

The innkeeper turned to Franz with an air that seemed to say, "Your friend is decidedly mad."

"My dear Albert," returned Franz, "your answer is sublime, and worthy the '*Let him die*,' of Corneille, only, when Horace made that answer, the safety of Rome was concerned; but, as for us, it is only to gratify a whim, and it would be ridiculous to risk our lives for so foolish a motive." Albert poured himself out a glass of *lacryma Christi*, which he sipped at intervals, muttering some unintelligible words.

"Well, Signor Pastrini," said Franz, "now that my companion is quieted, and you have seen how peaceful my intentions are, tell me who is this Luigi Vampa. Is he a shepherd or a nobleman?—young or old?—tall or short? Describe him, in order that, if we meet him by chance, like Bugaboo John or Lara, we may recognize him."— "You could not apply to any one better able to inform you on all these points, for I knew him when he was a child, and one day that I fell into his hands, going from Ferentino to Alatri, he, fortunately for me, recollected me, and set me free, not only without ransom, but made me a present of a very splendid watch, and related his history to me."

"Let us see the watch," said Albert.

Signor Pastrini drew from his fob a magnificent Bréguet, bearing the name of its maker, of Parisian manufacture, and a count's coronet.

"Hero it is," said he.—"*Peste*," returned Albert, "I compliment you on it; I have its fellow"—he took his watch from his waistcoat pocket—"and it cost me 3,000 francs."

"Let us hear the history," said Franz, motioning Signor Pastrini to seat himself.—"Your excellencies permit it?" asked the host.

"*Pardieu!*" cried Albert, "you are not a preacher, to remain standing!"

The host sat down, after having made each of them a respectful bow, which meant that he was ready to tell them all they wished to know concerning Luigi Vampa. "You tell me," said Franz, at the moment Signor Pastrini was about to open his mouth, "that you knew Luigi Vampa when he was a child—he is still a young man, then?"—"A young man? he is only two and twenty;—he will gain himself a reputation."

"What do you think of that, Albert?—at two and twenty to be thus famous?"—"Yes, and at his age, Alexander, Caesar, and Napoleon, who have all made some noise in the world, were quite behind him."

"So," continued Franz, "the hero of this history is only two and twenty?"

"Scarcely so much."

"Is he tall or short?"—"Of the middle height—about the same stature as his excellency," returned the host, pointing to Albert.

"Thanks for the comparison," said Albert, with a bow.

"Go on, Signor Pastrini," continued Franz, smiling at his friend's susceptibility. "To what class of society does he belong?"

"He was a shepherd-boy attached to the farm of the Count of San-Felice, situated between Palestrina and the lake of Gabri; he was born at Pampinara, and entered the count's service when he was five years old; his father was also a shepherd, who owned a small flock, and lived by the wool and the milk, which he sold at Rome. When quite a child, the little Vampa displayed a most extraordinary precocity. One day, when he was seven years old, he came to the curate of Palestrina, and asked to be taught to read; it was somewhat difficult, for he could not quit his flock; but the good curate went every day to say mass at a little hamlet too poor to pay a priest and which, having no other name, was called Borgo; he told Luigi that he might meet him on his return, and that then he would give him a lesson, warning him that it would be short, and that he must profit as much as possible by it. The child accepted joyfully. Every day Luigi led his flock to graze on the road that leads from Palestrina to Borgo; every day, at nine o'clock in the morning, the priest and the boy sat down on a bank by the wayside, and the little shepherd took his lesson out of the priest's breviary. At the end of three months he had learned to read. This was not enough—he must now learn to write. The priest had a writing teacher at Rome make three alphabets—one large, one middling, and one small; and pointed out to him that by the help of a sharp instrument he could trace the letters on a slate, and thus learn to write. The same evening, when the flock was safe at the farm, the little Luigi hastened to the smith at Palestrina, took a large nail, heated and sharpened it, and formed a sort of stylus. The next morning he gathered an armful of pieces of slate and began. At the end of three months he had learned to write. The curate, astonished at his quickness and intelligence, made him a present of pens, paper, and a penknife. This demanded new effort, but nothing compared to the first; at the end of a week he wrote as well with the pen as with the stylus. The curate related the incident to the Count of San Felice, who sent for the little shepherd, made him read and write before him, ordered his attendant to let him eat with the domestics, and to gave him two piastres a month. With this, Luigi purchased books and pencils. He applied his imitative powers to everything, and, like Giotto, when young, he drew on his slate sheep, houses, and trees. Then, with his knife, he began to carve all sorts of objects in wood; it was thus that Pinelli, the famous sculptor, had commenced.

"A girl of six or seven—that is, a little younger than Vampa—

tended sheep on a farm near Palestrina; she was an orphan, born at Valmontone, and was named Teresa. The two children met, sat down near each other, let their flocks mingle together, played, laughed, and conversed together; in the evening they separated the Count of San-Felice's flock from those of Baron Cervetri, and the children returned to their respective farms, promising to meet the next morning. The next day they kept their word, and thus they grew up together. Vampa was twelve, and Teresa eleven. And yet their natural disposition revealed itself. Beside his taste for the fine arts, which Luigi had carried as far as he could in his solitude, he was given to alternating fits of sadness and enthusiasm, was often angry and capricious, and always sarcastic. None of the lads of Pampinara, Palestrina, or Valmontone had been able to gain any influence over him, or even to become his companion. His disposition (always inclined to exact concessions rather than to make them) kept him aloof from all friendships. Teresa alone ruled by a look, a word, a gesture, this impetuous character, which yielded beneath the hand of a woman, and which beneath the hand of a man might have broken, but could never have been bended. Teresa was lively and gay, but coquettish to excess. The two piastres that Luigi received every month from the Count of San-Felice's steward, and the price of all the little carvings in wood he sold at Rome, were expended in earrings, necklaces, and gold hairpins. So that, thanks to her friend's generosity, Teresa was the most beautiful and the best-attired peasant near Rome. The two children grew up together, passing all their time with each other, and giving themselves up to the wild ideas of their different characters. Thus, in all their dreams, their wishes, and their conversations, Vampa saw himself the captain of a vessel, general of an army, or governor of a province. Teresa saw herself rich, superbly attired, and attended by a train of liveried domestics. Then, when they had thus passed the day in building castles in the air, they separated their flocks, and descended from the elevation of their dreams to the reality of their humble position.

"One day the young shepherd told the count's steward that he had seen a wolf come out of the Sabine mountains, and prowl around his flock. The steward gave him a gun; this was what Vampa longed for. This gun had an excellent barrel, made at Breschia, and carrying a ball with the precision of an English rifle; but one day the count broke the stock, and had then cast the gun aside. This, however, was nothing to a sculptor like Vampa; he examined the broken stock, calculated what change it would require to adapt the gun to his shoulder, and made a fresh stock, so beautifully carved that it would have fetched fifteen or twenty piastres, had he chosen to sell it. But nothing could be farther from his thoughts. For a long time a gun had been the young man's greatest ambition. In every country where independence has taken the place of liberty, the first desire of a manly heart is to possess a weapon, which at once renders him capable of defence or attack, and, by rendering its owner terrible, often makes him feared. From this moment Vampa devoted all his leisure time to perfecting himself in the use of his precious weapon; he purchased powder and ball, and everything served him for a mark—the trunk of some old and moss-grown olive-tree, that grew on the Sabine mountains; the fox, as he quitted his earth on some maranding excursion; the eagle that soared above their heads; and thus he soon became so expert, that Teresa overcame the terror she at first felt at the report, and amused herself by watching him direct the ball wherever he pleased, with as much accuracy as if he placed it by hand.

"One evening a wolf emerged from a pine-wood near which they were usually stationed, but the wolf had scarcely advanced ten yards ere he was dead. Proud of this exploit, Vampa took the dead animal on his shoulders, and carried him to the farm. These exploits had gained Luigi considerable reputation. The man of superior abilities always finds admirers, go where he will. He was spoken of as the most adroit, the strongest, and the most courageous *contadino* for ten leagues around; and although Teresa was universally allowed to be the most beautiful girl of the Sabines, no one had ever spoken to her of love, because it was known that she was beloved by Vampa. And yet the two young people had never declared their affection; they had grown together like two trees whose roots are mingled, whose branches intertwine, and whose intermingled perfume rises to the heavens. Only their wish to see each other had become a necessity, and they would have preferred death to a day's separation. Teresa was sixteen, and Vampa seventeen. About this time, a band of brigands that had established itself in the Lepini mountains began to be much spoken of. The brigands have never been really extirpated from the neighborhood of Rome. Sometimes a chief is wanted, but when a chief presents himself he rarely has to wait long for a band of followers.

"The celebrated Cucumetto, pursued in the Abruzzo, driven out of the kingdom of Naples, where he had carried on a regular war, had crossed the Garigliano, like Manfred, and had taken refuge on the banks of the Amasine between Sonnino and Juperno. He strove to collect a band of followers, and followed the footsteps of Decesaris and Gasperone, whom he hoped to surpass. Many young men of Palestrina, Frascati, and Pampinara disappeared. Their disappearance at first caused much disquietude; but it was soon known that they had joined Cucumetto. After some time Cucumetto became the object of universal attention; the most extraordinary traits of ferocious daring and brutality were related of him. One day he carried off a young girl, the daughter of a surveyor of Frosinone. The bandit's laws are positive; a young girl belongs first to him who carries her off, then the rest draw lots for her, and she is abandoned to their brutality until death relieves her sufferings. When their parents are sufficiently rich to pay a ransom, a messenger is sent to negotiate; the prisoner is hostage for the security of the messenger; should the ransom be refused, the prisoner is irrevocably lost. The young girl's lover was in Cucumetto's troop; his name was Carlini. When she recognized her lover, the poor girl extended her arms to him, and believed herself safe; but Carlini felt his heart sink, for he but too well knew the fate that awaited her. However, as he was a favorite with Cucumetto, as he had for three years faithfully served him, and as he had saved his life by shooting a dragoon who was about to cut him down, he hoped the chief would have pity on him. He took Cucumetto one side, while the young girl, seated at the foot of a huge pine that stood in the centre of the forest, made a veil of her picturesque head-dress to hide her face from the lascivious gaze of the bandits. There he told the chief all—his affection for the prisoner, their promises of mutual fidelity, and how every night, since he had been near, they had met in some neighboring ruins.

"It so happened that night that Cucumetto had sent Carlini to a village, so that he had been unable to go to the place of meeting. Cucumetto had been there, however, by accident, as he said, and had carried the maiden off. Carlini besought his chief to make an exception in Rita's favor, as her father was rich, and could pay a large ransom. Cucumetto seemed to yield to his friend's entreaties, and bade him find a shepherd to send to Rita's father at Frosinone. Carlini flew joyfully to Rita, telling her she was saved, and bidding her write to her father, to inform him what had occurred, and that her ransom was fixed at three hundred piastres. Twelve hours' delay was all that was granted—that is, until nine the next morning. The instant the letter was written, Carlini seized it, and hastened to the plain to find a messenger. He found a young shepherd watching his flock. The natural messengers of the bandits are the shepherds who live between the city and the mountains, between civilized and savage life. The boy undertook the commission, promising to be in Frosinone in less than an hour. Carlini returned, anxious to see his mistress, and announce the joyful intelligence. He found the troop in the glade, supping off the provisions exacted as contributions from the peasants; but his eye vainly sought Rita and Cucumetto among them. He inquired where they were, and was answered by a burst of laughter. A cold perspiration burst from every pore, and his hair stood on end. He repeated his question. One of the bandits rose, and offered him a glass filled with Orvietto, saying, 'To the health of the brave Cucumetto and the fair Rita.' At this moment Carlini heard a woman's cry; he divined the truth, seized the glass, broke it across the face of him who presented it, and rushed towards the spot whence the cry came. After a hundred yards he turned the corner of the thicket; he found Rita senseless in the arms of Cucumetto. At the sight of Carlini, Cucumetto rose, a pistol in each hand. The two brigands looked at each other for a moment—the one with a smile of lasciviousness on his lips, the other with the pallor of death on his brow. A terrible battle between the two men seemed imminent; but by degrees Carlini's features relaxed, his hand, which had grasped one of the pistols in his belt, fell to his side. Rita lay between them. The moon lighted the group.

"'Well,' said Cucumetto, 'have you executed your commission?'

"'Yes, captain,' returned Carlini. 'At nine o'clock to-morrow Rita's father will be here with the money.'—'It is well; in the meantime, we will have a merry night; this young girl is charming, and does credit to your taste. Now, as I am not egotistical, we will return to our comrades and draw lots for her.'—'You have determined, then, to abandon her to the common law?" said Carlini.

"'Why should an exception be made in her favor?'

"'I thought that my entreaties'—

"'What right have you, any more than the rest, to ask for an exception?'—'It is true.'—'But never mind,' continued Cucumetto, laughing, 'sooner or later your turn will come.' Carlini's teeth clinched convulsively.

"'Now, then,' said Cucumetto, advancing towards the other bandits, 'are you coming?'—'I follow you.'

"Cucemetto departed, without losing sight of Carlini, for, doubtless, he feared least he should strike him unawares; but nothing betrayed a hostile design on Carlini's part. He was standing, his arms folded, near Rita, who was still insensible. Cucumetto fancied for a moment the young man was about to take her in his arms and fly: but this mattered little to him now Rita had been his; and as for the money, three hundred piastres distributed among the band was so small a sum that he cared little about it. He continued to follow the path to the glade; but, to his great surprise, Carlini arrived almost as soon as himself. 'Let us draw lots! let us draw lots!' cried all the brigands, when they saw the chief.

"Their demand was fair, and the chief inclined his head in sign of acquiescence. The eyes of all shone fiercely as they made their demand, and the red light of the fire made them look like demons. The names of all, including Carlini, were placed in a hat, and the youngest of the band drew forth a ticket; the ticket bore the name of Diavolaccio. He was the man who had proposed to Carlini the health of their chief, and to whom Carlini replied by breaking the glass across his face. A large wound, extending from the temple to the mouth, was bleeding profusely. Diovalaccio, seeing himself thus favored by fortune, burst into a loud laugh. 'Captain,' said he, 'just now Carlini would not drink your health when I proposed it to him; propose mine to him, and let us see if he will be more condescending to you than to me.' Every one expected an explosion on Carlini's part; but to their great surprise, he took a glass in one hand and a flask in the other, and filling it,—'Your health, Diavolaccio,' said he calmly, and he drank it off without his hand trembling in the least. Then sitting down by the fire, 'My supper,' said he; 'my expedition has given me an appetite.'—'Well done, Carlini!' cried the brigands; 'that is acting like a good fellow;' and they all formed a circle round the fire, while Diavolaccio disappeared. Carlini ate and drank as if nothing had happened. The bandits looked on with astonishment at this singular conduct until they heard footsteps. They turned round, and saw Diavolaccio bearing the young girl in his arms. Her head hung back, and her long hair swept the ground. As they entered the circle, the bandits could perceive, by the firelight, the unearthly pallor of the young girl and of Diavolaccio. This apparition was so strange and so solemn, that every one rose, with the exception of Carlini, who remained seated, and ate and drank calmly. Diavolaccio advanced amidst the most profound silence, and laid Rita at the captain's feet. Then every one could understand the cause of the unearthly pallor in the young girl and the bandit. A knife was plunged up to the hilt in Rita's left breast. Every one looked at Carlini; the sheath at his belt was empty. 'Ah, ah,' said the chief, 'I now understand why Carlini stayed behind.' All savage natures appreciate a desperate deed. No other of the bandits would, perhaps, have done the same; but they all understood what Carlini had done. 'Now, then,' cried Carlini, rising in his turn, and approaching the corpse, his hand on the butt of one of his pistols, 'does any one dispute the possession of this woman with me?'— 'No,' returned the chief, 'she is thine.' Carlini raised her in his arms, and carried her out of the circle of firelight. Cucumetto placed his sentinels for the night, and the bandits wrapped themselves in their cloaks, and lay down before the fire. At midnight the sentinel gave the alarm, and in an instant all were on the alert. It was Rita's father, who brought his daughter's ransom in person. 'Here,' said he, to Cucumetto, 'here are three hundred piastres; give me back my child.' But the chief, without taking the money, made a sign to him to follow. The old man obeyed. They both advanced beneath the trees, through whose branches streamed the moonlight. Cucumetto stopped at last, and pointed to two persons grouped at the foot of a tree.

"'There,' said he, 'demand thy child of Carlini; he will tell thee what has become of her;' and he returned to his companions. The old man remained motionless; he felt that some great and unforeseen misfortune hung over his head. At length he advanced toward the group, the meaning of which he could not comprehend. As he approached, Carlini raised his head, and the forms of two persons became visible to the old man's eyes. A woman lay on the ground, her head resting on the knees of a man, who was seated by her; as he raised his head, the woman's face became visible. The old man recognized his child, and Carlini recognized the old man. 'I expected thee,' said the bandit to Rita's father.—'Wretch!' returned the old man, `what hast thou done?' and he gazed with terror on Rita, pale and bloody, a knife buried in her bosom. A ray of moonlight poured through the trees, and lighted up the face of the dead.—'Cucumetto had violated thy daughter,' said the bandit; 'I loved her, therefore I slew her; for she would have served as the sport of the whole band.' The old man spoke not, and grew pale as death. 'Now,' continued Carlini, 'if I have done wrongly, avenge her;' and withdrawing the knife from the wound in Rita's bosom, he held it out to the old man with one hand, while with the other he tore open his vest.—'Thou hast done well!' returned the old man in a hoarse voice; 'embrace me, my son.' Carlini threw himself, sobbing like a child, into the arms of his mistress's father. These were the first tears the man of blood had ever wept. 'Now,' said the old man, 'aid me to bury my child.' Carlini fetched two pickaxes; and the father and the lover began to dig at the foot of a huge oak, beneath which the young girl was to repose. When the grave was formed, the father kissed her first, and then the lover; afterwards, one taking the head, the other the feet, they placed her in the grave. Then they knelt on each until the grave was filled. Then, extending his hand, the old man said, 'I thank you, my son; and now leave me alone.'—'Yet'—replied Carlini.—'Leave me, I command you.' Carlini obeyed, rejoined his comrades, folded himself in his cloak, and soon appeared to sleep as soundly as the rest. It had been resolved the night before to change their encampment. An hour before daybreak, Cucumetto aroused his men, and gave the word to march. But Carlini would not quit the forest, without knowing what had become of Rita's father. He went toward the place where he had left him. He found the old man suspended from one of the branches of the oak which shaded his daughter's grave. He then took an oath of bitter vengeance over the dead body of the one and the tomb of the other. But he was unable to complete this oath, for two days afterwards, in an encounter with the Roman carbineers, Carlini was killed. There was some surprise, however, that, as he was with his face to the enemy, he should have received a ball between his shoulders. That astonishment ceased when one of the brigands remarked to his comrades that Cucumetto was stationed ten paces in Carlini's rear when he fell. On the morning of the departure from the forest of Frosinone he had followed Carlini in the darkness, and heard this oath of vengeance, and, like a wise man, anticipated it. They told ten other stories of this bandit chief, each more singular than the other. Thus, from Fondi to Perusia, every one trembles at the name of Cucumetto.

"These narratives were frequently the theme of conversation between Luigi and Teresa. The young girl trembled very much at hearing the stories; but Vampa reassured her with a smile, tapping the butt of his good fowling-piece, which threw its ball so well; and if that did not restore her courage, he pointed to a crow, perched on some dead branch, took aim, touched the trigger, and the bird fell dead at the foot of the tree. Time passed on, and the two young people had agreed to be married when Vampa should be twenty and Teresa nineteen years of age. They were both orphans, and had only their employers' leave to ask, which had been already sought and obtained. One day when they were talking over their plans for the future, they heard two or three reports of firearms, and then suddenly a man came out of the wood, near which the two young persons used to graze their flocks, and hurried towards them. When he came within hearing, he exclaimed, 'I am pursued; can you conceal me?' They knew full well that this fugitive must be a bandit; but there is an innate sympathy between the Roman brigand and the Roman peasant, and the latter is always ready to aid the former. Vampa, without saying a word, hastened to the stone that closed up the entrance to their grotto, drew it away, made a sign to the fugitive to take refuge there, in a retreat unknown to every one, closed the stone upon him, and then went and resumed his seat by Teresa. Instantly afterwards four carbineers, on horseback, appeared on the edge of the wood; three of them appeared to be looking for the fugitive, while the fourth dragged a brigand prisoner by the neck. The three carbineers looked about carefully on every side, saw the young peasants, and galloping up, began to question them. They had seen no one. 'That is very annoying,' said the brigadier; 'for the man we are looking for is the chief.'—'Cucumetto?' cried Luigi and Teresa at the same moment.

"'Yes,' replied the brigadier; 'and as his head is valued at a thousand Roman crowns, there would have been five hundred for you, if you had helped us to catch him.' The two young persons exchanged looks. The brigadier had a moment's hope. Five hundred Roman crowns are three thousand lire, and three thousand lire are a fortune for two poor orphans who are going to be married.

"'Yes, it is very annoying,' said Vampa; 'but we have not seen him.'

"Then the carbineers scoured the country in different directions, but in vain; then, after a time, they disappeared. Vampa then removed the stone, and Cucumetto came out. Through the crevices in the granite he had seen the two young peasants talking with the carbineers, and guessed the subject of their parley. He had read in the countenances of Luigi and Teresa their steadfast resolution not to surrender him, and he drew from his pocket a purse full of gold, which he offered to them. But Vampa raised his head proudly; as to Teresa, her eyes sparkled when she thought of all the fine gowns and gay jewellery she could buy with this purse of gold.

"Cucumetto was a cunning fiend, and had assumed the form of a brigand instead of a serpent, and this look from Teresa showed to him that she was a worthy daughter of Eve, and he returned to the forest, pausing several times on his way, under the pretext of saluting his protectors. Several days elasped, and they neither saw nor heard of Cucumetto. The time of the Carnival was at hand. The

Count of San-Felice announced a grand masked ball, to which all that were distinguished in Rome were invited. Teresa had a great desire to see this ball. Luigi asked permission of his protector, the steward, that she and he might be present amongst the servants of the house. This was granted. The ball was given by the count for the particular pleasure of his daughter Carmela, whom he adored. Carmela was precisely the age and figure of Teresa, and Teresa was as handsome as Carmela. On the evening of the ball Teresa was attired in her best, her most brilliant ornaments in her hair, and gayest glass beads,—she was in the costume of the women of Frascati. Luigi wore the very picturesque garb of the Roman peasant at holiday time. They both mingled, as they had leave to do, with the servants and peasants.

"The *festa* was magnificent; not only was the villa brilliantly illuminated, but thousands of colored lanterns were suspended from the trees in the garden; and very soon the palace overflowed to the terraces, and the terraces to the garden-walks. At each cross-path was an orchestra, and tables spread with refreshments; the guests stopped, formed quadrilles, and danced in any part of the grounds they pleased. Carmela was attired like a woman of Sonnino. Her cap was embroidered with pearls, the pins in her hair were of gold and diamonds, her girdle was of Turkey silk, with large embroidered flowers, her bodice and skirt were of cashmere, her apron of Indian muslin, and the buttons of her corset were of jewels. Two of her companions were dressed, the one as a woman of Nettuno, and the other as a woman of La Riecia. Four young men of the richest and noblest families of Rome accompanied them with that Italian freedom which has not its parallel in any other country in the world. They were attired as peasants of Albano, Velletri, Civita-Castellana, and Sora. We need hardly add that these peasant costumes, like those of the young women, were brilliant with gold and jewels.

"Carmela wished to form a quadrille, but there was one lady wanting. Carmela looked all around her, but not one of the guests had a costume similar to her own, or those of her companions. The count of San-Felice pointed out Teresa, who was hanging on Luigi's arm in a group of peasants. 'Will you allow me, father?' said Carmela.—'Certainly,' replied the count, 'are we not in Carnival time?'—Carmela turned towards the young man who was talking with her, and saying a few words to him, pointed with her finger to Teresa. The young man looked, bowed in obedience, and then went to Teresa, and invited her to dance in a quadrille directed by the count's daughter. Teresa felt a flush pass over her face; she looked at Luigi, who could not refuse his assent. Luigi slowly relinquished Teresa's arm, which he had held beneath his own, and Teresa, accompanied by her elegant cavalier, took her appointed place with much agitation in the aristocratic quadrille. Certainly, in the eyes of an artist, the exact and strict costume of Teresa had a very different character from that of Carmela and her companions; and Teresa was frivolous and coquettish, and thus the embroidery and muslins, the cashmere waist-girdles, all dazzled her, and the reflection of sapphires and diamonds almost turned her giddy brain.

"Luigi felt a sensation hitherto unknown arising in his mind. It was like an acute pain which gnawed at his heart, and then thrilled through his whole body. He followed with his eye each movement of Teresa and her cavalier; when their hands touched, he felt as though he should swoon: every pulse beat with violence, and it seemed as though a bell were ringing in his ears. When they spoke, although Teresa listened timidly and with downcast eyes to the conversation of her cavalier, as Luigi could read in the ardent looks of the good-looking young man that his language was that of praise, it seemed as if the whole world was turning round with him, and all the voices of hell were whispering in his ears ideas of murder and assassination. Then fearing that his paroxysm might get the better of him, he clutched with one hand the branch of a tree against which he was leaning, and with the other convulsively grasped the dagger with a carved handle which was in his belt, and which, unwittingly, he drew from the scaboard from time to time. Luigi was jealous! He felt that, influenced by her ambitions and coquettish disposition, Teresa might escape him.

"The young peasant girl, at first timid and scared, soon recovered herself. We have said that Teresa was handsome, but this is not all; Teresa was endowed with all those wild graces which are so much more potent than our affected and studied elegancies. She had almost all the honors of the quadrille, and if she were envious of the Count of San-Felice's daughter, we will not undertake to say that Carmela was not jealous of her. And with overpowering compliments her handsome cavalier led her back to the place whence he had taken her, and where Luigi awaited her. Twice or thrice during the dance the young girl had glanced at Luigi, and each time she saw that he was pale and that his features were agitated; once even the blade of his knife, half drawn from its sheath, had dazzled her eyes with its sinister glare. Thus, it was almost tremblingly that she resumed her lover's arm. The quadrille had been most perfect, and it was evident there was a great demand for a repetition, Carmela alone objecting to it, but the Count of San-Felice besought his daughter so earnestly, that she acceded. One of the cavaliers then hastened to invite Teresa, without whom it was impossible for the quadrille to be formed, but the young girl had disappeared. The truth was, that Luigi had not felt the strength to support another such trial, and, half by persuasion and half by force, he had removed Teresa toward another part of the garden. Teresa had yielded in spite of herself, but when she looked at the agitated countenance of the young man, she understood by his silence and trembling voice that something strange was passing within him. She herself was not exempt from internal emotion, and without having done anything wrong, yet fully comprehended that Luigi was right in reproaching her. Why she did not know, but yet she did not the less feel that these reproaches were merited. However, to Teresa's great astonishment, Luigi remained mute, and not a word escaped his lips the rest of the evening. When the chill of the night had driven away the guests from the gardens, and the gates of the villa were closed on them for the *festa* in-doors, he took Teresa quite away, and as he left her at her home, he said,—

"'Teresa, what were you thinking of as you danced opposite the young Countess of San-Felice?'—'I thought,' replied the young girl, with all the frankness of her nature, 'that I would give half my life for a costume such as she wore.'

"'And what said your cavalier to you?'—'He said it only depended on myself to have it, and I had only one word to say.'

"'He was right,' said Luigi. 'Do you desire it as ardently as you say?'—'Yes.'—'Well, then, you shall have it!'

"The young girl, much astonished, raised her head to look at him, but his face was so gloomy and terrible that her words froze to her lips. As Luigi spoke thus, he left her. Teresa followed him with her eyes into the darkness as long as she could, and when he had quite disappeared, she went into the house with a sigh.

"That night a memorable event occurred, due, no doubt, to the imprudence of some servant who had neglected to extinguish the lights. The Villa of San-Felice took fire in the rooms adjoining the very apartment of the lovely Carmela. Awakened in the night by the light of the flames, she sprang out of bed, wrapped herself in a dressing-gown, and attempted to escape by the door, but the corridor by which she hoped to fly was already a prey to the flames. She then returned to her room, calling for help as loudly as she could, when suddenly her window, which was twenty feet from the ground, was opened, a young peasant jumped into the chamber, seized her in his arms, and with superhuman skill and strength conveyed her to the turf of the grass-plot, where she fainted. When she recovered, her father was by her side. All the servants surrounded her, offering her assistance. An entire wing of the villa was burnt down; but what of that, as long as Carmela was safe and uninjured? Her preserver was everywhere sought for, but he did not appear, he was inquired after, but no one had seen him. Carmela was greatly troubled that she had not recognized him. As the count was immensely rich, excepting the danger Carmela had run,—and the marvellous manner in which she had escaped, made that appear to him rather a favor of providence than a real misfortune,—the loss occasioned by the conflagration was to him but a trifle.

"The next day, at the usual hour, the two young peasants were on the borders of the forest. Luigi arrived first. He came toward Teresa in high spirits, and seemed to have completely forgotten the events of the previous evening. The young girl was very pensive, but seeing Luigi so cheerful, she on her part assumed a smiling air, which was natural to her when she was not excited or in a passion. Luigi took her arm beneath his own, and led her to the door of the grotto. Then he paused. The young girl, perceiving that there was something extraordinary, looked at him steadfastly. 'Teresa,' said Luigi, 'yesterday evening you told me you would give all the world to have a costume similar to that of the count's daughter.'—'Yes,' replied Teresa with astonishment; 'but I was mad to utter such a wish.'—'And I replied, "Very well, you shall have it."'—'Yes,' replied the young girl, whose astonishment increased at every word uttered by Luigi, 'but of course your reply was only to please me.'

"'I have promised no more than I have given you, Teresa.' said Luigi proudly. 'Go into the grotto and dress yourself.' At these words he drew away the stone, and showed Teresa the grotto, lighted up by two wax lights, which burnt on each side of a splendid mirror; on a rustic table, made by Luigi, were spread out the pearl necklace and the diamond pins, and on a chair at the side was laid the rest of the costume.

"Teresa uttered a cry of joy, and, without inquiring whence this attire came, or even thanking Luigi, darted into the grotto, transformed into a dressing-room. Luigi pushed the stone behind her, for on the crest of a small adjacent hill which cut off the view toward Palestrina, he saw a traveller on horseback, stopping a moment, as if uncertain of his road, and thus presenting against the blue sky that perfect outline which is peculiar to distant objects in southern climes. When he saw Luigi, he put his horse into a gallop and advanced toward him. Luigi was not mistaken. The traveller, who was going from Palestrina to Tivoli, had mistaken his way; the young man directed him; but as at a distance of a quarter of a mile the road again divided into three ways, and on reaching these the traveller might again stray from his route, he begged Luigi to be his guide. Luigi threw his cloak on the ground, placed his carbine on his shoulder, and freed from his heavy covering, preceded the traveller with the rapid step of a mountaineer, which a horse can scarcely keep up with. In ten minutes Luigi and the traveller reached the cross-roads. On arriving there, with an air as majestic as that of an emperor, he stretched his hand towards that one of the roads which the traveller was to follow.—'That is your road, excellency, and now you cannot again mistake.'—'And here is your recompense,' said the traveller, offering the young herdsman some small pieces of money.

"'Thank you,' said Luigi, drawing back his hand; 'I render a service, I do not sell it.'—'Well,' replied the traveller, who seemed used to this difference between the servility of a man of the cities and the pride of the mountaineer, 'if you refuse wages, you will, perhaps, accept a gift.'—'Ah, yes, that is another thing.'—'Then,' said the traveller, 'take these two Venetian sequins and give them to your bride, to make herself a pair of earrings.'

"'And then do you take this poniard,' said the young herdsman; "you will not find one better carved between Albano and Civita-Castellana.'

"'I accept it,' answered the traveller, 'but then the obligation will be on my side, for this poniard is worth more than two sequins.'—"For a dealer perhaps; but for me, who engraved it myself, it is hardly worth a piastre.'

"'What is your name?' inquired the traveller.—'Luigi Vampa,' replied the shepherd, with the same air as he would have replied, Alexander, King of Macedon.—'And yours?'—'I,' said the traveller, 'am called Sinbad the Sailor.'" Franz d'Epinay started with surprise.—"Sinbad the Sailor," he said.

"Yes," replied the narrator; "that was the name which the traveller gave to Vampa as his own."

"Well, and what may you have to say against this name?" inquired Albert; "it is a very pretty name, and the adventures of the gentleman of that name amused me very much in my youth, I must confess."—Franz said no more. The name of Sinbad the Sailor, as may well be supposed, awakened in him a world of recollections, as had the name of the Count of Monte Cristo on the previous evening.—"Proceed!" said he to the host.

"Vampa put the two sequins haughtily into his pocket, and slowly returned by the way he had gone. As he came within two or three hundred paces of the grotto, he thought he heard a cry. He listened to know whence this sound could proceed. A moment afterwards he thought he heard his own name pronounced distinctly. The cry proceeded from the grotto. He bounded like a chamois, cocking his carbine as he went, and in a moment reached the summit of a hill opposite to that on which he had perceived the traveller. Thence cries for help came more distinctly to his ear. He east his eyes around him, and saw a man carrying off Teresa, as Nessus, the centaur, carried Dejanira. This man, who was hastening towards the wood, was already three-quarters of the way on the road from the grotto to the forest. Vampa measured the distance; the man was at least two hundred paces in advance of him, and there was not a chance of overtaking him. The young shepherd stopped, as if his feet had been rooted to the ground; then he put the butt of his carbine to his shoulder, took aim at the ravisher, followed him for a second in his track, and then fired. The ravisher stopped suddenly, his knees bent under him, and he fell with Teresa in his arms. The young girl rose instantly, but the man lay on the earth struggling in the agonies of death. Vampa then rushed towards Teresa; for at ten paces from the dying man her legs had failed her, and she had dropped on her knees, so that the young man feared that the ball that had brought down his enemy, had also wounded his betrothed. Fortunately, she was unscathed, and it was fright alone that had overcome Teresa. When Luigi had assured himself that she was safe and unharmed, he turned towards the wounded man. He had just expired, with clinched hands, his mouth in a spasm of agony, and his hair on end in the sweat of death. His eyes remained open and menacing. Vampa approached the corpse, and recognized Cucumetto. From the day on which the bandit had been saved by the two young peasants, he had been enamoured of Teresa, and had sworn she should be his. From that time he had watched them, and profiting by the moment when her lover had left her alone, had carried her off, and believed he at length had her in his power, when the ball, directed by the unerring skill of the young herdsman, had pierced his heart. Vampa gazed on him for a moment without betraying the slightest emotion; while, on the contrary, Teresa, shuddering in every limb, dared not approach the slain ruffian but by degrees, and threw a hesitating glance at the dead body over the shoulder of her lover. Suddenly Vampa turned toward his inistress:—'Ah,' said he—'good, good! You are dressed; it is now my turn to dress myself.'

"Teresa was clothed from head to foot in the garb of the Count of San-Felice's daughter. Vampa took Cucumetto's body in his arms and conveyed it to the grotto, while in her turn Teresa remained outside. If a second traveller had passed, he would have seen a strange thing,—a shepherdess watching her flock, clad in a cashmere gown, with ear-rings and necklace of pearls, diamond pins, and buttons of sapphires, emeralds, and rubies. He would, no doubt, have believed that he had returned to the times of Florian, and would have declared, on reaching Paris, that he had met an Alpine shepherdess seated at the foot of the Sabine Hill. At the end of a quarter of an hour Vampa quitted the grotto; his costume was no less elegant than that of Teresa. He wore a vest of garnet-colored velvet, with buttons of cut gold; a silk waistcoat covered with embroidery; a Roman scarf tied round his neck; a cartridge-box worked with gold, and red and green silk; sky-blue velvet breeches, fastened above the knee with diamond buckles; garters of deerskin, worked with a thousand arabesques, and a hat whereon hung ribbons of all colors; two watches hung from his girdle, and a splendid poniard was in his belt. Teresa uttered a cry of admiration. Vampa in this attire resembled a painting by Leopold Robert, or Schnetz. He had assumed the entire costume of Cucumetto. The young man saw the effect produced on his betrothed, and a smile of pride passed over his lips.—'Now,' he said to Teresa, 'are you ready to share my fortune, whatever it may be?'—'Oh, yes!' exclaimed the young girl enthusiastically.—'And follow me wherever I go?'—'To the world's end.'—'Then take my arm, and let us on; we have no time to lose.'—The young girl did so without questioning her lover as to where he was conducting her, for he appeared to her at this moment as handsome, proud, and powerful as a god. They went towards the forest, and soon entered it. We need scarcely say that all the paths of the mountain were known to Vampa; he therefore went forward without a moment's hesitation, although there was no beaten track, but he knew his path by looking at the trees and bushes, and thus they kept on advancing for nearly an hour and a half. At the end of this time they had reached the thickest of the forest. A torrent, whose bed was dry, led into a deep gorge. Vampa took this wild road, which, enclosed between two ridges, and shadowed by the tufted umbrage of the pines, seemed, but for the difficulties of its descent, that path to Avernus of which Virgil speaks. Teresa had become alarmed at the wild and deserted look of the plain around her, and pressed closely against her guide, not uttering a syllable; but as she saw him advance with even step and composed countenance, she endeavored to repress her emotion. Suddenly, about ten paces from them, a man advanced from behind a tree and aimed at Vampa.—'Not another step,' he said, 'or you are a dead man.'— 'What, then,' said Vampa, raising his hand with a gesture of disdain, while Teresa, no longer able to restrain her alarm, clung closely to him, 'do wolves rend each other?'—'Who are you?' inquired the sentinel.—'I am Luigi Vampa, shepherd of the San-Felice farm.'—'What do you want?'—'I would speak with your companions who are in the glade at Rocca Bianca.'—'Follow me, then,' said the sentinel; 'or, as you know your way, go first.'—Vampa smiled disdainfully at this precaution on the part of the bandit, went before Teresa, and continued to advance with the same firm and easy step as before. At the end of ten minutes the bandit made them a sign to stop. The two young persons obeyed. Then the bandit thrice imitated the cry of a crow; a croak answered this signal.—'Good!' said the sentry; 'you may now go on.'—Luigi and Teresa again set forward; as they went on Teresa clung tremblingly to her lover at the sight of weapons and the glistening of carbines through the trees. The retreat of Rocca Bianca was at the top of a small mountain, which no doubt in former days had been a volcano—an extinct volcano before the days when Remus and Romulus had deserted Alba to come and found the city of Rome. Teresa and Luigi reached the summit, and all at once found themselves in the presence of twenty bandits. 'Here is a young man who seeks and wishes to speak to you,' said the sentinel.—'What has he to say?' inquired the young man who was in command in the chief's absence.—'I wish to say that I am tired of a shepherd's life,' was Vampa's reply.—'Ah, I understand,' said the lieutenant; 'and you seek admittance into our ranks?'—'Welcome!' cried several bandits from Ferrusino, Pampinara, and Anagni, who had recognized Luigi Vampa.—'Yes, but I came to ask something more than to be your companion.'—'And what may that be?' inquired the bandits with astonishment.—'I come to ask to be your captain,' said the young man. The bandits shouted with laughter. 'And what have you done to aspire to this honor?' demanded the lieutenant.—'I have killed your chief, Cucumetto, whose dress I now wear; and I set fire to the villa

San Felice to procure a wedding-dress for my betrothed.' An hour afterwards Luigi Vampa was chosen captain, vice Cucumetto deceased."

"Well, my dear Albert," said Franz, turning towards his friend, "what think you of citizen Luigi Vampa?"

"I say he is a myth," replied Albert, "and never had an existence."

"And what may a myth be?" inquired Pastrini.

"The explanation would be too long, my dear landlord," replied Franz.

"And you say that Signor Vampa exercises his profession at this moment in the environs of Rome?"—"And with a boldness of which no bandit before him ever gave an example."

"Then the police have vainly tried to lay hands on him?"—"Why, you see, he has a good understanding with the shepherds in the plains, the fishermen of the Tiber, and the smugglers of the coast. They seek for him in the mountains, and he is on the waters; they follow him on the waters, and he is on the open sea; then they pursue him, and he has suddenly taken refuge in the islands, at Giglio, Guanouti, or Monte Cristo; and when they hunt for him there, he reappears suddenly at Albano, Tivoli, or La Riccia."

"And how does he behave towards travellers?"—"Alas! his plan is very simple. It depends on the distance he may be from the city, whether he gives eight hours, twelve hours, or a day wherein to pay their ransom; and when that time has elapsed he allows another hour's grace. At the sixtieth minute of this hour, if the money is not forthcoming, he blows out the prisoner's brains with a pistol-shot, or plants his dagger in his heart, and that settles the account."

"Well, Albert," inquired Franz of his companion, "are you still disposed to go to the Colosseum by the outer wall?"—"Quite so," said Albert, "if the way be picturesque." The clock struck nine as the door opened, and a coachman appeared. "Excellencies," said he, "the coach is ready."

"Well, then," said Franz, "let us to the Colosseum."

"By the Porta del Popolo or by the streets, your excellencies?"

"By the streets, *morbleu*, by the streets!" cried Franz.

"Ah, my dear fellow," said Albert, rising, and lighting his third cigar, "really, I thought you had more courage." So saying, the two young men went down the staircase, and got into the carriage.

XXXIV

The Colosseum

F RANZ HAD SO MANAGED his route, that during the ride to the Colosseum they passed not a single ancient ruin, so that no preliminary impression interfered to mitigate the colossal proportions of the gigantic building they came to admire. The road selected was a continuation of the Via Sistina; then, by cutting off the right angle of the street in which stands Santa Maria Maggiore, and proceeding by the Via Urbana and San Pietro in Vincoli, the travellers would find themselves directly opposite the Colosseum. This itinerary possessed another great advantage,—that of leaving Franz at full liberty to indulge his deep reverie upon the subject of Signor Pastrini's story, in which his mysterious host of Monte Cristo was so strangely mixed up. Seated with folded arms in a corner of the carriage, he continued to ponder over the singular history he had so lately listened to, and to ask himself an interminable number of questions touching its various circumstances, without, however, arriving at a satisfactory reply to any of them. One fact more than the rest brought his friend "Sinbad the Sailor" back to his recollection, and that was the mysterious sort of intimacy that seemed to exist between the brigands and the sailors; and Pastrini's account of Vampa's having found refuge on board the vessels of smugglers and fishermen, reminded Franz of the two Corsican bandits he had found supping so amicably with the crew of the little yacht, which had even deviated from its course and touched at Porto-Vecchio for the sole purpose of landing them. The very name assumed by his host of Monte Cristo, and again repeated by the landlord of the Hôtel de Loudres, abnodantly proved to him that his island friend was playing his philanthropic part on the shores of Plombino, Civita-Vecchia, Ostia, and Gaëta, as on those of Corsica, Tuscany, and Spain; and further, Franz bethought him of having heard his singular entertainer speak both of Tunis and Palermo, proving thereby how largely his circle of acquaintances extended.

But however the mind of the young man might be absorbed in these reflections, they were at once dispersed at the sight of the dark frowning ruins of the stupendous Colosseum, through the various openings of which the pale moonlight played and flickered like the unearthly gleam from the eyes of the wandering dead. The carriage stopped near the Meta Sudans; the door was opened, and the young men, eagerly alighting, found themselves opposite a *cicerone*, who appeared to have sprung up from the ground, so unexpected was his appearance.

The usual guide from the hotel having followed them, they had paid two conductors, nor is it possible, at Rome, to avoid this abundant supply of guides; besides the ordinary *cicerone*, who seizes upon you directly you set foot in your hotel, and never quits you while you remain in the city, there is also a special *cicerone* belonging to each monument—nay, almost to each part of a monument. It may, therefore, be easily imagined there is no scarcity of guides at the Colosseum, that wonder of all ages, which Martial thus eulogizes: "Let Memphis cease to boast the barbarous miracles of her pyramids, and the wonders of Babylon be talked of no more among us; all must bow to the superiority of the gigantic labor of the Cæsars, and the many voices of Faine spread far and wide the surpassing merits of this incomparable monument."

As for Albert and Franz, they essayed not to escape from their *ciceronian* tyrants; and, indeed, it would have been so much the more difficult to break their bondage, as the guides alone are permitted to visit these monuments with torches in their hands. Thus, then, the young men made no attempt at resistance, but blindly and confidingly surrendered themselves into the care and custody of their conductors. Albert had already made seven or eight similar excursions to the Colosseum, while his less favored companion trod for the first time in his life the classic ground forming the monument of Flavius Vespasian; and, to his credit be it spoken, his mind, even amid the glib loquacity of the guides, was duly and deeply touched with awe and enthusiastic admiration of all he saw; and certainly no adequate notion of these stupendous ruins can be formed save by such as have visited them, and more especially by moonlight, at which time the vast proportions of the building appear twice as large when viewed by the mysterious beans of a southern moonlit sky, whose rays are sufficiently clear and vivid to light the horizon with a glow equal to the soft twilight of an eastern clime. Scarcely, therefore, had the reflective Franz walked a hundred steps beneath the interior porticoes of the ruin, than, abandoning Albert to the guides (who would by no means yield their prescriptive right of carrying their victims through the routine regularly laid down, and as regularly followed by them, but dragged the unconscious visitor to the various objects with a pertinacity that admitted of no appeal, beginning, as a matter of course, with the Lions' Den, and finishing with Cæsar's "Podium,"), to escape a jargon and mechanical survey of the wonders by which he was surrounded, Franz ascended a half-dilapidated staircase, and, leaving them to follow their monotonous round, seated himself at the foot of a column, and immediately opposite a large aperture, which permitted him to enjoy a full and undisturbed view of the gigantic dimensions of the majestic ruin.

Franz had remained for nearly a quarter of an hour perfectly hidden by the shadow of the vast column at whose base he had found a resting-place, and from whence his eyes followed the motions of Albert and his guides, who, holding torches in their hands, had emerged from a vomitarium at the opposite extremity of the Colosseum, and then again disappeared down the steps conducting to the seats reserved for the Vestal virgins, resembling, as they glided along, some restless shades following the flickering glare of so many *ignes-fatui*. All at once his ear caught a sound resembling that of a stone rolling down the staircase opposite the one by which he had himself ascended. There was nothing remarkable in the circumstance of a fragment of granite giving way and falling heavily below; but it seemed to him that the substance that fell gave way beneath the pressure of a foot, and also that some one, who endeavored as much as possible to prevent his footsteps from being heard, was approaching the spot where he sat. Conjecture soon became certainty, for the figure of a man was distinctly visible to Franz, gradually emerging from the staircase opposite, upon which the moon was at that moment pouring a full tide of silvery brightness.

The stranger thus presenting himself was probably a person who, like Franz, preferred the enjoyment of solitude and his own thoughts to the frivolous gabble of the guides. And his appearance had nothing extraordinary in it; but the hesitation with which he proceeded, stopping and listening with anxious attention at every step he took, convinced Franz that he expected the arrival of some person. By a sort of instinctive impulse, Franz withdrew as much as possible behind his pillar. About ten feet from the spot where he and the stranger were, the roof had given way, leaving a large round opening, through which might be seen the blue vault of heaven, thickly studded with stars. Around this opening, which had, possibly, for ages permitted a free entrance to the brilliant moonbeams that now illumined the vast pile, grew a quantity of creeping plants, whose delicate green branches stood out in bold relief against the clear azure of the firmanent, while large masses of thick, strong fibrous shoots forced their way through the chasm, and hung floating to and fro like so many waving strings. The person whose mysterious arrival had attracted the attention of Franz stood in a kind of half-light, that rendered it impossible to distinguish his features, although his dress was easily made out. He wore a large brown mantle one fold of which, thrown over his left shoulder, served likewise to mask the lower part of his countenance, while the upper part was completely hidden by his broad-brimmed hat. The lower part of his dress was more distinctly visible by the bright rays of the moon, which, entering through the broken ceiling, shed their refulgent beams on feet cased in elegantly made boots of polished leather, over which descended fashionably cut trousers of black cloth.

From the imperfect means Franz had of judging, he could only come to one conclusion,—that the person whom he was thus watching certainly belonged to no inferior station of life. Some few minutes had elapsed, and the stranger began to show manifest signs of impatience, when a slight noise was heard outside the aperture in the roof, and almost immediately a dark shadow seemed to obstruct the flood of light that had entered it, and the figure of a man was clearly seen gazing with eager scrutiny on the immense space beneath him; then, as his eye caught sight of him in the mantle, he grasped a floating mass of thickly matted boughs, and glided down by their help to within three or four feet of the ground, and then leaped lightly on his feet. The man who had performed this daring act with so much indifference wore the Transtevere[1] costume. "I beg your excellency's pardon for keeping you waiting," said the man, in the Roman dialect, "but I don't think I'm many minutes after my time; ten o'clock has just struck on the Lateran."

"Say not a word about being late," replied the stranger in purest Tuscan; "'tis I who am too soon. But even if you had caused me to wait a little while, I should have felt quite sure that the delay was not occasioned by any fault of yours."

"Your excellency is perfectly right in so thinking," said the

[1] A district of Rome on the right bank of the Tiber.

man: "I came here direct from the Castle of St. Angelo, and I had an immense deal of trouble before I could get a chance to speak to Beppo."

"And who is Beppo?"—"Oh, Beppo is employed in the prison, and I give him so much a year to let me know what is going on within his holiness's castle."

"Indeed! You are a provident person, I see."—"Why, you see, no one knows what may happen. Perhaps some of these days I may be entrapped, like poor Peppino, and may be very glad to have some little nibbling mouse to gnaw the meshes of my net, and so help me out of prison."

"Briefly, what did you glean?"—"That two executions of considerable interest will take place the day after to-morrow at two o'clock, as is customary at Rome at the commencement of all great festivals. One of the culprits will be *mazzolato*;[1] he is an atrocious villain, who murdered the priest who brought him up, and deserves not the smallest pity. The other sufferer is sentenced to be *decapitato*;[2] and he, your excellency, is poor Peppino."

"The fact is, that you have inspired not only the pontifical government, but also the neighboring states, with such extreme fear, that they are glad of an opportunity of making an example."—"But Peppino did not even belong to my band; he was merely a poor shepherd, whose only crime consisted in furnishing us with provisions."

"Which makes him your accomplice to all intents and purposes. But mark the distinction with which he is treated; instead of being knocked on the head, as you would be if once they caught hold of you, he is simply sentenced to be guillotined, by which means, too, the amusements of the day are diversified, and there is a spectacle to please every spectator."

[1] Knocked on the head.
[2] Beheaded.

"Without reckoning the wholly unexpected one I am preparing to surprise them with."

"My good friend," said the man in the cloak, "excuse me for saying that you seem to me precisely in the mood to commit some wild or extravagant act."—"Perhaps I am; but one thing I have resolved on, and that is, to stop at nothing to restore a poor devil to liberty, who has got into this scrape solely from having served me. I should hate and despise myself as a coward did I desert the brave fellow in his present extremity."

"And what do you mean to do?"—"To surround the scaffold with twenty of my best men, who, at a signal from me, will rush forward directly Peppino is brought for execution, and, by the assistance of their stilettos, drive back the guard, and carry off the prisoner."

"That seems to me as hazardous as uncertain, and convinces me that my scheme is far better than yours."

"And what is your excellency's project?"—"Just this. I will so advantageously bestow 2,000 piastres, that the person receiving them shall obtain a respite till next year for Peppino; and during that year, another skilfully placed 1,000 piastres will afford him the means of escaping from his prison."

"And do you feel sure of succeeding?"

"*Pardieu!*" exclaimed the man in the cloak, suddenly expressing himself in French.

"What did your excellency say?" inquired the other.—"I said, my good fellow, that I would do more single-handed by the means of gold, than you and all your troop could effect with stilettos, pistols, carbines, and blunderbusses included. Leave me, then, to act, and have no fears for the result."

"At least, there can be no harm in myself and party being in readiness, in case your excellency should fail."—"None whatever. Take what precautions you please, if it is any satisfaction to you to do so; but rely upon my obtaining the reprieve I seek."

"Remember, the execution is fixed for the day after tomorrow, and that you have but one day to work in."—"And what of that? Is not a day divided into twenty-four hours, each hour into sixty minutes, and every minute sub-divided into sixty seconds? Now in 86,400 seconds very many things can be done."

"And how shall I know whether your excellency has succeeded or not?"

"Oh, that is very easily arranged. I have engaged the three lower windows at the Café Rospoli; should I have obtained the requisite pardon for Peppino, the two outside windows will be hung with yellow damasks, and the centre with white, having a large cross in red marked on it."

"And whom will you employ to carry the reprieve to the officer directing the execution?"—"Send one of your men, disguised as a penitent friar, and I will give it to him. His dress will procure him the means of approaching the scaffold itself, and he will deliver the official order to the officer, who, in his turn, will hand it to the executioner; in the meantime, it will be as well to acquaint Peppino with what we have determined on, if it be only to prevent his dying of fear or losing his senses, because in either case a very useless expense will have been incurred."

"Your excellency," said the man, "you are fully persuaded of my entire devotion to you, are you not?"—"Nay, I flatter myself that there can be no doubt of it," replied the cavalier in the cloak.

"Well, then, only fulfil your promise of rescuing Peppino, and henceforward you shall receive not only devotion, but the most absolute obedience from myself and those under me that one human being can render to another."

"Have a care how far you pledge yourself, my good friend, for I may remind you of your promise at some, perhaps, not very distant period, when I, in my turn, may require your aid and influence."—"Let that day come sooner or later, your excellency will find me what I have found you in this my heavy trouble; and if from the other end of the world you but write me word to do such or such a thing, you may regard it as done, for done it shall be, on the word and faith of"—

"Hush!" interrupted the stranger; "I hear a noise."

"'Tis some travellers, who are visiting the Colosseum by torch-light."

"'T'were better we should not be seen together; those guides are nothing but spies, and might possibly recognize you; and, however I may be honored by your friendship, my worthy friend, if once the extent of our intimacy were known, I am sadly afraid both my reputation and credit would suffer thereby."

"Well, then, if you obtain the reprieve?"

"The middle window at the Café Rospoli will be hung with white damask, bearing a red cross."—"And if you fail?"

"Then all three windows will have yellow draperies."—"And then?"

"And then, my good fellow, use your daggers in any way you please, and I further promise you to be there as a spectator of your prowess."

"We understand each other perfectly, then. Adieu, your excellency; depend upon me as firmly as I do upon you."

Saying these words, the Transteverin disappeared down the staircase, while his companion, muffling his features more closely than before in the folds of his mantle, passed almost close to Franz, and descended to the arena by an outward flight of steps. The next minute Franz heard himself called by Albert, who made the lofty building re-echo with the sound of his friend's name. Franz, however, did not obey the summons till he had satisfied himself that the two men whose conversation he had overheard were at a sufficient distance to prevent his encountering them in his descent. In ten minutes after the strangers had departed, Franz was on the road to the Piazza de Spazni, listening with studied indifference to the learned dissertation delivered by Albert, after the manner of Pliny and Calpurnius, touching the iron-pointed nets used to prevent the ferocious beasts from springing on the spectators. Franz let him proceed without interruption, and, in fact, did not hear what was said; he longed to be alone, and free to ponder over all that had occurred. One of the two men, whose mysterious meeting in the Colosseum he had so unintentionally witnessed, was an entire stranger to him, but not so the other; and though Franz had been unable to distinguish his features, from his being either wrapped in his mantle or obscured by the shadow, the tones of his voice had made too powerful an impression on him the first time he had heard them for him ever again to forget them, hear them when or where he might. It was more especially when this man was speaking in a manner half jesting, half bitter, that Franz's ear recalled most vividly the deep, sonorous, yet well-pitched voice that had addressed him in the grotto of Monte Cristo, and which he heard for the second time amid the darkness and ruined grandeur of the Colosseum. And the more he thought, the more entire was his conviction, that the person who wore the mantle was no other than his former host and entertainer, "Sinbad the Sailor."

Under any other circumstances, Franz would have found it impossible to resist his extreme curiosity to know more of so singular a personage, and with that intent have sought to renew their short acquaintance; but in the present instance, the confidential nature of the conversation he had overheard made him, with propriety judge that his appearance at such a time would be anything but agreeable. As we have seen, therefore, he permitted his former host to retire without attempting a recognition, but fully promising himself a rich indemnity for his present forbearance should chance afford him another opportunity. In vain did Franz endeavor to forget the many perplexing thoughts which assailed him; in vain did he court the refreshment of sleep. Slumber refused to visit his eyelids, and the night was passed in feverish contemplation of the chain of circumstances tending to prove the identity of the mysterious visitant to the Colosseum with the inhabitant of the grotto of

Monte Cristo; and the more he thought, the firmer grew his opinion on the subject. Worn out at length, he fell asleep at daybreak,
and did not awake till late. Like a genuine Frenchman, Albert had
employed his time in arranging for the evening's diversion; he had
sent to engage a box at the Teatro Argentino; and Franz, having a
number of letters to write, relinquished the carriage to Albert for
the whole of the day. At five o'clock Albert returned, delighted with
his day's work; he had been occupied in leaving his letters of introduction, and had received in return more invitations to balls and
routs than it would be possible for him to accept; besides this, he
had seen (as he called it) all the remarkable sights at Rome. Yes, in
a single day he had accomplished what his more serious-minded
companion would have taken weeks to effect. Neither had he
neglected to ascertain the name of the piece to be played that night
at the Teatro Argentino, and also what performers appeared in it.

The opera of "Parisina" was announced for representation, and
the principal actors were Coselli, Moriani, and La Specchia. The
young men, therefore, had reason to consider themselves fortunate
in having the opportunity of hearing one of the best works by the
composer of "Lucia di Lammermoor," supported by three of the
most renowned vocalists of Italy. Albert had never been able to
endure the Italian theatres, with their orchestras from which it is
impossible to see, and the absence of balconies, or open boxes; all
these defects pressed hard on a man who had had his stall at the
Bouffes, and had shared a lower box at the Opera. Still, in spite of
this, Albert displayed his most dazzling and effective costumes each
time he visited the theatres; but, alas, his elegant toilet was wholly
thrown away, and one of the most worthy representatives of Parisian
fashion had to carry with him the mortifying reflection that he had
nearly overrun Italy without meeting with a single adventure.

Sometimes Albert would affect to make a joke of his want of
success; but internally he was deeply wounded, and his self-love
immensely piqued, to think that Albert de Morcerf, the most

admired and most sought after of any young person of his day, should thus be passed over, and merely have his labor for his pains. And the thing was so much the more annoying, as, according to the characteristic modesty of a Frenchman. Albert had quitted Paris with the full conviction that he had only to show himself in Italy to carry all before him, and that upon his return he should astonish the Parisian world with the recital of his numerous love-affairs. Alas, poor Albert! none of those interesting adventures fell in his way; the lovely Genoese, Florentine, and Neapolitans were all faithful, if not to their husbands, at least to their lovers, and thought not of changing even for the splendid appearance of Albert de Morcerf; and all he gained was the painful conviction that the ladies of Italy have this advantage over those of France, that they are faithful even in their infidelity. Yet he could not restrain a hope that in Italy, as elsewhere, there might be an exception to the general rule. Albert, besides being an elegant, well-looking young man, was also possessed of considerable talent and ability; moreover, he was a viscount—a recently created one, certainly, but in the present day it is not necessary to go as far back as Noah in tracing a descent, and a genealogical tree is equally estimated, whether dated from 1399 or merely 1815; but to crown all these advantages, Albert de Morcerf commanded an income of 50,000 livres, a more than sufficient sum to render him a personage of considerable importance in Paris. It was therefore no small mortification to him to have visited most of the principal cities in Italy without having excited the most trifling observation. Albert, however, hoped to indemnify himself for all these slights and indifferences during the Carnival, knowing full well that among the different states and kingdoms in which this festivity is celebrated, Rome is the spot where even the wisest and gravest throw off the usual rigidity of their lives, and deign to mingle in the follies of this time of liberty and relaxation.

The Carnival was to commence on the morrow; therefore Albert had not an instant to lose in setting forth the programme of his hopes, expectations, and claims to notice. With this design he had engaged a box in the most conspicuous part of the theatre, and exerted himself to set off his personal attractions by the aid of the most rich and elaborate toilet. The box taken by Albert was in the first circle; although each of the three tiers of boxes is deemed equally aristocratic, and is, for this reason, generally styled the "nobility's boxes," and although the box engaged for the two friends was sufficiently capacious to contain at least a dozen persons, it had cost less than would be paid at some of the French theatres for one admitting merely four occupants. Another motive had influenced Albert's selection of his seat,—who knew but that, thus advantageously placed, he might not in truth attract the notice of some fair Roman, and an introduction might ensue that would procure him the offer of a seat in a carriage, or a place in a princely balcony, from which he might behold the gayeties of the Carnival? These united considerations made Albert more lively and anxious to please than he had hitherto been. Totally disregarding the business of the stage, he leaned from his box and began attentively scrutinizing the beauty of each pretty woman, aided by a powerful opera-glass; but, alas, this attempt to attract notice wholly failed: not even curiosity had been excited, and it was but too apparent that the lovely creatures, into whose good graces he was desirous of stealing, were all so much engrossed with themselves, their lovers, or their own thoughts, that they had not so much as noticed him or the manipulation of his glass.

The truth was, that the anticipated pleasures of the Carnival, with the "holy week" that was to succeed it, so filled every fair breast, as to prevent the least attention being bestowed even on the business of the stage. The actors made their entries and exits unobserved or unthought of; at certain conventional moments, the spectators would suddenly cease their conversation, or rouse themselves from their musings, to listen to some brilliant effort of Moriani's, a well-executed recitative by Coselli, or to join in loud applause at the wonderful powers of La Specchia; but that momentary excitement over, they quickly relapsed into their former state of preoccupation or interesting conversation. Towards the close of the first act, the door of a box which had been hitherto vacant was opened; a lady entered to whom Franz had been introduced in Paris, where, indeed, he had imagined she still was. The quick eye of Albert caught the involuntary start with which his friend beheld the new arrival, and, turning to him, he said hastily, "Do you know the woman who has just entered that box?"

"Yes; what do you think of her?"—"Oh, she is perfectly lovely—what a complexion! And such magnificent hair! Is she French?"—"No; a Venetian."—"And her name is—"—"Countess G—."

"Ah, I know her by name!" exclaimed Albert; "she is said to possess as much wit and cleverness as beauty. I was to have been presented to her when I met her at Madame Villefort's ball."

"Shall I assist you in repairing your negligence?" asked Franz.

"My dear fellow, are you really on such good terms with her as to venture to take me to her box?"—"Why, I have only had the honor of being in her society and conversing with her three or four times in my life; but you know that even such an acquaintance as that might warrant my doing what you ask." At that instant, the countess perceived Franz, and graciously waved her hand to him, to which he replied by a respectful inclination of the head. "Upon my word," said Albert, "you seem to be on excellent terms with the beautiful countess."

"You are mistaken in thinking so," returned Franz calmly; "but you merely fall into the same error which leads so many of our countrymen to commit the most egregious blunders,—I mean that of judging the habits and customs of Italy and Spain by our Parisian notions; believe me, nothing is more fallacious than to form any estimate of the degree of intimacy you may suppose existing among persons by the familiar terms they seem upon; there is a similarity of feeling at this instant between ourselves and the countess—

nothing more."—"Is there, indeed, my good fellow? Pray tell me, is it sympathy of heart?"

"No; of taste," continued Franz gravely.

"And in what manner has this congeniality of mind been evinced?"

"By the countess's visiting the Colosseum, as we did last night, by moonlight, and nearly alone."—"You were with her, then?"

"I was."—"And what did you say to her?"

"Oh, we talked of the illustrious dead of whom that magnificent ruin is a glorious monument!"

"Upon my word," cried Albert, 'you must have been a very entertaining companion alone, or all but alone, with a beautiful woman in such a place of sentiment as the Colosseum, and yet to find nothing better to talk about than the dead! All I can say is, if ever I should get such a chance, the living should be my theme."—"And you will probably find your theme ill-chosen."

"But," said Albert, breaking in upon his discourse, "never mind the past; let us only remember the present. Are you not going to keep your promise of introducing me to the fair subject of our remarks?"—"Certainly, directly the curtain falls on the stage."

"What a confounded time this first act takes. I believe, on my soul, that they never mean to finish it."—"Oh, yes, they will only listen to that charming finale. How exquisitely Coselli sings his part."

"But what an awkward, inelegant fellow he is."

"Well, then, what do you say to La Specchia? Did you ever see anything more perfect than her acting?"—"Why, you know, my dear fellow, when one has been accustomed to Malibran and Sontag, such singers as these don't make the same impression on you they perhaps do on others."

"At least, you must admire Moriani's style and execution." —"I never fancied men of his dark, ponderous appearance singing with a voice like a woman's."

"My good friend," said Franz, turning to him, while Albert continued to point his glass at every box in the theatre, "you seem
determined not to approve; you are really too difficult to please."
The curtain at length fell on the performances, to the infinite satisfaction of the Viscount of Morcerf, who seized his hat, rapidly
passed his fingers through his hair, arranged his cravat and wristbands, and signified to Franz that he was waiting for him to lead the
way. Franz, who had mutely interrogated the countess, and received
from her a gracious smile in token that he would be welcome,
sought not to retard the gratification of Albert's eager impatience,
but began at once the tour of the house, closely followed by Albert,
who availed himself of the few minutes required to reach the opposite side of the theatre to settle the height and smoothness of his
collar, and to arrange the lappets of his coat. This important task was
just completed as they arrived at the countess's box. At the knock,
the door was immediately opened, and the young man who was
seated beside the countess, in obedience to the Italian custom,
instantly rose and surrendered his place to the strangers, who, in
turn, would be expected to retire upon the arrival of other visitors.

Franz presented Albert as one of the most distinguished young
men of the day, both as regarded his position in society and extraordinary talents; nor did he say more than the truth, for in Paris and the
circle in which the viscount moved, he was looked upon and cited
as a model of perfection. Franz added that his companion, deeply
grieved at having been prevented the honor of being presented to
the countess during her sojourn in Paris, was most anxious to make
up for it, and had requested him (Franz) to remedy the past misfortune by conducting him to her box, and concluded by asking pardon
for his presumption in having taken it upon himself to do so. The
countess, in reply, bowed gracefully to Albert, and extruded her hand
with cordial kindness to Franz; then inviting Albert to take the vacant
seat beside her, she recommended Franz to take the next best, if he
wished to view the ballet, and pointed to the one behind her own

chair. Albert was soon deeply engrossed in discoursing upon Paris and Parisian matters, speaking to the countess of the various persons they both knew there. Franz perceived how completely he was in his element; and, unwilling to interfere with the pleasure he so evidently felt, took up Albert's glass, and began in his turn to survey the audience. Sitting alone, in the front of a box immediately opposite, but situated on the third row, was a woman of exquisite beauty, dressed in a Greek costume, which evidently, from the case and grace with which she wore it, was her national attire. Behind her, but in deep shadow, was the outline of a masculine figure; but the features of this latter personage it was not possible to distinguish. Franz could not forbear breaking in upon the apparently interesting conversation passing between the countess and Albert, to inquire of the former if she knew who was the fair Albanian opposite, since beauty such as hers was well worthy of being observed by either sex. "All I can tell about her," replied the countess, "is, that she has been at Rome since the beginning of the season; for I saw her where she now sits the very first night of the season, and since then she has never missed a performance. Sometimes she is accompanied by the person who is now with her, and at others she is merely attended by a black servant."

"And what do you think of her personal appearance?"—"Oh, I consider her perfectly lovely—she is just my idea of what Medora must have been."

Franz and the countess exchanged a smile, and then the latter resumed her conversation with Albert, while Franz returned to his previous survey of the house and company. The curtain rose on the ballet, which was one of those excellent specimens of the Italian school, admirably arranged and put on the stage by Heuri, who has established for himself a great reputation throughout Italy for his taste and skill in the choregraphic art—one of those masterly productions of grace, method, and elegance in which the whole *corps de ballet*, from the principal dancers to the humblest supernumerary, are all engaged on the stage at the same time; and a hundred and fifty persons may be seen exhibiting the same attitude, or elevating the same arm or leg with a simultaneous movement, that would lead you to suppose that but one mind, one act of volition, influenced the moving mass—the ballet was called "Poliska." However much the ballet might have claimed his attention, Franz was too deeply occupied with the beautiful Greek to take any note of it; while she seemed to experience an almost childlike delight in watching it, her eager, animated looks contrasting strongly with the utter indifference of her companion, who, during the whole time the piece lasted, never even moved, not even when the furious, crashing din produced by the trumpets, eymbals, and Chinese bells sounded their loudest from the orchestra. Of this he took no heed, but was, as far as appearances might be trusted, enjoying soft repose and bright celestial dreams. The ballet at length came to a close, and the curtain fell amid the loud, unanimous plaudits of an enthusiastic and delighted audience.

Owing to the very judicious plan of dividing the two acts of the opera with a ballet, the pauses between the performances are very short, the singers in the opera having time to repose themselves and change their costume, when necessary, while the dancers are execnting their pirouettes and exhibiting their graceful steps. The overture to the second act began; and, at the first sound of the leader's bow across his violin, Franz observed the sleeper slowly arise and approach the Greek girl, who turned around to say a few words to him, and then, leaning forward again on the railing of her box, she became as absorbed as before in what was going on. The countenance of the person who had addressed her remained so completely in the shade, that, though Franz tried his utmost, he could not distinguish a single feature. The curtain rose, and the attention of Franz was attracted by the actors; and his eyes turned from the box containing the Greek girl and her strange companion to watch the business of the stage.

Most of my readers are aware that the second act of "Parisina" opens with the celebrated and effective duet in which Parisina, while sleeping, betrays to Azzo the secret of her love for Ugo. The injured husband goes through all the emotions of jealousy, until conviction seizes on his mind, and then, in a frenzy of rage and indignation, he awakens his guilty wife to tell her that he knows her guilt, and to threaten her with his vengeance. This duet is one of the most beautiful, expressive, and terrible conceptions that has ever emanated from the fruitful pen of Donizetti. Franz now listened to it for the third time; yet its notes, so tenderly expressive and fearfully grand, as the wretched husband and wife give vent to their different griefs and passions, thrilled through the soul of Franz with an effect equal to his first emotions upon hearing it. Excited beyond his usual calm demeanor, Franz rose with the audience, and was about to join the loud, enthusiastic applause that followed; but suddenly his purpose was arrested, his hands fell by his sides, and the half-uttered "bravos" expired on his lips. The occupant of the box in which the Greek girl sat appeared to share the universal admiration that prevailed; for he left his seat to stand up in front, so that, his countenance being fully revealed, Franz had no difficulty in recognizing him as the mysterious inhabitant of Monte Cristo, and the very same person he had encountered the preceding evening in the ruins of the Colosseum, and whose voice and figure had seemed so familiar to him. All doubt of his identity was now at an end; his singular host evidently resided at Rome. The surprise and agitation occasioned by this full confirmation of Franz's former suspicion had no doubt imparted a corresponding expression to his features; for the countess, after gazing with a puzzled look at his face, burst into a fit of laughter, and begged to know what had happened. "Countess," returned Franz, totally unheeding her raillery, "I asked you a short time since if you knew any particulars respecting the Albanian lady opposite; I must now beseech you to inform me who and what is her husband?"

"Nay," answered the countess, "I know no more of him than yourself."—"Perhaps you never before noticed him?"

"What a question—so truly French! Do you not know that we Italians have eyes only for the man we love?"

"True," replied Franz.—"All I can say is," continued the countess, taking up the *lorgnette*, and directing it toward the box in question, "that the gentleman, whose history I am unable to furnish, seems to me as though he had just been dug up; he looks more like a corpse permitted by some friendly grave-digger to quit his tomb for a while, and revisit this earth of ours, than anything human. How ghastly pale he is!"

"Oh, he is always as colorless as you now see him," said Franz.

"Then you know him?" almost screamed the countess. "Oh, pray do, for heaven's sake, tell us all about—is he a vampire, or a resuscitated corpse, or what?"

"I fancy I have seen him before; and I even think he recognizes me."

"And I can well understand," said the countess, shrugging up her beautiful shoulders, as though an involuntary shudder passed through her veins, "that those who have once seen that man will never be likely to forget him." The sensation experienced by Franz was evidently not peculiar to himself; another, and wholly uninterested person, felt the same unaccountable awe and misgiving. "Well," inquired Franz, after the countess had a second time directed her *lorgnette* at the box, "what do you think of our opposite neighbor?"—"Why, that he is no other than Lord Ruthven himself in a living form." This fresh allusion to Byron[1] drew a smile to Franz's countenance; although he could but allow that if anything was likely to induce belief in the existence of vampires, it would be the presence of such a man as the mysterious personage before him.—"I must positively find out who and what he is," said Franz, rising from his seat.—"No, no," cried the

[1] Scott, of course: "The son of an ill-fated sire, and the father of a yet more unfortunate family, bore in his looks that east of inauspicious melancholy by which the physiognomists of that time pretended to distinguish those who were predestined to a violent and unhappy death,"—*The Abbot*6, ch. xxii.

countess; "you must not leave me. I depend upon you to escort me home. Oh, indeed, I cannot permit you to go."

"Is it possible," whispered Franz, "that you entertain any fear?"

"I'll tell you," answered the countess. "Byron had the most perfect belief in the existence of vampires, and even assured me that he had seen them. The description he gave me perfectly corresponds with the features and character of the man before us. Oh, he is the exact personification of what I have been led to expect! The coal-black hair, large bright, glittering eyes, in which a wild, unearthly fire seems burning, —the same ghastly paleness. Then observe, too, that the woman with him is altogether unlike all others of her sex. She is a foreigner—a stranger. Nobody knows who she is, or where she comes from. No doubt she belongs to the same horrible race he does, and is, like himself, a dealer in magical arts. I entreat of you not to go near him—at least to-night; and if to-morrow your curiosity still continues as great, pursue your researches if you will; but to-night you neither can nor shall. For that purpose I mean to keep you all to myself." Franz protested he could not defer his pursuit till the following day, for many reasons. "Listen to me," said the countess, "and do not be so very headstrong. I am going home. I have a party at my house to-night, and therefore cannot possibly remain till the end of the opera. Now, I cannot for one instant believe you so devoid of gallantry as to refuse a lady your escort when she even condescends to ask you for it."

There was nothing else left for Franz to do but to take up his hat, open the door of the box, and offer the countess his arm. It was quite evident, by her manner, that her uneasiness was not feigned; and Franz himself could not resist a feeling of superstitious dread—so much the stronger in him, as it arose from a variety of corroborative recollections, while the terror of the countess sprang from an instinctive belief, originally created in her mind by the wild tales she had listened to till she believed them truths. Franz could even feel her arm tremble as he assisted her into the carriage. Upon arriving at her hotel, Franz perceived that she had deceived him when she spoke of expecting company; on the contrary, her own return before the appointed hour seemed greatly to astonish the servants. "Excuse my little subterfuge," said the countess, in reply to her companion's half-reproachful observation on the subject; "but that horrid man had made me feel quite uncomfortable, and I longed to be alone, that I might compose my startled mind." Franz essayed to smile. "Nay," said she, "do not smile; it ill accords with the expression of your countenance, and I am sure it does not spring from your heart. However, promise me one thing."

"What is it?"—"Promise me, I say."

"I will do anything you desire, except relinquish my determination of finding out who this man is. I have more reasons than you can imagine for desiring to know who he is, from whence he came, and whither he is going."

"Where he comes from I am ignorant; but I can readily tell you where he is going to, and that is down below, without the least doubt."

"Let us only speak of the promise you wished me to make," said Franz.

"Well, then, you must give me your word to return immediately to your hotel, and make no attempt to follow this man to-night. There are certain affinities between the persons we quit and those we meet afterwards. For heaven's sake, do not serve as a conductor between that man and me. Pursue your chase after him to-morrow as eagerly as you please; but never bring him near me, if you would not see me die of terror. And now, good-night; go to your rooms, and try to sleep away all recollections of this evening. For my own part, I am quite sure I shall not be able to close my eyes." So saying, the countess quitted Franz, leaving him unable to decide whether she were merely amusing herself at his expense, or whether her fears and agitations were genuine.

Upon his return to the hotel, Franz found Albert in his dressing-gown and slippers, listlessly extended on a sofa, smoking a cigar. "My dear fellow," cried he, springing up, "is it really you? Why, I did not expect to see you before to-morrow."—"My dear Albert," replied Franz, "I am glad of this opportunity to tell you, once and forever, that you entertain a most erroneous notion concerning Italian women. I should have thought the continual failures you have met with in all your own love affairs might have taught you better by this time."

"Upon my soul, these women would puzzle the very Devil to read them aright. Why, here—they give you their hand—they press yours in return—they keep up a whispering conversation—permit you to accompany them home. Why, if a Parisian were to indulge in a quarter of these marks of flattering attention, her reputation would be gone forever."—"And the very reason why the women of this fine country put so little restraint on their words and actions, is because they live so much in public, and have really nothing to conceal. Besides, you must have perceived that the countess was really alarmed."

"At what? At the sight of that respectable gentleman sitting opposite to us in the same box with the lovely Greek girl? Now, for my part, I met them in the lobby after the conclusion of the piece; and hang me, if I can guess where you took your notions of the other world from. I can assure you that this hobgoblin of yours is a deuced fine-looking fellow—admirably dressed. Indeed, I feel quite sure, from the cut of his clothes, they are made by a first-rate Paris tailor—probably Blin or Humann. He was rather too pale, certainly; but then, you know, paleness is always looked upon as a strong proof of aristocratic descent and distinguished breeding." Franz smiled; for he well remembered that Albert particularly prided himself on the entire absence of color in his own complexion.

"Well, that tends to confirm my own ideas," said Franz, "that the countess's suspicions were destitute alike of sense and reason. Did he speak in your hearing? and did you catch any of his words?"

"I did; but they were uttered in the Romaic dialect. I knew that from the mixture of Greek words. I don't know whether I ever told you that when I was at college I was rather—rather strong in Greek."

"He spoke the Romaic language, did he?"—"I think so."

"That settles it," murmured Franz. "'Tis he, past all doubt."

"What do you say?"—"Nothing, nothing. But tell me, what were you thinking about when I came in?"

"Oh, I was arranging a little surprise for you."

"Indeed. Of what nature?"

"Why, you know it is quite impossible to procure a carriage."

"Certainly; and I also know that we have done all that human means afforded to endeavor to get one."

"Now, then, in this difficulty a bright idea has flashed across my brain." Franz looked at Albert as though he had not much confidence in the suggestions of his imagination. "I tell you what. Sir Franz," cried Albert, "you deserve to be called out for such a misgiving and incredulous glance as that you were pleased to bestow on me just now."—"And I promise to give you the satisfaction of a gentleman if your scheme turns out as ingenious as you assert."

"Well, then, hearken to me."—"I listen."

"You agree, do you not, that obtaining a carriage is out of the question?"—"I do."—"Neither can we procure horses?"

"True; we have offered any sum, but have failed."

"Well, now, what do you say to a cart? I dare say such a thing might be had."—"Very possibly."—"And a pair of oxen?"

"As easily found as the cart."—"Then you see, my good fellow, with a cart and a couple of oxen our business can be managed. The cart must be tastefully ornamented; and if you and I dress ourselves as Neapolitan reapers, we may get up a striking tablean, after the manner of that splendid picture by Leopold Robert. It would add greatly to the effect if the countess would join us in the costume of a peasant from Puzzoli or Sorrento. Our group would then be quite complete, more especially as the countess is quite beautiful enough to represent a madonna."

"Well," said Franz, "this time, Albert, I am bound to give you credit for having hit upon a most capital idea."

"And quite a national one, too," replied Albert with gratified pride. "A mere masque borrowed from our own festivities. Ha, ha, ye Romans! you thought to make us, unhappy strangers, trot at the heels of your processions, like so many lazzaroni, because no carriages or horses are to be had in your beggarly city. But you don't know us; when we can't have one thing we invent another."

"And have you communicated your triumphant idea to anybody?"

"Only to our host. Upon my return home I sent for him, and I then explained to him what I wished to procure. He assured me that nothing would be easier than to furnish all I desired. One thing I was sorry for; when I bade him have the horns of the oxen gilded, he told me there would not be time, as it would require three days to do that; so you see we must do without this little superfluity."— "And where is he now?"—"Who?"—"Our host."

"Gone out in search of our equipage; by to-morrow it might be too late."—"Then he will be able to give us an answer to-night."

"Oh, I expect him every minute." At this instant the door opened, and the head of Signor Pastrini appeared. "*Permesso?*" inquired he.

"Certainly—certainly," cried Franz. "Come in, mine host."— "Now, then," asked Albert eagerly, "have you found the desired cart and oxen?"

"Better than that!" replied Signor Pastrini, with the air of a man perfectly well satisfied with himself.

"Take care, my worthy host," said Albert, "*better* is a sure enemy to *well.*"—"Let your excellencies only leave the matter to me," returned Signor Pastrini in a tone indicative of unbounded self-confidence.

"But what *have* you done?" asked Franz. "Speak out, there's a worthy fellow."—"Your excellencies are aware," responded the landlord, swelling with importance, "that the Count of Monte Cristo is living on the same floor with yourselves!"

"I should think we did know it," exclaimed Albert, "since it is owing to that circumstance that we are packed into these small rooms, like two poor students in the back streets of Paris."—"Well, then, the Count of Monte Cristo, hearing of the dilemma in which you are placed, has sent to offer you seats in his carriage and two places at his windows in the Palazzo Rospoli." The friends looked at each other with unutterable surprise.

"But do you think," asked Albert, "that we ought to accept such offers from a perfect stranger?"—"What sort of person is this Count of Monte Cristo?" asked Franz of his host. "A very great nobleman, but whether Maltese or Sicilian I cannot exactly say; but this I know, that he is noble as a Borghese and rich as a gold-mine."—"It seems to me," said Franz, speaking in an undertone to Albert, "that if this person merited the high panegyrics of our land-lord, he would have conveyed his invitation through another chan-nel, and not permitted it to be brought to us in this unceremonious way. He would have written—or"—

At this instant some one knocked at the door. "Come in," said Franz. A servant, wearing a livery of considerable style and richness, appeared at the threshold, and, placing two cards in the landlord's hands, who forthwith presented them to the two young men, he said, "Please to deliver these, from the Count of Monte Cristo to Viscomte Albert de Morcerf and M. Franz d'Epinay. The Count of Monte Cristo," continued the servant, "begs these gentlemen's per-mission to wait upon them as their neighbor, and he will be hon-ored by an intimation of what time they will please to receive him."

"Faith, Franz," whispered Albert, "there is not much to find fault with here."—"Tell the count," replied Franz, "that we will do our-selves the pleasure of calling on him." The servant bowed and retired.

"That is what I call an elegant mode of attack," said Albert. "You were quite correct in what you said, Signor Pastrini. The Count of Monte Cristo is unquestionably a man of first-rate breeding and knowledge of the world."

"Then you accept his offer?" said the host.

"Of course we do," replied Albert. "Still, I must own I am sorry to be obliged to give up the cart and the group of reapers—it would have produced such an effect! And were it not for the windows at the Palazzo Rospoli, by way of recompense for the loss of our beautiful scheme, I don't know but what I should have held on by my original plan. What say you, Franz?"

"Oh, I agree with you; the windows in the Palazzo Rospoli alone decided me." The truth was, that the mention of two places in the Palazzo Rospoli had recalled to Franz the conversation he had overheard the preceding evening in the ruins of the Colosseum between the mysterious unknown and the Transteverin, in which the stranger in the cloak had undertaken to obtain the freedom of a condemned criminal; and if this muffled-up individual proved (as Franz felt sure he would) the same as the person he had just seen in the Teatro Argentino, then he should be able to establish his identity, and also to prosecute his researches respecting him with perfect facility and freedom. Franz passed the night in confused dreams respecting the two meetings he had already had with his mysterious tormentor, and in waking speculations as to what the morrow would produce. The next day must clear up every doubt; and unless his near neighbor and would-be friend, the Count of Monte Cristo, possessed the ring of Gyges, and by its power was able to render himself invisible, it was very certain he could not escape this time. Eight o'clock found Franz up and dressed, while Albert, who had not the same motives for early rising, was still soundly asleep. The first act of Franz was to summon his landlord, who presented himself with his accustomed obsequiousness.

"Pray, Signor Pastrini," asked Franz, "is not some execution appointed to take place to-day?"—"Yes, your excellency; but if your reason for inquiry is that you may procure a window to view it from, you are much too late."

"Oh, no," answered Franz, "I had no such intention; and even if

I had felt a wish to witness the spectacle, I might have done so from Monte Pineio—could I not?"

"Ah!" exclaimed mine host, "I did not think it likely your excellency would have chosen to mingle with such a rabble as are always collected on that hill, which, indeed, they consider as exclusively belonging to themselves."

"Very possibly I may not go," answered Franz; "but in case I feel disposed, give me some particulars of to-day's executions."

"What particulars would your excellency like to hear?"— "Why, the number of persons condemned to suffer, their names, and description of the death they are to die."

"That happens just lucky, your excellency! Only a few minutes ago they brought me the *tavolettas*."—"What are they?"

"Sort of wooden tablets hung up at the corners of streets the evening before an execution, on which is pasted up a paper containing the names of the condemned persons, their crimes, and mode of punishment. The reason for so publicly announcing all this is, that all good and faithful Catholics may offer up their prayers for the unfortunate culprits, and, above all, beseech of heaven to grant them a sincere repentance."—"And these tablets are brought to you that you may add your prayers to those of the faithful, are they?" asked Franz somewhat incredulously.

"Oh, dear, no, your excellency! I have not time for anybody's affairs but my own and those of my honorable guests; but I make an agreement with the man who pastes up the papers, and he brings them to me as he would the playbills, that in case any person staying at my hotel should like to witness an execution, he may obtain every requisite information concerning the time and place, etc."—"Upon my word, that is a most delicate attention on your part, Signor Pastrini," cried Franz.

"Why, your excellency," returned the landlord, chuckling and rubbing his hands with infinite complacency, "I think I may take upon myself to say I neglect nothing to deserve the support and patronage of the noble visitors to this poor hotel." —"I see that plainly enough, my most excellent host, and you may rely upon me to proclaim so striking a proof of your attention to your guests wherever I go. Meanwhile, oblige me by a sight of one of these *tacylettas*."

"Nothing can be easier than to comply with your excellency's wish," said the landlord, opening the door of the chamber; "I have caused one to be placed on the landing, close by your apartment." Then, taking the tablet from the wall, he handed it to Franz, who read as follows:—

"'The public is informed that on Wednesday, February 23d, being the first day of the Carnival, executions will take place in the Piazza del Popolo, by order of the Tribunal of the Rota, of two persons, named Andrea Rondola, and Peppino, otherwise called Rocca Priori; the former found guilty of the murder of a venerable and exemplary priest, named Don Cesare Torlini, canon of the church of St. John Lateran; and the latter convicted of being an accomplice of the atrocious and sanguinary bandit, Luigi Vampa, and his band. The first-named malefactor will be subjected to the *mazzuola*, the second culprit beheaded. The prayers of all good Christians are entreated for these unfortunate men, that it may please God to awaken them to a sense of their guilt, and to grant them a hearty and sincere repentance for their crimes.'"

This was precisely what Franz had heard the evening before in the ruins of the Colosseum. No part of the programme differed,— the names of the condemned persons, their crimes, and mode of punishment, all agreed with his previous information. In all probability, therefore, the Transteverin was no other than the bandit Luigi Vampa himself, and the man strouded in the mantle the same he had known as "Sinbad the Sailor," but who, no doubt, was still pursuing his philanthropic expedition in Rome, as he had already done at Porto-Vecchio and Tunis. Time was getting on, however, and Franz deemed it advisable to awaken Albert; but at the moment he prepared to proceed to his chamber, his friend entered the room in perfect costume for the day. The anticipated delights of the Carnival had so run in his head as to make him leave his pillow long before his usual hour. "Now, my excellent Signor Pastrini," said Franz, addressing his landlord, "since we are both ready, do you think we may proceed at once to visit the Count of Monte Cristo?"—"Most assuredly," replied he. "The Count of Monte Cristo is always an early riser; and I can answer for his having been up these two hours."

"Then you really consider we shall not be intruding if we pay our respects to him directly?"—'Oh, I am quite sure. I will take all the blame on myself if you find I have led you into an error."

"Well, then, if it he so; are you ready, Albert?"—'Perfectly."

"Let us go and return our best thanks for his courtesy."—'Yes, let us do so." The landlord preceded the friends across the landing, which was all that separated them from the apartments of the count, rang at the bell, and, upon the door being opened by a servant, said, "*I signori Francesi.*"

The domestic bowed respectfully, and invited them to enter. They passed through two rooms, furnished in a luxurious manner they had not expected to see under the roof of Signor Pastrini, and were shown into an elegantly fitted-up drawing-room. The richest Turkey carpets covered the floor, and the softest and most inviting couches, easy-chairs, and sofas, offered their high-piled and yielding cushions to such as desired repose or refreshment. Splendid paintings by the first masters were ranged against the walls, intermingled with magnificent trophies of war, while heavy curtains of costly tapestry were suspended before the different doors of the room. "If your excellencies will please to be seated," said the man, "I will let the count know that you are here."

And with these words he disappeared behind one of the tapestried *portières*. As the door opened, the sound of a *guzlu* reached the ears of the young men, but was almost immediately lost, for the rapid closing of the door merely allowed one rich swell of harmony to enter. Franz and Albert looked inquiringly at each other, then at the gorgeous furnishings of the apartment. Everything seemed more magnificent at a second view than it had done at their first rapid survey.

"Well," said Franz to his friend, "what think you of all this?"

"Why, upon my soul, my dear fellow, it strikes me that our elegant and attentive neighbor must either be some successful stock-jobber who has speculated in the fall of the Spanish funds, or some prince travelling *incog*."

"Hush, hush!" replied Franz; "we shall ascertain who and what he is—he comes!" As Franz spoke, he heard the sound of a door turning on its hinges, and almost immediately afterwards the tapestry was drawn aside, and the owner of all these riches stood before the two young men. Albert instantly rose to meet him, but Franz remained, in a manner, spellbound on his chair; for in the person of him who had just entered he recognized not only the mysterious visitant to the Colosseum, and the occupant of the box at the Teatro Argentino, but also his extraordinary host of Monte Cristo.

XXXV

La Mazzolata

"GENTLEMEN," SAID THE COUNT of Monte Cristo as he entered, "I pray you excuse me for suffering my visit to be anticipated; but I feared to disturb you by presenting myself earlier at your apartments; besides, you sent me word that you would come to me, and I have held myself at your disposal."

"Franz and I have to thank you a thousand times, count," returned Albert; "you extricated us from a great dilemma, and we were on the point of inventing a very fantastic vehicle when your friendly invitation reached us."—"Indeed," returned the count, motioning the two young men to sit down. "It was the fault of that blockhead Pastrini, that I did not sooner assist you in your distress. He did not mention a syllable of your embarrassment to me, when he knows that, alone and isolated as I am, I seek every opportunity of making the acquaintance of my neighbors. As soon as I learned I could in any way assist you, I most eagerly seized the opportunity of offering my services." The two young men bowed. Franz had, as yet, found nothing to say; he had come to no determination, and as nothing in the count's manner manifested the wish that he should recognize him, he did not know whether to make any allusion to the past, or wait until he had more proof; besides, although sure it was he who had been in the box the previous evening, he could not be equally positive that this was the man he had seen at the Colosseum. He resolved, therefore, to let things take their course without making any direct overture to the count. Moreover, he had this advantage, he was master of the count's secret, while the count had no hold on Franz, who had nothing to conceal. However, he resolved to lead the conversation to a subject which might possibly clear up his doubts.

"Count," said he, "you have offered us places in your carriage, and at your windows in the Rospoli Palace. Can you tell us where we can obtain a sight of the Piazza del Popolo?" —"Ah," said the count negligently, looking attentively at Morcerf, "is there not something like an execution upon the Piazza del Popolo?"

"Yes," returned Franz, finding that the count was coming to the point he wished.—"Stay, I think I told my steward yesterday to attend to this; perhaps I can render you this slight service also." He extended his hand, and rang the bell thrice. "Did you ever occupy yourself," said he to Franz, "with the employment of time and the means of simplifying the summoning your servants? I have. When I ring once, it is for my valet; twice, for my majordomo; thrice, for my steward,—thus I do not waste a minute or a word. Here he is." A man of about forty-five or fifty entered, exactly resembling the smuggler who had introduced Franz into the cavern; but he did not appear to recognize him. It was evident he had his orders. "Monsieur Bertuccio," said the count, "you have procured me windows looking on the Piazza del Popolo, as I ordered you yesterday?"— "Yes, excellency," returned the steward; "but it was very late."

"Did I not tell you I wished for one?" replied the count, frowning.

"And your excellency has one, which was let to Prince Loban-ieff; but I was obliged to pay a hundred"—

"That will do—that will do, Monsieur Bertuccio; spare these gentlemen all such domestic arrangements. You have the window, that is sufficient. Give orders to the coachman; and be in readiness on the stairs to conduct us to it." The steward bowed, and was about to quit the room. "Ah," continued the count, "be good enough to ask Pastrini if he has received the *tavoletta*, and if he can send us an account of the execution."

"There is no need to do that," said Franz, taking out his tablets; "for I saw the account, and copied it down."

"Very well, you can retire, M. Bertuccio; but let us know when breakfast is ready. These gentlemen," added he, turning to the two friends, "will, I trust, do me the honor to breakfast with me?"

"But, my dear count," said Albert, "we shall abuse your kindness."

"Not at all; on the contrary, you will give me great pleasure. You will, one or other of you, perhaps both, return it to me at Paris. M. Bertuccio, lay covers for three." He then book Franz's tablets out of his hand. "'We announce,' he read, in the same tone with which he would have read a newspaper, 'that to-day, the 23d of February, will be executed Andrea Rondolo, guilty of murder on the person of the respected and venerated Don Cesare Torlini, canon of the church of St. John Lateran, and Peppino, called Rocca Priori, convicted of complicity with the detestable bandit Luigi Vampa, and the men of his band.' Hum! 'The first will be *mazzolato*, the second *decapitato*.' "Yes," continued the count, "it was at first arranged in this way; but I think since yesterday some change has taken place in the order of the ceremony."

"Really?" said Franz.

"Yes, I passed the evening at the Cardinal Rospigliosi's, and there mention was made of something like a pardon for one of the two men."

"For Andrea Rondolo?" asked Franz.

"No," replied the count, carelessly; "for the other (he glanced at the tablets as if to recall the name), for Peppino, called Rocca Priori. You are thus deprived of seeing a man guillotined; but the *mazzuolu* still remains, which is a very curious punishment when seen for the first time, and even the second, while the other, as you must know, is very simple. The *mandaïa*[1] never fails, never trembles, never strikes thirty times ineffectually, like the soldier who beheaded the

[1] Guillotine.

Count of Chalais, and to whose tender mercy Richelieu had doubtless recommended the sufferer. Ah," added the count, in a contemptuous tone, "do not tell me of European punishments, they are in the infancy, or rather the old age, of cruelty."

"Really, count," replied Franz, "one would think that you had studied the different tortures of all the nations of the world."

"There are, at least, few that I have not seen," said the count coldly.

"And you took pleasure in beholding these dreadful spectacles?"

"My first sentiment was horror, the second indifference, the third curiosity."—"Curiosity—that is a terrible word."

"Why so? In life, our greatest preoccupation is death; is it not, then, curious to study the different ways by which the soul and body can part; and how, according to their different characters, temperaments and even the different customs of their countries, different persons bear the transition from life to death, from existence to annihilation? As for myself, I can assure you of one thing,—the more men you see die, the easier it becomes to die yourself; and in my opinion, death may be a torture, but it is not an expiation."

"I do not quite understand you," replied Franz; "pray explain your meaning, for you excite my curiosity to the highest pitch."

"Listen," said the count, and deep hatred mounted to his face, as the blood would to the face of any other. "If a man had by unheard-of and excruciating tortures destroyed your father, your mother, your betrothed,—a being who, when torn from you, left a desolation, a wound that never closes, in your breast,—do you think the reparation that society gives you is sufficient when it interposes the knife of the guillotine between the base of the occiput and the trapezal muscles of the murderer, and allows him who has caused us years of moral sufferings to escape with a few moments of physical pain?"

"Yes, I know," said Franz, "that human justice is insufficient to console us; she can give blood in return for blood, that is all; but you must demand from her only what it is in her power to grant."

"I will put another case to you," continued the count; "that where society, attacked by the death of a person, avenges death by death. But are there not a thousand tortures by which a man may be made to suffer without society taking the least cognizance of them, or offering him even the insufficient means of vengeance, of which we have just spoken? Are there not crimes for which the impalement of the Turks, the augers of the Persians, the stake and the brand of the Iroquois Indians, are inadequate tortures, and which are unpunished by society? Answer me, do not these crimes exist?"—"Yes," answered Franz; "and it is to punish them that duelling is tolerated."

"Ah, duelling," cried the count; "a pleasant manner, upon my soul, of arriving at your end when that end is vengeance! A man has carried off your mistress, a man has seduced your wife, a man has dishonored your daughter; he has rendered the whole life of one who had the right to expect from heaven that portion of happiness God has promised to every one of his creatures, an existence of misery and infamy; and you think you are avenged because you send a ball through the head, or pass a sword through the breast, of that man who has planted madness in your brain, and despair in your heart. And remember, moreover, that it is often he who comes off victorious from the strife, absolved of all crime in the eyes of the world. No, no," continued the count; "had I to avenge myself, it is not thus I would take revenge."

"Then you disapprove of duelling? You would not fight a duel?" asked Albert in his turn, astonished at this strange theory.

"Oh, yes," replied the count; "understand me, I would fight a duel for a trifle, for an insult, for a blow; and the more so that, thanks to my skill in all bodily exercises, and the indifference to danger I have gradually acquired, I should be almost certain to kill my man. Oh, I would fight for such a cause; but in return for a slow, profound, eternal torture, I would give back the same, were it possible; an eye for an eye, a tooth for a tooth, as the Orientalists say,—our masters in everything,—those favored creatures who have formed for themselves a life of dreams and a paradise of realities."

"But," said Franz to the count, "with this theory, which renders you at once judge and executioner of your own cause, it would be difficult to adopt a course that would forever prevent your falling under the power of the law. Hatred is blind; rage carries you away; and he who pours out vengeance runs the risk of lasting a bitter draught."

"Yes, if he be poor and inexperienced, not if he be rich and skilful; besides, the worst that could happen to him would be the punishment of which we have already spoken, and which the philanthropic French Revolution has substituted for being torn to pieces by horses or broken on the wheel. What matters this punishment, as long as he is avenged? On my word, I almost regret that in all probability this miserable Peppino will not be beheaded, as you might have had an opportunity then of seeing how short a time the punishment lasts, and whether it is worth even mentioning; but, really, this is a most singular conversation for the Carnival, gentlemen; how did it arise? Ah, I recollect, you asked for a place at my window; you shall have it; but let us first sit down to table, for here comes the servant to inform us that breakfast is ready." As he spoke, a servant opened one of the four doors of the apartment, saying—"*Al suo commodo!*" The two young men arose and entered the breakfast-room.

During the meal, which was excellent, and admirably served, Franz looked repeatedly at Albert, in order to observe the impressions which he doubted not had been made on him by the words of their entertainer; but whether with his usual carelessness he had paid but little attention to him, whether the explanation of the Count of Monte Cristo with regard to duelling had satisfied him, or whether the events which Franz knew of had had their effect on him alone, he remarked that his companion did not pay the least regard to them, but on the contrary ate like a man who for the last four or five months had been condemned to partake of Italian cookery—that is, the worst in the world. As for the count, he just touched the dishes; he seemed to fulfil the duties of a host by sitting down with his guests, and awaited their departure to be served with some strange or more delicate food. This brought back to Franz, in spite of himself, the recollection of the terror with which the count had inspired the Countess G——, and her firm conviction that the man in the opposite box was a vampire. At the end of the breakfast Franz took out his watch. "Well," said the count, "what are you doing?"—"You must excuse us, count," returned Franz, "but we have still much to do."

"What may that be?"

"We have no masks, and it is absolutely necessary to procure them."

"Do not concern yourself about that; we have, I think, a private room in the Piazza del Popolo; I will have whatever costumes you choose brought to us, and you can dress there."

"After the execution?" cried Franz.—"Before or after, whichever you please."

"Opposite the scaffold?"—"The scaffold forms part of the fête."

"Count, I have reflected on the matter," said Franz, "I thank you for your courtesy, but I shall content myself with accepting a place in your carriage and at your window at the Rospoli Palace, and I leave you at liberty to dispose of my place at the Piazza del Popolo."

"But I warn you, you will lose a very curious sight," returned the count.

"You will describe it to me," replied Franz, "and the recital from your lips will make as great an impression on me as if I had witnessed it. I have more than once intended witnessing an execution, but I have never been able to make up my mind; and you, Albert?"

"I," replied the viscount,—"I saw Castaing executed, but I think I was rather intoxicated that day, for I had quitted college the same morning, and we had passed the previous night at a tavern."

"Besides, it is no reason because you have not seen an execution at Paris, that you should not see one anywhere else; when you travel, it is to see everything. Think what a figure you will make when you are asked, 'How do they execute at Rome?' and you reply, 'I do not know'! And, besides, they say that the culprit is an infamous scoundrel, who killed with a log of wood a worthy canon who had brought him up like his own son. *Diable*, when a churchman is killed, it should be with a different weapon than a log, especially when he has behaved like a father. If you went to Spain, would you not see the bull-fights? Well, suppose it is a bull-fight you are going to see? Recollect the ancient Romans of the Circus, and the sports where they killed three hundred lions and a hundred men. Think of the eighty thousand applauding spectators, the sage matrons who took their daughters, and the charming Vestals who made with the thumb of their white hands the fatal sign that said, 'Come, despatch the dying.'"—"Shall you go, then, Albert?" asked Franz.

"*Ma foi*, yes; like you, I hesitated, but the count's eloquence decides me."—"Let us go, then," said Franz, "since you wish it; but on our way to the Piazza del Popolo, I wish to pass through the Corso. Is this possible, count?"

"On foot, yes; in a carriage, no."—"I will go on foot, then."

"Is it important that you should go that way?"

"Yes, there is something I wish to see."

"Well, we will go by the Corso. We will send the carriage to wait for us on the Piazza del Popolo, by the Strada del Babuino, for I shall be glad to pass, myself, through the Corso, to see if some orders I have given have been executed."

"Excellency," said a servant, opening the door, "a man in the dress of a penitent wishes to speak to you."—"Ah, yes," returned the count, "I know who he is, gentlemen; will you return to the salon? You will find good cigars on the centre table. I will be with you directly." The young men rose and returned into the salon, while the count, again apologizing, left by another door. Albert, who was a great smoker, and who had considered it no small sacrifice to be deprived of the cigars of the Café de Paris, approached the table, and uttered a cry of joy at perceiving some veritable *puros*.

"Well," asked Franz, "what think you of the Count of Monte Cristo?"—"What do I think?" said Albert, evidently surprised at such a question from his companion; "I think he is a delightful fellow, who does the honors of his table admirably; who has travelled much, read much, is, like Brutus, of the Stoic school, and moreover," added he, sending a volume of smoke up towards the ceiling, "that he has excellent cigars." Such was Albert's opinion of the count, and as Franz well knew that Albert professed never to form an opinion except upon long reflection, he made no attempt to change it. "But," said he, "did you observe one very singular thing?"—"What?"

"How attentively he looked at you."—"At me?"

"Yes."—Albert reflected. "Ah," replied he, sighing, "that is not very surprising; I have been more than a year absent from Paris, and my clothes are of a most antiquated cut; the count takes me for a provincial. The first opportunity you have, undeceive him, I beg, and tell him I am nothing of the kind." Franz smiled; an instant after the count entered.—"I am now quite at your service, gentlemen," said he. "The carriage is going one way to the Piazza del Popolo, and we will go another; and, if you please, by the Corso. Take some more of these cigars, M. de Morcerf."—"With all my heart," returned Albert; "Italian cigars are horrible. When you come to Paris, I will return all this."

"I will not refuse; I intend going there soon, and since you allow me, I will pay you a visit. Come, we have not any time to lose, it is half-past twelve—let us set off." All three descended; the coachman received his master's orders, and drove down the Via del Babuino. While the three gentlemen walked along the Piazza de Spagni and the Via Frattina, which led directly between the Fiano and Rospoli palaces, Franz's attention was directed towards the windows of that last palace, for he had not forgotten the signal agreed upon between the man in the mantle and the Transtevere peasant. "Which are your windows?" asked he of the count, with as much indifference as he could assume. "The three last," returned he, with a negligence evidently unaffected, for he could not imagine with what intention the question was put. Franz glanced rapidly towards the three windows. The side windows were hung with yellow damask, and the centre one with white damask and a red cross. The man in the mantle had kept his promise to the Transteverin, and there could now be no doubt that he was the count. The three windows were still untenanted. Preparations were making on every side: chairs were placed, scaffolds were raised, and windows were hung with flags. The masks could not appear: the carriages could not move about; but the masks were visible behind the windows, the carriages, and the doors.

Franz, Albert, and the count continued to descend the Corso. As they approached the Piazza del Popolo, the crowd became more dense, and above the heads of the multitude two objects were visible; the obelisk, surmounted by a cross, which marks the centre of the square, and in front of the obelisk, at the point where the three streets, del Babuino, del Corso, and di Ripetta, meet, the two uprights of the scaffold, between which glittered the curved knife of the *mandaïa*. At the corner of the street they met the count's steward, who was awaiting his master. The window, let at an exorbitant price, which the count had doubtless wished to conceal from his guests, was on the second floor of the great palace, situated between the Via del Babuino and the Monte Pincio. It consisted, as we have said, of a small dressing-room, opening into a bedroom, and, when the door of communication was shut, the inmates were quite alone. On chairs were laid elegant masquerade costumes of blue and white satin. "As you left the choice of your costumes to me," said the count to the two friends, "I have had these brought, as they will be the most worn this year; and they are most suitable, on account of the *confetti* (sweetmeats), as they do not show the flour."

Franz heard the words of the count but imperfectly, and he

perhaps did not fully appreciate this new attention to their wishes; for he was wholly absorbed by the spectacle that the Piazza del Popolo presented, and by the terrible instrument that was in the centre. It was the first time Franz had ever seen a guillotine,—we say guillotine, because the Roman *mandaïa* is formed on almost the same model as the French instrument.[1] The knife, which is shaped like a crescent, that cuts with the convex side, falls from a less height, and that is all the difference. Two men, seated on the movable plank on which the victim is laid, were eating their breakfasts, while waiting for the criminal. Their repast consisted apparently of bread and sausages. One of them lifted the plank, took out a flask of wine, drank some, and then passed it to his companion. These two men were the executioner's assistants. At this sight Franz felt the perspiration start forth upon his brow. The prisoners, transported the previous evening from the Carcere Nuovo to the little church of Santa Maria del Popolo, had passed the night, each accompanied by two priests, in a chapel closed by a grating, before which were two sentinels, who were relieved at intervals. A double line of carbineers, placed on each side of the door of the church, reached to the scaffold, and formed a circle around it, leaving a path about ten feet wide, and around the guillotine a space of nearly a hundred feet. All the rest of the square was paved with heads. Many women held their infants on their shoulders, and thus the children had the best view. The Monte Pincio seemed a vast amphitheatre filled with spectators; the balconies of the two churches at the corner of the Via del Babuino and the Via di Ripetta were crammed; the steps even seemed a parti-colored sea, that was impelled towards the portico; every niche in the wall held its living statue. What the count said was true—the most curious spectacle in life is that of death. And yet, instead of the silence and the solemnity demanded

[1] Dr. Guillotin got the idea of his famous machine from witnessing an execution in Italy.

by the occasion, laughter and jests arose from the crowd. It was evident that the execution was, in the eyes of the people, only the
commencement of the Carnival. Suddenly the tumult ceased, as if
by magic, and the doors of the church opened. A brotherhood of
penitents, clothed from head to foot in robes of gray sackcloth, with
holes for the eyes, and holding in their hands lighted tapers,
appeared first; the chief marched at the head. Behind the penitents
came a man of vast stature and proportions. He was naked, with the
exception of cloth drawers, at the left side of which hung a large
knife in a sheath, and he bore on his right shoulder a heavy iron
sledge-hammer. This man was the executioner. He had, moreover,
sandals bound on his feet by cords. Behind the executioner came,
in the order in which they were to die, first Peppino and then
Andrea. Each was accompanied by two priests. Neither had his eyes
bandaged. Peppino walked with a firm step, doubtless aware of what
awaited him. Andrea was supported by two priests. Each of them,
from time to time, kissed the crucifix a confessor held out to them.
At this sight alone Franz felt his legs tremble under him. He looked
at Albert—he was as white as his shirt, and mechanically cast away
his cigar, although he had not half smoked it. The count alone
seemed unmoved—nay, more, a slight color seemed striving to rise
in his pale cheeks. His nostrils dilated like those of a wild beast that
scents its prey, and his lips, half opened, disclosed his white teeth,
small and sharp like those of a jackal. And yet his features wore an
expression of smiling tenderness, such as Franz had never before
witnessed in them; his black eyes especially were full of kindness
and pity. However, the two culprits advanced, and as they
approached their faces became visible. Peppino was a handsome
young man of four or five and twenty, bronzed by the sun; he carried his head erect, and seemed on the watch to see on which side
his liberator would appear. Andrea was short and fat; his visage,
marked with brutal cruelty, did not indicate age; he might be thirty.
In prison he had suffered his beard to grow; his head fell on his

shoulder, his legs bent beneath him, and his movements were apparently automatic and unconscious.

"I thought." said Franz to the count, "that you told me there would be but one execution."—"I told you true," replied he coldly.

"And yet here are two culprits."

"Yes; but only one of these two is about to die; the other has many years to live."

"If the pardon is to come, there is no time to lose."

"And see, here it is," said the count. At the moment when Peppino reached the foot of the *mandaïa*, a priest arrived in some haste, forced his way through the soldiers, and, advancing to the chief of the brotherhood, gave him a folded paper. The piercing eye of Peppino had noticed all. The chief took the paper, unfolded it, and, raising his hand, "Heaven be praised, and his holiness also," said he in a loud voice; "here is a pardon for one of the prisoners!"

"A pardon!" cried the people with one voice—"a pardon!" At this cry Andrea raised his head. "Pardon for whom?" cried he.

Peppino remained breathless. "A pardon for Peppino, called Rocca Priori," said the principal friar. And he passed the paper to the officer commanding the carbineers, who read and returned it to him.

"For Peppino!" cried Andrea, who seemed roused from the torpor in which he had been plunged. "Why for him and not for me? We ought to die together. I was promised he should die with me. You have no right to put me to death alone. I will not die alone—I will not!" And he broke from the priests struggling and raving like a wild beast, and striving desperately to break the cords that bound his hands. The executioner made a sign, and his two assistants leaped from the scaffold and seized him. "What is going on?" asked Franz of the count; for, as all the talk was in the Roman dialect, he had not perfectly understood it. "Do you not see?" returned the count, "that this human creature who is about to die is furious that his fellow-sufferer does not perish with him? and, were he able, he would rather tear him to pieces with his teeth and nails than let him enjoy the life he himself is about to be deprived of. Oh, man, man—race of croc-odiles," cried the count, extending his clinched hands towards the crowd, "how well do I recognize you there, and that at all times you are worthy of yourselves!" Meanwhile Andrea and the two execu-tioners were struggling on the ground, and he kept exclaiming, "He ought to die!—he shall die!—I will not die alone!"

"Look, look," cried the count, seizing the young men's hands— "look, for on my soul it is curious. Here is a man who had resigned himself to his fate, who was going to the scaffold to die—like a cow-ard, it is true, but he was about to die without resistance. Do you know what gave him strength? —do you know what consoled him? It was, that another partook of his punishment—that another par-took of his anguish—that another was to die before him. Lead two sheep to the butcher's, two oxen to the slaughterhouse, and make one of them understand that his companion will not die; the sheep will bleat for pleasure, the ox will bellow with joy. But man—man, whom God created in his own image—man, upon whom God has laid his first, his sole commandment, to love his neighbor—man, to whom God has given a voice to express his thoughts—what is his first cry when he hears his fellowman is saved? A blasphemy. Honor to man, this masterpiece of nature, this king of the creation!" And the count burst into a laugh; a terrible laugh, that showed he must have suffered horribly to be able thus to laugh. However, the struggle still contin-ued, and it was dreadful to witness. The people all took part against Andrea, and twenty thousand voices cried, "Put him to death! put him to death!" Franz sprang back, but the count seized his arm, and held him before the window. "What are you doing?" said he. "Do you pity him? If you heard the cry of 'Mad dog!' you would take your gun—you would unhesitatingly shoot the poor beast, who, after all, was only guilty of having been bitten by another dog. And yet you pity a man who, without being bitten by one of his race, has yet murdered his benefactor; and who, now unable to kill any one, because his hands are bound, wishes to see his companion in captivity perish. No, no—look, look!"

The command was needless. Franz was fascinated by the horrible spectacle. The two assistants had borne Andrea to the scaffold, and there, in spite of his struggles, his bites, and his cries, had forced him to his knees. During this time the executioner had raised his mace, and signed to them to get out of the way; the criminal strove to rise, but, ere he had time, the mace fell on his left temple. A dull and heavy sound was heard, and the man dropped like an ox on his face, and then turned over on his back. The executioner let fall his mace, drew his knife, and with one stroke opened his throat, and mounting on his stomach, stamped violently on it with his feet. At every stroke a jet of blood sprang from the wound.

This time Franz could contain himself no longer, but sank, half fainting, into a seat. Albert, with his eyes closed, was standing grasping the window-curtains. The count was erect and triumphant, like the Avenging Angel!

XXXVI

The Carnival at Rome

W HEN FRANZ RECOVERED HIS senses, he saw Albert drinking a glass of water, of which, to judge from his pallor, he stood in great need; and the count, who was assuming his masquerade costume. He glanced mechanically towards the square—the scene was wholly changed; scaffold, executioners, victims, all had disappeared; only the people remained, full of noise and excitement. The bell of Monte Citorio, which only sounds on the pope's decease and the opening of the Carnival, was ringing a joyous peal. "Well," asked he of the count, "what has, then, happened?"—"Nothing," replied the count; "only, as you see, the Carnival has commenced. Make haste and dress yourself."—"In fact," said Franz, "this horrible scene has passed away like a dream."

"It is but a dream, a nightmare, that has disturbed you."

"Yes, that I have suffered; but the culprit?"

"That is a dream also; only he has remained asleep, while you have awakened; and who knows which of you is the most fortunate?"

"But Peppino—what has become of him?"—"Peppino is a lad of sense, who, unlike most men, who are happy in proportion as they are noticed, was delighted to see that the general attention was directed towards his companion. He profited by this distraction to slip away among the crowd, without even thanking the worthy priests who accompanied him. Decidedly man is an ungrateful and egotistical animal. But dress yourself; see, M. de Morcerf sets you the example. Albert was drawing on the satin pantaloon over his black trousers and varnished boots. "Well, Albert," said Franz. "do you feel much inclined to join the revels? Come, answer frankly."— "*Ma foi*, no" returned Albert. "But I am really glad to have seen such a sight; and I understand what the count said—that when you have once habituated yourself to a similar spectacle, it is the only one that causes you any emotion."

"Without reflecting that this is the only moment in which you can study character," said the count; "on the steps of the scaffold death tears off the mask that has been worn through life, and the real visage is disclosed. It must be allowed that Andrea was not very handsome, the hideous scoundrel! Come, dress yourselves, gentlemen, dress yourselves." Franz felt it would be ridiculous not to follow his two companions' example. He assumed his costume, and fastened on the mask that scarcely equalled the pallor of his own face. Their toilet finished, they descended; the carriage awaited them at the door, filled with sweetmeats and bouquets. They fell into the line of carriages. It is difficult to form an idea of the perfect change that had taken place. Instead of the spectacle of gloomy and silent death, the Piazza del Popolo presented a spectacle of gay and noisy mirth and revelry. A crowd of masks flowed in from all sides, emerging from the doors, descending from the windows. From every street and every corner drove carriages filled with clowns, harlequins, dominoes, mummers, pantomimists, Transteverins, knights, and peasants, screaming, fighting, gesticulating, throwing eggs filled with flour, confetti, nosegays, attacking, with their sarcasms and their missiles, friends and foes, companions and strangers, indiscriminately, and no one took offence, or did anything but laugh. Franz and Albert were like men who, to drive away a violent sorrow, have recourse to wine, and who, as they drink and become intoxicated, feel a thick veil drawn between the past and the present. They saw, or rather continued to see, the image of what they had witnessed; but little by little the general vertigo seized them, and they felt themselves obliged to take part in the noise and confusion. A handful of confetti that came from a neighboring carriage, and which, while it covered Morcerf and his two companions with dust, pricked his neck and that portion of his face uncovered by his mask like a hundred pins, incited him to join in the general combat, in which all the masks around him were engaged. He rose in his turn, and seizing handfuls of confetti and sweetmeats, with which the carriage was filled, cast them with all the force and skill he was master of.

The strife had fairly begun, and the recollection of what they had seen half an hour before was gradually effaced from the young men's minds, so much were they occupied by the gay and glittering procession they now beheld. As for the Count of Monte Cristo, he had never for an instant shown any appearance of having been moved. Imagine the large and splendid Corso, bordered from one end to the other with lofty palaces, with their balconies hung with carpets, and their windows with flags. At these balconies are three hundred thousand spectators—Romans, Italians, strangers from all parts of the world, the united aristocracy of birth, wealth, and genius. Lovely women, yielding to the influence of the scene, bend over their balconies, or lean from their windows, and shower down confetti, which are returned by bouquets; the air seems darkened with the falling confetti and flying flowers. In the streets the lively crowd is dressed in the most fantastic costumes—gigantic cabbages walk gravely about, buffaloes' heads bellow from men's shoulders, dogs walk on their hind legs; in the midst of all this a mask is lifted, and, as in Callot's Temptation of St. Anthony, a lovely face is exhibited, which we would fain follow, but from which we are separated by troops of fiends. This will give a faint idea of the Carnival at Rome. At the second turn the count stopped the carriage, and requested permission to withdraw, leaving the vehicle at their disposal. Franz looked up—they were opposite the Rospoli Palace. At the centre window, the one hung with white damask with a red cross, was a blue domino, beneath which Franz's imagination easily pictured the beautiful Greek of the Argentina. "Gentlemen," said the count, springing out, "when you are tired of being actors, and wish to become spectators of this scene, you know you have places at my windows. In the meantime, dispose of my coachman, my carriage, and my servants." We have forgotten to mention, that the count's coachman was attired in a bear-skin, exactly resembling Odry's in "The Bear and the Pasha;" and the two footmen behind were dressed up as green monkeys, with spring masks, with which they made grimaces at every one who passed. Franz thanked the count for his attention. As for Albert, he was busily occupied throwing bouquets at a carriage full of Roman peasants that was passing near him. Unfortunately for him, the line of carriages moved on again, and while he descended the Piazza del Popolo, the other ascended towards the Palazzo di Venezia. "Ah, my dear fellow," said he to Franz; "you did not see?"—"What?"

"There,—that calash filled with Roman peasants."—"No."

"Well, I am convinced they are all charming women."

"How unfortunate that you were masked, Albert," said Franz; "here was an opportunity of making up for past disappointments."

"Oh," replied he, half laughing, half serious; "I hope the Carnival will not pass without some amends in one shape or the other."

But, in spite of Albert's hope, the day passed unmarked by any incident, excepting two or three encounters with the carriage full of Roman peasants. At one of these encounters, accidentally or purposely, Albert's mask fell off. He instantly rose and cast the remainder of the bouquets into the carriage. Doubtless one of the charming females Albert had detected beneath their coquettish disguise was touched by his gallantry; for, as the carriage of the two friends passed her, she threw a bunch of violets. Albert seized it, and as Franz had no reason to suppose it was meant for him, he suffered

Albert to retain it. Albert placed it in his button-hole, and the carriage went triumphantly on.

"Well," said Franz to him; "here is the beginning of an adventure."—"Laugh if you please—I really think so. So I will not abandon this bouquet."

"*Pardieu*," returned Franz, laughing, "in token of your ingratitude." The jest, however, soon appeared to become earnest; for when Albert and Franz again encountered the carriage with the *contadini*, the one who had thrown the violets to Albert, clapped her hands when she beheld them in his button-hole. "Bravo, bravo," said Franz; "things go wonderfully. Shall I leave you? Perhaps you would prefer being alone?"—"No," replied he; "I will not be caught like a fool at a first disclosure by a rendezvous under the clock, as they say at the opera-balls. If the fair peasant wishes to carry matters any further, we shall find her, or rather, she will find us to-morrow; then she will give me some sign or other, and I shall know what I have to do."

"On my word," said Franz, "you are wise as Nestor and prudent as Ulysses, and your fair Circe must be very skilful or very powerful if she succeed in changing you into a beast of any kind." Albert was right; the fair unknown had resolved, doubtless, to carry the intrigue no farther; for although the young men made several more turns, they did not again see the calash, which had turned up one of the neighboring streets. Then they returned to the Rospoli Palace; but the count and the blue domino had also disappeared; the two windows, hung with yellow damask, were still occupied by the persons whom the count had invited. At this moment the same bell that had proclaimed the beginning of the mascherata sounded the retreat. The file on the Corso broke the line, and in a second all the carriages had disappeared. Franz and Albert were opposite the Via delle Maratte; the coachman, without saying a word, drove up it, passed along the Piazza di Spagni and the Rospoli Palace and stopped at the door of the hotel. Signor Pastrini came to the door to receive his guests. Franz hastened to inquire after the count, and to express regret that he had not returned in sufficient time; but Pastrini reassured him by saying that the Count of Monte Cristo had ordered a second carriage for himself, and that it had gone at four o'clock to fetch him from the Rospoli Palace. The count had, moreover, charged him to offer the two friends the key of his box at the Argentina. Franz questioned Albert as to his intentions; but Albert had great projects to put into execution before going to the theatre; and instead of making any answer, he inquired if Signor Pastrini could procure him a tailor. "A tailor," said the host; "and for what?"—"To make us between now and to-morrow two Roman peasant costumes," returned Albert. The host shook his head. "To make you two costumes between now and to-morrow? I ask your excellencies' pardon, but this is quite a French demand; for the next week you will not find a single tailor who would consent to sew six buttons on a waistcoat if you paid him a crown a piece for each button."—"Then I must give up the idea?"

"No; we have them ready-made. Leave all to me; and to-morrow, when you awake, you shall find a collection of costumes with which you will be satisfied."—"My dear Albert," said Franz, "leave all to our host; he has already proved himself full of resources; let us dine quietly, and afterwards go and see 'The Algerian Captive.'"

"Agreed," returned Albert; "but remember, Signor Pastrini, that both my friend and myself attach the greatest importance to having to-morrow the costumes we have asked for." The host again assured them they might rely on him, and that their wishes should be attended to; upon which Franz and Albert mounted to their apartments, and proceeded to disencumber themselves of their costumes. Albert, as he took off his dress, carefully preserved the bunch of violets; it was his token reserved for the morrow. The two friends sat down to table; but they could not refrain from remarking the difference between the Count of Monte Cristo's table and that of Signor Pastrini. Truth compelled Franz, in spite of the dislike he seemed to have taken to the count, to confess that the advantage was not on Pastrini's side. During dessert, the servant inquired at what time they wished for the carriage. Albert and Franz looked at each other, fearing really to abuse the count's kindness. The servant understood them. "His excellency the Count of Monte Cristo had," he said, "given positive orders that the carriage was to remain at their lordships' orders all day, and they could therefore dispose of it without fear of indiscretion."

They resolved to profit by the count's courtesy, and ordered the horses to be harnessed, while they substituted evening dress for that which they had on, and which was somewhat the worse for the numerous combats they had sustained. This precaution taken, they went to the theatre, and installed themselves in the count's box. During the first act, the Countess G— entered. Her first look was at the box where she had seen the count the previous evening, so that she perceived Franz and Albert in the place of the very person concerning whom she had expressed so strange an opinion to Franz. Her opera-glass was so fixedly directed towards them, that Franz saw it would be cruel not to satisfy her curiosity; and, availing himself of one of the privileges of the spectators of the Italian theatres, who use their boxes to hold receptions, the two friends went to pay their respects to the countess. Scarcely had they entered, when she motioned to Franz to assume the seat of honor. Albert, in his turn, sat behind.

"Well," said she, hardly giving Franz time to sit down, "it seems you have nothing better to do than to make the acquaintance of this new Lord Ruthven, and you are already the best friends in the world."

"Without being so far advanced as that, my dear countess," returned Franz, "I cannot deny that we have abused his good nature all day."

"All day?"—"Yes; this morning we breakfasted with him; we rode in his carriage all day, and now we have taken possession of his box."

"You know him, then?"—"Yes, and no."

"How so?"—"It is a long story."

"Tell it to me."—"It would frighten you too much."

"So much the more reason."—"At least wait until the story has a conclusion."

"Very well; I prefer complete histories; but tell me how you made his acquaintance? Did any one introduce you to him?"

"No; it was he who introduced himself to us."—"When?"

"Last night, after we left you."—"Through what medium?"

"The very prosaic one of our landlord."

"He is staying, then, at the Hotel de Londres with you?"

"Not only in the same hotel, but on the same floor."

"What is his name—for, of course, you know?"

"The Count of Monte Cristo."—"That is not a family name?"

"No, it is the name of the island he has purchased."

"And he is a count?"—"A Tuscan count."

"Well, we must put up with that," said the countess, who was herself from one of the oldest Venetian families. "What sort of a man is he?"

"Ask the Vicomte de Morcerf."

"You hear, M. de Morcerf, I am referred to you," said the countess.

"We should be very hard to please, madam," returned Albert, "did we not think him delightful. A friend of ten years' standing could not have done more for us, or with a more perfect courtesy."

"Come," observed the countess, smiling, "I see my vampire is only some millionaire, who has taken the appearance of Lara in order to avoid being confounded with M. de Rothschild; and you have seen her?"—"Her?"—"The beautiful Greek of yesterday."

"No; we heard, I think, the sound of her *guzla*, but she remained perfectly invisible."—"When you say invisible," interrupted Albert, "it is only to keep up the mystery; for whom do you take the blue domino at the window with the white curtains?"

"Where was this window with white hangings?" asked the countess.

"At the Rospoli Palace."

"The count had three windows at the Rospoli Palace?"

"Yes. Did you pass through the Corso?"—"Yes."

"Well, did you notice two windows hung with yellow damask, and one with white damask with a red cross? Those were the count's windows?"

"Why, he must be a nabob. Do you know what those three windows were worth?"—"Two or three hundred Roman crowns?"

"Two or three thousand."—"The deuce."

"Does his island produce him such a revenue?"

"It does not bring him a baiocco."—"Then why did he purchase it?"

"For a whim."—"He is an original, then?"

"In reality," observed Albert, "he seemed to me somewhat eccentric; were he at Paris, and a frequenter of the theatres, I should say he was a poor devil literally mad. This morning he made two or three exits worthy of Didier or Anthony." At this moment a fresh visitor entered, and, according to custom, Franz gave up his seat to him. This circumstance had, moreover, the effect of changing the conversation; an hour afterwards the two friends returned to their hotel. Signor Pastrini had already set about procuring their disguises for the morrow; and he assured them that they would be perfectly satisfied. The next morning, at nine o'clock, he entered Franz's room, followed by a tailor, who had eight or ten Roman peasant costumes on his arm; they selected two exactly alike, and charged the tailor to sew on each of their hats about twenty yards of ribbon, and to procure them two of the long silk sashes of different colors with which the lower orders decorate themselves on fête-days. Albert was impatient to see how he looked in his new dress—a jacket and breeches of blue velvet, silk stockings with clocks, shoes with buckles, and a silk waistcoat. This picturesque attire set him off to great advantage; and when he had bound the scarf around his waist, and when his hat, placed coquettishly on one side, let fall on his shoulder a stream of ribbons, Franz was forced to confess that costume has much to do with the physical superiority we accord to certain nations. The Turks used to be so picturesque with their long and flowing robes, but are they not now hideous with their blue frocks buttoned up to the chin, and their red caps, which make them look like a bottle of wine with a red seal? Franz complimented Albert, who looked at himself in the glass with an unequivocal smile of satisfaction. They were thus engaged when the Count of Monte Cristo entered.

"Gentlemen," said he, "although a companion is agreeable, perfect freedom is sometimes still more agreeable. I come to say that to-day, and for the remainder of the Carnival, I leave the carriage entirely at your disposal. The host will tell you I have three or four more, so that you will not inconvenience me in any way. Make use of it, I pray you, for your pleasure or your business."

The young men wished to decline, but they could find no good reason for refusing an offer which was so agreeable to them. The Count of Monte Cristo remained a quarter of an hour with them, conversing on all subjects with the greatest ease. He was, as we have already said, perfectly well acquainted with the literature of all countries. A glance at the walls of his salon proved to Franz and Albert that he was a connoisseur of pictures. A few words he let fall showed them that he was no stranger to the sciences, and he seemed much occupied with chemistry. The two friends did not venture to return the count the breakfast he had given them; it would have been too absurd to offer him in exchange for his excellent table the very inferior one of Signor Pastrini. They told him so frankly, and he received their excuses with the air of a man who appreciated their delicacy. Albert was charmed with the count's manners, and he was only prevented from recognizing him for a perfect gentleman by reason of his varied knowledge. The permission to do what he liked with the carriage pleased him above all, for the fair peasants had appeared in a most elegant carriage the preceding evening, and Albert was not sorry to be upon an equal footing with them. At half-past one they descended, the coachman and footman had put on their livery over their disguises, which gave them a more ridiculous appearance than ever, and which gained them the applause of Franz and Albert. Albert had fastened the faded bunch of violets to his button-hole. At the first sound of the bell they hastened into the Corso by the Via Vittoria. At the second turn, a bunch of fresh violets, thrown from a carriage filled with harlequins, indicated to Albert that, like himself and his friend, the peasants had changed their costume also; and whether it was the result of chance, or whether a similar feeling had possessed them both, while he had changed his costume they had assumed his.

Albert placed the fresh bouquet in his button-hole, but he kept the faded one in his hand; and when he again met the calash, he raised it to his lips, an action which seemed greatly to amuse not only the fair lady who had thrown it, but her joyous companions also. The day was as gay as the preceding one, perhaps even more animated and noisy; the count appeared for an instant at his window, but when they again passed he had disappeared. It is almost needless to say that the flirtation between Albert and the fair peasant continued all day. In the evening, on his return, Franz found a letter from the embassy, informing him that he would have the honor of being received by his holiness the next day. At each previous visit he had made to Rome, he had solicited and obtained the same favor; and incited as much by a religious feeling as by gratitude, he was unwilling to quit the capital of the Christian world without laying his respectful homage at the feet of one of St. Peter's successors who has set the rare example of all the virtues. He did not then think of the Carnival, for in spite of his condescension and touching kindness, one cannot incline one's self without awe before the venerable and noble old man called Gregory XVI. On his return from the Vatican, Franz carefully avoided the Corso; he brought away with him a treasure of pious thoughts, to which the mad gayety of the maskers would have been profanation.

At ten minutes past five Albert entered overjoyed. The harlequin had reassumed her peasant's costume, and as she passed she raised her mask. She was charming. Franz congratulated Albert, who received his congratulations with the air of a man conscious that they are merited. He had recognized by certain unmistakable signs, that his fair *incognita* belonged to the aristocracy. He had made up his mind to write to her the next day. Franz remarked, while he gave these details, that Albert seemed to have something to ask of him, but that he was unwilling to ask it. He insisted upon it, declaring beforehand that he was willing to make any sacrifice the other wished. Albert let himself be pressed just as long as friendship required, and then avowed to Franz that he would do him a great favor by allowing him to occupy the carriage alone the next day. Albert attributed to Franz's absence the extreme kindness of the fair peasant in raising her mask. Franz was not sufficiently egotistical to stop Albert in the middle of an adventure that promised to prove so agreeable to his curiosity and so flattering to his vanity. He felt assured that the perfect indiscretion of his friend would duly inform him of all that happened; and as, during three years that he had travelled all over Italy, a similar piece of good fortune had never fallen to his share, Franz was by no means sorry to learn how to act on such an occasion. He therefore promised Albert that he would content himself the morrow with witnessing the Carnival from the windows of the Rospoli Palace.

The next morning he saw Albert pass and repass, holding an enormous bouquet, which he doubtless meant to make the bearer of his amorous epistle. This belief was changed into certainly when Franz saw the bouquet (conspicuous by a circle of white camellias) in the hand of a charming harlequin dressed in rose-colored satin. The evening was no longer joy, but delirium. Albert nothing doubted but that the fair unknown would reply in the same manner. Franz anticipated his wishes by saying that the noise fatigued him, and that he should pass the next day in writing and looking over his journal. Albert was not deceived, for the next evening

Franz saw him enter triumphantly shaking a folded paper which he held by one corner. "Well," said he, "was I mistaken?"—"She has answered you!" cried Franz.

"Read." This word was pronounced in a manner impossible to describe. Franz took the letter, and read:—

Tuesday evening, at seven o'clock, descend from your carriage opposite the Via dei Pontefiel, and follow the Roman peasant who snatches your torch from you. When you arrive at the first step of the church of San Giacomo, be sure to fasten a knot of rose-colored ribbons to the shoulder of your harlequin costume, in order that you may be recognized. Until then you will not see me.

CONSTANCY AND DISCRETION.

"Well," asked he, when Franz had finished, "what do you think of that?"

"I think that the adventure is assuming a very agreeable appearance."

"I think so, also," replied Albert; "and I very much fear you will go alone to the Duke of Bracciano's ball." Franz and Albert had received that morning an invitation from the celebrated Roman banker. "Take care, Albert," said Franz. "All the nobility of Rome will be present; and if your fair *incognita* belong to the higher class of society, she must go there."

"Whether she goes there or not, my opinion is still the same," returned Albert. "You have read the letter?"—"Yes."

"You know how imperfectly the women of the *mezzo cito* are educated in Italy?" (This is the name of the lower class.)—"Yes."

"Well, read the letter again. Look at the writing, and find if you can, any blemish in the language or orthography." (The writing was, in reality, charming, and the orthography irreproachable.) "You are born to good fortune," said Franz, as he returned the letter

"Laugh as much as you will," replied Albert, "I am in love."—
"You alarm me," cried Franz. "I see that I shall not only go alone
to the Duke of Bracciano's, but also return to Florence alone."

"If my unknown be as amiable as she is beautiful," said Albert,
"I shall fix myself at Rome for six weeks, at least. I adore Rome,
and I have always had a great taste for archaeology."—"Come, two
or three more such adventures, and I do not despair of seeing you
a member of the Academy." Doubtless Albert was about to discuss
seriously his right to the academic chair when they were informed
that dinner was ready. Albert's love had not taken away his appetite.
He hastened with Franz to seat himself, free to recommence the
discussion after dinner. After dinner, the Count of Monte Cristo
was announced. They had not seen him for two days. Signor Pastrini informed them that business had called him to Civita Vecchia.
He had started the previous evening, and had only returned an
hour since. He was charming. Whether he kept a watch over himself, or whether by accident he did not sound the acrimonious
chords that in other circumstances had been touched, he was to-
night like everybody else. The man was an enigma to Franz. The
count must feel sure that Franz recognized him; and yet he had not
let fall a single word indicating any previous acquaintance between
them. On his side, however great Franz's desire was to allude to
their former interview, the fear of being disagreeable to the man
who had loaded him and his friend with kindness prevented him
from mentioning it. The count had learned that the two friends had
sent to secure a box at the Argentina Theatre, and were told they
were all let. In consequence, he brought them the key of his own—
at least such was the apparent motive of his visit. Franz and Albert
made some difficulty, alleging their fear of depriving him of it; but
the count replied that, as he was going to the Palli Theatre, the box
at the Argentina Theatre would be lost if they did not profit by it.
This assurance determined the two friends to accept it.

Franz had by degrees become accustomed to the count's pallor, which had so forcibly struck him at their first meeting. He could not refrain from admiring the severe beauty of his features, the only defect, or rather the principal quality of which was the pallor. Truly, a Byronic hero! Franz could not, we will not say see him, but even think of him without imagining his stern head upon Manfred's shoulders, or beneath Lara's helmet. His forehead was marked with the line that indicates the constant presence of bitter thoughts; he had the fiery eyes that seem to penetrate to the very soul, and the haughty and disdainful upper lip that gives to the words it utters a peculiar character that impresses them on the minds of those to whom they are addressed. The count was no longer young. He was at least forty; and yet it was easy to understand that he was formed to rule the young men with whom he associated at present. And, to complete his resemblance with the fantastic heroes of the English poet, the count seemed to have the power of fascination. Albert was constantly expatiating on their good fortune in meeting such a man. Franz was less enthusiastic; but the count exercised over him also the ascendency a strong mind always acquires over a mind less domineering. He thought several times of the project the count had of visiting Paris; and he had no doubt but that, with his eccentric character, his characteristic face, and his colossal fortune, he would produce a great effect there. And yet he did not wish to be at Paris when the count was there. The evening passed as evenings mostly pass at Italian theatres; that is, not in listening to the music, but in paying visits and conversing. The Countess G— wished to revive the subject of the count, but Franz announced he had something far newer to tell her; and, in spite of Albert's demonstrations of false modesty, he informed the countess of the great event which had preoccupied them for the last three days. As similar intrigues are not uncommon in Italy, if we may credit travellers, the countess did not manifest the least incredulity, but congratulated Albert on his success. They promised, upon separating, to meet at the Duke of Bracciano's ball, to which all Rome was invited. The heroine of the bouquet kept her word; she gave Albert no sign of her existence the morrow or the day after.

At length Tuesday came, the last and most tumultuous day of the Carnival. On Tuesday, the theatres open at ten o'clock in the morning, as Lent begins after eight at night. On Tuesday, all those who through want of money, time, or enthusiasm, have not been to see the Carnival before, mingle in the gayety, and contribute to the noise and excitement. From two o'clock till five Franz and Albert followed in the fête, exchanging handfuls of confetti with the other carriages and the pedestrians, who crowded amongst the horses' feet and the carriage wheels without a single accident, a single dispute, or a single fight. The fêtes are veritable pleasure days to the Italians. The author of this history, who has resided five or six years in Italy, does not recollect to have ever seen a ceremony interrupted by one of those events so common in other countries. Albert was triumphant in his harlequin costume. A knot of rose-colored ribbons fell from his shoulder almost to the ground. In order that there might be no confusion, Franz wore his peasant's costume.

As the day advanced, the tumult became greater. There was not on the pavement, in the carriages, at the windows, a single tongue that was silent, a single arm that did not move. It was a human storm, made up of a thunder of cries, and a hail of sweetmeats, flowers, eggs, oranges, and nosegays. At three o'clock the sound of fireworks, let off on the Piazza del Popolo and the Piazza di Venezia (heard with difficulty amid the din and confusion) announced that the races were about to begin. The races, like the *moccoli*, are one of the episodes peculiar to the last days of the Carnival. At the sound of the fireworks the carriages instantly broke ranks, and retired by the adjacent streets. All these evolutions are executed with an inconceivable address and marvellous rapidity, without the police interfering in the matter. The pedestrians ranged themselves against the walls; then the trampling of horses and the clashing of steel were heard. A detachment of carbineers, fifteen abreast, galloped up the

Corso in order to clear it for the *barberi*. When the detachment arrived at the Piazza di Venezia, a second volley of fireworks was discharged, to announce that the street was clear. Almost instantly in the midst of a tremendous and general outcry, seven or eight horses, excited by the shouts of three hundred thousand spectators, passed by like lightning. Then the Castle of Saint Angelo fired three cannon to indicate that number three had won. Immediately, without any other signal, the carriages moved on, flowing on towards the Corso, down all the streets, like torrents pent up for a while which again flow into the parent river; and the immense stream again continued its course between its two granite banks.

A new source of noise and movement was added to the crowd The sellers of *moccoletti* entered on the scene. The *moccoli*, or *moccoletti*, are candles which vary in size from the pascal taper to the rushlight, and which give to each actor in the great final scene of the Carnival two very serious problems to grapple with,—first how to keep his own *moccoletto* alight; and, secondly, how to extinguish the *moccoletti* of others. The *moccoletto* is like life: man has found but one means of transmitting it, and that one comes from God. But he has discovered a thousand means of taking it away, and the devil has somewhat aided him. The *moccoletto* is kindled by approaching it to a light. But who can describe the thousand means of extinguishing the *moccoletto?*—the gigantic bellows, the monstrous extinguishers, the superhuman fans. Every one hastened to purchase *moccoletti*—Franz and Albert among the rest.

The night was rapidly approaching; and already, at the cry of "*Moccoletti!*" repeated by the shrill voices of a thousand vendors, two or three stars began to burn among the crowd. It was a signal. At the end of ten minutes fifty thousand lights glittered, descending from the Palazzo di Venezia to the Piazza del Popolo, and mounting from the Piazzo del Popolo to the Palazzo di Venezia. It seemed like the fête of jack-o'-lanterns. It is impossible to form any idea of it without having seen it. Suppose that all the stars had descended from the sky and mingled in a wild dance on the face of the earth, the whole accompanied by cries that were never heard in any other part of the world. The *facchino* follows the prince, the Transteverin the citizen, every one blowing, extinguishing, relighting. Had old Æolus appeared at this moment, he would have been proclaimed king of the *moccoli*, and Aquilo the heir-presumptive to the throne This battle of folly and flame continued for two hours; the Corso was light as day; the features of the spectators on the third and fourth stories were visible. Every five minutes Albert took out his watch; at length it pointed to seven. The two friends were in the Via dei Pontefici. Albert sprang out, bearing his *moccoletto* in his hand. Two or three masks strove to knock his *moccoletto* out of his hand; but Albert, a first-rate pugilist, sent them rolling in the street, one after the other, and continued his course towards the church of San Giacomo. The steps were crowded with masks, who strove to snatch each other's torches. Franz followed Albert with his eyes, and saw him mount the first step. Instantly a mask, wearing the well-known costume of a peasant woman, snatched his *moccoletto* from him without his offering any resistance. Franz was too far off to hear what they said; but, without doubt, nothing hostile passed, for he saw Albert disappear arm-in-arm with the peasant girl. He watched them pass through the crowd for some time, but at length he lost sight of them in the Via Macello. Suddenly the bell that gives the signal for the end of the Carnival sounded, and at the same instant all the *moccoletti* were extinguished as if by enchantment. It seemed as though one immense blast of the wind had extinguished every one. Franz found himself in utter darkness. No sound was audible save that of the carriages that were carrying the maskers home; nothing was visible save a few lights that burnt behind the windows. The Carnival was over.

XXXVII

The Catacombs
of Saint Sebastian

I N HIS WHOLE LIFE, perhaps, Franz had never before experienced
so sudden an impression, so rapid a transition from gayety to
sadness, as in this moment. It seemed as though Rome, under
the magic breath of some demon of the night, had suddenly
changed into a vast tomb. By a chance, which added yet more to
the intensity of the darkness, the moon, which was on the wane,
did not rise until eleven o'clock, and the streets which the young
man traversed were plunged in the deepest obscurity. The distance
was short, and at the end of ten minutes his carriage, or rather the
count's, stopped before the Hôtel de Londres. Dinner was waiting,
but as Albert had told him that he should not return so soon, Franz
sat down without him. Signor Pastrini, who had been accustomed
to see them dine together, inquired into the cause of his absence,
but Franz merely replied that Albert had received on the previous
evening an invitation which he had accepted. The sudden extinc-
tion of the *moccoletti*, the darkness which had replaced the light, and
the silence which had succeeded the turmoil, had left in Franz's
mind a certain depression which was not free from uneasiness. He
therefore dined very silently, in spite of the officions attention of his
host, who presented himself two or three times to inquire if he
wanted anything.

Franz resolved to wait for Albert as late as possible. He ordered the carriage, therefore, for eleven o'clock, desiring Signor Pastrini to inform him the moment that Albert returned to the hotel. At eleven o'clock Albert had not come back. Franz dressed himself, and went out, telling his host that he was going to pass the night at the Duke of Bracciano's. The house of the Duke of Bracciano is one of the most delightful in Rome, the duchess, one of the last heiresses of the Colonnas, does its honors with the most consummate grace, and thus their fêtes have a European celebrity. Franz and Albert had brought to Rome letters of introduction to them, and their first question on his arrival was to inquire the whereabouts of his travelling companion. Franz replied that he had left him at the moment they were about to extinguish the *moccoli*, and that he had lost sight of him in the Via Macello. "Then he has not returned?" said the duke.—"I waited for him until this hour," replied Franz.

"And do you know whither he went?"—"No, not precisely; however, I think it was something very like a rendezvous."

"*Diavolo!*" said the duke, "this is a bad day, or rather a bad night, to be out late; is it not, countess?" These words were addressed to the Countess G—, who had just arrived, and was leaning on the arm of Signor Torlonia, the duke's brother.—"I think, on the contrary, that it is a charming night," replied the countess, "and those who are here will complain of but one thing—its too rapid flight."

"I am not speaking," said the duke with a smile, "of the persons who are here; the men run no other danger than that of falling in love with you, and the women of falling ill of jealousy at seeing you so lovely; I meant persons who were out in the streets of Rome."— "Ah," asked the countess, "who is out in the streets of Rome at this hour, unless it be to go to a ball?"

"Our friend, Albert de Morcerf, countess, whom I left in pursuit of his unknown about seven o'clock this evening," said Franz, "and whom I have not seen since."

"And don't you know where he is?"—"Not at all."

"Is he armed?"—"He is in masquerade."

"You should not have allowed him to go," said the duke to Franz; "you, who know Rome better than he does."—"You might as well have tried to stop number three of the *barberi*, who gained the prize in the race to-day," replied Franz; "and then, moreover, what could happen to him?"

"Who can tell? The night is gloomy, and the Tiber is very near the Via Macello." Franz felt a shudder run through his veins at observing that the feeling of the duke and the countess was so much in unison with his own personal disquietude. "I informed them at the hotel that I had the honor of passing the night here, duke," said Franz, "and desired them to come and inform me of his return."—"Ah," replied the duke, "here, I think, is one of my servants who is seeking you."

The duke was not mistaken; when he saw Franz, the servant came up to him. "Your excellency," he said, "the master of the Hôtel de Londres has sent to let you know that a man is waiting for you with a letter from the Viscount of Morcerf."—"A letter from the viscount!" exclaimed Franz.

"Yes."—"And who is the man?"

"I do not know."—"Why did he not bring it to me here?"

"The messenger did not say."—"And where is the messenger?"

"He went away directly he saw me enter the ball-room to find you."

"Oh," said the countess to Franz, "go with all speed—poor young man! Perhaps some accident has happened to him."

"I will hasten," replied Franz.

"Shall we see you again to give us any information?" inquired the countess.—"Yes, if it is not any serious affair, otherwise I cannot answer as to what I may do myself."

"Be prudent, in any event," said the countess.

"Oh, pray be assured of that." Franz took his hat and went away in haste. He had sent away his carriage with orders for it to fetch him at two o'clock; fortunately the Palazzo Bracciano, which is on one side in the Corso, and on the other in the Square of the Holy Apostles, is hardly ten minutes' walk from the Hôtel de Londres. As he came near the hotel, Franz saw a man in the middle of the street. He had no doubt that it was the messenger from Albert. The man was wrapped up in a large cloak. He went up to him, but, to his extreme astonishment, the stranger first addressed him. "What wants your excellency of me?" inquired the man, retreating a step or two, as if to keep on his guard.

"Are not you the person who brought me a letter," inquired Franz, "from the Viscount of Morcerf?"

"Your excellency lodges at Pastrini's hotel?"—"I do."

"Your excellency is the travelling companion of the viscount?"

"I am."—"Your excellency's name"—

"Is the Baron Franz d'Epinay."

"Then it is to your excellency that this letter is addressed."

"Is there any answer?" inquired Franz, taking the letter from him.

"Yes—your friend at least hopes so."—"Come up-stairs with me, and I will give it to you."—"I prefer waiting here," said the messenger, with a smile.

"And why?"

"Your excellency will know when you have read the letter."

"Shall I find you here, then?"—"Certainly."

Franz entered the hotel. On the staircase he met Signor Pastrini. "Well?" said the landlord.—"Well—what?" responded Franz.

"You have seen the man who desired to speak with you from your friend?" he asked of Franz.—"Yes, I have seen him," he replied, "and he has handed this letter to me. Light the candles in my apartment, if you please." The innkeeper gave orders to a servant to go before Franz with a light. The young man had found Signor Pastrini looking very much alarmed, and this had only made him the more anxious to read Albert's letter; and so he went instantly towards the waxlight, and unfolded it. It was written and signed by Albert. Franz read it twice before he could comprehend what it contained. It was thus worded:—

MY DEAR FELLOW,—The moment you have received this, have the kindness to take the letter of credit from my pocket-book, which you will find in the square drawer of the secretary; add your own to it, if it be not sufficient. Run to Torlonia, draw from him instantly four thousand plastres, and give them to the bearer. It is urgent that I should have this money without delay. I do not say more, relying on you as you may rely on me. Your friend,

ALBERT DE MORCERF.

P.S.—I now believe in Italian banditti.

Below these lines were written, in a strange hand, the following in Italian:—

Se alle sei della mattina le quattro mile plastre non sono nelle mile mani, alla sette il conte Alberto avrà cessato di vivere.

LUIGI VAMPA.

"If by six in the morning the four thousand pilastres are not in my hands, by seven o'clock the Count Albert will have ceased to live."
This second signature explained everything to Franz, who now understood the objection of the messenger to coming up into the apartment; the street was safer for him. Albert, then, had fallen into the hands of the famous bandit chief, in whose existence he had for so long a time refused to believe. There was no time to lose. He hastened to open the secretary, and found the pocket-book in the drawer, and in it the letter of credit. There were in all six thousand piastres, but of these six thousand Albert had already expended three

thousand. As to Franz, he had no letter of credit, as he lived at Florence, and had only come to Rome to pass seven or eight days; he had brought but a hundred louis, and of these he had not more than fifty left. Thus seven or eight hundred piastres were wanting to them both to make up the sum that Albert required. True, he might in such a case rely on the kindness of Signor Torlonia. He was, therefore, about to return to the Palazzo Bracciano without loss of time, when suddenly a luminous idea crossed his mind. He remembered the Count of Monte Cristo. Franz was about to ring for Signor Pastrini, when that worthy presented himself. "My dear sir," he said, hastily, "do you know if the count is within?"

"Yes, your excellency; he has this moment returned."

"Is he in bed?"—"I should say no."

"Then ring at his door, if you please, and request him to be so kind as to give me an audience." Signor Pastrini did as he was desired, and returning five minutes after, he said,—"The count awaits your excellency." Franz went along the corridor, and a servant introduced him to the count. He was in a small room which Franz had not yet seen, and which was surrounded with divans. The count came towards him. "Well, what good wind blows you hither at this hour?" said he; "have you come to sup with me? It would be very kind of you."

"No; I have come to speak to you of a very serious matter."

"A serious matter," said the count, looking at Franz with the earnestness usual to him; "and what may it be?"

"Are we alone?"—"Yes," replied the count, going to the door, and returning. Franz gave him Albert's letter. "Read that," he said. The count read it.

"Well, well!" said he.

"Did you see the postscript?"—"I did, indeed.

"'Se alle sei della mattina le quattro mile pilastre non sono nelle mie mani, alla sette il conte Alberto avrà cessalo di vivere.

"'LUIGI VAMPA.'"

"What think you of that?" inquired Franz.

"Have you the money he demands?"

"Yes, all but eight hundred piastres." The count went to his secretary, opened it, and pulling out a drawer filled with gold, said to Franz,—"I hope you will not offend me by applying to any one but myself."

"You see, on the contrary, I come to you first and instantly," replied Franz.—"And I thank you; have what you will;" and he made a sign to Franz to take what he pleased.

"Is it absolutely necessary, then, to send the money to Luigi Vampa?" asked the young man, looking fixedly in his turn at the count—"Judge for yourself," replied he. "The postscript is explicit."

"I think that if you would take the trouble of reflecting, you could find a way of simplifying the negotiation," said Franz.

"How so?" returned the count, with surprise.

"If we were to go together to Luigi Vampa, I am sure he would not refuse you Albert's freedom."

"What influence can I possibly have over a bandit?"

"Have you not just rendered him a service that can never be forgotten?"—"What is that?"

"Have you not saved Peppino's life?"

"Well, well," said the count, "who told you that?"

"No matter; I know it." The count knit his brows, and remained silent an instant. "And if I went to seek Vampa, would you accompany me?"

"If my society would not be disagreeable."—"Be it so. It is a lovely night, and a walk without Rome will do us both good."

"Shall I take any arms?"—"For what purpose?"

"Any money?"

"It is useless. Where is the man who brought the letter?"

"In the street."

"He awaits the answer?"—"Yes."

"I must learn where we are going. I will summon him hither."

"It is useless; he would not come up."—"To your apartments, perhaps; but he will not make any difficulty at entering mine." The count went to the window of the apartment that looked on to the street, and whistled in a peculiar manner. The man in the mantle quitted the wall, and advanced into the middle of the street. "*Salite!*" said the count, in the same tone in which he would have given an order to his servant. The messenger obeyed without the least hesitation but rather with alacrity, and, mounting the steps at a bound entered the hotel; five seconds afterwards he was at the door of the room. "Ah, it is you, Peppino," said the count. But Peppino, instead of answering, threw himself on his knees, seized the count's hand, and covered it with kisses. "Ah," said the count, "you have, then, not forgotten that I saved your life; that is strange, for it is a week ago."—"No, excellency; and never shall I forget it," returned Peppino, with an accent of profound gratitude.

"Never? That is a long time; but it is something that you believe so. Rise and answer." Peppino glanced anxiously at Franz. "Oh, you may speak before his excellency," said he; "he is one of my friends. You allow me to give you this title?" continued the count in French; "it is necessary to excite this man's confidence."

"You can speak before me," said Franz; "I am a friend of the count's."

"Good!" returned Peppino. "I am ready to answer any questions your excellency may address to me."

"How did the Viscount Albert fall into Luigi's hands?"

"Excellency, the Frenchman's carriage passed several times the one in which was Teresa."—"The chief's mistress?"

"Yes. The Frenchman threw her a bonquet; Teresa returned it— all this with the consent of the chief, who was in the carriage."

"What?" cried Franz, "was Luigi Vampa in the carriage with the Roman peasants?"—"It was he who drove, disguised as the coachman," replied Peppino.—"Well?" said the count.

"Well, then, the Frenchman took off his mask; Teresa, with the chief's consent, did the same. The Frenchman asked for a rendezvous; Teresa gave him one—only, instead of Teresa, it was Beppo who was on the steps of the church of San Giacomo."—"What!" exclaimed Franz, "the peasant girl who snatched his *moccoletto* from him"—

"Was a lad of fifteen," replied Peppino. "But it was no disgrace to your friend to have been deceived; Beppo has taken in plenty of others."—"And Beppo led him outside the walls?" said the count.

"Exactly so; a carriage was waiting at the end of the Via Macello. Beppo got in, inviting the Frenchman to follow him, and he did not wait to be asked twice. He gallantly offered the right-hand seat to Beppo, and sat by him. Beppo told him he was going to take him to a villa a league from Rome; the Frenchman assured him he would follow him to the end of the world. The coachman went up the Via di Ripetta and the Porta San Paola; and when they were two hundred yards outside, as the Frenchman became somewhat too forward, Beppo put a brace of pistols to his head, the coachman pulled up and did the same. At the same time, four of the band, who were concealed on the banks of the Almo, surrounded the carriage. The Frenchman made some resistance, and nearly strangled Beppo; but he could not resist five armed men, and was forced to yield. They made him get out, walk along the banks of the river, and then brought him to Teresa and Luigi, who were waiting for him in the catacombs of St. Sebastian."

"Well," said the count, turning towards Franz, "it seems to me that this is a very likely story. What do you say to it?"—"Why, that I should think it very amusing," replied Franz, "if it had happened to any one but poor Albert."

"And, in truth, if you had not found me here," said the count, "it might have proved a gallant adventure which would have cost your friend dear; but now, be assured, his alarm will be the only serious consequence."—"And shall we go and find him?" inquired Franz.

"Oh, decidedly, sir. He is in a very picturesque place—do you know the catacombs of St. Sebastian?"

"I was never in them, but I have often resolved to visit them."

"Well, here is an opportunity made to your hand, and it would be difficult to contrive a better. Have you a carriage?"—"No."

"That is of no consequence; I always have one ready, day and night."

"Always ready?"

"Yes. I am a very capricious being, and I should tell you that sometimes when I rise, or after my dinner, or in the middle of the night, I resolve on starting for some particular point, and away I go." The count rang, and a footman appeared. "Order out the carriage," he said, "and remove the pistols which are in the holsters. You need not awaken the coachman; Ali will drive." In a very short time the noise of wheels was heard, and the carriage stopped at the door. The count took out his watch. "Half-past twelve," he said. "We might start at five o'clock and be in time, but the delay may cause your friend to pass an uneasy night, and therefore we had better go with all speed to extricate him from the hands of the infidels. Are you still resolved to accompany me?"—"More determined than ever."—"Well, then, come along."

Franz and the count went downstairs, accompanied by Peppino. At the door they found the carriage. Ali was on the box, in whom Franz recognized the dumb slave of the grotto of Monte Cristo. Franz and the count got into the carriage. Peppino placed himself beside Ali, and they set off at a rapid pace. Ali had received his instructions, and went down the Corso, crossed the Campo Vaccino, went up the Strada San Gregorio, and reached the gates of St. Sebastian. Then the porter raised some difficulties, but the Count of Monte Cristo produced a permit from the governor of Rome, allowing him to leave or enter the city at any hour of the day or night; the portcullis was therefore raised, the porter had a louis for his trouble, and they went on their way. The road which the carriage now traversed was the ancient Appian Way, and bordered with tombs. From time to time, by the light of the moon, which began to rise, Franz imagined that he saw something like a sentinel appear at various points among the ruins, and suddenly retreat into the darkness on a signal from Peppino. A short time before they reached the Baths of Caracalla the carriage stopped, Peppino opened the door, and the count and Franz alighted.

"In ten minutes," said the count to his companion, "we shall be there."

He then took Peppino aside, gave him an order in a low voice, and Peppino went away, taking with him a torch, brought with them in the carriage. Five minutes elapsed, during which Franz saw the shepherd going along a narrow path that led over the irregular and broken surface of the Campagna; and finally he disappeared in the midst of the tall red herbage, which seemed like the bristling mane of an enormous lion. "Now," said the count, "let us follow him." Franz and the count in their turn then advanced along the same path, which, at the distance of a hundred paces, led them over a declivity to the bottom of a small valley. They then perceived two men conversing in the obscurity. "Ought we to go on?" asked Franz of the count; "or shall we wait awhile?"—"Let us go on; Peppino will have warned the sentry of our coming." One of the two men was Peppino, and the other a bandit on the lookout. Franz and the count advanced, and the bandit saluted them. "Your excellency," said Peppino, addressing the count, "if you will follow me, the opening of the catacombs is close at hand."—"Go on, then," replied the count. They came to an opening behind a clump of bushes and in the midst of a pile of rocks, by which a man could scarcely pass. Peppino glided first into this crevice; after they got along a few paces the passage widened. Peppino paused, lighted his torch, and turned to see if they came after him. The count first reached an open space and Franz followed him closely. The passageway sloped in a gentle descent, enlarging as they proceeded; still Franz and the count were compelled to advance in a stooping posture, and were scarcely able to proceed abreast of one another. They went on a hundred and fifty paces in this way, and then were stopped by, "Who comes there?" At the same time they saw the reflection of a torch on a carbine barrel.

"A friend!" responded Peppino; and, advancing alone towards the sentry, he said a few words to him in a low tone; and then he, like the first, saluted the nocturnal visitors, making a sign that they might proceed.

Behind the sentinel was a staircase with twenty steps. Franz and the count descended these, and found themselves in a mortuary chamber. Five corridors diverged like the rays of a star, and the walls, dug into niches, which were arranged one above the other in the shape of coffins, showed that they were at last in the catacombs. Down one of the corridors, whose extent it was impossible to determine, rays of light were visible. The count laid his hand on Franz's shoulder. "Would you like to see a camp of bandits in repose?" he inquired.—"Exceedingly," replied Franz.

"Come with me, then, Peppino, put out the torch." Peppino obeyed, and Franz and the count were in utter darkness, except that fifty paces in advance of them a reddish glare, more evident since Peppino had put out his torch, was visible along the wall. They advanced silently, the count guiding Franz as if he had the singular faculty of seeing in the dark. Franz himself, however, saw his way more plainly in proportion as he went on towards the light, which served in some manner as a guide. Three arcades were before them, and the middle one was used as a door. These arcades opened on one side into the corridor where the count and Franz were, and on the other into a large square chamber, entirely surrounded by niches similar to those of which we have spoken. In the midst of this chamber were four stones, which had formerly served as an altar, as was evident from the cross which still surmounted them. A lamp, placed at the base of a pillar, lighted up with its pale and flickering flame the singular scene which presented itself to the eyes of the two visitors concealed in the shadow. A man was seated with his elbow leaning on the column, and was reading with his back turned to the arcades, through the openings of which the newcomers contemplated him. This was the chief of the band, Luigi Vampa. Around him, and in groups, according to their fancy, lying in their mantles, or with their backs against a sort of stone bench, which went all round the columbariumn, were to be seen twenty brigands or more, each having his carbine within reach. At the other end, silent, scarcely visible, and like a shadow, was a sentinel, who was walking up and down before a grotto, which was only distinguishable because in that spot the darkness seemed more dense than elsewhere. When the count thought Franz had gazed sufficiently on this picturesque tableau, he raised his finger to his lips, to warn him to be silent, and, ascending the three steps which led to the corridor of the columbarium, entered the chamber by the middle arcade, and advanced towards Vampa, who was so intent on the book before him that he did not hear the noise of his footsteps.

"Who comes there?" cried the sentinel, who was less abstracted, and who saw by the lamp-light a shadow approaching his chief. At this challenge, Vampa rose quickly, drawing at the same moment a pistol from his girdle. In a moment all the bandits were on their feet, and twenty carbines were levelled at the count. "Well," said he in a voice perfectly calm, and no muscle of his countenance disturbed, "well, my dear Vampa, it appears to me that you receive a friend with a great deal of ceremony."—"Ground arms," exclaimed the chief, with an imperative sign of the hand, while with the other he took off his hat respectfully; then, turning to the singular personage who had caused this scene, he said, "Your pardon, your excellency, but I was so far from expecting the honor of a visit, that I did not really recognize you."

"It seems that your memory is equally short in everything, Vampa," said the count, "and that not only do you forget people's faces, but also the conditions you make with them."—"What conditions have I forgotten, your excellency?" inquired the bandit, with the air of a man who, having committed an error, is anxious to repair it.

"Was it not agreed," asked the count, "that not only my person, but also that of my friends, should be respected by you?"

"And how have I broken that treaty, your excellency?"—"You have this evening carried off and conveyed hither the Vicomte Albert de Morcerf. Well," continued the count, in a tone that made Franz shudder, "this young gentleman is one of *my friends*—this young gentleman lodges in the same hotel as myself—this young gentleman has been up and down the Corso for eight hours in my private carriage, and yet, I repeat to you, you have carried him off, and conveyed him hither, and," added the count, taking the letter from his pocket, "you have set a ransom on him, as if he were an utter stranger."

"Why did you not tell me all this—you?" inquired the brigand chief, turning towards his men, who all retreated before his look. "Why have you caused me thus to fail in my word towards a gentleman like the count, who has all our lives in his hands? By heavens, if I thought one of you knew that the young gentleman was the friend of his excellency, I would blow his brains out with my own hand!"—"Well," said the count, turning towards Franz, "I told you there was some mistake in this."

"Are you not alone?" asked Vampa with uneasiness.

"I am with the person to whom this letter was addressed, and to whom I desired to prove that Luigi Vampa was a man of his word. Come, your excellency," the count added, turning to Franz, "here is Luigi Vampa, who will himself express to you his deep regret at the mistake he has committed." Franz approached, the chief advancing several steps to meet him. "Welcome among us, your excellency," he said to him; "you heard what the count just said, and also my reply; let me add that I would not for the four thousand piastres at which I had fixed your friend's ransom, that this had happened."—"But," said Franz, looking round him uneasily, "where is the viscount?—I do not see him."

"Nothing has happened to him, I hope," said the count frowningly.

"The prisoner is there," replied Vampa, pointing to the hollow space in front of which the bandit was on guard, "and I will go myself and tell him he is free." The chief went towards the place he had pointed out as Albert's prison, and Franz and the count followed him. "What is the prisoner doing?" inquired Vampa of the sentinel.

"*Ma foi*, captain," replied the sentry, "I do not know; for the last hour I have not heard him stir."—"Come in, your excellency," said Vampa. The count and Franz ascended seven or eight steps after the chief, who drew back a bolt and opened a door. Then, by the gleam of a lamp, similar to that which lighted the columbarium, Albert was to be seen wrapped up in a cloak which one of the bandits had lent him, lying in a corner in profound slumber. "Come," said the count, smiling with his own peculiar smile, "not so bad for a man who is to be shot at seven o'clock tomorrow morning." Vampa looked at Albert with a kind of admiration; he was not insensible to such a proof of courage.

"You are right, your excellency," he said; "this must be one of your friends." Then going to Albert, he touched him on the shoulder, saying, "Will your excellency please to awaken?" Albert stretched out his arms, rubbed his eyelids, and opened his eyes. "Oh," said he, "is it you, captain? You should have allowed me to sleep. I had such a delightful dream. I was dancing the galop at Torlonia's with the Countess G——." Then he drew his watch from his pocket, that he might see how time sped.

"Half-past one only," said he. "Why the devil do you rouse me at this hour?"—"To tell you that you are free, your excellency."

"My dear fellow," replied Albert, with perfect ease of mind, "remember, for the future, Napoleon's maxim, 'Never awaken me but for bad news;' if you had let me sleep on, I should have finished my galop, and have been grateful to you all my life. So, then, they have paid my ransom?"

"No, your excellency."—"Well, then, how am I free?"

"A person to whom I can refuse nothing has come to demand you."

"Come hither?"—"Yes, hither."

"Really? Then that person is a most amiable person." Albert looked around and perceived Franz. "What," said he, "is it you, my dear Franz, whose devotion and friendship are thus displayed?"—"No, not I," replied Franz, "but our neighbor, the Count of Monte Cristo."

"Oh, my dear count," said Albert gayly, arranging his cravat and wristbands, "you are really most kind, and I hope you will consider me as under eternal obligations to you, in the first place for the carriage, and in the next for this visit," and he put out his hand to the count, who shuddered as he gave his own, but who nevertheless did give it. The bandit gazed on this scene with amazement; he was evidently accustomed to see his prisoners tremble before him, and yet here was one whose gay temperament was not for a moment altered; as for Franz, he was enchanted at the way in which Albert had sustained the national honor in the presence of the bandit. "My dear Albert," he said, "if you will make haste, we shall yet have time to finish the night at Torlonia's. You may conclude your interrupted galop, so that you will owe no ill-will to Signor Luigi, who has, indeed, throughout this whole affair acted like a gentleman."—"You are decidedly right, and we may reach the Palazzo by two o'clock. Signor Luigi," continued Albert, "is there any formality to fulfil before I take leave of your excellency?"

"None, sir," replied the bandit, "you are as free as air."

"Well, then, a happy and merry life to you. Come, gentlemen, come."

And Albert, followed by Franz and the count, descended the staircase, crossed the square chamber, where stood all the bandits, hat in hand. "Peppino," said the brigand chief, "give me the torch."

"What are you going to do?" inquired the count.

"I will show you the way back myself," said the captain; "that is the least honor that I can render to your excellency." And taking the lighted torch from the hands of the herdsman, he preceded his guests, not as a servant who performs an act of civility, but like a king who precedes ambassadors. On reaching the door, he bowed. "And now, your excellency," added he, "allow me to repeat my apologies, and I hope you will not entertain any resentment at what has occurred."

"No, my dear Vampa," replied the count; "besides, you compensate for your mistake in so gentlemanly a way, that one almost feels obliged to you for having committed them."

"Gentlemen," added the chief, turning towards the young men, "perhaps the offer may not appear very tempting to you; but if you should ever feel inclined to pay me a second visit, wherever I may be, you shall be welcome." Franz and Albert bowed. The count went out first, then Albert. Franz paused for a moment. "Has your excellency anything to ask me?" said Vampa with a smile.

"Yes, I have," replied Franz; "I am curious to know what work you were perusing with so much attention as we entered."

"Cæsar's 'Commentaries,'" said the bandit; "it is my favorite work."

"Well, are you coming?" asked Albert.

"Yes," replied Franz, "here I am," and he, in his turn, left the caves. They advanced to the plain. "Ah, your pardon," said Albert, turning round; "will you allow me, captain?" And he lighted his cigar at Vampa's torch. "Now, my dear count," he said, "let us on with all the speed we may. I am enormously anxious to finish my night at the Duke of Bracciano's." They found the carriage where they had left it. The count said a word in Arabic to Ali, and the horses went off at great speed. It was just two o'clock by Albert's watch when the two friends entered into the dancing-room. Their return was quite an event, but as they entered together, all uneasiness on Albert's account ceased instantly. "Madame," said the Viscount of Morcerf, advancing towards the countess, "yesterday you were so condescending as to promise me a galop; I am rather late in claiming this gracious promise, but here is my friend, whose character for veracity you well know, and he will assure you the delay arose from no fault of mine." And as at this moment the orchestra gave the signal for the waltz, Albert put his arm round the waist of the countess, and disappeared with her in the whirl of dancers. In the meanwhile Franz was considering the singular shudder that had passed over the Count of Monte Cristo at the moment when he had been, in some sort, forced to give his hand to Albert.

XXXVIII

The Compact

THE FIRST WORDS THAT Albert uttered to his friend, on the following morning, contained a request that Franz would accompany him on a visit to the count; true, the young man had warmly and energetically thanked the count on the previous evening; but services such as he had rendered could never be too often acknowledged. Franz, who seemed attracted by some invisible influence towards the count, in which terror was strangely mingled, felt an extreme reluctance to permit his friend to be exposed alone to the singular fascination that this mysterious personage seemed to exercise over him, and therefore made no objection to Albert's request, but at once accompanied him to the desired spot, and, after a short delay, the count joined them in the salon. "My dear count," said Albert, advancing to meet him, "permit me to repeat the poor thanks I offered last night, and to assure you that the remembrance of all I owe to you will never be effaced from my memory; believe me, as long as I live, I shall never cease to dwell with grateful recollection on the prompt and important service you rendered me; and also to remember that to you I am indebted even for my life."—"My very good friend and excellent neighbor," replied the count, with a smile, "you really exaggerate my trifling exertions. You owe me nothing but some trifle of 20,000 francs, which you have been saved out of your travelling expenses, so that there is not much of a score between us;—but you must really permit me to congratulate you on the ease and unconcern with which you resigned yourself to your fate, and the perfect indifference you manifested as to the turn events might take."

"Upon my word," said Albert, "I deserve no credit for what I could not help, namely, a determination to take everything as I found it, and to let those bandits see, that although men get into troublesome scrapes all over the world, there is no nation but the French that can smile even in the face of grim Death himself. All that, however, has nothing to do with my obligations to you, and I now come to ask you whether, in my own person, my family, or connections, I can in any way serve you? My father, the Comte de Morcerf, although of Spanish origin, possesses considerable influence, both at the court of France and Madrid, and I unhesitatingly place the best services of myself, and all to whom my life is dear, at your disposal."—"Monsieur de Morcerf," replied the count, "your offer, far from surprising me, is precisely what I expected from you, and I accept it in the same spirit of hearty sincerity with which it is made;—nay, I will go still further, and say that I had previously made up my mind to ask a great favor at your hands."—"Oh, pray name it."

"I am wholly a stranger to Paris—it is a city I have never yet seen."

"Is it possible," exclaimed Albert, "that you have reached your present age without visiting the finest capital in the world? I can scarcely credit it."

"Nevertheless, it is quite true; still, I agree with you in thinking that my present ignorance of the first city in Europe is a reproach to me in every way, and calls for immediate correction; but, in all probability, I should have performed so important, so necessary a duty, as that of making myself acquainted with the wonders and beauties of your justly celebrated capital, had I known any person who would have introduced me into the fashionable world, but unfortunately I possessed no acquaintance there, and, of necessity, was compelled to abandon the idea."

"So distinguished an individual as yourself," cried Albert, "could scarcely have required an introduction."—"You are most kind; but as regards myself, I can find no merit I possess, save that, as a millionaire, I might have become a partner in the speculations of M. Aguado and M. Rothschild; but as my motive in travelling to your capital would not have been for the pleasure of dabbling in stocks, I stayed away till some favorable chance should present itself of carrying my wish into execution. Your offer, however, smooths all difficulties, and I have only to ask you, my dear M. de Morcerf" (these words were accompanied by a most peculiar smile), "whether you undertake, upon my arrival in France, to open to me the doors of that fashionable world of which I know no more than a Huron or a native of Cochin-China?"

"Oh, that I do, and with infinite pleasure," answered Albert; "and so much the more readily as a letter received this morning from my father summons me to Paris, in consequence of a treaty of marriage (my dear Franz, do not smile, I beg of you) with a family of high standing, and connected with the very cream of Parisian society."

"Connected by marriage, you mean," said Franz, laughingly.

"Well, never mind how it is," answered Albert, "it comes to the same thing in the end. Perhaps by the time you return to Paris, I shall be quite a sober, staid father of a family! A most edifying representative I shall make of all the domestic virtues—don't you think so? But as regards your wish to visit our fine city, my dear count, I can only say that you may command me and mine to any extent you please."—"Then it is settled," said the count; "and I give you my solemn assurance that I only waited an opportunity like the present to realize plans that I have long meditated." Franz did not doubt that these plans were the same concerning which the count had dropped a few words in the grotto of Monte Cristo, and while the count was speaking the young man watched him closely,

hoping to read something of his purpose in his face, but his countenance was inscrutable especially when, as in the present case, it
was veiled in a sphinx-like smile. "But tell me now, count,"
exclaimed Albert, delighted at the idea of having to chaperon so
distinguished a person as Monte Cristo; "tell me truly whether you
are in earnest, or if this project of visiting Paris is merely one of the
chimerical and uncertain air castles of which we make so many in
the course of our lives, but which, like a house built on the sand, is
liable to be blown over by the first puff of wind?"

"I pledge you my honor," returned the count, "that I mean to
do as I have said; both inclination and positive necessity compel me
to visit Paris."—"When do you propose going thither?"

"Have you made up your mind when you shall be there yourself?"

"Certainly I have; in a fortnight or three weeks' time, that is to
say, as fast as I can get there!"

"Nay," said the count: I will give you three months ere I join you,
you see I make an ample allowance for all delays and difficulties."

"And in three months' time," said Albert, "you will be at my
house?"

"Shall we make a positive appointment for a particular day and
hour?" inquired the count; "only let me warn you that I am proverbial for my punctilious exactitude in keeping my engagements."

"Day for day, hour for hour," said Albert; "that will suit me to a
dot."—"So be it, then," replied the count, and extending his hand
towards a calendar, suspended near the chimney-piece, he said, "to-
day is the 21st of February;" and drawing out his watch, added, "it
is exactly half-past ten o'clock. Now promise me to remember this,
and expect me the 21st of May at the same hour in the forenoon."

"Capital," exclaimed Albert; "your breakfast shall be waiting."

"Where do you live?"—"No. 27, Rue du Helder."

"Have you bachelor's apartments there? I hope my coming will
not put you to any inconvenience."—"I reside in my father's house

but occupy a pavilion at the farther side of the court-yard, entirely separated from the main building."

"Quite sufficient," replied the count, as, taking out his tablets, he wrote down "No. 27, Rue du Helder, 21st May, half-past ten in the morning." "Now then," said the count, returning his tablets to his pocket, "make yourself perfectly easy; the hand of your time-piece will not be more accurate in marking the time than myself."— "Shall I see you again ere my departure?" asked Albert.

"That depends; when do you leave?"

"To-morrow evening, at five o'clock."—"In that case I must say adieu to you, as I am compelled to go to Naples, and shall not return hither before Saturday evening or Sunday morning. And you, baron," pursued the count, addressing Franz, "do you also depart to-morrow?"—"Yes."

"For France?"

"No, for Venice; I shall remain in Italy for another year or two."

"Then we shall not meet in Paris?"

"I fear I shall not have that honor."—"Well, since we must part," said the count, holding out a hand to each of the young men, "allow me to wish you both a safe and pleasant journey." It was the first time the hand of Franz had come in contact with that of the mysterious individual before him, and unconsciously he shuddered at its touch, for it felt cold and icy as that of a corpse. "Let us understand each other," said Albert; "it is agreed—is it not?—that you are to be at No. 27, in the Rue du Helder, on the 21st of May, at half past ten in the morning, and your word of honor passed for your punctuality?"

"The 21st of May, at half-past ten in the morning, Rue du Helder, No. 27," replied the count. The young men then rose, and bowing to the count, quitted the room. "What is the matter?" asked Albert of Franz, when they had returned to their own apartments; "you seem more than commonly thoughtful."—"I will confess to you, Albert," replied Franz, "the count is a very singular person, and the appointment you have made to meet him in Paris fills me with a thousand apprehensions."

"My dear fellow," exclaimed Albert, "what can there possibly be in that to excite uneasiness? Why, you must have lost your senses."—"Whether I am in my senses or not," answered Franz, "that is the way I feel."

"Listen to me, Franz," said Albert; "I am glad that the occasion has presented itself for saying this to you, for I have noticed how cold you are in your bearing towards the count, while he, on the other hand, has always been courtesy itself to us. Have you anything particular against him?"

"Possibly."

"Did you ever meet him previously to coming hither?"—"I have."

"And where?"—"Will you promise me not to repeat a single word of what I am about to tell you?"

"I promise."

"Upon your honor?"

"Upon my honor."—"Then listen to me." Franz then related to his friend the history of his excursion to the Island of Monte Cristo, and of his finding a party of smugglers there, and the two Corsican bandits with them. He dwelt with considerable force and energy on the almost magical hospitality he had received from the count, and the magnificence of his entertainment in the grotto of the "Thousand and One Nights." He recounted, with circumstantial exactitude, all the particulars of the supper, the hashish, the statues, the dream, and how, at his awakening, there remained no proof or trace of all these events, save the small yacht, seen in the distant horizon driving under full sail toward Porto-Vecchio. Then he detailed the conversation overheard by him at the Colosseum, between the count and Vampa, in which the count had promised to obtain the release of the bandit Peppino,—an engagement which, as our readers are aware, he most faithfully fulfilled. At last he

arrived at the adventure of the preceding night, and the embarrassment in which he found himself placed by not having sufficient
cash by six or seven hundred piastres to make up the sum required,
and finally of his application to the count and the picturesque and
satisfactory result that followed. Albert listened with the most profound attention. "Well," said he, when Franz had concluded, "what
do you find to object to in all you have related? The count is fond
of travelling, and, being rich, possesses a vessel of his own. Go but
to Portsmouth or Southampton, and you will find the harbors
crowded with the yachts belonging to such of the English as can
afford the expense, and have the same liking for this amusement.
Now, by way of having a resting-place during his excursions, avoiding the wretched cookery—which has been trying its best to poison me during the last four months, while you have manfully
resisted its effects for as many years,—and obtaining a bed on
which it is possible to slumber, Monte Cristo has furnished for
himself a temporary abode where you first found him; but, to prevent the possibility of the Tuscan government taking a fancy to his
enchanted palace, and thereby depriving him of the advantages naturally expected from so large an outlay of capital, he has wisely
enough purchased the island, and taken its name. Just ask yourself,
my good fellow, whether there are not many persons of our aquain-
tance who assume the names of lands and properties they never in
their lives were masters of?"—"But," said Franz, "the Corsican bandits that were among the crew of his vessel?"

"Why, really the thing seems to me simple enough. Nobody
knows better than yourself that the bandits of Corsica are not
rogues or thieves, but purely and simply fugitives, driven by some
sinister motive from their native town or village, and that their fel-
lowship involves no disgrace or stigma; for my own part, I protest
that, should I ever go to Corsica, my first visit, ere even I presented
myself to the mayor or prefect, should be to the bandits of
Colomba, if I could only manage to find them; for, on my

conscience, they are a race of men I admire greatly."—"Still," persisted Franz, "I suppose you will allow that such men as Vampa and
his band are regular villains, who have no other motive than plunder when they seize your person. How do you explain the influence the count evidently possessed over those ruffians?"

"My good friend, as in all probability I owe my present safety
to that influence, it would ill become me to search too closely into
its source; therefore, instead of condemning him for his intimacy
with outlaws, you must give me leave to excuse any little irregular-
ity there may be in such a connection; not altogether for preserving my life, for my own idea was that it never was in much danger,
but certainly for saving me 4,000 piastres, which, being translated,
means neither more nor less than 24,000 livres of our money—a
sum at which, most assuredly, I should never have been estimated
in France, proving most indisputably," added Albert with a laugh,
"that no prophet is honored in his own country."—"Talking of
countries," replied Franz, "of what country is the count, what is his
native tongue, whence does he derive his immense fortune, and
what were those events of his early life—a life as marvellous as
unknown—that have tinctured his succeeding years with so dark
and gloomy a misanthropy? Certainly these are questions that, in
your place, I should like to have answered."

"My dear Franz," replied Albert, "when, upon receipt of my letter, you found the necessity of asking the count's assistance, you
promptly went to him, saying. 'My friend Albert de Morcerf is in
danger; help me to deliver him.' Was not that nearly what you said?"

"It was."—"Well, then, did he ask you, 'Who is M. Albert de
Morcerf? how does he come by his name—his fortune? what are
his means of existence? what is his birthplace? of what country is
he a native?' Tell me, did he put all these questions to you?"

"I confess he asked me none."—"No; he merely came and freed
me from the hands of Signor Vampa, where, I can assure you, in spite
of all my outward appearance of ease and unconcern, I did not very

particularly care to remain. Now, then, Franz, when, for services so promptly and unhesitatingly rendered, he but asks me in return to do for him what is done daily for any Russian prince or Italian nobleman who may pass through Paris—merely to introduce him into society—would you have me refuse? My good fellow, you must have lost your senses to think it possible I could act with such coldblooded policy." And this time it must be confessed that, contrary to the usual state of affairs in discussions between the young men, the effective arguments were all on Albert's side.—"Well," said Franz with a sigh, "do as you please, my dear viscount, for your arguments are beyond my powers of refutation. Still, in spite of all, you must admit that this Count of Monte Cristo is a most singular personage."—"He is a philanthropist," answered the other; "and no doubt his motive in visiting Paris is to compete for the Monthyon prize, given, as you are aware, to whoever shall be proved to have most materially advanced the interests of virtue and humanity. If my vote and interest can obtain it for him, I will readily give him the one and promise the other. And now, my dear Franz, let us talk of something else. Come, shall we take our luncheon, and then pay a last visit to St. Peter's?" Franz silently assented; and the following afternoon, at half-past five o'clock, the young men parted, Albert de Morcerf to return to Paris, and Franz d'Epinay to pass a fortnight at Venice. But, ere he entered his travelling carriage, Albert, fearing that his expected guest might forget the engagement he had entered into, placed in the care of a waiter at the hotel a card to be delivered to the Count of Monte Cristo, on which, beneath the name of Vicomte Albert de Morcerf, he had written in pencil—"27, Rue du Helder, on the 21st May, half-past ten A.M."

XXXIX

The Guests

IN THE HOUSE IN the Rue du Helder, where Albert had invited the Count of Monte Cristo, everything was being prepared on the morning of the 21st of May to do honor to the occasion. Albert de Morcerf inhabited a pavilion situated at the corner of a large court, and directly opposite another building, in which were the servants' apartments. Two windows only of the pavilion faced the street; three other windows looked into the court, and two at the back into the garden. Between the court and the garden, built in the heavy style of the imperial architecture, was the large and fashionable dwelling of the Count and Countess of Morcerf. A high wall surrounded the whole of the hotel, surmounted at intervals by vases filled with flowers, and broken in the centre by a large gate of gilded iron, which served as the carriage entrance. A small door, close to the lodge of the concierge, gave ingress and egress to the servants and masters when they were on foot.

It was easy to discover that the delicate care of a mother, unwilling to part from her son, and yet aware that a young man of the viscount's age required the full exercise of his liberty, had chosen this habitation for Albert. There were not lacking, however, evidences of what we may call the intelligent egoism of a youth who is charmed with the indolent, careless life of an only son, and who lives as it were in a gilded cage. By means of the two windows looking into the street, Albert could see all that passed; the sight of what is going on is necessary to young men, who always want to see the world traverse their horizon, even if that horizon is only a public thoroughfare Then, should anything appear to merit a more minute examination, Albert de Morcerf could follow up his researches by means of a small gate, similar to that close to the concierge's door, and which merits a particular description. It was a little entrance that seemed never to have been opened since the house was built, so entirely was it covered with dust and dirt; but the well-oiled hinges and locks told quite another story. This door was a mockery to the concierge, from whose vigilance and jurisdiction it was free, and, like that famous portal in the "Arabian Nights," opening at the "*Sesame*" of Ali Baba, it was wont to swing backward at a cabalistic word or a concerted tap from without from the sweetest voices or whitest fingers in the world. At the end of a long corridor, with which the door communicated, and which formed the antechamber, was, on the right, Albert's breakfast-room, looking into the court, and on the left the salon, looking into the garden. Shrubs and creeping plants covered the windows, and hid from the garden and court these two apartments, the only rooms into which, as they were on the ground-floor, the prying eyes of the curious could penetrate. On the floor above were similar rooms, with the addition of a third, formed out of the antechamber; these three rooms were a salon, a boudoir, and a bedroom. The salon down-stairs was only an Algerian divan, for the use of smokers. The boudoir up-stairs communicated with the bedchamber by an invisible door on the staircase; it was evident that every precaution had been taken. Above this floor was a large *atelier*, which had been increased in size by pulling down the partitions—a pandemonium, in which the artist and the dandy strove for preeminence. There were collected and piled up all Albert's successive caprices, hunting-horns, bass-viols, flutes—a whole orchestra, for Albert had had not a taste but a fancy for music; easels, palettes, brushes, pencils—for music had been succeeded by painting; foils, boxing-gloves, broadswords, and single-sticks—for, following the example of the fashionable young men of the time, Albert de Morcerf cultivated, with far more perseverance than music and drawing, the three arts that complete a dandy's education, i.e., fencing, boxing, and single-stick; and it was here that he received Grisier, Cook, and Charles Leboncher. The rest of the furniture of this privileged apartment consisted of old cabinets, filled with Chinese porcelain and Japanese vases, Lucca della Robbia faïence, and Palissy platters; of old arm-chairs, in which perhaps had sat Henry IV. or Sully, Louis XIII. or Richelieu—for two of these arm-chairs, adorned with a carved shield, on which were engraved the fleur-de-lis of France on an azure field, evidently came from the Louvre, or, at least, some royal residence. Over these dark and sombre chairs were thrown splendid stuffs, dyed beneath Persia's sun, or woven by the fingers of the women of Calcutta or of Chandernagor What these stuffs did there, it was impossible to say; they awaited, while gratifying the eyes, a destination unknown to their owner himself; in the meantime they filled the place with their golden and silky reflections. In the centre of the room was a Roller and Blanchet "baby grand" piano in rosewood, but holding the potentialities of an orchestra in its narrow and sonorous cavity, and groaning beneath the weight of the chefs-d'œuvre of Beethoven, Weber, Mozart, Haydn Grétry, and Porpora. On the walls, over the doors, on the ceiling, were swords, daggers, Malay creeses, maces, battle-axes; gilded, damasked, and inlaid suits of armor; dried plants, minerals, and stuffed birds, their flame-colored wings outspread in motionless flight, and their beaks forever open. This was Albert's favorite lounging place

However, the morning of the appointment, the young man had established himself in the small salon down-stairs. There, on a table surrounded at some distance by a large and luxurious divan, every species of tobacco known,—from the yellow tobacco of Petersburg to the black of Sinai, and so on along the scale from Maryland and Porto-Rico, to Latakïa,—was exposed in pots of crackled earthenware of which the Dutch are so fond; beside them, in boxes of fragrant wood, were ranged, according to their size and quality, pueros, regalias, havanas, and manillas; and, in an open cabinet, a collection of German pipes, of chibouques, with their amber mouth-pieces ornamented with coral, and of narghiles, with their long tubes of morocco, awaiting the caprice or the sympathy of the smokers. Albert had himself presided at the arrangement, or, rather, the symmetrical derangement, which, after coffee, the guests at a break fast of modern days love to contemplate through the vapor that escapes from their mouths, and ascends in long and fanciful wreaths to the ceiling. At a quarter to ten, a valet entered; he composed, with a little groom named John, and who only spoke English, all Albert's establishment, although the cook of the hotel was always at his service, and on great occasions the count's chasseur also. This valet, whose name was Germain, and who enjoyed the entire confidence of his young master, held in one hand a number of papers, and in the other a packet of letters, which he gave to Albert. Albert glanced carelessly at the different missives, selected two written in a small and delicate hand, and enclosed in scented envelopes, opened them and perused their contents with some attention. "How did these letters come?" said he.

"One by the post, Madame Danglars' footman left the other."

"Let Madame Danglars know that I accept the place she offers me in her box. Wait; then, during the day, tell Rosa that when I leave the Opera I will sup with her as she wishes. Take her six bottles of different wine—Cyprus, sherry, and Malaga, and a barrel of Ostend oysters; get them at Borel's, and be sure you say they are for me."

"At what o'clock, sir, do you breakfast?"

"What time is it now?"—"A quarter to ten."

"Very well, at half past ten. Debray will, perhaps, be obliged to go to the minister—and besides" (Albert looked at his tablets), "it is the hour I told the count, 21st May, at half past ten; and though I do not much rely upon his promise, I wish to be punctual. Is the countess up yet?"—"If you wish, I will inquire."

"Yes, ask her for one of her liqueur cellarets, mine is incomplete; and tell her I shall have the honor of seeing her about three o'clock, and that I request permission to introduce some one to her." The valet left the room. Albert threw himself on the divan, tore off the cover of two or three of the papers, looked at the theatre announcements, made a face seeing they gave an opera, and not a ballet; hunted vainly amongst the advertisements for a new tooth-powder of which he had heard, and threw down, one after the other, the three leading papers of Paris, muttering, "These papers become more and more stupid every day." A moment after, a carriage stopped before the door, and the servant announced M. Lucien Debray. A tall young man, with light hair, clear gray eyes, and thin and compressed lips, dressed in a blue coat with beautifully carved gold buttons, a white neckcloth, and a tortoiseshell eye-glass suspended by a silken thread, and which, by an effort of the superciliary and zygomatic muscles, he fixed in his eye, entered, with a half-official air, without smiling or speaking. "Good-morning, Lucien, good-morning," said Albert; "your punctuality really alarms me. What do I say? punctuality! You, whom I expected last, you arrive at five minutes to ten, when the time fixed was half-past! Has the ministry resigned?" —"No, my dear fellow," returned the young man, seating himself on the divan; "reassure yourself; we are tottering always, but we never fall, and I begin to believe that we shall pass into a state of immobility, and then the affairs of the Peninsula will completely consolidate us."

"Ah, true; you drive Don Carlos out of Spain." —"No, no, my dear fellow, do not confound our plans. We take him to the other side of the French frontier, and offer him hospitality at Bourges."

"At Bourges?" —"Yes, he has not much to complain of; Bourges is the capital of Charles VII. Do you not know that all Paris knew it yesterday, and the day before it had already transpired on the Bourse, and M. Danglars (I do not know by what means that man contrives to obtain intelligence as soon as we do) made a million!"

"And you another order, for I see you have a blue ribbon at your button-hole."—"Yes; they sent me the order of Charles III.," returned Debray, carelessly.

"Come, do not affect indifference, but confess you were pleased to have it."—"Oh, it is very well as a finish to the toilet. It looks very neat on a black coat buttoned up."

"And makes you resemble the Prince of Wales or the Duke of Reichstadt."—"It is for that reason you see me so early."

"Because you have the order of Charles III., and you wish to announce the good news to me?"—"No, because I passed the night writing letters,—five and twenty despatches. I returned home at daybreak, and strove to sleep; but my head ached, and I got up to have a ride for an hour. At the Bois de Boulogne, *ennui* and hunger attacked me at once,—two enemies who rarely accompany each other, and who are yet leagued against me, a sort of Carlo-republican alliance. I then recollected you gave a breakfast this morning, and here I am. I am hungry, feed me; I am bored, amuse me."

"It is my duty as your host," returned Albert, ringing the bell, while Lucien turned over, with his gold-mounted cane, the papers that lay on the table. "Germain, a glass of sherry and a biscuit. In the meantime, my dear Lucien, here are cigars—contraband, of course—try them, and persuade the minister to sell us such instead of poisoning us with cabbage leaves."—"*Peste*, I will do nothing of the kind; the moment they come from government you would find them execrable. Besides, that does not concern the home but the financial department. Address yourself to M. Humann, section of the indirect contributions, corridor A., No. 26."

"On my word," said Albert, "you astonish me by the extent of your knowledge. Take a cigar."—"Really, my dear Albert," replied Lucien, lighting a manilla at a rose-colored taper that burnt in a beautifully enamelled stand—"how happy you are to have nothing to do. You do not know your own good fortune!"

"And what would you do, my dear diplomatist," replied

Morcerf, with a slight degree of irony in his voice, "if you did nothing? What? private secretary to a minister, plunged at once into European cabals and Parisian intrigues; having kings, and, better still, queens, to protect, parties to unite, elections to direct; making more use of your cabinet with your pen and your telegraph than Napoleon did of his battle-fields with his sword and his victories; possessing five and twenty thousand francs a year, besides your place; a horse, for which Château-Renaud offered you four hundred louis, and which you would not part with; a tailor who never disappoints you; with the opera, the jockey-club, and other diversions, can you not amuse yourself? Well, I will amuse you."—
"How?" "By introducing to you a new acquaintance."

"A man or a woman?"—"A man."

"I know so many men already."—"But you do not know this man."

"Where does he come from—the end of the world?"

"Farther still, perhaps."

"The deuce! I hope he does not bring our breakfast with him."

"Oh, no; our breakfast comes from my father's kitchen. Are you hungry?"

"Humiliating as such a confession is, I am. But I dined at M. de Villefort's and lawyers always give you very bad dinners. You would think they felt some remorse; did you ever remark that?"

"Ah, depreciate other persons' dinners; you ministers give such splendid ones."—"Yes; but we do not invite people of fashion. If we were not forced to entertain a parcel of country boobies because they think and vote with us, we should never dream of dining at home, I assure you."

"Well, take another glass of sherry and another biscuit."

"Willingly. Your Spanish wine is excellent. You see we were quite right to pacify that country."—"Yes; but Don Carlos?"

"Well, Don Carlos will drink Bordeaux, and in ten years we will marry his son to the little queen."

"You will then obtain the Golden Fleece, if you are still in the ministry."—"I think, Albert, you have adopted the system of feeding me on smoke this morning."

"Well, you must allow it is the best thing for the stomach; but I hear Beauchamp in the next room; you can dispute together, and that will pass away the time."—"About what?" "About the papers."

"My dear friend," said Lucien with an air of sovereign contempt, "do I ever read the papers?"

"Then you will dispute the more."

"M. Beauchamp," announced the servant. "Come in, come in," said Albert, rising and advancing to meet the young man. "Here is Debray, who detests you without reading you, so he says."

"He is quite right," returned Beauchamp; "for I criticise him without knowing what he does. Good-day, commander!"

"Ah, you know that already," said the private secretary, smiling and shaking hands with him.

"*Pardieu*?"—"And what do they say of it in the world?"

"In which world? we have so many worlds in the year of grace 1838."

"In the entire political world, of which you are one of the leaders."

"They say that it is quite fair, and that sowing so much red, you ought to reap a little blue."—"Come, come, that is not bad!" said Lucien. "Why do you not join our party, my dear Beauchamp? With your talents you would make your fortune in three or four years."

"I only await one thing before following your advice; that is, a minister who will hold office for six months. My dear Albert, one word, for I must give poor Lucien a respite. Do we breakfast or dine? I must go to the Chamber, for our life is not an idle one."

"You only breakfast; I await two persons, and the instant they arrive we shall sit down to table."

XL

The Breakfast

"AND WHAT SORT OF persons do you expect to breakfast?" said Beauchamp.

"A gentleman, and a diplomatist."

"Then we shall have to wait two hours for the gentleman, and three for the diplomatist. I shall come back to dessert; keep me some strawberries, coffee, and cigars. I shall take a cutlet on my way to the Chamber."—"Do not do anything of the sort; for were the gentleman a Montmorency, and the diplomatist a Metternich, we will breakfast at eleven; in the meantime, follow Debray's example, and take a glass of sherry and a biscuit."

"Be it so; I will stay; I must do something to distract my thoughts."

"You are like Debray, and yet it seems to me that when the minister is out of spirits, the opposition ought to be joyous."

"Ah, you do not know with what I am threatened. I shall hear this morning that M. Danglars make a speech at the Chamber of Deputies, and at his wife's this evening I shall hear the tragedy of a peer of France. The devil take the constitutional government, and since we had our choice, as they say, at least, how could we choose that?"

"I understand; you must lay in a stock of hilarity."

"Do not run down M. Danglars' speeches," said Debray; "he votes for you, for he belongs to the opposition."

"*Pardieu*, that is exactly the worst of all. I am waiting until you send him to speak at the Luxembourg, to laugh at my case."

"My dear friend," said Albert to Beanchamp, "it is plain that the affairs of Spain are settled, for you are most desperately out of humor this morning. Recollect that Parisian gossip has spoken of a marriage between myself and Mlle. Engénie Danglars; I cannot in conscience therefore, let you run down the speeches of a man who will one day say to me, 'Vicomte, you know I give my daughter two millions.'"

"Ah, this marriage will never take place," said Beauchamp. "The king has made him a baron, and can make him a peer, but he cannot make him a gentleman, and the Count of Morcerf is too aristocratic to consent, for the paltry sum of two million francs, to a *mésalliance*. The Viscount of Morcerf can only wed a marchioness."

"But two million francs make a nice little sum," replied Morcerf.

"It is the social capital of theatre on the boulevard, or a railroad from the Jardin des Plantes to La Râpée."

"Never mind what he says, Morcerf," said Debray, "do you marry her. You marry a money-bag label, it is true; well, but what does that matter? It is better to have a blazon less and a figure more on it. You have seven martlets on your arms; give three to your wife and you will still have four; that is one more than M. de Guise had who so nearly became King of France, and whose cousin was Emperor of Germany."

"On my word, I think you are right, Lucien," said Albert absently.

"To be sure; besides, every millionaire is as noble as a bastard— that is, he can be."—"Do not say that, Debray," returned Beauchamp, laughing, "for here is Château-Renaud, who, to cure you of your mania for paradoxes, will pass the sword of Renaud de Montauban, his ancestor, through your body."

"He will sully it then," returned Lucien; "for I am low—very low."

"Oh, heavens," cried Beauchamp, "the minister quotes Béranger; what shall we come to next?"—"M. de Château-Renaud—M. Maximilian Morrel," said the servant, announcing two fresh guests.

"Now, then, to breakfast," said Beauchamp; "for, if I remember, you told me you only expected two persons, Albert."

"Morrel," muttered Albert—"Morrel—who is he?" But before he had finished, M. de Château-Renaud, a handsome young man of thirty, gentleman all over,—that is, with the figure of a Guiche and the wit of a Mortemart,—took Albert's hand. "My dear Albert," said he, "let me introduce to you M. Maximilian Morrel, captain of Spahis, my friend; and what is more—however the man speaks for himself—my preserver. Salute my hero, viscount." And he stepped on one side to give place to a young man of refined and dignified bearing, with large and open brow, piercing eyes, and black mustache, whom our readers have already seen at Marseilles, under circumstances sufficiently dramatic not to be forgotten. A rich uniform, half French, half Oriental, set off his graceful and stalwart figure, and his broad chest was decorated with the order of the Legion of Honor. The young officer bowed with easy and elegant politeness. "Monsieur," said Albert with affectionate courtesy, "the Count of Château-Renaud knew how much pleasure this introduction would give me; you are his friend, be ours also."

"Well said," interrupted Château-Renaud; "and pray that, if you should ever be in a similar predicament, he may do as much for you as he did for me."—"What has he done?" asked Albert.

"Oh, nothing worth speaking of," said Morrel; "M. de Château-Renaud exaggerates."—"Not worth speaking of?" cried Château-Renaud; "life is not worth speaking of!—that is rather too philosophical, on my word, Morrel. It is very well for you, who risk your life every day, but for me, who only did so once"—

"We gather from all this, baron, that Captain Morrel saved your life."—"Exactly so."

"On what occasion?" asked Beauchamp.

"Beauchamp, my good fellow, you know I am starving," said Debray; "do not set him off on some long story."—"Well, I do not prevent your sitting down to table," replied Beauchamp, "Château-Renaud can tell us while we eat our breakfast."

"Gentlemen," said Morcerf, "it is only a quarter past ten, and I expect some one else."—"Ah, true—a diplomatist!" observed Debray.

"Diplomat or not, I don't know; I only know that he charged himself on my account with a mission, which he terminated so entirely to my satisfaction, that had I been king, I should have instantly created him knight of all my orders, even had I been able to offer him the Golden Fleece and the Garter."

"Well, since we are not to sit down to table," said Debray, "take a glass of sherry, and tell us all about it."

"You all know that I had the fancy of going to Africa."

"It is a road your ancestors have traced for you," said Albert gallantly.

"Yes, but I doubt that your object was like theirs—to rescue the Holy Sepulchre."—"You are quite right, Beauchamp," observed the young aristocrat. "It was only to fight as an amateur. I cannot bear duelling since two seconds, whom I had chosen to arrange an affair, forced me to break the arm of one of my best friends, one whom you all know—poor Franz d'Epinay."

"Ah, true," said Debray, "you did fight some time ago;—about what?"

"The devil take me, if I remember," returned Château-Renaud. "But I recollect perfectly one thing, that, being unwilling to let such talents as mine sleep, I wished to try upon the Arabs the new pistols that had been given to me. In consequence I embarked for Oran, and went from thence to Constantine, where I arrived just in time to witness the raising of the siege. I retreated with the rest, for eight and forty hours. I endured the rain during the day, and the cold during the night tolerably well, but the third morning my horse died of cold. Poor brute—accustomed to be covered up and to have a stove in the stable, the Arabian finds himself unable to bear ten degrees of cold in Arabia." "That's why you want to purchase my English horse," said Debray; "you think he will bear the cold better."

"You are mistaken, for I have made a vow never to return to Africa."

"You were very much frightened, then?" asked Beauchamp.

"Well, yes, and I had good reason to be so," replied Château-Renaud. "I was retreating on foot, for my horse was dead. Six Arabs came up, full gallop, to cut off my head. I shot two with my double-barrelled gun, and two more with my pistols, but I was then disarmed, and two were still left; one seized me by the hair (that is why I now wear it so short, for no one knows what may happen), the other swung a yataghan, and I already felt the cold steel on my neck, when this gentleman whom you see here charged them, shot the one who held me by the hair, and cleft the skull of the other with his sabre. He had assigned himself the task of saving a man's life that day; chance caused that man to be myself. When I am rich I will order a statue of Chance from Klagmann or Marochetti."

"Yes," said Morrel, smiling, "it was the 5th of September, the anniversary of the day on which my father was miraculously preserved; therefore, as far as it lies in my power, I endeavor to celebrate it by some"—

"Heroic action," interrupted Château-Renaud. "I was chosen. But that is not all—after rescuing me from the sword, he rescued me from the cold, not by sharing his cloak with me, like St. Martin, but by giving me the whole; then from hunger by sharing with me—guess what?"

"A Strasbourg pie?" asked Beauchamp.

"No, his horse; of which we each of us ate a slice with a hearty appetite. It was very hard."—"The horse?" said Morcerf, laughing.

"No, the sacrifice," returned Château-Renaud; "ask Debray if he would sacrifice his English steed for a stranger?"—"Not for a stranger," said Debray, "but for a friend I might, perhaps."

"I divined that you would become mine, count," replied Morrel; "besides, as I had the honor to tell you, heroism or not, sacrifice or not, that day I owed an offering to bad fortune in recompense for the favors good fortune had on other days granted to us."

"The history to which M. Morrel alludes," continued Château-Renaud, "is an admirable one, which he will tell you some day when you are better acquainted with him; to-day let us fill our stomachs, and not our memories. What time do you breakfast, Albert?"

"At half-past ten."

"Precisely?" asked Debray, taking out his watch.

"Oh, you will give me five minutes' grace," replied Morcerf, "for I also expect a preserver."—"Of whom?"

"Of myself," cried Morcerf; "*parbleu*, do you think I cannot be saved as well as any one else, and that there are only Arabs who cut off heads? Our breakfast is a philanthropic one, and we shall have at table—at least, I hope so—two benefactors of humanity."—"What shall we do?" said Debray; "we have only one Monthyon prize."

"Well, it will be given to some one who has done nothing to deserve it," said Beauchamp; "that is the way the Academy mostly escapes from the dilemma."—"And where does he come from?" asked Debray. "You have already answered the question once, but so vaguely that I venture to put it a second time."

"Really," said Albert, "I do not know; when I invited him three months ago, he was then at Rome, but since that time, who knows where he may have gone?"

"And you think him capable of being exact?" demanded Debray.

"I think him capable of everything."

"Well, with the five minutes' grace, we have only ten left."

"I will profit by them to tell you something about my guest."

"I beg pardon," interrupted Beauchamp; "are there any materials for an article in what you are going to tell us?"

"Yes, and for a most curious one."—"Go on, then, for I see I shall not get to the Chamber this morning, and I must make up for it."

"I was at Rome during the last Carnival."

"We know that," said Beauchamp.

"Yes, but what you do not know is that I was carried off by bandits."

"There are no bandits," cried Debray.

"Yes there are, and most hideous, or rather most admirable ones, for I found them ugly enough to frighten me."—"Come, my dear Albert," said Debray, "confess that your cook is behindhand, that the oysters have not arrived from Ostend or Mareunes, and that, like Madame de Maintenon, you are going to replace the dish by a story. Say so at once; we are sufficiently well-bred to excuse you, and to listen to your history, fabulous as it promises to be."

"And I say to you, fabulous as it may seem, I tell it as a true one from beginning to end. The brigands had carried me off, and conducted me to a gloomy spot, called the Catacombs of Saint Sebastian."

"I know it," said Château-Renaud; "I narrowly escaped catching a fever there."

"And I did more than that," replied Morcerf, "for I caught one. I was informed that I was prisoner until I paid the sum of 4,000 Roman crowns—about 24,000 francs. Unfortunately, I had not above 1,500. I was at the end of my journey and of my credit. I wrote to Franz—and were he here he would confirm every word— I wrote then to Franz that if he did not come with the four thousand crowns before six, at ten minutes past I should have gone to join the blessed saints and glorious martyrs in whose company I had the honor of being; and Signor Luigi Vampa, such was the name of the chief of these bandits, would have scrupulously kept his word."

"But Franz did come with the four thousand crowns," said Château-Renaud. "A man whose name is Franz d'Epinay or Albert de

Morcerf has not much difficulty in procuring them."—"No, he arrived accompanied simply by the guest I am going to present to you."

"Ah, this gentleman is a Hercules killing Cacus, a Perscus freeing Andromeda."—"No, he is a man about my own size."

"Armed to the teeth?"—"He had not even a knitting-needle."

"But he paid your ransom?"

"He said two words to the chief and I was free."—"And they apologized to him for having carried you off?" said Beauchamp.

"Just so."—"Why, he is a second Ariosto."

"No, his name is the Count of Monte Cristo."

"There is no Count of Monte Cristo," said Debray.

"I do not think so," added Château-Renaud, with the air of a man who knows the whole of the European nobility perfectly.

"Does any one know anything of a Count of Monte Cristo?"

"He comes possibly from the Holy Land, and one of his ancestors possessed Calvary, as the Mortemarts did the Dead Sea."

"I think I can assist your researches," said Maximilian. "Monte Cristo is a little island I have often heard spoken of by the old sailors my father employed—a grain of sand in the centre of the Mediterranean, an atom in the infinite."—"Precisely!" cried Albert. "Well, he of whom I speak is the lord and master of this grain of sand, of this atom; he has purchased the title of count somewhere in Tuscany."

"He is rich, then?"—"I believe so."

"But that ought to be visible."

"That is what deceives you, Debray."

"I do not understand you."

"Have you read the 'Arabian Nights'?"

"What a question!"—"Well, do you know if the persons you see there are rich or poor, if their sacks of wheat are not rubies or diamonds? They seem like poor fishermen, and suddenly they open some mysterious cavern filled with the wealth of the Indies."

"Which means?"

"Which means that my Count of Monte Cristo is one of those fishermen. He has even a name taken from the book, since he calls himself Sinbad the Sailor, and has a cave filled with gold."

"And you have seen this cavern, Morcerf?" asked Beauchamp.

"No, but Franz has; for heaven's sake, not a word of this before him. Franz went in with his eyes blindfolded, and was waited on by mutes and by women to whom Cleopatra was a painted strumpet. Only he is not quite sure about the women, for they did not come in until after he had taken hashish, so that what he took for women might have been simply a row of statues."

The two young men looked at Morcerf as if to say,—"Are you mad, or are you laughing at us?"—"And I also," said Morrel thoughtfully, "have heard something like this from an old sailor named Penelon."

"Ah," cried Albert, "it is very lucky that M. Morrel comes to aid me; you are vexed, are you not, that he thus gives a clew to the labyrinth?"

"My dear Albert," said Debray, "what you tell us is so extraordinary."

"Ah, because your ambassadors and your consuls do not tell you of them—they have no time. They are too much taken up with interfering in the affairs of their countrymen who travel."—"Now you get angry, and attack our poor agents. How will you have them protect you? The Chamber cuts down their salaries every day, so that now they have scarcely any. Will you be ambassador, Albert? I will send you to Constantinople."

"No, lest on the first demonstration I make in favor of Mehemet Ali, the Sultan send me the bowstring, and make my secretaries strangle me."

"You say very true," responded Debray.—"Yes," said Albert, "but this has nothing to do with the existence of the Count of Monte Cristo."

"*Pardieu*, every one exists."

"Doubtless, but not in the same way; every one has not black slaves, a princely retinue, an arsenal of weapons that would do credit to an Arabian fortress, horses that cost six thousand francs apiece, and Greek mistresses."—"Have you seen the Greek mistress?"

"I have both seen and heard her. I saw her at the theatre, and heard her one morning when I breakfasted with the count."—"He eats, then?"—"Yes; but so little, it can hardly be called eating."

"He must be a vampire."—"Laugh, if you will; the Countess G— who knew Lord Ruthven, declared that the count was a vampire."

"Ah, capital," said Beauchamp. "For a man not connected with newspapers, here is the pendant to the famous sea-serpent of the *Constitutionnel*."—"Wild eyes, the iris of which contracts or dilates at pleasure," said Debray; "facial angle strongly developed, magnificent forehead, livid complexion, black beard, sharp and white teeth, politeness unexceptionable."

"Just so, Lucien," returned Morcerf; "you have described him feature for feature. Yes, keen and cutting politeness. This man has often made me shudder; and one day that we were viewing an execution, I thought I should faint, more from hearing the cold and calm manner in which he spoke of every description of torture, than from the sight of the executioner and the culprit."—"Did he not conduct you to the ruins of the Colosseum and suck your blood?" asked Beauchamp.

"Or, having delivered you, make you sign a flaming parchment, surrendering your soul to him as Esau did his birthright?"—"Rail on, rail on at your case, gentlemen," said Morcerf, somewhat piqued. "When I look at you Parisians, idlers on the Boulevard de Gand or the Bois de Boulogne, and think of this man, it seems to me we are not of the same race."

"I am highly flattered," returned Beauchamp. "At the same time," added Château-Renaud, "your Count of Monte Cristo is a very fine fellow, always excepting his little arrangements with the Italian banditti."—"There are no Italian banditti," said Debray.

"No vampire," cried Beauchamp. "No Count of Monte Cristo," added Debray. "There is half-past ten striking, Albert."

"Confess you have dreamed this, and let us sit down to breakfast," continued Beauchamp. But the sound of the clock had not died away when Germain announced, "His excellency the Count of Monte Cristo." The involuntary start every one gave proved how much Morcerf's narrative had impressed them, and Albert himself could not wholly refrain from manifesting sudden emotion. He had not heard a carriage stop in the street, or steps in the antechamber; the door had itself opened noiselessly. The count appeared, dressed with the greatest simplicity, but the most fastidious dandy could have found nothing to cavil at in his toilet. Every article of dress—hat, coat, gloves, and boots—was from the first makers. He seemed scarcely five and thirty. But what struck everybody was his extreme resemblance to the portrait Debray had drawn. The count advanced, smiling, into the centre of the room, and approached Albert, who hastened towards him, holding out his hand in a ceremonial manner: "Punctuality," said Monte Cristo, "is the politeness of kings, according to one of your sovereigns, I think; but it is not the same with travellers. However, I hope you will excuse the two or three seconds I am behindhand; five hundred leagues are not to be accomplished without some trouble, and especially in France, where, it seems, it is forbidden to beat the postilions."

"My dear count," replied Albert, "I was announcing your visit to some of my friends, whom I had invited in consequence of the promise you did me the honor to make, and whom I now present to you. They are the Count of Château-Renaud, whose nobility goes back to the twelve peers, and whose ancestors had a place at the Round Table; M. Lucien Debray, private secretary to the minister of the interior; M. Beauchamp, an editor of a paper, and the terror of the French government, but of whom, in spite of his national celebrity, you perhaps have not heard in Italy, since his paper is prohibited there; and M. Maximilian Morrel, captain of Spahis."

At this name the count, who had hitherto saluted every one with courtesy, but at the same time with coldness and formality, stepped a pace forward, and a slight tinge of red colored his pale cheeks. "You wear the uniform of the new French conquerors, monsieur," said he; "it is a handsome uniform." No one could have said what caused the count's voice to vibrato so deeply, and what made his eye flash, which was in general so clear, lustrous, and limpid when he pleased. "You have never seen our Africans, count?" said Albert. "Never," replied the count, who was by this time perfectly master of himself again.

"Well, beneath this uniform beats one of the bravest and noblest hearts in the whole army."

"Oh, M. de Morcerf," interrupted Morrel.

"Let me go on, captain. And we have just heard," continued Albert, "of a new deed of his, and so heroic a one, that, although I have seen him to-day for the first time, I request you to allow me to introduce him as my friend." At these words it was still possible to observe in Monte Cristo the concentrated look, changing color, and slight trembling of the eyelid that show emotion. "Ah, you have a noble heart," said the count: "so much the better." This exclamation, which corresponded to the count's own thought rather than to what Albert was saying, surprised everybody, and especially Morrel, who looked at Monte Cristo with wonder. But, at the same time, the intonation was so soft that, however strange the speech might seem, it was impossible to be offended at it. "Why should he doubt it?" said Beauchamp to Château-Renaud.

"In reality," replied the latter, who, with his aristocratic glance and his knowledge of the world, had penetrated at once all that was penetrable in Monte Cristo, "Albert has not deceived us, for the count is a most singular being. What say you, Morrel?"—"*Ma foi*, he has an open look about him that pleases me, in spite of the singular remark he has made about me."

"Gentlemen," said Albert, "Germain informs me that breakfast is ready. My dear count, allow me to show you the way." They passed silently into the breakfast room, and every one took his place. "Gentlemen," said the count, seating himself, "permit me to make a confession which must form my excuse for any improprieties I may commit. I am a stranger, and a stranger to such a degree, that this is the first time I have ever been at Paris. The French way of living is utterly unknown to me, and up to the present time I have followed the Eastern customs, which are entirely in contrast to the Parisian. I beg you, therefore, to excuse if you find anything in me too Turkish, too Italian, or too Arabian. Now, then, let us breakfast."

"With what an air he says all this," muttered Beauchamp; "decidedly he is a great man."—"A great man in his own country," added Debray.

"A great man in every country, M. Debray," said Château-Renaud. The count was, it may be remembered, a most temperate guest. Albert remarked this, expressing his fears lest, at the outset, the Parisian mode of life should displease the traveller in the most essential point. "My dear count," said he, "I fear one thing and that is, that the fare of the Rue du Helder is not so much to your taste as that of the Piazza di Spagni. I ought to have consulted you on the point, and have had some dishes prepared expressly."—"Did you know me better," returned the count, smiling, "you would not give one thought of such a thing for a traveller like myself, who has successively lived on maccaroni at Naples, polenta at Milan, olla podrida as Valencia, pilau at Constantinople, karrick in India, and swallows' nests in China. I eat everywhere, and of everything, only I eat but little; and to-day, that you reproach me with my want of appetite, is my day of appetite, for I have not eaten since yesterday morning."

"What," cried all the guests, "you have not eaten for four and twenty hours?"—"No," replied the count; "I was forced to go out of my road to obtain some information near Nîmes, so that I was somewhat late, and therefore I did not choose to stop."

"And you ate in your carriage?" asked Morcerf.—"No, I slept, as I generally do when I am weary without having the courage to amuse myself, or when I am hungry without feeling inclined to eat."

"But you can sleep when you please, monsieur?" said Morrel.

"Yes."—"You have a recipe for it?"—"An infallible one."

"That would be invaluable to us in Africa, who have not always any food to eat, and rarely anything to drink."—"Yes," said Monte Cristo; "but, unfortunately, a recipe excellent for a man like myself would be very dangerous applied to an army, which might not awake when it was needed."

"May we inquire what is this recipe?" asked Debray.—"Oh, yes," returned Monte Cristo; "I make no secret of it. It is a mixture of excellent opium, which I fetched myself from Canton in order to have it pure, and the best hashish which grows in the East—that is, between the Tigris and the Euphrates. These two ingredients are mixed in equal proportions, and formed into pills. Ten minutes after one is taken, the effect is produced. Ask Baron Franz d'Epinay; I think he tasted them one day'

"Yes," replied Morcerf, "he said something about it to me."

"But," said Beauchamp, who, as became a journalist, was very incredulous, "you always carry this drug about you?"—"Always."

"Would it be an indiscretion to ask to see those precious pills?" continued Beauchamp, hoping to take him at a disadvantage.— "No, monsieur," returned the count; and he drew from his pocket a marvellous casket, formed out of a single emerald and closed by a golden lid which unscrewed and gave passage to a small greenish coloured pellet about the size of a pea. This ball had an acrid and penetrating odor. There were four or five more in the emerald, which would contain about a dozen. The casket passed around the table, but it was more to examine the admirable emerald than to see the pills that it passed from hand to hand. "And is it your cook who prepares these pills?" asked Beanchamp.

"Oh, no, monsieur," replied Monte Cristo; "I do not thus betray my enjoyments to the vulgar. I am a tolerable chemist, and prepare my pills myself"

"This is a magnificent emerald, and the largest I have ever seen," said Château-Renaud, "although my mother has some remarkable family jewels.'

"I had three similar ones," returned Monte Cristo. "I gave one to the Sultan, who mounted it in his sabre; another to our holy father the Pope, who had it set in his tiara, opposite to one nearly as large, though not so fine, given by the Emperor Napoleon to his predecessor, Pius VII. I kept the third for myself, and I had it hollowed out, which reduced its value, but rendered it more commodious for the purpose I intended." Every one looked at Monte Cristo with astonishment; he spoke with so much simplicity that it was evident he spoke the truth, or that he was mad. However, the sight of the emerald made them naturally incline to the former belief. "And what did these two sovereigns give you in exchange for these magnificent presents?" asked Debray.—"The Sultan, the liberty of a woman," replied the count; "the Pope, the life of a man; so that once in my life I have been as powerful as if heaven had brought me into the world on the steps of a throne."

"And it was Peppino you saved, was it not?" cried Morcerf; "it was for him that you obtained pardon?"

"Perhaps," returned the count, smiling.

"My dear count, you have no idea what pleasure it gives me to hear you speak thus," said Morcerf. "I had announced you beforehand to my friends as an enchanter of the 'Arabian Nights,' a wizard of the Middle Ages; but the Parisians are so subtle in paradoxes that they mistake for caprices of the imagination the most incontestable truths, when these truths do not form a part of their daily existence. For example, here is Debray who reads, and Beauchamp who prints, every day, 'A member of the Jockey Club has been stopped and robbed on the Boulevard;' 'four persons have been assassinated in the Rue St. Denis' or 'the Faubourg St. Germain;'

'ten, fifteen, or twenty thieves, have been arrested in a *café* on the Boulevard du Temple, or in the Thermes de Julien,'—and yet these same men deny the existence of the bandits in the Maremma, the Campagna di Romana, or the Pontine Marshes. Tell them yourself that I was taken by bandits, and that without your generous intercession I should now have been sleeping in the Catacombs of St. Sebastian, instead of receiving them in my humble abode in the Rue du Helder."

"Ah," said Monte Cristo, "you promised me never to mention that circumstance."—"It was not I who made that promise," cried Morcerf; "it must have been some one else whom you have rescued in the same manner, and whom you have forgotten. Pray speak of it, for I shall not only, I trust, relate the little I do know, but also a great deal I do not know."

"It seems to me," returned the count, smiling, "that you played a sufficiently important part to know as well as myself what happened."—"Well, you promise me, if I tell all I know, to relate, in your turn, all that I do not know?"—"That is but fair," replied Monte Cristo.

"Well," said Morcerf, "for three days I believed myself the object of the attentions of a masque, whom I took for a descendant of Tullia or Poppoea, while I was simply the object of the attentions of a *contadina*, and I say *contadina* to avoid saying peasant girl. What I know is, that, like a fool, a greater fool than he of whom I spoke just now, I mistook for this peasant girl a young bandit of fifteen or sixteen, with a beardless chin and slim waist, and who, just as I was about to imprint a chaste salute on his lips, placed a pistol to my head, and, aided by seven or eight others, led, or rather dragged me, to the Catacombs of St. Sebastian, where I found a highly educated brigand chief perusing Cæsar's 'Commentaries,' and who deigned to leave off reading to inform me, that unless the next morning, before six o'clock, four thousand piastres were paid into his account at his banker's, at a quarter past six I should have ceased to exist. The letter is still to be seen, for it is in Franz d'Epinay's possession, signed by me, and with a postscript of M. Luigi Vampa. This is all I know, but I know not, count, how you contrived to inspire so much respect in the bandits of Rome, who ordinarily have so little respect for anything. I assure you, Franz and I were lost in admiration."

"Nothing more simple," returned the count. "I had known the famous Vampa for more than ten years. When he was quite a child, and only a shepherd, I gave him a few gold pieces for showing me my way, and he, in order to repay me, gave me a poniard, the hilt of which he had carved with his own hand, and which you may have seen in my collection of arms. In after years, whether he had forgotten this interchange of presents, which ought to have cemented our friendship, or whether he did not recollect me, he sought to take me, but, on the contrary, it was I who captured him and a dozen of his band. I might have handed him over to Roman justice, which is somewhat expeditious, and which would have been particularly so with him; but I did nothing of the sort—I suffered him and his band to depart."

"With the condition that they should sin no more," said Beauchamp, laughing. "I see they kept their promise."

"No, monsieur," returned Monte Cristo, "upon the simple condition that they should respect myself and my friends. Perhaps what I am about to say may seem strange to you, who are socialists, and vaunt humanity and your duty to your neighbor, but I never seek to protect a society which does not protect me, and which I will even say, generally occupies itself about me only to injure me; and thus by giving them a low place in my esteem, and preserving a neutrality towards them, it is society and my neighbor who are indebted to me."—"Bravo," cried Château-Renaud; "you are the first man I ever met sufficiently courageous to preach egotism. Bravo, count, bravo!"

"It is Frank, at least," said Morrel. "But I am sure that the count does not regret having once deviated from the principles he has so boldly avowed."—"How have I deviated from those principles, monsieur?" asked Monte Cristo, who could not help looking at Morrel with so much intensity, that two or three times the young man had been unable to sustain that clear and piercing glance.

"Why, it seems to me," replied Morrel, "that in delivering M. de Morcerf, whom you did not know, you did good to your neighbor and to society."—"Of which he is the brightest ornament," said Beauchamp, drinking off a glass of champagne.

"My dear count," cried Morcerf, "you are at fault—you, one of the most formidable logicians I know—and you must see it clearly proved that instead of being an egotist, you are a philanthropist. Ah, you call yourself Oriental, a Levantine, Maltese, Indian, Chinese; your family name is Monte Cristo; Sinbad the Sailor is your baptismal appellation, and yet the first day you set foot in Paris you instinctively display the greatest virtue, or rather the chief defect, of us eccentric Parisians,—that is, you assume the vices you have not, and conceal the virtues you possess."—"My dear vicomte," returned Monte Cristo, "I do not see, in all I have done, anything that merits, either from you or these gentlemen, the pretended eulogies I have received. You were no stranger to me, for I knew you from the time I gave up two rooms to you, invited you to breakfast with me, lent you one of my carriages, witnessed the Carnival in your company, and saw with you from a window in the Piazza del Popolo the execution that affected you so much that you nearly fainted. I will appeal to any of these gentlemen, could I leave my guest in the hands of a hideous bandit, as you term him? Besides, you know, I had the idea that you could introduce me into some of the Paris salons when I came to France. You might some time ago have looked upon this resolution as a vague project, but to-day you see it was a reality, and you must submit to it under penalty of breaking your word."

"I will keep it," returned Morcerf; "but I fear that you will be much disappointed, accustomed as you are to picturesque events and fantastic horizons. Amongst us you will not meet with any of those episodes with which your adventurous existence has so familiarized you; our Chimborazo is Mortmartre, our Himalaya is Mount Valérien, our Great Desert is the Plain of Grenelle, where they are now boring an artesian well to water the caravans. We have plenty of thieves, though not so many as is said; but these thieves stand in far more dread of a policeman than a lord. France is so prosaic, and Paris so civilized a city, that you will not find in its eighty-five departments—I say eighty-five, because I do not include Corsica—you will not find, then, in these eighty-five departments a single hill on which there is not a telegraph, or a grotto in which the commissary of police has not put up a gas-lamp. There is but one service I can render you, and for that I place myself entirely at your orders, that is, to present, or make my friends present, you everywhere; besides, you have no need of any one to introduce you—with your name, and your fortune, and your talent" (Monte Cristo bowed with a somewhat ironical smile) "you can present yourself everywhere, and be well received. I can be useful in one way only—if knowledge of Parisian habits, of the means of rendering yourself comfortable, or of the bazaars, can assist, you may depend upon me to find you a fitting dwelling here. I do not dare offer to share my apartments with you, as I shared yours at Rome— I, who do not profess egotism, but am yet egotist *par excellence*; for, except myself, these rooms would not hold a shadow more, unless that shadow were feminine."—"Ah," said the count, "that is a most conjugal reservation; I recollect that at Rome you said something of a projected marriage. May I congratulate you?"

"The affair is still in projection."—"And he who says in 'projection,' means already decided," said Debray.

"No," replied Morcerf, "my father is most anxious about it; and I hope, ere long, to introduce you, if not to my wife, at least to my betrothed—Mademoiselle Eugénie Danglars."—"Eugénie Danglars," said Monte Cristo; "tell me, is not her father Baron Danglars?"

"Yes," returned Morcerf; "a baron of a new creation."—"What

matter," said Monte Cristo, "if he has rendered the State services which merit this distinction?"

"Enormous ones," answered Beauchamp. "Although in reality a Liberal, he negotiated a loan of six millions for Charles X., in 1829, who made him a baron and chevalier of the Legion of Honor; so that he wears the ribbon, not, as you would think, in his waistcoat-pocket, but at his button-hole."—"Ah," interrupted Morcerf, laughing, "Beauchamp, Beauchamp, keep that for the *Corsaire* or the *Charivari*, but spare my future father-in-law before me." Then, turning to Monte Cristo, "You just now spoke his name as if you knew the baron?"

"I do not know him," returned Monte Cristo; "but I shall probably soon make his acquaintance, for I have a credit opened with him by the house of Richard & Blount, of London, Arstein & Eskeles of Vienna, and Thomson & French at Rome." As he pronounced the two last names, the count glanced at Maximilian Morrel. If the stranger expected to produce an effect on Morrel, he was not mistaken—Maximilian started as if he had been electrified. "Thomson & French," said he; "do you know this house, monsieur?"—"They are my bankers in the capital of the Christian world," returned the count quietly. "Can my influence with them be of any service to you?"—"Oh, count, you could assist me perhaps in researches which have been, up to the present, fruitless. This house, in past years, did ours a great service, and has, I know not for what reason, always denied having rendered us this service."

"I shall be at your orders," said Monte Cristo, bowing.

"But," continued Morcerf, "*à propos* of Danglars,—we have strangely wandered from the subject. We were speaking of a suitable habitation for the Count of Monte Cristo. Come, gentlemen, let us all propose some place. Where shall we lodge this new guest in our great capital?"

"Faubourg Saint-Germain," said Château-Renaud. "The count will find there a charming hotel, with a court and garden."

"Bah, Château-Renaud," returned Debray, "you only know

your dull and gloomy Faubourg Saint-Germain; do not pay any attention to him, count—live in the Chaussée d'Antin, that's the real centre of Paris."—"Boulevard de l'Opéra," said Beauchamp; "the second floor—a house with a balcony. The count will have his cushions of silver cloth brought there, and as he smokes his chibouque, see all Paris pass before him."

"You have no idea, then, Morrel?" asked Château-Renaud; "you do not propose anything."—"Oh, yes," returned the young man, smiling; "on the contrary, I have one, but I expected the count would be tempted by one of the brilliant proposals made him, yet as he has not replied to any of them, I will venture to offer him a suite of apartments in a charming hotel, in the Pompadour style, that my sister has inhabited for a year, in the Rue Meslay."

"You have a sister?" asked the count.—"Yes, monsieur, a most excellent sister."—"Married?"—"Nearly nine years,"—"Happy?" asked the count again.

"As happy as it is permitted to a human creature to be," replied Maximilian. "She married the man she loved, who remained faithful to us in our fallen fortunes—Emmanuel Herbaut." Monte Cristo smiled imperceptibly. "I live there during my leave of absence," continued Maximilian; "and I shall be, together with my brother-in-law Emmanuel, at the disposition of the count, whenever he thinks fit to honor us."—"One minute," cried Albert, without giving Monte Cristo the time to reply. "Take care, you are going to immure a traveller, Sinbad the Sailor, a man who comes to see Paris; you are going to make a patriarch of him."

"Oh, no," said Morrel; "my sister is five and twenty, my brother-in-law is thirty, they are gay, young, and happy. Besides, the count will be in his own house, and only see them when he thinks fit to do so."—"Thanks, monsieur," said Monte Cristo; "I shall content myself with being presented to your sister and her husband, if you will do me the honor to introduce me; but I cannot accept the offer of any one of these gentlemen, since my habitation is already prepared."

"What," cried Morcerf; "you are, then, going to an hotel—that will be very dull for you."

"Was I so badly lodged at Rome?" said Monte Cristo smiling.

"*Parbleu*, at Rome you spent fifty thousand piastres in furnishing your apartments, but I presume that you are not disposed to spend a similar sum every day."—"It is not that which deterred me," replied Monte Cristo; "but as I determined to have a house to myself, I sent on my valet de chambre, and he ought by this time to have bought the house and furnished it."

"But you have, then, a valet de chambre who knows Paris?" said Beauchamp.—"It is the first time he has ever been in Paris. He is black, and cannot speak," returned Monte Cristo.

"It is Ali!" cried Albert, in the midst of the general surprise.

"Yes, Ali himself, my Nubian mute, whom you saw, I think, at Rome."

"Certainly," said Morcerf; "I recollect him perfectly. But how could you charge a Nubian to purchase a house, and a mute to furnish it?—he will do everything wrong."

"Undeceive yourself, monsieur," replied Monte Cristo; "I am quite sure, that, on the contrary, he will choose everything as I wish. He knows my tastes, my caprices, my wants. He has been here a week, with the instinct of a hound, hunting by himself. He will arrange everything for me. He knew that I should arrive to-day at ten o'clock; he was waiting for me at nine at the Barrière de Fontainebleau. He gave me this paper; it contains the number of my new abode; read it yourself," and Monte Cristo passed a paper to Albert. "Ah, that is really original," said Beauchamp.

"And very princely," added Château-Renaud.

"What, do you not know your house?" asked Debray.

"No," said Monte Cristo; "I told you I did not wish to be behind my time; I dressed myself in the carriage, and descended at the viscount's door." The young men looked at each other; they did not know if it was a comedy Monte Cristo was playing, but every word he uttered had such an air of simplicity, that it was impossible to suppose what he said was false—besides, why should he tell a falsehood? "We must content ourselves, then," said Beauchamp, "with rendering the count all the little services in our power. I, in my quality of journalist, open all the theatres to him."—"Thanks, monsieur," returned Monte Cristo, "my steward has orders to take a box at each theatre."

"Is your steward also a Nubian?" asked Debray.

"No, he is a countryman of yours, if a Corsican is a countryman of any one's. But you know him, M. de Morcerf."

"Is it that excellent M. Bertuccio, who understands hiring windows so well?"—"Yes, you saw him the day I had the honor of receiving you; he has been a soldier, a smuggler—in fact, everything. I would not be quite sure that he has not been mixed up with the police for some trifle—a stab with a knife, for instance."

"And you have chosen this honest citizen for your steward," said Debray. "Of how much does he rob you every year?"

"On my word," replied the count, "not more than another. I am sure he answers my purpose, knows no impossibility, and so I keep him."—"Then," continued Château-Renaud, "since you have an establishment, a steward, and a hotel in the Champs Elysées, you only want a mistress." Albert smiled. He thought of the fair Greek he had seen in the count's box at the Argentina and Valle theatres. "I have something better than that," said Monte Cristo; "I have a slave. You procure your mistresses from the opera, the Vandeville, or the Variétés; I purchased mine at Constantinople; it cost me more, but I have nothing to fear."—"But you forget," replied Debray, laughing, "that we are Franks by name and franks by nature, as King Charles said, and that the moment she puts her foot in France your slave becomes free."

"Who will tell her?"—"The first person who sees her."

"She only speaks Romaic."—"That is different."

"But at least we shall see her," said Beauchamp, "or do you keep ennuchs as well as mutes?"——"Oh, no," replied Monte Cristo; "I do not carry brutalism so far. Every one who surrounds me is free to quit me, and when they leave me will no longer have any need of me or any one else; it is for that reason, perhaps, that they do not quit me." They had long since passed to dessert and cigars.

"My dear Albert," said Debray, rising, "it is half-past two. Your guest is charming, but you leave the best company to go into the worst sometimes. I must return to the minister's. I will tell him of the count, and we shall soon know who he is."——"Take care," returned Albert; "no one has been able to accomplish that."

"Oh, we have three millions for our police; it is true they are almost always spent beforehand, but, no matter, we shall still have fifty thousand francs to spend for this purpose."

"And when you know, will you tell me?"

"I promise you. *Au revoir*, Albert. Gentlemen, good-morning."

As he left the room, Debray called out loudly, "My carriage."

"Bravo," said Beauchamp to Albert; "I shall not go to the Chamber, but I have something better to offer my readers than a speech of M. Danglars."——"For heaven's sake, Beauchamp," returned Morcerf, "do not deprive me of the merit of introducing him everywhere. Is he not peculiar?"

"He is more than that," replied Château-Renaud; "he is one of the most extraordinary men I ever saw in my life. Are you coming, Morrel?"——"Directly I have given my card to the count, who has promised to pay us a visit at Rue Meslay, No. 14."——"Be sure I shall not fail to do so," returned the count, bowing. And Maximilian Morrel left the room with the Baron de Château-Renaud, leaving Monte Cristo alone with Morcerf.

XLI

The Presentation

WHEN ALBERT FOUND HIMSELF alone with Monte Cristo, "My dear count," said he, "allow me to commence my services as *cicerone* by showing you a specimen of a bachelor's apartment. You, who are accustomed to the palaces of Italy, can amuse yourself by calculating in how many square feet a young man who is not the worst lodged in Paris can live. As we pass from one room to another, I will open the windows to let you breathe." Monte Cristo had already seen the breakfast-room and the salon on the ground-floor. Albert led him first to his atelier, which was, as we have said, his favorite apartment. Monte Cristo quickly appreciated all that Albert had collected here—old cabinets, Japanese porcelain, Oriental stuffs, Venetian glass, arms from all parts of the world—everything was familiar to him; and at the first glance he recognized their date, their country, and their origin. Morcerf had expected he should be the guide; on the contrary, it was he who, under the count's guidance, followed a course of archæology, mineralogy, and natural history. They descended to the first floor; Albert led his guest into the salon. The salon was filled with the works of modern artists; there were landscapes by Dupré, with their long reeds and tall trees, their lowing oxen and marvellous skies; Delacroix's Arabian cavaliers, with their long white burnovses, their shining belts, their damasked arms, their horses, who tore each other with their teeth while their riders contended fiercely with their maces; aquarelles of Boulanger, representing Notre Dâme de Paris with that vigor that makes the artist the rival of the poet; there were paintings by Diaz, who makes his flowers more beautiful than flowers, his suns more brilliant than the sun; designs by Decamp, as vividly colored as those of Salvator Rosa, but more poetic; pastels by Giraud and Müller, representing children like angels and women with the features of a virgin; sketches torn from the album of Danzats' "Travels in the East," that had been made in a few seconds on the saddle of a camel, or beneath the dome of a mosque—in a word, all that modern art can give in exchange and as recompense for the art lost and gone with ages long since past.

Albert expected to have something new this time to show to the traveller, but, to his great surprise, the latter, without seeking for the signatures, many of which, indeed, were only initials, named instantly the author of every picture in such a manner that it was easy to see that each name was not only known to him, but that each style associated with it had been appreciated and studied by him. From the salon they passed into the bed-chamber; it was a model of taste and simple elegance. A single portrait, signed by Leopold Robert, shone in its carved and gilded frame. This portrait attracted the Count of Monte Cristo's attention, for he made three rapid steps in the chamber, and stopped suddenly before it. It was the portrait of a young woman of five or six and twenty, with a dark complexion, and light and lustrous eyes, veiled beneath long lashes. She wore the picturesque costume of the Catalan fisherwomen, a red and black bodice, and golden pins in her hair. She was looking at the sea, and her form was outlined on the blue ocean and sky. The light was so faint in the room that Albert did not perceive the pallor that spread itself over the count's visage, or the nervous heaving of his chest and shoulders. Silence prevailed for an instant, during which Monte Cristo gazed intently on the picture.

"You have there a most charming mistress, viscount," said the count in a perfectly calm tone; "and this costume—a ball costume, doubtless—becomes her admirably."

"Ah, monsieur," returned Albert, "I would never forgive you this mistake if you had seen another picture beside this. You do not know my mother; she it is whom you see here. She had her portrait painted thus six or eight years ago. This costume is a fancy one, it appears, and the resemblance is so great that I think I still see my mother the same as she was in 1830. The countess had this portrait painted during the count's absence. She doubtless intended giving him an agreeable surprise; but, strange to say, this portrait seemed to displease my father, and the value of the picture, which is, as you see, one of the best works of Leopold Robert, could not over-come his dislike to it. It is true, between ourselves, that M. de Morcerf is one of the most assiduous peers at the Luxembourg, a general renowned for theory, but a most mediocre amateur of art. It is different with my mother, who paints exceedingly well, and who, unwilling to part with so valuable a picture, gave it to me to put here, where it would be less likely to displease M. de Morcerf, whose portrait, by Gros, I will also show you. Excuse my talking of family matters, but as I shall have the honor of introducing you to the count, I tell you this to prevent you making any allusions to this picture. The picture seems to have a malign influence, for my mother rarely comes here without looking at it, and still more rarely does she look at it without weeping. This disagreement is the only one that has ever taken place between the count and countess, who are still as much united, although married more than twenty years, as on the first day of their wedding."

Monte Cristo glanced rapidly at Albert, as if to seek a hidden meaning in his words, but it was evident the young man uttered them in the simplicity of his heart. "Now," said Albert, "that you have seen all my treasures, allow me to offer them to you, unworthy as they are. Consider yourself as in your own house, and to put

yourself still more at your case, pray accompany me to the apartments of M. de Morcerf, to whom I wrote from Rome an account
of the services you rendered me, and to whom I announced your
promised visit, and I may say that both the count and countess anxiously desire to thank you in person. You are somewhat *blasé* I
know, and family scenes have not much effect on Sinbad the Sailor,
who has seen so many others. However, accept what I propose to
you as an initiation into Parisian life—a life of politeness, visiting,
and introductions." Monte Cristo bowed without making any
answer; he accepted the offer without enthusiasm and without
regret, as one of those conventions of society which every gentleman looks upon as a duty. Albert summoned his servant, and
ordered him to acquaint M. and Madame de Morcerf of the arrival
of the Count of Monte Cristo. Albert followed him with the count.
When they arrived at the antechamber, above the door was visible
a shield, which, by its rich ornaments and its harmony with the rest
of the furniture, indicated the importance the owner attached to
this blazon. Monte Cristo stopped and examined it attentively.

"Azure seven merlets, or, placed bender," said he. "These are,
doubtless, your family arms? Except the knowledge of blazons, that
enables me to decipher them, I am very ignorant of heraldry—I, a
count of a fresh creation, fabricated in Tuscany by the aid of a commandery of St. Stephen, and who would not have taken the trouble
had I not been told that when you travel much it is necessary. Besides,
you must have something on the panels of your carriage, to escape
being searched by the custom-house officers. Excuse my putting such
a question to you."—"It is not indiscreet," returned Morcerf, with the
simplicity of conviction. "You have guessed rightly. These are our
arms, that is, those of my father, but they are, as you see, joined to
another shield, which has gules, a silver tower, which are my mother's.
By her side I am Spanish, but the family of Morcerf is French, and, I
have heard, one of the oldest of the south of France."

"Yes," replied Monte Cristo, "these blazons prove that. Almost all the armed pilgrims that went to the Holy Land took for their arms either a cross, in honor of their mission, or birds of passage, in sign of the long voyage they were about to undertake, and which they hoped to accomplish on the wings of faith. One of your ancestors had joined the Crusades, and supposing it to be only that of St. Louis, that makes you mount to the thirteenth century, which is tolerably ancient."—"It is possible," said Morcerf; "my father has in his study a genealogical tree which will tell you all that, and on which I made commentaries that would have greatly edified Hozier and Jaucourt. At present I no longer think of it, and yet I must tell you that we are beginning to occupy ourselves greatly with these things under our popular government."

"Well, then, your government would do well to choose from the past something better than the things that I have noticed on your monuments, and which have no heraldic meaning whatever. As for you, viscount," continued Monte Cristo to Morcerf, "you are more fortunate than the government, for your arms are really beautiful, and speak to the imagination. Yes, you are at once from Provence and Spain; that explains, if the portrait you showed me be like, the dark hue I so much admired on the visage of the noble Catalan." It would have required the penetration of Œdipus or the Sphinx to have divined the irony the count concealed beneath these words, apparently uttered with the greatest politeness. Morcerf thanked him with a smile, and pushed open the door above which were his arms, and which, as we have said, opened into the salon. In the most conspicuous part of the salon was another portrait. It was that of a man, from five to eight and thirty, in the uniform of a general officer, wearing the double epaulet of heavy bullion, that indicates superior rank, the ribbon of the Legion of Honor around his neck, which showed he was a commander, and on the right breast, the star of a grand officer of the order of the Saviour, and on the left that of the grand cross of Charles III:, which proved that the person represented by the picture had served in the wars of Greece and Spain, or, what was just the same thing as regarded decorations, had fulfilled some diplomatic mission in the two countries.

Monte Cristo was engaged in examining this portrait with no less care than he had bestowed upon the other, when another door opened, and he found himself opposite to the Count of Morcerf in person. He was a man of forty to forty-five years, but he seemed at least fifty, and his black mustache and eyebrows contrasted strangly with his almost white hair, which was cut short, in the military fashion. He was dressed in plain clothes, and wore at his button-hole the ribbons of the different orders to which he belonged. He entered with a tolerably dignified step, and some little haste. Monte Cristo saw him advance towards him without making a single step. It seemed as if his feet were rooted to the ground, and his eyes on the Count of Morcerf. "Father," said the young man, "I have the honor of presenting to you the Count of Monte Cristo, the gener-ous friend whom I had the good fortune to meet in the critical sit-uation of which I have told you."—"You are most welcome, monsieur," said the Count of Morcerf, saluting Monte Cristo with a smile; "and monsieur has rendered our house, in preserving its only heir, a service which insures him our eternal gratitude." As he said these words, the Count of Morcerf pointed to a chair, while he seated himself in another opposite the window.

Monte Cristo, in taking the seat Morcerf offered him, placed himself in such a manner as to remain concealed in the shadow of the large velvet curtains, and read on the careworn and livid fea-tures of the count a whole history of secret griefs written in each wrinkle time had planted there. "The countess," said Morcerf, "was at her toilet when she was informed of the visit she was about to receive. She will, however, be in the salon in ten minutes."—"It is a great honor to me," returned Monte Cristo, "to be thus, on the first day of my arrival in Paris, brought in contact with a man whose merit equals his reputation, and to whom fortune has for once been equitable, but has she not still on the plains of Metidja, or in the mountains of Atlas, a marshal's staff to offer you?"

"Oh," replied Morcerf, reddening slightly, "I have left the service, monsieur. Made a peer at the Restoration, I served through the first campaign under the orders of Marshal Bourmont. I could, therefore, expect a higher rank, and who knows what might have happened had the elder branch remained on the throne? But the Revolution of July was, it seems, sufficiently glorious to allow itself to be ungrateful, and it was so for all services that did not date from the imperial period. I tendered my resignation, for when you have gained your epaulets on the battle-field, you do not know how to manœuvre on the slippery grounds of the salons. I have hung up my sword, and cast myself into politics. I have devoted myself to industry; I study the useful arts. During the twenty years I served, I often wished to do so, but I had not the time."—"These are the ideas that render your nation superior to any other," returned Monte Cristo. "A gentleman of high birth, possessor of an ample fortune, you have consented to gain your promotion as an obscure soldier, step by step—this is uncommon; then become general, peer of France, commander of the Legion of Honor, you consent to again commence a second apprenticeship, without any other hope or any other desire than that of one day becoming useful to your fellow-creatures; this, indeed, is praiseworthy,—nay, more, it is sublime." Albert looked on and listened with astonishment; he was not used to see Monte Cristo give vent to such bursts of enthusiasm. "Alas," continued the stranger, doubtless to dispel the slight cloud that covered Morcerf's brow, "we do not act thus in Italy; we grow according to our race and our species, and we pursue the same lines, and often the same uselessness, all our lives."

"But, monsieur," said the Count of Morcerf, "for a man of your merit, Italy is not a country, and France opens her arms to receive you; respond to her call. France will not, perhaps, be always ungrateful. She treats her children ill, but she always welcomes strangers."

"Ah, father," said Albert with a smile, "it is evident you do not know the Count of Monte Cristo; he despises all honors, and contents himself with those written on his passport."—"That is the most just remark," replied the stranger, "I ever heard made concerning myself."

"You have been free to choose your career," observed the Count of Moreerf, with a sigh; "and you have chosen the path strewed with flowers."—"Precisely, monsieur," replied Monte Cristo, with one of those smiles that a painter could never represent or a physiologist analyze.

"If I did not fear to fatigue you," said the general, evidently charmed with the count's manners, "I would have taken you to the Chamber; there is a debate very curious to those who are strangers to our modern senators."

"I shall be most grateful, monsieur, if you will, at some future time, renew your offer, but I have been flattered with the hope of being introduced to the countess, and I will therefore wait."—"Ah, here is my mother," cried the viscount. Monte Cristo turned round hastily, and saw Madame de Morcerf at the entrance of the salon, at the door opposite to that by which her husband had entered, pale and motionless; when Monte Cristo turned round, she let fall her arm, which for some unknown reason had been resting on the gilded door-post. She had been there some moments, and had heard the last words of the visitor. The latter rose and bowed to the countess, who inclined herself without speaking. "Ah, good heavens, madame," said the count, "are you ill, or is it the heat of the room that affects you?"

"Are you ill, mother?" cried the viscount, springing towards her. She thanked them both with a smile. "No," returned she, "but I feel some emotion on seeing, for the first time, the man without whose intervention we should have been in tears and desolation. Monsieur," continued the countess, advancing with the majesty of a queen, "I owe to you the life of my son, and for this I bless you. Now

I thank you for the pleasure you give me in thus affording me the opportunity of thanking you as I have blessed you, from the bottom of my heart." The count bowed again, but lower than before; he was even paler than Mercédès. "Madame," said he, "the count and yourself recompense too generously a simple action. To save a man, to spare a father's feelings, or a mother's sensibility, is not to do a good action, but a simple deed of humanity." At these words, uttered with the most exquisite sweetness and politeness, Madame de Morcerf replied. "It is very fortunate for my son, monsieur, that he found such a friend, and I thank God that things are thus." And Mercédès raised her fine eyes to heaven with so fervent an expression of gratitude, that the count fancied he saw tears in them. M. de Morcerf approached her. "Madame," said he, "I have already made my excuses to the count for quitting him, and I pray you to do so also. The sitting commences at two; it is now three, and I am to speak."

"Go, then, and monsieur and I will strive our best to forget your absence," replied the countess, with the same tone of deep feeling. "Monsieur," continued she, turning to Monte Cristo, "will you do us the honor of passing the rest of the day with us?"—"Believe me, madame, I feel most grateful for your kindness, but I got out of my travelling carriage at your door this morning, and I am ignorant how I am installed in Paris, which I scarcely know; this is but a tri-fling inquietude, I know, but one that may be appreciated."

"We shall have the pleasure another time," said the countess; "you promise that?" Monte Cristo inclined himself without answering, but the gesture might pass for assent. "I will not detain you, monsieur," continued the countess; "I would not have our gratitude become indiscreet or importunate."

"My dear count," said Albert, "I will endeavor to return your politeness at Rome, and place my coupé at your disposal until your own be ready."

"A thousand thanks for your kindness, viscount," returned the Count of Monte Cristo; "but I suppose that M. Bertuccio has suitably employed the four hours and a half I have given him, and that I shall find a carriage of some sort ready at the door." Albert was used to the count's manner of proceeding; he knew that, like Nero, he was in search of the impossible, and nothing astonished him, but wishing to judge with his own eyes how far the count's orders had been executed, he accompanied him to the door of the house. Monte Cristo was not deceived. As soon as he appeared in the Count of Morcerf's antechamber, a footman, the same who at Rome had brought the count's card to the two young men, and announced his visit, sprang into the vestibule, and when he arrived at the door the illustrious traveller found his carriage awaiting him. It was a coupé of Koller's building, and with horses and harness for which Drake had, to the knowledge of all the lions of Paris, refused on the previous day seven hundred guineas. "Monsieur," said the count to Albert, "I do not ask you to accompany me to my house, as I can only show you a habitation fitted up in a hurry, and I have, as you know, a reputation to keep up as regards not being taken by surprise. Give me, therefore, one more day before I invite you; I shall then be certain not to fail in my hospitality."

"If you ask me for a day, count, I know what to anticipate; it will not be a house I shall see, but a palace. You have decidedly some genius at your control."

"*Ma foi*, spread that idea," replied the Count of Monte Cristo, putting his foot on the velvet-lined steps of his splendid carriage, "and that will be worth something to me among the ladies." As he spoke, he sprang into the vehicle, the door was closed, but not so rapidly that Monte Cristo failed to perceive the almost imperceptible movement which stirred the curtains of the apartment in which he had left Madame de Morcerf. When Albert returned to his mother, he found her in the boudoir reclining in a large velvet armchair, the whole room so obscure that only the shining spangle, fastened here and there to the drapery, and the angles of the gilded frames of the pictures, showed with some degree of brightness in the

gloom. Albert could not see the face of the countess, as it was covered with a thin veil she had put on her head, and which fell over her
features in misty folds, but it seemed to him as though her voice had
altered. He could distinguish amid the perfumes of the roses and
heliotropes in the flower-stands, the sharp and fragrant odor of
volatile salts, and he noticed in one of the chased cups on the mantle-piece the countess's smelling-bottle, taken from its shagreen case,
and exclaimed in a tone of uneasiness, as he entered,—"My dear
mother, have you been ill during my absence?"

"No, no, Albert, but you know these roses, tuberoses, and
orange-flowers throw out at first, before one is used to them, such
violent perfumes."

"Then, my dear mother," said Albert, putting his hand to the
bell, "they must be taken into the antechamber. You are really ill,
and just now were so pale as you came into the room"—

"Was I pale, Albert?"—"Yes; a pallor that suits you admirably,
mother, but which did not the less alarm my father and myself."

"Did your father speak of it?" inquired Mercédès eagerly.

"No, madame; but do you not remember that he spoke of the
fact to you?"

"Yes, I do remember," replied the countess. A servant entered,
summoned by Albert's ring of the bell. "Take these flowers into the
anteroom or dressing-room," said the viscount; "they make the
countess ill." The footman obeyed his orders. A long pause ensued,
which lasted until all the flowers were removed. "What is this name
of Monte Cristo?" inquired the countess, when the servant had
taken away the last vase of flowers; "is it a family name, or the name
of the estate, or a simple title?"—"I believe, mother, it is merely a
title. The count purchased an island in the Tuscan Archipelago, and,
as he told you to-day, has founded a commandery. You know the
same thing was done for Saint Stephen of Florence, Saint George,
Constantinian of Parma, and even for the Order of Malta. Except
this, he has no pretension to nobility, and calls himself a chance

count, although the general opinion at Rome is that the count is a man of very high distinction."

"His manners are admirable," said the countess; "at least, as far as I could judge in the few minutes he remained here." "They are perfect, mother, so perfect, that they surpass by far all I have known in the leading aristocracy of the three proudest nobilities of Europe—the English, the Spanish, and the German." The countess paused a moment; then, after a slight hesitation, she resumed,—"You have seen, my dear Albert—I ask the question as a mother—you have seen M. de Monte Cristo in his house, you are quicksighted, have much knowledge of the world, more tact than is usual at your age, do you think the count is really what he appears to be?"—"What does he appear to be?"

"Why, you have just said,—a man of high distinction."

"I told you, my dear mother, he was esteemed such."

"But what is your own opinion, Albert?"

"I must tell you that I have not come to any decided opinion respecting him, but I think him a Maltese."

"I do not ask you of his origin, but what he is."—"Ah, what he is; that is quite another thing. I have seen so many remarkable things in him, that if you would have me really say what I think, I shall reply that I really do look upon him as one of Byron's heroes, whom misery has marked with a fatal brand; some Manfred, some Lara, some Werner, one of those wrecks, as it were, of some ancient family, who, disinherited of their patrimony, have achieved one by the force of their adventurous genius, which has placed them above the laws of society."

"You say"—

"I say that Monte Cristo is an island in the midst of the Mediterranean, without inhabitants or garrison, the resort of smugglers of all nations, and pirates of every flag. Who knows whether or not these industrious worthies do not pay to their feudal lord some dues for his protection?"

"That is possible," said the countess, reflecting.

"Never mind," continued the young man, "smuggler or not, you must agree, mother dear, as you have seen him, that the Count of Monte Cristo is a remarkable man, who will have the greatest success in the salons of Paris. Why, this very morning, in my rooms, he made his *entrée* amongst us by striking every man of us with amazement, not even excepting Château-Renaud."—"And what do you suppose is the count's age?" Inquired Mercédès, evidently attaching great importance to this question.

"Thirty-five or thirty-six, mother."

"So young,—it is impossible," said Mercédès, replying at the same time to what Albert said as well as to her own private reflection.

"It is the truth, however. Three or four times he has said to me, and certainly without the slightest premeditation, 'at such a period I was five years old, at another ten years old, at another twelve,' and I, induced by curiosity, which kept me alive to these details, have compared the dates, and never found him inaccurate. The age of this singular man, who is of no age, is then, I am certain, thirty-five. Besides, mother, remark how vivid his eye, how raven-black his hair, and his brow, though so pale, is free from wrinkles,—he is not only vigorous, but also young." The countess bent her head, as if beneath a heavy wave of bitter thoughts. "And has this man displayed a friendship for you, Albert?" she asked with a nervous shudder.

"I am inclined to think so."—"And—do—you—like—him?"

"Why, he pleases me in spite of Franz d'Epinay, who tries to convince me that he is a being returned from the other world." The countess shuddered. "Albert," she said, in a voice which was altered by emotion, "I have always put you on your guard against new acquaintances. Now you are a man, and are able to give me advice; yet I repeat to you, Albert, be prudent."—"Why, my dear mother, it is necessary, in order to make your advice turn to account that I should know beforehand what I have to distrust. The count never plays, he only drinks pure water tinged with a little sherry, and is so rich that he cannot, without intending to laugh at me, try to borrow money. What, then, have I to fear from him?"

"You are right," said the countess, "and my fears are weakness, especially when directed against a man who has saved your life. How did your father receive him, Albert? It is necessary that we should be more than complaisant to the count. M. de Morcerf is sometimes occupied, his business makes him reflective, and he might, without intending it"—

"Nothing could be in better taste than my father's demeanor, madame," said Albert; "nay, more, he seemed greatly flattered at two or three compliments which the count very skilfully and agreeably paid him with as much ease as if he had known him these thirty years. Each of these little tickling arrows must have pleased my father," added Albert with a laugh. "And thus they parted the best possible friends, and M. de Morcerf even wished to take him to the Chamber to hear the speakers." The countess made no reply. She fell into so deep a revery that her eyes gradually closed. The young man, standing up before her, gazed upon her with that filial affection which is so tender and endearing with children whose mothers are still young and handsome. Then, after seeing her eyes closed, and hearing her breathe gently, he believed she had dropped asleep, and left the apartment on tiptoe, closing the door after him with the utmost precaution. "This devil of a fellow," he muttered, shaking his head; "I said at the time he would create a sensation here, and I measure his effect by an infallible thermometer. My mother has noticed him, and he must therefore, perforce, be remarkable." He went down to the stables, not without some slight annoyance, when he remembered that the Count of Monte Cristo had laid his hands on a "turnout" which sent his bays down to second place in the opinion of connoisseurs. "Most decidedly," said he, "men are not equal, and I must beg my father to develop this theorem in the Chamber of Peers."

XLII

Monsieur Bertuccio

MEANWHILE THE COUNT HAD arrived at his house; it had taken him six minutes to perform the distance, but these six minutes were sufficient to induce twenty young men who knew the price of the equipage they had been unable to purchase themselves, to put their horses in a gallop in order to see the rich foreigner who could afford to give 20,000 francs apiece for his horses. The house Ali had chosen, and which was to serve as a town residence to Monte Cristo, was situated on the right hand as you ascend the Champs Elysées. A thick clump of trees and shrubs rose in the centre, and masked a portion of the front; around this shrubbery two alleys, like two arms, extended right and left, and formed a carriage-drive from the iron gates to a double portico, on every step of which stood a porcelain vase, filled with flowers. This house, isolated from the rest, had, besides the main entrance, another in the Rue Ponthieu. Even before the coachman had hailed the concierge, the massy gates rolled on their hinges—they had seen the count coming and at Paris, as everywhere else, he was served with the rapidity of lightning. The coachman entered and traversed the half-circle without slackening his speed, and the gates were closed ere the wheels had ceased to sound on the gravel. The carriage stopped at the left side of the portico, two men presented themselves at the carriage-window; the one was Ali, who, smiling with an expression of the most sincere joy, seemed amply repaid by a mere look from Montage Cristo. The other bowed respectfully, and offered his arm to assist the count in descending. "Thanks, M. Bertuccio," said the count, springing lightly up the three steps of the portico; "and the notary?"—"He is in the small salon, excellency," returned Bertuccio.

"And the cards I ordered to be engraved as soon as you knew the number of the house?"—"Your excellency, it is done already. I have been myself to the best engraver of the Palais Royal, who did the plate in my presence. The first card struck off was taken, according to your orders, to the Baron Danglars, Rue de la Chaussée d'Antin, No. 7; the others are on the mantle-piece of your excellency's bedroom."

"Good; what o'clock is it?"—"Four o'clock." Monte Cristo gave his hat, cane, and gloves to the same French footman who had called his carriage at the Count of Morcerf's, and then he passed into the small salon, preceded by Bertuccio, who showed him the way. "These are but indifferent marbles in this antechamber," said Monte Cristo. "I trust all this will soon be taken away." Bertuccio bowed. As the steward had said, the notary awaited him in the small salon. He was a simple-looking lawyer's clerk, elevated to the extraordinary dignity of a provincial scrivener. "You are the notary empowered to sell the country house that I wish to purchase, monsieur?" asked Monte Cristo.— "Yes, count," returned the notary.—"Is the deed of sale ready?"—"Yes, count."—"Have you brought it?"—"Here it is."

"Very well: and where is this house that I purchase?" asked the count carelessly, addressing himself half to Bertuccio, half to the notary. The steward made a gesture that signified. "I do not know." The notary looked at the count with astonishment. "What!" said he, "does not the count know where the house he purchases is situated?"

"No," returned the count.—"The count does not know?"

"How should I know? I have arrived from Cadiz this morning.

I have never before been at Paris, and it is the first time I have ever even set my foot in France."—"Ah, that is different; the house you purchase is at Auteuil." At these words Bertuccio turned pale. "And where is Auteuil?" asked the count.—"Close by here, monsieur," replied the notary—"a little beyond Passy; a charming situation, in the heart of the Bois de Boulogne."—"So near as that?" said the count; "but that is not in the country. What made you choose a house at the gates of Paris, M. Bertuccio?"

"I," cried the steward with a strange expression. "His excellency did not charge me to purchase this house. If his excellency will recollect—if he will think"—

"Ah, true," observed Monte Cristo; "I recollect now. I read the advertisement in one of the papers, and was tempted by the false title, 'a country house.'"

"It is not yet too late," cried Bertuccio, eagerly; "and if your excellency will intrust me with the commission, I will find you a better at Enghien, at Fontenay-aux-Roses, or at Bellevue."

"Oh, no," returned Monte Cristo, negligently; "since I have this, I will keep it."

"And you are quite right," said the notary, who feared to lose his fee. "It is a charming place, well supplied with spring-water and fine trees; a comfortable habitation, although abandoned for a long time, without reckoning the furniture, which, although old, is yet valuable, now that old things are so much sought after. I suppose the count has the tastes of the day?"

"To be sure," returned Monte Cristo; "it is very convenient, then?"

"It is more—it is magnificent."

"*Peste*, let us not lose such an opportunity," returned Monte Cristo. "The deed, if you please, Mr. Notary." And he signed it rapidly, after having first run his eye over that part of the deed in which were specified the situation of the house and the names of the proprietors. "Bertuccio," said he, "give fifty-five thousand francs to monsieur." The steward left the room with a faltering step, and returned with a bundle of bank-notes, which the notary counted like a man who never gives a receipt for money until after he is sure it is all there. "And now," demanded the count, "are all the forms complied with?"

"All, sir."—"Have you the keys?"

"They are in the hands of the concierge, who takes care of the house; but here is the order I have given him to install the count in his new possessions."—"Very well;" and Monte Cristo made a sign with his hand to the notary, which said, "I have no further need of you; you may go."

"But," observed the honest notary, "the count is, I think, mistaken; it is only fifty thousand francs, everything included."

"And your fee?"—"Is included in this sum."

"But have you not come from Auteuil here?"

"Yes, certainly."—"Well, then, it is but fair that you should be paid for your loss of time and trouble," said the count; and he made a gesture of polite dismissal. The notary left the room backwards, and bowing down to the ground; it was the first time he had ever met a similar client. "See this gentleman out," said the count to Bertuccio. And the steward followed the notary out of the room. Scarcely was the count alone, when he drew from his pocket a book closed with a lock, and opened it with a key which he wore round his neck, and which never left him. After having sought for a few minutes, he stopped at a leaf which had several notes, and compared them with the deed of sale, which lay on the table. "'Auteuil, Rue de la Fontaine, No. 28;' it is indeed the same," said he; "and now, am I to rely upon an avowal extorted by religious or physical terror? However, in an hour I shall know all. Bertuccio!" cried he, striking a light hammer with a pliant handle on a small gong. "Bertuccio!" The steward appeared at the door. "Monsieur Bertuccio," said the count, "did you never tell me that you had travelled in France?"—"In some parts of France—yes, excellency?"

"You know the environs of Paris, then?"

"No, excellency, no," returned the steward, with a sort of nervous trembling, which Monte Cristo, a connoisseur in all emotions, rightly attributed to great disquietude.—"It is unfortunate," returned he, "that you have never visited the environs, for I wish to see my new property this evening, and had you gone with me, you could have given me some useful information."—"To Auteuil!" cried Bertuccio, whose copper complexion became livid—"I go to Auteuil?"

"Well, what is there surprising in that? When I live at Auteuil, you must come there, as you belong to my service." Bertuccio hung down his head before the imperious look of his master, and remained motionless, without making any answer. "Why, what has happened to you?—are you going to make me ring a second time for the carriage?" asked Monte Cristo, in the same tone that Louis XIV. pronounced the famous, "I have been almost obliged to wait." Bertuccio made but one bound to the ante-chamber, and cried in a hoarse voice—"His excellency's horses!" Monte Cristo wrote two or three notes, and, as he sealed the last, the steward appeared. "Your excellency's carriage is at the door," said he.

"Well, take your hat and gloves," returned Monte Cristo.

"Am I to accompany you, your excellency?" cried Bertuccio.

"Certainly, you must give the orders, for I intend residing at the house." It was unexampled for a servant of the count's to dare to dispute an order of his, so the steward, without saying a word, followed his master, who got into the carriage, and signed to him to follow, which he did, taking his place respectfully on the front seat.

XLIII

The House at Auteuil

ONTE CRISTO NOTICED, AS they descended the staircase, that Bertuccio signed himself in the Corsican manner; that is, had formed the sign of the cross in the air with his thumb, and as he seated himself in the carriage, muttered a short prayer. Any one but a man of exhaustless thirst for knowledge would have had pity on seeing the steward's extraordinary repugnance for the count's projected drive without the walls; but the count was too curious to let Bertuccio off from this little journey. In twenty minutes they were at Auteuil; the steward's emotion had continued to augment as they entered the village. Bertuccio, crouched in the corner of the carriage, began to examine with a feverish anxiety every house they passed. "Tell them to stop at Rue de la Fontaine, No. 28," said the count, fixing his eyes on the steward, to whom he gave this order. Bertuccio's forehead was covered with perspiration; however, he obeyed, and, leaning out of the window, he cried to the coachman,—"Rue de la Fontaine, No. 28." No. 28 was situated at the extremity of the village; during the drive night had set in, and darkness gave the surroundings the artificial appearance of a scene on the stage. The carriage stopped, the footman sprang off the box, and opened the door. "Well," said the count, "you do not get out, M. Bertuccio—you are going to stay in the carriage, then? What are you thinking of this evening?" Bertuccio sprang out, and offered his shoulder to the count, who, this time, leaned upon it as he descended the three steps of the carriage. "Knock," said the count, "and announce me." Bertuccio knocked, the door opened, and the concierge appeared. "What is it?" asked he.

"It is your new master, my good fellow," said the footman. And he held out to the concierge the notary's order.

"The house is sold, then?" demanded the concierge; "and this gentleman is coming to live here?"

"Yes, my friend," returned the count; "and I will endeavor to give you no cause to regret your old master."—"Oh, monsieur," said the concierge, "I shall not have much cause to regret him, for he came here but seldom; it is five years since he was here last, and he did well to sell the house, for it did not bring him in anything at all."

"What was the name of your old master?" said Monte Cristo.

"The Marquis of Saint Méran. Ah, I am sure he has not sold the house for what he gave for it."

"The Marquis of Saint-Méran!" returned the count. "The name is not unknown to me; the Marquis of Saint-Méran!" and he appeared to meditate.—"An old gentleman," continued the concierge, "a stanch follower of the Bourbons; he had an only daughter, who married M. de Villefort, who had been the king's attorney at Nimes, and afterwards at Versailles." Monte Cristo glanced at Bertuccio, who became whiter than the wall against which he leaned to prevent himself from falling. "And is not this daughter dead?" demanded Monte Cristo; "I fancy I have heard so."—"Yes, monsieur, one and twenty years ago; and since then we have not seen the poor marquis three times."

"Thanks, thanks," said Monte Cristo, judging from the steward's utter prostration that he could not stretch the cord further without danger of breaking it. "Give me a light."

"Shall I accompany you, monsieur?"

"No, it is unnecessary; Bertuccio will show me a light." And

Monte Cristo accompanied these words by the gift of two gold pieces, which produced a torrent of thanks and blessings from the concierge. "Ah, monsieur," said he, after having vainly searched on the mantle-piece and the shelves, "I have not got any candles."— "Take one of the carriage-lamps, Bertuccio," said the count, "and show me the apartments." The steward obeyed in silence, but it was easy to see, from the manner in which the hand that held the light trembled, how much it cost him to obey. They went over a tolerably large ground-floor; a second floor consisted of a salon, a bath-room, and two bedrooms; near one of the bedrooms they came to a winding staircase that led down to the garden.

"Ah, here is a private staircase," said the count; "that is convenient. Light me, M. Bertuccio, and go first; we will see where it leads to."—"Monsieur," replied Bertuccio, "it leads to the garden."

"And, pray, how do you know that?"

"It ought to do so, at least."

"Well, let us be sure of that." Bertuccio sighed, and went on first; the stairs did, indeed, lead to the garden. At the outer door the steward paused. "Go on, Monsieur Bertuccio," said the count. But he who was addressed stood there, stupefied, bewildered, stunned; his haggard eyes glanced around, as if in search of the traces of some terrible event, and with his clinched hands he seemed striving to shut out horrible recollections. "Well," insisted the count. "No, no," cried Bertuccio, setting down the lantern at the angle of the interior wall. "No, monsieur, it is impossible; I can go no farther."

"What does this mean?" demanded the irresistible voice of Monte Cristo.—"Why, you must see, your excellency," cried the steward, "that this is not natural; that, having a house to purchase, you purchase it exactly at Auteuil, and that, purchasing it at Auteuil, this house should be No. 28, Rue de la Fontaine. Oh, why did I not tell you all? I am sure you would not have forced me to come. I hoped your house would have been some other one than this; as if there was not another house at Auteuil than that of the assassination!"—"What, what!" cried

Monte Cristo, stopping suddenly, "what words do you utter? Devil of a man, Corsican that you are—always mysteries or superstitions. Come, take the lantern, and let us visit the garden; you are not afraid of ghosts with me, I hope?" Bertuccio raised the lantern, and obeyed. The door, as it opened, disclosed a gloomy sky, in which the moon strove vainly to struggle through a sea of clouds that covered her with billows of vapor which she illumined for an instant, only to sink into obscurity. The steward wished to turn to the left. "No, no, monsieur," said Monte Cristo. "What is the use of following the alleys? Here is a beautiful lawn; let us go on straight forwards."

Bertuccio wiped the perspiration from his brow, but obeyed; however, he continued to take the left hand. Monte Cristo, on the contrary, took the right hand; arrived near a clump of trees, he stopped. The steward could not restrain himself. "Move, monsieur—move away, I entreat you; you are exactly in the spot!"

"What spot?"—"Where he fell."

"My dear Monsieur Bertuccio," said Monte Cristo, laughing, "control yourself; we are not at Sartena or at Corte. This is not a Corsican arbor, but an English garden; badly kept, I own, but still you must not calumniate it for that."

"Monsieur, I implore you do not stay there!"—"I think you are going mad, Bertuccio," said the count coldly. "If that is the case, I warn you, I shall have you put in a lunatic asylum."

"Alas, excellency," returned Bertuccio, joining his hands, and shaking his head in a manner that would have excited the count's laughter, had not thoughts of a superior interest occupied him, and rendered him attentive to the least revelation of this timorous conscience. "Alas, excellency, the evil has arrived!"

"M. Bertuccio," said the count, "I am very glad to tell you, that while you gesticulate, you wring your hands and roll your eyes like a man possessed by a devil who will not leave him; and I have always observed, that the devil most obstinate to be expelled is a secret. I knew you were a Corsican. I knew you were gloomy, and always brooding over some old history of the vendetta; and I overlooked that in Italy, because in Italy those things are thought nothing of. But in France they are considered in very bad taste; there are gendarmes who occupy themselves with such affairs, judges who condemn, and scaffolds which avenge." Bertuccio clasped his hands, and as, in all these evolutions, he did not let fall the lantern, the light showed his pale and altered countenance. Monte Cristo examined him with the same look that, at Rome, he had bent upon the execution of Andrea, and then, in a tone that made a shudder pass through the veins of the poor steward,—"The Abbé Busoni, then told me an untruth," said he, "when, after his journey in France, in 1829, he sent you to me, with a letter of recommendation, in which he enumerated all your valuable qualities. Well, I shall write to the abbé; I shall hold him responsible for his *protégé's* misconduct, and I shall soon know all about this assassination. Only I warn you, that when I reside in a country, I conform to all its code, and I have no wish to put myself within the compass of the French laws for your sake."

"Oh, do not do that, excellency; I have always served you faithfully," cried Bertuccio, in despair. "I have always been an honest man, and, as far as lay in my power, I have done good."

"I do not deny it," returned the count; "but why are you thus agitated? It is a bad sign; a quiet conscience does not occasion such paleness in the cheeks, and such fever in the hands of a man."

"But, your excellency," replied Bertuccio hesitatingly, "did not the Abbé Busoni, who heard my confession in the prison at Nimes, tell you that I had a heavy burden upon my conscience?"—"Yes; but as he said you would make an excellent steward, I concluded you had stolen—that was all."

"Oh, your excellency," returned Bertuccio in deep contempt.

"Or, as you are a Corsican, that you had been unable to resist the desire of making a 'stiff,' as you call it."—"Yes, my good master," cried Bertuccio, casting himself at the count's feet, "it was simply vengeance—nothing else."—"I understand that, but I do not understand what it is that galvanizes you in this manner."—"But, monsieur, it is very natural," returned Bertuccio, "since it was in this house that my vengeance was accomplished."—"What! my house?"—"Oh, your excellency, it was not yours, then."—"Whose, then? The Marquis de Saint-Méran, I think, the concierge said. What had you to revenge on the Marquis de Saint-Méran?"— "Oh, it was not on him, monsieur; it was on another."

"This is strange," returned Monte Cristo, seeming to yield to his reflections, "that you should find yourself without any preparation in a house where the event happened that causes you so much remorse."—"Monsieur," said the steward, "it is fatality, I am sure. First, you purchase a house at Auteuil—this house is the one where I have committed an assassination; you descend to the garden by the same staircase by which he descended; you stop at the spot where he received the blow; and two paces farther is the grave in which he had just buried his child. This is not chance, for chance, in this case, is too much like providence."

"Well, amiable Corsican, let us suppose it is providence. I always suppose anything people please, and, besides, you must concede something to diseased minds. Come, collect yourself, and tell me all"—"I have related it but once, and that was to the Abbé Busoni. Such things," continued Bertuccio, shaking his head, "are only related under the seal of confession."—"Then," said the count, "I refer you to your confessor. Turn Chartreux or Trappist, and relate your secrets, but, as for me, I do not like any one who is alarmed by such phantasms, and I do not choose that my servants should be afraid to walk in the garden of an evening. I confess I am not very desirous of a visit from the commissary of police, for, in Italy, justice is only paid when silent—in France she is paid only when she speaks. *Peste*, I thought you somewhat Corsican, a great deal smuggler, and an excellent steward; but I see you have other strings to your bow. You are no longer in my service, Monsieur Bertuccio."

"Oh, your excellency, your excellency!" cried the steward,

struck with terror at this threat, "if that is the only reason I cannot remain in your service, I will tell all, for if I quit you, it will only be to go to the scaffold."—"That is different," replied Monte Cristo; "but if you intend to tell an untruth, reflect it were better not to speak at all."

"No, monsieur, I swear to you, by my hopes of salvation, I will tell you all, for the Abbé Busoni himself only knew a part of my secret; but, I pray you, go away from that plane-tree. The moon is just bursting through the clouds, and there, standing where you do, and wrapped in that cloak that conceals your figure, you remind me of M. de Villefort."—"What!" cried Monte Cristo, "it was M. de Villefort?"—"Your excellency knows him?"—"The former royal attorney at Nimes?"—"Yes."—"Who married the Marquis of Saint-Méran's daughter?"—"Yes."—"Who enjoyed the reputation of being the most severe, the most upright, the most rigid magistrate on the bench?"—"Well, monsieur," said Bertuccio, "this man with this spotless reputation"—"Well?"—"Was a villain."—"Bah." replied Monte Cristo, "impossible!"—'It is as I tell you."—"Ah, really," said Monte Cristo. "Have you proof of this?"—"I had it."—"And you have lost it; how stupid!"—"Yes; but by careful search it might be recovered."—"Really," returned the count, "relate it to me, for it begins to interest me." And the count, humming an air from "Lucia," went to sit down on a bench, while Bertuccio followed him, collecting his thoughts. Bertuccio remained standing before him.

XLIV

The Vendetta

"A T WHAT POINT SHALL I begin my story, your excellency?" asked Bertuccio.—"Where you please," returned Monte Cristo, "since I know nothing at all of it."

"I thought the Abbé Busoni had told your excellency."

"Some particulars, doubtless, but that is seven or eight years ago, and I have forgotten them."

"Then I can speak without fear of tiring your excellency."

"Go on, M. Bertuccio; you will supply the want of the evening papers."

"The story begins in 1815."

"Ah," said Monte Cristo, "1815 is not yesterday."

"No, monsieur, and yet I recollect all things as clearly as if they had happened but then. I had a brother, an elder brother, who was in the service of the emperor; he had become lieutenant in a regiment composed entirely of Corsicans. This brother was my only friend; we became orphans—I at five, he at eighteen. He brought me up as if I had been his son, and in 1814 he married. When the emperor returned from the Island of Elba, my brother instantly joined the army, was slightly wounded at Waterloo, and retired with the army beyond the Loire."—"But that is the history of the Hundred Days,

M. Bertuccio," said the count; "unless I am mistaken, it has been already written."

"Excuse me, excellency, but these details are necessary, and you promised to be patient."—"Go on; I will keep my word."

"One day we received a letter. I should tell you that we lived in the little village of Rogliano, at the extremity of Cape Corso. This letter was from my brother. He told us that the army was disbanded, and that he should return by Châteauroux, Clermont-Ferrand, Le Puy, and Nîmes; and, if I had any money, he prayed me to leave it for him at Nîmes, with an innkeeper with whom I had dealings."—"In the smuggling line?" said Monte Cristo.

"Eh, your excellency? Every one must live."—"Certainly; go on."

"I loved my brother tenderly, as I told your excellency, and I resolved not to send the money, but to take it to him myself. I possessed a thousand francs. I left five hundred with Assunta, my sister-in-law, and with the other five hundred I set off for Nîmes. It was easy to do so, and as I had my boat and a lading to take in at sea, everything favored my project. But, after we had taken in our cargo, the wind became contrary, so that we were four or five days without being able to enter the Rhône. At last, however, we succeeded, and worked up to Arles. I left the boat between Bellegarde and Beaucaire, and took the road to Nîmes."

"We are getting to the story now?"

"Yes, your excellency; excuse me, but, as you will see, I only tell you what is absolutely necessary. Just at this time the famous massacres took place in the south of France. Three brigands, called Trestaillon, Truphemy, and Graffan, publicly assassinated everybody whom they suspected of Bonapartism. You have doubtless heard of these massacres, your excellency?"—"Vaguely; I was far from France at that period. Go on."

"As I entered Nîmes, I literally waded in blood; at every step you encountered dead bodies and bands of murderers, who killed, plundered, and burned. At the sight of this slaughter and devastation I became terrified, not for myself—for I, a simple Corsican fisherman, had nothing to fear; on the contrary, that time was most favorable for us smugglers—but for my brother, a soldier of the empire, returning from the army of the Loire, with his uniform and his epaulets, there was everything to apprehend. I hastened to the innkeeper. My misgivings had been but too true. My brother had arrived the previous evening at Nîmes, and, at the very door of the house where he was about to demand hospitality, he had been assassinated. I did all in my power to discover the murderers, but no one durst tell me their names, so much were they dreaded. I then thought of that French justice of which I had heard so much, and which feared nothing, and I went to the king's attorney."—"And this king's attorney was named Villefort?" asked Monte Cristo carelessly.

"Yes, your excellency; he came from Marseilles, where he had been deputy-procureur. His zeal had procured him advancement, and he was said to be one of the first who had informed the government of the departure from the Island of Elba."—"Then," said Monte Cristo, "you went to him?"

"'Monsieur,' I said, 'my brother was assassinated yesterday in the streets of Nimes, I know not by whom, but it is your duty to find out. You are the representative of justice here, and it is for justice to avenge those she has been unable to protect.'—'Who was your brother?' asked he.—'A lieutenant in the Corsican battalion.'—'A soldier of the usurper, then?'—'A soldier of the French army.'—'Well,' replied he, 'he has smitten with the sword, and he has perished by the sword.'—"You are mistaken, monsieur,' I replied; 'he has perished by the poniard.'—'What do you want me to do?' asked the magistrate.—'I have already told you—avenge him.'—'On whom?'—'On his murderers.'—'How should I know who they are?'—'Order them to be sought for.'—'Why, your brother has been involved in a quarrel, and killed in a duel. All these old soldiers commit excesses which were tolerated in the time of the emperor, but which are not suffered now, for the people here do not like soldiers of such disorderly conduct.'— 'Monsieur,' I replied, 'it is not for myself that I entreat your interference—I should grieve for him or avenge him; but my poor brother had a wife, and were anything to happen to me, the poor creature would perish from want, for my brother's pay alone kept her. Pray, try and obtain a small government pension for her.'

"'Every revolution has its catastrophes,' returned M. de Villefort; 'your brother has been the victim of this. It is a misfortune, and government owes nothing to his family. If we are to judge by all the vengeance that the followers of the usurper exercised on the partisans of the king, when, in their turn, they were in power, your brother would be to-day, in all probability, condemned to death. What has happened is quite natural, and in conformity with the law of reprisals.'—'What,' cried I, 'do you, a magistrate, speak thus to me?'—'All these Corsicans are mad, on my honor,' replied M. de Villefort; 'they fancy that their countryman is still emperor. You have mistaken the time, you should have told me this two months ago, it is too late now. Go now, at once, or I shall have you put out.'

"I looked at him an instant to see if there was anything to hope from further entreaty. But he was a man of stone. I approached him, and said in a low voice, 'Well, since you know the Corsicans so well, you know that they always keep their word. You think that it was a good deed to kill my brother, who was a Bonapartist, because you are a royalist. Well, I, who am a Bonapartist also, declare one thing to you, which is, that I will kill you. From this moment I declare the vendetta against you, so protect yourself as well as you can, for the next time we meet your last hour has come.' And before he had recovered from his surprise, I opened the door and left the room."

"Well, well," said Monte Cristo, "such an innocent looking person as you are to do those things, M. Bertuccio, and to a king's attorney at that! But did he know what was meant by the terrible word 'vendetta'?"

"He knew so well, that from that moment he shut himself in his house, and never went out unattended, seeking me high and low. Fortunately, I was so well concealed that he could not find me. Then he became alarmed, and dared not stay any longer at Nîmes, so he solicited a change of residence, and, as he was in reality very influential, he was nominated to Versailles. But, as you know, a Corsican who has sworn to avenge himself cares not for distance, so his carriage, fast as it went, was never above half a day's journey before me, who followed him on foot. The most important thing was, not to kill him only—for I had an opportunity of doing so a hundred times—but to kill him without being discovered—at least, without being arrested. I no longer belonged to myself, for I had my sister-in-law to protect and provide for. For three months I watched M. de Villefort, for three months he took not a step out-of-doors without my following him. At length I discovered that he went mysteriously to Auteuil. I followed him thither, and I saw him enter the house where we now are, only, instead of entering by the great door that looks into the street, he came on horseback, or in his carriage, left the one or the other at the little inn, and entered by the gate you see there." Monte Cristo made a sign with his head to show that he could discern in the darkness the door to which Bertuccio alluded. "As I had nothing more to do at Versailles, I went to Auteuil, and gained all the information I could. If I wished to surprise him, it was evident this was the spot to lie in wait for him. The house belonged, as the concierge informed your excellency, to M. de Saint-Méran, Villefort's father-in-law. M. de Saint-Méran lived at Marseilles, so that this country house was useless to him, and it was reported to be let to a young widow, known only by the name of 'the baroness.'

"One evening, as I was looking over the wall, I saw a young and handsome woman who was walking alone in that garden, which was not overlooked by any windows, and I guessed that she was awaiting M. de Villefort. When she was sufficiently near for me to distinguish her features, I saw she was from eighteen to nineteen, tall and very fair. As she had a loose muslin dress on, and as nothing concealed her figure, I saw she would ere long become a mother. A few moments after, the little door was opened and a man entered. The young woman hastened to meet him, they threw themselves into each other's arms, embraced tenderly, and returned together to the house. The man was M. de Villefort; I fully believed that when he went out in the night he would be forced to traverse the whole of the garden alone."—"And," asked the count, "did you ever know the name of this woman?"—"No, excellency," returned Bertuccio; "you will see that I had no time to learn it."—"Go on."

"That evening," continued Bertuccio, "I could have killed the procurer, but as I was not sufficiently acquainted with the neighborhood, I was fearful of not killing him on the spot, and that if his cries were overheard I might be taken; so I put it off until the next occasion, and in order that nothing should escape me, I took a chamber looking into the street bordered by the wall of the garden. Three days after, about seven o'clock in the evening, I saw a servant on horseback leave the house at full gallop, and take the road to Sèvres. I concluded that he was going to Versailles, and I was not deceived. Three hours later, the man returned covered with dust, his errand was performed, and ten minutes after, another man on foot, muffled in a mantle, opened the little door of the garden, which he closed after him. I descended rapidly; although I had not seen Villefort's face, I recognized him by the beating of my heart. I crossed the street, and stopped at a post placed at the angle of the wall, and by means of which I had once before looked into the garden. This time I did not content myself with looking, but I took my knife out of my pocket, felt that the point was sharp, and sprang over the wall. My first care was to run to the door; he had left the key in it, taking the simple precaution of turning it twice in the lock. Nothing, then, preventing my escape by this means, I examined the grounds. The garden was long and narrow; a stretch of smooth turf extended down the middle, and at the corners were clumps of trees with thick and massy foliage, that made a background for the shrubs and flowers. In order to go from the door to the house, or from the house to the door, M. de Villefort would be obliged to pass by one of these clumps of trees.

"It was the end of September; the wind blew violently. The faint glimpses of the pale moon, hidden momentarily by masses of dark clouds that were sweeping across the sky, whitened the gravel walks that led to the house, but were unable to pierce the obscurity of the thick shrubberies, in which a man could conceal himself without any fear of discovery. I hid myself in the one nearest to the path Villefort must take, and scarcely was I there when, amidst the gusts of wind, I fancied I heard groans; but you know, or rather you do not know, your excellency, that he who is about to commit an assassination fancies that he hears low cries perpetually ringing in his ears. Two hours passed thus, during which I imagined I heard moans repeatedly. Midnight struck. As the last stroke died away, I saw a faint light shine through the windows of the private staircase by which we have just descended. The door opened, and the man in the mantle reappeared. The terrible moment had come, but I had so long been prepared for it that my heart did not fail in the least. I drew my knife from my pocket again, opened it, and made ready to strike. The man in the mantle advanced towards me, but as he drew near I saw that he had a weapon in his hand. I was afraid, not of a struggle, but of a failure. When he was only a few paces from me, I saw that what I had taken for a weapon was only a spade. I was still unable to divine for what reason M. de Villefort had this spade in his hands, when he stopped close to the thicket where I was, glanced round, and began to dig a hole in the earth. I then perceived that he was hiding something under his mantle, which he laid on the grass in order to dig more freely. Then, I confess, curiosity mingled with hatred; I wished to see what Villefort was going to do there, and I remained motionless, holding my breath. Then an idea crossed my mind, which was confirmed when I saw the procureur lift from under his mantle a box, two feet long, and six or eight inches deep. I let him place the box in the hole he had made, then, while he stamped with his feet to remove all traces of his occupation, I rushed on him and plunged my knife into his breast, exclaiming,—'I am Giovanni Bertuccio; thy death for my brother's; thy treasure for his widow; thou seest that my vengeance is more complete than I had hoped.' I know not if he heard these words; I think he did not, for he fell without a cry. I felt his blood gush over my face, but I was intoxicated, I was delirious, and the blood refreshed, instead of burning me. In a second I had disinterred the box; then, that it might not be known I had done so, I filled up the hole, threw the spade over the wall, and rushed through the door, which I double-locked, carrying off the key."

"Ah," said Monte Cristo, "it seems to me this was nothing but murder and robbery."—"No, your excellency," returned Bertuccio; "it was a vendetta followed by restitution."

"And was the sum a large one?"—"It was not money."

"Ah, I recollect," replied the count; "did you not say something of an infant?"—"Yes, excellency; I hastened to the river, sat down on the bank, and with my knife forced open the lock of the box.

In a fine linen cloth was wrapped a new-born child. Its purple visage, and its violet-colored hands showed that it had perished from suffocation, but as it was not yet cold, I hesitated to throw it into the water that ran at my feet. After a moment I fancied that I felt a slight pulsation of the heart, and as I had been assistant at the hospital at Bastia, I did what a doctor would have done—I inflated the lungs by blowing air into them, and at the expiration of a quarter of an hour, it began to breathe, and cried feebly. In my turn I uttered a cry, but a cry of joy. 'God has not cursed me then,' I cried, 'since he permits me to save the life of a human creature, in exchange for the life I have taken away.'"

"And what did you do with the child?" asked Monte Cristo. "It was an embarrassing load for a man seeking to escape."—"I had not for a moment the idea of keeping it, but I knew that at Paris there was an asylum where they receive such creatures. As I passed the city gates I declared that I had found the child on the road, and I inquired where the asylum was; the box confirmed my statement, the linen proved that the infant belonged to wealthy parents, the blood with which I was covered might have proceeded from the child as well as from any one else. No objection was raised, but they pointed out the asylum, which was situated at the upper end of the Rue d'Enfer, and after having taken the precaution of cutting the linen in two pieces, so that one of the two letters which marked it was on the piece wrapped around the child, while the other remained in my possession, I rang the bell, and fled with all speed. A fortnight after I was at Rogliano, and I said to Assunta,—'Console thyself, sister; Israel is dead, but he is avenged.' She demanded what I meant, and when I had told her all,—'Giovanni,' said she, 'you should have brought this child with you; we would have replaced the parents it has lost, have called it Benedetto, and then, in consequence of this good action, God would have blessed us.' In reply I gave her the half of the linen I had kept in order to reclaim him if we became rich."

"What letters were marked on the linen?" said Monte Cristo.

"An H and an N, surmounted by a baron's coronet."

"By heaven, M. Bertuccio, you make use of heraldic terms; where did you study heraldry?"—"In your service, excellency, where everything is learned."—"Go on; I am curious to know two things."

"What are they, your excellency?"—"What became of this little boy? for I think you told me it was a boy, M. Bertuccio."

"No, excellency, I do not recollect telling you that."

"I thought you did; I must have been mistaken."

"No, you were not, for it was in reality a little boy. But your excellency wished to know two things; what was the second?"

"The second was the crime of which you were accused when you asked for a confessor, and the Abbé Busoni came to visit you at your request in the prison at Nîmes."

"The story will be very long, excellency."—"What matter? you know I take but little sleep, and I do not suppose you are very much inclined for it either." Bertuccio bowed, and resumed his story.

"Partly to drown the recollections of the past that haunted me, partly to supply the wants of the poor widow, I eagerly returned to my trade of smuggler, which had become more easy since that relaxation of the laws which always follows a revolution. The southern districts were ill-watched in particular, in consequence of the disturbances that were perpetually breaking out in Avignon, Nîmes, or Uzés. We profited by this respite on the part of the government to make friends every where. Since my brother's assassination in the streets of Nîmes, I had never entered the town; the result was that the innkeeper with whom we were connected, seeing that we would no longer come to him, was forced to come to us, and had established a branch to his inn, on the road from Bellegarde to Beaucaire, at the sign of the Pont du Gard. We had thus, at Aigues-Mortes, Martigues, or Bouc, a dozen places where we left our goods, and where, in case of necessity, we concealed ourselves from the gendarmes and custom-house officers. Smuggling is a profitable trade, when a certain degree of vigor and intelligence is employed; as for myself, brought up in the mountains, I had a double motive for fearing the gendarmes and custom-house officers, as my appearance before the judges would cause an inquiry, and an inquiry always looks back into the past. And in my past life they might find something far more grave than the selling of smuggled cigars, or barrels of Brandy without a permit. So, preferring death to capture, I accomplished the most astonishing deeds, and which, more than once, showed me that the too great care we take of our bodies is the only obstacle to the success of those projects which require rapid decision, and vigorous and determined execution. In reality, when you have once devoted your life to your enterprises, you are no longer the equal of other men, or, rather, other men are no longer your equals, and whosoever has taken this resolution, feels his strength and resources doubled."

"Philosophy, M. Bertuccio," interrupted the count; "you have done a little of everything in your life."—"Oh, excellency."

"No, no; but philosophy at half-past ten at night is somewhat late; yet I have no other observation to make, for what you say is correct, which is more than can be said for all philosophy."

"My journeys became more and more extensive and more productive. Assunta took care of all, and our little fortune increased. One day as I was setting off on an expedition, 'Go,' said she; 'at your return I will give you a surprise.' I questioned her, but in vain; she would tell me nothing, and I departed. Our expedition lasted nearly six weeks; we had been to Lucca to take in oil, to Leghorn for

English cottons, and we ran our cargo without opposition, and returned home full of joy. When I entered the house, the first thing I beheld in the middle of Assunta's chamber was a cradle that might be called sumptuous compared with the rest of the furniture, and in it a baby seven or eight months old. I uttered a cry of joy; the only moments of sadness I had known since the assassination of the procureur were caused by the recollection that I had abandoned this child. For the assassination itself I had never felt any remorse. Poor Assunta had guessed all. She had profited by my absence, and furnished with the half of the linen, and having written down the day and hour at which I had deposited the child at the asylum, had set off for Paris, and had reclaimed it. No objection was raised, and the infant was given up to her. Ah, I confess, your excellency, when I saw this poor creature sleeping peacefully in its cradle, I felt my eyes filled with tears. 'Ah, Assunta,' cried I, 'you are an excellent woman, and heaven will bless you.'"—"This," said Monte Cristo, "is less correct than your philosophy,—it is only faith."

"Alas, your excellency is right," replied Bertuccio. "and God made this infant the instrument of our punishment. Never did a perverse nature declare itself more prematurely, and yet it was not owing to any fault in his bringing up. He was a most lovely child, with large blue eyes, of that deep color that harmonizes so well with the blond complexion; only his hair, which was too light, gave his face a most singular expression, and added to the vivacity of his look, and the malice of his smile. Unfortunately, there is a proverb which says that 'red is either altogether good or altogether bad.' The proverb was but too correct as regarded Benedetto, and even in his infancy he manifested the worst disposition. It is true that the indulgence of his foster-mother encouraged him. This child, for whom my poor sister would go to the town, five or six leagues off, to purchase the earliest fruits and the most tempting sweetmeats, preferred to Palma grapes or Genoese preserves, the chestnuts stolen from a neighbor's orchard, or the dried apples in his loft, when he could eat as well of the nuts and apples that grew in my garden. One day, when Benedetto was about five or six, our neighbor Vasilio, who, according to the custom of the country, never locked up his purse or his valuables—for, as your excellency knows, there are no thieves in Corsica—complained that he had lost a louis out of his purse; we thought he must have made a mistake in counting his money, but he persisted in the accuracy of his statement. One day, Benedetto, who had been gone from the house since morning, to our great anxiety, did not return until late in the evening, dragging a monkey after him, which he said he had found chained to the foot of a tree. For more than a month past, the mischievous child, who knew not what to wish for, had taken it into his head to have a monkey. A boatman, who had passed by Rogliano, and who had several of these animals, whose tricks had greatly diverted him, had, doubtless, suggested this idea to him. 'Monkeys are not found in our woods chained to trees,' said I; 'confess how you obtained this animal.' Benedetto maintained the truth of what he had said, and accompanied it with details that did more honor to his imagination than to his veracity. I became angry; he began to laugh, I threatened to strike him, and he made two steps backwards. 'You cannot beat me,' said he; 'you have no right, for you are not my father.'

"We never knew who had revealed this fatal secret, which we had so carefully concealed from him; however, it was this answer, in which the child's whole character revealed itself, that almost terrified me, and my arm fell without touching him. The boy triumphed, and this victory rendered him so audacious, that all the money of Assunta, whose affection for him seemed to increase as he became more unworthy of it, was spent in caprices she knew not

how to contend against, and follies she had not the courage to prevent. When I was at Rogliano everything went on properly, but no
sooner was my back turned than Benedetto became master, and
everything went ill. When he was only eleven, he chose his companions from among the young men of eighteen or twenty, the
worst characters in Bastia, or, indeed, in Corsica, and they had
already, for some mischievous pranks, been several times threatened
with a prosecution. I became alarmed, as any prosecution might be
attended with serious consequences. I was compelled, at this
period, to leave Corsica on an important expedition; I reflected for
a long time, and with the hope of averting some impending misfortune, I resolved that Benedetto should accompany me. I hoped
that the active and laborious life of a smuggler, with the severe discipline on board, would have a salutary effect on his character,
which was now well-nigh, if not quite, corrupt. I spoke to
Benedetto alone, and proposed to him to accompany me, endeavoring to tempt him by all the promises most likely to dazzle the
imagination of a child of twelve. He heard me patiently, and when
I had finished, burst out laughing.

"'Are you mad, uncle?' (he called me by this name when he was
in good humor); 'do you think I am going to change the life I lead
for your mode of existence—my agreeable indolence for the hard
and precarious toil you impose on yourself? exposed to the bitter
frost at night, and the scorching heat by day, compelled to conceal
yourself, and when you are perceived, receive a volley of bullets, all
to earn a paltry sum? Why, I have as much money as I want; mother
Assunta always furnishes me when I ask for it! You see that I should
be a fool to accept your offer.' The arguments, and his audacity, perfectly stupefied me. Benedetto rejoined his associates, and I saw him
from a distance point me out to them as a fool."

"Sweet child," murmured Monte Cristo.

"Oh, had he been my own son," replied Bertuccio, "or even my nephew, I would have brought him back to the right road, for the knowledge that you are doing your duty gives you strength, but the idea that I was striking a child whose father I had killed, made it impossible for me to punish him. I gave my sister, who constantly defended the unfortunate boy, good advice, and as she confessed that she had several times missed money to a considerable amount, I showed her a safe place in which to conceal our little treasure for the future. My mind was already made up. Benedetto could read, write, and cipher perfectly, for when the fit seized him, he learned more in a day than others in a week. My intention was to enter him as a clerk in some ship, and without letting him know anything of my plan, to convey him some morning on board; by this means his future treatment would depend upon his own conduct. I set off for France, after having fixed upon the plan. Our cargo was to be landed in the Gulf of Lyons, and this was a difficult thing to do because it was then the year 1829. The most perfect tranquillity was restored, and the vigilance of the custom-house officers was redoubled, and their strictness was increased at this time, in consequence of the fair at Beaucaire.

"Our expedition made a favorable beginning. We anchored our vessel—which had a double hold, where our goods were concealed—amidst a number of other vessels that bordered the banks of the Rhône from Beaucaire to Arles. On our arrival we began to discharge our cargo in the night, and to convey it into the town, by the help of the innkeeper with whom we were connected. Whether success rendered us imprudent, or whether we were betrayed, I know not; but one evening, about five o'clock, our little cabin-boy came breathlessly, to inform us that he had seen a detachment of custom-house officers advancing in our direction. It was not their proximity that alarmed us, for detachments were constantly patrolling along the banks of the Rhône, but the care, according to the boy's account, that they took to avoid being seen. In an instant we were on the alert, but it was too late; our vessel was surrounded, and amongst the custom-house officers I observed several gendarmes, and, as terrified at the sight of their uniforms as I was brave at the sight of any other, I sprang into the hold, opened a port, and dropped into the river, dived, and only rose at intervals to breathe, until I reached a ditch that had recently been made from the Rhône to the canal that runs from Beaucaire to Aigues-Mortes. I was now safe, for I could swim along the ditch without being seen, and I reached the canal in safety. I had designedly taken this direction. I have already told your excellency of an innkeeper from Nîmes who had set up a little tavern on the road from Bellegarde to Beaucaire."—"Yes," said Monte Cristo, "I perfectly recollect him; I think he was your colleague."

"Precisely," answered Bertuccio; "but he had, seven or eight years before this period, sold his establishment to a tailor at Marseilles, who, having almost ruined himself in his old trade, wished to make his fortune in another. Of course, we made the same arrangements with the new landlord that we had with the old; and it was of this man that I intended to ask shelter."—"What was his name?" inquired the count, who seemed to become somewhat interested in Bertuccio's story.

"Gaspard Caderousse; he had married a woman from the village of Carconte, and whom we did not know by any other name than that of her village. She was suffering from malarial fever, and seemed dying by inches. As for her husband, he was a strapping fellow of forty, or five and forty, who had more than once, in time of danger, given ample proof of his presence of mind and courage."—"And you say," interrupted Monte Cristo, "that this took place towards the year"—

"1829, your excellency."—"In what month?"—"June."

"The beginning or the end?"—"The evening of the 3d."

"Ah," said Monte Cristo, "the evening of the 3d of June, 1829. Go on."

"It was from Caderousse that I intended demanding shelter, and, as we never entered by the door that opened onto the road, I resolved not to break through the rule, so climbing over the garden-hedge, I crept amongst the olive and wild fig trees, and fearing that Caderousse might have some guest, I entered a kind of shed in which I had often passed the night, and which was only separated from the inn by a partition, in which holes had been made in order to enable us to watch an opportunity of announcing our presence. My intention was, if Caderousse was alone, to acquaint him with my presence, finish the meal the custom-house officers had interrupted, and profit by the threatened storm to return to the Rhône, and ascertain the state of our vessel and its crew. I stepped into the shed, and it was fortunate I did so, for at that moment Caderousse entered with a stranger.

"I waited patiently, not to overhear what they said, but because I could do nothing else; besides, the same thing had occurred often before. The man who was with Caderousse was evidently a stranger to the South of France; he was one of those merchants who come to sell jewellery at the Beaucaire fair, and who during the month the fair lasts, and during which there is so great an influx of merchants and customers from all parts of Europe, often have dealings to the amount of 100,000 to 150,000 francs. Caderousse entered hastily. Then, seeing that the room was, as usual, empty, and only guarded by the dog, he called to his wife, 'Hello, Carconte,' said he, 'the worthy priest has not deceived us; the diamond is real.' An exclamation of joy was heard, and the staircase creaked beneath a feeble step. 'What do you say?' asked his wife, pale as death.

"'I say that the diamond is real, and that this gentleman, one of the first jewellers of Paris, will give us 50,000 francs for it. Only, in order to satisfy himself that it really belongs to us, he wishes you to relate to him, as I have done already, the miraculous manner in which the diamond came into our possession. In the meantime please to sit down, monsieur, and I will fetch you some refreshment.' The jeweller examined attentively the interior of the inn and the apparent poverty of the persons who were about to sell him a diamond that seemed to have come from the casket of a prince. 'Relate your story, madame,' said he, wishing, no doubt, to profit by the absence of the husband, so that the latter could not influence the wife's story, to see if the two recitals tallied.

"'Oh,' returned she, 'it was a gift of heaven. My husband was a great friend, in 1814 or 1815, of a sailor named Edmond Dantès. This poor fellow, whom Caderousse had forgotten, had not forgotten him, and at his death he bequeathed this diamond to him.'— 'But how did he obtain it?' asked the jeweller; 'had he it before he was imprisoned?'—'No, monsieur; but it appears that in prison he made the acquaintance of a rich Englishman, and as in prison he fell sick, and Dantès took the same care of him as if he had been his brother, the Englishman, when he was set free, gave this stone to Dantès, who, less fortunate, died, and, in his turn, left it to us, and charged the excellent abbé, who was here this morning, to deliver it.'—'The same story,' muttered the jeweller; 'and improbable as it seemed at first, it may be true. There's only the price we are not agreed about'—'How not agreed about?' said Caderousse. 'I thought we agreed for the price I asked.'—'That is,' replied the jeweller, 'I offered 40,000 francs.'—'Forty thousand,' cried La Carconte; 'we will not part with it for that sum. The abbé told us it was worth 50,000 without the setting.'

"'What was the abbé's name?' asked the indefatigable

questioner.—'The Abbé Busoni,' said La Carconte.—'He was a foreigner?'—'An Italian, from the neighborhood of Mantua, I believe.'—'Let me see this diamond again,' replied the jeweller; 'the first time you are often mistaken as to the value of a stone.' Caderousse took from his pocket a small case of black shagreen, opened, and gave it to the jeweller. At the sight of the diamond, which was as large as a hazel-nut, La Carconte's eyes sparkled with cupidity."

"And what did you think of this fine story, eavesdropper?" said Monte Cristo; "did you credit it?"

"Yes, your excellency. I did not look on Caderousse as a bad man, and I thought him incapable of committing a crime, or even a theft."

"That did more honor to your heart than to your experience, M. Bertuccio. Had you known this Edmond Dantès, of whom they spoke?"

"No, your excellency, I had never heard of him before, and never but once afterwards, and that was from the Abbé Busoni himself, when I saw him in the prison at Nîmes."—"Go on."

"The jeweller took the ring, and drawing from his pocket a pair of steel pliers and a small set of copper scales, he took the stone out of its setting, and weighed it carefully. 'I will give you 45,000,' said he, 'but not a sou more; besides, as that is the exact value of the stone, I brought just that sum with me.'—'Oh, that's no matter,' replied Caderousse, 'I will go back with you to fetch the other 5,000 francs.'—'No,' returned the jeweller, giving back the diamond and the ring to Caderousse—'no, it is worth no more, and I am sorry I offered so much, for the stone has a flaw in it, which I had not seen. However, I will not go back on my word, and I will give 45,000.'—'At least, replace the diamond in the ring,' said La Carconte sharply.—'Ah, true,' replied the jeweller, and he reset the stone.—'No matter,' observed Caderousse, replacing the box in his

pocket, 'some one else will purchase it.'—'Yes,' continued the jeweller; 'but some one else will not be so easy as I am, or content himself with the same story. It is not natural that a man like you should
possess such a diamond. He will inform against you. You will have
to find the Abbé Busoni; and abbés who give diamonds worth two
thousand louis are rare. The law would seize it, and put you in
prison; if at the end of three or four months you are set at liberty,
the ring will be lost, or a false stone, worth three francs, will be
given you, instead of a diamond worth 50,000 or perhaps 55,000
francs; from which you must allow that one runs considerable risk
in purchasing.' Caderousse and his wife looked eagerly at each
other.—'No,' said Caderousse, 'we are not rich enough to lose
5,000 francs.'—'As you please, my dear sir,' said the jeweller; 'I had,
however, as you see, brought you the money in bright coin.' And he
drew from his pocket a handful of gold, and held it sparkling before
the dazzled eyes of the innkeeper, and in the other hand he held a
packet of bank-notes.

"There was evidently a severe struggle in the mind of Caderousse; it was plain that the small shagreen case, which he turned
over and over in his hand, did not seem to him commensurate in
value to the enormous sum which fascinated his gaze. He turned
towards his wife. 'What do you think of this?' he asked in a low
voice.—'Let him have it—let him have it,' she said. 'If he returns to
Beaucaire without the diamond, he will inform against us, and, as
he says, who knows if we shall ever again see the Abbé Busoni?—
in all probability we shall ever again see him.'—'Well, then, so I
will!' said Caderonsse; 'so you may have the diamond for 45,000
francs. But my wife wants a gold chain, and I want a pair of silver
buckles.' The jeweller drew from his pocket a long that box, which
contained several samples of the articles demanded. 'Here,' he said,
'I am very straightforward in my dealings—take your choice.' The

woman selected a gold chain worth about five louis, and the husband a pair of buckles, worth perhaps fifteen francs.—'I hope you will not complain now?' said the jeweller.

"'The abbé told me it was worth 50,000 francs,' muttered Caderousse. 'Come, come—give it to me! What a strange fellow you are,' said the jeweller, taking the diamond from his hand. 'I give you 45,000 francs—that is, 2,500 livres of income,—a fortune such as I wish I had myself, and you are not satisfied!'—'And the five and forty thousand francs,' inquired Caderousse in a hoarse voice, 'where are they? Come—let us see them.'—'Here they are,' replied the jeweller; and he counted out upon the table 15,000 francs in gold, and 30,000 francs in bank-notes.

"'Wait while I light the lamp,' said La Carconte; 'it is growing dark, and there may be some mistake.' In fact, night had come on during this conversation, and with night the storm which had been threatening for the last half-hour. The thunder growled in the distance; but it was apparently not heard by the jeweller, Caderousse or La Carconte, absorbed as they were all three with the demon of gain. I myself felt a strange kind of fascination at the sight of all this gold and all these bank-notes; it seemed to me that I was in a dream, and, as it always happens in a dream, I felt myself riveted to the spot. Caderousse counted and again counted the gold and the notes, then handed them to his wife, who counted and counted them again in her turn. During this time, the jeweller made the diamond play and sparkle in the lamplight, and the gem threw out jets of light which made him unmindful of those which—precursors of the storm—began to play in at the windows. 'Well,' inquired the jeweller, 'is the cash all right?'

"'Yes,' said Caderousse. 'Give me the pocket-book, La Carconte, and find a bag somewhere.'

"La Carconte went to a cupboard, and returned with an old

leathern pocket-book and a bag. From the former she took some greasy letters, and put in their place the bank-notes, and from the bag took two or three crowns of six livres each, which, in all probability, formed the entire fortune of the miserable couple. 'There,' said Caderousse; 'and now, although you have wronged us of perhaps 10,000 francs, will you have your supper with us? I invite you with good will.'—'Thank you,' replied the jeweller, 'it must be getting late, and I must return to Beaucaire—my wife will be getting uneasy.' He drew out his watch, and exclaimed, '*Marbleu*, nearly nine o'clock—why, I shall not get back to Beaucaire before midnight! Goodnight, my friends. If the Abbé Busoni should by any accident return, think of me.'—'In another week you will have left Beaucaire,' remarked Caderousse, 'for the fair ends in a few days.'—'True, but that makes no difference. Write to me at Paris, to M. Joannes, in the Palais Royal, arcade Pierre, No. 45. I will make the journey on purpose to see him, if it is worth while.' At this moment there was a tremendous clap of thunder, accompanied by a flash of lightning so vivid, that it quite eclipsed the light of the lamp.

"'See here,' exclaimed Caderousse. 'You cannot think of going out in such weather as this.'—'Oh, I am not afraid of thunder,' said the jeweller.—'And then there are robbers,' said La Carconte. 'The road is never very safe during fair time.'—'Oh, as to the robbers,' said Joannes, 'here is something for them;' and he drew from his pocket a pair of small pistols, loaded to the muzzle. 'Here,' said he, 'are dogs who bark and bite at the same time, they are for the two first who shall have a longing for your diamond, Friend Caderousse.'

"Caderousse and his wife again interchanged a meaning look. It seemed as though they were both inspired at the same time with some horrible thought. 'Well, then, a good journey to you,' said Caderousse.—'Thanks,' replied the jeweller. He then took his cane, which he had placed against an old cupboard, and went out. At the moment when he opened the door, such a gust of wind came in that the lamp was nearly extinguished. 'Oh,' said he, 'this is very nice weather, and two leagues to go in such a storm.'—'Remain,' said Caderousse. 'You can sleep here.'—'Yes; do stay,' added La Carconte in a tremulous voice; 'we will take every care of you.'—'No; I must sleep at Beaucaire. So, once more, good-night.' Caderousse followed him slowly to the threshold. 'I can see neither heaven nor earth,' said the jeweller, who was outside the door. 'Do I turn to the right, or to the left hand?'—'To the right,' said Caderousse. 'You cannot go wrong—the road is bordered by trees on both sides.'—'Good—all right,' said a voice almost lost in the distance. 'Close the door,' said La Carconte; 'I do not like open doors when it thunders.'—'Particularly when there is money in the house, eh?' answered Caderousse, double-locking the door.

"He came into the room, went to the cupboard, took out the bag and pocket-book, and both began, for the third time, to count their gold and bank-notes. I never saw such an expression of cupidity as the flickering lamp revealed in those two countenances. The woman, especially, was hideous; her usual feverish tremulousness was intensified, her countenance had become livid, and her eyes resembled burning coals. 'Why,' she inquired in a hoarse voice, 'did you invite him to sleep here to-night?'—'Why?' said Caderousse with a shudder; 'why, that he might not have the trouble of returning to Beaucaire.'—'Ah,' responded the woman, with an expression impossible to describe; 'I thought it was for something else.'—'Woman, woman—why do you have such ideas?' cried Caderousse; 'or, if you have them, why don't you keep them to yourself?'—'Well,' said La Carconte, after a moment's pause, 'you are not a man.'—'What do you mean?' added Caderousse.—'If you had been a man, you would not have let him go from here.'—'Woman!'—'Or else he should not have reached Beaucaire.'—'Woman!'—'The road takes a turn—he is obliged to follow it—while alongside of the canal there is a shorter road.'—'Woman!—you offend the good God. There—listen!' And at this moment there was a tremendous peal of thunder, while the livid lightning illumined the room, and the thunder, rolling away in the distance, seemed to withdraw unwillingly from the cursed abode. 'Mercy!' said Caderousse, crossing himself.

"At the same moment, and in the midst of the terrifying silence which usually follows a clap of thunder, they heard a knocking at the door. Caderousse and his wife started and looked aghast at each other. 'Who's there?' cried Caderousse, rising, and drawing up in a heap the gold and notes scattered over the table, and which he covered with his two hands.—'It is I,' shouted a voice. 'And who are you?'—'Eh, *pardieu*, Joannes, the jeweller.'—'Well, and you said I offended the good God,' said La Carconte with a horrid smile. 'Why, the good God sends him back again.' Caderousse sank pale and breathless into his chair. La Carconte, on the contrary, rose, and going with a firm step towards the door, opened it, saying, as she did so—'Come in, dear M. Joannes.'—'*Ma foi*,' said the jeweller, drenched with rain, 'I am not destined to return to Beaucaire to-night. The shortest follies are best, my dear Caderousse. You offered me hospitality, and I accept it, and have returned to sleep beneath your friendly roof.' Caderousse stammered out something, while he wiped away the sweat that started to his brow. La Carconte doubled-locked the door behind the jeweller.

XLV

The Rain of Blood

"A S THE JEWELLER RETURNED to the apartment, he cast, around him a scrutinizing glance—but there was nothing to excite suspicion, if it did not exist, or to confirm it, if it were already awakened. Caderousse's hands still grasped the gold and bank-notes, and La Carconte called up her sweetest smiles while welcoming the reappearance of their guest. 'Well, well,' said the jeweller, 'you seem, my good friends, to have had some fears respecting the accuracy of your money, by counting it over so carefully directly I was gone.'—'Oh, no,' answered Caderousse, 'that was not my reason, I can assure you; but the circumstances by which we have become possessed of this wealth are so unexpected, as to make us scarcely credit our good fortune, and it is only by placing the actual proof of our riches before our eyes that we can persuade ourselves that the whole affair is not a dream.' The jeweller smiled.—'Have you any other guests in your house?' inquired he.—'Nobody but ourselves,' replied Caderousse; 'the fact is, we do not lodge travellers—indeed, our tavern is so near the town, that nobody would think of stopping here.'—'Then I am afraid I shall very much inconvenience you.'—'Inconvenience us? Not at all, my dear sir,' said La Carconte in her most gracious manner. 'Not at all, I assure you.'— 'But where will you manage to stow me?'—'In the chamber overhead.'—'Surely that is where you yourselves sleep?'—'Never mind that; we have a second bed in the adjoining room.' Caderousse stared at his wife with much astonishment.

"The jeweller, meanwhile, was humming a song as he stood warming his back at the fire La Carconte had kindled to dry the wet garments of her guest; and this done, she next occupied herself in arranging his supper, by spreading a napkin at the end of the table, and placing on it the slender remains of their dinner, to which she added three or four fresh-laid eggs. Caderousse had once more parted with his treasure—the bank-notes notes were replaced in the pocket-book, the gold put back into the bag, and the whole carefully locked in the cupboard. He then began pacing the room with a pensive and gloomy air, glancing from time to time at the jeweller, who stood reeking with the steam from his wet clothes, and merely changing his place on the warm hearth, to enable the whole of his garments to be dried.

"'There,' said La Carconte, as she placed a bottle of wine on the table, 'supper is ready whenever you are.'—'And you?' asked Joannes.—'I don't want any supper,' said Caderousse.—'We dined so very late,' hastily interposed La Carconte.—'Then it seems I am to eat alone,' remarked the jeweller.—'Oh, we shall have the pleasure of waiting upon you,' answered La Carconte, with an eager attention she was not accustomed to manifest even to guests who paid for what they took.

"From time to time Caderousse darted on his wife keen, searching glances, but rapid as the lightning flash. The storm still continued. 'There, there,' said La Carconte; 'do you hear that? Upon my word, you did well to come back.'—'Nevertheless' replied the jeweller, 'if by the time I have finished my supper the tempest has at all abated, I shall make another start.'—'It's the mistral,' said Caderousse, 'and it will be sure to last till to-morrow morning.' He sighed heavily.—'Well,' said the jeweller, as he placed himself at table, 'all I can say is, so much the worse for those who are abroad.'—'Yes,' chimed in La Carconte, 'they will have a wretched night of it.'

"The jeweller began eating his supper, and the woman, who was ordinarily so querulous and indifferent to all who approached her, was suddenly transformed into the most smiling and attentive hostess. Had the unhappy man on whom she lavished her assiduities been previously acquainted with her, so sudden an alteration might well have excited suspicion in his mind, or at least have greatly astonished him. Caderousse, meanwhile, continued to pace the room in gloomy silence, sedulously avoiding the sight of his guest; but as soon as the stranger had completed his repast, the agitated innkeeper went eagerly to the door and opened it. 'I believe the storm is over,' said he. But as if to contradict his statement, at that instant a violent clap of thunder seemed to shake the house to its very foundation, while a sudden gust of wind, mingled with rain, extinguished the lamp be held in his hand. Trembling and awe-struck, Caderousse hastily shut the door and returned to his guest, while La Carconte lighted a candle by the smouldering ashes that glimmered on the hearth. 'You must be tired,' said she to the jeweller; 'I have spread a pair of white sheets on your bed; go up when you are ready, and sleep well.'

"Joannes stayed for a while to see whether the storm seemed to abate in its fury, but a brief space of time suffered to assure him that, instead of diminishing, the violence of the rain and thunder momentarily increased; resigning himself, therefore, to what seemed inevitable, he bade his host good-night, and mounted the stairs. He passed over my head and I heard the flooring creak beneath his footsteps. The quick, eager glance of La Carconte followed him as he ascended, while Caderousse, on the contrary, turned his back, and seemed most anxiously to avoid even glancing at him.

"All these circumstances did not strike me as painfully at the time as they have since done; in fact, all that had happened (with the exception of the story of the diamond, which certainly did wear an air of improbability), appeared natural enough, and called for neither apprehension nor mistrust; but, worn out as I was with fatigue, and fully purposing to proceed onwards directly the tempest abated, I determined to obtain a few hours' sleep. Overhead I could accurately distinguish every movement of the jeweller, who, after making the best arrangements in his power for passing a comfortable night, threw himself on his bed, and I could hear it creak and groan beneath his weight. Insensibly my eyelids grew heavy, deep sleep stole over me, and having no suspicion of anything wrong, I sought not to shake it off. I looked into the kitchen once more and saw Caderousse sitting by the side of a long table upon one of the low wooden stools which in country places are frequently used instead of chairs; his back was turned towards me, so that I could not see the expression of his countenance—neither should I have been able to do so had he been placed differently, as his head was buried between his two hands. La Carconte continued to gaze on him for sometime, then shrugging her shoulders, she took her seat immediately opposite to him. At this moment the expiring embers threw up a fresh flame from the kindling of a piece of wood that lay near, and a bright light flashed over the room. La Carconte still kept her eyes fixed on her husband, but as he made no sign of changing his position, she extended her hard, bony hand, and touched him on the forehead.

"Caderousse shuddered. The woman's lips seemed to move, as though she were talking; but because she merely spoke in an undertone, or my senses were dulled by sleep, I did not catch a word she uttered. Confused sights and sounds seemed to float before me, and gradually I fell into a deep, heavy slumber. How long I had been in this unconscious state I know not, when I was suddenly aroused by the report of a pistol, followed by a fearful cry. Weak and tottering footsteps resounded across the chamber above me, and the next instant a dull, heavy weight seemed to fall

powerless on the staircase. I had not yet fully recovered consciousness, when again I heard groans, mingled with half-stifled cries, as
if from persons engaged in a deadly struggle. A cry more prolonged
than the others and ending in a series of groans effectually roused
me from my drowsy lethargy. Hastily raising myself on one arm. I
looked around, but all was dark; and it seemed to me as if the rain
must have penetrated through the flooring of the room above, for
some kind of moisture appeared to fall, drop by drop, upon my
forehead, and when I passed my hand across my brow, I felt that it
was wet and clammy.

"To the fearful noises that had awakened me had succeeded the
most perfect silence—unbroken, save by the footsteps of a man
walking about in the chamber above. The staircase creaked, he
descended into the room below, approached the fire and lit a candle. The man was Caderousse—he was pale and his shirt was all
blood. Having obtained the light, he hurried up-stairs again, and
once more I heard his rapid and uneasy footsteps. A moment later
he came down again, holding in his hand the small shagreen case,
which he opened, to assure himself it contained the diamond,—
seemed to hesitate as to which pocket he should put it in, then, as
if dissatisfied with the security of either pocket, he deposited it in
his red handkerchief, which he carefully rolled round his head.
After this he took from his cupboard the bank-notes and gold he
had put there, thrust the one into the pocket of his trousers, and
the other into that of his waistcoat, hastily tied up a small bundle
of linen, and rushing towards the door, disappeared in the darkness
of the night.

"Then all became clear and manifest to me, and I reproached
myself with what had happened, as though I myself had done the
guilty deed. I fancied that I still heard faint moans, and imagining
that the unfortunate jeweller might not be quite dead, I determined to go to his relief, by way of atoning in some slight degree,
not for the crime I had committed, but for that which I had not

endeavored to prevent. For this purpose I applied all the strength I possessed to force an entrance from the cramped spot in which I lay to the adjoining room; the poorly fastened boards which alone divided me from it yielded to my efforts, and I found myself in the house. Hastily snatching up the lighted candle, I hurried to the staircase; about midway a body was lying quite across the stairs. It was that of La Carconte. The pistol I had heard had doubtless been fired at her. The shot had frightfully lacerated her throat, leaving two gaping wounds from which, as well as the mouth, the blood was pouring in floods. She was stone dead. I strode past her, and ascended to the sleeping chamber, which presented an appearance of the wildest disorder. The furniture had been knocked over in the deadly struggle that had taken place there, and the sheets, to which the unfortunate jeweller had doubtless clung, were dragged across the room. The murdered man lay on the floor, his head leaning against the wall, and about him was a pool of blood which poured forth from three large wounds in his breast; there was a fourth gash, in which a long table knife was plunged up to the handle.

"I stumbled over some object; I stooped to examine—it was the second pistol, which had not gone off, probably from the powder being wet. I approached the jeweller, who was not quite dead, and at the sound of my footsteps and the creaking of the floor, he opened his eyes, fixed them on one with an anxious and inquiring gaze, moved his lips as though trying to speak, then, overcome by the effort, fell back and expired. This appalling sight almost bereft me of my senses, and finding that I could no longer be of service to any one in the house, my only desire was to fly. I rushed towards the staircase, clutching my hair and uttering a groan of horror. Upon reaching the room below, I found five or six custom-house officers, and two or three gendarmes—all heavily armed. They threw themselves upon me. I made no resistance; I was no longer master of my senses. When I strove to speak, a few inarticulate sounds alone escaped my lips.

"As I noticed the significant manner in which the whole party pointed to my blood-stained garments, I involuntarily surveyed myself, and then I discovered that the thick warm drops that had so bedewed me as I lay beneath the staircase must have been the blood of La Carconte. I pointed to the spot where I had concealed myself. 'What does he mean?' asked a gendarme. One of the officers went to the place. I directed. 'He means,' replied the man upon his return, 'that he got in that way;' and he showed the hole I had made when I broke through.

"Then I saw that they took me for the assassin. I recovered force and energy enough to free myself from the hands of those who held me, while I managed to stammer forth—'I did not do it! Indeed, indeed I did not!' A couple of gendarmes held the muzzles of their carbines against my breast.—'Stir but a step,' said they, 'and you are a dead man.'—'Why should you threaten me with death,' cried I, 'when I have already declared my innocence?'—'Tush, tush,' cried the men; 'keep your innocent stories to tell to the judge at Nîmes. Meanwhile, come along with us; and the best advice we can give you is to do so unresistingly.' Alas, resistance was far from my thoughts. I was utterly overpowered by surprise and terror; and without a word I suffered myself to be handcuffed and tied to a horse's tail, and thus they took me to Nîmes.

"I had been tracked by a customs-officer, who had lost sight of me near the tavern; feeling certain that I intended to pass the night there, he had returned to summon his comrades, who just arrived in time to hear the report of the pistol, and to take me in the midst of such circumstantial proofs of my guilt as rendered all hopes of proving my innocence utterly futile. One only chance was left me, that of beseeching the magistrate before whom I was taken to cause every inquiry to be made for the Abbé Busoni, who had stopped at the inn of the Pont du Gard on that morning. If Caderousse had invented the story relative to the diamond, and there existed no such person as the Abbé Busoni, then, indeed. I was lost past redemption, or, at least, my life hung upon the feeble chance of Caderousse himself being apprehended and confessing the whole truth. Two months passed away in hopeless expectation on my part, while I must do the magistrate the justice to say that he used every means to obtain information of the person I declared could exculpate me if he would. Caderousse still evaded all pursuit, and I had resigned myself to what seemed my inevitable fate. My trial was to come on at the approaching assizes; when, on the 8th of September—that is to say, precisely three months and five days after the events which had perilled my life—the Abbé Busoni, whom I never ventured to believe I should see, presented himself at the prison doors, saying he understood one of the prisoners wished to speak to him; he added, that having learned at Marseilles the particulars of my imprisonment, he hastened to comply with my desire. You may easily imagine with what eagerness I welcomed him, and how minutely I related the whole of what I had seen and heard. I felt some degree of nervousness as I entered upon the history of the diamond, but, to my inexpressible astonishment, he confirmed it in every particular, and to my equal surprise, he seemed to place entire belief in all I said. And then it was that, won by his mild charity, seeing that he was acquainted with all the habits and customs of my own country, and considering also that pardon for the only crime of which I was really guilty might come with a double power from lips so benevolent and kind, I besought him to receive my confession, under the seal of which I recounted the Auteuil affair in all its details, as well as every other transaction of my life. That which I had done by the impulse of my best feelings produced the same effect as though it had been the result of calculation. My voluntary confession of the assassination at Auteuil proved to him that I had not committed that of which I stood accused. When he quitted me, he bade me be of good courage, and to rely upon his doing all in his power to convince my judges of my innocence.

"I had speedy proofs that the excellent abbé was engaged in my behalf, for the rigors of my imprisonment were alleviated by many trifling though acceptable indulgences, and I was told that my trial was to be postponed to the assizes following those now being held. In the interim it pleased providence to cause the apprehension of Caderousse, who was discovered in some distant country, and brought back to France, where he made a full confession, refusing to make the fact of his wife's having suggested and arranged the murder any excuse for his own guilt. The wretched man was sentenced to the galleys for life, and I was immediately set at liberty."

"And then it was, I presume," said Monte Cristo, "that you came to me as the bearer of a letter from the Abbé Busoni?"—"It was, your excellency; the benevolent abbé took an evident interest in all that concerned me.

"'Your mode of life as a smuggler,' said he to me one day, 'will be the ruin of you; if you get out, don't take it up again.'—'But how,' inquired I, 'am I to maintain myself and my poor sister?'

"'A person, whose confessor I am,' replied he, 'and who entertains a high regard for me, applied to me a short time since to procure him a confidential servant. Would you like such a post? If so, I will give you a letter of introduction to him.'—'Oh, father,' I exclaimed, 'you are very good.'

"'But you must swear solemnly that I shall never have reason to repent my recommendation.' I extended my hand, and was about to pledge myself by any promise he would dictate, but he stopped me. 'It is unnecessary for you to bind yourself by any vow,' said he; 'I know and admire the Corsican nature too well to fear you. Here, take this,' continued he, after rapidly writing the few lines I brought to your excellency, and upon receipt of which you deigned to receive me into your service, and proudly I ask whether your excellency has ever had cause to repent having done so?"— "No," replied the count; "I take pleasure in saying that you have served me faithfully, Bertuccio; but you might have shown more confidence in me."—"I, your excellency?"—"Yes; you. How comes it, that having both a sister and an adopted son, you have never spoken to me of either?"—"Alas, I have still to recount the most distressing period of my life. Anxious as you may suppose I was to behold and comfort my dear sister, I lost no time in hastening to Corsica, but when I arrived at Rogliano I found a house of mourning, the consequences of a scene so horrible that the neighbors remember and speak of it to this day. Acting by my advice, my poor sister had refused to comply with the unreasonable demands of Benedetto, who was continually tormenting her for money, as long as he believed there was a sou left in her possession. One morning that he had demanded money, threatening her with the severest consequences if she did not supply him with what he desired, he disappeared and remained away all day, leaving the kind-hearted Assunta, who loved him as if he were her own child, to weep over his conduct and bewail his absence. Evening came, and still, with all the patient solicitude of a mother, she watched for his return.

"As the eleventh hour struck, he entered with a swaggering air, attended by two of the most dissolute and reckless of his boon companions. She stretched out her arms to him, but they seized hold of her, and one of the three—none other than the accursed Benedetto exclaimed,—'Put her to torture and she'll soon tell us where her money is.'

"It unfortunately happened that our neighbor, Vasilio, was at Bastia, leaving no person in his house but his wife; no human creature beside could hear or see anything that took place within our dwelling. Two held poor Assunta, who, unable to conceive that any harm was intended to her, smiled in the face of those who were soon to become her executioners. The third proceeded to barricade the doors and windows, then returned, and the three united in stifling the cries of terror incited by the sight of these preparations, and then dragged Assunta feet foremost towards the brazier, expecting to wring from her an avowal of where her supposed treasure was secreted. In the struggle her clothes caught fire, and they were obliged to let go their hold in order to preserve themselves from sharing the same fate. Covered with flames, Assunta rushed wildly to the door, but it was fastened; she flew to the windows, but they were also secured; then the neighbors heard frightful shrieks; it was Assunta calling for help. The cries died away in groans, and next morning, as soon as Vasilio's wife could muster up courage to venture abroad, she caused the door of our dwelling to be opened by the public authorities, when Assunta, although dreadfully burnt, was found still breathing; every drawer and closet in the house had been forced open, and the money stolen. Benedetto never again appeared at Rogliano, neither have I since that day either seen or heard anything concerning him.

"It was subsequently to these dreadful events that I waited on your excellency, to whom it would have been folly to have mentioned Benedetto, since all trace of him seemed entirely lost; or of my sister, since she was dead."—"And in what light did you view the occurrence?" inquired Monte Cristo.—"As a punishment for the crime I had committed," answered Bertuccio. "Oh, those Villeforts are an accursed race!"—"Truly they are," murmured the count in a lugubrious tone.

"And now," resumed Bertuccio, "your excellency may, perhaps, be able to comprehend that this place, which I revisit for the first time—this garden, the actual scene of my crime—must have given rise to reflections of no very agreeable nature, and produced that gloom and depression of spirits which excited the notice of your excellency, who was pleased to express a desire to know the cause. At this instant a shudder passes over me as I reflect that possibly I am now standing on the very grave in which lies M. de Villefort, by whose hand the ground was dug to receive the corpse of his child."—"Everything is possible," said Monte Cristo, rising from the bench on which he had been sitting; "even," he added in an inaudible voice, "even that the procureur be not dead. The Abbé Busoni did right to send you to me," he went on in his ordinary tone, "and you have done well in relating to me the whole of your history, as it will prevent my forming any erroneous opinions concerning you in future. As for that Benedetto, who so grossly belied his name, have you never made any effort to trace out whither he has gone, or what has become of him?"

"No; far from wishing to learn whither he has betaken himself, I should shun the possibility of meeting him as I would a wild beast. Thank God, I have never heard his name mentioned by any person, and I hope and believe he is dead."—"Do not think so, Bertuccio," replied the count; "for the wicked are not so easily disposed of, for God seems to have them under his special watch-care to make of them instruments of his vengeance."

"So be it," responded Bertuccio, "all I ask of heaven is that I may never see him again. And now, your excellency," he added, bowing his head, "you know everything—you are my judge on earth, as the Almighty is in heaven; have you for me no words of consolation?"—"My good friend, I can only repeat the words addressed to you by the Abbé Busoni. Villefort merited punishment for what he had done to you, and, perhaps, to others. Benedetto, if still living, will become the instrument of divine retribution in some way or other, and then be duly punished in his turn. As far as you yourself are concerned, I see but one point in which you are really guilty. Ask yourself, wherefore, after rescuing the infant from its living grave, you did not restore it to its mother? There was the crime, Bertuccio—that was where you became really culpable."

"True, excellency, that was the crime, the real crime, for in that I acted like a coward. My first duty, directly I had succeeded in recalling the babe to life, was to restore it to its mother; but, in order to do so, I must have made close and careful inquiry, which would, in all probability, have led to my own apprehension; and I clung to life, partly on my sister's account, and partly from that feeling of pride inborn in our hearts of desiring to come off untouched and victorious in the execution of our vengeance. Perhaps, too, the natural and instinctive love of life made me wish to avoid endangering my own. And then, again, I am not as brave and courageous as was my poor brother." Bertuccio hid his face in his hands as he uttered these words, while Monte Cristo fixed on him a look of inscrutable meaning. After a brief silence, rendered still more solemn by the time and place, the count said, in a tone of melancholy wholly unlike his usual manner, "In order to bring this conversation to a fitting termination (the last we shall ever hold upon this subject), I will repeat to you some words I have heard from the lips of the Abbé Busoni. For all evils there are two remedies—time and silence. And now leave me, Monsieur Bertuccio, to walk alone here in the garden. The very circumstances which inflict on you, as a principal in the tragic scene enacted here, such painful emotions, are to me, on the contrary, a source of something like contentment, and serve but to enhance the value of this dwelling in my estimation. The chief beauty of trees consists in the deep shadow of their umbrageous boughs, while fancy pictures a moving multitude of shapes and forms flitting and passing beneath that shade. Here I have a garden laid out in such a way as to afford the fullest scope for the imagination, and furnished with thickly grown trees, beneath whose leafy screen a visionary like myself may conjure up phantoms at will. This to me, who expected but to find a blank enclosure surrounded by a straight wall, is I assure you, a most agreeable surprise. I have no fear of ghosts, and I have never heard it said that so much harm had been done by the dead during six thousand years as is wrought by the living in a single day. Retire within, Bertuccio, and tranquilize your mind. Should your confessor be less indulgent to you in your dying moments than you found the Abbé Busoni, send for me, if I am still on earth, and I will soothe your ears with words that shall effectually calm and soothe your parting soul ere it goes forth to traverse the ocean called eternity."

Bertuccio bowed respectfully, and turned away, sighing heavily. Monte Cristo, left alone, took three or four steps onwards, and murmured, "Here, beneath this plane-tree, must have been where the infant's grave was dug. There is the little door opening into the garden. At this corner is the private staircase communicating with the sleeping apartment. There will be no necessity for me to make a note of these particulars, for there, before my eyes, beneath my feet, all around me, I have the plan sketched with all the living reality of truth." After making the tour of the garden a second time, the count re-entered his carriage, while Bertuccio, who perceived the thoughtful expression of his master's features, took his seat beside the driver without uttering a word. The carriage proceeded rapidly towards Paris.

That same evening, upon reaching his abode in the Champs Elysées, the Count of Monte Cristo went over the whole building with the air of one long acquainted with each nook or corner. Nor, although preceding the party, did he once mistake one door for another, or commit the smallest error when choosing any particular corridor or staircase to conduct him to a place or suite of rooms he desired to visit. Ali was his principal attendant during this nocturnal survey. Having given various orders to Bertuccio relative to the improvements and alterations he desired to make in the house, the count, drawing out his watch, said to the attentive Nubian, "It is half-past eleven o'clock; Haidee will soon be here. Have the French attendants been summoned to await her coming?" Ali extended his hands towards the apartments destined for the fair Greek, which were so effectually concealed by means of a tapestried entrance, that it would have puzzled the most curious to have divined their existence. Ali, having pointed to the apartments, held up three fingers of his right hand, and then, placing it beneath his head, shut his eyes, and feigned to sleep. "I understand," said Monte Cristo, well acquainted with Ali's pantomime; "you mean to tell me that three female attendants await their new mistress in her sleeping-chamber." Ali, with considerable animation, made a sign in the affirmative.

"Madame will be tired to-night," continued Monte Cristo, "and will, no doubt, wish to rest. Desire the French attendants not to weary her with questions, but merely to pay their respectful duty and retire. You will also see that the Greek servants hold no communication with those of this country." Ali bowed. Just at that moment voices were heard hailing the concierge. The gate opened, a carriage rolled down the avenue, and stopped at the steps. The count hastily descended, presented himself at the already opened carriage door, and held out his hand to a young woman, completely enveloped in a green silk mantle heavily embroidered with gold. She raised the hand extended towards her to her lips, and kissed it with a mixture of love and respect. Some few words passed between them in that sonorous language in which Homer makes his gods converse. The young woman spoke with an expression of deep tenderness, while the count replied with an air of gentle gravity. Preceded by Ali, who carried a rose-colored flambeau in his hand, the new-comer, who was no other than the lovely Greek who had been Monte Cristo's companion in Italy, was conducted to her apartments; while the count retired to the pavilion reserved for himself. In another hour every light in the house was extinguished, and it might have been thought that all its inmates slept.

XLVI

Unlimited Credit

ABOUT TWO O'CLOCK THE following day a calash, drawn by a pair of magnificent English horses, stopped at the door of Monte Cristo, and a person dressed in a blue coat, with buttons of a similar color, a white waistcoat, over which was displayed a massive gold chain, brown trousers, and a quantity of black hair descending so low over his eyebrows as to leave it doubtful whether it were not artificial, so little did its jetty glossiness assimilate with the deep wrinkles stamped on his features—a person, in a word, who, although evidently past fifty, desired to be taken for not more than forty, bent forwards from the carriage door, on the panels of which were emblazoned the armorial bearings of a baron, and directed his groom to inquire at the porter's lodge whether the Count of Monte Cristo resided there, and if he were within. While waiting, the occupant of the carriage surveyed the house, the garden as far as he could distinguish it, and the livery of servants who passed to and fro, with an attention so close as to be somewhat impertinent. His glance was keen, but showed cunning rather than intelligence; his lips were straight, and so thin that, as they closed, they were drawn in over the teeth; his cheekbones were broad and projecting, a never-failing proof of audacity and craftiness: while the flatness of his forehead, and the enlargement of the back of his skull, which rose much higher than his large and coarsely shaped ears, combined to form a phys-iognomy anything but prepossessing, save in the eyes of such as con-sidered that the owner of so splendid an equipage must needs be all that was admirable and enviable, more especially when they gazed on the enormous diamond that glittered in his shirt, and the red ribbon that depended from his button-hole.

The groom, in obedience to his orders, tapped at the window of the porter's lodge, saying, "Pray, does not the Count of Monte Cristo live here?"—"His excellency does reside here," replied the concierge; "but"—added he, glancing an inquiring look at Ali. Ali returned a sign in the negative. "But what?" asked the groom.

"His excellency does not receive visitors to-day."—"Then here is my master's card,—the Baron Danglars. You will take it to the count, and say that, although in haste to attend the Chamber, my master came out of his way to have the honor of calling upon him."

"I never speak to his excellency," replied the concierge; "the valet de chamber will carry your message." The groom returned to the carriage. "Well?" asked Danglars. The man, somewhat crestfallen by the rebuke he had received, repeated what the concierge had said. "Bless me," murmured Baron Danglars, "this must surely be a prince instead of a count by their styling him 'excellency,' and only venturing to address him by the medium of his valet de chamber. However, it does not signify; he has a letter of credit on me, so I must see him when he requires his money."

Then throwing himself back in his carriage, Danglars called out to his coachman, in a voice that might be heard across the road, "To the Chamber of Deputies."

Apprised in time of the visit paid him, Monte Cristo had, from behind the blinds of his pavilion, as minutely observed the baron, by means of an excellent lorgnette, as Danglars himself had scruti-nized the house, garden, and servants. "That fellow has a decidedly bad countenance," said the count in a tone of disgust, as he shut up his glass into its ivory case. "How comes it that all do not retreat in aversion at sight of that flat, receding, serpent-like forehead, round, vulture-shaped head, and sharp-hooked nose, like the beak of a buzzard? Ali," cried he, striking at the same time on the brazen gong. Ali appeared. "Summon Bertuccio," said the count. Almost immediately Bertuccio entered the apartment. "Did your excellency desire to see me?" inquired he. "I did," replied the count. "You no doubt observed the horses standing a few minutes since at the door?"—"Certainly, your excellency. I noticed them for their remarkable beauty."

"Then how comes it," said Monte Cristo with a frown, "that, when I desired you to purchase for me the finest pair of horses to be found in Paris, there is another pair, fully as fine as mine, not in my stables?" At the look of displeasure, added to the angry tone in which the count spoke, Ali turned pale and held down his head. "It is not your fault, my good Ali," said the count in the Arabic language, and with a gentleness none would have thought him capable of showing, either in voice or face—"it is not your fault. You do not understand the points of English horses." The countenance of poor Ali recovered its serenity. "Permit me to assure your excellency," said Bertuccio, "that the horses you speak of were not to be sold when I purchased yours." Monte Cristo shrugged his shoulders. "It seems, sir steward," said he, "that you have yet to learn that all things are to be sold to such as care to pay the price."

"His excellency is not, perhaps, aware that M. Danglars gave 16,000 francs for his horses?"—"Very well. Then offer him double that sum; a banker never loses an opportunity of doubling his capital."

"Is your excellency really in earnest?" inquired the steward. Monte Cristo regarded the person who durst presume to doubt his words with the look of one equally surprised and displeased. "I have to pay a visit this evening," replied he. "I desire that these horses, with completely new harness, may be at the door with my carriage." Bertuccio bowed, and was about to retire; but when he reached the door, he paused, and then said, "At what o'clock does your excellency wish the carriage and horses to be ready?"—"At five o'clock," replied the count.

"I beg your excellency's pardon," interposed the steward in a deprecating manner, "for venturing to observe that it is already two o'clock."

"I am perfectly aware of that fact," answered Monte Cristo calmly. Then, turning towards Ali, he said, "Let all the horses in my stables be led before the windows of your young lady, that she may select those she prefers for her carriage. Request her also to oblige me by saying whether it is her pleasure to dine with me; if so, let dinner be served in her apartments. Now leave me, and desire my valet de chambre to come hither." Scarcely had Ali disappeared when the valet entered the chamber. "Monsieur Baptistin," said the count, "you have been in my service one year, the time I generally give myself to judge of the merits of demerits of those about me. You suit me very well." Baptistin bowed low. "It only remains for me to know whether I also suit you?"—"Oh, your excellency!" exclaimed Baptistin eagerly.

"Listen, if you please, till I have finished speaking," replied Monte Cristo. "You receive 1,500 francs per annum for your services here—more than many a brave subaltern, who continually risks his life for his country, obtains. You live in a manner far superior to many clerks who work ten times harder than you do for their money. Then, though yourself a servant, you have other servants to wait upon you, take care of your clothes, and see that your linen is duly prepared for you. Again, you make a profit upon each article you purchase for my toilet, amounting in the course of a year to a sum equalling your wages."—"Nay, indeed, your excellency."

"I am not condemning you for this, Monsieur Baptistin; but let your profits end here. It would be long indeed ere you would find so lucrative a post as that you have now the good fortune to fill. I neither ill-use nor ill-treat my servants by word or action. An error I readily forgive, but wilful negligence or forgetfulness, never. My commands are ordinarily short, clear, and precise; and I would rather be obliged to repeat my words twice, or even three times, than they should be misunderstood. I am rich enough to know whatever I desire to know, and I can promise you I am not wanting in curiosity. If, then, I should learn that you had taken upon yourself to speak of me to any one favorably or unfavorably, to comment on my actions, or watch my conduct, that very instant you would quit my service. You may now retire. I never caution my servants a second time—remember that." Baptistin bowed, and was proceeding towards the door. "I forgot to mention to you," said the count, "that I lay yearly aside a certain sum for each servant in my establishment; those whom I am compelled to dismiss lose (as a matter of course) all participation in this money, while their portion goes to the fund accumulating for those domestics who remain with me, and among whom it will be divided at my death. You have been in my service a year, your fund has already begun to accumulate—let it continue to do so."

This address, delivered in the presence of Ali, who, not understanding one word of the language in which it was spoken, stood wholly unmoved, produced an effect on M. Baptistin only to be conceived by such as have occasion to study the character and disposition of French domestics. "I assure your excellency," said he, "that at least it shall be my study to merit your approbation in all things, and I will take M. Ali as my model."—"By no means," replied the count in the most frigid tones; "Ali has many faults mixed with most excellent qualities. He cannot possibly serve you as a pattern for your conduct, not being, as you are, a paid servant, but a mere slave—a dog, who, should he fail in his duty towards me, I should not discharge from my service, but kill." Baptistin opened his eyes with astonishment.

"You seem incredulous," said Monte Cristo, who repeated to Ali in the Arabic language what he had just been saying to Baptistin in French. The Nubian smiled assentingly to his master's words, then, kneeling on one knee, respectfully kissed the hand of the count. This corroboration of the lesson he had just received put the finishing stroke to the wonder and stupefaction of M. Baptistin. The count then motioned the valet de chambre to retire, and to Ali to follow to his study, where they conversed long and earnestly together. As the hand of the clock pointed to five the count struck thrice upon his gong. When Ali was wanted one stroke was given, two summoned Baptistin, and three Bertuccio. The steward entered. "My horses," said Monte Cristo.

"They are at the door harnessed to the carriage as your excellency desired. Does your excellency wish me to accompany him?"—"No, the coachman, Ali, and Baptistin will go." The count descended to the door of his mansion, and beheld his carriage drawn by the very pair of horses he had so much admired in the morning as the property of Danglars. As he passed them he said,— "They are extremely handsome certainly, and you have done well to purchase them, although you were somewhat remiss not to have procured them sooner."—"Indeed, your excellency, I had very considerable difficulty in obtaining them, and, as it is, they have cost an enormous price."

"Does the sum you gave for them make the animals less beautiful?" inquired the count, shrugging his shoulders.—"Nay, if your excellency is satisfied, it is all that I could wish. Whither does your excellency desire to be driven?"

"To the residence of Baron Danglars, Rue de la Chaussée d'Antin." This conversation had passed as they stood upon the terrace, from which a flight of stone steps led to the carriage-drive. As Bertuccio, with a respectful bow, was moving away, the count called him back. "I have another commission for you, M. Bertuccio," said he; "I am desirous of having an estate by the seaside in Normandy—for instance, between Havre and Bonlogne. You see I give you a wide range. It will be absolutely necessary that the place you may select have a small harbor, creek, or bay, into which my corvette can enter and remain at anchor. She draws only fifteen feet. She must be kept in constant readiness to sail immediately I think proper to give the signal. Make the requisite inquiries for a place of this description, and when you have met with an eligible spot, visit it, and if it possess the advantages desired, purchase it at once in your own name. The corvette must now, I think, be on her way to Fécamp, must she not?"

"Certainly, your excellency; I saw her put to sea the same evening we quitted Marseilles."—"And the yacht."—"Was ordered to remain at Martigues."—"'Tis well. I wish you to write from time to time to the captains in charge of the two vessels so as to keep them on the alert."—"And the steamboat?"—"She is at Chalons?"—"Yes."—"The same orders for her as for the two sailing vessels."—"Very good."—"When you have purchased the estate I desire, I want constant relays of horses at ten leagues apart along the northern and southern road."—"Your excellency may depend upon me." The count made a gesture of satisfaction, descended the terrace steps, and sprang into his carriage, which was whirled along swiftly to the banker's house. Danglars was engaged at that moment, presiding over a railroad committee. But the meeting was nearly concluded when the name of his visitor was announced. As the count's title sounded on his ear he rose, and addressing his colleagues, who were members of one or the other Chamber, he said,— "Gentlemen, pardon me for leaving you so abruptly; but a most ridiculous circumstance has occurred, which is this,—Thomson & French, the Roman bankers, have sent to me a certain person calling himself the Count of Monte Cristo, and have given him an unlimited credit with me. I confess this is the drollest thing I have ever met with in the course of my extensive foreign transactions, and you may readily suppose it has greatly roused my curiosity. I took the trouble this morning to call on the pretended count,—if he were a real count he wouldn't be so rich. But, would you believe it, 'He was not receiving.' So the master of Monte Cristo gives himself airs befitting a great millionaire or a capricious beauty. I made inquiries, and found that the house in the Champs Elysées is his own property, and certainly it was very decently kept up. But," pursued Danglars with one of his sinister smiles, "an order for unlimited credit calls for something like caution on the part of the banker to whom that order is given. I am very anxious to see this man. I suspect a hoax is intended, but the instigators of it little knew whom they had to deal with. 'They laugh best who laugh last!'"

Having delivered himself of this pompons address, uttered with a degree of energy that left the baron almost out of breath, he bowed to the assembled party and withdrew to his drawing-room, whose sumptuous furnishings of white and gold had caused a great sensation in the Chaussée d'Antin. It was to this apartment he had desired his guest to be shown, with the purpose of overwhelming him at the sight of so much luxury. He found the count standing before some copies of Albano and Fattore that had been passed off to the banker as originals; but which, mere copies as they were, seemed to feel their degradation in being brought into juxtaposition with the gaudy colors that covered the ceiling. The count turned round as he heard the entrance of Danglars into the room. With a slight inclination of the head, Danglars signed to the count to be seated, pointing significantly to a gilded arm-chair, covered with white satin embroidered with gold. The count sat down. "I have the honor, I presume, of addressing M. de Monte Cristo."

The count bowed. "And I of speaking to Baron Danglars, chevalier of the Legion of Honor, and member of the Chamber of Deputies?"

Monte Cristo repeated all the titles he had read on the baron's card.

Danglars felt the irony and compressed his lips. "You will, I trust, excuse me, monsieur, for not calling you by your title when I first addressed you," he said, "but you are aware that we are living under a popular form of government, and that I am myself a representative of the liberties of the people."—"So much so," replied Monte

Cristo, "that while you call yourself baron you are not willing to call anybody else count."

"Upon my word, monsieur," said Danglars with affected carelessness, "I attach no sort of value to such empty distinctions; but the fact is, I was made baron, and also chevalier of the Legion of Honor, in return for services rendered, but"—

"But you have discarded your titles after the example set you by Messrs. de Montmorency and Lafayette? That was a noble example to follow, monsieur."

"Why," replied Danglars, "not entirely so; with the servants,—you understand."—"I see; to your domestics you are 'my lord,' the journalists style you 'monsieur,' while your constituents call you 'citizen.' These are distinctions very suitable under a constitutional government. I understand perfectly." Again Danglars bit his lips; he saw that he was no match for Monte Cristo in an argument of this sort, and he therefore hastened to turn to subjects more congenial.

"Permit me to inform you, count," said he, bowing, "that I have received a letter of advice from Thomson & French, of Rome."

"I am glad to hear it, baron,—for I must claim the privilege of addressing you after the manner of your servants. I have acquired the bad habit of calling persons by their titles from living in a country where barons are still barons by right of birth. But as regards the letter of advice, I am charmed to find that it has reached you; that will spare me the troublesome and disagreeable task of coming to you for money myself. You have received a regular letter of advice?"

"Yes," said Danglars, "but I confess I didn't quite comprehend its meaning."—"Indeed?"

"And for that reason I did myself the honor of calling upon you, in order to beg for an explanation."—"Go on, monsieur. Here I am, ready to give you any explanation you desire."

"Why," said Danglars, "in the letter—I believe I have it about me"—here he felt in his breast-pocket—"yes, here it is. Well, this letter gives the Count of Monte Cristo unlimited credit on our house."

"Well, baron, what is there difficult to understand about that?"

"Merely the term *unlimited*—nothing else, certainly."—"Is not that word known in France? The people who wrote are Anglo-Germans, you know."

"Oh, as for the composition of the letter, there is nothing to be said; but as regards the competency of the document, I certainly have doubts."—"Is it possible?" asked the count, assuming an air and tone of the utmost simplicity and candor. "Is it possible that Thomson & French are not looked upon as safe and solvent bankers? Pray tell me what you think, baron, for I feel uneasy, I can assure you, having some considerable property in their hands."

"Thomson & French are perfectly solvent," replied Danglars, with an almost mocking smile: "but the word *unlimited*, in financial affairs, is so extremely vague."

"Is, in fact, unlimited," said Monte Cristo.

"Precisely what I was about to say," cried Danglars. "Now what is vague is doubtful; and it was a wise man who said, 'when in doubt, keep out.'"

"Meaning to say," rejoined Monte Cristo, "that however Thomson & French may be inclined to commit acts of imprudence and folly, the Baron Danglars is not disposed to follow their example."

"Not at all."

"Plainly enough. Messrs. Thomson & French set no bounds to their engagements, while those of M. Danglars have their limits; he is a wise man, according to his own showing."

"Monsieur," replied the banker, drawing himself up with a haughty air, "the extent of my resources has never yet been questioned."

"It seems, then, reserved for me," said Monte Cristo coldly, "to be the first to do so."—"By what right, sir?"

"By right of the objections you have raised, and the explanations you have demanded, which certainly must have some motive."

Once more Danglars bit his lips. It was the second time he had been worsted, and this time on his own ground. His forced politeness sat awkwardly upon him, and approached almost to impertinence. Monte Cristo, on the contrary, preserved a graceful suavity of demeanor, aided by a certain degree of simplicity he could assume at pleasure, and thus possessed the advantage.

"Well, sir," resumed Danglars, after a brief silence, "I will endeavor to make myself understood, by requesting you to inform me for what sum you propose to draw upon me?"—"Why, truly," replied Monte Cristo, determined not to lose an inch of the ground he had gained, "my reason for desiring an 'unlimited' credit was precisely because I did not know how much money I might need."

The banker thought the time had come for him to take the upper hand. So throwing himself back in his arm-chair, he said, with an arrogant and purse-proud air,—"Let me beg of you not to hesitate in naming your wishes; you will then be convinced that the resources of the house of Danglars, however limited, are still equal to meeting the largest demands; and were you even to require a million"—

"I beg your pardon," interposed Monte Cristo.

"I said a million," replied Danglars, with the confidence of ignorance.

"But could I do with a million?" retorted the count. "My dear sir, if a trifle like that could suffice me, I should never have given myself the trouble of opening an account. A million? Excuse my smiling when you speak of a sum I am in the habit of carrying in my pocket-book or dressing-case." And with these words Monte Cristo took from his pocket a small case containing his visiting cards, and drew forth two orders on the treasury for 500,000 francs each, payable at sight to the bearer. A man like Danglars was wholly inaccessible to any gentler method of correction. The effect of the present revelation was stunning; he trembled and was on the verge of apoplexy. The pupils of his eyes, as he gazed at Moute Cristo, dilated horribly.

"Come, come," said Monte Cristo, "confess honestly that you have not perfect confidence in Thomson & French. I understand,

and foreseeing that such might be the case, I took, in spite of my ignorance of affairs, certain precautions. See, here are two similar letters to that you have yourself received; one from the house of Arstein & Eskeles of Vienna, to Baron Rothschild, the other drawn by Baring of London, upon M. Laffitte. Now, sir, you have but to say the word, and I will spare you all uneasiness by presenting my letter of credit to one or other of these two firms." The blow had struck home, and Danglars was entirely vanquished; with a trembling hand he took the two letters from the count, who held them carelessly between finger and thumb, and proceeded to scrutinize the signatures, with a minuteness that the count might have regarded as insulting, had it not suited his present purpose to mislead the banker. "Oh, sir," said Danglars, after he had convinced himself of the authenticity of the documents he held, and rising as if to salute the power of gold personified in the man before him,— "three letters of unlimited credit! I can be no longer mistrustful, but you must pardon me, my dear count, for confessing to some degree of astonishment."

"Nay," answered Monte Cristo, with the most gentlemanly air, 'tis not for such trifling sums as these that your banking house is to be incommoded. Then, you can let me have some money, can you not?"

"Whatever you say, my dear count; I am at your orders."

"Why," replied Monte Cristo, "since we matually understand each other—for such I presume is the case?" Danglars bowed assentingly. "You are quite sure that not a lurking doubt or suspicion lingers in your mind?"—"Oh, my dear count," exclaimed Danglars, "I never for an instant entertained such a feeling towards you."

"No, you merely wished to be convinced, nothing more; but now that we have come to so clear an understanding, and that all distrust and suspicion are laid at rest, we may as well fix a sum as the probable expenditure of the first year, suppose we say six millions to"—

"Six millions!" gasped Danglars—"so be it."

"Then, if I should require more," continued Monte Cristo in a careless manner, "why, of course, I should draw upon you; but my present intention is not to remain in France more than a year, and during that period I scarcely think I shall exceed the sum I mentioned. However, we shall see. Be kind enough, then, to send me 500,000 francs to-morrow. I shall be at home till midday, or if not, I will leave a receipt with my steward."

"The money you desire shall be at your house by ten o'clock to-morrow morning, my dear count," replied Danglars. "How would you like to have it? in gold, silver, or notes?"—"Half in gold, and the other half in bank-notes, if you please," said the count, rising from his seat.

"I must confess to you, count," said Danglars, "that I have hitherto imagined myself acquainted with the degree of all the great fortunes of Europe, and still wealth such as yours has been wholly unknown to me. May I presume to ask whether you have long possessed it?"—"It has been in the family a very long while," returned Monte Cristo, "a sort of treasure expressly forbidden to be touched for a certain period of years, during which the accumulated interest has doubled the capital. The period appointed by the testator for the disposal of these riches occurred only a short time ago, and they have only been employed by me within the last few years. Your ignorance on the subject, therefore, is easily accounted for. However, you will be better informed as to me and my possessions ere long." And the count, while pronouncing these latter words, accompanied them with one of those ghastly smiles that used to strike terror into poor Franz d'Epinay.

"With your tastes, and means of gratifying them," continued Danglars, "you will exhibit a splendor that must effectually put us poor miserable millionaires quite in the shade. If I mistake not you are an admirer of paintings, at least I judged so from the attention you appeared to be bestowing on mine when I entered the room.

If you will permit me, I shall be happy to show you my picture gallery, composed entirely of works by the ancient masters—warranted as such. Not a modern picture among them. I cannot endure the modern school of painting."—"You are perfectly right in objecting to them, for this one great fault—that they have not yet had time to become old."

"Or will you allow me to show you several fine statues by Thor-waldsen, Bartoloni, and Canova?—all foreign artists, for, as you may perceive, I think but very indifferently of our French sculptors."

"You have a right to be unjust to them, monsieur; they are your compatriots."

"But all this may come later, when we shall be better known to each other. For the present, I will confine myself (if perfectly agreeable to you) to introducing you to the Baroness Danglars—excuse my impatience, my dear count, but a client like you is almost like a member of the family." Monte Cristo bowed, in sign that he accepted the proffered honor; Danglars rang and was answered by a servant in a showy livery. "Is the baroness at home?" inquired Danglars.—"Yes, my lord," answered the man.

"And alone?"—"No, my lord, madame has visitors."

"Have you any objection to meet any persons who may be with madame, or do you desire to preserve a strict *incognito*?"—"No, indeed," replied Monte Cristo with a smile, "I do not arrogate to myself the right of so doing."

"And who is with madame?—M. Debray?" inquired Danglars, with an air of indulgence and good-nature that made Monte Cristo smile, acquainted as he was with the secrets of the banker's domestic life.

"Yes, my lord," replied the servant, "M. Debray is with madame." Danglars nodded his head; then, turning to Monte Cristo, said, "M. Lucien Debray is an old friend of ours, and private secretary to the Minister of the Interior. As for my wife, I must tell you, she lowered herself by marrying me, for she belongs to one of the most ancient families in France. Her maiden name was De Servières, and her first husband was Colonel the Marquis of Nargonne."

"I have not the honor of knowing Madame Danglars; but I have already met M. Lucien Debray."—"Ah, indeed?" said Danglars; "and where was that?"—"At the house of M. de Morcerf."—"Ah, ha, you are acquainted with the young viscount, are you?"—"We were together a good deal during the Carnival at Rome."—"True, true," cried Danglars. "Let me see; have I not heard talk of some strange adventure with bandits or thieves hid in ruins, and of his having had a miraculous escape? I forget how, but I know he used to amuse my wife and daughter by telling them about it after his return from Italy."

"Her ladyship is waiting to receive you, gentlemen," said the servant, who had gone to inquire the pleasure of his mistress. "With your permission," said Danglars, bowing, "I will precede you, to show you the way."

"By all means," replied Monte Cristo; "I follow you."

XLVII

The Dappled Grays

THE BARON, FOLLOWED BY the count, traversed a long series of apartments, in which the prevailing characteristics were heavy magnificence and the gaudiness of ostentations wealth, until he reached the bondoir of Madame Danglars—a small octagonal-shaped room, hung with pink satin, covered with white Indian muslin. The chairs were of ancient workmanship and materials; over the doors were painted sketches of shepherds and shepherdesses, after the style and manner of Boucher; and at each side pretty medallions in crayons, harmonizing well with the furnishings of this charming apartment, the only one throughout the great mansion in which any distinctive taste prevailed. The truth was, it had been entirely overlooked in the plan arranged and followed out by M. Danglars and his architect, who had been selected to aid the baron in the great work of improvement solely because he was the most fashionable and celebrated decorator of the day. The decorations of the boudoir had then been left entirely to Madame Danglars and Lucien Debray. M. Danglars, however, while possessing a great admiration for the antique, as it was understood during the time of the Directory, entertained the most sovereign contempt for the simple elegance of his wife's favorite sitting-room, where, by the way, he was never permitted to intrude, unless, indeed, he excused his own appearance by ushering in some more agreeable visitor than himself; and even then he had rather the air and manner of a person who was himself introduced, than that of being the presenter of another, his reception being cordial or frigid, in proportion as the person who accompanied him chanced to please or displease the baroness.

Madame Danglars (who, although past the first bloom of youth, was still strikingly handsome) was now seated at the piano, a most elaborate piece of cabinet and inlaid work, while Lucien Debray, standing before a small work-table, was turning over the pages of an album. Lucien had found time, preparatory to the count's arrival, to relate many particulars respecting him to Madame Danglars. It will be remembered that Monte Cristo had made a lively impression on the minds of all the party assembled at the breakfast given by Albert de Morcerf; and although Debray was not in the habit of yielding to such feelings, he had never been able to shake off the powerful influence excited in his mind by the impressive look and manner of the count, consequently the description given by Lucien to the baroness bore the highly-colored tinge of his own heated imagination. Already excited by the wonderful stories related of the count by De Morcerf, it is no wonder that Madame Danglars eagerly listened to, and fully credited, all the additional circumstances detailed by Debray. This posing at the piano and over the album was only a little ruse adopted by way of precaution. A most gracious welcome and unusual smile were bestowed on M. Danglars; the count, in return for his gentlemanly bow, received a formal though graceful courtesy, while Lucien exchanged with the count a sort of distant recognition, and with Danglars a free and easy nod.

"Baroness," said Danglars, "give me leave to present to you the Count of Monte Cristo, who has been most warmly recommended to me by my correspondents at Rome. I need but mention one fact to make all the ladies in Paris court his notice, and that is, that he has come to take up his abode in Paris for a year, during which brief period he proposes to spend six millions of money. That means balls, dinners, and lawn parties without end, in all of which I trust the count will remember us, as he may depend upon it we shall him, in our own humble entertainments." In spite of the gross flattery and coarseness of this address. Madame Dauglars could not forbear gazing with considerable interest on a man capable of expending six millions in twelve months, and who had selected Paris for the scene of his princely extravagance. "And when did you arrive here?" inquired she.

"Yesterday morning, madame."—"Coming, as usual, I presume, from the extreme end of the globe? Pardon me—at least such I have heard is your custom."

"Nay, madame. This time I have merely come from Cadiz."

"You have selected almost unfavorable moment for your first visit. Paris is a horrible place in summer. Balls, parties, and fêtes are over; the Italian opera is in London; the French opera everywhere except in Paris. As for the Théâtre Français, you know, of course, that it is nowhere. The only amusements left us are the indifferent races at the Champ de Mars and Satory. Do you propose entering any horses at either of these races, count?"

"I shall do whatever they do at Paris, madame, if I have the good fortune to find some one who will initiate me into the prevalent ideas of amusement."

"Are you fond of horses, count?"

"I have passed a considerable part of my life in the East, madame, and you are doubtless aware that the Orientals value only two things—the fine breeding of their horses and the beauty of their women."—"Nay, count," said the baroness, "it would have been somewhat more gallant to have placed the ladies first."

"You see, madame, how rightly I spoke when I said I required a preceptor to guide me in all my sayings and doings here." At this instant the favorite attendant of Madame Danglars entered the boudoir; approaching her mistress, she spoke some words in an

undertone. Madame Danglars turned very pale, then exclaimed,—
"I cannot believe it; the thing is impossible."

"I assure you, madame." replied the woman, "it is as I have said." Turning impatiently towards her husband, Madame Danglars demanded, "Is this true?"

"Is what true, madame?" inquired Danglars, visibly agitated.

"What my maid tells me."—"But what does she tell you?"

"That when my coachman was about to harness the horses to my carriage, he discovered that they had been removed from the stables without his knowledge. I desire to know what is the meaning of this?"

"Be kind enough, madame, to listen to me," said Danglars.

"Oh, yes; I will listen, monsieur, for I am most curious to hear what explanation you will give. These two gentlemen shall decide between us; but, first, I will state the case to them. Gentlemen," continued the baroness, "among the ten horses in the stables of Baron Danglars, are two that belong exclusively to me—a pair of the handsomest and most spirited creatures to be found in Paris. But to you, at least, M. Debray, I need not give a further description, because to you my beautiful pair of dappled grays were well known. Well, I had promised Madame de Villefort the loan of my carriage to drive to-morrow to the Bois; but when my coachman goes to fetch the grays from the stables they are gone—positively gone. No doubt M. Danglars has sacrificed them to the selfish consideration of gaining some thousands of paltry francs. Oh, what a detestable crew they are, these mercenary speculators!"

"Madame," replied Danglars, "the horses were not sufficiently quiet for you; they were scarcely four years old, and they made me extremely uneasy on your account."

"Nonsense," retorted the baroness; "you could not have entertained any alarm on the subject, because you are perfectly well aware that I have had for a month in my service the very best coachman in Paris. But, perhaps, you have disposed of the coachman as well as the horses?"

"My dear love, pray do not say any more about them, and I promise you another pair exactly like them in appearance, only more quiet and steady." The baroness shrugged her shoulders with an air of ineffable contempt, while her husband, affecting not to observe this unconjugal gesture, turned towards Monte Cristo, and said,—"Upon my word, count, I am quite sorry not to have met you sooner. You are setting up an establishment, of course?"

"Why, yes," replied the count.

"I should have liked to have made you the offer of these horses. I have almost given them away, as it is; but, as I before said, I was anxious to get rid of them upon any terms. They were only fit for a young man."

"I am much obliged by your kind intentions towards me," said Monte Cristo; "but this morning I purchased a very excellent pair of a carriage-horses, and I do not think they were dear. There they are. Come, M. Debray, you are a connoisseur, I believe, let me have your opinion upon them." As Debray walked towards the window, Danglars approached his wife. "I could not tell you before others," said he in a low tone, "the reason of my parting with the horses; but a most enormous price was offered me this morning for them. Some madman or fool, bent upon ruining himself as fast as he can, actually sent his steward to me to purchase them at any cost; and the fact is, I have gained 16,000 francs by the sale of them. Come, don't look so angry, and you shall have 4,000 francs of the money to do what you like with, and Engénie shall have 2,000. There, what do you think now of the affair? Wasn't I right to part with the horses?" Madame Danglars surveyed her husband with a look of withering contempt.

"Great heavens?" suddenly exclaimed Debray.

"What is it?" asked the baroness.

"I cannot be mistaken; there are your horses! The very animals were were speaking of, harnessed to the count's carriage!"—"My dappled grays?" demanded the baroness, springing to the window. "'Tis indeed they!" said she. Danglars looked absolutely stupefied. "How very singular," cried Monte Cristo with well-feigned astonishment.

"I cannot believe it," murmured the banker. Madame Danglars whispered a few words in the ear of Debray, who approached Monte Cristo, saying, "The baroness wishes to know what you paid her husband for the horses."

"I scarcely know," replied the count; "it was a little surprise prepared for me by my steward, and cost me—well, somewhere about 30,000 francs." Debray conveyed the count's reply to the baroness. Poor Danglars looked so crestfallen and discomfited that Monte Cristo assumed a pitying air towards him. "See," said the count, "how very ungrateful women are. Your kind attention, in providing for the safety of the baroness by disposing of the horses, does not seem to have made the least impression on her. But so it is; a woman will often, from mere willfulness, prefer that which is dangerous to that which is safe. Therefore, in my opinion, my dear baron, the best and easiest way is to leave them to their fancies, and allow them to act as they please, and then, if any mischief follows, why, at least, they have no one to blame but themselves." Danglars made no reply; he was occupied in anticipations of the coming scene between himself and the baroness, whose frowning brow, like that of Olympic Jove, predicted a storm. Debray, who perceived the gathering clouds, and felt no desire to witness the explosion of Madame Danglars' rage, suddenly recollected an appointment, which compelled him to take his leave; while Monte Cristo, unwilling by prolonging his stay to destroy the advantages he hoped to obtain, made a farewell bow and departed, leaving Danglars to endure the angry reproaches of his wife.

"Excellent," murmured Monte Cristo to himself, as he came away. "All has gone according to my wishes. The domestic peace of this family is henceforth in my hands. Now, then, to play another master-stroke, by which I shall gain the heart of both husband and wife—delightful! Still," added he, "amid all this, I have not yet been presented to Mademoiselle Eugénie Danglars, whose acquaintance

I should have been glad to make. But," he went on with his peculiar smile, "I am here in Paris, and have plenty of time before me—by and by will do for that." With these reflections he entered his carriage and returned home. Two hours afterwards, Madame Danglars received a most flattering epistle from the count, in which he entreated her to receive back her favorite "dappled grays," protesting that he could not endure the idea of making his entry into the Parisian world of fashion with the knowledge that his splendid equipage had been obtained at the price of a lovely woman's regrets. The horses were sent back wearing the same harness she had seen on them in the morning; only, by the count's orders, in the centre of each rosette that adorned either side of their heads, had been fastened a large diamond.

To Danglars Monte Cristo also wrote, requesting him to excuse the whimsical gift of a capricious millionaire, and to beg the baroness to pardon the Eastern fashion adopted in the return of the horses.

During the evening, Monte Cristo quitted Paris for Auteuil, accompanied by Ali. The following day, about three o'clock, a single blow struck on the gong summoned Ali to the presence of the count. "Ali," observed his master, as the Nubian entered the chamber, "you have frequently explained to me how more than commonly skilful you are in throwing the lasso, have you not?" Ali drew himself up proudly, and then returned a sign in the affirmative. "I thought I did not mistake. With your lasso you could stop an ox?" Again Ali repeated his affirmative gesture. "Or a tiger?" Ali bowed his head in token of assent. "A lion even?" Ali sprung forwards, imitating the action of one throwing the lasso; then of a strangled lion.

"I understand," said Monte Cristo; "you wish to tell me you have hunted the lion?" Ali smiled with triumphant pride as he signified that he had indeed both chased and captured many lions. "But do you believe you could arrest the progress of two horses rushing forwards with ungovernable fury?" The Nubian smiled. "It is well," said Monte Cristo. "Then listen to me. Ere long a carriage will dash past here, drawn by the pair of dappled gray horses you saw me with yesterday; now, at the risk of your own life, you must manage to stop those horses before my door."

Ali descended to the street, and a marked a straight line on the pavement immediately at the entrance of the house, and then pointed out the line he had traced to the count, who was watching him. The count patted him gently on the shoulder, his usual mode of praising Ali, who, pleased and gratified with the commission assigned him, walked calmly towards a projecting stone forming the angle of the street and house, and, seating himself thereon, began to smoke his chibouque, while Monte Cristo re-entered his dwelling, perfectly assured of the success of his plan. Still, as five o'clock approached, and the carriage was momentarily expected by the count, the indication of more than common impatience and uneasiness might be observed in his manner. He stationed himself in a room commanding a view of the street, pacing the chamber with restless steps, stopping merely to listen from time to time for the sound of approaching wheels, then to cast an anxious glance on Ali; but the regularity with which the Nubian puffed forth the smoke of his chibouque proved that he at least was wholly absorbed in the enjoyment of his favorite occupation. Suddenly a distant sound of rapidly advancing wheels was heard, and almost immediately a carriage appeared, drawn by a pair of wild, ungovernable horses, while the terrified coachman strove in vain to restrain their furious speed.

In the vehicle was a young woman and a child of about seven or eight clasped in each other's arms. Terror seemed to have deprived them even of the power of uttering a cry. The carriage creaked and rattled as it flew over the rough stones, and the slightest obstacle under the wheels would have caused disaster; but it kept on in the middle of the road, and those who saw it pass uttered cries of terror.

Ali suddenly cast aside his chibouque, drew the lasso from his pocket, threw it so skilfully as to catch the forelegs of the near horse in its triple fold, and suffered himself to be dragged on for a few steps by the violence of the shock, then the animal fell over on the pole, which snapped, and therefore prevented the other horse from pursuing its way. Gladly availing himself of this opportunity, the coachman leaped from his box; but Ali had promptly seized the nostrils of the second horse, and held them in his iron grasp, till the breast, snorting with pain, sunk beside his companion. All this was achieved in much less time than is occupied in the recital. The brief space had, however, been sufficient for a man, followed by a number of servants, to rush from the house before which the accident had occurred, and, as the coachman opened the door of the carriage, to take from it a lady who was convulsively grasping the cushions with one hand, while with the other she pressed to her bosom the young boy, who had lost consciousness.

Monte Cristo carried them both to the salon, and deposited them on a sofa. "Compose yourself, madame," said he; "all danger is over." The woman looked up at these words, and, with a glance far more expensive than any entreaties could have been, pointed to her child, who still continued insensible. "I understand the nature of your alarms, madame," said the count, carefully examining the child, "but I assure you there is not the slightest occasion for uneasiness; your little charge has not received the least injury; his insensibility is merely the effects of terror, and will soon pass."—"Are you quite sure you do not say so to tranquillize my fears? See how deadly pale he is! My child, my darling Edward; speak to your mother—open your dear eyes and look on me once again! Oh, sir, in pity send for a physician; my whole fortune shall not be thought too much for the recovery of my boy."

With a calm smile and a gentle wave of the hand, Monte Cristo signed to the distracted mother to lay aside her apprehensions; then, opening a casket that stood near, he drew forth a phial of Bohemian glass incrusted with gold, containing a liquid of the color of blood, of which he let fall a single drop on the child's lips. Scarcely had it reached them, ere the boy, though still pale as marble, opened his eyes, and eagerly gazed around him. At this, the delight of the mother was almost frantic. "Where am I?" exclaimed she; "and to whom am I indebted for so happy a termination to my late dreadful alarm?"—"Madame," answered the count, "you are under the roof of one who esteems himself most fortunate in having been able to save you from a further continuance of your sufferings."

"My wretched curiosity has brought all this about." pursued the lady. "All Paris rung with the praises of Madame Danglars' beautiful horses, and I had the folly to desire to know whether they really merited the high praise given to them."—"Is it possible," exclaimed the count with well-feigned astonishment, "that these horses belong to the baroness?"

"They do, indeed. May I inquire if you are acquainted with Madame Danglars?"

"I have that honor; and my happiness at your escape from the danger that threatened you is redoubled by the consciousness that I have been the unwilling and the unintentional cause of all the peril you have incurred. I yesterday purchased these horses of the baron; but as the baroness evidently regretted parting with them, I ventured to send them back to her, with a request that she would gratify me by accepting them from my hands."

"You are, then, doubtless, the Count of Monte Cristo, of whom Hermine has talked to me so much?"

"You have rightly guessed, madame," replied the count.

"And I am Madame Héloise de Villefort." The count bowed with the air of a person who hears a name for the first time. "How grateful will M. de Villefort be for all your goodness; "How thankfully will he acknowledge that to you alone he owes the existence of his wife and child! Most certainly, but for the prompt assistance of your intrepid servant, this dear child and myself must both have perished."— "Indeed, I still shudder at the fearful danger you were placed in."

"I trust you will allow me to recompense worthily the devotion of your man."

"I beseech you, madame," replied Monte Cristo, "not to spoil Ali, either by too great praise or rewards. I cannot allow him to acquire the habit of expecting to be recompensed for every trifling service he may render. Ali is my slave, and in saving your life he was but discharging his duty to me."

"Nay," interposed Madame de Villefort, on whom the authoritative style adopted by the count made a deep impression, "nay, but consider that to preserve my life he has risked his own."

"His life, madame, belongs not to him; it is mine, in return for my having myself saved him from death." Madame de Villefort made no further reply; her mind was utterly absorbed in the contemplation of the person who, from the first instant she saw him, had made so powerful an impression on her. During the evident preoccupation of Madame de Villefort, Monte Cristo scrutinized the features and appearance of the boy she kept folded in her arms, lavishing on him the most tender endearments. The child was small for his age, and unnaturally pale. A mass of straight black hair, defying all attempts to train or curl it, fell over his projecting forehead, and hung down to his shoulders, giving increased vivacity to eyes already sparkling with a youthful love of mischief and foundness for every forbidden enjoyment. His mouth was large, and the lips, which had not yet regained their color, were particularly thin; in fact, the deep and crafty look, giving a predominant expression to the child's face, belonged rather to a boy of twelve or fourteen than to one so young. His first movement was to free himself by a violent push from the encircling arms of his mother, and to rush forward to the casket from whence the count had taken the phial of elixir; then, without asking permission of any one, he proceeded, in all the willfulness of a spoiled child unaccustomed to restrain either whims or caprices, to pull the corks out of all the bottles.

"Touch nothing, my little friend," cried the count eagerly; "some of those liquids are not only dangerous to taste, but even to inhale."

Madame de Villefort became very pale, and seizing her son's

arm, drew him anxiously toward her; but, once satisfied of his safety, she also cast a brief but expressive glance on the casket, which was not lost upon the count. At this moment Ali entered. At sight of him Madame de Villefort uttered an expression of pleasure, and, holding the child still closer towards her, she said, "Edward, dearest, do you see that good man? He has shown very great courage and resolution, for he exposed his own life to stop the horses that were running away with us, and would certainly have dashed the carriage to pieces. Thank him, then, my child, in your very best manner; for, had he not come to our aid, neither you nor I would have been alive to speak our thanks." The child stuck out his lips and turned away his head in a disdainful manner, saying, "He's too ugly."

The count smiled as if the child bade fair to realize his hopes, while Madame de Villefort reprimanded her son with a gentleness and moderation very far from conveying the least idea of a fault having been committed. "This lady," said the count, speaking to Ali in the Arabic language, "is desirous that her son should thank you for saving both their lives; but the boy refuses, saying you are too ugly." Ali turned his intelligent countenance towards the boy, on whom he gazed without any apparent emotion; but the spasmodic working of the nostrils showed to the practised eye of Monte Cristo that the Arab had been wounded to the heart.

"Will you permit me to inquire," said Madame de Villefort, as she arose to take her leave, "whether you usually reside here?"

"No, I do not," replied Monte Cristo; "it is a small place I have purchased quite lately. My place of abode is No. 30, Avenue des Champs Elysées; but I see you have quite recovered from your fright, and are, no doubt, desirous of returning home. Anticipating your wishes, I have desired the same horses you came with to be put to one of my carriages, and Ali, he whom you think so very ugly," continued he, addressing the boy with a smiling air, "will have the honor of driving you home, while your coachman remains here to attend to the necessary repairs of your calash. As soon as that important business is concluded, I will have a pair of my own horses harnessed to convey it direct to Madame Danglars."

"I dare not return with those dreadful horses," said Madame de Villefort.

"You will see," replied Monte Cristo, "that they will be as different as possible in the hands of Ali. With him they will be gentle and docile as lambs." Ali had, indeed, given proof of this; for, approaching the animals, who had been got upon their legs with considerable difficulty, he rubbed their foreheads and nostrils with a sponge soaked in aromatic vinegar, and wiped off the sweat and foam that covered their mouths. Then, commencing a loud whistling noise, he rubbed them well all over their bodies for several minutes; then, undisturbed by the noisy crowd collected round the broken carriage, Ali quietly harnessed the pacified animals to the count's chariot, took the reins in his hands, and mounted the box, when to the utter astonishment of those who had witnessed the ungovernable spirit and maddened speed of the same horses, he was actually compelled to apply his whip in no very gentle manner before he could induce them to start; and even then all that could be obtained from the celebrated "dappled grays," now changed into a couple of dull, sluggish, stupid brutes, was a slow, pottering pace, kept up with so much difficulty that Madame de Villefort was more than two hours returning to her residence in the Faubourg St. Honoré.

Scarcely had the first congratulations upon her marvellous escape been gone through when she wrote the following letter to Madame Danglars:—

DEAR HERMINE,—I have just had a wonderful escape from the most imminent danger, and I owe my safety to the very Count of Monte Cristo we were talking about yesterday, but whom I little expected to see to-day. I remember how unmercifully I laughed at what I considered your eulogistic and exaggerated praises of him; but I have now ample cause to admit that your enthusiastic description of this wonderful man fell far short of his merits. Your horses got as far as Ranelagh, when they darted forward like mad things, and galloped away at so fearful a rate, that there seemed no other prospect for myself and my poor Edward but that of being dashed to pieces against the first object that impeded their progress, when a strange-looking man,—an Arab, a negro, or a Nubian, at least a black of some nation or other,—at a signal from the count, whose domestic he is, suddenly seized and stopped the infuriated animals, even at the risk of being trampled to death himself; and certainly he must have had a most wonderful escape. The count then hastened to us, and took us into his house, where he speedily recalled my poor Edward to life. He sent us home in his own carriage. Yours will be returned to you to-morrow. You will find your horses in bad condition, from the results of this accident; they seem thoroughly stupefied, as if sulky and vexed at having been conquered by man. The count, however, has commissioned me to assure you that two or three days' rest, with plenty of barley for their sole food during that time, will bring them back to as fine, that is as terrifying, a condition as they were in yesterday. Adieu! I cannot return you many thanks for the drive of yesterday; but, after all, I ought not to blame you for the misconduct of your horses, more especially as it procured me the pleasure of an introduction to the Count of Monte Cristo,—and certainly that illustrious personage, apart from the millions he is said to be so very anxious to dispose of, seemed to me one of those curiously interesting problems I, for one, delight in solving at any risk, even if it were to necessitate another drive to the Bois behind your horses. Edward endured the accident with miraculous courage—he did not utter a single cry, but fell lifeless into my arms; nor did a tear fall from his eyes after it was over. I doubt not you will consider these praises the result of blind maternal affection; but there is a soul of iron in that delicate, fragile body. Valentine sends many affectionate remembrances to your dear Eugénie. I embrace you with all my heart.

HÉLOÏSE DE VILLEFORT.

P.S.—Do pray contrive some means for me to meet the Count of Monte Cristo at your house. I must and will see him again. I have just made M. de Villefort promise to call on him, and I hope the visit will be returned.

That night the adventure at Auteuil was talked of everywhere. Albert related it to his mother; Château-Renaud recounted it at the Jockey Club, and Debray detailed it at length in the salons of the minister; even Beauchamp accorded twenty lines in his journal to the relation of the count's courage and gallantry, thereby celebrating him as the greatest hero of the day in the eyes of all the feminine members of the aristocracy. Vast was the crowd of visitors and inquiring friends who left their names at the residence of Madame de Villefort, with the design of renewing their visit at the right moment, of hearing from her lips all the interesting circumstances of this most romantic adventure. As for M. de Villefort, he fulfilled the predictions of Héloïse to the letter,—donned his dress suit, drew on a pair of white gloves, ordered the servants to attend the carriage dressed in their full livery, and drove that same night to No. 30 in the Avenue des Champs-Elysées.

XLVIII

Ideology

I F THE COUNT OF MONTE Cristo had been for a long time familiar with the ways of Parisian society, he would have appreciated better the significance of the step which M. de Villefort had taken. Standing well at court, whether the king regnant was of the elder or younger branch, whether the government was doctrinaire, liberal, or conservative; looked upon by all as a man of talent, since those who have never experienced a political check are generally so regarded; hated by many, but warmly supported by others, without being really liked by anybody, M. de Villefort held a high position in the magistracy, and maintained his eminence like a Harlay or a Molé. His drawing-room, under the regenerating influence of a young wife and a daughter by his first marriage, scarcely eighteen, was still one of the well-regulated Paris salons where the worship of traditional customs and the observance of rigid etiquette were carefully maintained. A freezing politeness, a strict fidelity to government principles, a profound contempt for theories and theorists, a deep-seated hatred of ideality,—these were the elements of private and public life displayed by M. de Villefort.

He was not only a magistrate, he was almost a diplomatist. His relations with the former court, of which he always spoke with dignity and respect, made him respected by the new one, and he knew so many things, that not only was he always carefully considered, but sometimes consulted. Perhaps this would not have been so had it been possible to get rid of M. de Villefort; but, like the feudal barons who rebelled against their sovereign, he dwelt in an impregnable fortress. This fortress was his post as king's attorney, all the advantages of which he exploited with marvellous skill, and which he would not have resigned but to be made deputy, and thus to replace neutrality by opposition. Ordinarily M. de Villefort made and returned very few visits. His wife visited for him, and this was the received thing in the world, where the weighty and multifarious occupations of the magistrate were accepted as an excuse for what was really only calculated pride, a manifestation of professed superiority—in fact, the application of the axiom, "Pretend to think well of yourself, and the world will think well of you," an axiom a hundred times more useful in society nowadays than that of the Greeks, "Know thyself," a knowledge for which, in our days, we have substituted the less difficult and more advantageous science of knowing others.

To his friends M. de Villefort was a powerful protector; to his enemies, he was a silent, but bitter opponent; for those who were neither the one nor the other, he was a statue of the law-made man. He had a haughty bearing, a look either steady and impenetrable or insolently piercing and inquisitorial. Four successive revolutions had built and cemented the pedestal upon which his fortune was based. M. de Villefort had the reputation of being the least curious and the least wearisome man in France. He gave a ball every year, at which he appeared for a quarter of an hour only,—that is to say, five and forty minutes less than the king is visible at his balls. He was never seen at the theatres, at concerts, or in any place of public resort. Occasionally, but seldom, he played at whist, and then care was taken to select partners worthy of him—sometimes they were ambassadors, sometimes archbishops, or sometimes a prince, or a president, or some dowager duchess. Such was the man whose carriage had just now stopped before the Count of Monte Cristo's door. The valet de chambre announced M. de Villefort at the moment when the count, leaning over a large table, was tracing on a map the route from St. Petersburg to China.

The procureur entered with the same grave and measured step he would have employed in entering a court of justice. He was the same man, or rather the development of the same man, whom we have heretofore seen as assistant attorney at Marseilles. Nature, according to her way, had made no deviation in the path he had marked out for himself. From being slender he had now become meagre; once pale, he was now yellow; his deep-set eyes were hollow, and the gold spectacles shielding his eyes seemed to be an integral portion of his face. He dressed entirely in black, with the exception of his white tie, and his funeral appearance was only mitigated by the slight line of red ribbon which passed almost imperceptibly through his button-hole, and appeared like a streak of blood traced with a delicate brush. Although master of himself, Monte Cristo scrutinized with irrepressible curiosity the magistrate whose salute he returned, and who, distrustful by habit, and especially incredulous as to social prodigies, was much more disposed to look upon "the noble stranger," as Monte Cristo was already called, as an adventurer in search of new fields, or an escaped criminal, rather than as a prince of the Holy See, or a sultan of the Thousand and One Nights.

"Sir," said Villefort, in the squeaky tone assumed by magistrates in their oratorical periods, and of which they cannot, or will not, divest themselves in society, "sir, the signal service which you yesterday rendered to my wife and son has made it a duty for me to offer you my thanks. I have come, therefore, to discharge this duty, and to express to you my overwhelming gratitude." And as he said this, the "eye severe" of the magistrate had lost nothing of its habitual arrogance. He spoke in a voice of the procureur-general, with the rigid inflexibility of neck and shoulders which caused his flatterers to say (as we have before observed) that he was the living statue of the law.

"Monsieur," replied the count, with a chilling air, "I am very happy to have been the means of preserving a son to his mother, for they say that the sentiment of maternity is the most holy of all; and the good fortune which occurred to me, monsieur, might have enabled you to dispense with a duty which, in its discharge, confers an undoubtedly great honor; for I am aware that M. de Villefort is not usually lavish of the favor which he now bestows on me,—a favor which, however estimable, is unequal to the satisfaction which I have in my own consciousness." Villefort, astonished at this reply, which he by no means expected, started like a soldier who feels the blow levelled at him over the armor he wears, and a curl of his disdainful lip indicated that from that moment he noted in the tablets of his brain that the Count of Monte Cristo was by no means a highly bred gentleman. He glanced around, in order to seize on something on which the conversation might turn, and seemed to fall easily on a topic. He saw the map which Monte Cristo had been examining when he entered, and said, "You seem geographically engaged, sir? It is a rich study for you, who, as I learn, have seen as many lands as are delineated on this map."—"Yes, sir," replied the count; "I have sought to make of the human race, taken in the mass, what you practise every day on individuals—a physiological study. I have believed it was much easier to descend from the whole to a part than to ascend from a part to the whole. It is an algebraic axiom, which makes us proceed from a known to an unknown quantity, and not from an unknown to a known; but sit down, sir, I beg of you."

Monte Cristo pointed to a chair, which the procureur was obliged to take the trouble to move forwards himself, while the count merely fell back into his own, on which he had been kneeling when M. Villefort entered. Thus the count was halfway turned towards his visitor, having his back towards the window, his elbow resting on the geographical chart which furnished the theme of conversation for the moment,—a conversation which assumed, as in the case of the interviews with Danglars and Morcerf, a turn analogous to the persons, if not to the situation. "Ah, you philosophize," replied Villefort, after a moment's silence, during which, like a wrestler who encounters a powerful opponent, he took breath; "well, sir, really, if, like you, I had nothing else to do, I should seek a more amusing occupation."—"Why, in truth, sir," was Monte Cristo's reply, "man is but an ugly caterpillar for him who studies him through a solar microscope; but you said, I think, that I had nothing else to do. Now, really, let me ask, sir, have you?—do you believe you have anything to do? or to speak in plain terms, do you really think that what you do deserves being called anything?"

Villefort's astonishment redoubled at this second thrust so forcibly made by his strange adversary. It was a long time since the magistrate had heard a paradox so strong, or rather, to say the truth more exactly, it was the first time he had ever heard of it. The procureur exerted himself to reply. "Sir," he responded, "you are a stranger, and I believe you say yourself that a portion of your life has been spent in Oriental countries, so you are not aware how human justice, so expeditious in barbarous countries, takes with us a prudent and well-studied course."—"Oh, yes—yes, I do, sir; it is the *pede claudo* of the ancients. I know all that, for it is with the justice of all countries especially that I have occupied myself—it is with the criminal procedure of all nations that I have compared natural justice, and I must say, sir, that it is the law of primitive nations, that is, the law of retaliation, that I have most frequently found to be according to the law of God."

"If this law were adopted, sir," said the procureur, "it would greatly simplify our legal codes, and in that case the magistrates would not (as you just observed) have much to do."— "It may, perhaps, come to this in time," observed Monte Cristo; "you know that human inventions march from the complex to the simple, and simplicity is always perfection."

"In the meanwhile," continued the magistrate, "our codes are in full force, with all their contradictory enactments derived from Gallic customs, Roman laws, and Frank usages; the knowledge of all which, you will agree, is not to be acquired without extended labor; it needs tedious study to acquire this knowledge, and, when acquired, a strong power of brain to retain it."—"I agree with you entirely, sir; but all that even you know with respect to the French code, I know, not only in reference to that code, but as regards the codes of all nations. The English, Turkish, Japanese, Hindu laws, are as familiar to me as the French laws, and thus I was right, when I said to you, that relatively (you know that everything is relative, sir)—that relatively to what I have done, you have very little to do; but that relatively to all I have learned, you have yet a great deal to learn."

"But with what motive have you learned all this?" inquired Villefort, in astonishment. Monte Cristo smiled. "Really, sir," he observed, "I see that in spite of the reputation which you have acquired as a superior man, you look at everything from the material and vulgar view of society, beginning with man, and ending with man—that is to say, in the most restricted, most narrow view which it is possible for human understanding to embrace."—"Pray, sir, explain yourself," said Villefort, more and more astonished, "I really do—not—understand you—perfectly."

"I say, sir, that with the eyes fixed on the social organization of nations, you see only the springs of the machine, and lose sight of the sublime workman who makes them act; I say that you do not recognize before you and around you any but those office-holders whose commissions have been signed by a minister or king; and that the men whom God has put above those office-holders, ministers, and kings, by giving them a mission to follow out, instead of a post to fill—I say that they escape your narrow, limited field of observation. It is thus that human weakness fails, from its debilitated and imperfect organs. Tobias took the angel who restored him to light for an ordinary young man. The nations took Attila, who was doomed to destroy them, for a conqueror similar to other conquerors, and it was necessary for both to reveal their missions, that they might be known and acknowledged; one was compelled to say, 'I am the angel of the Lord'; and the other, 'I am the hammer of God,' in order that the divine essence in both might be revealed."—"Then," said Villefort, more and more amazed, and really supposing he was speaking to a mystic or a madman, "you consider yourself as one of those extraordinary beings whom you have mentioned?"

"And why not?" said Monte Cristo coldly.

"Your pardon, sir," replied Villefort, quite astounded, "but you will excuse me if, when I presented myself to you, I was unaware that I should meet with a person whose knowledge and understanding so far surpass the usual knowledge and understanding of men. It is not usual with us corrupted wretches of civilization to find gentlemen like yourself, possessors, as you are, of immense fortune—at least, so it is said —and I beg you to observe that I do not inquire, I merely repeat;—it is not usual, I say, for such privileged and wealthy beings to waste their time in speculations on the state of society, in philosophical reveries, intended at best to console those whom fate has disinherited from the goods of this world."

"Really, sir," retorted the count, "have you attained the eminent situation in which you are, without having admitted, or even without having met with exceptions? and do you never use your eyes, which must have acquired so much finesse and certainty, to divine, at a glance, the kind of man by whom you are confronted? Should not a magistrate be not merely the best administrator of the law, but the most crafty expounder of the chicanery of his profession, a steel probe to search hearts, a touchstone to try the gold which in each soul is mingled with more or less of alloy?"

"Sir," said Villefort, "upon my word, you overcome me. I really never heard a person speak as you do."

"Because you remain eternally encircled in a round of general conditions, and have never dared to raise your wings into those upper spheres which God has peopled with invisible or exceptional beings."——"And you allow then, sir, that spheres exist, and that these marked and invisible beings mingle amongst us?"

"Why should they not? Can you see the air you breathe, and yet without which you could not for a moment exist?"

"Then we do not see those beings to whom you allude?"

"Yes, we do; you see them whenever God pleases to allow them to assume a material form. You touch them, come in contact with them, speak to them, and they reply to you."

"Ah," said Villefort, smiling, "I confess I should like to be warned when one of these beings is in contact with me."

"You have been served as you desire, monsieur, for you were warned just now, and I now again warn you."

"Then you yourself are one of these marked beings?"

"Yes, monsieur, I believe so; for until now, no man has found himself in a position similar to mine. The dominions of kings are limited either by mountains or rivers, or a change of manners, or an alteration of language. My kingdom is bounded only by the world, for I am not an Italian, or a Frenchman, or a Hindu, or an American, or a Spaniard—I am a cosmopolite. No country can say it saw my birth. God alone knows what country will see me die. I adopt all customs, speak all languages. You believe me to be a Frenchman, for I speak French with the same facility and purity as yourself. Well, Ali, my Nubian, believes me to be an Arab; Bertuccio, my steward, takes me for a Roman; Haidee, my slave, thinks me a Greek. You may, therefore, comprehend, that being of no country, asking no protection from any government, acknowledging no man as my brother, not one of the scruples that arrest the powerful, or the obstacles which paralyze the weak, paralyzes or arrests me. I have only two adversaries—I will not say two conquerors, for with perseverance I subdue even them,—they are time and distance. There is a third, and the most terrible—that is my condition as a mortal being. This alone can stop me in my onward career, before I have attained the goal at which I aim, for all the rest I have reduced to mathematical terms. What men call the chances of fate—namely, ruin, change, circumstances—I have fully anticipated, and if any of these should overtake me, yet it will not overwhelm me. Unless I die, I shall always be what I am, and therefore it is that I utter the things you have never heard, even from the mouths of kings—for kings have need, and other persons have fear of you. For who is there who does not say to himself, in a society as incongruously organized as ours, 'Perhaps some day I shall have to do with the king's attorney'?"

"But can you not say that, sir? The moment you become an inhabitant of France, you are naturally subjected to the French law."—"I know it, sir," replied Monte-Cristo; "but when I visit a country I begin to study, by all the means which are available, the men from whom I may have anything to hope or to fear, till I know them as well as, perhaps better than, they know themselves. It follows from this, that the king's attorney, be he who he may, with whom I should have to deal, would assuredly be more embarrassed than I should."

"That is to say," replied Villefort with hesitation, "that human nature being weak, every man, according to your creed, has committed faults."—"Faults or crimes," responded Monte Cristo with a negligent air.

"And that you alone, amongst the men whom you do not recognize as your brothers—for you have said so," observed Villefort in a tone that faltered somewhat—"you alone are perfect."

"No, not perfect," was the count's reply; "only impenetrable, that's all. But let us leave off this strain, sir, if the tone of it is displeasing to you; I am no more disturbed by your justice than are you by my second-sight."

"No, no,—by no means," said Villefort, who was afraid of seeming to abandon his ground. "No; by your brilliant and almost sublime conversation you have elevated me above the ordinary level; we no longer talk, we rise to dissertation. But you know how the theologians in their collegiate chairs, and philosophers in their controversies, occasionally say cruel truths; let us suppose for the moment that we are theologizing in a social way, or even philosophically, and I will say to you, rude as it may seem, 'My brother, you sacrifice greatly to pride; you may be above others, but above you there is God.'"

"Above us all, sir," was Monte Cristo's response, in a tone and with an emphasis so deep, that Villfort involuntarily shuddered. "I have my pride for men—serpents always ready to threaten every one who would pass without crushing them under foot. But I lay aside that pride before God, who has taken me from nothing to make me what I am."

"Then, count, I admire you," said Villefort, who, for the first time in this strange conversation, used the aristocratic form to the unknown personage, whom, until now, he had only called monsieur. "Yes, and I say to you, if you are really strong, really superior, really pious, or impenetrable, which you were right in saying amounts to the same thing—then be proud, sir, for that is the characteristic of predominance. Yet you have unquestionably some ambition."

"I have, sir."—"And what may it be?"

"I too, as happens to every man once in his life, have been taken by Satan into the highest mountain in the earth, and when there he showed me all the kingdoms of the world, and as he said before, so said he to me, 'Child of earth, what wouldst thou have to make thee adore me?' I reflected long, for a gnawing ambition had long preyed upon me, and then I replied, 'Listen,—I have always heard of providence, and yet I have never seen him, or anything that resembles him, or which can make me believe that he exists. I wish to be providence myself, for I feel that the most beautiful, noblest, most sublime thing in the world, is to recompense and punish.' Satan bowed his head, and groaned. 'You mistake,' he said, 'providence does exist, only you have never seen him, because the child of God is as invisible as the parent. You have seen nothing that resembles him, because he works by secret springs, and moves by hidden ways. All I can do for you is to make you one of the agents of that providence.' The bargain was concluded. I may sacrifice my soul, but what matters it?" added Monte Cristo. "If the thing were to do again, I would again do it." Villefort looked at Monte Cristo with extreme amazement. "Count," he inquired, "have you any relations?"—"No, sir, I am alone in the world."

"So much the worse."—"Why?" asked Monte Cristo.

"Because then you might witness a spectacle calculated to break down your pride. You say you fear nothing but death?"

"I did not say that I feared it; I only said that death alone could check the execution of my plans."—"And old age?"

"My end will be achieved before I grow old."—"And madness?"

"I have been nearly mad; and you know the axiom,—*non bis in idem*. It is an axiom of criminal law, and, consequently, you understand its full application."—"Sir," continued Villefort, "there is something to fear besides death, old age, and madness. For instance, there is apoplexy—that lightning-stroke which strikes but does not destroy you, and yet which brings everything to an end. You are still yourself as now, and yet you are yourself no longer; you who, like Ariel, verge on the angelic, are but an inert mass, which, like Caliban, verges on the brutal; and this is called in human tongues, as I tell you, neither more nor less than apoplexy. Come, if so you will, count, and continue this conversation at my house, any day you may be willing to see an adversary capable of understanding and anxious to refute you, and I will show you my father, M. Noirtier de Villefort, one of the most fiery Jacobins of the French Revolution; that is to say, he had the most remarkable audacity, seconded by a most powerful organization—a man who has not, perhaps, like yourself seen all the kingdoms of the earth, but who has helped to overturn one of the greatest; in fact, a man who believed himself, like you, one of the envoys, not of God, but of a supreme being; not of providence, but of fate. Well, sir, the rupture of a blood-vessel on the lobe of the brain has destroyed all this, not in a day, not in an hour, but in a second. M. Noirtier, who, on the previous night, was the old Jacobin, the old senator, the old Carbonaro, laughing at the guillotine, the cannon, and the dagger—M. Noirtier, playing with revolutions—M. Noirtier, for whom France was a vast chess-board, from which pawns, rooks, knights, and queens were to disappear, so that the king was checkmated—M. Noirtier, the redoubtable, was the next morning 'poor M. Noirtier,' the helpless old man, at the tender mercies of the weakest creature in the household, that is, his grandchild, Valentine; a dumb and frozen carcass, in fact, living painlessly on, that time may be given for his frame to decompose without his consciousness of its decay."

"Alas, sir," said Monte Cristo, "this spectacle is neither strange to my eye nor my thought. I am something of a physician, and have, like my fellows, sought more than once for the soul in living and in dead matter; yet, like providence, it has remained invisible to my eyes, although present to my heart. A hundred writers since Socrates, Seneca, St. Augustine, and Gall, have made, in verse and prose, the comparison you have made, and yet I can well understand that a father's sufferings may effect great changes in the mind of a son. I will call on you, sir, since you bid me contemplate, for the advantage of my pride, this terrible spectacle, which must have been so great a source of sorrow to your family."

"It would have been so unquestionably, had not God given me so large a compensation. In contrast with the old man, who is dragging his way to the tomb, are two children just entering into life—Valentine, the daughter by my first wife—Mademoiselle Renée de Saint-Méran—and Edward, the boy whose life you have this day saved."

"And what is your deduction from this compensation, sir?" inquired Monte Cristo.—"My deduction is," replied Villefort, "that my father, led away by his passions, has committed some fault unknown to human justice, but marked by the justice of God. That

God, desirous in his mercy to punish but one person, has visited this justice on him alone." Monte Cristo, with a smile on his lips, uttered in the depths of his soul a groan which would have made Villefort fly had he but heard it. "Adieu, sir," said the magistrate, who had risen from his seat; "I leave you, bearing a remembrance of you—a remembrance of esteem, which I hope will not be disagreeable to you when you know me better; for I am not a man to bore my friends, as you will learn. Besides, you have made an eternal friend of Madame de Villefort." The count bowed, and contented himself with seeing Villefort to the door of his cabinet, the procureur being escorted to his carriage by two footmen, who, on a signal from their master, followed him with every mark of attention. When he had gone, Monte Cristo breathed a profound sigh, and said,—"Enough of this poison, let me now seek the antidote." Then sounding his bell, he said to Ali, who entered, "I am going to madam's chamber—have the carriage ready at one o'clock."

XLIX

Haidee

I T WILL BE RECOLLECTED that the new, or rather old, acquaintances of the Count of Monte Cristo, residing in the Rue Meslay, were no other than Maximilian, Julie, and Emmanuel. The very anticipations of delight to be enjoyed in his forthcoming visits—the bright, pure gleam of heavenly happiness it diffused over the almost deadly warfare in which he had voluntarily engaged, illumined his whole countenance with a look of ineffable joy and calmness, as, immediately after Villefort's departure, his thoughts flew back to the cheering prospect before him, of tasting, at least, a brief respite from the fierce and stormy passions of his mind. Even Ali, who had hastened to obey the count's summons, went forth from his master's presence in charmed amazement at the unusual animation and pleasure depicted on features ordinarily so stern and cold; while, as though dreading to put to flight the agreeable ideas hovering over his patron's meditations, whatever they were, the faithful Nubian walked on tiptoe towards the door, holding his breath, lest its faintest sound should dissipate his master's happy reverie.

It was noon, and Monte Cristo had set apart one hour to be passed in the apartments of Haidee, as though his oppressed spirit

required a gradual succession of calm and gentle emotions to prepare his mind to receive full and perfect happiness, in the same
manner as ordinary natures demand to be inured by degrees to the
reception of strong or violent sensations. The young Greek, as we
have already said, occupied apartments wholly unconnected with
those of the count. The rooms had been fitted up in strict accordance with Oriental ideas; the floors were covered with the richest
carpets Turkey could produce; the walls hung with brocaded silk of
the most magnificent designs and texture; while around each chamber luxurious divans were placed, with piles of soft and yielding
cushions, that needed only to be arranged at the pleasure or con-
venience of such as sought repose. Haidee had three French maids,
and one who was a Greek. The first three remained constantly in a
small waiting-room, ready to obey the summons of a small golden
bell, or to receive the orders of the Romaic slave, who knew just
enough French to be able to transmit her mistress's wishes to the
three other waiting-women; the latter had received most peremp-
tory instructions from Monte Cristo to treat Haidee with all the
deference they would observe to a queen.

The young girl herself generally passed her time in the chamber
at the farther end of her apartments. This was a sort of boudoir, circular, and lighted only from the roof, which consisted of rose-colored
glass. Haidee was reclining upon soft downy cushions, covered with
blue satin spotted with silver; her head, supported by one of her
exquisitely moulded arms, rested on the divan immediately behind
her, while the other was employed in adjusting to her lips the coral
tube of a rich narghile, through whose flexible pipe she drew the
smoke fragrant by its passage through perfumed water. Her attitude,
though perfectly natural for an Eastern woman, would, in a European, have been deemed too full of coquettish straining after effect.
Her dress, which was that of the women of Epirus, consisted of a pair

of white satin trousers, embroidered with pink roses, displaying feet so exquisitely formed and so delicately fair, that they might well have been taken for Parian marble, had not the eye been undeceived by their movements as they constantly shifted in and out of a pair of little slippers with upturned toes, beautifully ornamented with gold and pearls. She wore a blue and white-striped vest, with long open sleeves, trimmed with silver loops and buttons of pearls, and a sort of bodice, which, closing only from the centre to the waist, exhibited the whole of the ivory throat and upper part of the bosom; it was fastened with three magnificent diamond clasps. The junction of the bodice and drawers was entirely concealed by one of the many-colored scarfs, whose brilliant hues and rich silken fringe have rendered them so precious in the eyes of Parisian belles. Tilted on one side of her head she had a small cap of gold-colored silk, embroidered with pearls; while on the other a purple rose mingled its glowing colors with the luxuriant masses of her hair, of which the blackness was so intense that it was tinged with blue. The extreme beauty of the countenance, that shone forth in loveliness that mocked the vain attempts of dress to augment it, was peculiarly and purely Grecian; there were the large, dark, melting eyes, the finely formed nose, the coral lips, and pearly teeth, that belonged to her race and country. And, to complete the whole, Haidee was in the very springtide and fulness of youthful charms—she had not yet numbered more than twenty summers.

Monte Cristo summoned the Greek attendant, and bade her inquire whether it would be agreeable to her mistress to receive his visit. Haidee's only reply was to direct her servant by a sign to withdraw the tapestried curtain that hung before the door of her boudoir, the framework of the opening thus made serving as a sort of border to the graceful tableau presented by the young girl's picturesque attitude and appearance. As Monte Cristo approached, she leaned upon the elbow of the arm that held the narghile, and extending to him her other hand, said, with a smile of captivating sweetness, in the sonorous language spoken by the women of Athens and Sparta, "Why demand permission ere you enter? Are you no longer my master, or have I ceased to be your slave?" Monte Cristo returned her smile. "Haidee," said he, "you well know."—"Why do you address me so coldly—so distantly?" asked the young Greek. "Have I by any means displeased you? Oh, if so, punish me as you will; but do not—do not speak to me in tones and manner so formal and constrained."

"Haidee," replied the count, "you know that you are now in France, and are free."

"Free to do what?" asked the young girl.

"Free to leave me."

"Leave you? Why should I leave you?"—"That is not for me to say; but we are now about to mix in society—to visit and be visited."

"I don't wish to see anybody but you."—"And should you see one whom you could prefer, I would not be so unjust"—

"I have never seen any one I preferred to you, and I have never loved any one but you and my father."—"My poor child," replied Monte Cristo, "that is merely because your father and myself are the only men who have ever talked to you."

"I don't want anybody else to talk to me. My father said I was his 'joy'—you style me your 'love,'—and both of you have called me 'my child.'"—"Do you remember your father, Haidee?" The young Greek smiled. "He is here, and here," said she, touching her eyes and her heart. "And where am I?" inquired Monte Cristo laughingly.

"You?" cried she, with tones of thrilling tenderness, "you are everywhere!" Monte Cristo took the delicate hand of the young girl in his, and was about to raise it to his lips, when the simple child of nature hastily withdrew it, and presented her cheek. "You now understand, Haidee," said the count, "that from this moment you are absolutely free; that here you exercise unlimited sway, and are at liberty to lay aside or continue the costume of your country, as it may suit your inclination. Within this mansion you are absolute mistress of your actions, and may go abroad or remain in your apartments as may seem most agreeable to you. A carriage waits your orders, and Ali and Myrtho will accompany you whithersoever you desire to go. There is but one favor I would entreat of you."—"Speak."

"Guard carefully the secret of your birth. Make no allusion to the past; nor upon any occasion be induced to pronounce the names of your illustrious father or ill-fated mother."—"I have already told you, my lord, that I shall see no one."

"It is possible, Haidee, that so perfect a seclusion, though conformable with the nabits and customs of the East, may not be practicable in Paris. Endeavor, then, to accustom yourself to our manner of living in these northern climes, as you did to those of Rome, Florence, Milan, and Madrid; it may be useful to you one of these days, whether you remain here or return to the East." The young girl raised her tearful eyes towards Monte Cristo, as she said with touching earnestness, "Whether *we* return to the East, you mean to say, my lord, do you not?"

"My child," returned Monte Cristo, "you know full well that whenever we part, it will be no fault or wish of mine; the tree forsakes not the flower—the flower falls from the tree."

"My lord," replied Haidee, "I never will leave you, for I am sure I could not exist without you."—"My poor girl, in ten years I shall be old, and you will be still young."

"My father had a long white beard, but I loved him; he was sixty years old, but to me he was handsomer than all the fine youths I saw."—"Then tell me, Haidee, do you believe you shall be able to accustom yourself to our present mode of life?"

"Shall I see you?"—"Every day."

"Then what do you fear, my lord?"

"You might find it dull."

"No, my lord. In the morning, I shall rejoice in the prospect of your coming, and in the evening dwell with delight on the happiness I have enjoyed in your presence; then too, when alone, I can call forth mighty pictures of the past, see vast horizons bounded only by the towering mountains of Pindus and Olympus. Oh, believe me, that when three great passions, such as sorrow, love, and gratitude fill the heart, *ennui* can find no place."—"You are a worthy daughter of Epirus, Haidee, and your charming and poetical ideas prove well your descent from that race of goddesses who claim your country as their birthplace. Depend on my care to see that your youth is not blighted, or suffered to pass away in ungenial solitude; and of this be well assured, that if you love me as a father, I love you as a child."

"You are wrong, my lord. The love I have for you is very different from the love I had for my father. My father died, but I did not die. If you were to die, I should die too." The count, with a smile of profound tenderness, extended his hand, and she carried it to her lips. Monte Cristo, thus attuned to the interview he proposed to hold with Morrel and his family, departed, murmuring as he went these lines of Pindar, "Youth is a flower of which love is the fruit; happy is he who, after having watched its silent growth, is permitted to gather and call it his own." The carriage was prepared according to orders, and stepping lightly into it, the count drove off at his usual rapid pace.

L

The Morrel Family

IN A VERY FEW minutes the count reached No. 7 in the Rue Meslay. The house was of white stone, and in a small court before it were two small beds full of beautiful flowers. In the concierge that opened the gate the count recognized Coclès; but as he had but one eye, and that eye had become somewhat dim in the course of nine years, Coclès did not recognize the count. The carriages that drove up to the door were compelled to turn, to avoid a fountain that played in a basin of rockwork,—an ornament that had excited the jealousy of the whole quarter, and had gained for the place the appellation of "The Little Versailles." It is needless to add that there were gold and silver fish in the basin. The house, with kitchens and cellars below, had above the ground-floor, two stories and attics. The whole of the property, consisting of an immense workshop, two pavilions at the bottom of the garden, and the garden itself, had been purchased by Emmanuel, who had seen at a glance that he could make of it a profitable speculation. He had reserved the house and half the garden, and building a wall between the garden and the workshops, had let them upon lease with the pavilions at the bottom of the garden. So that for a trifling sum he was as well lodged, and as perfectly shut out from observation, as the inhabitants of the finest mansion in the Faubourg St. Germain. The breakfast-room was finished in oak; the salon in mahogany, and the furnishings were of blue velvet; the bed-room was in citronwood and green damask. There was a study for Emmanuel, who never studied, and a music-room for Julie, who never played. The whole of the second story was set apart for Maximilian; it was precisely similar to his sister's apartments, except that for the breakfast-parlor he had a billiard-room, where he received his friends. He was superintending the grooming of his horse, and smoking his cigar at the entrance of the garden, when the count's carriage stopped at the gate.

Coclès opened the gate, and Baptistin, springing from the box, inquired whether Monsieur and Madame Herbault and Monsieur Maximilian Morrel would see his excellency the Count of Monte Cristo. "The Count of Monte Cristo?" cried Morrel, throwing away his cigar and hastening to the carriage; "I should think we would see him. Ah, a thousand thanks, count, for not having forgotten your promise." And the young officer shook the count's hand so warmly, that Monte Cristo could not be mistaken as to the sincerity of his joy, and he saw that he had been expected with impatience, and was received with pleasure. "Come, come," said Maximilian, "I will serve as your guide; such a man as you are ought not to be introduced by a servant. My sister is in the garden plucking the dead roses; my brother is reading his two papers, the *Presse* and the *Débats*, within six steps of her; for wherever you see Madame Herbault, you have only to look within a circle of four yards and you will find M. Emmanuel, and 'reciprocally,' as they say at the Polytechnic School." At the sound of their steps a young woman of twenty to five and twenty, dressed in a silk morning gown, and busily engaged in plucking the dead leaves off a noisette rose-tree, raised her head. This was Julie, who had become, as the clerk of the house of Thomson & French had predicted, Madame Emmanuel Herbault. She uttered a cry of surprise at the sight of a stranger, and Maximilian began to laugh. "Don't disturb yourself, Julie," said he. "The count has only been two or three days in Paris, but he already knows what a fashionable woman of the Marais is, and if he does not, you will show him."

"Ah, monsieur," returned Julie, "it is treason in my brother to bring you thus, but he never has any regard for his poor sister. Penelon, Penelon!" An old man, who was digging busily at one of the beds, stuck his spade in the earth, and approached, cap in hand, striving to conceal a quid of tobacco he had just thrust into his cheek. A few locks of gray mingled with his hair, which was still thick and matted, while his bronzed features and determined glance well suited an old sailor who had braved the heat of the equator and the storms of the tropics. "I think you hailed me, Mademoiselle Julie?" said he. Penelon had still preserved the habit of calling his master's daughter "Mademoiselle Julie," and had never been able to change the name to Madame Herbault. "Penelon," replied Julie, "go and inform M. Emmanuel of this gentleman's visit, and Maximilian will conduct him to the salon." Then, turning to Monte Cristo,—"I hope you will permit me to leave you for a few minutes," continued she; and without awaiting any reply, disappeared behind a clump of trees, and escaped to the house by a lateral alley.

"I am sorry to see," observed Monte Cristo to Morrel, "that I cause no small disturbance in your house."—"Look there," said Maximilian, laughing; "there is her husband changing his jacket for a coat. I assure you, you are well known in the Rue Meslay."

"Your family appears to be a very happy one," said the count, as if speaking to himself.

"Oh, yes, I assure you, count, they want nothing that can render them happy; they are young and cheerful, they are tenderly attached to each other, and with twenty-five thousand francs a year they fancy themselves as rich as Rothschild."—"Five and twenty thousand francs is not a large sum, however," replied Monte Cristo, with a tone so sweet and gentle, that it went to Maximilian's heart like the voice of a father; "but they will not be content with that. Your brother-in-law is a barrister? a doctor?"

"He was a merchant, monsieur, and had succeeded to the business of my poor father. M. Morrel, at his death, left 500,000 francs, which were divided between my sister and myself, for we were his only children. Her husband, who, when he married her, had no other patrimony than his noble probity, his first-rate ability, and his spotless reputation, wished to possess as much as his wife. He labored and toiled until he had amassed 250,000 francs; six years sufficed to achieve this object. Oh, I assure you, sir, it was a touching spectacle to see these young creatures, destined by their talents for higher stations, toiling together, and through their unwillingness to change any of the customs of their paternal house, taking six years to accomplish what less scrupulous people would have effected in two or three. Marseilles resounded with their well-earned praises. At last, one day, Emmanuel came to his wife, who had just finished making up the accounts. 'Julie,' said he to her, 'Coclès has just given me the last rouleau of a hundred francs; that completes the 250,000 francs we had fixed as the limits of our gains. Can you content yourself with the small fortune which we shall possess for the future? Listen to me. Our house transacts business to the amount of a million a year, from which we derive an income of 40,000 francs. We can dispose of the business, if we please, in an hour, for I have received a letter from M. Delaunay, in which he offers to purchase the good-will of the house, to unite with his own, for 300,000 francs. Advise me what I had better do.'—'Emmanuel,' returned my sister, 'the house of Morrel can only be carried on by a Morrel. Is it not worth 300,000 francs to save our father's name from the chances of evil fortune and failure?'—'I thought so,' replied Emmanuel; 'but I wished to have your advice.'—'This is my counsel:—Our accounts are made up and our bills paid; all we have to do is to stop the issue of any more, and close our office.' This was done instantly. It was three o'clock; at a quarter past, a merchant presented himself to insure two ships; it was a clear profit of 15,000 francs. 'Monsieur,' said Emmanuel, 'have the goodness to address yourself to M. Delaunay. We have quitted business.'—"How long?' inquired the astonished merchant. 'A quarter of an hour,' was the reply. And this is the reason, monsieur," continued Maximilian, "of my sister and brother-in-law having only 25,000 francs a year."

Maximilian had scarcely finished his story, during which the count's heart had swelled within him, when Emmanuel entered wearing a hat and coat. He saluted the count with the air of a man who is aware of the rank of his guest; then, after having led Monte Cristo around the little garden, he returned to the house. A large vase of Japan porcelain, filled with flowers that loaded the air with their perfume, stood in the salon. Julie, suitably dressed, and her hair arranged (she had accomplished this feat in less than ten minutes), received the count on his entrance. The songs of the birds were heard in an aviary hard by, and the branches of laburnums and rose acacias formed an exquisite framework to the blue velvet curtains. Everything in this charming retreat, from the warble of the birds to the smile of the mistress, breathed tranquillity and repose. The count had felt the influence of this happiness from the moment he entered the house, and he remained silent and pensive, forgetting that he was expected to renew the conversation, which had ceased after the first salutations had been exchanged. The silence became almost painful when, by a violent effort, tearing himself from his pleasing reverie—"Madame," said he at length, "I pray you to excuse my emotion, which must astonish you who are only accustomed to the happiness I meet here; but contentment is so new a sight to me, that I could never be weary of looking at yourself and your husband."

"We are very happy, monsieur," replied Julie; "but we have also known unhappiness, and few have ever undergone more bitter sufferings than ourselves." The count's features displayed an expression of the most intense curiosity.

"Oh, all this is a family history, as Château-Renaud told you the other day," observed Maximilian. "This humble picture would have but little interest for you, accustomed as you are to behold the pleasures and the misfortunes of the wealthy and illustrious; but such as we are, we have experienced bitter sorrows."—"And God has poured balm into your wounds, as he does into those of all who are in affliction?" said Monte Cristo inquiringly.

"Yes, count," returned Julie, "we may indeed say he has, for he has done for us what he grants only to his chosen; he sent us one of his angels." The count's cheeks became scarlet, and he coughed, in order to have an excuse for putting his handkerchief to his mouth. "Those born to wealth, and who have the means of gratifying every wish," said Emmanuel, "know not what is the real happiness of life, just as those who have been tossed on the stormy waters of the ocean on a few frail planks can alone realize the blessings of fair weather."

Monte Cristo rose, and without making any answer (for the tremulousness of his voice would have betrayed his emotion) walked up and down the apartment with a slow step.

"Our magnificence makes you smile, count," said Maximilian, who had followed him with his eyes. "No, no," returned Monte Cristo, pale as death, pressing one hand on his heart to still its throbbings, while with the other he pointed to a crystal cover, beneath which a silken purse lay on a black velvet cushion. "I was wondering what could be the significance of this purse, with the paper at one end and the large diamond at the other."—"Count," replied Maximilian, with an air of gravity, "those are our most precious family treasures."

"The stone seems very brilliant," answered the count.

"Oh, my brother does not allude to its value, although it has been estimated at 100,000 francs; he means, that the articles contained in this purse are the relics of the angel I spoke of just now."

"This I do not comprehend; and yet I may not ask for an explanation, madame," replied Monte Cristo, bowing. "Pardon me, I had no intention of committing an indiscretion."—"Indiscretion,—oh, you make us happy by giving us an excuse for expatiating on this subject. If we wanted to conceal the noble action this purse commemorates, we should not expose it thus to view. Oh, would we could relate it everywhere, and to every one, so that the emotion of our unknown benefactor might reveal his presence."

"Ah, really," said Monte Cristo, in a half-stifled voice.

"Monsieur," returned Maximilian, raising the glass cover, and respectfully kissing the silken purse, "this has touched the hand of a man who saved my father from suicide, us from ruin, and our name from shame and disgrace,—a man by whose matchless benevolence we poor children, doomed to want and wretchedness, can at present hear every one envying our happy lot. This letter" (as he spoke, Maximilian drew a letter from the purse and gave it to the count)— "this letter was written by him the day that my father had taken a desperate resolution, and this diamond was given by the generous unknown to my sister as her dowry." Monte Cristo opened the letter, and read it with an indescribable feeling of delight. It was the letter written (as our readers know) to Julie, and signed "Sinbad the Sailor." "Unknown you say, is the man who rendered you this service—unknown to you?"

"Yes; we have never had the happiness of pressing his hand," continued Maximilian. "We have supplicated heaven in vain to grant us this favor, but the whole affair has had a mysterious meaning that we cannot comprehend—we have been guided by an invisible hand,—a hand as powerful as that of an enchanter."

"Oh," cried Julie, "I have not lost all hope of some day kissing that hand, as I now kiss the purse which he has touched. Four years ago, Penelon was at Trieste—Penelon, count, is the old sailor you saw in the garden, and who, from quartermaster, has become gardener—Penelon, when he was at Trieste, saw on the quay an Englishman, who was on the point of embarking on board a yacht, and he recognized him as the person who called on my father the fifth of June, 1829, and who wrote me this letter on the fifth of September. He felt convinced of his identity, but he did not venture to address him."—"An Englishman," said Monte Cristo, who grew uneasy at the attention with which Julie looked at him. "An Englishman you say?"

"Yes," replied Maximilian, "an Englishman, who represented himself as the confidential clerk of the house of Thomson & French, at Rome. It was this that made me start when you said the other day, at M. de Morcerf's, that Messrs. Thomson & French were your bankers. That happened, as I told you, in 1829. For God's sake, tell me, did you know this Englishman?'

"But you tell me, also, that the house of Thomson & French have constantly denied having rendered you this service?"—"Yes."

"Then is it not probable that this Englishman may be some one who, grateful for a kindness your father had shown him, and which he himself had forgotten, has taken this method of requiting the obligation?"

"Everything is possible in this affair, even a miracle."

"What was his name?" asked Monte Cristo.

"He gave no other name," answered Julie, looking earnestly at the count, "than that at the end of his letter—'Sinbad the Sailor.'"

"Which is evidently not his real name, but a fictitious one."

Then, noticing that Julie was struck with the sound of his voice,—

"Tell me," continued he, "was he not about my height, perhaps a little taller, with his chin imprisoned, as it were, in a high cravat; his coat closely buttoned up, and constantly taking out his pencil?"

"Oh, do you then know him?" cried Julie, whose eyes sparkled with joy.—"No," returned Monte Cristo, "I only guessed. I knew a Lord Wilmore, who was constantly doing actions of this kind."

"Without revealing himself?"

"He was an eccentric being, and did not believe in the existence of gratitude."—"Oh, heaven," exclaimed Julie, clasping her hands, "in what did he believe, then?"

"He did not credit it at the period when I knew him," said Monte Cristo, touched to the heart by the accents of Julie's voice; "but, perhaps, since then he has had proofs that gratitude does exist."

"And do you know this gentleman, monsieur?" inquired Emmanuel.

"Oh, if you do know him," cried Julie, "can you tell us where he is—where we can find him? Maximilian—Emmanuel—if we do but discover him, he must believe in the gratitude of the heart!" Monte Cristo felt tears start into his eyes, and he again walked hastily up and down the room.—"In the name of heaven," said Maximilian, "if you know anything of him, tell us what it is."— "Alas," cried Monte Cristo, striving to repress his emotion, "if Lord Wilmore was your unknown benefactor, I fear you will never see him again. I parted from him two years ago at Palermo, and he was then on the point of setting out for the most remote regions; so that I fear he will never return."

"Oh, monsieur, this is cruel of you," said Julie, much affected; and the young lady's eyes swam with tears.

"Madame," replied Monte Cristo gravely, and gazing earnestly on the two liquid pearls that trickled down Julie's cheeks, "had Lord Wilmore seen what I now see, he would become attached to life, for the tears you shed would reconcile him to mankind;" and he held out his hand to Julie, who gave him hers, carried away by the look and accent of the count. "But," continued she, "Lord Wilmore had a family or friends, he must have known some one, can we not—"

"Oh, it is useless to inquire," returned the count; "perhaps, after all, he was not the man you seek for. He was my friend; he had no secrets from me, and if this had been so he would have confided in me."

"And he told you nothing?"—"Not a word."

"Nothing that would lead you to suppose?"—"Nothing."

"And yet you spoke of him at once."

"Ah, in such a case one supposes"—

"Sister, sister," said Maximilian, coming to the count's aid, "monsieur is quite right. Recollect what our excellent father so often told us, 'It was no Englishman that thus saved us.'" Monte Cristo started. "What did your father tell you, M. Morrel?" said he eagerly.

"My father thought that this action had been miraculously performed—he believed that a benefactor had arisen from the grave to save us. Oh, it was a touching superstition, monsieur, and although I did not myself believe it, I would not for the world have destroyed my father's faith. How often did he muse over it and pronounce the name of a dear friend—a friend lost to him forever; and on his death-bed, when the near approach of eternity seemed to have illumined his mind with supernatural light, this thought, which had until then been but a doubt, became a conviction, and his last words were, 'Maximilian, it was Edmond Dantès!'" At these words the count's paleness, which had for some time been increasing, became alarming; he could not speak; he looked at his watch like a man who has forgotten the hour, said a few hurried words to Madame Herbault, and pressing the hands of Emmanuel and Maximilian,— "Madame," said he, "I trust you will allow me to visit you occasionally; I value your friendship, and feel grateful to you for your welcome, for this is the first time for many years that I have thus yielded to my feelings;" and he hastily quitted the apartment.

"This Count of Monte Cristo is a strange man," said Emmanuel.

"Yes," answered Maximilian, "but I feel sure he has an excellent heart, and that he likes us."

"His voice went to my heart," observed Julie; "and two or three times I fancied that I had heard it before."

LI

Pyramus and Thisbe

ABOUT TWO-THIRDS OF the way along the Faubourg Saint-Honoré, and in the rear of one of the most imposing mansions in this rich neighborhood, where the various houses vie with each other for elegance of design and magnificence of construction, extended a large garden, where the wide-spreading chestnut-trees raised their heads high above the walls in a solid rampart, and with the coming of every spring scattered a shower of delicate pink and white blossoms into the large stone vases that stood upon the two square pilasters of a curiously wrought iron gate, that dated from the time of Louis XII. This noble entrance, however, in spite of its striking appearance and the graceful effect of the geraniums planted in the two vases, as they waved their variegated leaves in the wind and charmed the eye with their scarlet bloom, had fallen into utter disuse. The proprietors of the mansion had many years before thought it best to confine themselves to the possession of the house itself, with its thickly planted court-yard, opening into the Faubourg Saint-Honoré, and to the garden shut in by this gate, which formerly communicated with a fine kitchen-garden of about an acre. For the demon of speculation drew a line, or in other words projected a street, at the farther side of the kitchen-garden. The street was laid out, a name was chosen and posted up on an iron plate, but before construction was begun, it occurred to the possessor of the property that a handsome sum might be obtained for the ground then devoted to fruits and vegetables, by building along the line of the proposed street, and so making it a branch of communication with the Faubourg Saint-Honoré itself, one of the most important thoroughfares in the city of Paris.

In matters of speculation, however, though "man proposes," "money disposes." From some such difficulty the newly named street died almost in birth, and the purchaser of the kitchen-garden, having paid a high price for it, and being quite unable to find any one willing to take his bargain off his hands without a considerable loss, yet still clinging to the belief that at some future day he should obtain a sum for it that would repay him, not only for his past out-lay, but also the interest upon the capital locked up in his new acquisition, contented himself with letting the ground temporarily to some market-gardeners, at a yearly rental of 500 francs. And so, as we have said, the iron gate leading into the kitchen-garden had been closed up and left to the rust, which bade fair before long to eat off its hinges, while to prevent the ignoble glances of the dig-gers and delvers of the ground from presuming to sully the aristo-cratic enclosure belonging to the mansion, the gate had been boarded up to a height of six feet. True, the planks were not so closely adjusted but that a hasty peep might be obtained through their interstices; but the strict decorum and rigid propriety of the inhabitants of the house left no grounds for apprehending that advantage would be taken of that circumstance.

Horticulture seemed, however, to have been abandoned in the deserted kitchen-garden; and where cabbages, carrots, radishes, pease, and melons had once flourished, a scanty crop of lucerne alone bore evidence of its being deemed worthy of cultivation. A small, low door gave egress from the walled space we have been describing into the projected street, the ground having been aban-doned as unproductive by its various renters, and had now fallen so completely in general estimation as to return not even the one-half per cent it had originally paid. Towards the house the chestnut-trees we have before mentioned rose high above the wall, without in any way affecting the growth of other luxuriant shrubs and flowers that eagerly pressed forward to fill up the vacant spaces, as though asserting their right to enjoy the boon of light and air. At one corner, where the foliage became so thick as almost to shut out day, a large stone bench and sundry rustic seats indicated that this sheltered spot was either in general favor or particular use by some inhabitant of the house, which was faintly discernible through the dense mass of verdure that partially concealed it, though situated but a hundred paces off.

Whoever had selected this retired portion of the grounds as the boundary of a walk, or as a place for meditation, was abundantly justified in the choice by the absence of all glare, the cool, refreshing shade, the screen it afforded from the scorching rays of the sun, that found no entrance there even during the burning days of hottest summer, the incessant and melodious warbling of birds, and the entire removal from either the noise of the street or the bustle of the mansion. On the evening of one of the warmest days spring had yet bestowed on the inhabitants of Paris, might be seen negligently thrown upon the stone bench, a book, a parasol, and a work-basket, from which hung a partly embroidered cambric handkerchief, while at a little distance from these articles was a young woman, standing close to the iron gate, endeavoring to discern something on the other side by means of the openings in the planks,—the earnestness of her attitude and the fixed gaze with which she seemed to seek the object of her wishes, proving how much her feelings were interested in the matter. At that instant the little side-gate leading from the waste ground to the street was noiselessly opened, and a tall, powerful young man appeared. He was dressed in a common gray blouse and velvet cap, but his carefully arranged hair, beard and mustache, all of the richest and glossiest black, ill accorded with his plebeian attire. After casting a rapid glance around him, in order to assure himself that he was unobserved, he entered by the small gate, and, carefully closing and securing it after him, proceeded with a hurried step towards the barrier.

At the sight of him she expected, though probably not in such a costume, the young woman started in terror, and was about to make a hasty retreat. But the eye of love had already seen, even through the narrow chinks of the wooden palisades, the movement of the white robe, and observed the fluttering of the blue sash. Pressing his lips close to the planks, he exclaimed, "Don't be alarmed, Valentine—it is I!" Again the timid girl found courage to return to the gate, saying, as she did so, "And why do you come so late to-day? It is almost dinner-time, and I had to use no little diplomacy to get rid of my watchful mother-in-law, my too-devoted maid, and my troublesome brother, who is always teasing me about coming to work at my embroidery, which I am in a fair way never to get done. So pray excuse yourself as well as you can for having made me wait, and, after that, tell me why I see you in a dress so singular that at first I did not recognize you." "Dearest Valentine," said the young man, "the difference between our respective stations makes me fear to offend you by speaking of my love, but yet I cannot find myself in your presence without longing to pour forth my soul, and tell you how fondly I adore you. If it be but to carry away with me the recollection of such sweet moments, I could even thank you for chiding me, for it leaves me a gleam of hope, that if you did not expect me (and that indeed would be worse than vanity to suppose), at least I was in your thoughts. You asked me the cause of my being late, and why I come disguised. I will candidly explain the reason of both, and I trust to your goodness to pardon me. I have chosen a trade."

"A trade? Oh, Maximilian, how can you jest at a time when we have such deep cause for uneasiness?"—"Heaven keep me from jesting with that which is far dearer to me than life itself! But listen to me, Valentine, and I will tell you all about it. I became weary of ranging fields and scaling walls, and seriously alarmed at the idea suggested by you, that if caught hovering about here your father would very likely have me sent to prison as a thief. That would compromise the honor of the French army, to say nothing of the fact that the continual presence of a captain of Spahis in a place where no warlike projects could be supposed to account for it might well create surprise; so I have become a gardener, and, consequently, adopted the costume of my calling."

"What excessive nonsense you talk, Maximilian!"

"Nonsense? Pray do not call what I consider the wisest action of my life by such a name. Consider, by becoming a gardener I effectually screen our meetings from all suspicion or danger."

"I beseech of you, Maximilian, to cease trifling, and tell me what you really mean."—"Simply, that having ascertained that the piece of ground on which I stand was to let, I made application for it, was readily accepted by the proprietor, and am now master of this fine crop of lucerne. Think of that, Valentine! There is nothing now to prevent my building myself a little but on my plantation, and residing not twenty yards from you. Only imagine what happiness that would afford me. I can scarcely contain myself at the bare idea. Such felicity seems above all price—as a thing impossible and unattainable. But would you believe that I purchase all this delight, joy, and happiness, for which I would cheerfully have surrendered ten years of my life, at the small cost of 500 francs per annum, paid quarterly? Henceforth we have nothing to fear. I am on my own ground, and have an undoubted right to place a ladder against the wall, and to look over when I please, without having any apprehensions of being taken off by the police as a suspicious character. I may also enjoy the precious privilege of assuring you of my fond, faithful, and unalterable affection, whenever you visit your favorite bower, unless, indeed, it offends your pride to listen to professions of love from the lips of a poor workingman, clad in a blouse and cap." A faint cry of mingled pleasure and surprise escaped from the lips of Valentine, who almost instantly said, in a saddened tone, as though some envious cloud darkened the joy which illumined her heart, "Alas, no, Maximilian, this must not be, for many reasons. We should presume too much on our own strength, and, like others, perhaps, be led astray by our blind confidence in each other's prudence."

"How can you for an instant entertain so unworthy a thought, dear Valentine? Have I not, from the first blessed hour of our acquaintance, schooled all my words and actions to your sentiments and ideas? And you have, I am sure, the fullest confidence in my honor. When you spoke to me of experiencing a vague and indefinite sense of coming danger, I placed myself blindly and devotedly at your service, asking no other reward than the pleasure of being useful to you; and have I ever since, by word or look, given you cause of regret for having selected me from the numbers that would willingly have sacrificed their lives for you? You told me, my dear Valentine, that you were engaged to M. d'Epinay, and that your father was resolved upon completing the match, and that from his will there was no appeal, as M. de Villefort was never known to change a determination once formed. I kept in the background, as you wished, and waited, not for the decision of your heart or my own, but hoping that providence would graciously interpose in our behalf, and order events in our favor. But what cared I for delays or difficulties, Valentine, as long as you confessed that you loved me, and took pity on me? If you will only repeat that avowal now and then, I can endure anything."

"Ah, Maximilian, that is the very thing that makes you so bold, and which renders me at once so happy and unhappy, that I frequently ask myself whether it is better for me to endure the harshness of my mother-in-law, and her blind preference for her own child, or to be, as I now am, insensible to any pleasure save such as I find in these meetings, so fraught with danger to both."

"I will not admit that word," returned the young man; "it is at once cruel and unjust. Is it possible to find a more submissive slave than myself? You have permitted me to converse with you from time to time, Valentine, but forbidden my ever following you in your walks or elsewhere—have I not obeyed? And since I found means to enter this enclosure to exchange a few words with you through this gate—to be close to you without really seeing you— have I ever asked so much as to touch the hem of your gown or tried to pass this barrier which is but a trifle to one of my youth and strength? Never has a complaint or a murmur escaped me. I have been bound by my promises as rigidly as any knight of olden times. Come, come, dearest Valentine, confess that what I say is true, lest I be tempted to call you unjust."

"It is true," said Valentine, as she passed the end of her slender fingers through a small opening in the planks, and permitted Maximilian to press his lips to them, "and you are a true and faithful friend; but still you acted from motives of self-interest, my dear Maximilian, for you well knew that from the moment in which you had manifested an opposite spirit all would have been ended between us. You promised to bestow on me the friendly affection of a brother. For I have no friend but yourself upon earth, who am neglected and forgotten by my father, harassed and persecuted by my mother-in-law, and left to the sole companionship of a paralyzed and speechless old man, whose withered hand can no longer press mine, and who can speak to me with the eye alone, although there still lingers in his heart the warmest tenderness for his poor grandchild. Oh, how bitter a fate is mine, to serve either as a victim or an enemy to all who are stronger than myself, while my only friend and supporter is a living corpse! Indeed, indeed, Maximilian, I am very miserable, and if you love me it must be out of pity."

"Valentine," replied the young man, deeply affected, "I will not say you are all I love in the world, for I dearly prize my sister and brother-in-law; but my affection for them is calm and tranquil, in no manner resembling what I feel for you. When I think of you my heart beats fast, the blood burns in my veins, and I can hardly breathe; but I solemnly promise you to restrain all this ardor, this fervor and intensity of feeling, until you yourself shall require me to render them available in serving or assisting you. M. Franz is not expected to return home for a year to come, I am told; in that time many favorable and unforeseen chances may befriend us. Let us, then, hope for the best; hope is so sweet a comforter. Meanwhile, Valentine, while reproaching me with selfishness, think a little what you have been to me—the beautiful but cold resemblance of a marble Venus. What promise of future reward have you made me for all the submission and obedience I have evinced?—none whatever. What granted me?—scarcely more. You tell me of M. Franz d'Epinay, your betrothed lover, and you shrink from the idea of being his wife; but tell me, Valentine, is there no other sorrow in your heart? You see me devoted to you, body and soul, my life and each warm drop that circles round my heart are consecrated to your service; you know full well that my existence is bound up in yours—that were I to lose you I would not outlive the hour of such crushing misery; yet you speak with calmness of the prospect of your being the wife of another! Oh, Valentine, were I in your place, and did I feel conscious, as you do, of being worshipped, adored, with such a love as mine, a hundred times at least should I have passed my hand between these iron bars, and said, 'Take this hand, dearest Maximilian, and believe that, living or dead, I am yours—yours only, and forever!'" The poor girl made no reply, but her lover could plainly hear her sobs and tears. A rapid change took place in the young man's feelings. "Dearest, dearest Valentine," exclaimed he, "forgive me if I have offended you, and forget the words I spoke if they have unwittingly caused you pain."

"No, Maximilian, I am not offended," answered she; "but do you not see what a poor, helpless being I am, almost a stranger and an outcast in my father's house, where even he is seldom seen; whose will has been thwarted, and spirits broken, from the age of ten years, beneath the iron rod so sternly held over me; oppressed, mortified, and persecuted, day by day, hour by hour, minute by minute, no person has cared for, even observed my sufferings, nor have I ever breathed one word on the subject save to yourself. Outwardly and in the eyes of the world, I am surrounded by kindness and affection; but the reverse is the case. The general remark is, 'Oh, it cannot be expected that one of so stern a character as M. Villefort could lavish the tenderness some fathers do on their daughters. What though she has lost her own mother at a tender age, she has had the happiness to find a second mother in Madame de Villefort.' The world, however, is mistaken; my father abandons me from utter indifference, while my mother-in-law detests me with a hatred so much the more terrible because it is veiled beneath a continual smile."—"Hate you, sweet Valentine," exclaimed the young man; "how is it possible for any one to do that?"

"Alas," replied the weeping girl, "I am obliged to own that my mother-in-law's aversion to me arises from a very natural source— her overweening love for her own child, my brother Edward."

"But why should it?"—"I do not know; but, though unwilling to introduce money matters into our present conversation, I will just say this much—that her extreme dislike to me has its origin there; and I much fear she envies me the fortune I enjoy in right of my mother, and which will be more than doubled at the death of M. and Mme. de Saint-Méran, whose sole heiress I am. Madame de Villefort has nothing of her own, and hates me for being so richly endowed. Alas, how gladly would I exchange the half of this wealth for the happiness of at least sharing my father's love. God knows, I would prefer sacrificing the whole, so that it would obtain me a happy and affectionate home."

"Poor Valentine!"

"I seem to myself as though living a life of bondage, yet at the same time am so conscious of my own weakness that I fear to break the restraint in which I am held, lest I fall utterly helpless. Then, too, my father is not a person whose orders may be infringed with impunity; protected as he is by his high position and firmly established reputation for talent and unswerving integrity, no one could oppose him; he is all-powerful even with the king; he would crush you at a word. Dear Maximilian, believe me when I assure you that if I do not attempt to resist my father's commands it is more on your account than my own."

"But why, Valentine, do you persist in anticipating the worst,— why picture so gloomy a future?"

"Because I judge it from the past."

"Still, consider that although I may not be, strictly speaking, what is termed an illustrious match for you, I am, for many reasons, not altogether so much beneath your alliance. The days when such distinctions were so nicely weighed and considered no longer exist in France, and the first families of the monarchy have intermarried with those of the empire. The aristocracy of the lance has allied itself with the nobility of the cannon. Now I belong to this last-named class; and certainly my prospects of military preferment are most encouraging as well as certain. My fortune, though small, is free and unfettered, and the memory of my late father is respected in our country, Valentine, as that of the most upright and honorable merchant of the city; I say our country, because you were born not far from Marseilles."

"Don't speak of Marseilles, I beg of you, Maximilian; that one word brings back my mother to my recollection—my angel mother, who died too soon for myself and all who knew her; but who, after watching over her child during the brief period allotted to her in this world, now, I fondly hope, watches from her home in heaven. Oh, if my mother were still living, there would be nothing to fear, Maximilian, for I would tell her that I loved you, and she would protect us."

"I fear, Valentine," replied the lover, "that were she living I should never have had the happiness of knowing you; you would then have been too happy to have stooped from your grandeur to bestow a thought on me."

"Now it is you who are unjust, Maximilian," cried Valentine; "but there is one thing I wish to know."

"And what is that?" inquired the young man, perceiving that Valentine hesitated.

"Tell me truly, Maximilian, whether in former days, when our fathers dwelt at Marseilles, there was ever any misunderstanding between them?"—"Not that I am aware of," replied the young man, "unless, indeed, any ill-feeling might have arisen from their being of opposite parties—your father was, as you know, a zealous partisan of the Bourbons, while mine was wholly devoted to the emperor; there could not possibly be any other difference between them. But why do you ask?"

"I will tell you," replied the young girl, "for it is but right you should know. Well, on the day when your appointment as an officer of the Legion of Honor was announced in the papers, we were all sitting with my grandfather, M. Noirtier; M. Danglars was there also—you recollect M. Danglars, do you not, Maximilian, the banker, whose horses ran away with my mother-in-law and little brother, and very nearly killed them? While the rest of the company were discussing the approaching marriage of Mademoiselle Danglars, I was reading the paper to my grandfather; but when I came to the paragraph about you, although I had done nothing else but read it over to myself all the morning (you know you had told me all about it the previous evening), I felt so happy, and yet so nervous, at the idea of speaking your name aloud, and before so many people, that I really think I should have passed it over, but for the fear that my doing so might create suspicions as to the cause of my silence; so I summoned up all my courage, and read it as firmly and as steadily as I could."

"Dear Valentine!"

"Well, would you believe it? directly my father caught the

sound of your name he turned round quite hastily, and, like a poor silly thing, I was so persuaded that every one must be as much affected as myself by the utterance of your name, that I was not surprised to see my father start, and almost tremble; but I even thought (though that surely must have been a mistake) that M. Danglars trembled too."

"'Morrel, Morrel,' cried my father, 'stop a bit;' then knitting his brows into a deep frown, he added, 'surely this cannot be one of the Morrel family who lived at Marseilles, and gave us so much trouble from their violent Bonapartism—I mean about the year 1815.'—'Yes,' replied M. Danglars, 'I believe he is the son of the old shipowner.'"

"Indeed," answered Maximilian; "and what did your father say then, Valentine?"—"Oh, such a dreadful thing, that I don't dare to tell you."

"Always tell me everything," said Maximilian with a smile.

"'Ah,' continued my father, still frowning, 'their idolized emperor treated these madmen as they deserved; he called them 'food for powder,' which was precisely all they were good for; and I am delighted to see that the present government have adopted this salutary principle with all its pristine vigor; if Algiers were good for nothing but to furnish the means of carrying so admirable an idea into practice, it would be an acquisition well worthy of struggling to obtain. Though it certainly does cost France somewhat dear to assert her rights in that uncivilized country.'"

"Brutal politics, I must confess," said Maximilian; "but don't attach any serious importance, dear, to what your father said. My father was not a bit behind yours in that sort of talk. 'Why,' said he, 'does not the emperor, who has devised so many clever and efficient modes of improving the art of war, organize a regiment of lawyers, judges, and legal practitioners, sending them in the hottest fire the enemy could maintain, and using them to save better men?' You see, my dear, that for picturesque expression and generosity of spirit there is not much to choose between the language of either party. But what did M. Danglars say to this outburst on the part of the procureur?"

"Oh, he laughed, and in that singular manner so peculiar to himself—half-malicious, half-ferocious; he almost immediately got up and took his leave; then, for the first time, I observed the agitation of my grandfather, and I must tell you, Maximilian, that I am the only person capable of discerning emotion in his paralyzed frame. And I suspected that the conversation that had been carried on in his presence (for they always say and do what they like before the dear old man, without the smallest regard for his feelings) had made a strong impression on his mind; for, naturally enough, it must have pained him to hear the emperor he so devotedly loved and served spoken of in that depreciating manner."

"The name of M. Noirtier," interposed Maximilian, "is celebrated throughout Europe; he was a statesman of high standing, and you may or may not know, Valentine, that he took a leading part in every Bonapartist conspiracy set on foot during the restoration of the Bourbons."—"Oh, I have often heard whispers of things that seem to me most strange—the father a Bonapartist, the son a Royalist; what can have been the reason of so singular a difference in parties and politics? But to resume my story; I turned towards my grandfather, as though to question him as to the cause of his emotion; he looked expressively at the newspaper I had been reading. 'What is the matter, dear grandfather?' said I, 'are you pleased?' He gave me a sign in the affirmative. 'With what my father said just now?' He returned a sign in the negative. 'Perhaps you liked what M. Danglars said?' Another sign in the negative. 'Oh, then, you were glad to hear that M. Morrel (I didn't dare to say Maximilian) had been made an officer of the Legion of Honor?' He signified assent; only think of the poor old man's being so pleased to think that you, who were a perfect stranger to him, had been made an officer of the Legion of Honor! Perhaps it was a mere whim on his part, for he is falling, they say, into second childhood, but I love him for showing so much interest in you."

"How singular," murmured Maximilian; "your father hates me, while your grandfather, on the contrary—What strange feelings are aroused by politics."

"Hush," cried Valentine, suddenly; "some one is coming!" Maximilian leaped at one bound into his crop of lucerne, which he began to pull up in the most ruthless way, under the pretext of being occupied in weeding it.

"Mademoiselle, mademoiselle!" exclaimed a voice from behind the trees. "Madame is searching for you everywhere; there is a visitor in the drawing-room."

"A visitor?" inquired Valentine, much agitated; "who is it?"

"Some grand personage—a prince I believe they said—the Count of Monte Cristo."

"I will come directly," cried Valentine aloud. The name of Monte Cristo sent an electric shock through the young man on the other side of the iron gate, to whom Valentine's "I am coming" was the customary signal of farewell. "Now, then," said Maximilian, leaning on the handle of his spade, "I would give a good deal to know how it comes about that the Count of Monte Cristo is acquainted with M. de Villefort."

LII

Toxicology

I T WAS REALLY THE Count of Monte Cristo who had just
arrived at Madame de Villefort's for the purpose of returning
the procureur's visit, and at his name, as may be easily imagined, the whole house was in confusion. Madame de Villefort, who
was alone in her drawing-room when the count was announced,
desired that her son might be brought thither instantly to renew his
thanks to the count; and Edward, who heard this great personage
talked of for two whole days, made all possible haste to come to
him, not from obedience to his mother, or out of any feeling of
gratitude to the count, but from sheer curiosity, and that some
chance remark might give him the opportunity for making one of
the impertinent speeches which made his mother say,—"Oh, that
naughty child! But I can't be severe with him, he is really *so* bright."

After the usual civilities, the count inquired after M. de Villefort. "My husband dines with the chancellor," replied the young
lady; "he has just gone, and I am sure he'll be exceedingly sorry
not to have had the pleasure of seeing you before he went." Two
visitors who were there when the count arrived, having gazed at
him with all their eyes, retired after that reasonable delay which
politeness admits and curiosity requires. "What is your sister Valentine doing?" inquired Madame de Villefort of Edward; "tell some

one to bid her come here, that I may have the honor of introducing her to the count."

"You have a daughter, then, madame?" inquired the count; "very young, I presume?"—"The daughter of M. de Villefort by his first marriage," replied the young wife, "a fine well-grown girl."

"But melancholy," interrupted Master Edward, snatching the feathers out of the tail of a splendid parroquet that was screaming on its gilded perch, in order to make a plume for his hat. Madame de Villefort merely cried,—"Be still, Edward!" She then added,—"This young madcap is, however, very nearly right, and merely re-echoes what he has heard me say with pain a hundred times; for Mademoiselle de Villefort is, in spite of all we can do to rouse her, of a melancholy disposition and taciturn habit, which frequently injure the effect of her beauty. But what detains her? Go, Edward, and see."

"Because they are looking for her where she is not to be found."

"And where are they looking for her?"

"With grandpapa Noirtier."

"And do you think she is not there?"—"No, no, no, no, no, she is not there," replied Edward, singing his words.

"And where is she, then? If you know, why don't you tell?"

"She is under the big chestnut-tree," replied the spoiled brat, as he gave, in spite of his mother's commands, live flies to the parrot, which seemed keenly to relish such fare. Madame de Villefort stretched out her hand to ring, intending to direct her waiting-maid to the spot where she would find Valentine, when the young lady herself entered the apartment. She appeared much dejected; and any person who considered her attentively might have observed the traces of recent tears in her eyes.

Valentine, whom we have in the rapid march of our narrative presented to our readers without formally introducing her, was a tall and graceful girl of nineteen, with bright chestnut hair, deep blue eyes, and that reposeful air of quiet distinction which characterized her

mother. Her white and slender fingers, her pearly neck, her cheeks
tinted with varying hues, reminded one of the lovely Englishwomen
who have been so poetically compared in their manner to the grace-
fulness of a swan. She entered the apartment, and seeing near her
stepmother the stranger of whom she had already heard so much,
saluted him without any girlish awkwardness, or even lowering her
eyes, and with an elegance that redoubled the count's attention. He
rose to return the salutation. "Mademoiselle de Villefort, my daugh-
ter-in-law," said Madame de Villefort to Monte Cristo, leaning back
on her sofa and motioning towards Valentine with her hand. "And
M. de Monte Cristo, King of China, Emperor of Cochin-China,"
said the young imp, looking slyly towards his sister.

Madame de Villeforte at this really did turn pale, and was very
nearly angry with this household plague, who answered to the
name of Edward; but the count, on the contrary, smiled, and
appeared to look at the boy complacently, which caused the maternal heart to bound again with joy and enthusiasm.

"But, madame," replied the count, continuing the conversation,
and looking by turns at Madame de Villefort and Valentine, "have I not
already had the honor of meeting yourself and mademoiselle before?
I could not help thinking so just now; the idea came over my mind,
and as mademoiselle entered the sight of her was an additional ray of
light thrown on a confused remembrance; excuse the remark."—"I
do not think it likely, sir; Mademoiselle de Villefort is not very fond of
society, and we very seldom go out," said the young lady.

"Then it was not in society that I met with mademoiselle or
yourself, madame, or this charming little merry boy. Besides, the
Parisian world is entirely unknown to me, for, as I believe I told
you, I have been in Paris but very few days. No,—but, perhaps, you
will permit me to call to mind—stay!" The count placed his hand
on his brow as if to collect his thoughts. "No—it was somewhere—
away from here—it was—I do not know—but it appears that this
recollection is connected with a lovely sky and some religious fête;

mademoiselle was holding flowers in her hand, the interesting boy was chasing a beautiful peacock in a garden, and you, madame, were under the trellis of some arbor. Pray come to my aid, madame; do not these circumstances appeal to your memory?"

"No, indeed," replied Madame de Villefort; "and yet it appears to me, sir, that if I had met you anywhere, the recollection of you must have been imprinted on my memory."

"Perhaps the count saw us in Italy," said Valentine timidly.

"Yes, in Italy; it was in Italy most probably," replied Monte Cristo; "you have travelled then in Italy, mademoiselle?"

"Yes; madame and I were there two years ago. The doctors, anxious for my lungs, had prescribed the air of Naples. We went by Bologna, Perugia, and Rome."—"Ah, yes—true, mademoiselle," exclaimed Monte Cristo, as if this simple explanation was sufficient to revive the recollection he sought. "It was at Perugia on Corpus Christi Day, in the garden of the Hôtel des Postes, when chance brought us together; you, Madame de Villefort, and her son; I now remember having had the honor of meeting you."

"I perfectly well remember Perugia, sir, and the Hôtel des Postes, and the festival of which you speak," said Madame de Villefort, "but in vain do I tax my memory, of whose treachery I am ashamed, for I really do not recall to mind that I ever had the pleasure of seeing you before."

"It is strange, but neither do I recollect meeting with you," observed Valentine, raising her beautiful eyes to the count.

"But I remember it perfectly," interposed the darling Edward.

"I will assist your memory, madame," continued the count; "the day had been burning hot; you were waiting for horses, which were delayed in consequence of the festival. Mademoiselle was walking in the shade of the garden, and your son disappeared in pursuit of the peacock."

"And I caught it, mamma, don't you remember?" interposed Edward, "and I pulled three such beautiful feathers out of his tail."

"You, madame, remained under the arbor; do you not remember, that while you were seated on a stone bench, and while, as I told you, Mademoiselle de Villefort and your young son were absent, you conversed for a considerable time with somebody?"

"Yes, in truth, yes," answered the young lady, turning very red, "I do remember conversing with a person wrapped in a long woollen mantle; he was a medical man, I think."—"Precisely so, madame; this man was myself; for a fortnight I had been at that hotel, during which period I had cured my valet de chambre of a fever, and my landlord of the jaundice, so that I really acquired a reputation as a skilful physician. We discoursed a long time, madame, on different subjects; of Perugino, of Raffaelle, of manners, customs, of the famous aquatofana, of which they had told you, I think you said, that certain individuals in Perugia had preserved the secret."

"Yes, true," replied Madame de Villefort, somewhat uneasily, "I remember now."

"I do not recollect now all the various subjects of which we discoursed, madame," continued the count with perfect calmness; "but I perfectly remember that, falling into the error which others had entertained respecting me, you consulted me as to the health of Mademoiselle de Villefort."—"Yes, really, sir, you were in fact a medical man," said Madame de Villefort, "since you had cured the sick."

"Molière or Beaumarchais would reply to you, madame, that it was precisely because I was not, that I had cured my patients; for myself, I am content to say to you that I have studied chemistry and the natural sciences somewhat deeply, but still only as an amateur, you understand."—At this moment the clock struck six. "It is six o'clock," said Madame de Villefort, evidently agitated. "Valentine, will you not go and see if your grandpapa will have his dinner?" Valentine rose, and saluting the count, left the apartment without speaking.

"Oh, madame," said the count, when Valentine had left the room, "was it on my account that you sent Mademoiselle de Villefort away?"

"By no means," replied the young lady quickly; "but this is the hour when we usually give M. Noirtier the unwelcome meal that sustains his pitiful existence. You are aware, sir, of the deplorable condition of my husband's father?"

"Yes, madame, M. de Villefort spoke of it to me—a paralysis, I think."

"Alas, yes; the poor old gentleman is entirely helpless; the mind alone is still active in this human machine, and that is faint and flickering, like the light of a lamp about to expire. But excuse me, sir, for talking of our domestic misfortunes; I interrupted you at the moment when you were telling me that you were a skilful chemist."—"No, madame, I did not say as much as that," replied the count with a smile; "quite the contrary. I have studied chemistry because, having determined to live in eastern climates, I have been desirous of following the example of King Mithridates."

"*Mithridates rex Ponticus*," said the young scamp, as he tore some beautiful portraits out of a splendid album, "the individual who took cream in his cup of poison every morning at breakfast."

"Edward, you naughty boy," exclaimed Madame de Villefort, snatching the mutilated book from the urchin's grasp; "you are positively past bearing; you really disturb the conversation; go, leave us, and join your sister Valentine in dear grandpapa Noirtier's room."

"The album," said Edward sulkily.

"What do you mean?—the album!"—"I want the album."

"How dare you tear out the drawings?"

"Oh, it amuses me."—"Go—go at once."

"I won't go unless you give me the album," said the boy, seating himself doggedly in an arm-chair, according to his habit of never giving way.—"Take it, then, and pray disturb us no longer," said Madame de Villefort, giving the album to Edward, who then went towards the door, led by his mother. The count followed her with his eyes.

"Let us see if she shuts the door after him," he muttered. Madame de Villefort closed the door carefully after the child, the count appearing not to notice her; then casting a scrutinizing glance around the chamber, the young wife returned to her chair, in which she seated herself. "Allow me to observe, madame," said the count, with that kind tone he could assume so well, "you are really very severe with that dear clever child."—"Oh, sometimes severity is quite necessary," replied Madame de Villefort, with all a mother's real firmness.

"It was his Cornelius Nepos that Master Edward was repeating when he referred to King Mithridates," continued the count, "and you interrupted him in a quotation which proves that his tutor has by no means neglected him, for your son is really advanced for his years."

"The fact is, count," answered the mother, agreeably flattered, "he has great aptitude, and learns all that is set before him. He has but one fault, he is somewhat wilful; but really, on referring for the moment to what he said, do you truly believe that Mithridates used these precautions, and that these precautions were efficacious?"

"I think so, madame, because I myself have made use of them, that I might not be poisoned at Naples, at Palermo, and at Smyrna—that is to say, on three several occasions when, but for these precautions, I must have lost my life."—"And your precautions were successful?"

"Completely so."—"Yes, I remember now your mentioning to me at Perugia something of this sort."

"Indeed?" said the count with an air of surprise, remarkably well counterfeited; "I really did not remember."—"I inquired of you if poisons acted equally, and with the same effect, on men of the North as on men of the South; and you answered me that the cold and sluggish habits of the North did not present the same aptitude as the rich and energetic temperaments of the natives of the South."

"And that is the case," observed Monte Cristo. "I have seen Russians devour, without being visibly inconvenienced, vegetable substances which would infallibly have killed a Neapolitan or an Arab."—"And you really believe the result would be still more sure with us than in the East, and in the midst of our fogs and rains a man would habituate himself more easily than in a warm latitude to this progressive absorption of poison?"

"Certainly; it being at the same time perfectly understood that he should have been duly fortified against the poison to which he had not been accustomed."—"Yes, I understand that; and how would you habituate yourself, for instance, or rather, how did you habituate yourself to it?"—"Oh, very easily. Suppose you knew beforehand the poison that would be made use of against you; suppose the poison was, for instance, brucine"—

"Brucine is extracted from the false angostura,[1] is it not?" inquired Madame de Villefort.—"Precisely, madame," replied Monte Cristo; "but I perceive I have not much to teach you. Allow me to compliment you on your knowledge; such learning is very rare among ladies."

"Oh, I am aware of that," said Madame de Villefort; "but I have a passion for the occult sciences, which speak to the imagination like poetry, and are reducible to figures, like an algebraic equation; but go on, I beg of you; what you say interests me to the greatest degree."

"Well," replied Monte Cristo, "suppose, then, that this poison was brucine, and you were to take a milligramme the first day, two milligrammes the second day, and so on. Well, at the end of ten days you would have taken a centigramme; at the end of twenty days, increasing another milligramme, you would have taken three hundred centigrammes; that is to say, a dose which you would support without inconvenience, and which would be very dangerous for any other person who had not taken the same precautions as yourself. Well, then, at the end of a month, when drinking water from the same carafe, you would kill the person who drank with you, without your perceiving, otherwise than from slight inconvenience, that there was any poisonous substance mingled with this water."

[1] *Brucœa ferruginea.*

"Do you know any other counter-poisons?"—"I do not."

"I have often read, and read again, the history of Mithridates," said Madame de Villefort in a tone of reflection, "and had always considered it a fable."

"No, madame, contrary to most history, it is true; but what you tell me, madame, what you inquire of me, is not the result of a chance query, for two years ago you asked me the same questions, and said then, that for a very long time this history of Mithridates had occupied your mind."

"True, sir. The two favorite studies of my youth were botany and mineralogy, and subsequently, when I learned that the use of simples frequently explained the whole history of a people, and the entire life of individuals in the East, as flowers betoken and symbolize a love affair, I have regretted that I was not a man, that I might have been a Flamel, a Fontana, or a Cabanis."

"And the more, madame," said Monte Cristo, "as the Orientals do not confine themselves, as did Mithridates, to make a cuirass of his poisons, but they also made them a dagger. Science becomes, in their hands, not only a defensive weapon, but still more frequently an offensive one; the one serves against all their physical sufferings, the other against all their enemies. With opium, belladonna, brucaea, snake-wood, and the cherry-laurel, they put to sleep all who stand in their way. There is not one of those women, Egyptian, Turkish, or Greek, whom here you call 'good women,' who do not know how, by means of chemistry, to stupefy a doctor, and in psychology to amaze a confessor."—"Really," said Madame de Villefort, whose eyes sparkled with strange fire at this conversation.

"Oh, yes, indeed, madame," continued Monte Cristo, "the secret dramas of the East begin with a love philtre and end with a death potion—begin with paradise and end with—hell. There are as many elixirs of every kind as there are caprices and peculiarities in the physical and moral nature of humanity; and I will say further—the art of these chemists is capable with the utmost precision to

accommodate and proportion the remedy and the bane to yearn-
ings for love or desires for vengeance."

"But, sir," remarked the young woman, "these Eastern societies,
in the midst of which you have passed a portion of your existence,
are as fantastic as the tales that come from their strange land. A man
can easily be put out of the way there, then; it is, indeed, the Bagdad and Bassora of the 'Thousand and One Nights.' The sultans and
viziers who rule over society there, and who constitute what in
France we call the government, are really Haroun-al-Raschids and
Giaffars, who not only pardon a poisoner, but even make him a
prime minister, if his crime has been an ingenious one, and who,
under such circumstances, have the whole story written in letters
of gold, to divert their hours of idleness and ennui."

"By no means, madame; the fanciful exists no longer in the East.
There, disguised under other names, and concealed under other
costumes, are police agents, magistrates, attorneys-general, and
bailiffs. They hang, behead, and impale their criminals in the most
agreeable possible manner; but some of these, like clever rogues,
have contrived to escape human justice, and succeed in their fraud-
ulent enterprises by cunning stratagems. Amongst us a simpleton,
possessed by the demon of hate or cupidity, who has an enemy to
destroy, or some near relation to dispose of, goes straight to the grocer's or druggist's, gives a false name, which leads more easily to his
detection than his real one, and under the pretext that the rats prevent him from sleeping, purchases five or six grammes of arsenic—
if he is really a cunning fellow, he goes to five or six different
druggists or grocers, and thereby becomes only five or six times
more easily traced;—then, when he has acquired his specific, he
administers duly to his enemy, or near kinsman, a dose of arsenic
which would make a mammoth or mastodon burst, and which,
without rhyme or reason, makes his victim utter groans which
alarm the entire neighborhood. Then arrive a crowd of policemen
and constables. They fetch a doctor, who opens the dead body, and

collects from the entrails and stomach a quantity of arsenic in a spoon. Next day a hundred newspapers relate the fact, with the names of the victim and the murderer. The same evening the grocer or grocers, druggist or druggists, come and say, 'It was I who sold the arsenic to the gentleman;' and rather than not recognize the guilty purchaser, they will recognize twenty. Then the foolish criminal is taken, imprisoned, interrogated, confronted, confounded, condemned, and cut off by hemp or steel; or if she be a woman of any consideration, they lock her up for life. This is the way in which you Northerns understand chemistry, madame. Desrues was, however, I must confess, more skilful."

"What would you have, sir?" said the lady, laughing; "we do what we can. All the world has not the secret of the Medicis or the Borgias."

"Now," replied the count, shrugging his shoulders, "shall I tell you the cause of all these stupidities? It is because, at your theatres, by what at least I could judge by reading the pieces they play, they see persons swallow the contents of a phial, or suck the button of a ring, and fall dead instantly. Five minutes afterwards the curtain falls, and the spectators depart. They are ignorant of the consequences of the murder; they see neither the police commissary with his badge of office, nor the corporal with his four men; and so the poor fools believe that the whole thing is as easy as lying. But go a little way from France—go either to Aleppo or Cairo, or only to Naples or Rome, and you will see people passing by you in the streets—people erect, smiling, and fresh-colored, of whom Asmodeus, if you were holding on by the skirt of his mantle, would say, 'That man was poisoned three weeks ago; he will be a dead man in a month.'"

"Then," remarked Madame de Villefort, "they have again discovered the secret of the famous aquatofana that they said was lost at Perugia."

"Ah, but madame, does mankind ever lose anything? The arts change about and make a tour of the world; things take a different name, and the vulgar do not follow them—that is all; but there is always the same result. Poisons act particularly on some organ or another—one on the stomach, another on the brain, another on the intestines. Well, the poison brings on a cough, the cough an inflammation of the lungs, or some other complaint catalogued in the book of science, which, however, by no means precludes it from being decidedly mortal; and if it were not, would be sure to become so, thanks to the remedies applied by foolish doctors, who are generally bad chemists, and which will act in favor of or against the malady, as you please; and then there is a human being killed according to all the rules of art and skill, and of whom justice learns nothing, as was said by a terrible chemist of my acquaintance, the worthy Abbé Adelmonte of Taormina, in Sicily, who has studied these national phenomena very profoundly."

"It is quite frightful, but deeply interesting," said the young lady, motionless with attention. "I thought, I must confess, that these tales, were inventions of the Middle Ages."

"Yes, no doubt, but improved upon by ours. What is the use of time, rewards of merit, medals, crosses, Monthyon prizes, if they do not lead society towards more complete perfection? Yet man will never be perfect until he learns to create and destroy; he does know how to destroy, and that is half the battle."

"So," added Madame de Villefort, constantly returning to her object, "the poisons of the Borgias, the Medicis, the Renés, the Ruggieris, and later, probably, that of Baron de Trenck, whose story has been so misused by modern drama and romance"—

"Were objects of art, madame, and nothing more," replied the count. "Do you suppose that the real savant addresses himself stupidly to the mere individual? By no means. Science loves eccentricities, leaps and bounds, trials of strength, fancies, if I may be allowed so to term them. Thus, for instance, the excellent Abbé Adelmonte, of whom I spoke just now, made in this way some marvellous experiments."

"Really?"

"Yes; I will mention one to you. He had a remarkably fine garden, full of vegetables, flowers, and fruit. From amongst these vegetables he selected the most simple—a cabbage, for instance. For three days he watered this cabbage with a distillation of arsenic; on the third, the cabbage began to droop and turn yellow. At that moment he cut it. In the eyes of everybody it seemed fit for table, and preserved its wholesome appearance. It was only poisoned to the Abbé Adelmonte. He then took the cabbage to the room where he had rabbits—for the Abbé Adelmonte had a collection of rabbits, cats, and guinea-pigs, fully as fine as his collection of vegetables, flowers, and fruit. Well, the Abbé Adelmonte took a rabbit, and made it eat a leaf of the cabbage. The rabbit died. What magistrate would find, or even venture to insinuate, anything against this? What procureur has ever ventured to draw up an accusation against M. Magendie or M. Flourens, in consequence of the rabbits, cats, and guinea-pigs they have killed?—not one. So, then, the rabbit dies, and justice takes no notice. This rabbit dead, the Abbé Adelmonte has its entrails taken out by his cook and thrown on the dunghill; on this dunghill is a hen, who, pecking these intestines, is in her turn taken ill, and dies next day. At the moment when she is struggling in the convulsions of death, a vulture is flying by (there are a good many vultures in Adelmonte's country); this bird darts on the dead fowl, and carries it away to a rock, where it dines off its prey. Three days afterwards, this poor vulture, which has been very much indisposed since that dinner, suddenly feels very giddy while flying aloft in the clouds, and falls heavily into a fish-pond. The pike, eels, and carp eat greedily always, as everybody knows— well, they feast on the vulture. Now suppose that next day, one of these eels, or pike, or carp, poisoned at the fourth remove, up at your table. Well, then, your guest will be poisoned remove, and die, at the end of eight or ten days, o intestines, sickness, or abscess of the pylorus. The d body and say with an air of profound learning, 'The subject has died of a tumor on the liver, or of typhoid fever!'"

"But," remarked Madame de Villefort, "all these circumstances which you link thus to one another may be broken by the least accident; the vulture may not see the fowl, or may fall a hundred yards from the fish-pond."

"Ah, that is where the art comes in. To be a great chemist in the East, one must direct chance; and this is to be achieved."—Madame de Villefort was in deep thought, yet listened attentively. "But," she exclaimed, suddenly, "arsenic is indelible, indestructible; in whatso-ever way it is absorbed, it will be found again in the body of the victim from the moment when it has been taken in sufficient quan-tity to cause death."

"Precisely so," cried Monte Cristo—"precisely so; and this is what I said to my worthy Adelmonte. He reflected, smiled, and replied to me by a Sicilian proverb, which I believe is also a French proverb, 'My son, the world was not made in a day—but in seven. Return on Sun-day.' On the Sunday following I did return to him. Instead of having watered his cabbage with arsenic, he had watered it this time with a solution of salts, having their basis in strychnine, *strychnos colubrina*, as the learned term it. Now, the cabbage had not the slightest appearance of disease in the world, and the rabbit had not the smallest distrust; yet, five minutes afterwards, the rabbit was dead. The fowl pecked at the rabbit, and the next day was a dead hen. This time we were the vul-tures, so we opened the bird, and this time all special symptoms had disappeared, there were only general symptoms. There was no pecu-liar indication in any organ—an excitement of the nervous system—that was it; a case of cerebral congestion—nothing more. The fowl had not been poisoned—she had died of apoplexy. Apoplexy is rare dis-ease among fowls, I believe, but very common among men." Madame de Villefort appeared more and more thoughtful.

"It is very fortunate," she observed, "that such substances could only be prepared by chemists; otherwise, all the world would be poisoning each other."—"By chemists and persons who have a taste for chemistry," said Monte Cristo carelessly.

"And then," said Madame de Villefort, endeavoring by a struggle, and with effort, to get away from her thoughts, "however skilfully it is prepared, crime is always crime, and if it avoid human scrutiny, it does not escape the eye of God. The Orientals are stronger than we are in cases of conscience, and, very prudently, have no hell—that is the point."

"Really, madame, this is a scruple which naturally must occur to a pure mind like yours, but which would easily yield before sound reasoning. The bad side of human thought will always be defined by the paradox of Jean Jacques Rousseau,—you remember,—the mandarin who is killed five hundred leagues off by raising the tip of the finger. Man's whole life passes in doing these things, and his intellect is exhausted by reflecting on them. You will find very few persons who will go and brutally thrust a knife in the heart of a fellow-creature, or will administer to him, in order to remove him from the surface of the globe on which we move with life and animation, that quantity of arsenic of which we just now talked. Such a thing is really out of rule—eccentric or stupid. To attain such a point, the blood must be heated to thirty-six degrees, the pulse be, at least, at ninety, and the feelings excited beyond the ordinary limit. But suppose one pass, as is permissible in philology, from the word itself to its softened synonym, then, instead of committing an ignoble assassination you make an 'elimination;' you merely and simply remove from your path the individual who is in your way, and that without shock or violence, without the display of the sufferings which, in the case of becoming a punishment, make a martyr of the victim, and a butcher, in every sense of the word, of him who inflicts them. Then there will be no blood, no groans, no convulsions, and above all, no consciousness of that horrid and compromising moment of accomplishing the act,—then one escapes the clutch of the human law, which says, 'Do not disturb society!' This is the mode in which they manage these things, and succeed in Eastern climes, where there are grave and phlegmatic persons who care very little for the questions of time in conjunctures of importance."—"Yet conscience remains," remarked Madame de Villefort in an agitated voice, and with a stifled sigh.

"Yes," answered Monte Cristo, "happily, yes, conscience does remain; and if it did not, how wretched we should be! After every action requiring exertion, it is conscience that saves us, for it supplies us with a thousand good excuses, of which we alone are judges; and these reasons, howsoever excellent in producing sleep, would avail us but very little before a tribunal, when we were tried for our lives. Thus Richard III., for instance, was marvellously served by his conscience after the putting away of the two children of Edward IV.; in fact, he could say, 'These two children of a cruel and persecuting king, who have inherited the vices of their father, which I alone could perceive in their juvenile propensities—these two children are impediments in my way of promoting the happiness of the English people, whose unhappiness they (the children) would infallibly have caused.' Thus was Lady Macbeth served by her conscience, when she sought to give her son, and not her husband (whatever Shakspeare may say), a throne. Ah, maternal love is a great virtue, a powerful motive—so powerful that it excuses a multitude of things, even if, after Duncan's death, Lady Macbeth had been at all pricked by her conscience."

Madame de Villefort listened with avidity to these appalling maxims and horrible paradoxes, delivered by the count with that ironical simplicity which was peculiar to him. After a moment's silence, the lady inquired, "Do you know, my dear count," she said, "that you are a very terrible reasoner, and that you look at the world through a somewhat distempered medium? Have you really measured the world by scrutinies, or through alembics and crucibles? For you must indeed be a great chemist, and the elixir you administered to my son, which recalled him to life almost instantaneously"—

"Oh, do not place any reliance on that, madame; *one* drop of that elixir sufficed to recall life to a dying child, but three drops would have impelled the blood into his lungs in such a way as to have produced most violent palpitations; six would have suspended his respiration, and caused syncope more serious than that in which he was; ten would have destroyed him. You know, madame, how suddenly I snatched him from those phials which he so imprudently touched?"—"Is it then so terrible a poison?"

"Oh, no. In the first place, let us agree that the word poison does not exist, because in medicine use is made of the most violent poisons, which become, according as they are employed, most salutary remedies."

"What, then, is it?"

"A skilful preparation of my friend's the worthy Abbé Adelmonte, who taught me the use of it."—"Oh," observed Madame de Villefort, "it must be an admirable anti-spasmodic."

"Perfect, madame, as you have seen," replied the count; "and I frequently make use of it—with all possible prudence though, be it observed," he added with a smile of intelligence.

"Most assuredly," responded Madame de Villefort in the same tone. "As for me, so nervous, and so subject to fainting-fits, I should require a Doctor Adelmonte to invent for me some means of breathing freely and tranquillizing my mind, in the fear I have of dying some fine day of suffocation. In the meanwhile, as the thing is difficult to find in France, and your abbé is not probably disposed to make a journey to Paris on my account, I must continue to use Monsieur Planché's anti-spasmodics; and mint and Hoffman's drops are among my favorite remedies. Here are some lozenges which I have made up on purpose; they are compounded doubly strong." Monte Cristo opened the tortoise-shell box, which the lady presented to him, and inhaled the odor of the lozenges with the air of an amateur who thoroughly appreciated their composition. "They are indeed exquisite," he said; "but as they are necessarily submitted to the process of deglutition—a function which it is frequently impossible for a fainting person to accomplish—I prefer my own specific."

"Undoubtedly, and so should I prefer it, after the effects I have seen produced; but of course it is a secret, and I am not so indiscreet as to ask it of you."—"But I," said Monte Cristo, rising as he spoke—"I am gallant enough to offer it you."

"How kind you are."—"Only remember one thing—a small dose is a remedy, a large one is poison. One drop will restore life, as you have seen; five or six will inevitably kill, and in a way the more terrible inasmuch as, poured into a glass of wine, it would not in the slightest degree affect its flavor. But I say no more, madame; it is really as if I were prescribing for you." The clock struck half-past six, and a lady was announced, a friend of Madame de Villefort, who came to dine with her.—"If I had had the honor of seeing you for the third or fourth time, count, instead of only for the second," said Madame de Villefort: "if I had had the honor of being your friend, instead of only having the happiness of being under an obligation to you, I should insist on detaining you to dinner, and not allow myself to be daunted by a first refusal."

"A thousand thanks, madame," replied Monte Cristo, "but I have an engagement which I cannot break. I have promised to escort to the Académie a Greek princess of my acquaintance who has never seen your grand opera, and who relies on me to conduct her thither."

"Adieu, then, sir, and do not forget the prescription."

"Ah, in truth, madame, to do that I must forget the hour's conversation I have had with you, which is indeed impossible." Monte Cristo bowed, and left the house. Madame de Villefort remained immersed in thought. "He is a very strange man," she said, "and in my opinion is himself the Adelmonte he talks about." As to Monte Cristo, the result had surpassed his utmost expectations. "Good," said he, as he went away; "this is a fruitful soil, and I feel certain that the seed sown will not be cast on barren ground." Next morning, faithful to his promise, he sent the prescription requested.

GATEWAY MOVIE CLASSICS
CLASSIC NOVELS THAT INSPIRED CLASSIC MOVIES

The Scarlet Pimpernel by Baroness Orczy
Beau Geste by P.C. Wren
Ben-Hur: A Tale of the Christ by Lew Wallace
Quo Vadis by Henryk Sienkiewicz

Errol Flynn Double Feature!
      The Sea Hawk by Rafael Sabatini
      Captain Blood by Rafael Sabatini

Alexandre Dumas's Swashbuckling Adventures
      The Three Musketeers
      The Man in the Iron Mask
      The Count of Monte Cristo, two volumes

COMING ATTRACTIONS.........

Scaramouche by Rafael Sabatini
The Prisoner of Zenda by Anthony Hope
Bulldog Drummond by Henry Cyril "Sapper" MacNeil

Classics from H. Rider Haggard
      King Solomon's Mines
      She
      Allan Quatermain and the Lost City of Gold